CONTENTS: I

ACKNOWLEDGEMENTS

I owe a huge debt of gratitude to my friends:

Rachel Roy, my beta reader and supporter
J.M. Ney-Grimm, my mentor for graphics and publishing
Sandy Manning, my writing partner and first reader

COPYRIGHT

ISBN-13: 978-0692589809 (Trilka Press)
ISBN-10: 0692589805

PERMISSIONS

Scripture quotations from The Authorized (King James) Version. Rights in the Authorized Version in the United Kingdom are vested in the Crown. Reproduced by permission of the Crown's patentee, Cambridge University Press.

PRIDE'S CHILDREN

A novel of obsession, betrayal, and love

ALICIA BUTCHER EHRHARDT

DEDICATION

For Bill, Life Companion,
without whose constant support
none of this
would have happened.

BOOK ONE

PURGATORY

Purgatory is where you pay for your sins

DISCLAIMER

PRIDE'S CHILDREN is FICTION

With one exception*, any resemblance of CHARACTER NAMES
to names of actual persons is purely coincidental.
LOCATIONS may be real; no attempt has been made to ensure
they are accurate.
The PLOT is my own invention, based on real life and tabloid stories.
PUBLICATIONS quoted are either fictional, or used in a fictional
manner.

*Wayne Blackburn has graciously allowed me to name one of the
villains after him. He is NOT the character.

❧ PROTHALAMION ❧

DEPARTMENT OF CELEBRITIES

OCTOBER 23, 2006

MIXED~UP MARRIAGE?

BY D. LIEBJA HUNTER

Schadenfreude: knickers in a twist—publicly?

The world was shocked, nay, stunned, by the recent revelation that, even as his pregnant fiancée, America's Sweetheart Bianca Doyle, lay supine in a hospital bed at the California Regional Women's Hospital in Burbank, on complete bedrest to forestall the premature birth of his twin daughters, Irish Megastar Andrew O'Connell, seen last March dedicating his winning statuette at the Academy Awards to Ms. Doyle, was secretly married to best-selling author K. Beth Winter, many years his senior.

The happy couple met in February 2005 here in New York on the set of *Night Talk*, with Dana…

THE NEW YORKER

~ 1 ~

ഈ CHAPTER ONE ഌ
To ride the fickle horse of fame

...the LORD gave, and the LORD hath taken away; blessed be the name of the LORD.

Job 1:21, KJV

"... guests tomorrow will be actor Andrew O'Connell, star of the blockbuster medieval epic *Roland*, and best-selling author of *Prairie Fires* K. Beth Winter. So—that's it for today. Good night, New York!"

Dana Lewiston, *Night Talk*, 2/24/05

KARY
New York City; February 25, 2005; 11 P.M.

I, KARENNA ELIZABETH Ashe, being of sound mind, do... *But that's it, isn't it? Being here proves I am* not *of sound mind.* She wished, for the nth time, she had not agreed to tonight's interview. *They have Laura Hillenbrand—isn't that enough?* But, "...we need more people like you"—meaning 'damaged like you'—"to speak up..." The handwritten note from *Night Talk*'s host put the burden of duty on psyche and skeleton held together by spider's silk. Dana didn't know what she asked for. *But I know. Winter dies tonight. Of exposure.*

"Kary? Are you okay?"

"I'm fine. Why?" Kary felt like her own straitjacket, hugging herself tightly with goose-bumped arms.

"You seemed alarmed." Elise's face was a study in tact. "Then you went further into that head of yours."

Dear Elise, worrying about her difficult hermit author. Kind Elise, who hadn't demanded tiresome explanations: Why not a suburban book signing? Why national television? *And why now?* As

~ 3 ~

response, Kary nodded toward the plate-glass window separating WMRC-NY's third-floor greenroom from the clear New York night, where streetlights battled the erratic illumination of neon signs under an almost-full moon.

Elise joined her, gazed warily at the skyline. "What?"

It was automatic, halfway through the first decade of the twenty-first century. "No. Down." Below, across the avenue, a knot of pedestrians encircled a figure in a puffy red parka whose arm was being held and dusted off by a second figure in a Navy peacoat. "Must be black ice." Kary pointed. "The red one fell. He hit his head. He lay so still for so long I thought he was dead. I would've called 911—" She shrugged. "But then people got to him, and he came back to life, so I started drafting a new will—"

Elise made a sound of disbelief. "A will?"

"Death? Resurrection? Life changes? Wills?" Logical train of thought? *Am I going to be this incoherent tonight? Oh, God.*

"Ah. Perfect sense. Of course." Elise glanced up to where the ticking wall clock's minute hand jerked to 11:10. "Aren't you hungry?" She gestured with a mug of decaf at the spread of pastries, square blue Fiji water bottles, and the ubiquitous coffeepot.

Hollow, yes. Hungry, no. The acrid aroma of coffee nauseated Kary. Elise had insisted on picking her up at the airport, getting her settled at the hotel, and taking her out. They had chatted desultorily in the taxicab. *I should try harder to be polite—I come so infrequently.* "Dinner's still with me. I'm fine."

"Makeup okay? I told them not too much."

Kary's hand started toward her cheek; she restrained herself. "It's fine. Thanks."

"This show is way too late—" Elise's head snapped round at sudden music.

Kary heard the faint tinny sound of Beethoven. *Für Elise.* 'If composers write for you, what you gonna do?' was the agent's standard joke about her ringtone. As Elise went to dig out the devil's communication device from her gargantuan handbag, Kary turned back to the window, but the sidewalk Samaritans had dispersed.

"What? I told you not to call—" Elise took her cellphone conflict to the far corner.

Kary caught muted acrimony, but not the words. Then placation, promise, a hang-up snap.

"Kary…" Elise was back.

Kary braced herself, drew the half-smile on her lips. *Here it comes.*

"I know I promised to take you back to the hotel…"

"But something's wrong."

"My daughter's been in an accident—minor," Elise hastened. "She couldn't track her dad down, she's all shook up— She just got her license—"

"You have to go. Of course."

"I hate to leave you. If it were anything less—"

She touched Elise's arm in reassurance. "Family comes first." A stab of envy that Elise had a teenager and a husband to go home to. "I'm already here. What can go wrong?" *Don't worry; I won't bolt—I gave my word.*

The vertical worry-lines in Elise's forehead relaxed. "I'll arrange with the staff to take you—"

"I'll get a cab, Elise. I'm a grown woman. Go!" Kary kept her tone light. "It was very sweet of you to come with me." She helped Elise with her coat, bundled her out, clicked the door shut.

She leaned both palms on the door's cool steel, exhaled. She ordered her fingers not to go for the doorknob. Her forearm nerves fizzled with electricity. *I have no right to feel abandoned.*

Quiet. The ritual would help. She stood straight, took three deliberate breaths, centered herself. *Light, sound.* She located the switch, cut the buzzing overhead fluorescents that overpowered the table lamps' gentle glow. The remaining soft sibilance of too-dry air through ductwork, she reclassified to white noise. Better. She suppressed the urge to flee, folded herself into the pearl-gray velveteen armchair cube in the expensively noncommittal room.

She focused her mind on the clock, instructed tension to ratchet down as every tock marked the death of a second. *You've lectured to auditoria full of med students—how can this be worse?* But that was years ago…

She closed her eyes and expanded her quiet zone, attending to each extraneous stimulus before consigning it to oblivion. Relax. Breathe. Release. Breath *in,* adrenaline metabolites *out* with the cleansing flow. Breath *in…*

Kary startled as the door banged open.

The producer, a pixie of a young woman with cropped black hair held back by her headset, wafted in, hovering inches above the floor. Her gaze flickered around. "Ms. Carter…?"

"Family emergency. Problems?"

"It's always frantic before live TV." The producer snorted delicately. "Listen, I'm sorry it's short notice, but will you mind terribly being first?"

Kary's stomach muscles clenched. "No. Of course not," she lied. Will you mind being executed a half-hour earlier? What was the producer's name? *Damn this brain.*

"Andrew O'Connell's late." The producer tapped her wristwatch. "He can't possibly make it—it's eleven twenty."

"Already...?" Icy roads? Accident? What if he doesn't show and I have to be coherent for a whole hour? *The outcome will be the same.* Shh. *Quiet.* Panic never went far. *Silly Panic.*

The producer's head swiveled at the sound of footsteps and voices from the hallway.

"Your missing guest?" *Salvation?*

The producer darted to the door. "Phew! Now you won't have to rush." Quick peek at her watch, head shake. "Cutting it awfully close. I gotta run." Hesitation. "Is there anything you need? Dana insisted—"

A last meal? Final cigarette? Eleventh hour reprieve? "I'm fine. Go."

"Can I flip the monitor on for you?" The producer flitted toward the plasma screen TV, reached for the ON switch.

"No!" Too sharp? *Quiet.* "Thanks. I'll just rest till you want me."

The producer nodded and whizzed out, leaving the door open again. *Rats.* Melly! *That* was the producer's name.

So much energy so lavishly squandered. Kary's lips compressed a smile. Well—*I* know where *I* am in the pecking order. She lowered her eyelids, breathed out a molecule at a time.

Remember: you're not here for you.

ANDREW

ANDREW O'CONNELL scrambled after the WMRC-NY staffer, entourage at his heels. Damn meetings. Damn slippery night traffic. Last time he trusted someone else's estimates of travel time. He was acutely aware the show had started. No way around that. Unprofessional, being late and not warmed up. *A reputation I do not need.*

The corridor's chessboard pattern—man-size black and white squares—keyed the memories of his other visit. Greenroom? To his left? There. Sharp girl, Dana, but fair, if memory served him. *Will she treat me the same?* The corner of his mouth curled. *Cynic.*

"We're ready for you, Mr. O'Connell," the producer greeted him, peeling him away from his escort. She stole a quick glance at her watch. "Five minutes."

He heard relief underlying briskness. Little bit of a thing. Wedding ring. Pity. New? *Promised I'd be here, didn't I?* He knew that was dangerously disingenuous. "Ye'll be wanting me in there?" He gestured toward the doorway. Wouldn't do to worry about the lads—George's bailiwick.

"Too late. Dana needs you in the wings," she said, as she hurried him past, down the short corridor to stage left. He caught a passing glimpse of a straight-backed woman, legs tucked under her in an armchair, her eyes closed. Short pale hair and soft gray top, flowered skirt wrapped about her. Dana's other guest, the mysterious writer?

The producer hustled him toward a chair at curtain's edge.

"Thanks. I'd rather be standing." A knight on the back rank, surrounded by purposeful chaos: he liked having these few moments to himself. Anticipation tingled the backs of his hands, and his fingers itched to light a fag. *Americans and their damned regulations.* Maybe he'd quit when there was no stress in his life.

The producer deserted him without a word, scurried into the fray. The smallish studio thrummed. Five tiers, sixty, a hundred people? College students, middle-aged couples, retirees. Packed house. *All mine.*

The usual painful Klieg lights spotlit the magnificent Dana, in full monologue, striding about for the audience, milking them for delighted groans. Black lamé slit to the thigh and impossibly high heels, with one arm covered to the wrist and the other naked. No jewelry he could see, except for sparkles at her ears. *Ah, Dana.* Stunning—and aware of it. Too bad she was off-limits—a longtime live-in boyfriend. Now that he had more currency, he asked George to check; George gave him the look, said, in the irritating manner of nailed-down men, 'Ye'll only be in New York for one night, lad.' *So I should spend it alone?*

Dana must like living on the edge—*Night Talk* was one of a tiny minority of shows that didn't pre-tape at a reasonable hour. Which wasn't an excuse. He caught the exact moment she *knew* he was there—she drew herself taller, squared her shoulders. If she played hardball later, well, he deserved it. *Her show, boyo.*

His attention was distracted by a mouse of a hair-and-makeup girl apologetically interrupting him to dull whatever shine there might be on his face—he wished he'd had time to shower and shave: scruffy was accidental, unless ye believed the yellow sheets—and to run a comb through what Bridget used to call his 'shaggy blond mess.' He wouldn't find Bridget in the audience— *Slash that line of thought off at the root.*

Makeup girl was followed by an equally meek microphone tech; by the time he looked up Dana dominated center stage, going to commercial with a mite of a lead-in: "Don't go away—when we come back—*Andrew O'Connell.*"

Dana's gorgeous closeup was replaced on the studio monitor by a commercial plugging a cruise line. Without even a glance in his direction, Dana strode to the dais, assumed her throne, and, while worker bees surrounded her, crossed her lovely leg toward him as high as TV allowed. Curious how most male talk show hosts hid behind desks. The women universally flaunted themselves.

He found himself evaluating the scene as a set before "Action!" *Hell, still plenty of time.* This was his first chance for a direct comparison of 'before' and 'now.' Devil of a trick figuring out what had changed. Fifteen months ago, almost to the day, he'd been here doing promos for FAL, a week before its opening. Before the harrowing period for award nominations, small victories, smashed hopes. By industry reckoning, it was a reasonable success—and vanished, as most did. But there was camaraderie, a we're-all-in-this-together feeling from staff on the TV shows where he plugged the film.

They would never have left me alone before, put up with me being late. No, the producer wasn't new—but her deference was. *Shite.* Same for makeup girl and mike tech. Now they wore masks. *Shite.* He'd been kicked upstairs. He craved fame—and the universe was slapping his face with it.

His heart rate, which had been settling, ticked into high gear. It meant, subtly or no, that he'd lost the ability to take people at face value, trust his intuition. And it put the earlier meeting with the record label execs in a different light, their CD deal, the offered tour. He knew they were interested in the band only because of him and his sudden notoriety, but he thought the execs sincere about the music: his lyrics, his and George's quirky melodies, the band's complex rhythms. *So be it.* The music came first. He'd take one, then, for the band, for them tolerating his 'day job.' If suckers came because of *him*—and stayed for the sound, good enough.

Now Dana was back from the break, and he readied himself. He willed his pulse, if not slow, somehow voluntary. He fisted his hands, then stretched his fingers as far back as they would go, twisted the signet on his right ring finger around and settled it, expelled all the air from his lungs. *They want entertainment?* Well, he'd have to provide, wouldn't he?

A few more jokes, and then Dana clipped the arm of her chair with the edge of her hand, rose pneumatically, pivoted, and to rising applause and catcalls, gave them what they wanted. "Here he is—" dragged-out pause, "Andrew *O'Connell!*"

Hell, it's still good. He stopped trying not to grin, gathered himself up, launched himself across the stage. The audience went wild. He chose two red-headed women in the second row, waved. As he neared Dana, a wicked idea grew. Last time she'd granted him a no-fuss, no-muss air-kiss. *Well, we'll be seeing about that.* He calculated angles to the TV cameras, bet himself she tangoed. Dana extended a welcoming hand.

To hell with safe choices. He closed two steps, grasped her hand, pulled it up and around her to twirl her into the crook of his arm in a swirl of cooperative skirt. He bent her way back, leaned down to soft lips and a hint of ...Shalimar? An infinite second; he reversed, spun her upright, steadied her. When he released her, the crowd erupted.

"Hey! *I* thought we were just *friends!*" Dana said, eyebrows raised, industrial-strength lipstick unsmeared. She patted her mane back into perfection.

Good girl; it'd take more than that to rattle *her.* Shame the hair was so stiff. "That *was* just friends, luv." He achieved the precise aggrieved hurt tone he was aiming for, pouted his bottom lip. Couldn't *possibly* compromise her ratings.

Her gaze assessed his measure. She gave him three slow claps. "*You* get the reputation you deserve." She shook her head and chuckled, took her seat.

He dropped into the guest chair, mugged for a front row bevy of college blondes in tight turtlenecks, let the moment stretch. Then he turned his attention to the host of *Night Talk.*

Good enough for ye? "Grandmother O'Connell says I never get a lick amiss."

BIANCA

Hollywood Hills, California; 8:45 P.M. PST

"YOU OKAY, BABE? YOU haven't said a word."

"Look, Michael, I'm going to get screwed again—can we not talk about it?" Bianca Doyle gazed out the side window of the limo, but her focus was not on the occasional streetlights nor the well-set mansions lining Alameda East up towards The Hills. She reviewed the meeting mercilessly. She *hadn't* done anything wrong.

True, Thomas Pentell had insisted on an early dinner at *Les Clés*, almost too early for this Dior—she lengthened her neck, lifted her chin—cleavage only worked if you showed it. Cleavage, and the cosmetics to make her black eyes, hair, and lashes prove her one of the most beautiful women in the world.

Pentell'd made her wait until they were finished. 'Sorry, my sweet.' He lit up one of his awful cigars, finally got it puffing foul smoke, his excuse for choosing the private club. 'The studio just won't go for it: you have no directing experience, the script is a patchwork, and you know after the last two…'

He knew perfectly well you did what you got—Hollywood was hell on women—if they sent you crap, you acted the crap out of it.

If the studio'd put *any* money behind distribution… Before that they couldn't get enough of me, *America's Sweetheart*, remember?

She probed the exchange seared into her memory: 'It's high concept, Tom. Francis is working on it—'

'People don't want to see a movie about a pervert. C'mon. Nude photos of children?'

'Even if he wrote *Alice in Wonderland*?'

'Biopics are dead. And, by the way, they hate the title.'

'*Dodgson*? It's a working title for God's sake, Tom.' Charles Lutwidge *Dodgson*? Lewis *Carroll*? *Hello*?

She *knew* Pentell wouldn't be meeting with her if he wasn't interested. 'But the *angle*, Tom. Did he tell stories to the Liddell girls to cover his affair with their governess, did he go after Miss Prickett to hide a thing for little girls, or—'

'Or was he just too innocent? Tell me something I *don't* know.'

She hadn't gotten through to Pentell until she played her hole card. If—

"C'mon, Bi," Michael interrupted her replay again. "He said 'yes.' Pentell is going to get the studio execs to let you direct."

Were you even there, Michael? "*If*, Michael. If. If I get O'Connell. If I get that dumb-ass Francis to get off his butt and finish the script. If I produce it for peanuts." She turned away in disgust.

"But you said you had O'Connell—"

For someone claiming to run a production company, Michael was as dumb as a rock. What had she ever seen in him? "What I *said* was that he was *interested* in the *part*. Which isn't the same as having signed on the dotted line." And if the damn Branford Studios hadn't dragged its heels, it would have been a done deal last year at the Academy Awards dinner, when she'd had five minutes to pitch Andrew O'Connell right when he was smarting from being gracious about *First at Lies* losing every award but cinematography. "Now, after *Roland*, he'll be completely out of reach."

"But *Roland* was released too late for consideration for this year's awards."

"Thank God for small favors!" Huge favors. What were its producers thinking when they couldn't manage to edit *Roland* in time for a limited release before New Year's? Idiots. By *next* year, no one would remember, not the Academy anyway.

"You'll have plenty of time to talk to O'Connell up in Maine next month."

"New Hampshire." Is it really that hard, Michael, to remember where my next movie is? *Men are fools. Damn fools. All of them.*

"Whatever—you can do it."

One chance—the boonies—closed set— She had a mountain of work ahead of her. O'Connell had been alone at the Academy ceremonies—no 'significant other'? *Be damned if he's not eating out of my hand by the time New Hampshire's a wrap.*

The limousine whispered on, usually the most calming of sounds, windshield wipers whisking away the beginnings of a light winter mist. She forced herself to relax into the soothing leather with its faint aroma of saddle soap, but they were already turning into their cul-de-sac.

Then everything went horribly wrong: the limo turned on its approach, and, through the rain-dribbled side window, her gaze locked onto her mansion, a floating wraith pale and insubstantial at the end of the drive. She gripped the armrest as warmth drained from her body. A ghost house. *Everything I've worked for is a dream.*

"Bianca? What is it?"

A switch somewhere activated. The long line of Mission California arches sprang to life. She blinked.

"Nothing." She shuddered, pulled the shawl closer. "Turn up the heat."

"But we're almost home—"

She glared at him. "And get that timer fixed. Immediately." She never again wanted the illusion of a dead set.

Michael shrugged, adjusted the heat. He checked the security system, clicked the remote in his pocket; the gate swung open. Thankfully, he kept his mouth shut.

The driver pulled up to the front steps, stopped. He came round to open the door. Michael stepped out, carefully scanning the area around the brilliantly-lit entrance before opening the umbrella and offering her his hand.

She quashed the tiny fear. Michael was good at this now. No fans here—though there had been a small crowd outside *Les Clés*, if not fans, then gawky tourists who would settle for any celebrity.

Leaving the club, Michael had known to allow just a few autographs—napkins, maps, even an actual autograph book—and a couple snapshots, before motioning the limousine forwards for her gracious escape. Fans didn't argue with Michael Hendricks; even in Armani something about his bearing screamed 'ex action star.' Here, home, safe—but she leaned lightly on his hand and made the effort graceful, gave him a peck on the cheek. "Thank you, Michael." Too bad there were no cameras.

She inhaled the heavy fragrance of massed night-blooming *huele-de-noche* flanking the entrance. *This is mine—my Tara—whatever it takes.*

"Bi? You're getting wet." Michael had dismissed car and driver; he waited, annoyance evident in the pointed way he held the umbrella.

She let him guide her up the steps to where, on cue, the door opened. She said '*Buenas noches*' to whichever uniformed maid had evening duty, handed the girl her wrap. "Don't be too long," she threw back over her shoulder as she strode away. She could hear Michael ordering ice for a nightcap. Which irritated her all over again. Must he drink every night? Her Papi had *his* every single night—and look where that landed him. *Men.* Would it be too much to hope that the damned Irishman O'Connell didn't drink?

For that was where the solution lay; she could visualize him and that sandy hair so clearly in the scenes Francis had finished. Lewis Carroll: the Reverend Charles Lutwidge Dodgson, writer, cleric— *and what else?*

ANDREW

Night Talk, **New York City**

"…THEN YOU PLAYED A gay prep-school math teacher accused of propositioning a student. *First at Lies* for director Don Neilsson." Dana recrossed her leg. "Bit of a stretch for you?" The proffered thigh was tan, firm.

"Aye, that 'twas." Andrew gnawed at a fingernail, waited for the chuckles to subside.

"Because you're straight?" She leaned in close, her manner inviting confidences.

The audience rustled forward in their seats.

"No." He knew what she wanted. *Ham.* "Because I'm god-awful at maths."

Open laughter.

She straightened, serious now. "*I* thought you deserved the Oscar."

"It was a great role, and an incredible honor to be nominated." The loser's obligatory reply. *Can we not go down that path, luv?*

"*Speaking* of great roles…" Dana grinned.

"Aye…?" He couldn't help himself—his smile widened of its own volition.

A swell of cheering.

Dana held off for the sound to die down, spoke to the TV viewers at home. "If you haven't been to the movies recently—you have a very special treat in store." She shifted her gaze back to him. "*Roland* has been out…?"

"Four weeks." Four unreal, heart-stopping weeks in which he hadn't slept twice in the same bed.

"Rumor is you almost didn't take the role. What changed your mind?"

"The period ones—when they're bad…" He shrugged. "Norm— our director Norm Endleson—he swore he wouldn't let them cut corners."

Dana faced the center camera which obediently went to closeup. "For the two people in the universe who don't know the plot— one's a guy who thinks it's a chick flick, the other's a girl who hates blood-and-guts macho movies—*Roland* is based on the French epic poem *The Song of Roland*."

"It's a *chanson de geste*." The dialect of Bagnéres-de-Bigorre brought a sharp pang of loss to his tongue.

"Hey, pretty good French for an Irishman."

"If ye tongue can twist about the Gaelic, *French* is a snap."

"Twisting tongue, eh…?" Her tone carried a full load of innuendo. She rocked her body suggestively, Groucho Marx'd her eyebrows.

Laughter rippled through the studio.

Dana waved in the general direction of her audience. "We did it in high school—the poem's *unbelievably* boring,"

"Ah—it's a bit stylized—"

"*Bor—ing.*"

Have it yer way, woman. He sipped his coffee, set the mug back down. "There were no *talk* shows back then."

Appreciative chuckles.

Dana conceded that one, settled in. "Eleventh century, right?"

"Well, the *chanson* is, but Roland's campaign was before Charlemagne's coronation as Holy Roman Emperor at Christmas 800 A. D."

"So the actual legend had centuries to develop." She nodded, gestured with an open hand for him to continue. "Roland's a French knight—"

"—sent to accept the Moors' surrender at Zaragoza in Spain."

"A cocky bastard." Dana's glance was pointed.

Titters.

He accepted the compliment with a shrug. "Aye. But loyal. He's betrayed and ambushed escorting the Moors' tribute through the Pyrenees—"

"The critics complain it's gory."

"Some of the blood's mine." That odd moment when ye *know* ye've been cut…

"Didn't someone get the sack for slashing your arm open?"

"Well, now, there's how the rumors get started. Josh—that's our weapons trainer—was working me, the ground was a wee bit mucky and I slipped, and, well, me arm and his sword decided to occupy the same piece of space."

"He was fired?"

Andrew shook his head. "The papers, they made it out so. *I* think the lad was feeling bad enough about it: he chewed me out royally while they sewed me up like a quilt. Are ye wanting to see the scar?"

Dana leered. "Too bad it's only your arm."

"I've better scars—" He jumped up, setting the coffee mug awobble. He reached one hand for the bottom edge of his sweater, the other for the waistband of his jeans.

Dana shot out a warding hand. "Decent?"

"Ah. No." He plopped back into the chair.

The crowd sniggered.

Dana rolled her eyes. "What was it like, working with Richard D'Anzio as Charlemagne and Peter Hyland as the Saracen chief?"

"I followed around after them like a puppy, ye know? It was heady breathing the same air."

"The testosterone must have been thick."

"Clouds of it. Peter's sixty but ye must be watching him every second or he's lopping yer head off *and* stealing the scene. No, really, they're so professional it raises the level of the whole shoot. They cut though the bull—" he caught himself, decided what the hell, "the bullshite that bedevils some projects."

"The film's texture's incredibly rich, down to the tiniest details."

"Norm had the castle ready when we got there. He's a perfectionist—don't think he slept for six months."

"The credits listed a gigantic crew."

"Thousands, not counting extras." *Everyone of them family.* "But I was the one having the most fun." Something cold surrounded his heart.

"*If* you call months of sword fighting, hard riding, and hand-to-hand combat, fun. And that's *before* the shooting started. Endleson put you through hell, didn't he?" Dana's tone was envy, regret, longing. "Living in a castle, using a privy in *winter*…?"

How did she, of all the interviewers, know? *It doesn't exist any more, the tent city gone, the stables empty once more.* He dragged himself back. He sensed the absence of sound that meant an audience in rapt attention. "It's—" he cleared his throat, "it's about keeping the anachronisms from creeping in. Ye'd be thinking the feudal lords had it good—but those castles are *cold*. Still find meself adjusting me codpiece—" He started to reach, made eye contact with the middle of the third row. "Ah. Can't be doing that on national telly, can we now?"

Laughter.

Dana interlaced her fingers around her knee, smiled. "It's the role of a lifetime, isn't it?"

"Have pity on me—I'm but five-and-thirty."

"You know what I mean."

He leaned forward and for one brief shining moment felt against his skin coarse wool; under his palm cool chainmail, sweaty leather; beneath him the great black stallion. His hand clutched ghost reins. "I would have traded in me children after me for it."

Thick silence—as if they were separated from the expectant rows by solid glass.

A camera zoomed in shattering the spell. Dana's head went up as she seemed to catch a signal. "More later, but you brought us a clip, didn't you?"

Catcalls and whistles.

The clip screen whirred up.

Andrew blinked eyes suddenly gritty. *Careful, boyo, ye're getting tired. Ye let her in much too close.* He checked the screen. "Roland's off to Spain, pledging to bring Aude's brother Oliver back in one piece."

> Foot soldiers. Archers. King. Knights, horses, squires. Martial score. The camera went long, dwelling on the army filling the castle courtyard...
>
> ...Oliver standing in his stirrups, impatient...
>
> ...Aude's face full of foreboding...
>
> ...Roland mounting, slipping her token into the neck of his tunic.
>
> Long shot pull back: the traitor Ganelon watching from a tower window as the army streamed out of the courtyard.
>
> Music swelling...

The clip ended, the screen sank behind them.

Applause rose, subsided.

Dana's gaze was on him again. "His lady, Aude, avenges him—in a love story without Roland being alone with her once."

He picked up the coffee cup to give his hands something to control. "They managed."

"Aude is played by the astonishingly medieval Allison Ryers."

"Aye." Fierce Aude in the snowy garden, her duenna discreet by the ice-covered fountain. *Ye'll never see her again.* His breath came rough. He heard Peter Hyland's dry steady voice in his mind: *'Get a grip, man.'* "Norm extracted her bodily from a tapestry at the Louvre." The Pyrenees faded into shadows. He raised the cup to his lips.

"Did you have an affair with your co-star?"

Andrew choked on his coffee. *Come again?* "Ah...?"

"The tabloids said—"

"She's married, for Christ's sake!"

"You've been joined in print to every actress you've shared a screen with."

"It sells papers." He made his inflection flat, let his gaze caress from breast to thigh to high-heels and slowly back to her delighted face. "I like beautiful women. Sometimes they like me."

From the far side of the stage where his band lounged, George squawked the bass.

Laughter and applause.

"Any plans to take one home?"

He widened his eyes, dropped his jaw. "Ye offerin'?" He knew the camera focus was so short the folks at home could count pores, gave it full value: he narrowed his eyes, paused long, tilted his head, raised his lashes, let the corner of his mouth curl. "This Brian of yers—he any good with a sword?"

KARY

"MS. WINTER, IT'S TIME."

Karenna Ashe couldn't trust her voice. She nodded, obediently got to her feet. She clutched *Yorktown Harbor* for a shield. Was this how Marie Antoinette felt when the jailer came for her? *I can't do this. God, I'm so tired.*

Something slowed the nerve impulses to her legs; she followed Melly by remote control until Melly stopped before a chair in the wings. Kary caught her first sight of the packed auditorium. This was how the crowd waited for the queen's head. *Millions of people will watch this. Live.*

The single canvas-backed chair stood in a little circle of parquet. Rushing air overcooled her skin, muffled the sound from the audience, the speakers. A dead spot. *Intentional?*

Out on stage, the host of *Night Talk* bantered with the actor, who lounged with his arm over the back of the chair as relaxed and confident as a Serengeti lion. She wondered what his movie was about. Obviously successful. Or was it an act? *I can't follow that—I'll be as stiff as a stick.*

The follicles on Kary's forearms contracted, making each little hair stand straight up. She dissociated, monitoring, from a place outside herself, her more gruesome physiological reactions to panic.

She contemplated the third response possibility: not fight or flight—invisibility. *Authors are people whose prose flows like warmed honey, not impostors like me who struggle with every word.*

Melly looked concerned. "Do you want me to stay?"

Kary heard herself say, "No. Thanks." She knew her smile stank. And that the producer couldn't afford to take notice. *I'll come across as an idiot.*

"Back in a sec then."

Kary saw, rather than heard, the audience laughing—something the actor said?

What would happen if I walked away, grabbed my coat, took the elevator down, hailed a taxi? *Nothing.* They'd manage: Dana would keep the actor talking—the audience'd like that, he already had them eating out of his hand. Elise would spin it, probably get better publicity. *No one will know what I look like, no one will ask me again to do the impossible.*

Impossible? *You are incredibly self-indulgent.* And what's worse, you're a coward. Exhaustion hasn't kept you secluded; fear has. Ordinary— common— Fear.

Her knees turned to quicksand; she was grateful for the chair.

The fear-beast crouched at her feet, clinging monkey-child, its claws embedded in her flesh. She stroked its head. Face the fear, reassure it. Dance with the fear. Surely Dana has plenty of tricks for inarticulate guests—I can't be the first. You should never meet the author, anyway: it ruins the book.

She bowed her head, closed her eyes. The eight-hundred-page brick weighed her solidly in place.

Fear is for children.

∽ CHAPTER TWO ∾
Daughter of Jairus

"Are you ready?" Jake spoke quietly from the covered wagon's seat.

I will never be ready. Meggie surveyed the wasted, wretched landscape, turning slowly to burn this place into her memory: to the east, interminably flat, ochre grasses hid the wheels, floating the wagons on an endless swell-less sea; southward, a faint band of green marked the borders of the Platte; north and west rose mountains so dark and tall crossing them must be impossible; and behind her, sentinels, the gnarly scrub oak and the great rock shaded the darker rectangle where her heart was buried.

She climbed the schooner's step.

Jake twitched reins in hand. "Giddyap."

She would not need to look again.

K. Beth Winter, Prairie Fires, Ch. 18.

...in other 'news' Irish actor ANDREW O'CONNELL has joined the ranks of actors who think they can sing, who dump personal money on vanity tours. His voice scarred by smoke, he fronts an Irish pub band, the *DEADLY NIGHTSHADES*, who should hang on to their day jobs. Not ready for big time.

www.musicpetes, Archives, 2004

ANDREW
Night Talk, NYC; February 25; 11:30 P.M. (cont.)

"IF ALL THE CRITICS SAY I'm entirely the wrong fellow for it." Andrew shrugged as he answered Dana's question, 'What makes you sign on to a project?' *That was easy enough.*

"Afraid of getting typecast?"

"Deathly."

"You're filming in America next." Dana hunkered down, elbows propped on the arms of her chair, hands clasped attentively in her lap. "*Incident at Bunker Hill* for director Grant Sykes. You're the villain."

"They told me I'd be playing the hero!" *Beat.* "A loyal Englishman!"

Laughter and whistling from the upper decks.

"Irish, eh?" He pretended to be surprised. "Ye can burn me in effigy later—may be I'm not very good at it."

Appreciative chuckles.

"Who else is starring?"

"John Robbins." He paused for the clapping and catcalls. Popular lad, Johnnie. "And Peter." It would be good to be around Peter again. "Lots of horses."

"Aren't you forgetting someone?"

"Eh?"

"The beautiful Miss Bianca Doyle?" Dana cocked her head, smirked. "You were seen deep in conversation with her at last year's Academy Award ceremonies..."

"We were *talking* about a *role*." Not the right time for that one yet. "Ye'd be thinking they'd let me have me fun first. I've met her *once*." *Vultures.* The verbal fencing was trickier than that with a sword—at least ye knew then who ye were trying to kill. "Even I need more time than that."

She leaned in closer. "You'll get a chance for a lot more *talking* soon."

Ah. It's a scoop ye'll be wanting. He'd been a minnow last time. Now she honored him as top prey. All in good fun, of course— Dana would not antagonize guests. Why had he thought women were easier? She was displaying signs of the shark: sharp teeth— embedded in his flesh, quick darting in and out—with a chunk of that flesh as her prize. He let the pause lengthen—dead air was *her* problem.

A derisive squawk from George's bass.

Dana cast a glance in the band's direction, chuckled in concession. "You'll let us know?"

"The minute there's a contract to put ink on." *And the bloody thing is public.*

"We'll be waiting for it anxiously." Dana acknowledged the swell of applause. "Now, tell us about your band, the *Deadly Night-shades.*"

Hooting from the crowd.

"They're all very shy fellows."

Laughter.

"You've been playing together a long time."

"Since we were barely out of nappies." *And never enough time any more.*

"You'd just finished your first US tour when *Roland* hit."

"Aye."

"You realize future tickets'll be bought by women who want to see Roland in the flesh, who've never heard you sing and who don't give a damn if you can?"

Roland changed everything. *Not even the band was safe.* "If they like what they're hearing—the big *if*—they'll be coming back. We're getting ready to cut another CD. We managed to move more than fifty of the first one; that encouraged the lads."

Scattered applause; a few people waved CD cases.

Dana caught a cue from the producer on the sidelines. "And you'll all have to wait, folks—time for a word from our sponsors. When we come back, novelist K. Beth Winter!"

The camera rolled back, the monitor switched to commercial.

Dana stretched her neck, cracked her vertebrae. "It always gets me, the tension." The shark smiled at him unapologetically. "Four minutes. Need anything?"

"Nope." *Damn American smoking laws.* He deposited his mug on the table, shifted gratefully in a chair that had become a prison. He was the momentary eye in a hurricane of frenetic activity. Privacy—versus the publicity clauses in his contract. It left a metallic taste, as if he'd had a gun in his mouth. Since *Roland*—offers to be sifted and winnowed. Bianca Doyle directing *Dodgson* was but a faint possibility. She was one of many in the Hollywood firmament: competent at women's emotions, sleek, taut-bodied, sexually free, available—interchangeable.

In the wings, the woman from the greenroom sat bowed over a book.

Stage fright? Prayer? What was *she* hiding?

~ ~ ~

ANDREW SCOOTED HIMSELF out of the hot seat to the adjacent chair. He scanned the audience, gave three blondes using their CD cases as mirrors to attract his attention a wave and nod. In a previous life he could've talked to them, made a date; now he'd be lucky if they kept their shirts on. It complicated things. A staffer replaced his mug with a steaming one; the countdown reprised. Behind them, Dana's mobile face in closeup filled the audience's giant TV monitors. *Me turn to observe.*

"We're back! Still to come, Andrew O'Connell and his band—the *Deadly Nightshades*," Dana said. "But now, my other guest this evening is a woman who's not used to the limelight, not because she doesn't deserve it, but because, as I hope she'll tell us, she can't take much of it. Four years ago her first book, *Prairie Fires*, rocketed to the top of the best-seller lists like a bomb out of the blue; when it was followed by *Thunder at Creek Station*, the world discovered a major new talent—a writing voice of liquid gold. Tonight we're honored to present her first interview ever.

"So without further introduction," Dana stood to lead the clapping, angled her head, "here to tell us about her new novel, *Yorktown Harbor*, is K. Beth Winter!"

He rose, clapped along with the crowd, focused on the author. She came out of the blocks well, with a determined stride, and the grace which bespoke little-girl ballet lessons. A long clean line. Clothes—minimalist, expensive, barely adorned with flat gold earstuds. She seemed surprised by the applause, but smiled and waved her free hand before accepting a cheek brush from Dana.

For a moment he had her full attention. She was unexpectedly tall, only an inch or two shorter in low-heeled gray boots than his six feet-two. Steady gray-green eyes under straight pale eyebrows held his gaze in assessment. She inclined her head, offered her hand. "It's a pleasure to meet you, Mr. O'Connell."

He took the slim hand in both of his, raised it to his lips: cool, short nails, no polish, no rings. A writer's hand. "The pleasure is all mine."

Something felt odd. What?

She broke contact first. Dana gestured at the chairs. The author sat, folded her long legs sideways toward him, politely faced their host. He settled in for a listen.

The monitor image bracketed the two women. Then, as the applause continued unabated, the cameras switched, giving him a chance to examine her in closeup. She had a fine skull—she would still be beautiful when she was ninety. Older than he. Forties? A faint blush colored her winter-pale skin. So, embarrassed by the attention. Why? George had discovered the name was a pseudonym, located not even the customary writer's vanity photo on a dust jacket.

A puzzle. None of the markers of the sophisticate. He'd bet a lot of money the short hair was neither dyed nor lacquered. Lip gloss, mascara on what were probably, from her coloring, very pale lashes... Why did he always have to be so curious? He'd never see her again. The usual answer was 'grist for the mill,' that it all connected somewhere in the recesses of his terminally nosy brain.

A grownup? Someday he might want to be like her—but certainly not now.

Everything perfect in her life.

KARY

SHE COULDN'T HAVE moved if she'd wanted to, but the guest armchair enclosed and supported her like a full-body cast. Her gaze swept over the audience which wouldn't stop clapping. Many of them stood. That people had liked her stories was evident from Elise's sales reports, unreal numbers she had swallowed with a grain of salt knowing returns from bookstores hadn't yet been factored in. She had let Elise's staff handle any fan mail. The advances she discounted: publishers must have needed someone to fill a niche. But these were real people, and the roar was enthusiastic, not polite.

To her right, the actor clapped along with the crowd. She retained an impression of muscled bulk in jeans and hand-knit fisherman's sweater, sandy lion's mane, eyes of intense blue. Dana was no help; if anything, she seemed to be encouraging the unmerited response.

You might as well enjoy it: the damage was done the instant a TV camera broadcast your image. She hoped Charles wasn't watching. She gripped right wrist with left hand over the hardcover in her lap, and awaited the Inquisition.

Dana grinned. "This is a coup for us, Ms. Winter." She reached for a hardcover edition of *Prairie Fires* on the end table, held it up. "I took it on vacation with me and stayed up half the night to finish."

Kary glanced at the TV monitor; the cover filled the screen. "Please. Call me Kary." *Another nail in my coffin? As if it matters.* Her throat needed clearing. Stupid nerves. "Sorry for the missed sleep."

"I don't even like historical fiction!" Dana shook her head as if amused at herself. "What made you choose to write about the wagon trains—and the women who settled the West?"

"My public library." *This I can do.* With an effort, she ignored lights, cameras, audience. She focused on their host: the younger woman would guide her through. "I chanced on a book called *Women's Diaries of the Westward Journey*, by Lillian Schlissel. These pioneer women crossing the country in covered wagons put more in their journals than they realized."

"How so? Didn't they record what happened?"

"It's more complicated than that. They'd make entries such as 'stopped for one day', 'caught up with the train later.'"

"But not why?"

Perceptive. "No. From these fragments Lillian deduced the women were birthing babies, dying in childbirth, and losing children and husbands to disease, snake-bite, drowning—the obstacles imposed by the imperative to get across the prairies before winter hit."

"If I lost a child I'd be damn sure to record it," Dana said.

"On paper?" *As if you could forget.* "It was too painful. Lillian's description of little crosses by the roadside makes you weep." *So many didn't survive.* Her shoulders rose, dropped. "And they couldn't indulge weakness. Not then, not when they got to the new lands."

"The rest?" Dana's thumb and forefinger held far apart measured a fat book.

"Journals, letters, government archives—lots of people helped." Kary shrugged again. *Nobody wants to hear about research.* "I've tried to acknowledge all of them in the credits."

"Critics complained you pandered to mass markets by giving these women sex lives."

"Most were young and healthy." With her free hand, Kary reached for the mug beside her. She sipped, had a flash of gratitude for whoever had filled it with iced water. *Steady now.* She met and held Dana's gaze. "They *had* sex lives."

Chuckles from the audience.

"Margaret Mitchell based Scarlett O'Hara on her grandmother. Did you have any real-life models for Meggie and Jake?"

Insightful of Dana. "My father's sister told me tales of growing up on a farm in the Midwest. I tried to imagine what distinguished the hardy souls who survived from those who didn't make it—and from the ones who remained behind. Besides luck, of course."

"A kind of loving ruthlessness?"

Kary nodded.

"You struck a chord—it became one of the most-read books in America." Dana exhibited the second hardcover book for the viewers. "Then came *Thunder at Creek Station.* Another bestseller." Dana angled her head. "An Alabama town during the Civil War—a bit of overlap with *Gone with the Wind?*"

"From a less romantic perspective on the war." *Nitpicking, maybe, but important.* "Some people want to understand what *Mammy's* life was like."

Dana's eyebrows arched. "Caring for a series of spoiled brats." Her manner closed the topic.

Appreciative chuckles.

"And this is...?" Dana gestured at the thick book in Kary's lap.

Host's prerogative: keep it moving. Kary presented the product.

Dana held up the new volume like a Lectionary, arrayed for her congregation. The only thing missing was a prayer. "*Yorktown Harbor.* It'll be in stores...?"

"Tomorrow." She knew it would sound self-serving, being on a talk show immediately before the book's release. If she'd postponed again it could have been safely out. *All accidental.* But it would please her publishers no end, and they'd been obliged to have so much patience.

More thunderous applause.

Dana intoned, from the back cover, "'A virtual time machine to the last major battle of the Revolutionary War—which might have gone either way.'"

"Professor Elyonnes exaggerates." But his letter had warmed her heart.

"Would you...?" Dana returned the book reverently.

The neck of Kary's sweater was too warm. The request gave her an excuse to break eye contact. She managed not to drop the pen tendered, opened the tome, and inscribed it 'To Dana. *Memorare.* Kary.'

Dana placed the book next to the others; the TV monitor briefly displayed the three volumes side by side. She leaned forward, clasped her hands in front of her heart. "It takes you a very long time to write these stories, doesn't it? And there is a very special understanding in their pages of pain, exhaustion, and sacrifice." Her voice was low, full of solicitude. "Would you tell our viewers why?"

The time has come to do some good—or look like an idiot. Kary took a deep breath, banished extraneous thoughts. "The people I write about have active, impassioned lives. They work hard, push through adversity, achieve great things. I honor their lives by writing about them, since I can no longer *be* them. My life is exactly the opposite: to get anything done at all, I parcel out my energy and time like a miser, curtail all other expenditures except for writing.

"I have the mysterious illness known variously as CFS—Chronic Fatigue Syndrome, ME—myalgic encephalomyelitis, chronic mono." She paused. "Or, humorously, Yuppie flu." *There. Might as well be naked.* Dana's 'Ms. Winter' was well-meaning but utterly futile. Name, face, profession—and now disease—for fifty million viewers. One of them would connect the dots. *It is done.*

"But there's nothing funny about it," Dana said.

"Nope. Not much." *I chose to come. No one forced me.* But— 'We need people to see what it's really like'—from her support group. And they were right. *Why me?* Because you've found a way to make an impact in spite of... *So be it.*

"It causes you pain, and extreme fatigue, and brain fog, and—"

Let's keep it light, okay? "I particularly mind the 'dog collar' effect." She grabbed her throat, stuck out her tongue, mimed choking.

Dana's head jerked back. "The what?"

"The neck's lymph glands—they swell up, make it hard to keep my head level—like a tight dog collar." *Enough gruesome details?* "It's one of my warnings—it means 'go to bed this instant, you've pushed yourself past another damn limit.'"

Titters from the audience, a snort from the actor.

She'd forgotten they were there.

"I'm curious." Dana leaned in further, lowered her clasped hands to her lap. "Why, given all that it costs you, are you willing to spend your allotment of energy on *writing?*"

The crux. "Because I can. Because even if I can only work in one-page increments, there is something of me left." *I won't say, 'What else can I do?'* She heard 'victim' in her earnest tone, lightened it. "And sometimes I have good days!"

"But it's hard."

Why is Dana pushing? It's bad enough having to live it. "Flannery O'Connor didn't stop writing because of pain. Frieda Kahlo didn't stop painting." *Wait—that implies I think I'm in their category.* "They are my role models; I aspire to what they achieved." Somehow that was worse. *Try again.* "You just can't let these things take what's left of you."

"Or they win?" Dana's voice was quiet and reasonable.

Kary let the accumulated tension out with a whoosh of stale air. Dana understood. "Or they win." She glanced toward the audience, smiled. "Can't have that."

A smattering of applause.

"How do you stay so cheerful?" Dana probed, her needle of a voice looking for the vein and the rush of blood.

"I find little ways." *I can't volunteer at the soup kitchen.* Or build houses for the homeless. Or even promise to be there every Wednesday at the same time to read to the third graders. *I can't deal with people.* What Dana did so effortlessly would wipe Kary out. She raised her shoulders, feeling the stretch. "I can't afford the energy to get angry about it." *Or the aftereffects of adrenaline.* "I cheat. A lot."

"You cheat?"

The last thing I want is intelligent sympathy. Or pity. "I don't mow the lawn, or clean house, or anything useful like that. And I don't do many interviews."

Laughter.

"And you are getting better."

"I wish I could say that."

"But you've finished three novels, and you're here." Dana spoke with fierce conviction. "You're better."

Kary was taken aback. *What does she want?* "Some people have improved, a few seem completely recovered; I've regained some control by napping several times a day..." She could not give false hope. "I'm sorry—that's all most of us manage." *Dana doesn't understand.*

Dana hid her face with her palms; then she shook herself, steepled her fingers under her chin. "I apologize. When I heard of all you've done, I wanted..." She gestured with her hands out, fingers spread wide. She faced the audience, spoke directly into the camera. "Those of you who are regulars know I rarely talk about myself. I'm more of a 'what you see is what you get' kind of gal. But tonight I *had* to have Kary—Ms. Winter—on, for a very personal reason." She turned to Kary, eyes bright. "My baby sister's one of your biggest fans. She's had CFS for five years."

Kary let her eyes close for a moment. It all made sense now. *I'm so worried about myself, I forgot why I came. Selfish, selfish.* "I'm so sorry to hear that." *The poor child!*

"Chrissy watches me every night." Dana blinked fast, visibly pulled herself together. "We're all looking for a cure." Her gaze shifted to the TelePrompTer. "Oops! Time for our break."

The audience began to clap.

"And when we come back, hold on to your hats, because Andrew O'Connell and his band, the *Deadly Nightshades*, will be singing their hearts out for you!"

Applause rose, fell.

On the silent monitor a woman in the first commercial mouthed about her deodorant. Kary was drained down to the base of her spine, to the aching muscles in her thighs. She shoved the nascent headache to the edge of her skull.

I used to be a physician. But what can I do for Chrissy? Not one damned thing.

~ ~ ~

FROM CENTER OF attention, Kary transitioned to 'stage prop.'

The makeup girl scurried in to blot her forehead, administer a benediction in the form of a layer of powder. The actor walked off with the producer, gesticulating as he talked. Dana's input was required elsewhere...

Kary closed her eyes, sank deeply into the chair. Trying to block external stimuli and her own disorganized thoughts, she drew air into her lungs and imagined pulling it all the way down to her soles.

A crisp, "Two minutes, please!" broke through the background. She opened her eyes to a worried Dana.

"You okay?" Dana asked. "Chrissy'll kill me if you have a relapse."

"Don't worry." Way too late now. The fear-beast purred at her feet. The new world looked exactly like the old one. *Of course it does.* "Even if I do, thanks for the national exposure."

"Andrew'll take the next ten minutes," Dana said. "After him and the last break, a ten minute wrap—but if you're not up to it..."

"I've come this far." *If I don't try to move, no one will know that I can't.* She fought the paralysis and the sense of doom. *Snap out of it, for heaven's sake!* "Besides, now I'm curious."

"You and every woman in America." Dana seemed relieved, turned to answer a crewman's question.

TV hype? Kary knew nothing about Andrew O'Connell. Why hadn't she watched Dana interview him? *You have to stop being so self-centered.*

In the lull, the television monitor displayed an image of Andrew half-perched on a high black stool, holding an acoustic guitar. He was in animated discussion with the producer, who gave a quick nod of assent and hurried off camera.

The monitor went to closeup. He seemed perfectly at home on screen. The shaggy hair was a good cut, overgrown. His gaze roved: band to audience to Dana. Kary's breath caught: he'd inherited darker brows and 'smutty-finger' lashes surrounding the Irish blue, but camera and lighting emphasized them beyond all fairness. *What a treasure for an actor.*

"Five, four, three…"

As the cameras went live, the man on the screen faced the camera head-on, his fingers picking the strings in quiet rhythm. His ring flashed red as the stone caught the light. "I like to tell people a wee story about how I came to write me songs." The tip of his tongue wet his lips. "This one is a little thing I wrote, don't know who for yet, but she's out there somewhere, and I'm hoping she's listening tonight." He smiled, a lost look came over his face, his eyes gazed far off into the distance. "It's called 'The mother of my child'…"

Kary startled. *From a rock band?*

The crowd cheered; catcalls and whistles; an expectant hush.

The music pickup brought out the haunting melody; the pit of her stomach went queasy. His voice, backed by the bass, was rough, the band's music full of unexpected Celtic harmonics.

> *"He throws a ball,*
> *she's always there to catch…"*

Did he have any idea what they'd cost him, wife, child? His vision was unattainable illusion.

> *"…She'll take my soul,*
> *she'll give it back to me.*
> *The mother of my child."*

He kept his gaze lowered, repeated the refrain twice with the band soft behind him.

Kary's heart syncopated. *Why should I care?*

It's just a song.

It's his *job* to tug heartstrings. *It's just a song.*

✒ CHAPTER THREE ✑
"... if he shall gain the whole world ... "
(Mark 8:36, KJV)

...from the French/Spanish border where Norman Endleson is filming ROLAND due out by Christmas: he should have heeded warnings about headstrong ANDREW O'CONNELL, whose demands brought production to a near standstill more than once. O'Connell's clumsiness with a sword nearly cost an extra's life, and he seems equally adept at slicing himself up...
www.insidefilms, Archives, 2004

...rumors of ROLAND post-production holdups delaying the release till after New Year's, dashing hopes of Academy noms for the monstrously expensive epic...
www.insidefilms, Archives, 2004

BIANCA
Hollywood Hills, CA; February 25; 9 P.M. PST

BIANCA DRAGGED THE star sapphires from her earlobes as she strode towards her dressing suite with the uniformed maid in tow. Papi's dancing-ballerina jewelry box should have given her a lift, but instead it added to her sense of impotence. She stowed the earrings, slamming the lid and sending the dancer's legs jittering.

The maid held out a sleek nightgown sheath in ice-blue satin like a tributary offering. She departed with an armload of lingerie, her skinny peasant braids knitted together with red yarn making a 'U' across her back.

Calm down—they're all bastards. The gilt-and-marble bathroom designed for silent film idol Noira Matthews reminded her of who *she* was. She reached for her electric toothbrush, polished each tooth with care. It left behind a trace of too-sweet wintergreen. *Great—dessert.*

She sat herself erect in front of the lit mirror. One by one she dug out the long hairpins, dropped them on the dressing table. Thick hair pooled about her shoulders. *Time to work.* She ran her fingers through it, massaged her scalp. She reached for the brush. Gently, then harder, she pulled it through, long luxurious strokes. She shook her head, admired the silk-curtain sway; reluctantly, she braided the glossy hank loosely for the night. Jean-Pierre constantly proclaimed, '*Always* to bed beautiful.' *Whatever it costs—I'm worth it.*

She fondled her skin, inspecting up close the smooth brow, the delicate skin under eyes so dark brown they were black; she could hear Jean-Pierre's voice: 'You make the crease so many times, then the skin it marks—save for the camera.' She feathered in the final eye cream. And again, 'Softly, chérie. No *frottage.*' She inclined her head and lengthened her neck, switching the lights to the harsh 'Daylight' setting. That was *not* a tiny wrinkle.

Tonight the ritual scared her: she would be thirty in a year.

Fact: she could do, in front of the camera, anything a director wanted.

Fact: Grant Sykes chose *her* for *Incident at Bunker Hill.*

One last look in the full-length mirrors. *They are* not *replacing me with sixteen-year-old starlets.*

Michael was already propped up in bed, in silk PJ boxers which exposed the tanned abs he was so proud of. He stretched a palm out like an invitation on a silver platter. She ignored him, piled pillows on her side. *Lousy timing. As usual.* She scooped up the stack of papers from her nightstand, tucked another pillow behind her lower back. More nitwit romantic comedies. She discarded each grommeted script after a few pages. "Crap!"

"Who's your fallback?"

"What are you talking about?"

"If you can't get O'Connell? Face it, babe, even if you seduce him in New Hampshire, you gotta have a backup—"

"I don't know, Michael. I wanted him for *Dodgson* the minute I saw *Sun over Water. Before* the Irish 'Best Actor.' If the damn studio—" Despair licked at her heart. *So many of Them!*

Michael yawned widely enough for her to hear his jaw pop. "You had no script. And they couldn't be sure he'd break out."

And I'm not bankable any more? *'Easy, princess.' Papi's voice. 'Pick your* own *time.'* She clamped her teeth on the edges of her tongue, exhaled. She made it a joke: "Whose side are you on any-way?"

"Just don't want you hurt, babe. Don't get a rep for being diffi-cult, not in this climate."

And be like you? Without enough ambition or talent to move to the A-list? With a laughingstock of a 'production company'—the kept man's out? She suppressed the barb from her voice with diffi-culty. "They respond to *power*, Michael. Nothing else."

Michael patted the bed by his thigh, idly flicked the plasma-screen TV on. "C'mere." He thumbed the remote, channel-surfing. "Speak of the devil—"

Andrew was in her bedroom on a tall black stool. Life-size. He plucked the guitar, spoke to her without sound.

Glance at the *Night Talk* logo bottom right, then the clock. *Damn!* She'd missed half the show. She pinched Michael. "Un-mute."

"What was that for?"

Andrew looked so young, alone in the world. He began to sing soundlessly.

She wrested the TV remote from Michael, turned the volume high. She caught the last line of a verse. Andrew O'Connell gazed straight at her, blue eyes wide and innocent, and sang the refrain in a lilting Irish accent, '...*The mother of my child.*'

Her back arched as an icy hand grabbed the root of her spine, deep in her pelvis.

"Hey, not so loud." Michael gave her a proprietary pat, reached towards the remote.

With an effort, she controlled the urge to claw him, lowered the volume the tiniest smidgen, leaned closer. She crouched there as Andrew sang to her all his hopes and yearnings for the woman who would fill his life, bear his child. Her hand crept up to cover her mouth. He repeated the refrain twice, so raw and vulnerable her throat ached for him.

The camera went for an extreme close-up as Andrew broke eye contact, turned introspectively to his guitar. Sandy hair flopped down over one eye, curled over the neck of his sweater.

What a dynasty we'd make.

On screen, Andrew leapt up suddenly, his face alive and mischie-vous, and flung the stool off camera. He launched his band into something livelier. Bianca muted, sank into the pillows watching his body move, until the song ended and 'A message from our sponsors' hijacked the screen. She hated commercials.

Michael stirred, his gaze still on his reading, reaching for her to use the time to get started.

She propelled herself off the bed, escaped to the bathroom, secured the door.

She slid out of the negligee. Her body posed itself for her approval in the triple mirror, posture and attitude honed by coaching and practice, her right leg bent just so.

Her instrument. Taut and muscled, just the right hint of firmness under a thin softening layer: in repose, female. She worked hard for the perfect effect. She'd seen women body builders in person, once, and they disgusted her: unnatural women's heads on men's bodies, their breasts either empty from total absence of body fat—or fake.

She cradled her breasts like her best custom underwire bra. The nipples stiffened obediently, tightening the skin. Perfectly formed, perfectly proportioned B cups, heavy. The gift that convinced her God meant her to be on a pedestal. She remembered the terror of that pregnancy, when they swelled and all she could think of was sag, the relief when Nate was four weeks premature and she could get that idiot doctor to suppress the horrible dripping milk.

Andrew would know to support them, gentle them, never press them out of shape. She rested her palms on the marble countertop and locked gazes with her mirror-image. *He needs me. Endleson's a fluke, but I know everybody. And with him by my side, no one will ever say No again.* Her twin smiled back in complete understanding and accord: fair trade. A month! She had a whole month with him in some one-horse town. If that wasn't Fate…

Sideways, she scrutinized her flank in the unforgiving center mirror. She imagined Andrew's hands encircling her waist, his hand under hers, skimming her flat belly, sliding downwards…

Oh, bleep! *Andrew.* She yanked the silky sheath over her head, hurried back to the bedroom.

Michael was reading, hadn't bothered to turn the sound on. Without looking up he said, "You're missing the show."

She nestled into her pillows, seized the remote, unmuted the TV to a close-up of an older woman. Hippie type—like Mother—no makeup. The woman was saying, "—with these *huge* backstories."

The camera cut to Dana Lewiston's response, and then to Andrew and his laugh that captured you and promised you'd have more fun with him than with anyone else in the world. He parried

Dana's movie questions masterfully in his honeyed Irish accent—so unlike Roland's.

Stupid audience lapped it up. Bianca tuned them out. When the credits rolled, she blanked the screen before the sponsors began selling to the masses.

Predictable Michael perked up. "What? He get you with that hokey line? 'Mother of my child'?" He turned on his side, walked his fingers down her torso, stroking like one of those spiders that has to coax the female into readiness. "You ready to turn that lovely body back into a baby-making machine?"

Bianca glanced at the frame on the nightstand with its ridiculous school-photo background of autumn leaves. *'Bird in hand, princess,' Papi said.* Thank God the house belonged to her alone, and an untouchable trust kept it that way forever. "We've had this discussion, Michael. I'd lose half my fans."

"The offer stands." He did his asinine evil chuckle, insinuated his hand between her legs, caressed her inner thigh from groin to knee.

She didn't push him away—he had his uses—but her mind flooded with images of a doomed IRA terrorist's rough tenderness before going out in a spray of bullets, a battle-worn knight triumphant a moment before the tide turned for all eternity.

She wasn't thinking of Michael Hendricks as they made love.

Why not *me?*

KARY

Night Talk, NYC; February 26; 12:15 A.M.

ALL ALONG THEIR INNER margin, Kary's arms ached. Breathing came shallow. How could he *possibly* know about watching Big Bird with your warm child enfolded in your lap?

"*...the mother of my child.*" Andrew's voice trailed off with the last note. On the giant monitor, he looked up, out, as if he expected to see his true love on the other side of the camera's window to the world. Longing battled desolation in his intelligent eyes. He blinked, woken from the dream; the camera focus zoomed out to show the band.

Kary shuddered, took her first deep breath in hours.

Applause shattered the audience's idolatrous hush. Security personnel edged closer.

He jumped up, a different person. "And that's all I'm saying about that!"

It has *to be an act.*

He tossed the stool to a stage-hand, traded the guitar for an electric one. Mike in hand, he challenged them, "Listen up—I'll be wanting every last one of ye on the chorus!"

The cheering continued.

He shook the guitar by its skinny neck. "This one's for all ye dancers!" The band fed him power, lightning to a rod, broke into a foot-stomping Irish country ballad that set the audience clapping, and more than one girl dancing crazily in the aisles.

Invisible tendrils uncoiled themselves from Kary's heart and vaporized as if cauterized. Her foot shared the beat. *This* she'd expect of a rock band.

After three frenzied verses he yelled, "I can't hear ye!" until the cheering fans encored the refrain, "Ye love 'em, ye leave 'em/Ye never get to keep 'em," to his full satisfaction—it took three tries.

Lays it on with a backhoe! This territory she could visit safely; she blocked out the other. *Good for him!* Shaking her head at the profligate expenditure of energy, she couldn't avoid grinning. Now, if she could only bottle the excess...

Andrew twanged a last discord, laughed out loud at the catcalls and whistling, signaled 'Cut!', waited for relative calm.

"Me true-blue session mates." His wide smile said he reveled in sharing the accolades.

"Casey Collins! We fought over the same girls in school. I won." Andrew smirked. "But *he* got the drums. Damn!" Casey skimmed his sticks over drums and cymbals.

"Sean O'Neill! That bass is mine—Lord knows whose bed he left *his* under. Plays mean Uilleann pipes." Sean beamed.

"Barry FitzGerald on keyboards and Ganley flute. He's new—I don't know anything bad about him—yet!"

"And last *and* worst, George Cosgrave! Half the songs are his fault." He shook his fist at the increase in the pandemonium. "Our first guitars were rubber bands stretched 'cross shoe boxes. We were lads of five." George riffed the bass, returned the fist salute.

King of the hill, Andrew's affection seemed genuine. *And why not?*

The monitor cut to commercial, Kary's gaze shifted to the man on the soundstage. A stagehand brought him a towel, retrieved it when he finished wiping his face and neck. What was the verse, Jeremiah 13:1? Would that cloth ever be laundered again?

Andrew regained the dais at 'Thirty seconds!' He cocked his eyebrows at Kary, plunked down into the center seat she'd vacated. He drained a bottle of Evian. Faint odor of damp wool, man-sweat.

'On air' lit.

Dana went for the jugular. "Kary, what's your biggest fear as a writer?"

Kary was caught off guard. *Me first?* She found a raspy version of her voice. "Appearing ridiculous. Farce instead of drama." Clearing her throat—*have to remove that annoying habit*—steadied her. "My first drafts read like soap operas."

"And you eliminate melodrama how?"

"When I'm successful, you mean?" Someone clapped; Kary glanced toward the audience, back to Dana. "By digging deeper into the characters, asking 'why' over and over. Characters are never as simple they first appear."

"Do all your characters come from you?"

"If *I* had grown up *them*." *Why didn't I pick an easier fear?* She was aware of Andrew's intent gaze. "I end up with these *huge* backstories."

Andrew chuckled in sympathy.

Dana, piranha-ready, swung toward the sound. "You're basically in the same business, right? Your reputation says you're almost obsessive about your preparation."

"Almost?"

Audience titters.

Dana gave him a sly look. "Tell us something *new* about *Roland*."

He drew in breath, released it in a whoosh. "All right, then." He paused in the far-off stare of one remembering. "Sometimes, when the scientists, they dig up old human bones," his voice was an intimate rumble, "they find calluses, where the muscles stressed the bones, strengthened them—"

"Like an archer—" Kary froze, as in one well-oiled movement Andrew's head swiveled until his vivid blue eyes were focused quizzically on hers. She hadn't intended to voice the thought.

"Like a blacksmith?" Dana's louder voice drew Andrew's attention back to his host.

Kary dared a glance while Andrew's gaze remained politely on Dana: thick biceps bulged his fisherman's sweater. Earned, then, not a gym; he was proud of them.

"Aye. Josh practiced me on the crossbow till I'd be hitting the target at two hundred metres, worked me with the broadsword, ye know? If I died now, me bones'd pass for a warrior's. Boggles the mind, eh?"

A burst of applause.

"It does—" Dana responded to a throat-cutting gesture from her producer. "And we're out of time. Best wishes to both of you, at either end of the same war."

Dana raised her chin, faced her audience, quieted them with open palms until she could finish. "For info on Andrew and the *Deadly Nightshades* in concert, and to keep track of where he's filming, check out www.aocorner.ie. Great website." She nodded toward Andrew.

He echoed the nod. "Couple of good fans back home—do a fantastic job."

Dana thanked him, turned to Kary. "In stores and Amazon Friday." Dana lifted her copy of *Yorktown Harbor*, cover forward. "And *Thunder at Creek Station* is coming out in paperback...?"

Kary relaxed in relief. "This month." *It's over.* A fizz of elation: she'd survived.

But Dana hadn't finished. She addressed the audience again, linking her words to Kary by a wide sweep of her hand. "If you're always exhausted, and your brain doesn't work, and everything hurts—there are CFS links on our website, at www.wmrcnow/CFS, and operators standing by the 800 number hotline on your screens."

Every eye seemed directed at Kary, immobilizing her, poster child for a disease. *"Look at the freak lady, mommy!"* Skewered, marginalized, classified—discounted. Forever marked down, not a woman but a symbol. *"Poor dear—she writes such interesting books, considering..."*

On camera, oblivious Dana got the last word. "Thanks to our guests, writer K. Beth Winter, and actor Andrew O'Connell and his band, the *Deadly Nightshades*." Her royal wave released her viewers. "Good night, New York!" Behind her, the monitor rolled credits over panned images of the applauding audience.

Dana meant so well. Kary carved a smile out of ice.

For a few minutes I was almost normal.

ANDREW

ANDREW STRETCHED WITH a sense of satisfaction. *Well, boyo, another one gone without making too big an ass of yerself.* He knew the drill: Dana'd be furiously occupied for a couple minutes with tech stuff. Most of the studio audience were gathering their coats, heading for the exits; a number collected before the stage, as close as the watchful uniformed security let them, but expectant, well-mannered.

The producer darted over to take his mike and transmitter; she whispered in his ear. He said, "Good. Thanks." His plan was coming together.

Next step. He turned to the writer.

She sat rigid, unseeing, gripping the *Night Talk* mug.

He said, "Kary?" as the producer reached for Kary's clip-on.

Sharp inhale, polite smile. "Yes?" She put the mug on the table, let the producer unclip the mike as a child might wait for adults to care for her. She leaned back, gripped the chair arms. "Thank you, Melly."

He examined Kary's face. Confusion? *This one becomes still when stressed, hard to read.* Sheep in headlights? "It gets easier."

"What? What does?"

That was better. The inward focus was replaced by an awareness of her surroundings. She was actually looking at him. "Interviews, shows..."

"I'm not planning any more." She shook herself, shivered. Ghost of smile. "I've done my part."

Now that he was out from under pressure, he put pieces together: 'first interview,' 'support group,' the graciousness, nerves. She'd claimed illness—but she didn't *look* ill. Fragile, yes; like the bone-china shepherdesses his mother so loved. "Satisfy a bit of curiosity?"

"If you can keep it to yourself—it's been a tough night." Her forearms lay quiet along the arms of the chair; her fingers stretched, calmed.

"Ye were something else before ye were a writer. Am I right?" *Nosy, nosy.* Make it mutual? "Me, a bartender—or anything ye might be wanting."

"I trained as a neonatologist." Precise. Uninflected. She was watching his eyes.

"'Winter' is a pseudonym."

"Yes."

Ah! "Ye let Dana out ye." *For a cause.*

"Technically, Dana didn't. But someone will." She shrugged it off.

"It means that much?"

She cocked her head, self-deprecating but good-humored. *"From those to whom much has been given—"*

"Much is required?" His eyes narrowed reflexively. How could she say that? Years: med school, residence, internship, practice. All down the crapper. Start all over—reach the level where talk shows wanted ye. *She has guts.*

Dana's approach interrupted his prying. Her post-show wrap finished, she beamed down at them. He recognized the type, surrendered to Dana's smile: Dana's guests were again worth noticing. She ran long fingers through her hair, grabbing handfuls and tugging, hard. "Ready?"

"Trying to pull it out?" Kary sounded alarmed.

"Nope. Loosens the scalp."

He watched, amused. Women! "Now what?"

Dana evaluated the small crowd. "Audience members get a few minutes for autographs?"

"No problem." George and the guys were headed over. Least he could do—these folks stood in line in the cold.

"Kary? You up to it?" Dana tipped her head toward the waiting fans.

"I'm positive I know whose signature they want." Kary smiled at him, but he had the sense the portcullis was dropped, the castle secured.

She's making me awkward, like a schoolboy. Refreshing. "Wait a bit." He met Kary's gaze, glanced up at Dana. "Me agent's throwing a little party at *Mallory's*. Just friends. I was hoping ye'd both come." He trotted out his ace. "Dana, Melly's having Brian bring yer sister."

Dana blinked several times. "Chrissy'll love that."

He had achieved the right touch. *Good.* "If Kary comes, they could talk..." He appealed to Kary. "Ye're probably tired—but..."

She considered so long he thought he'd lost her.

Prolonged exhalation, nod. "I think I can manage. My plane doesn't leave until late tomorrow. New Hampshire's only a short flight."

"There's a trooper."

"On the condition I don't have to stay till the wee hours."

"Cross me heart—the minute ye've had it, ye're out." He made the child's sign before he could catch himself. "Okay?" He'd make time to talk to her later. That settled, he popped to his feet. "Bring on the Christians."

Kary remained rooted.

Aha! "Ye've never done autographs, have ye?"

"Am I that obvious?"

He chuckled. "It won't hurt. Much." He bowed, offered his hand. "Come here to me."

She laughed and shook her head as if to a wayward beau with wheedling ways, put her hand in his. But she didn't need actual support. Her hand was as light as one of the baby birds he used to try to rescue, all feathers and no substance. She stood up as models did, in a single fluid motion, retrieved her hand with an inclination of thanks.

They walked side by side toward his rowdy mates at the barricades where a table was set up for Kary. He wasn't surprised to notice a substantial portion of the crowd wanting her autograph.

He welcomed his obligations: his fans awaited, young and old; he was there. As usual, some of the pretty ones hung back, hoping to leave a lasting impression. It was twenty minutes before the final fan was escorted to the studio door, squealing happily to her friends with Andrew's pen in her hand.

He shook his head with regret as she left. *What a bloody waste.*

KARY

Mallory's Bar and Grill, NYC

"*ROLAND! ROLAND!*" A ragged roar of applause from women in glitter, men in black tie, the shockwave hit Kary's ears like a physical blow as Andrew swung open the door from *Mallory's* kitchen into the upper East Side bar and grill, and held it for Dana and for her. '*In the jungle, the mighty jungle...*' floated through her head.

His eyebrows arched, but he didn't seem fazed; his smile encompassed everyone.

The king entering the Great Hall? She shook her head. *This is a little party?* She should have anticipated this. At the WMRC dock, George Cosgrave had shepherded them into the heated limo so quickly she hadn't time to get cold in the brittle black New York night, but the chauffeur delivered them, not to the front entrance, but to the alley behind the restaurant. *For safety?*

Escaping the maelstrom was her first thought. Too soon for people to suss out who she was—they'd either been getting ready for the party or already here drinking when *Night Talk* blew her cover. If she could dissociate herself from the man of the hour, she could still avoid detection. She touched Andrew's arm. "Dana and I have to find her sister." She attracted Dana's attention. *Great—trading one celebrity for another.* "Okay with you, Dana?"

Dana locked arms. "We'll raid the buffet. I'm starved."

"Keep a chair for me," he said. "There's a pile o' people I have to make nice with. I'm the ram on the auction block." His petitioners bore him away, but not before he had grabbed the maitre d' and handed Dana and Kary over.

The restaurant matched Kary's mental image of an old gentlemen's club: heavy dark furniture, hunter-green flocked wallpaper above the wainscotting, photos of celebrities and politicians in massive gilded frames. To one side, five servers presided over a display worthy of Versailles. *Elaborate. And expensive.*

From a booth toward the front, she kept up with Andrew's progress: the fisherman's sweater stood out easily from the crowd. He poached a beer from a passing waiter, grazed from group to group without letting any claim him.

"Pours it on rather thick, doesn't he?" Dana's attention alternated between the knot with Andrew at its center, and the entrance. "There's Chrissy!"

Dana took charge. Mother-hen-like, with Brian as footman, she snagged a waiter and supervised delivery of 'two of everything.' She pampered Chrissy and Kary impartially. "If I don't, Chrissy won't eat enough to keep a mouse alive."

Kary had to raise her voice to be heard. "Do you know all these people?"

"Producers, agents, gossip columnists." Dana returned a wave from a tall brunette in a jade cocktail dress. "Hangers-on. Yeah, most of them. But they're here to talk to Andrew, so enjoy your dinner."

"Fine with me."

Dana's head snapped up as Brian looked horrified. "Oh, God. I can't believe I said that!"

Brian, who had seated Dana by the wall 'to hide her from view,' hung his head. "You just called Kary 'small potatoes.'"

Chrissy laughed. "Foot in mouth?"

"Sorry, Kary. They're all too accustomed to me being outrageous. I didn't mean—"

"I did." The food restored her—she hadn't realized how long it had been since dinner—but she didn't belong here. The familiar ache starting between her shoulder blades warned her she was on time borrowed at exorbitant interest.

He invited me for one thing. She turned to Chrissy. How old was the girl? Twenty-three? Twenty-four? There was something wan about the face, a stillness about the body, as if someone had taken a Dana and smoothed away not only a few years but all of the verve. "Tired?"

"I'll pay for it tomorrow." Chrissy disavowed the cost with a shrug.

"It gets better."

"For everyone?"

"For most people." An exaggeration? "How long...?"

"Since my third year of college. Thought I'd come down with mono."

"Kissing someone, I presume?"

Chrissy laughed. "Yeah. But it never went away. I had to drop out—thought it would just be for the semester, but it was four years before I could go back. I'm only taking two courses a term, and I'll finally be finished next year. But I'm positive I'll never get a job—who'd want someone who can't work?"

"You don't have to work to be valuable." It had been so hard to believe that.

"And most people who've even heard of CFS think it's contagious, like AIDS."

"There'll be things you can do... Eventually..." *I'm not offering much relief, am I?* Helplessness fought with anger. She used to love nights like this in the city.

"And now that I'm old enough to drink legally, alcohol makes me sick!" Chrissy said.

You've got fight, kid. "I understand. I miss Tequila Sunrises." She held up the crisp chilled Sauvignon Blanc. "That gets better too— I'm up to an occasional half-glass of wine—"

Chrissy looked up past Kary's head, and her eyes lit up. Kary turned.

"Everyone wants a piece of me!" growled Andrew. "Are ye okay?" Guinness in hand, he collected a chair, turned it around and sat on it backward. "George, bring it over. Ye know George?"

"We came together?" Kary said.

"Ah. Right ye are." He got them all squeezed together, with one arm around Chrissy's shoulder. "Got it? George's documenting the whole thing."

"All here." George patted a fancy digital camera.

Kary said, "Shouldn't you be in the picture?"

"Aye, George. Here. Take us a few more."

A tiny remote control and a table-top tripod emerged from the camera bag. George insisted they say 'Guinness'—"So there won't be any silly smiles"—fitted himself into an imaginary space between Chrissy and Kary, snapped a quick bunch.

"Not too bored?" Andrew asked Kary. "Want me to introduce ye around?"

"Don't you dare. This is far better."

"Eh?"

"Where else can I still observe these people in their natural habitat?"

"Collecting specimens?" His brogue thickened. "Ye'll be pinning us up on the wall like wasps?"

"'Fess up. You like the idea."

He waved his free hand, including with the gesture everything in sight. "This *is* me territory."

Chrissy's gaze never left the actor's face, adoration plain. Kary kicked herself, steered the conversation in the right direction, and got out of it.

Andrew exerted himself, shared faintly naughty anecdotes, got Chrissy laughing and blushing at the same time. He focused on Chrissy as if she were the only person in the known universe.

An endearing trait. It must make him quite irresistible.

"Hey, there you are! Come on, you gotta meet—" A pudgy hand descended onto Andrew's shoulder. Andrew whirled, captured a plump wrist. "Watch it! Ouch!"

"Sorry, Maury. Act first, think later." He didn't sound sorry.

Some instinct made Kary glance at George; she caught the tail end of a suppressed grin. George mimed using the edge of his hand as an imaginary saw. She got it: last man who tried that lost his arm up past the elbow.

"Hey, Maury," Andrew said. "Meet me new friends."

~ 44 ~

Kary imagined the agent calculating their present value to him—zero—adding to it just the right dollop of worth as 'friends of Andrew.'

Maury cranked up the smile. "Dana. From the TV show, right?"

"Do ye need a new agent, Kary?" Andrew said. "I'm sure Maury'd be thrilled to take ye on."

The agent all but danced with impatience. "Sure thing." Out came the ever-ready card.

"Elise Carter's my agent." Kary stowed the card in her purse. "Do you know her?"

Maury shook his head. "Sorry. No."

"I'll be sure to call you if Elise and I come to a parting of the ways." She gave Andrew what she hoped was a stern glance.

Andrew's eyes opened very wide. Blameless. *Right.*

George chuckled.

Dana whispered with Chrissy. Kary recognized the signs: Chrissy was running on fumes. Dana chose the moment to make their escape.

"Must ye?" Andrew rose. He shook Brian's hand.

"I'm afraid so." Dana smoothed Chrissy's hair. "My fault. Early call."

"But thank you so much," Chrissy said. "It was wonderful meeting Kary."

Kary hugged her. "Keep your spirits up."

"I'll try. I promise."

Andrew kissed Chrissy's cheek, Dana's hand. "Be seeing ye."

"Ditto." Dana let George help with her coat, while Maury, chastened, held Chrissy's.

Kary's gaze followed Chrissy as Dana and Brian plowed a path for her to the door. A tap on her arm. Andrew.

"Gotta go. Maury's leading me to the slaughter." He appealed to George. "Stay with Kary, won't ye?"

"I've been trying to get rid of ye for hours," George said. "Unlike ye, *I* can read, and I want to talk about her books. Begone."

"Hey, a fan." Andrew stood. "Aye, then. Back in half a mo... I'm *coming*, Maury." A quick wave, and he'd plunged into the sea of supplicants.

"God, the din!" Kary covered her ears. "Is it always this chaotic?"

"Since *Roland*," George said. "I mean, people stopped him on the street before, but we never needed bodyguards."

"Is your band on tour?"

"Later this year. He flew us in for the show. Likes to share the wealth." George wagged his head. "The lads are catching the Dublin express tomorrow night. First class. They pamper ye so, it's embarrassing."

"You're not going to Ireland?"

George hesitated. "Well, ah; Andy's asked me to stay on a bit, be a sort of manager…"

She examined him critically. "Let me see… You've always done it for the band, and he needs you to keep things straight." *And he's put you on salary, which makes you horribly uncomfortable.* "You're the solid friend who knew him when."

George smiled wryly. "Aye. He thinks I can help with the vultures."

Kary glanced at Andrew, corralled against the far end of the bar by the birds of prey: men in suits, young women in dresses skimpy as camisoles. His stance had 'alpha lion' written all over.

George followed her line of sight, made a harrumphing sound.

"What?" Kary said. Andrew leaned a slip of paper on a suit's back, scribbled while conversing intently with a tiny frosted blonde in red sequins. "He looks happy enough."

"The ladies have taken him on."

"Are you jealous?"

"Me? Lord above, no. Fiona'd have me head."

"Fiona?" She coaxed his story out: running the farm for his ailing father, band member when 'the lads' got together around Andrew's increasingly demanding schedule. He retrieved a photo from his wallet: an Irish beauty with fiery ringlets, dimples, and a determined mouth. "She's beautiful, George."

"Is this how ye get yer material? Getting the other person to spill his secrets?"

"I wish." She stretched her neck and shoulders discreetly, exhaled. She should have left when Dana left. *But is* one *party too much to ask?*

The top of Andrew's head was all that remained visible. The schmoozing was as much required in his career as acting. He'd made no promises; she'd been foolish to expect a chance for intelligent conversation. *What was I thinking—he isn't coming back any time soon.*

"Tough break—getting sick, I mean," George said.

The sympathy in his voice, too close to pity, stiffened her resolve. *Time to go.* "You learn to live with it." She shrugged. "Which reminds me—it's been lovely speaking with you." She gathered the shreds of energy, rose, offered her hand. "You said you liked the books."

George got to his feet. "Very much."

"They wouldn't exist."

ANDREW

"...THEY EDITED IT OUT, but he never wore *that* shirt again." Andrew was finishing a story when George tapped his shoulder.

Kary stood quietly to one side. "I've come to say good night. It was very kind of you to make it possible for me to meet Chrissy—she's had a tough break."

"Ye're leaving?" *Damn, I didn't get opportunity to talk with her again.*

"George said you're all going barhopping; you won't even miss me."

"Hang a bit." He had a quick word with George. George headed for the kitchen. "The limo'll take ye back to yer hotel."

"I'll get a taxi, Mr. O'Connell. Don't worry about me. I'm a grown woman."

"That's yer excuse?"

It made her laugh.

The 'Mr. O'Connell' widened an intangible chasm between them: she was pulling away, returning to her world. "The driver bloke is sitting around doing nothing until we leave. It'll take him two shakes. Come, George already went to get him."

He guided her through the kitchen with its strong scent of pine cleaner, quiet clatter of cleaning crew. He waited outside with her in the frigid air. Their breath made tiny clouds.

"Thank you for a wonderful time."

"Nothing to it. Maury arranged everything."

"The buffet was excellent, but I meant the conversations."

"Good, eh?" What the hell was it about her? He didn't want her to leave yet.

"You guys are outrageous."

"Do ye *have* to pull a Cinderella?"

Something flashed across her eyes, disappeared. "Don't you have to get back to your guests? You'll freeze solid."

Serenity. She exuded calm. Everyone else was so frantic, everyone else wanted something. He held out both hands to her. "They can wait."

He expected her to place her hands in his. Instead, she received his hands as she might a gift, scrutinized his palms, gently turned his hands over, felt his calluses with her thumbs. The ruby in his uncle's ring gleamed in the glow of the street lamp. She examined the backs of his hands. He resisted the urge to move.

"Me worst feature." His large square hands—stubby fingers, nails chewed—lay captive in her slender ones. Her left ring finger had a faint indentation at the base. "What are ye doing?"

"Memorizing you." Her tone was light. "I don't want to forget anything—I probably won't see you again." She released him. "Good hands." She crossed her arms over her coat, tucked her hands under against a sudden gust.

Tire crunch. The limousine rounded the corner, purred to a stop. George climbed out, held the door.

Andrew handed her into the limo. *Last chance, lad.* "The film I'm doing next, about yer Independence War?"

She settled into the rear seat. Her eyes were level with his. "Yes?"

"We're filming in New England. That's close to ye, isn't it? Might I visit sometime?"

"Of course. That would be lovely." She smiled her goodbye, and he backed out. She turned to George. "Good night, George. You're a lucky man."

George grinned, closed the limousine's door with a firm clunk.

As the car floated away, she looked back and waved.

Andrew felt watched. Three fans stood patiently in the icy night. He signed what they thrust at him, told them to go home and get warm. He let George hustle him back inside.

He had the distinctly unsettled sensation of having made a mistake.

❧ CHAPTER FOUR ❧
Death's Day

...Never by me shall Frankish valour fail!
Rather I'll die than shame shall me attain.
Therefore strike on, the Emperour's love to gain.
> *The Song of Roland*, LXXXVI, 1090
> trans. by Charles Scott Moncrief, London, 1919

Pain comes on cat paws
Padding across your person
To prove you're alive.
> Tahiro Mizuki,
> trans.by R. Heath

...Pseudonym revealed: K. Beth Winter, best-selling author of *Prairie Fires* and others; on *Night Talk*; N.H. native Dr. Karenna Elizabeth Ashe talked with Dana Lewiston about the ravages the 'Yuppie Flu' has wreaked in her life...
> *Star!*, State of the Union, Feb. 26

KARY

NYC; February 26; 11 A.M.

KARY KNEW IT MUST BE a dream, but she was loath to wake herself up. Ethan, all grown up, shared a horse-drawn carriage with her on Central Park South toward Columbus Circle; the midsummer sun setting behind him shadowed his face. The hooves of the carriage horse clacked rhythmically. As a child he'd always begged for the tourist ride—why not now? He said, "You'll be glad in the end."

A more insistent tattoo, impossible to integrate, and the dream became untenable. Kary released it reluctantly and opened her eyes.

Red LEDs glowed ten-fifty in the dim room. The knocking was the kind that resulted in worried hotel employees with master keys. "Coming," she called out. The wisp of Ethan evanesced as she sat on the edge of the unfamiliar bed. *He was so real.* "Just a minute!"

She opened the door and stared.

Elise, immaculate and professional in mid-calf coat and scarf, black leather boots, eyed her. "You forgot."

"Plane doesn't leave until six."

"Checkout is noon."

"Late departure—all arranged—last night."

"And where were you last night?" Elise dumped briefcase and Bergdorf Goodman shopping bag on the Queen Anne chair by the suite's desk, opened the heavy outer draperies to let in brilliantly excessive sunlight. "I called *five* times. They said you weren't in yet—and then I had to cope with teenage tantrums and tears and it really *was* too late to call."

Kary escaped into the bathroom, ran water in the sink. Her nose wrinkled: her well back home lacked chlorine. When the water didn't get colder she visualized a mile-long maze of copper pipe threaded through the walls of a heated hotel, gave up. How far to the ice machine? Probably not worth it. Her head was full of cotton batting, consequence of the deal with the devil: sleep in, and be muddled half the next day; or don't sleep—and be a zombie. *Wonderful.* Sluggish, sluggish, sluggish—and no better for awareness. It would improve, though maybe not today. *Time for the daily struggle.* Stretching every joint ritually helped put the pain into its own box, limited. Pre-measured meds in little plastic cases made her feel like an old woman. She assessed, with wisdom born of experience, added extra ibuprofen to the mix, swallowed her pills with a mouthful of tepid tap water. Set the mental timer: thirty minutes to find real food—or hit the emergency protein bar in her purse. She made a face at the stranger in the mirror.

"Where were you after the show, Kary? I should have been there. I almost hopped the LIRR back into Manhattan."

Kary covered a yawn with the back of her hand. "Good morning to you, too." She ambled to the door, retrieved a *New York Times.* Puzzled, she looked both ways down the corridor. "That's funny." There'd been a *State of the Union* with the *Times* on her few previous trips to meet with her agent. She glanced at Elise. "That bad?" She spied the newspaper stuffed down beside a gift-wrapped package in the department store bag. She located the paragraph, flinched. Her ribcage stopped processing air. *You knew it could happen. Would happen.*

"You okay?"

No matter how you braced for it. Eight years of hiding—gone in a few thoughtless words. "They got most of it right."

"Lots of authors write under pseudonyms."

At least the article didn't list her among the hangers-on at *Mallory's*. "Now everyone knows why I'm slow."

Elise didn't respond.

Don't know how I'll react, do you? Kary tried to keep the bitterness out of her expression and voice. "Relax. I knew what I was doing. What'd you think of the show?"

"You were fine," Elise said. "You wouldn't believe the calls I've gotten already this morning. I think it's time to map out more—"

Kary winced, shaded her eyes. Trust Elise to push. "No."

"Stay another day or two. I have several interviews lined up. You can start small, keep them brief—"

God, how she missed New York. *Should have done so much more when I had the chance—but who knew then the promise was so finite?* "No."

"Why not? You said you'd have the new book by June, in time for the ABA—"

Thank God Joe insisted on contracts with no deadlines. "Elise. I said *might*."

"How's it coming? Are you writing? This isn't—?" Elise rummaged around the crumpled typed sheets in the wastebasket by the desk, looked up, horrified.

Kind of Elise to keep a leash on her impatience. "It's just scratch paper—I can't think on screen—it's not priceless." *I must be the most frustrating author she represents.* "It's at the mountains-of-notes stage." *It's at the I-can't-even-decide-what-to-write stage.* She exhaled, girded for battle.

"Do you have a logline?"

"I'm thinking about it."

"Maybe it'll do you good to do a short tour—"

"I can write—or I can be a performing monkey." She knew she was being unfair, but she could feel the withdrawals from the energy bank—ka-ching! *Plan: Shower. Pack—at least everything went. Schedule, food—soon, nap—the VIP lounge at Kennedy? Maybe? If not, eye-mask and earplugs for the plane. Not a speck of spare* stamina for the Metropolitan. *All I want to do is go home. Pathetic.* "Do you want the book or not?"

Elise inspected her with shrewd eyes. "So where *were* you?"

Memory, his hands in hers, scalded. *What on earth was I thinking?* Kary kept her attention on her hands. In the hall, housekeeper vacuum cleaners murdered any possibility of late sleep. "I went to a party for that nice young actor, Andrew O'Connell, from the show? Dana and I went."

"You went to a party with Andrew O'Connell?" Elise's rising tone mixed envy with disbelief.

"He invited Dana's sister Chrissy to meet me."

Elise was shaking her head.

"What? He has lovely manners." Was that so hard to believe? "Have you seen his movie, *Roland*?" And he's an attractive man— to the whole world. He can afford it. *Could I? In another life?* They'd been equals for all of ten minutes—while he focused on her. In the limo: 'Close your eyes—you have a bit of time,' and he and George and Dana kept their voices low. An opportunity wasted— but a most necessary break. *Ah, well—* It was already fading. She *had* to capture it. She went to the desk, grabbed paper and pen, started with the image of a laughing Andrew O'Connell with his arm through Dana's on one side, hers on the other, escorting them to the limousine... *I should have done this last night.*

"Kary."

"Just a sec." On her tongue, the piquant pure bite of *Moët & Chandon*, brut; a hot hors d'oeuvre, shrimp and Parmesan and curry...

"Kary!"

She'd forgotten she wasn't alone. Enough detail to reconstruct later. "Sorry—you woke the beast." She interlaced her fingers, reached out, up luxuriously, then rested her hands, fingers still tightly clasped, on the top of her head. "Remember the ubiquitous AOL CDs? Little mirrors. I saw a sculpture once, a rose, made with cracked CD pieces."

"So?"

"That's me. Shiny sharp shards of a broken mind—maybe I can turn them into art."

"Normal people don't get lost like you do."

"You *do* realize I live among imaginary people?" Her head was clearing. Reality intruded—and the present. Face reality. Manage reality. "Breakfast?"

"Lunch."

"You didn't answer. Have you seen his movie, *Roland*?"

Elise stared at her fixedly, a curious smile turning up the corners of her mouth. "Have I seen his movie, *Roland*?" she mimicked. "*I* don't go to the movies. *I* read books. But *I* went to see *Roland* on a dare—with my sister. And I went back again. All by myself."

"That good, huh?"

"*That* good."

"Is it out on video?"

Elise gaped at her. "Are you for real? It's still in the theaters, opening in new countries every week. It won't be 'out on video' for months." She shook her head. "When you get back to your tiny little town, look it up in your tiny little local cinema—and then call me if it isn't there."

BIANCA

Beverly Hills, CA; March 1; 1 P.M.

THE MAITRE D' WAS properly deferential. "Good afternoon, Ms. Doyle. Ms. Illstrom is waiting for you."

So this was the famous *Restaurant Myatelle*. Bianca nodded her thanks. The advantage of being fashionably late. Loads of light through the window wall bounced off the chrome and glass tables. Trendy today, gone tomorrow. *Probably won't even be here next time Tonya returns.* Bianca followed the man past the tiny precious micro-square of velvet grass and the monstrosity of a chrome fountain spewing random bursts of spray. She was acutely conscious of the flattering glances sent her way. *I look good—I work for it.* Hollywood gave nothing away free.

Tonya squealed, jumped up, and wrapped her in a bear hug.

Bianca hugged back, pretended to pout. "God, Toe, you look great. I work out every day, but you feel like granite!"

"Eight shows a week'll do it, Bi."

They still had it, 'Bee' and 'Toe' with Francis 'The Mat,' outcasts together since high school in Beverly Hills. *We showed 'em.*

Tonya grinned, held her at arm's length. "You don't look so bad yourself."

"Sit, sit. Tell me all." Bianca sat, ran fingertips over the heavy linen napkin in her lap with approval. "The reviews are fabulous."

"Finally, eh?" Tonya pulled clippings from her Hermès bag to share.

"Didn't see some of these." Bianca flipped through the stack, reading. "'Bout time."

Tonya glowed.

"When are you moving back to L. A., Toe? I need my best friend."

"I'm still your best friend, Bi." Toe gave her the 'serious' look. "But I'm East Coast now."

"Is it a man? Tell me you found a man."

"Eh, one or two. New Yorkers." Tonya rolled her eyes. "I should never have let you steal Michael."

"*Let* me? You *said* it would never work, him here, you there. You practically threw him at me!"

"You know that's not what I meant, Bi. For heaven's sake, he used me to get to you."

Bianca hmm'd. Five years ago Michael looked like he was going somewhere. *What a bust.*

"Where is he anyway?"

"Something came up." Bianca rolled *her* eyes up. Why had he insisted on coming, anyway? "He's in the lobby, glued to his cellphone."

"Nope. I'm right here."

She jumped. "Michael!" *He* knows *it drives me crazy when he sneaks up like that.*

"Hey, Toe. Heard you're doing good." Michael smothered Tonya. He grabbed a chair, joined them. He leaned back, taking up half the aisle.

Showoff.

"Hey yourself—thanks. How's business?" Tonya favored him with all her attention. *So like her to put the man first.*

"Couldn't be better—ask Bianca."

Who cares about his stupid company? "So he tells me." People at other tables were staring. *So he's handsome—too bad he never learned to act.* And did Toe have to make such a spectacle of herself with him?

"Hey." Tonya unfolded a strip of newsprint with Helena Van Sant's picture and *Hell's Angeles* header. "You guys made Hell's column."

"Oh?" Michael glanced at the blurb. "It was just dinner with Tom Pentell—" A waiter interrupted with menus.

Tonya turned coy, flapped theater lashes. "Can you stay, Michael?"

Bianca smiled over gritted teeth. Tonya was perfectly willing to let Michael spoil their only chance to talk. "Sorry—he's got some big meeting."

"They can wait for a few minutes." Michael checked his Rolex. "Oops! Guess they already did. Gotta go." He gave Tonya a peck on the lips. "Come more often. We miss you."

"It's a short plane ride," Tonya said severely.

Michael brushed Bianca's hair aside, kissed her nape.

Why couldn't he ever remember she hated anyone touching her hair after she got it settled just right around her face?

"I'll send the car back; he should be here before you two stop gabbing."

"Do you have to? Can't *you* take the taxi?"

"Doesn't make sense to have the driver sitting idle, does it now, pet?"

"What if I want to leave?" Damn it, Michael; don't make me beg.

"No worries. Toe'll take care of you." Michael had the nerve to grin. "Bye, ladies. Be kind to me behind my back. I'll have a word with the maitre d'."

"Michael, don't—"

Tonya's gaze tracked Michael's disappearing back. "What was that all about?"

"Nothing."

"Michael not paying you enough attention? He has a business to run, you know, and you're on location half the time."

"It's nothing." She had Michael on a string—he knew which side of his bread had butter. "Can we get on with lunch?"

"Are you in a rush, Bi?" Tonya's eyes narrowed. "I thought we had all afternoon."

"He has no sense of time." Bianca opened her menu. "Let's order—these places take forever to bring food."

"Hungry?"

With nothing but a protein shake for breakfast? "Famished."

"Ms. Illstrom." The waiter presented a notebook and pen, inclined his head towards a table by the window where an older woman in rose-colored Chanel occupied the seat opposite a deeply-tanned gentleman with silver hair and working buttonholes on his sleeves.

Great. Now they'd have to deal with fans.

Toe smiled at the couple, began writing on the small spiral-bound page. The woman took it as an invitation.

"I just *had* to tell you how thrilled we were to see you in New York last week in the *New Follies*. The dancing was breathtaking, and you have such a beautiful voice."

"That's very kind. I'm glad you enjoyed it." Tonya signed with a flourish.

"Delightful meeting you, Ms. Illstrom." The woman's gracious nod included Bianca. "Ms. Doyle."

Bianca nodded, seethed. *My* town, and *she's* the one with the classy fans? Thank God she's no competition for my roles.

The woman walked back to her table with the indefinable authority of old money. Bianca watched, stored. "You don't get many chances to observe her kind out here."

Tonya's gaze went from Bianca, to the fan, back to Bianca. "It'll be centuries before you have to walk like that for the camera."

"Dunno." Bianca inhaled deeply. "Can't play 'young and beautiful' forever."

"Is that why you want to direct?"

She didn't like Tonya's undertone. And not even, 'You'll always be beautiful, Bi'? "I want control, Toe. *I* want the final say on how I look on film."

The waiter clinked dishes, placed a basket of fresh croissants on the table. It reminded Bianca this was a public place.

Chicken Marrakesh for Tonya, *Salmon Provençe avec Haricôts Verts* for her. Fancy names for simple food. At least they'd have the sense to bring it without a gram of fat. She frowned. "Please take the bread away."

The waiter looked confused.

Bianca handed him the breadbasket. "Pan. Porfavor. No."

"Si, señorita." He left, taking the offending calories with him.

"They should all learn English."

Tonya pretended PC shock. "Bianca!"

"And *you* don't need bread." She poured Toe a half-glass of brut champagne. "Pretend you like it—pretend you're happy for me." She found herself smiling expectantly.

"You didn't."

"That dinner with Tom—Branford Studios?"

Tonya's eyebrows arched.

"They don't think I'm qualified. Tom tried to talk Francis into letting someone else do his script."

"But...?"

"Francis is holding out for me as Miss Prickett—says he needs to spice it up a bit or it won't fly at the box office, and *I'm* holding out for the director's slot, and…," Bianca wagged her head. *Dear Francis.* Toe would understand. *He owes me that much.*

"And? I can practically see feathers sticking out of your mouth, Bi."

"*And* I finally got Tom to agree that *if* I can get a big enough star to do the tortured ol' Reverend Dodgson, they'll let me take a stab at it." Tom Pentell wasn't much of a mentor, but he had taught her one thing: never let them see you hurting. *They'll have to reckon with me.* It was hard to hide triumph. *That would show Pentell.*

"Don't count your chickens. Has he…?"

"Not yet. I'm working on him. I talked to him *once*, for a whole five minutes." He kissed her hand; she *knew* that predatory alpha-male look, hooded eyes that saw her naked. "He was salivating." She conjured up his scent: *man*—cigarettes and musk. "I've been talking with his agent. He's on my side, too, doesn't want Andrew typecast." *There: Andrew.*

"Too bad you didn't sign him up before *Roland* came out. Then you'd really be sitting pretty, wouldn't you?"

"And if *Roland* flopped?" Obscure period pieces were a huge risk. "Thank God it missed the Academy deadline."

"Good point. Would've skyrocketed his asking price. Did you make him a firm offer?"

"Just firm enough he should feel obligated…"

"What does Michael think?"

Who cares what Michael thinks? "He says Andrew's too physical to play Dodgson. Michael's so *wrong*." Bianca shivered in anticipation. *C'mon, Toe.* "And…?"

"What? Oh, my God! You're doing that Revolutionary War thing with him, aren't you?"

"Uh huh."

"He won't know what hit him."

Finally! Tonya's admiration soothed Bianca's jangled nerves.

"Wouldn't we make a great couple?" She could imagine herself glittering beside him at the Academy Awards.

"You can't be serious!"

"Why not?" *I can give him the inside track.* "Think of the power we'd command."

"You're nuts, Bi. Michael is the best thing that ever happened to you." Toe's disapproving tone and pursed lips always reminded

Bianca of a prune. "What you need is to settle down and give Michael some kids."

"He's not interested."

"He worships the ground you walk on."

He likes living in the lap of luxury. "You care more about Michael than about me."

"I'm on your side, Bi. It's a pipe dream. I'd hate to see you lose Michael, you know, like the dog that drops his bone when he sees his reflection with a bigger bone?"

"Fine. Forget it."

"If anyone could do it on sheer willpower, Bi, you could. But you barely know the guy!"

"You're right. Just a crazy idea."

"Gossip columns would have a field day."

So she'd have to handle the media. *What else is new?* Stupid critics couldn't act their way out of a paper bag. "I said forget it."

"He's got a pretty raunchy reputation."

"Toe, just drop it, okay?" *Why did I open my mouth?* She dropped her pitch, exaggerated to make Toe laugh. "Anyway, I'm playing his *daughter.*" It didn't matter.

Toe'll come around when it's all over and I have what I want.

KARY

Sanctuary, Mt. Fire, Enfield, New Hampshire; March 4

"THIS IS NOT A GOOD time. Goodbye, Charles." It hardly qualified as an emergency. His comment stung: 'Gotta hand it to you, Kary—you go from J. D. Salinger to Monica Lewinski—couldn't you start by doing a signing in a bookstore, like normal people?'

Kary clicked the phone's receiver softly into its kitchen-counter cradle. *At least I had a week.* He was not allowed here, his ruffled feathers and damaged ego were *not* her problem. Her New Hampshire hill, and the house built into the granite wall, were *her* Sanctuary. Phantasmagorical New York had faded. Finally.

The first good morning's work in ages awaited editing, a neat pile on the coffee table.

Outside her windows a chorus cawed. Noisy birds—she had work to do.

Where were we? Ah, fire. On her haunches by the fireplace, she gave a log the final poke, settling it satisfactorily into its role as backdrop for the nice little blaze. What *were* the ravens so agitated about? *I should get started.* She went instead to the window, coming in to minor mayhem midway through the story: a bird with a dilemma.

The unbroken snow cover was glazed with sun-melted, night-hardened ice. In the center of a circle of watchful shiny black eyes, a lone raven's beak gripped a tasty morsel. *Roadkill? Prey?* Too big to swallow—but if he put it down to peck off a smaller piece, one of his mates would steal it. Already it was too late—alerted by the ruckus, more and more ravens were arriving. The raven with the prize took wing, but a shadow above and one below kept pace, miniature Blue Angels. The trio flew out of sight—she would not see the morality play end.

Loud knocking on her front door interrupted her reverie. *What the—?* The doorbell rang once, twice, continuously. A lost traveller, but—who'd be so impatient at ten a.m.? She made herself walk to the door against a crescendo of banging. The heavy oak door—had she remembered to throw the deadbolt? She leaned on the door, picked up thudding vibrations from the wood. Thank God the bolt was securely set into the doorframe. *How strong* are *deadbolts?*

The thumping stopped; Kary dared the peephole, while movie images where the assassin shot through it into the target's brain ran through her mind. Her heartbeat doubled, her heart thrashing wildly in her chest like a frenzied squirrel trying to escape. The fish-eye lens distorted a tall hefty man in a too-tight yellow parka, no hat. A nondescript maroon sedan boxed her pickup into its bay of plowed snow at the end of her gravel drive; she'd had no occasion to clear the hood. Exit blocked. Maybe he'd assume she wasn't home.

"Open up! I ain't leaving till you talk to me. Smoke's rising. You in there—open the damn door!"

The panic room to her left, its entrance disguised by a wall hanging? She'd made fun of the previous owner's conversion of the natural cave in the granite, used it for cold storage. Did the emergency phone even work? The door vibrated as the pounding started up again. She flinched, retreated. Could she cower in a hole behind a steel door? *Trapped?*

She couldn't. *Ever.* She jumped. The front door boomed as if a large weight had been hurled at it. *One of the boulders lining the drive?* Fear drove her toward the kitchen phone. *No one knows.* If the door broke, if he followed her, could she circle around through the living room and still slip...? She dialed the emergency number with useless fingers, connected with a disembodied voice, gave a panicked account of herself.

"Calm down, Ma'am. Ma'am? Ma'am?"

"Yes, I'm here." Kary stared, hypnotized, out the kitchen window; the sedan's trunk now stood open. "He's coming back."

"Stay by the phone. Are you okay? I've dispatched an officer—"

"He's heading toward me with some kind of a pipe—the jack handle from the *car*—" The window shattered; glass shards sprayed over sink, counter, floor. Her mouth went dry, she couldn't move; she had never been this terrified. The kitchen smelled of the cinnamon she'd sprinkled on her hot cereal. Part of herself dissociated to record in slow motion and vivid color. *For heaven's sake—will I watch my own murder? And do* what *with it?*

Adrenaline cleared her mind. *Adrenaline can be your friend.* She set the frantic receiver gently on the counter. How long would the police be? *No idea.* Would they come from Enfield? Or further, from Hanover or Lebanon? *I could be dead.*

She ignored the yelling, started thinking logically in spite of the hammering of blood in her eardrums. The window was too high, the man too fat. He hadn't brought a weapon—why else the tire iron? Her icy calm would have pleased the dispatcher. She scooped the contents of the knives drawer into a dishtowel. *No point in giving him any help.* She left out the largest. *What had she done to bring down this incoherent rage upon herself?* Later. Time for that later.

She was surprised how efficiently her mind considered escape routes: if he broke in, she wanted out. The pickup was useless. Unless he moved his car—to reach the kitchen window? She pocketed the keys from the kitchen hook. It would have to be the woods. She knew her woods.

Something hard smashed at the deadbolt. The frame around the lock was splintering, but held. She trusted it long enough to grab winter gear, snowshoes, from the coat closet, stuffed the bundle of knives and the wicked kitchen shears into the backpack. *No time to be angry now.* She'd take the door out from the lower level: it was unreachable from the front.

She clattered down the stairs, sat on the bottom step to order her fingers to lace her boots. If he got in, he'd waste precious time deciding where she was—the lower level was not the first place he'd search. She put the long knife at her side. If she had to use it, if he grabbed her, his short parka left his legs and groin, with the femoral arteries, vulnerable. *Lovely.*

She buckled a snowshoe. No point going out if she couldn't get away—her footprints would lead him straight to her, and he was big enough to bull his way through snow faster than she could. She reached for the second snowshoe. Would he trash the house? Too late—and she couldn't carry anything that would slow her down. *Mostly* everything was replaceable. She would not think about it. She stood. Coat, pack. Knife, keys.

The unnerving yelling and clatter from upstairs stopped suddenly. Was he looking for an easier entry? She'd be far away before he got in... And heard the sirens.

Her legs shook. She sat abruptly, placed the knife carefully on the step. *Primum non nocere*? It made no sense to do *him* no harm first, if he was meaning to harm *her*. She put her head between her knees to keep from throwing up.

The doorbell rang insistently. How could an inanimate object sound so different? "Police! Open up!"

Her head jerked up. If she didn't hurry, they'd finish the job on her front door, now there was no need. She grimaced at the irony, tore at the speed laces, climbed the stairs on rubber legs. She opened the door, was shoved aside. A police cruiser blocked the sedan. A cop with a gun assessed her, dashed off to secure the premises. She called after him, waited until he returned.

"Ma'am, are you all right?"

"There was only one guy. He won't be hard to find."

"Ma'am?"

"Silly man was wearing city shoes."

The cop chuckled. "Yeah. Chief caught him. First big drift." A second, then a third cruiser pulled up, lights and sirens yapping at the long-over emergency. Behind, a Land Rover deposited a man in a plaid jacket, plaid deerstalker cap.

Kary ran her hand down the splintered frame of the wounded door. She was shaking, couldn't stop herself. Reaction, of course. At her feet a decorative boulder from the flowerbed border lay like an extracted tooth, its place in the jaw a dark gaping hole.

The police officer stopped for a second. "EMTs on their way, Ma'am."

Oh God, no. But the officer had gone.

"Kary? Are you all right?"

She exhaled. "Joe. What are you—?"

"Chief knows I'm your lawyer—gave me a call on his way out. They said the EMTs—"

"Joe, stop them."

"Not sure I can—"

"You have to. There's nothing wrong with me. He didn't make it in, I don't want the fuss."

Joe stared. "They should check you out."

"No." She crossed her arms, went to sit by the fire as if she could still walk. "I'll see my own doctor." He needn't know she already had an appointment for a routine physical, and she'd decide then if there was any reason to bring any of this up. *So many of 'them'— pick my battles.* "And get them to turn off their toys."

Joe disappeared. Blessed silence descended. She covered her face, felt the fire's radiance penetrate the thin skin on the back of her hands, her body's only source of heat.

"Kary?"

She lifted her head. Her shoulders screamed at the burden. "What did he want?"

"Who? Oh, the man... Said he just wanted to talk to you. Wants you to recall every copy of *Creek Station*, said you slandered him and his town. He meant libel—"

"What's his name?"

"Tompkins Van. His driver's license gives an address in Little Creek Harbor, Georgia. Says his friends call him 'Sully,' you know, because of the 'Van.'" Joe realized what he'd said. "Legally, he hasn't a leg to stand on."

Every writer's nightmare. "Creek Station is in *Tennessee*. Tom O'Sullivan isn't real. He's a wizened old man... He's *black*."

"Exactly." Joe's distress furrowed his brow. "It's my fault, Kary, I was the one who talked you into the show. He'd never've been able to find you if—"

"I chose to go." *But does Fate have to be so vengeful?* She took a deep breath. It would go faster if she left the men to sort it out. "Feeling guilty? Good. Help me. Get rid of these guys—let them gather their evidence, get them out of my house. Block the window somehow. There's cardboard in the pantry." The fire couldn't handle the stream of frozen wind past her back from the broken window to the open door. "Call Lucy. Her number's on the bulletin board. Ask her please for me to come deal with the mess."

"Sure, but—"

"*Tell them*: he didn't get into the house. The knives on the stairs are mine. I never used them. Do your lawyer thing. Just thank them and make them leave."

"Are you pressing charges?"

She looked at him sharply. "Why wouldn't I?"

"Publicity?"

It gave her but a moment's pause. "Damn the publicity. Will I have to appear in court?"

Joe was shaking his head, trying to keep from laughing. "Not if he pleads out."

"Fine. What?"

"Did anyone ever tell you you'd make a top-notch general?"

She stared at him.

"Okay, okay. Give me a few minutes."

The phone rang. *What now?* She would've let the machine take it, but one of the officers with their sloppy boots brought the living room handset over. How did they keep from contaminating a real crime scene? "Says she's your agent, Ma'am."

"Thank you." *Not now!* Kary took the proffered phone. "Elise?" Joe paused mid-step, turned. *Nosy.*

"Who answered the phone?" Elise asked.

"They're fixing my kitchen window." Kary's teeth chattered violently. She gestured Joe back toward the fray. "What's up?"

"I called to ask how the new book's coming, and to see if you're ready to tackle another interview."

"Elise—"

"It'll be incredibly easy. She'll come to your house to—"

My house? "I don't think so." The literal truth would serve. "I had a good writing day, was just about to start revising." She heard a choked laugh. *Damn it, Joe. Go away.* She turned away from him, covered one ear. "After I took a little snowshoe walk. Had my boots on and everything."

"See. You're in the pink, it won't even be as hard—"

"No."

Out of the corner of her eye Kary saw Joe head out the door, closing it behind him. It stopped the icy flow, but not the cold.

"It's the New York Times Magazine—"

"This is not a good time, Elise." *Would she ever stop saying that?*

"All right, then. When *you're* ready." Elise exhaled exasperation. "Sales are up thirty percent since the show. You're hot right now."

The most sought-after author in America. *Stupid punny mind.* "Tell her thanks, would you?"

"Maybe later?"

"When I'm ready. Sure."

She sank into the sofa cushions, overlapped the split front of the Peruvian *ruana* around herself, stared at the flame dancers, listened to the pine sap pop. It smelled clean.

A gust of cold warned her the door had opened again, but it was too much trouble to turn her head. She heard air escaping as Joe's weight compressed the armchair cushion. "All taken care of."

"Did I say thank you?" She'd been inexcusably rude. Charles would've turned the whole incident into high drama.

"You're welcome. The glazier will be here in an hour. Lucy can let him in."

"Drink?"

"Sure. You?"

"Brandy." Exhaustion widened her yawn. "A tiny bit."

Impossible that the clock hadn't reached eleven. The house seemed subdued, a boxer after a losing fight. That was the wrong image—they'd won. Boxers were excited after winning a fight. She took her snifter to the window. The raven nation had flown, no sight of victory or defeat.

"You'd be safer living in town, you know."

Kary closed her eyes, inhaled the chilly air deep.

"Kary. You shouldn't be alone after all this."

He really was a dear. He must be as tired as she was. She shook herself. "I'm going upstairs to take a nap. I'll get the door repaired. Tomorrow. Promise. Poor thing, it took a beating. But it's safe, isn't it?" The lock *had* held.

"You have your friend in town—Zoë? Couldn't you stay with her a couple days?"

"Flee the field?" The idea made her smile even as she shuddered. "Zoë's household is—a little chaotic? Teenage boys, hockey sticks, skis—and her husband works at home."

"If... I have a spare bedroom. Nobody would bother you there. Ah..."

She inspected his face: Joseph Farentz, Esq., was blushing.

"It's a lovely offer, Joe, and I *do* appreciate it—but how could I work? And it's not likely this one crazy man is the beginning of a long string of intruders, is it?"

"I knew you'd say that. I have another idea. Listen. Don't judge."

"Fine." She put on her rapt face.

"Your entrance... From the road? I was in the Army: it's a perfect defensive position, I mean, it only needs a fence...."

"Fine. I'll have someone come out and look in the spring—"

"Now."

"In the dead of winter?"

"I know Tim down at the building supply store. It's a slow time. They can send a team out here—"

"Fine."

"It's better than posting an armed guard." He was utterly serious. "And he can fix the door."

"Fine." He seemed startled she wasn't fighting him. She brought the phone. "Here." She didn't dare sit down again. Capacity for movement was draining so quickly she was afraid she wouldn't make it upstairs. The sooner he was satisfied...

As Joe made arrangements, Lucy arrived. Sweet, competent, dour, silent Lucy, who took one look and went to get a broom. Tires on gravel announced the arrival of the glass truck.

Kary escorted Joe to the door. "It's supposed to snow again to-night," he said. "Eighteen inches."

"Good." All traces of the day would disappear. She waved as he backed up, turned. She bent down, replaced the boulder in its socket.

None of this was *its* fault.

~ ~ ~

Hanover, N.H.; March 8

KARY STARED AT THE ceiling fluorescents, breathed medicated air as normally as she could under the circumstances.

"Everything looks okay. You can get dressed now." Dr. Yolanda Moreno peeled latex gloves, clicked the searchlight off. "Come on back to my office."

Kary shivered. One down, how many more to go? Sometimes it sucked, being a grownup. But it'd be another year before the re-peat—and Susan would stop nagging. She tucked her jeans into mid-calf boots, pulled her fuchsia turtleneck over her head. She re-freshed her lip gloss and ran fingers through her hair under the im-personal observation of a small oval mirror.

Dr. Moreno waited in her office down the hall. She waved Kary in as she finished the phone call she had slipped into the hiatus. "So, how was the trip?" The dilapidated tweed armchair and a smoky bayberry candle completed the transformation from examin-ing room to a world of equals. The physician set the file she'd been reading to one side.

Kary preferred her air clean. *So many stupid little side effects.* She massaged the tightness in the middle of her forehead as she considered. "Not *too* bad."

"How many writing days did it cost you?" Dr. Moreno asked shrewdly.

"It was worth it." All right. Three. Or four. But she'd needed a break anyway. And she was back to writing again. Sort of. She hadn't remembered how the lack of a new plot always brought back all the old insecurities. "Did you see the show?"

"No. Sorry. Medical journals to catch up on... Too busy to watch much TV." Dr. Moreno consulted the remaining file on her blotter. "Blood pressure's up a bit, but your labs are fine, HDL 70," she looked up, "that's quite good."

"Carefully chosen genes." Kary didn't explain that her blood pressure was still reacting to an actual fight-or-flight incident—it wouldn't help, and it would just involve one more person. *She* would decide what was 'medically relevant.'

"Still walking?"

"At least every other day." What if she'd been outside when he came? *Stop it!*

"The report came from the pain specialist. He says you've tried everything short of narcotics. He *recommended* narcotics."

No. "We've wrestled it down to a dull roar." Most of the time.

"You don't have to be worried about getting addicted, you know?"

"Gets me too fuzzy-headed. I can't write." *Can't think. Can't plan. Can't wake up.* "Stretching helps."

Dr. Moreno dipped her head conceding defeat. "I think the trip did you good, overall. You seem," the physician searched for the right expression, "lighter." She fixed Kary with kindly X-ray eyes. "When you first came I worried that you were too...resigned?"

A crippled ship limping into port? "I've been afraid to take a chance. It's good to know I can survive."

"Understandable. How about some other risks? You're still an attractive woman, Kary."

"For heaven's sake. That's all behind me. Besides, where would I meet anyone?"

"Your support group? Church?"

"One sick person per family is quite enough." *Someone healthy won't want me.* And the thought of taking care of someone ill, like Joe... No. Things were best left as they were.

"Join a writer's group. Take a class." She peered over her reading glasses. "Life drawing?"

Right. "I'll think about it." Yolanda Moreno was almost a friend, but she didn't get it, living with uncertainty, not being able to count on yourself, never knowing where the bad parts would be.

"Just remember, if you do, be careful."

"Dr. Moreno! I'm Catholic." *And I don't need any more pain.* It occurred to her she'd never mentioned Ethan to her New Hampshire physician.

"Don't act so surprised. So am I. In Guadalajara, where I come from, we call the accidental late babies *santanazos,* after Saint Ann—tradition says the Virgin Mary was a very late child." Dr. Moreno stood and Kary followed suit.

"According to the Church, I'm still married."

"Whatever gets you through the dark nights. But don't forget it's just an excuse."

~ ~ ~

Sanctuary; **March 14; 3** P.M.

"WE MISSED YOU AT THE support group last weekend." Joe's concerned voice was staticky on the kitchen receiver.

She should get a new phone. What if it hadn't worked...? *You have to stop this.* "I was too tired." The group's in-joke drew a chuckle, but lately she'd been considering whether the diminishing returns were worth the monthly trip into Hanover, the loss of an afternoon, the slowness of her brain the following morning. *But—they kept me sane. And from turning into a complete recluse.* A flash of white outside her window made her jump. *Keep this up and you will be moving to town.* What was a white cat doing on the cord that hung the bird feeder from the overhead balcony?

"Well, the gang just wanted me to tell you 'nice job.' About the show."

"You didn't tell them about the intruder, did you?" They would worry, ply her with interminable questions. It was bad enough Joe would be horrified at the new hanging file dated yesterday labeled 'Intrusion.'

"I didn't think you would want me to."

She reached the window, squinted. Not a cat. An incredibly rarer gift: an albino squirrel. An omen? *Of what?* It behaved like all its kind, baffled by the clear plastic hemisphere protecting the seeds. It didn't know it was special. Recessive trait. *Pity.*

"Kary? Are you there?"

"My drive wasn't plowed till last night." Sanctuary wasn't destroyed, only desecrated. She sighed. Why did she feel imprisoned when she was the one person who could get in and out at will?

"So we'll see you next time?"

"Mother Nature willing." Poor Joe—he didn't dare ask if she was safe. She'd been happy not to be forced to make the decision: church, lunch, support group—all unreachable with a foot of wind-blown snow on her quarter-mile driveway. *Safety is an illusion.* You can't let what happened keep you locked up in the house.

"Are you writing?"

Can't sleep, ergo can't write. If only she'd gotten a new book well started before New York. She would've had something to drag her back to work. "Yes." Technically true. *Sitting at my desk counts—ask any writer.* Why did his concern irritate her? The phantom squirrel dematerialized, like the Cheshire Cat, but tail last. Her retinal cones reacted to a flicker as it scampered into the trees, leaving a faint paw trail—proof of existence?

"I'll leave you to it, then."

"Thanks, Joe." Equally idiotic to be bereft when he hung up. *Get a grip. You've dug yourself out of deeper holes.* She *had* dealt with the intrusion: her way. In writing. A mercilessly Jesuitical self-review: anger at herself, for panicking, then for letting him goad her to fury. Disbelief at her willingness to disembowel. Contempt that she couldn't force herself calm. And then amusement for not subjugating her emotions when being stalked and threatened in her own home. All of it writer's coin, saved for a future book. Definitely not normal. Normal people vanquish their fears. *I roll myself into a ball à la armadillo—and relish them.*

It was past three-thirty; the mailman would have come. She was fine. *Time to prove it.* Taking the pickup would only beg the question. Besides, a walk at the bracing twenty-two degrees would do her good.

She resisted the CCTV screen by the keypad; she wasn't going to check for bogeymen every time she went outside. The unbroken white blanket to either side of the drive was a more reliable indicator that no human lurked. Small animal tracks were crisp, delicate. On her eastern horizon Mt. Cardigan stood beacon; thick snow capped the blinding peak like white feathers a Bald Eagle.

She dreaded her first sight of the bottom of the driveway, but snow hid all traces of rawness of earth where the work crew had come, fenced, vanished, in a day. The gate, its twin posts skirted with white around their bases and topped by miniature Mt. Kilimanjaros, belonged as if it had always barred the entrance.

She brushed off the mailbox lid. Two days' mail—and it almost filled the metal bin in the gate. The world invaded, each letter a homunculus demanding attention. Not hers, but she'd have to repackage and mail it: Elise's office coped with fan mail. *Or hate mail?* How much would a letter bomb weigh? *Cut it out.* She hefted the single package. Lightweight. Smudged return address. She made out WMRC.

A DVD. How thoughtful. And a note from Dana: the show's hotline for CFS fielded hundreds of calls; they forwarded the mail to Elise. Kary shivered. *We were all so needy when we were first diagnosed.*

She whipped around at a loud plop: a branch had randomly dumped its snowload. *How would you handle this before? With no more than a glance. Coward.* Lengthening shadows, and the cheep of the chickadees as they found a perch for the night, reminded her the short day would leave her in penumbra once the sun slid behind her hill. She stuffed the DVD into the backpack's outer pocket.

It was far colder as she trudged back up.

Daylight went. She turned on interior lights, feeling, for the first time, illumined as if on stage. She quashed thoughts of a frozen faceless audience. There would be no changes: she would *not* have drapes installed. She inserted the DVD in the player, scavenged an early lasagna dinner, put her feet up, and clicked the TV on. *Let's see how bad you were.*

Andrew first; he twirled Dana on screen, a Dana who appeared genuinely startled. Not scripted then. Impulsive. *Arrogant bastard.* His leonine grace hadn't been nearly as evident with him sprawled in the guest chair.

The last time I danced was with Charles at Susan's wedding. A frigid formality he abandoned as soon as decent.

She played Andrew's interview with an abrupt consciousness of how rude she had been to not watch. *You would've looked the fool had Dana made reference to it.* The fisherman's sweater emphasized Andrew's quick eyes, quirky smile. She was suddenly and uncomfortably aware of him as a man. He said something about keeping the anachronisms out. He set up the clip, the TV zoomed in. And Kary was yanked into the early Middle Ages.

Roland, stiff in chainmail and leather, head uncovered. His left hand, gauntleted, rested on a dagger's hilt. The courtyard of the castle echoed with the sounds of men and horses. Snow lay trampled on the ground, pure in corners and ridges atop guard walls and turrets. At Roland's flank a huge war horse fidgeted, as eager to be off as its master. Roland laid his ungloved hand on its muzzle, gazed into the beast's eyes, murmured calming words. It snorted, Roland laughed.

Kary put her fork down. This couldn't be the same man. Not impersonation. Incarnation—someone else inhabited Andrew O'Connell's body. Someone dark-haired, from another time.

He turned, his scabbard clanking against his leg. His expression gentled. The ermine-edged hood of the woman's cloak fell back to reveal white skin, soft honey eyes with pale lashes and brows, and a dressed mass of Titian curls. "My lady."

"I trust my lord will be victorious," Aude said. Her gaze rose in mute appeal, darted toward a mounted knight who carried Charlemagne's standard and struggled to keep his own horse steady.

Roland's gaze followed, returned to his lady's face. "I pledge thee I will safeguard his life with my own." He held her small hand in his bare one, his other hand beneath.

Aude blinked back a hint of mist as she smiled up, placed in his hand a reliquary.

He opened it to exhibit a lone lock of her hair.

"Godspeed. May Blessed Mary accompany you."

Surrounded by an army, the two were alone.

The acrid tomato-sauce aroma made Kary's stomach queasy. She pushed the plate away. Her heart ached for the tiny perfect lady.

Aude stepped back to join her shadowed duenna. A friar and acolytes moved to the forefront. King, Roland, army knelt in the slush for the sonorous Latin blessing.

Squires helped impatient warriors mount, the courtyard alive with the repressed energy of an army hungry for battle. They streamed out the gatehouse and over the causeway, banners crackling, trumpets blaring the march.

From a castle tower a grizzled knight kept watch.

Kary took her barely-touched plate to the kitchen. She reset to the beginning of the clip, played it again. She savored details: Roland's instant control over his horse. His lips repeating the friar's Latin, 'In nomine Patris et Filii et Spiritus Sancti.' Crossing himself correctly and devoutly, with just enough careless speed to show the familiarity of the gesture, enough impatience to mark the formulaic. His cocky confidence quelling his lady's fears. A wordless signal to his squire fluidly initiating the purposeful chaos of the army's departure.

Nameless longing filled her. The phone book was in the kitchen drawer. Past four. Too late for an afternoon showing. *I don't want to drive back alone in the dark.*

The movie theater in Lebanon listed three films. The first was *Roland.*

~ ~ ~

Hanover; March 15; 2 P.M.

SHE WENT EARLY THE next afternoon, after an unquiet night of dreams, and a barren morning. Writing three novels had taught her to expect the deserts, but not how to find water from the rock. Maybe the movie would spark something.

She located the theater after unfamiliar icy turns. Why had no film in her five years in New Hampshire seemed worth the effort?

The theater held fewer than twenty people: retirees, a college student, two young women munching popcorn with its pervasive 'butter-flavored' enticement. A couple of them watched curiously as she took her seat. *What if they recognize me?* But they all turned away, indifferent. The lights dimmed. The screen flashed a reminder to turn off cellphones. She jammed hers into the bottom of her purse. *Let's get this over with.* The clip should have prepared her. It had not.

The music rumbled over her, a paean to military might, lust for war. It pulled from her, unwanted, hope: for victory, for safe home-coming, for glory. A great weight pressed her into her seat.

Roland radiated purpose. His passage left strength among his men. Scarred from the siege of Zaragoza, he returned victorious to escort the king to the treaty table. His success warranted optimism: the Moors had capitulated, the tribute was a fair ransom for the city. Roland accepted the honor of guiding it securely back to France, worried about the weather in the pass at Roncevaux, dispatched scouts and posted sentries. He told no one but the king his plans. Drummers led the rearguard; Roland's troops marched confidently in half-cadence.

He was already doomed. She knew what Roland did not: his fos-ter father, under guise of assistance, had wormed the route out of the king. She hoped against hope he would prevail, that the story would end differently, through sheer force of will, good triumph over evil.

His face registered progression from alertness to readiness for combat: when Marsile, on horseback, revealed himself, Roland snapped to battle command-er. The Moor challenged him, mockingly, to 'blow your Oliphant.' Roland's face displayed proper indig-nation. He refused Oliver's plea, to 'summon our lord Charles,' because it was 'meant to lure our liege to ambush.'

I know too much.

The engagement was a blur, no quarter, no sur-render. An enemy's lucky sword thrust slit Oliver's throat as he stepped in to protect Roland's back, and Roland's hope died with Oliver's warm spurting blood. Only the blackness of no moon paused the fight.

Her throat was so tight. She dug out tissues blindly, grateful for the dark.

He salvaged what he could, encouraged and joked with his ill-fated men in the glow of the watchfires. By Oliver's body, he pulled the reliquary from his tunic, caressed Aude's copper tendril. He sliced a lock from Oliver's blond mane with his dagger, cut from his own dark head a sweat-dampened curl. His finger rubbed the strands roughly, entwining them. He searched out the young cleric, tucked the reliquary on its riband into the boy's robe as if investing him with a scapular. 'Tell my lady... tell her if I do not return, my last thoughts were of her.'

His smile broke her heart. The movie alternated scenes between Roland's band, and the trial of the traitor in Charlemagne's great hall, giving the illusion—which she knew to be only that—of a simultaneity in time.

Conflict resumed at first light. Slow-welling blood soaked Roland's chain mail shirt over a hasty bandage.

The subclavian? Sepsis would kill him if battle did not. She fought to proscribe his death even as he faced it. *He is too beautiful to die.*

The Moorish vizier, Marsile, dared him to single combat. Roland's countenance clearly showed he knew it was a ruse when he undertook the challenge. A hundred archers ringed the clearing. The ritualized contest was as formal as a court dance.

Kary's heart sank with each mounted pass.

When he could not unhorse Roland, Marsile cocked his head, and Veillantif went down with three arrows through his eye. Roland nimbly leapt clear, ducked into the Moor's charge, and, even as the scimitar's last slash carved his chest, sent his opponent's head rolling.

She couldn't breathe.

Roland stumbled, caught the sword Durandal's tip under his chin. He commended his soul to God, begged forgiveness of his lady. Archers raised their bows, nocked their arrows. His last sight was the hundred arrows, released by a Moorish shout. He fell on his sword, that the Moors not be able to claim his death.

Kary shared his last sensation, the slam of the arrow swarm as the sword won the race.

The movie's parallel track ended with the king's swift justice: the knight entrusted with Ganelon's sword during the trial beheaded the traitor as he knelt at Charlemagne's feet. Vengeance brought the lady Aude grim satisfaction, but no comfort. As she passed, the young cleric on his knees lifted his bowed head. Her bleak visage, as she surrendered her life to the cloister, hauntingly marked her for untimely death.

The soaring angelic voices of a boy choir filled Kary's head as the credits rolled, but with the house lights came panic. She made it to her feet somehow, fumbled with coat, tissues, purse. Her throat hurt. She didn't know where to look. She blinked hard. She held on to the backs of the seats, escaped to the ladies' room, took refuge in a stall where tears coursed down her cheeks.

When she judged everyone must have left, she came out, splashed her face with cold water, held wet paper towels to her eyes. The last thing she needed was someone asking if she was all right.

ᕱ CHAPTER FIVE ᕱ
"... his feet part of iron and part of clay."
(Daniel 2:33, KJV)

...Huge crowds of ANDREW O'CONNELL fans were disappointed at the London première for ROLAND as the jouster himself made a brusque choreographed appearance surrounded by bodyguards, arriving when the showing was almost over, and staying barely long enough to answer a few questions from carefully pre-selected reporters...

www.londontells.uk, Archives, 2004

MARCH 12: *Incident at Bunker Hill* filming starts on the Ides of March! We welcome reports from Boston extras and crew. This could be Andrew's best movie ever.
Production moves to southern New Hampshire next month. Local readers might want to scope out the call for extras in the Dartmouth College paper.

www.AOCORNER

...GRANT SYKES' miscasting of Irishman ANDREW O'CONNELL as Col. Strathmore purely for box-office strategy practically guarantees a caricature of Anglo/American relationships at the opening of the Revolutionary War, crippling what could have been a promising film...

March 15, www.historicalfilms.uk

KARY
Sanctuary, **Enfield, N.H.; March 15; 8 P.M. (cont.)**

SHE DROVE HOME IN A daze through the last of the winter dusk. The shadowy white hills on either side of plowed I-89 merged before her eyes with images of the Pyrenees in winter, swirling flakes covering the bodies of fallen warriors, hiding the blood with patient layers of new snow. Her local road guided itself. Her teeth chattered; she had forgotten to turn on the heat. She wouldn't have known what to do if the gate remote hadn't worked.

The driveway was a dark gash in the snow, the turns icy in her headlights. Behind the trees, foot soldiers lay in wait. The pickup nosed into its accustomed spot. She jerked it to a stop.

She carried in a load of firewood, constructed a pyramid of tinder with frozen hands. She fed the fire mechanically until flames lapped against the back log. She left the blaze only long enough to make cocoa.

Light annoyed her. She clicked off the solitary lamp; the kitchen nightlight limned the door. Outside, the full moon divided the world into sharp black and almost white. She hunkered to stare, unseeing, her hands around the hot mug.

The flames became Roland's last campfire. She visualized Roland, surrounded by wounded men, Oliver's slashed and exsanguinated body already an alabaster statue stretched stiff on the snow. The young novice protesting. Roland, impatient: 'Thou art no use—thou canst even shrive us.' His face softening. 'Thine is the harder task. Carry word to my lord Charles of my foster father's treachery—or on the morrow we die in vain. Go with God, silent as the night owl.'

The phone interrupted her fugue state. She didn't bother with a light, navigated in the penumbra. She checked the blue illuminated Caller ID display. Why couldn't she keep her internal alarm signals from firing whenever the girls called?

"Hi, Mom."

"Hi, honey." Susan's indomitable cheeriness reassured her instantly. "Everyone okay?"

"Peachy. The Rockies dumped a mile of snow on Colorado. You should see the snowman Stephen and I made in the yard. It took us an hour, then I plonked him in the tub with all his boats while I tumbled his snowsuit dry. I think he had snow up his nose."

More snow. "Kiss him for me."

"Will do. Where were you? I called a couple times earlier. You don't usually write in the afternoon. Did you go to the doctor?"

"No. Did that last Tuesday."

"About time. Shopping?"

"If you must know, I drove into town for a movie."

Something flitted past the picture window. Bat? Owl? Kary shivered.

"Oh? What did you see?"

"*Roland*. Have you seen it?" Was her voice steady enough?

"Me? No. You know I hate violent movies. The reviews said it was really gory. Why that one?"

"The actor I was on *Night Talk* with—Andrew O'Connell—he was in it. Did you see the show?" Could I have a more inane conversation?

"No. I'm really sorry. But Betty next door said you were so sophisticated... She couldn't believe it was you."

"Why not?"

"Because I told her you won't even come out here to see us—I'm coming, Stephen!" Susan's voice trailed off, returned. "She said she couldn't see you as anybody's mother. We have a *lot* of talking to do when we all come out in August."

"August?"

"Like *every* year? Between Greg's summer classes and Fall Term? This isn't working—you're too far away."

"Oh?" Kary heard wailing in the background.

"Sorry, Mom, gotta go. Talk later. Love ya." And the phone went dead.

"Love you, too, honey." Kary leaned her forehead on the cool wall. She cradled the receiver on her third try.

Her stomach complained. She ignored it, knowing from long experience hunger would eventually give up. But she needed warmth. She waited impatiently for the microwave to reheat her untouched cocoa, picked her way through ghostly figures back to the dream.

She relived the initial onslaught of the ambushers. Outnumbered by the thousands, Oliver urged Roland to blow Oliphant, 'Summon our lord Charles to our aid.' Roland assessed the tight valley walls, reports of a massed horde beyond the ridges. 'I would not call my liege to ambush. Courage, my brother. They will learn to fear good Christian knights.' Oliver laughed; the battle turned in their favor as the men caught their spirit, fought on into dusk's lengthening shadows.

Roland dodged the arc of a scimitar, ran its bearer through, turned at a tiny gasp and a spurt of hot blood: the tip of the Saracen blade found, by worst luck, the joint betwixt Oliver's helmet and his shirt of mail. Oliver sank to his knees, struggled to raise his sword arm, failed—and died. Roland savagely cleared a space around them. His gaze encompassed the fighting, betrayed brief surety of doom. He kissed Oliver's forehead and laid him gently on the blood-soaked muck, threw himself into the fray possessed by demons.

Kary frantically examined Roland's choices; none made him responsible for the debacle. Barring the traitor's delays, Roland's contingent, with its heavily laden pack mules, should have been long past the narrow defile before the pursuing Saracens arrived. Roland had discussed strategy only with King Charles and his own lieutenants; Ganelon wormed information from the monarch on pretext of aiding his stepson.

Once he connected ambuscade to Ganelon's foreknowledge, Roland stayed behind, to certain death, not to guard treasure, but to ensure the cleric would get through with his warning.

Kary crouched in the gloom with Roland's men, the warmth of his reassurance dispelling dread. Doom receded to only one of many possible futures, except in Roland's unguarded eyes when a tree branch creaked loudly, fractured, and fell.

Roland was everywhere as the light deserted and the survivors huddled in their hastily-constructed camp. He directed the stowing of his Lord's rightful tribute from the Saracens. He conferred with sentries, leaving each bolstered and cheered with a word or a clap on the arm. He spoke to the injured, closed the eyes of the soldier who died holding his hand. He laughed with the men, shared a meager meal of bread and mead. He sharpened Durandal methodically, alternating sides, with an even pressure sliding the stone from hilt to tip.

Kary could find no flaw: Roland took each fork in the path of his destiny with a calm able heart, a man on whose shoulders command lay lightly. A supremely intelligent man, always thinking, always calculating risks. The ultimate fighting man, favored by God and his sovereign. Tested by a deity who exacted a high price for His favor. Medieval man, never questioning fate's blows, because he lived in a fixed cosmos where his place was preordained. Going with good cheer to his final battle.

It broke at first light. Kary hid in the woods with the disobedient young cleric. On Veillantif, Roland wielded Durandal with miraculous ferocity. Wave on wave, attackers fell. Where man and horse, one, charged, the victory went to the Franks, and the men rallied joyously.

But each one fell, overpowered, till Roland alone survived.

Three times Roland stormed the Moorish ranks to reach the mounted Moorish vizier directing the assault. Three times he failed, his great black stallion slipping on bloody bodies.

Roland bellowed his frustrated fury. 'Marsile! Coward, show thyself!' A whistle shrilled; Roland's arm rested wearily as the Saracens drew back into a silent ring. Marsile cantered into the circle. The two combatants clashed, time and again, without issue, each protected by his God, until through sheer bravado, Roland pressed close enough to nick his opponent's shoulder. Marsile's countenance changed. He retreated a pace, signaled with his damaged arm. Three archers raised their bows; Roland's mount gave way beneath him. He leapt clear; three arrows protruded from Veillantif's left eye.

A sigh escaped from the massed Moors. Kary knew: the Saracen had craved the great warhorse as prize. Roland touched the beast with tenderness, rose. The archers raised their bows; again Marsile signed to them.

The battle of champions renewed in a frenzy that could not last. Thrice the vizier attacked, three times Roland fought him to a standstill.

Finally, one God stumbled.

Rage made Marsile take a chance, rage was his undoing. He rushed his staggering opponent, using his mount's massive bulk as a battering ram. Roland, forced back, saw his opening, stepped into the attack, received the Moor's blow, but slipped his sword into the gap. The Moorish chieftain's head flew from his shoulders even as his body was borne past. The head rolled to a stop glaring up at an archer; Marsile had lost his place in legend.

Roland, mortally wounded, fell forward, catching his own throat on blood-stained Durandal, dead before the hundred arrows pierced his body. In the confusion, the young cleric stole away, carrying the story's ending to the courts of the Christian king.

Kary's face was wet, but she could not remember how it got that way.

SHE HAD NO IDEA WHAT time she'd floundered up to bed, but the sun was high when she woke, and her writing time long vanished.

She descended, drained. The steel band round her temples loosened but slowly to the largest dose she dared of her morning meds; she forced herself to wash them down with a huge glass of icewater, and to somehow swallow an untasted breakfast bar to keep the painkillers from shredding the lining of her stomach. Brilliant sunlight pounded through the window, hurt her eyes.

A notebook waited on the kitchen table. She could still write. *Not likely.*

She fled the light, crouched on a footstool in the great room by last night's dead fire, covered her eyes with both hands. There was no answer in the ashes. She couldn't see the ground from here, but she was certain the snow blanket below would be littered with corpses, and that the raven which darted past was come to pick them clean. Tears flooded her unfocused eyes.

Stop it, Kary, you're being ridiculous. It was a movie, a fake. The corpses got up, had a beer, washed the blood off. Served her right for not getting out more. The twisting in your gut, my dear, is simple lust. *For a man who, if he ever existed, died over twelve hundred years ago, a man in love with another woman.*

Phew. Nothing like a good hard lump of reality to remind you of your place in the scheme of things.

She shook her head wryly, reached for another notebook mute on the coffee table.

But the idea bank was closed. She tossed the pen on the table, went down to her office. Check email—biggest time-waster of all. Nothing new. A flagged message from a week before reminded her Ronnie was skiing in Jackson Hole with college friends.

Mountains. Cold. Why had they chosen to film the ambush in winter? Surely the Pyrenees would be impassable in winter? Cut it out, Kary, you're wallowing. No. Professional curiosity. Interested in the screenwriter's choices. Right.

She caved. She opened her browser; cursed—or was it blessed?—Elise's insistence on a high-speed internet connection—'You absolutely must have it for research'; Googled 'Roland +movie.' Five million plus.

Am I really that naïve? She had no idea. Fine. Visit the official site. Get it out of her system. She watched four different Quicktime movie trailers, read every scrap. She gave up trying to discipline herself, followed links to dozens of unofficial sites, gorged.

Each still from the movie brought back a scene, but now the shock of discovery was replaced by an intensity of yearning for the moment to last forever, to avoid the coming fate. She wanted to crawl into the pictures, change history.

Roland by the icy fountain with Aude. But the camera framed only him, in closeup. He gazed at Kary with a love so pure and happy her heart constricted. That the look was not for her helped not at all.

Hours later, past nightfall, when the iBook's alert system asked her, again, in her own voice, to 'Get up and touch your toes'—one of Elise's suggestions for writers stiff after long working sessions—she pushed back her chair.

Her head reeled from the contradictory reviews. 'Too gory for the PG-set.' 'An extraordinary tour-de-force.' 'A movie that exults in sickening savagery.' 'An unbelievable perversion of the glories of chivalry.' 'If you can see only one film this year, make it *Roland.*' You're right about that one. 'The total annihilation of *The Song of Roland.*' Not true. Not true at all. The epic poem corrupted history, turned it all stately and stark. The film returned legend to its bloody roots.

God, Kary, listen to yourself. What would good solid Joe think? People your age don't react like this. Blame the moviemakers for manipulating emotions with music. Be happy—it means you're coming back to life.

Who would it hurt? You haven't had the energy to be attracted to a man—and what woman wouldn't be attracted to this one? And judging from all the posts, she shared this incubus with millions of women.

She tackled the computer grimly, to force closure. She clicked on the official link, ordered the soundtrack of the Hans Maarlinko score, put the iBook to sleep.

A thought cut deep: What if you die tonight, and Susan goes back through the History folder on your browser, and sees where you've been? Her cheeks hot, she woke the computer, deleted the trail of links, cleaned out the caches and the cookies.

Eschewing the treacherous fire, she finally heeded a commonsense requirement for food. She knew she would pay for the orgy with lost writing days. She made herself drink extra water, stretch—it might help. Marginally. In bed, she read Dorothy Sayers, deliberately choosing a section on bell changes in *The Nine Tailors*, until her eyes closed.

~ ~ ~

March 21; 3 P.M.

NEVER TALK ABOUT unfinished work, the books advised. Kary snorted—there was nothing to talk about. *Was I a three-book wonder?* How easily eight years of daily writing practice disappeared. *Liar. I deliberately let Elise think I was writing.*

At least there was no signed contract, nor an advance like a huge bolus of indigestible food.

Her peaceful refuge turned into fortress when the gate went up. Now it girded for war, ants scrambling madly to defend the breaches. Her head hurt more than it usually did. She stretched her neck vainly looking for the crack that would relieve the tension. *This has got to stop. It's absurd. I'm absurd.*

The telephone shattered the murky silence. Zoë. A blessing in disguise? "Hey," said Zoë. "Long time no talk. Sorry—I meant to call sooner, but it's end of term, and the undergraduates are all needy, and I just got the final written, and—"

"Stop!" Kary laughed. "Feels good when it's someone else's problems."

"Oh?"

"The usual." She envied Zoë's boundless literary energy which, despite a full life as a professor, managed a mystery a year.

"Specifically?"

For the life of her she could think of nothing to say.

"How was your trip?" Zoë asked suspiciously.

"Better than expected. Did you see the show?" Kary oscillated on the bar stool at her kitchen counter, tiny sharp motions back and forth. She fan-folded a sheet of pink paper from the telephone pad.

"Of course." Zoë chuckled. "Never seen Dana Lewiston so respectful. Funny pairing you with an actor, but *Night Talk* guests don't interact much, so I guess it doesn't matter."

"He was nice." Kary bent the paper accordion into an arch. "Have you seen his movie, *Roland*?"

"Me? During a school term? Not my kind of film, anyway. Too gory, all those chopped-up bodies."

"You should see it. The gore is almost incidental. It's a very moral story."

"Young arrogant fool gets himself and his army slaughtered because he's too stubborn to call for help? I know the story, Kary. I teach Lit for a living. Maybe when it comes out on video. What have they done, turned it into a Hollywood romance, sex and all?"

"No." *Would I have seen it four times if it was? I have got to be out of my mind.* The man selling matinee tickets recognized her. She ran into the old gentleman again. He smiled conspiratorially. 'Good, isn't it?' 'It won't be on the big screen much longer,' she'd said, incapable of meeting his gaze. She stared instead at a life-size poster of Roland in the lobby. 'It has such beautiful production values.' Sex wouldn't have been appropriate. She marveled at the director's clout. "Young love told in flashbacks. With restraint." Lovers with their whole lives ahead of them, no need to take that risk. "Not so much as Romeo and Juliet."

"In the poem she just dies—that always seemed so unrealistic."

Kary's heart beat with Aude's, denuded of hope, dispossessed of her future, destitute of dreams. Mute at the king's right hand, unable to stop the novice murdering Roland with words. Desolate for the unexpected love which crept into the arranged betrothal of the king's ward to his favorite knight. Despoiled of plans to pray for him on his sorties, rejoice in each triumphant return. To give him sons, see them squires at court. To watch her beloved rise in the king's esteem, seasoned by each commission. To share the estates and honors which would surely follow. The banns had already been posted.

Emboldened by despair, Aude exceeded her woman's place, shamed her king and guardian into an unwanted public trial. Castle sanctuary to fortress in shambles. Like mine.

"Kary?"

Kary started, caught her breath. "She takes the veil after she avenges him. But she doesn't look long for this world."

"Pretty melodramatic. They always distort history to appeal to the teeny-boppers."

"It's not like that at all. It transports you to the Middle Ages. Come see it with me."

"It's still in theaters? I thought it came out ages ago."

"It's playing in Lebanon. You'll like it."

Zoë snorted. "Kary, I hate to tell you this, but you sound obsessed." Shrewdly, "How many times have you seen this thing?"

Kary squashed the miniature pink arch with her forefinger. "Four."

"Why?"

Why indeed? "Because it is so beautiful, and he does it so well." *For a writer, I'm woefully inarticulate.*

There was a long silence at the other end. "He's a movie star, Kary. And considerably younger than you are."

"I'm not interested in him, Zoë." Am I? She forced her mind away from the absurdity. "It's a beautiful story." I met him; he was friendly; it's enough. *I doubt he even remembers me.*

Another awkward pause from Zoë. "I ran in to that guy from your support group, Joe something-or-other. Didn't you say he'd invited you out?"

"Joseph Farentz, Esquire. He's my lawyer." Plaid. "For heaven's sake, Zoë! He's so old."

"He's younger than you are."

"You know what I mean. He acts so old."

"Illness can do that to you. I'd think you two had a lot in common. He likes you."

"I can't, Zoë. In the eyes of the church I'm still married."

"If you're so scrupulous, get an annulment."

"No grounds—Charles tried." Protection from Mother Church. It annoyed the hell out of him.

"You can always get an annulment. Anyway, I wasn't suggesting you sleep with the guy. Just go on a date."

Act my age, you mean. My sick age. "Sure. I'll think about it. When I see him. If he asks." At least Joe knows the score. "How are Tony and the boys?"

A pregnant pause: Zoë recognized 'No Trespassing' signs when she heard them. "Tony took the boys skiing. They got their Boy Scout skiing badges, he brought home a broken leg." She sounded absurdly proud.

"At least he doesn't drive to work."

"You wouldn't believe the status conveyed on a middle-aged man who breaks both leg bones avoiding an idiot beginner on a double black diamond run!"

Kary hmm'd. "Weekend warriors." *Ethan never got that badge...* Enough. She locked that door.

"You need to get out of the house more, Kary."

"I went for the mail," she offered. "It's freezing out there."

"I know. Like walking a dog, but on your schedule."

"And at my pace." Kary ran her fingers over the cellophane-wrapped plastic square from today's mail, stood it against the back-splash.

"You should come to my graduate seminar."

"Maybe some day."

"You're impossible. Lunch one of these days?"

"Give me a few more weeks?"

"Sure—I'm spending spring break writing—we'll have plenty to trade."

And I'll have the beginning of something to show you and Elise? When she hung up, she spent time examining the word Zoë used. Obsession. Susan would agree with Zoë.

Kary craved talk, about Roland, the movie, the music. Maybe Ronnie would understand, would have seen it. But Ronnie might also pity.

Roland looked deep into her soul from the jewel-case cover. The intelligence in the eyes frightened her, the bane of women of her kind since long before Rochester bewitched Jane Eyre. She flipped the case, read the back, slit the cellophane without volition, slid the CD into the player.

The crash of martial music returned her to the opening scene, a clashing show of swordsmanship where Roland disarmed his foster father in mock combat. Ganelon bowed, his hatred quickly veiled; Roland cloaked his own contempt in courtesy.

Outside, crepuscular shadows lengthened as they had at Ronce-vaux. Kary lost herself in the soundtrack, entranced before the fire again, grinding the story ever deeper into her bones.

~ ~ ~

March 22

KARY FACED HER Doppelgänger with the deep purple circles under its eyes. Light from the bathroom skylight fell vertically, il-luminating the odd mote. The mirror reflected truth, not vanity.

She had grown a second head, like Mrs. Grales, the old tomato woman in *A Canticle for Leibowitz*. Kary's Rachel was primevally innocent, too—and could not grasp the foolishness of inhabiting an aging body. Amputation followed by cautery would be the only choice, but she needed to cut deep, dissecting carefully down to the root to keep from nicking the carotid. *At least then the pains will be phantom.* She smiled wearily at her reflection: Rachel had no language. Rachel couldn't write.

She was surprised it had taken this long to crave knowledge of *Andrew*: his type of actor inhabited a character with his whole self, rather than bring his wonderful self to a film. Her tattered sense of dignity walled off avatar from actor.

Why? He looked so different as Roland, with his hair darkened and cut in a medieval bowl—like Charlton Heston in *The Warlord*—that would make anyone less masculine resemble a page boy. The medium she'd met on Dana's show hid his deep-running waters under a hand-knit Irish sweater. *Where did the depths come from?*

I didn't know I could still be smitten. I should thank him for that. Idiot! He's not involved. Just you. Her mouth tasted acrid. Thank God you had no idea when you met him: you would have made an utter ass of yourself. Even more than you already did.

It must be excised. She couldn't allow *anything* this much power over her.

He was flesh and blood, this actor. Well, he must have iron- and clay-bound feet. He would be like all the members of his exotic class: talented but spoiled, charming but fickle, successful precisely because he connected with millions.

She had proscribed internet links to Andrew O'Connell. Now she clicked on the websites remorselessly: bio, filmography, articles, live-interview transcripts with screen captures. The degree of exposure to public view made her cringe sympathetically—he couldn't put on a pound without the world commenting. *Goes with the territory.* Photos: posed, candid, artistically nude.

The official website for the *Deadly Nightshades* posted lyrics, memorabilia, tour dates. He co-wrote most songs. *Of course.* She wondered who was the Bridget in an early love song. She ordered their CD from an Irish distributor, wincing as she left an electronic trail.

She scoured the tongue-wagging pairing him with actresses and hangers-on. No marriages, no children. *Why not?* A perfectly sane woman reporter in Oregon admitted to seeing *Roland* forty-seven times. *My obsessions are molehills.*

He left no critic unpolarized: sycophantic, stalwart, or poisonous—had they no lives of their own? She found herself minutely leaning toward his side, but only because no human short of Stalin could be as bad as some of the websites portrayed him. Oddly enough, his main fan website, AOCORNER, presented every incident from both sides, determined to be unbiased. Yes, he'd been in a brawl at a pub; along with the sensational lead, they posted the followup from the local paper indicating a drunk had been charged for assault, the pub owner praised Andrew for 'protecting the property'—and Andrew refused to press charges.

It was an odd biography, composed of modern epistolary evidence: transcripts of live interviews, newspaper and magazine articles, and the uncensored internet comments, barely short of libel, of anyone who took license to write.

Easy to spot promise in the picture of him at eight—or had the article found the one photograph with the impish smile? Mother's little hellion? Handsome young dime-a-dozen men couldn't necessarily act. Or was the man ordinary, and his acting the source of apparent beauty? *I'm in too deep to be impartial.*

AOCORNER posted only Andrew's words alongside the images of him with beautiful young women. No gossip. A wary privacy seemed the result of years of getting slammed. She found the answer to a niggling question: why *Night Talk*—and not a dominant New York talk show? Loyalty—to the interviewer who had him on when he was nobody.

Very well. Encouraged voyeurism plus clinical detachment exposed the problem: he had been appointed bad boy, scapegoat, for others to live vicariously—in safety. *His life is charmed—mine is boring.* He was young and handsome and free of obligations, rich. Athletic and healthy. So healthy.

To give him credit, it took years to reach his current pinnacle: he'd earned it. His movie roles progressed from bit to minor to major to lead—talent? Or stubbornness, and, as he said in an interview, 'the ability to hit the mark'? She bought DVDs of them all; didn't want any more *Roland*s lurking.

Pain warned she had overextended herself: if she didn't get in some longer walks *now* she would endure weeks of aching before she built back her capacity to move. She put his CD in the portable player, headed out the door. She didn't even try to obstruct the memories evoked by his voice. Untrained, sometimes solo, sometimes with backup, personal songs.

Any man alive has one story in him.

Climbing was good pain, stretching pain, moving pain. *Mother of My Child* ambushed her as she reached the summit. He sang alone on her mountaintop. It only took four repetitions to memorize. She committed sacrilege: she let her mind weave subtle harmonies above and below the too-simple melody line, changing it, owning it. She sang with him—who would hear?

As in *Pride and Prejudice*, would he be in want of a wife? Was *he* ready? A wife fertile, beautiful, young. There'd be no shortage of starlets eager to fill the role. Chilled to shivers, she unplugged the earbuds, hiked home silently by a different path.

Nights and days lost their distinctness, and only the clock yoked her to time. Writing was on hold. Indefinitely. *So be it.*

Time for mail came, and the mailer bore the entire collection of DVDs. Damn Amazon's efficiency. *I must not be the only one who's ordered them.* Something minute loosened his hold. She was ravenous.

Maybe attraction was fair: the early movies all included scenes of male nudity, rear view. It reminded her of the time when, an adjunct teaching anatomy for a term, she had used Princeton's gym, observed the young student-athletes with their perfect chiseled bodies, and asked herself curiously if they turned her on. The response, even then, had been, 'What would we talk about? They are so *young.* Maybe when they grow up.'

But she was fascinated by indications of the growth of craft, of the discernment behind his choices. Mere male beauty would have palled. As comfortable in his body as a Serengeti lion, camera or no.

He will be in Hanover. Might as well be Tanzania. She'd been in a movie, once. Her college roommate dared her. They stood in line under a blazing Berkeley sun for hours. A callback led to two fourteen-hour days of excruciating boredom, the extras fenced away from the food set out for the crew—and from *any* contact with the cast. The general public was blocks away, behind security tape. She was permitted to walk in front of the star for her big scene: a nanosecond in the final cut immortalized her at seventeen in a 1940s shirtwaist.

Each movie she viewed caused pain. Necessary pain.

A moment in *Sun over Water.* His character—assassin? terrorist? freedom fighter?—listens as his superiors debate. He is coiled so tightly a blast is imminent—but she had to watch it three times before she knew how. Draped over a sofa, as much marble as the Pietà, he allowed himself a tiny tic: his left eye twitched, a trigger for the explosive action that left six men dead.

She watched them all, implacably, as many times as it took. A last meal before the execution. Her brain was mush. Time to lance the boil. *Time to call Aunt Ruth.*

Ruth herself picked up the phone. "Kary, what a nice surprise! How's my favorite niece?"

Your only niece. But she smiled. "Bless me, Aunt Ruth, for I have sinned."

"Have a juicy one for me, dear?"

God, she'd missed Ruth. "Yes, but I can't give you details. I'd lose your respect forever."

"Hmm. A man, then?"

"You are psychic. But no, not a real one, anyway." *Why not me?* Because.

"What have you done, gone and fallen for one of your creations again, like Jake?"

"You are balm from Gilead, Aunt Ruth. Besides, everyone falls in love with Jake. That's the point."

"When *I* can't sleep, I spend some time with him, and I feel rested."

"Jake puts you to sleep? Great."

Ruth paused before answering. "And this other one, he sleeps with you?"

Bullseye. "If only."

"Chances?"

"None."

Ruth sighed. "I hate to see you hurt."

"I did it to myself."

"On purpose?"

"No." Kary exhaled. "Yes. Not initially." She took the plunge, fishing for absolution. "I wallowed." *I did everything but pick up the phone.* It was good Ruth couldn't see the flush of shame creeping up her neck.

"Unlike you, dear."

"What do you want—I'm weak."

"Human," Ruth said.

"Fine."

"Are you writing, dear?"

Ruth always understood. "Not yet, but I think there's a candle in the forest."

"Is there a real one somewhere?"

"Don't I wish." She *knew* Ruth would agree about Joe.

"Come see me some time. I miss you. Saw you on the TV set, told all my friends." A longer pause. "Was he the one?"

Kary swallowed. Technically, no—the man she had fallen for was twelve centuries dead. "Him? No. I barely met him."

"Okay, then." Ruth's voice sounded tired. "Don't be too long coming out, Kary."

"I miss you, too, Aunt Ruth."

"Give my love to the girls." And out of nowhere, vehemently, "I never did like that Charles."

Going with the torrent and the scathing self-criticism drew the barb. Her own isolation, being between books, left her armorless. *Roland swept over that beach like a riptide: fight it, I exhaust myself and drown. Be patient, swim parallel to shore; when the undertow weakens, I can crawl ashore.* She dissected the obsession with a writer's objectivity, encased it in a Zen bubble exiled to the outermost limit of her self. Sated, satiated, gorged, her fascination faltered. An overabundance of fuel calcined the wick.

The realization she was but one of millions of women snagged by an actor's charisma freed her. *He won't miss one of us, and I refuse to be part of a harem.*

She collected all the pieces of her folly—CD, movie DVDs, the DVD from the show. She packed them neatly into one of her manuscript boxes. She couldn't decide what to write on it, left it blank. She placed the box in one of the drawers in her living room wall unit, pushed the drawer in with a sense of closure. When she was ready, she would decide whether to throw it out. *Surgery successful.*

Perversely, the seed for Akiiya's story—and a working title, *Hostages to Fortuna*—came from a rabid fan website: Andrew O'Connell could do no wrong. *No one is perfect.* What kind of personality let devotion paralyze judgment? What were the repercussions to the one enthralled? How did it lead to humans sacrificed for a cause?

She found notebook and favorite pen, raced to container the deluge.

BIANCA

Hollywood Hills; April 8

"WHERE IS THE MEAT?" Bianca enunciated to the uniformed maid. "*¿La carne?*"

"*El señor* Michael *se la llevó.*"

Dammit. Couldn't they follow one instruction? *She's mine.* Bianca pivoted towards the aviary. The fiery sunset cast a hellish glow on the shadows; it only impressed tourists too stupid to know its cause was smog. "Michael, I clearly told the girl to bring that to *me.*" She snatched the plate, took her place at the aviary's wire mesh wall. Nevermore was on her favorite perch. The raven did her little dance, short steps to each side, head bobs, tiny wing flaps.

"You were on the phone."

Bianca cawed softly. The bird answered. "See, she wants *me.*" Bianca fed Nevermore beak-sized chunks of horsemeat. Nevermore took them delicately, cawing with pleasure. "She says she had a very boring day."

"I wish you wouldn't keep her in a cage." Michael wrapped his handkerchief around his fingers—Nevermore had pecked him again.

Smart bird. "She's fine."

"You care more for that bird than for me."

"That's absurd, Michael. She's just a bird." Nevermore tolerated no one else's touch but hers. *Serves him right.* She stroked the bird's wing, imitated the raven's croak in her lowest register, enjoying the sensation deep in her throat. Nevermore appreciated her voice—one of the many things that distinguished her from the pack, deciding factor in several choice roles. Bianca knew her voice enthralled Michael; he hated her using it on Nevermore almost as much as he hated her insistence on keeping the bird she bought from a street urchin in Calexico. 'Let her free; it's probably illegal.' *Wimp. What would Nevermore do by herself?* "You can't take the Lear."

"I need it," Michael whined. "Look, I talked to Grant. You're prime property. He's sending his plane for you."

"Like cargo?" She barely kept her voice under control. *I paid for the jet; not your stupid company.* Why couldn't she say it out loud? *'Only fishwives screech, princess.'* "When were you going to tell me?"

"Be reasonable, babe. This way I can come visit you once in a while—"

"From Canada?" Bianca preened the bird's flight feathers with a perfect scarlet nail-tip. *Over my dead body.* "Don't come, Michael."

"Ruins your concentration, eh?"

"I mean it. Don't come." Bianca allowed the raven the last misshapen cube, watched her take flight, settle on a higher branch for the night. *Damn Michael. How much is it going to cost to untangle our finances?* "Concentrate on whatever it is you need to get your documentary filmed."

"Walk me out?"

Your bags are packed? Cold fury made it easy to avoid a scene. She let him kiss her on the colonnaded portico, lit as brightly as a night set. *'Always keep matters in your own hands, Bibi. Choose your time.'* Anyone watching would think she was mollified.

Anyone watching would be dead wrong.

KARY

Sanctuary; Monday, April 25; 11 A.M.

THIS WAS THE GOOD part. Revising. Rewriting. Kary sat at the big dining room table looking out: yellow-green foothills, emerald hills, and as backdrop the three-thousand foot snow-topped gray-green Mt. Cardigan. She needed mountains.

The birds and squirrels arguing over the feeder were pure happiness. They lived in the present, she wrote in the present.

On an impulse she'd taken out her watercolors and a tiny brush. It turned out eerily well, the two by three inch landscape painting of K'Tae in a ridiculously ornate frame. A view from a rocky promontory, across an inlet of the sea, to steep craggy implacable mountains with no green, no rivers, no snow. K'Tae had almost no free-running fresh water. K'Tae was not like Arrakis in *Dune*: here there was water in plenty—for those who could afford the expensive desalinization farms along the coast...

Three-quarters through her 'first act,' Akiiya the enforcer, Akiiya of the long red braid, was starting to talk back. *Good.*

The rebel group which captured Akiiya traveled light. They kept her hands tied; a short rope to Myrian's belt told her what they thought of her. It was not time to strangle Myrian with the rope; it was time to learn. To learn why the rebels fought hopelessly against a government fist-in-glove with Akiiya's Federation forces.

Kary struggled to polish the images; to select the exact words; to find the tightest, most transparent way to let Akiiya's story breathe.

The doorbell chimed; she jumped. K'Tae evaporated. *Damn.* How long would it take before her heart reacted without skipping beats? Stupid physiological responses—desensitization? Maybe she'd get Zoë to stand at the gate and ring the bell. The mailman wasn't due for hours. *Who on earth?*

A man. Shaggy dark hair, stocky. Head down; she couldn't see his face. Black leather jacket and pants, helmet under his arm. Next to him a massive black-and-chrome motorcycle. A delivery?

She pushed the intercom button. "Who is it?"

He looked up. Her heart stopped.

Andrew O'Connell.

❧ CHAPTER SIX ❧

Gathering his fools in one basket to see what would hatch

...at the awards luncheon ANDREW O'CONNELL was spotted hitting on tablemate LISETTE BOUDREAU. In the market for a child bride? Despite her mature endowments, the actress is still shy of her sixteenth. Ever-vigilant Papa Boudreau interrupted the tryst-to-be, leaving Lisette wistful. O'Connell disingenuously claimed not to know she was a minor...

> www.wayneblackburn, Archives, 2004

Note yesterday's customary distortion on Blackburn's website—Lisette's first big role, not surprising Andrew didn't know her, she's dressed to the nines—and looked beautiful.

> www.AOCORNER, Archives, 2004

—Are BD and MH breaking up? He's left for an extended period to do a documentary in Canada; sources say the star is determined not to let her private life interfere with her work—

> April 11, www.whereandhow

KARY

Sanctuary; **Monday, April 25; 1 P.M. (cont.)**

THE NEXT HEARTBEAT hurt as adrenaline surged. *My God, why do you torture me?*

"It's Andrew, Dr. Ashe," he said into the grating. "There was no getting yer phone number, so I gambled ye'd be home."

Her racing mind wrested control of her voice back from panic. "Ah— Of course. Come right up." She stared stupidly at the screen as the gates obeyed the electronic signal. *This isn't a DVD you can pause.* Thirty seconds for a quarter mile. *I've got thirty seconds.* His hair—she hadn't recognized him before she spoke. Images flooded her mind: Roland kneeling at Oliver's side—her thumbs touching Andrew's calloused hands in hers at the restaurant—Andrew on the black stool singing 'Mother of my child'— The approaching reverberation stopped the flow. *Open the door, Kary.*

The big Harley roared into view, spraying gravel as he skidded theatrically to the end of the drive. He kicked out the stand, balanced his helmet on the seat, shook out a shoulder-length mane. He padded up the stone walk, stopped by the stoop with his eyes level with hers. "Hi."

Her face was rigid plastic, the smile painted on. *Behave yourself. You can do this*—treat him as you would one of the med students you used to lecture to. *Don't let him smell fear.* "Hi yourself. This is an unexpected pleasure. What brings you to my kingdom?"

"The movie. *Bunker Hill.* Remember?"

A flicker of uncertainty in his eyes galvanized her. "Sorry! Where are my manners?" She backed up to allow him to enter. *Deal with it.* Like a lion tamer proving to herself mastery over the beast, she turned, walked down the short hall to the Great Room; prickling skin over the sixth cervical vertebra told her he followed. *One slip...* 'Research' taught her he suffered fools relatively patiently, deceit—not at all. *For his sake, keep it cordial, keep it brief, and he need never know about the crazy woman.*

She wasn't surprised when, like most first-time visitors, he continued past her to the windows. Below, early dogwoods bloomed around the modest patch of grass, with a spot of snowdrops and deep purple crocuses. Beyond—New Hampshire.

"Incredible!" His head swiveled in both directions. "What a view!"

She joined him. He occupied more space than she remembered. *You will not reach out to touch him—that woman is dead.* "You see why I call it my kingdom."

"I didn't know this part of the States had such great tracts without a body in 'em until I came up here." He let his gaze rove over the wall of green. "Naught on yer horizon but trees." His tone implied approval.

Not: 'Aren't ye lonely?' *Kindred soul?* "Is it as green as Ireland?"

"Aye. No. A different kind of green. Ireland's rolling meadows and misty mountains." He smiled and cocked his head, a now-familiar motion.

Act normal. "Here. Let me take your jacket." Underneath the black leather, the well-remembered ivory cableknit. He exuded the faint aroma of lanolin; nursing mothers used... *Get hold of yourself.* Her arms cradled the heat of the heavy coat, but by the time she had slid the girls' parkas to one side, and made her fingers insert a hanger, her composure was locked in. *It's but a courtesy call—he keeps casual promises. He is your guest, Karenna Ashe. If you make him uncomfortable in any way, I'll never forgive you.* When she rejoined him her exterior was calm. "How *did* you find me?"

"Wasn't easy. I coaxed yer address from yer agent. She hem'd and haw'd—people do have trouble saying no to me—I told her ye said—" Lop-sided grin. "But I didn't push me luck for a phone." His fingers were hooked under the bottom of his sweater, as if to keep his hands from wandering, while his thumbs stroked the edge. "She said she'd call."

"Shame on you—Irish charm." *Of course.* He bewitched Elise. Her own naïveté in New York b.A.—before Andrew—rose to haunt her. *What an innocent I was.*

He folded himself into the overstuffed chair she offered. "I asked around a bit." He dipped his head with a sideways wag. "People up here are either woefully ignorant, or dreadfully protective of ye."

"The latter, I'm afraid." She sat on the sofa's arm, caressed a cross-stitched cushion with jittery fingers. She forced herself not to use it as a shield. "Apparently, when *Creek Station* came out, some people took offense at how I portrayed one of the Southern characters." *Keep it simple.* "I passed a terrifying fifteen minutes while the police removed a large angry gentleman intent on demolishing my front door. Ergo, the fence and the security camera."

"After the show."

She shrugged; it wasn't a question. *If anyone knows...* "I live alone, but, Green Mountain Boys or no, I refuse to get a gun."

"Heard about 'em when I read up for this part." Open friendly smile, relaxed as a child's. "Ethan Allen and such."

"You've done your homework." *Am I really pulling this off?* She nested the pillows. "Would you like something to drink?"

He tilted forward on the edge of the chair with his hands clasped between his knees. "Would ye be having any of that good American beer?"

Shy? She hadn't anticipated that. "Certainly."

He rose. "Don't get up. I'll fetch it. What'll I get ye?"

"Come pick it out yourself." She guided him to the wall hanging, hooked the unobtrusive thread loop from the right over the equally unobtrusive hanger on the left, pushed to release the spring lock, and stepped aside as the slab door pivoted. She heard behind her his sharp intake of breath. She reached in, flicked the switch, fought an unaccustomed claustrophobia. "The man who designed the house widened a natural cave. It's fifty-five year round. Is that cold enough, or do you need an ice cube?"

"In *beer?*" He stared at her with shocked eyes. "Ah. I see. Ye're joshing me." He popped in, examined the offerings closely, brought out his selection—and spent a moment running his finger down the nearly-invisible installation seam.

"You should've seen your face." *He's teasable.* He accompanied her into the kitchen. "In-house joke. But isn't it colder than Guinness in pubs in Ireland?" *Ack!—damn brain.* Would he notice she knew his favorite? Shades of *Misery.* She added ice to an insulated mug, filled it with cold water from the refrigerator tap.

He opened the beer. "Water?" He rested a palm on the counter, his face a comical look of pure horror.

He looked so domestic she needed him *out* of her kitchen. *Now.* "Come on back—I'll light a fire—to kill the chill." She talked over her shoulder as she led the way back. "Can't tolerate much alcohol, I'm afraid—and I still have work to do." *Damn. That's exactly the wrong thing to say.*

ANDREW

DAMN—WHAT DID I DO? He settled back into the armchair warily—took a sip of the Samuel Adams Boston Lager. Had he been right to chance coming? 'Snap judgment,' George said once, 'will get ye in trouble some day, Andy boy.' His antennae were quivering. As he surveyed the room with its stunning view, his gaze was drawn by the single untidiness: papers spread out on the dining table. "Christ," he said. "Ye're working. I've come a'bargin' in heedless as a lost lambín!" As bad as the invading fan. He clambered to his feet, bottle in hand. *When will ye learn to think first?*

She looked up at him from where she knelt by the massive fireplace, glanced over at the table. "That," she dismissed his concerns, "will wait." She seemed to find his discomfiture amusing. "I don't have many rules here—but one of them is 'Live human over inanimate object any day.'" She turned back to her task, refusing his offer of help. She built an elaborate structure of crisscrossed kindling boxed by split logs, finally lit a match. When it was going to her satisfaction, she dusted her hands on her jeans, sat back on her heels to inspect her creation. "I love my fires." She took her seat as he did, but rested her arms on her knees, captivated by the flames. When she looked at him again, warmth from the fire pinked her cheeks. "I'm glad you felt free to come." She tucked her jeaned legs under her on the sofa, leaving her brogues on the rug. "Shed the boots? We're rather informal here."

"Ye're sure?" His toes seconded the motion; they'd had a busy morning.

"Yup. Think I'm upwind."

"Thanks a lot."

"Even Christ had dirty feet. Didn't keep him from getting invited places."

"Good enough for him..." He pulled the boots off, set them round the side of the chair, inquired with his eyebrows. He lifted grateful stockinged feet onto the table. "Aaah!" He wiggled his toes. "Ye know how to make a man welcome."

She sipped her water, ensconced herself into the pillows. "Indulge 'em like children—let 'em do whatever they want."

"Yer next novel?" he asked cautiously, jerking his head toward the table. Every writer he'd met since *Roland* couldn't wait to cast him in 'the perfect role.' "What's it about?" *Politeness requirement fulfilled?*

She broke eye contact to search for the answer out the window. "It's... Well..." Gallic shrug. "A clash of cultures."

He leaned forward to encourage her. *Would she bite?* Might as well give her the opening, get it over with. "How's it going?"

Awkward pause. "Sorry. I can never discuss them until I've dug out the story." She squirmed. "I think it's going well." Her tone was the locking of a strongbox. "Are you allowed to talk about your movie?"

"Allowed?"

"Contractual obligations?"

He realized he had no idea of the constraints she wrote under. "When it comes out they'll be wanting me on tour—*most* publicity is good publicity. Don't leak the ending?"

"Then don't tell me."

No special privileges? He found himself studying her through narrowed eyes, wondering again why illness implied 'recluse.' Most women wheedled. *She had depths, this one.* He was beginning to enjoy this. "All right then. Well—the 'Incident' is fiction—but it's about the war erupting, and folk having to decide: allegiance to old King George—or risk siding with the upstarts. Johnnie—John Robbins—is this impatient young gentleman farmer who joins the rebels." He drew on the lager, savored the aromatic aftertaste on his palate. "I'm the British colonel commanding the district garrison. Loyalty—and its cost. The colonials made tough choices."

She kept her gaze on him as she echoed his sip. "And Bianca Doyle's your—daughter? Aren't you a bit young to be playing father roles?"

The local newspapers played it up? "Makeup makes a crusty old codger of me." He scowled, wrinkled his brow. "Besides, in those days I'd be agèd enough for a grown daughter."

"But isn't she close to thirty?"

"Eh?" His eyebrows rose. *Cattiness?* He suppressed the twitch starting at the left corner of his mouth.

"Oh, God." She rolled her eyes up, shook her head, hid behind her hands. It took a moment before she could face him.

A blush? So, not a saint. Refreshing. "Dunno. And I'd never ask, now, would I?"

"Not if you were brought up right!"

"I *was*, never fear." *Not that it took.* "Grant Sykes's satisfied. We'll see when she arrives." Looking 'young and beautiful' was Bianca's problem. She wasn't an important role, anyway.

"She's not here?"

"Grant's a tidy director. She had no scenes in Boston."

"Oh."

"*As* I was saying, when I was so rudely interrupted?"

She pouted penitently, interlocked her fingers primly in her lap like an attentive schoolgirl. "Proceed, please."

Good. She could laugh at herself. He raised the bottle in assent. "Colonel Strathmore—that's me—forbids her to see young Winston—that's Johnnie—but her sympathies are shifting. It's complicated because me freed slave—Peter Hyland—doesn't trust the insurgents..." He let the cool bitter liquid slide down his throat. Not bad—for colonials. The big room, the fire, the view, and the perceptive questions conspired with the lager to soothe him into his story. It amused him, how safe and peaceful she made it seem.

Since when do I crave peace?

BIANCA

Incident at Bunker Hill set, Hanover, N.H.

FINALLY! AND WHERE THE hell is Grant?
Bianca's pulse quickened, as the limousine which met her at the unbelievably dinky 'Lebanon International Airport'—and where they got *that* title she couldn't imagine—pulled to a stop someplace in the sticks of this New Hampshire town deemed unchanged enough since the Revolution to be usable for Grant's latest epic. Her dialogue was safely memorized, even though they'd change it at whim—as usual. Her part needed more—now that she was here, she could work on Grant.

"Here we are, Miss Doyle," the white-haired chauffeur said unnecessarily as he opened the limo door for her. "This is where they told me to bring you."

She checked around for a center of activity along the row of double-wide trailers. Where was *here*?

The door to the nearest trailer popped open, delivering the standard female minion with a clipboard. "Afternoon, Miss Doyle." The young woman in typical shorts, T-shirt, and work boots consulted the clipboard. "You're in this one."

I don't give a rat's ass. "Where are they filming right now?" Bianca kept her voice even and pleasant, the same way she kept her voice even and 'tired' when the limo driver had tried to point out the sights of the town of Hanover and the tacky square which seemed to be the middle of Dartmouth. Students meandering across the streets made the drive even more frustrating. At least she'd been spared a chatterer in the back with her, and the driver had gotten the idea, and limited himself to the few major tourist points. She wanted into the nitty-gritty, she wanted to be on set—the first set, wherever Grant was directing. And she wanted to greet her father. "And how do I get there?"

"There you are," said a voice behind her.

Bianca whirled around, her hierarchy detectors in full swing. Resonant pitch. Male. Tall. Addressing her familiarly—talent. Too young for Andrew. *Ah.* The wonder boy. "Hi?" Yup. She right-sized the smile. "John?"

"Yes, Ma'am."

"Oh God—*please* don't!" Gawky and gangly and loose-limbed as a newborn colt. In farmer-boy colonial clothes, tricorn hat in hand. *I'm supposed to fall for this?* She pouted prettily, curtsied.

"I— What should—?" He cleared his adolescent throat.

She rescued him graciously. "I'm Bianca. Very nice to meet you." She put her hand out, got in return a huge, ever-so-slightly damp one attached to the most beautiful young man she had seen this close in a while. Camera-loving cheekbones, full lips, tidy ears—the girls would drool over him, and the awkwardness would only add to his charm. Good choice. She'd heard he was straight. Not that it mattered.

He blushed. "Grant asked me to—"

"Oh, good." Grant must be filming with Andrew. She turned to the clipboard girl, waved at car, chauffeur, and the pile of luggage accumulating on the grass. She couldn't wait for Wardrobe, to see if her input had improved her costumes. Luckily the historical period allowed women to show their 'bosoms.' *Ridiculous word.* "Can you—?"

"I'll get it squared away. Anything special, Miss Doyle?"

"Thank you. No. I'll get it later. Or somebody will." She smiled at the girl, thanked the chauffeur quickly—wouldn't do to get a reputation as uppity when it was so easy to avoid—and turned her attention back to her love interest. She would be kissing him. Chastely—but Grant would also film it as near-porn—in case he decided the final cut needed spicing up. John seemed respectful enough—would he be fiery enough? *Again, my job.* A shiver of content. Her whole body felt alive. *Finally.* "Ready—I can't wait."

But she was fit to be tied by the time the puppy delivered her to where Grant was wrapping up the scene. Waste of a walk—she should've been practicing how to manage the confining skirts and bodice of the period.

He'd insisted—'Grant said you wanted to see everything'—on walking her around what seemed like the whole town—'and he said it would be better if you waited until they were done, because, uh, everyone would stop working...' She knew exactly what Grant meant—everyone would turn around and babble and it *would* delay the filming if they were almost done—but it was infuriating. She *needed* to see every scene, to shadow Grant's every step, and she was running out of sweetness. It didn't help that each time John checked his cellphone there was a fresh delay—sometimes this business drove you bonkers. The light had definitely turned to 'late afternoon'—and wouldn't hold. They *had* to be done: dusk scenes were the pits to film outdoors; Grant knew better than to try.

"They're in the big field behind the barn." John pointed down the dirt lane. As they walked, he marked the site plan he'd been making for her. "I have to go that way, anyway. Gotta get ready for to-night—"

"Hey there, missy! How was the trip?" Grant, down-home-and-hearty, with that shock of unruly gray hair he played with constantly while directing and even more stupid goatee. He held her hands, kissed her on each cheek. "Thanks for taking care of my girl," he said to John, who blushed. Again.

"He showed me *everything*." She thanked John with a big smile she almost meant. And where the devil was O'Connell? "Andrew?"

"He's not in this scene." John reached out to hand her the map. "He took off on his motorcycle."

Grant folded his arms, unconcerned. "He wanted to scope out the countryside before he requires bodyguards."

"Oh?" The idiot colt had known the whole time—and hadn't thought to mention it? *I could have mined him for information.* She'd deal with *him*, later. "So, which scene was this?" *Could* Grant tell her interest had suddenly dropped? She didn't think so. Acting was a useful profession.

I need so many things from him.

KARY

Sanctuary

"—MISBEHAVING BRITISH redcoats, and battles—big show, cannon and horses and—" He lifted his arms expansively to include everything.

"You make it sound like a party." Kary knew her voice was wistful. *If the shoot revolves around you.*

"Aye. There's good people I've worked with on other films. A grand chaotic party for weeks, months."

"How long will it be for this one?"

"First day or two of June—and we're done."

And then it vanishes forever. "Gigantic letdown when it's over?"

"Aye. The wrap's wild. All the footage has to be in before they strike the sets, return the houses to the locals..."

"What then?"

"On to the next one, unless I'm lucky enough—or unlucky enough, I guess—to be having time off. Then I go home to Ireland, drink, appease the band, work on the farm and let me ma boss me around."

The mantelpiece clock chimed. She started to raise her hand, hesitated a fraction of a second, changed her mind again. *He might as well see the* real *me.* She let her hand finish its journey to 'Stop!' before counting on extended fingers to four. He looked curious. "Just one of my little crush—crutches." *Whatever you do, Karenna Ashe, don't minimize.* "I lose track."

"Can't believe I've been here an hour. We're shooting night scenes; makeup'll want me head. And ye've let me monopolize the conversation." He checked his watch, reached for the boots. "I've exhausted ye."

"Dead giveaway." She focused. *Almost out of danger.* "Slurred speech. Damn this brain. Some days I'm incoherent by sundown. But I can't remember a time I've enjoyed more."

"Are ye always so direct?"

"When I'm tired. Easier." *There; no deceit.* She produced a fractured smile. "Your reaction tells me it pleased you."

He grinned. "Aye."

I've earned a tiny defiance. "Why should I deny both of us that small pleasure?" *Watch it!*

He chuckled. "Aye. Indeed." He stood, appraised her view with appreciation. "It's a grand place ye're having here."

She got to her feet, walked him to the door in her socks. She retrieved his coat, grabbed her boots and backpack from the closet, stepped out onto the stoop to escape as he filled her entranceway while swinging the heavy leather jacket around his shoulders. *Too close, too close!* It wasn't going to help to remember him in the cave, in her kitchen, by the fire, putting his feet on her table... *I had no choice.* Liar. End it here. She didn't trust her voice.

He followed her out, enclosed again in black, took the single step down. "Boots?"

"Mail call," slipped out. *Shit. Why not 'Going for a walk to clear my head'?*

"Ahh. I'll give ye a ride down." He brought the shiny helmet back from where he'd perched it on the bike's seat. "Guests get the helmet."

"You're kidding."

"Perfectly safe—I won't go above the speed limit."

Find an excuse. Say goodbye. "I—"

"Ye can't be a chicken."

She tied her boots, shouldered the pack. So much less fuss to reach for the protective head gear.

He mounted, cranked the starter, twisted round to give her a hand. "Hold tight," he said unnecessarily, bringing her arms around him once she was seated.

How did I get myself into this? She gripped his torso as he roared off. The helmet blocked her side view, and his hair whipped in her face. The gravel drive, rough in the pickup, was rutted and erratic. The big bike fishtailed on the 'S' turn. Her hold tightened spasmodically, the median nerves along her inner arms a subdermal receiving antenna for his laughter. *You are hugging Andrew O'Connell. Satisfied?*

He helped her dismount at the gate. "Too much for ye?"

"No." *Tachycardia isn't fatal.*

"I'm due back or I'd be taking ye for a spin."

She removed the helmet, held it out to him. When he took it, she ran fingers through her hair, extracted a sheaf of envelopes from the mail drop. She brandished them as the gate swung open to a touch of the button on the key fob. "Plenty more paperwork back at the ranch." A few more seconds and she'd be free.

"I've had a lovely time."

Thank God. "It was lovely having you." She impressed a memory: modern knight, armor, steed. Absurd a grown man should possess lashes that thick.

"I was wondering..." He hugged the helmet to his chest with both arms. "Would it be all right if I come back? Sets get a bit crowded sometimes now." His voice gave the 'now' a peculiar odd little twist. His gaze flicked from her eyes to something extraordinarily compelling on the empty road beyond the gate.

He needs me? "Of course. Anytime." She slammed mental doors on clamoring warning bells. "Do you know your schedule in advance? May I offer you dinner?"

His smile returned as if refilled from an unclamped artery. "Are ye better in the mornings?"

"Usually." *Kary, don't.* "Why?"

"Friday I don't need to be reporting to makeup till eleven."

Far too late to resist the big clumsy lion cub. "Breakfast at eight early enough?"

"Can I bring supplies? So ye aren't going to extra trouble."

She had to laugh. "The idea of Andrew O'Connell wandering the Shopper's aisles, buying eggs and stopping traffic for miles? Almost worth it. But no. Thanks. My housekeeper keeps me in groceries."

Tanned skin crinkled around his eyes. *Celtic blue. Stop it.* He trapped her hand between his. "I'll not be interfering with yer work?"

"So?" Skin on electrified skin. *Stop that.* With her hand captive, she managed a nonchalant shrug with difficulty.

He raised his prey to his lips before releasing it. "Sure ye wouldn't be needing a ride up?"

She waved him off, forcing her voice light. "Haven't taken today's hike."

Her eyes followed the black figure until it vanished around a curve. *Can* I promise a haven? One of my med students; they never succeeded in flustering me, even when I was younger than they. A friend's grownup child. *Pure maternal instinct.*

Her knees insisted she sit on a stump. Mount Fire had risen to twice as high.

ANDREW

Bunker Hill, **Hanover; Wednesday, April 27; 9** P.M.

"WAKEUP CALL'S AT SIX."

"'Night, George." Just as well George begged off coming in— they had filmed until late in the crisp New Hampshire spring night, and Andrew ached down to his smallest bone. He stretched wearily, cracking as much of his backbone as would cooperate. Beer, smoke, shower, bed. Get up before dawn; do it again. *A good tired.* He was as satisfied as he ever got.

"Hello, Andrew," said a seductive voice.

He froze in the narrow hallway of his trailer, halfway through peeling his T-shirt off. *What the hell?*

"In here." The voice quavered.

A child? The bedroom. Senses on hyperalert, he wrenched the shirt down. Autopilot dropped him into the fighter's crouch, hands up. He oozed forward. The door stood an inch ajar. He burst into the tiny room.

The girl in the flimsy pink negligee parodied an older woman's sexual display. Exaggerated makeup. Reek of 'White Diamonds.'

Anger rose like an uncontrolled cobra. "What the bloody hell are ye doing here?"

"I, I wanted…".

"Don't move." Did that terrify her? *Good.*

She shrank into the pillows.

Fourteen? If that. *Damn!* He got the hell out, jerked the door closed. The window? Too small for her to crawl through. He took the trailer steps in a single bound, yelled to George Cosgrave's receding back.

Andrew paced the minuscule living room, chain-smoking, while George called Security. A field day—the media would have a fucking field day. *Lisette looked twenty.* Damn women.

Ted Silver, Head of Security, arrived in minutes. Together the three men entered the hallway, with Andrew inches behind Silver. Sounds of sobbing seeped through the door.

Silver twisted the knob—locked. "Security. Open up, miss." Silver's tone carried calm authority. "You're only making things worse for yourself." No answer. "Don't make me get the master key."

Master key? *It's a god-damned trailer, for Crissakes.* But Andrew's fury crested and he felt himself slipping into damage-control mode and away from wanting to shred the interloper, bury the body.

Silver raised a finger to his lips. "Come on, young lady. I have other things to do."

Scuffling noises from within. "Don't come in. Just a minute." Clunks, a zipper.

"Steady, Andy," George muttered. "Ye look like ye'd rip the door from the hinges."

Simple for George—he wasn't gossip-column fodder. Andrew pushed past him, located a cigarette. He threw himself on the couch, force-focused on the lazy plume of rising gray smoke.

The door opened a crack. Silver shoved it, yanked the girl into the living room between himself and George.

Jail bait with a blue backpack. Heavy tear-streaked mascara, tight black jeans, red spaghetti-strap top, clogs. *A child playing dress-up.* Andrew throttled rage. Let George and Silver do the talking.

"Have you any idea how much trouble you're in, sneaking into Mr. O'Connell's trailer?" Silver said. "Do you know we can charge you with criminal trespass?"

The girl's eyes appealed to Andrew.

He glowered. She flinched. *Good.*

She picked George's as the friendliest face. "I'm sorry." She started to whimper. "I just wanted..."

"I know what ye wanted, child," George said. "Do yer parents have the slightest notion where ye are?"

The girl visibly diminished in Silver's grasp as the enormity sunk in. "Oh, God! They'll kill me!"

"Should've thought of that first, miss." Silver faced Andrew. "Do you want to press charges?"

Christ, no. "Get her the hell out of here."

Silver hurried the girl through the doorway and down the steps. They heard him call for backup, the girl blubbering. *By the book.*

"I'd better go along," George said. "Keep ye out of this."

"Thanks, George." Lingering perfume made his head throb. He massaged the muscle between his brows. He couldn't even fix these things himself. "Tell Grant—keep it quiet otherwise?" *The last thing I need....*

When they'd gone, blessedly without sirens or lights, he opened the fridge, extracted a beer, downed aspirin with the bitter brew. His fingers probed the pack for another fag.

And things were going so well.

BIANCA

Bunker Hill; April 27; 10 P.M. (cont.)

THIS HAS GONE FAR enough.

She'd seen Grant; the night ended to Grant's satisfaction. *Andrew should be in a good mood.* Anticipation—almost as good as the instant before the cameras rolled. Bianca took her moment, knocked on Andrew's trailer door.

The door was yanked open as if he'd been laying in wait. "What hap— ?" Andrew filled the doorframe, his long hair loose around his shoulders. "Uh— hullo?"

Not exactly the welcome she planned for. His boots were dusty, his jeans well-worn, as if he hadn't bathed in days. *Foreigners.* "Hi yourself." Best not to give him too many options. "Can I come in?" *And who is he expecting this late?* "Won't take long."

He hesitated. Then, like he couldn't come up with an excuse, he moved aside.

Don't jump all over yourself inviting me in. She walked up the steps past him into a living room mirror-image of hers: short couch, armchair at either end, end tables, coffee table, wall sconces for practicality. Kitchenette beyond—probably nothing in the half-sized refrigerator but beer. Institutional chic—no personal touches like hers. *Men.* Maybe in the bedroom? Finagle a peek in there? "Lots of room."

"Don't spend much time here."

You call that an opening? "Where do you run lines?" He stood so still and huge it warmed the insides of her thighs—and spooked her. *Am I talking to myself?* "That's why I came. But not tonight." Damn him. She'd gotten more reaction out of gay guys.

"Anywhere. Outside." That seemed to unblock something. "Here. Let me get ye a beer. Let's sit in the deck chairs—it's stuffy inside."

Ah—does he have someone in here? She shrugged one shoulder. "It's a beautiful night." *Shit. How the hell am I supposed to seduce a guy in full view of the world?* And found herself outside in one of his chairs on the grass beside the entrance before she had a chance to do more than bump into him while they maneuvered in the small space.

His neck cracked as he peered into the edges of the dark. "Better."

Better for who? *Freezing out here.* What was he hiding? *Shit. Complications.* But there'd been not a drop of gossip. "It'll do." She raised the beer he'd opened for her. "Cheers."

"Something about lines?"

He wasn't going to let this rest, get acquainted? *Fine.* "Day after tomorrow. Friday afternoon. We're doing some of your scenes with me, in town—" *Aren't you the big professional, always prepared?* "Don't want to look like an idiot."

"Ah. Right." Dismissive tone.

Could he care a little? *Asshole.* "I'm off book. When?"

"Ah—right. I'm sorry. Grant's got me meeting meself coming back." He took a swig, scanned the dirt road like he was hoping the solution would show up there. "Friday morning? Before makeup?"

"No time tomorrow?"

"Not if it goes like today." He ran a hand through hair riffled by the breeze. He was spared further response by the sight of a red-headed man hurrying towards them. "Give me a sec."

"I just want to set a time—"

"I know. Wait." He met the intruder halfway, spoke rapidly, got an answer. The men joined her, remained standing. "Bianca, this is me manager, George."

She made getting up appear easy. "Nice to meet you." There went tonight—anyone else would've deep-sixed the help. *Idiots.* "Looks like you two have something you need to do. Friday morning? Takes them a while to get me ready—they want me at ten. Eight, then?" Barely enough time for a quick run-through. *Damn— there goes my beauty sleep.* They should've done it all by now, but the big star was 'busy.' *Out riding the damn motorcycle?*

George raised his eyebrows to Andrew. "Friday morning? Aren't ye—?"

"Ah, damn... Just a sec, George." Andrew stretched rudely, faced her. "Here—I'll find ye. Sometime tomorrow. After dinner? We can work in one of the tents for an hour or two. Might not be until late."

He'd find time? Wonderful. "It'll have to do." *What the hell was so serious they looked like a funeral?* "Goodnight, then." Warm smile now—counteract the sting. She nodded. "George." She took her time, made damn sure her walk gave them something to think about.

And thank you so much for making me feel important.

❦ CHAPTER SEVEN ❧

Who claimeth Sanctuary shall fast and pray, and toll the bells for forty days

WRITER CONQUERS ILLNESS
PWC (person with chronic fatigue) Sandraty Koel Eitch-kin said, 'She (Ashe) could do so much good (but) she never even answered my letter.' Bestseller Ashe (K. Beth Winter, *Prairie Fires*) refused this reporter's interview request.

B. J. Elsay, 'Model Roles,' *Art/Culture*, 4/20

...America's Sweetheart, BIANCA DOYLE, the roman-tic lead in GRANT SYKES' Revolutionary War epic, may be ANDREW O'CONNELL's latest victim. The ac-tor has a rep for lovin' and leavin' his costars—not that any complain...

April 25, www.StarryTips

And, behold, there came a great wind from the wilder-ness, and smote the four corners of the house, and it fell upon the young men, and they are dead...

Job 1:19, KJV

ANDREW
Bunker Hill; Wednesday, April 27; 11:20 P.M. (cont.)

"PROBLEMS?" GEORGE folded his arms, stared after Bianca un-til she moved beyond range of the lights.

"Christ, haven't I enough?" Andrew raked his hair with the fin-gers of both hands. *Worst is, Bianca's right to call me on it.*

Forget her—he had more immediate problems. Did the night have eyes? *Shite.* He hauled George into the trailer, yanked the door shut.

"Easy, lad." George nodded toward the entrance. "Security's sending a couple of rent-a-cops to lift the girl's prints." His forehead furrowed in distaste. "Glad she isn't me daughter. She'll be grounded till she's twenty."

Andrew couldn't shake the image of the girl splayed out on his pillow—no worse than precociously sexualized adverts on billboards—but wrong, *wrong. Christ.* Followed in his mind by a terrified child in smeared black eyes. "How old?"

"Thirteen."

"Damn." Would shite hit the media when some 'journalist' needed his mark? *And I can't do a thing.* Andrew raided the fridge for two beers, commandeered the farthest armchair. "I left it unlocked."

"Silver's pissed she got anywhere near." George's neutral inflection refused to assign blame. "And—ye left it unlocked."

"Never needed lock me doors before." He couldn't sit; took his bottle to the kitchen for a replacement, tried to see through the dark outside, repeated at the three windows in the living room. He jerked the door open. No obvious lurker. "What did Security *do?*"

George clasped hands behind his neck, leaned back expansively. "Stop pacing about like a caged lion."

"A thirteen-year-old girl, for Crissakes!" He threw himself in the chair. "Nobody missed her?"

"Told her parents she was studying at a friend's." George grimaced. "Silver let a female officer put the fear o' God in her. Full police workup—photos, prints, statement—kid's blubbering like a drowned rat. Confiscated the pack, and the—ah, negligee? Older sister's. The parents came storming in—mother screaming 'what did he do to my baby,' father furious for looking a fool in the middle of the night to retrieve her from 'some movie-star's bed.' No lawyer, thank the good Lord—no time, I'd be guessing. They saw *Roland*, her and her friends—said she was old enough to be Aude—"

"Dammit—Allison Ryers is twenty-four and has two kids!"

"She *looks* young?"

"Which is why they cast her!" He needed to break something. *Easy, boyo. Control.* "Are the friends in?"

"She said not—wanted to impress them on the morrow."

"So it blows up tomorrow? Christ!"

"I *think* not. Silver tells her, he should be passing her on to the authorities. 'The only thing between you and real trouble, young lady, is Mr. O'Connell's reluctance to be dragged into the spotlight.'" George copied Silver's accent. "'You've embarrassed my security force, as well as your parents. I have no idea what to do with you.' The father starts sputtering. *Eejit.* I suggested a compromise: Silver keeps all the evidence—and a signed confession. We use nothing unless word gets out—at which point all hell breaks loose, and she gets breaking-and-entering, trespass, harassment, stalking, indecent exposure, attempted entrapment..."

Too many people involved already. "Will the rest of 'em keep their bloody yaps shut?"

"Silver's mortified enough about *his* reputation—I trust so."

"Thanks, George." *A bloody conspiracy.* Contained? "Don't know what I'd do without ye."

"Get in a lot *more* trouble?" George bent forward, elbows on his thighs, hands linked. "Ye're lucky in one way."

"This is luck?"

"Because she was inside, the timeline's clean—I told Silver no more than maybe twenty, thirty seconds from ye saying goodnight to calling me back."

He envisioned the headlines: *Actor caught in bed with child.* Truth be damned. "They'll say ye lied for me."

"Ye're 'news'—this won't be the last time." George picked up his beer, put it down carefully without drinking. "Should've seen this coming: the job's getting too big for me, Andy. A professional team—"

"—Would have me a beast on display." He shook his head wearily. *Last thing I want is handlers.* "It's bad enough."

"Fine. I'll do me best. But I decide when it's to be kicked up."

"*We* decide." The adrenaline was fading, scouring him empty. A few hours sleep. Pour the rage onto tomorrow's film. "When needs be."

Hope the hell Grant understands.

BIANCA

Bunker Hill; Thursday, April 28; 11 P.M.

WHAT A HUGE DIFFERENCE twenty-four hours make. Last night still stung.

Bianca closed her eyes to block out the white tent around them, the hard folding chair, their scripts on the paper tablecloth over a long table, people in the background doing something with the food tables, the miscellaneous smells of lasagna and fried chicken and

Salisbury steak—ugh!—lingering from dinner. Someone had positioned a heater near where she and Andrew took up residence, and the warmth radiated to her right side. 'Satisfied?' he'd asked. "No—never!" She opened her eyes: he was smiling.

"Again?" He'd showered before seeking her out and his hair dried as they worked, settling into thick natural waves. Without makeup, the dark brown contrasted oddly with his lighter eyebrows.

"No. It's the right stopping point," she conceded reluctantly while stretching her arms sideways and wriggling her fingers. Two solid hours of fighting with her 'father' and she was smiling—much more like it. "We can't do anything else without blocking and a set. Just—I never like being bumped back into normal life. Coffee?"

"This late?"

"Decaf—something warm?"

"Tea for now—beer later."

"I'll go." A tiny disappointment: he hadn't invited her to share that beer. She collected the beverages, sat down, appraised him over the rim of the food-service cup as she sipped. With luck, she'd have a couple minutes. "Was this so horrible?"

"Ah—sorry about last night."

"I caught you at a bad time." She maintained eye contact, hoping he'd spill something. *Something I can work with.*

"Not yer fault." He shrugged, covered his mouth with the back of his arm to hide a yawn. "It's been crazy."

"It's *always* crazy." *Now or never.* "Anything specific?"

He became very still. "Why?"

Uh oh. What had she stirred up? "No reason. Sometimes sharing helps." She included the tent, the set, the film with a raise of her shoulder. "At the end, it's our faces on the screen. Nobody else quite gets it."

He snorted a laugh, watched her closely. "They don't."

Was he weighing whether it was safe to trust her? *Damn poker face.* When he remained silent a few seconds too long, she cast about for the right thing to say. "What's so important we couldn't do this tomorrow morning?"

"Ah—something wants doing." He started gathering his papers.

Shit. Wrong choice. He was so tight. "Before you go, have another minute?"

"What do ye need?"

I need you to stop being a bastard. "Can we talk a bit, about *Dodgson?*" She put appeal into her voice and eyes, begged a little.

"Of course."

Finally. So, he was still interested. "I've got funding."

"Ah?"

"Branford Studios. If I can get it all together." *And if you cooperate.*

"An intriguing idea."

You said the same thing a year ago. "The script's done."

"Fine. Send it to me agent." He patted his shirt pocket to check for pens, looked around to see if he'd left anything. "I'll be getting back to ye."

"I—" She reached down to her tote bag. "I brought you a copy." *There—he couldn't refuse.*

"So. Ye *are* organized." He took the script, placed it on the top of his pile. "Ah— I can't promise anything—"

"Read it if you get a moment." She got up, shouldered her bag. *Time to exit—on my terms.* "That was good. See you tomorrow." She could hear Papi's voice as she walked away.

'The power player is the first to leave.'

ANDREW

Sanctuary; Friday, April 29; 8 A.M.

ANDREW PULLED UP TO Kary's gate at eight, scanned his perimeter before removing his helmet. *All clear.* The unseasonable warmth promised by the weatherman, perfect for outdoor filming, brought cloudless blue skies. He faced the camera, reached for the buzzer.

"Hallo. You can come up," said a male voice as the gates began their pivot.

Damn! Too early for casual visitors. *Did she invite someone to meet me?* He'd anticipated an easy continuation of their prior talk.

His guard was still up when he pulled into position next to a maroon van which paralleled Kary's pickup. He wondered what was going on as the door was opened by a tall blond man in sweat clothes and sneakers. Andrew assessed automatically: salon sun streaks, sculpted chest muscles that came from a gym, tanning-booth bronze. *A fan?*

"Come in. I am Paalo. She will one minute be."

No blink of recognition. No offered hand. Scandinavian? Writer lady likes strapping young lads? *Mind yer own business, boyo.*

Paalo springboked down the steps to the lower level three at a time. As he disappeared, Kary's head popped into sight.

She adjusted a navy-blue sweatshirt over leotard and tights as she ascended. She emanated the rootbeer aroma of Ben Gay. "Sorry," she said to Andrew with no trace of embarrassment. "We're running late this morning."

Paalo returned, gigantic duffel in hand. "I will miss you, Kary."

"You'll love New York." Kary opened her arms to him, gave him a bear hug. "Email me, OK?"

"But of course." Paalo leaned in to peck her cheek. "Be well." He shouldered the bag, let himself out with a final wave. Van engine rev, wheels on gravel, silence.

Andrew kept his face noncommittal.

"He's a dear." She bestirred herself from staring at the door. "Today took us longer—this was our last time." She made a wry mouth. "Even in a hermitage, nothing lasts forever."

It's yer home. "Ye needn't explain."

She extended interlocked fingers toward the ceiling, rotated her shoulders. "Paalo is—was—my torturer: he racks my spine. Thanks to him today I can walk. He'll be hell to replace." She nodded toward the kitchen. "Come. You hungry? Nothing's started, but I'm fast, I was up at five to write, and I'm starved."

"Can I help?" *Must ye be top dog everywhere? And ye have a dirty mind.*

In the kitchen she moved fluidly, her height an advantage in reaching dishes from upper shelves. She put him in charge of corn muffins and the toaster oven while she cooked.

They took their plates to an octagonal cedar table with umbrella and cushioned swivel chairs on the wide encircling verandah. The warm morning saturated his senses: pine-scented air, low droning of insects, daffodil explosions at the edges of the grass patch. Harsh sun lit tiny laugh lines around her eyes. She exuded the calm contentment of a woman in her rightful place as they tucked into cheese omelets and a rasher of bacon, muffins, clover honey. She diverted his attempts to talk with 'Eat while your food is hot' until they finished and she brewed him the hazelnut-flavored coffee he opted for. She settled into her chair, smiled broadly at her domain. "And how's your filming going?"

"Not bad. Grant's pleased with the rushes."

"You?"

Perceptive. "Not me call—do it however Grant wants." Did she understand process? "Got me dander up, reading British officers' letters home—protecting the colonists. Same's Ireland."

"Pax Britannica?"

"Justifies me vicious choices."

"Your fans won't like it."

"Tough cookies."

Delicate snort. "When do you covet a part?"

"Aye. Covet." Writerly precision. "When I'll be dragging a character through hell."

Quick down-up of her chin.

"I'm an actor, not a movie star. I want roles which need laboring at."

"Perfectionist?"

"Me *flaws* are recorded for all time." Didn't she have the same problem? "I don't want me grandkids saying, 'Look at grandda's funny movie.'"

"Not much chance of that—*Roland* was so *good.*"

The earnestness, echo of masses, triggered his fight-or-flight response. *Damn.* "Aye. We needn't be ashamed of that one." Had she heard the wariness?

Her gaze switched to the trees circling the yard as her index finger toyed with her lower lip. "Didn't I hear mention of a cast and crew of *thousands?*"

Gently pricking his ego balloon? *Relax, boyo; stop imagining a hunter behind every tree.* "Aye."

He relaxed, found himself telling her stories about the people: the wrangler more concerned with the welfare of animals than actors, the lad charged with making buckets of fake blood, the woman who spent a day teaching medieval banquet etiquette for a scene which lasted two minutes. He poked fun at himself for good measure. It seemed hours later when he linked his hands behind his head, stretched his shoulders. "So, did ye get any usable stories?" He kept his tone facetious, watched her expression. Would he regret his candor?

"Tons. Glad I'm not a journalist. Not obligated to share."

"I'll not be seeing meself in print?"

She looked away.

"Well?"

Troubled eyes met his gaze. "It's… Everything is grist for the mill." She searched for words. "Some day you might find a—a resonance in a character…"

"A ghost?"

"A distillation." Widespread hands encompassed empty air. "A seed. An inspiration." She folded her fingers before her chin. "Not much action in my life—isolated as I am. Your words trigger images and ideas for one of the characters I'm struggling with… But it won't be you. I don't know *you*."

"I can live with that." *Fair enough.* "What *are* ye writing?"

"I'm trying something different." She flushed.

Careful—she's wondering whether she *can trust* ye. "How so?"

"I'm fleshing out a science fiction idea wedged in my mind. I decided what the heck."

"Science fiction? After historical novels? Yer agent will be having conniption fits."

She grinned ruefully. "Elise thinks I'm shooting myself in the foot. 'After all you've done to establish yourself, you can't be serious, Kary!'" Her shoulders denied responsibility. "I blamed it on illness: 'Look, Elise, my brain chose this, and that's that!'"

"Went over well, I presume?"

"Elise is coming around. But *I* have the opportunity to fall flat on my face."

"Take it."

"Oh, I am."

"Is it true? About yer illness?" Overstepping the boundary? Or would she lecture?

Her head bobbed like a bobble doll on a dashboard. "Requires more energy to fight my brain than to give in. Hope it doesn't decide to do a Western next."

He laughed with her. "Do ye write out here?"

She sighed. "Can't. The squirrels are circus artists. My office is downstairs."

"Might I see it? I *may* be playing a writer next." He gave Bianca's script a guilty thought. "I've no image how ye novelists work."

She hesitated. "It's rather plain…"

Put yer foot in it, lad? "Never mind me. Ma says I let me mouth flap before me brain's engaged."

Again a small flicker in her eyes. "It's okay. Come on, I'll show you. But I'm warning you, it's not very exciting." She led down stairs carved into the mountain granite to a dancing-school size room with random-width oak plank flooring, a practice barre anchored to full-length mirrors on the left, glass walls before them and to the right. An expensive sound system dossed under the stairs. "This is my moving room."

Big, bare. *Curious.* He glanced about as they crossed to a door on the far side which opened to an office with floor-to-ceiling off-white drapes, desk with executive chair, file cabinets, iBook attached to a large monitor, printer. Two spare shelves kept a scant selection of books at hand. A monk's cell. "Doesn't even appear as if anyone worked here."

"Doesn't, does it? Used to be the tiniest things distracted me, so I keep everything Spartan. The current book in the computer, printouts in the cabinet, and that's it."

"Okay." *If ye say so.*

She opened the nearest file drawer to reveal tidy labelled folders. "See?"

"Not at all what I envisioned for a writer's den." He half expected to find a computer cable with a plug for a socket in her head. "It's so *austere.*"

"I warned you." She made a small huffing sound. "Nothing here diverts me from my own little world."

He peered around. The only personal objects were a decorated pottery tumbler filled with pens, and a fossil fish with a burnt Sienna matte wall-mounted in a shadow-box frame. The stark surroundings exacted a shiver. "I need props. *Lots* of props."

Her compressed lips suppressed a smile. "Don't you ever get so focused people think you've turned to stone?"

"Aye...?"

"You block external stimuli. I can't. This room does it for me."

Ah. "Ye're not really here." Any more than a cyborg is.

"No."

"I get it." He touched the chair back. "Might I?"

"Go ahead."

He visualized himself writing at her desk. He stored sense-impressions: no smells; no food—unless she had something in her desk drawer? No sound—this computer setup lacked fans and motor sounds—or were they off? He scrutinized the room—no radio or CD player; no speakers in the corners or on the shelves. He evaluated the kinesthetics of working from one spot as he fiddled with the chair adjustments, fingered the keyboard, found the books at a convenient distance. He put a hand out, opened a file drawer, rifled through hanging files and manila folders. He lifted one edge of the drapes, let it drop—they blocked the expected ground-level view of the garden and the birdfeeder. He spun around twice for good luck. "Not half-way bad."

He leaned into the chair, placed hands on the armrests, turned to face his hostess with a half-formed question, to find she had gone rigid. *Ah—damned thoughtlessness.* Most people found it amusing when he mucked about with their things, absorbing a gestalt—but she wasn't 'most people.' "Why'd ye let me? I've messed up yer settings."

She blinked several times, drew an audible breath. "Don't worry—easy to fix; Stephen loves to spin."

"Stephen?"

"My daughter Susan's boy—he's four."

Why not 'grandson'?

KARY

KARY LISTENED TO herself babble with a growing sense of horror. *What in God's name was I thinking?* The physical reality of Andrew O'Connell touching, *touching…* Her carefully constructed bubble exploded. *I can never work in here again.* She had to get him out. Out—that was the salvation. *Of course.* Out—where nothing carried tinges of the past. Pent-up breath released. "How would you like to see my 'mountain'?"

"Aye." He sprang up. "Can I put things back?"

"I'll get it later." She waited for him to exit, sealed her inner sanctum with a discrete click, and headed for the stairs. Had she kept her voice steady?

"What did ye mean by 'moving' room?"

His question came from further behind her than she expected. She stopped with her foot on the lowest tread. *I was so close.* She turned, saw her room through an actor's awareness of space: a stage.

He stood in the exact center of the polished floor, glancing around as if measuring. "Dance studio?"

Dear God. "Sort of. Exercise room. Music room." *Get him out of here. Now.* Never had she been more grateful for her medical training: first rule of being an intern was icy outward calm—never let the Attending Physician on rounds see your indecision or panic. She indicated the built-in cabinet with a rock-steady hand. "Mats and stuff in there."

With a last glance to the garden, he rejoined her. "Do ye listen to music when ye write?"

Safe topic—was he still taking data about what 'writers' did? "Wish I could. But my stupid brain only handles one thing at a time."

He backtracked to examine her music setup, paused to flip through her CDs. He held up a Mary Chapin Carpenter with a quizzical look.

She breathed easier, starting to understand his need to sniff everything. *He didn't expect this privilege to be repeated, so he had to store it all. It wasn't personal—he was working.* "Soft rock—for washing dishes."

He nodded as if he knew.

Try to imagine him scrubbing pots. "You don't do dishes."

"Somebody else's job unless I'm camping, and then it's a quick rub with a bit of clean sand."

"Yuck!"

"Soap's a recent invention." He pulled out another CD. "I like ABBA. Ye dance?"

If only he didn't keep needling the trigger points! How could she have thought she had a handle on her reactions? "Haven't danced with anyone for years." *For heaven's sake, Kary, shut up!*

He stuck his lower lip out, cocked his head. "Ye should try it. Unless it's...?"

"Dangerous? No. Not any more." *He must think I'm nuts. Why did I bring him down here?* Enough. She reaffirmed her decision, hard fought, to make this his last visit. She lifted her eyebrows to feign indifference. "Shall we?" She headed up the steps, forcing him to follow.

ANDREW

ANDREW RECOGNIZED the symptoms of invaded turf. Why had she accommodated him then? Thought he'd be content with a cursory peek? But he needed full immersion... He bent for one last glimpse below, intrigued by an image of Dr. Karenna Ashe's trim muscular legs stretched on the barre. People didn't go to the bother and expense of a barre unless they used it. And how old was she, precisely? Cosmopolitan one moment, two years old the next.

She waited, composed and unreadable, at the landing. "Give me a minute to change—" She checked her wristwatch as an alarm beeped. "Ah—I forgot. Must call Elise before the day starts piling up on her."

"Take yer time, Dr. Ashe." He glanced around at paintings, framed photographs, *objects d'art* on shelving and wall units around the fireplace. Somehow, she didn't seem the type to employ a decorator. Ye could tell so much from what people kept near them—if they made their own choices. "Okay if I wander?"

"Go ahead." She retrieved a manila folder from the coffee table. "Ten minutes, tops. And call me Kary." Soft ballet flats made pale swish sounds as she vanished up the granite stairs.

For the most part he contented himself with looking: her collection included bright Mexican pottery vases filled with silk flowers, clay warrior gods, a bronze horse. A painting of a doorway contrasted with one of a window with lace curtains that would have been at home in his parish in Athenry. He smiled at a cheesy tourist replica of the Eiffel Tower. Each must have a story, each looked at home. He hefted a glass globe embedded with brilliant glass *millefiori*, as his other hand reached for one of the photographs in a mosaic frame.

"My grandfather's." Bare feet had silenced her approach. She stood behind him holding socks. "Elise wasn't..."

He replaced the heavy orb carefully, inspected the photo he held—a family at the beach: a younger Kary, an older bearded man, two leggy long-haired girls, a young boy. "Beautiful picture," he said lamely. "Which one's Susan?"

She reached out a finger, tapped the laughing blonde. "My eldest."

He pointed to the dark-haired girl.

"Ronnie. Veronica."

He nodded. "They're older now?"

"Twenty-five and twenty-two."

"Husband?"

"Ex."

"I'm sorry." How many women would keep the ex on display?

"He couldn't take my being ill." Wry twist of lips.

The snapshot froze a slice of happiness forever. *Pity about the divorce.* "And yer boy?" Susan's arm circled her shaggy tow-headed brother. "Is he at university now?"

"We lost Ethan five years ago this past December."

Andrew looked up from the photograph to find her hugging herself, eyes brimming. "God on high. I didn't know."

"How could you?" She sniffed, blew out a long exhalation. "I miss him." She blinked hard, regained control of her voice. "He would have loved to meet you, tell all his friends. That boy in *Roland* reminded me of him. He was like that. All open. A wonderfully sunny child." Tears threatened again.

Hostages to fortune. *How do ye live if yer child is dead?* "I am so sorry."

Shaky laugh. "Just when you think you have it neatly tucked away."

"I should not be so nosy. I am truly sorry to remind..." The photograph in his hands weighed a ton.

"Don't be. I never want to forget anything about him." She gently restored the icon to its shrine, kept her gaze on its portrayal of a perfect family. "It was quick. One day he was a normal twelve-year-old, riding his bike, doing homework, pestering his sisters. The next he was stumbling into things, clumsy. They diagnosed a glio— a brain tumor. Where they couldn't touch it. One of the horrors of being MDs—we knew exactly what his chances were. Three months later he was gone."

He put his arm awkwardly round her shoulders, and she leaned on him for a moment's comfort. *When there is none.*

She inhaled deeply, pulled away. "Thanks."

'Better no word than the wrong word,' floated idiotically through his head.

KARY

I AM ETHAN'S MOTHER. Serenity settled, deep inside her core. Kary reached into the hall closet for her backpack and a windbreaker. She knew who she was. *And Susan's mother and Ronnie's mother. I am a writer. I have my own place in the universe.* She thanked God she was over the foolishness. "Come. The air will clear my head."

"Shall I carry that for ye?"

"Part of my exercise program. But thanks." She sat on the doorstep to tie her boots while Andrew watched with a half smile. *What's so amusing? Other women don't take him hiking?* It didn't matter. Spring had sprung: the chartreuse leaf tips of the sweet gum sheltering her pickup contrasted with the hunter-green of the old growth pine background behind the white dogwood blossoms and the beginning pink blooms of her one crabapple; after all these years she still wondered why her brain had such a hard time making the decision to go outside.

He gave her a hand up. "Which way?"

She shouldered the pack. "This was once a summer camp; all paths lead to the summit." *And gaining elevation first makes coming back so much easier.*

"Lead on—I'll follow ye."

Movement felt good, a place to dump the adrenaline before it started to fester. *Careful. Enough to dissipate the tension—and no more.* She realized, with a *frisson* of pride, that she hadn't worried about intruders in a while; she'd have to remember to thank Joe. The hilltop, at under half an hour, was a prudent distance. When they got down, she'd say goodbye, plead exhaustion if he seemed to linger—not likely: he had his obligations. She'd nap, think about Ethan for a while, take another nap. *He didn't know—I live surrounded by pictures of the kids all the time.* She wouldn't have energy left for editing, not tonight, but then there hadn't been much for writing this morning, not with knowing Paalo was leaving her— and all that implied—and knowing that *he* was coming. Men—they all churned her mind.

Ethan had never been in New Hampshire—that helped. The house in Princeton that was full of memories of him—lost to her forever, even if it hadn't been full of other bad memories. Best not to think of those—they didn't deserve time. And the photographs of Ethan doing homework at her table in the tiny apartment on Witherspoon—thank God she found the energy to take those—had she had a premonition? And the hospital, well, that was seared into her heart, when she could bear to go there. Ethan wouldn't want her remembering only that part, though it was her memories of the little boy grown too soon into a man, and their long talks, which she treasured.

For now, hike. Ethan would chastise her if she wallowed. *I promised him I wouldn't.* Not often, anyway.

The trail she chose twisted and turned as they climbed, wending its way up the west side of the hill through the new greenness, across streamlets, among the mixed conifers and budding deciduous oaks and maples. The forenoon penumbra kept the air cool in the shadows, and the insect chirps and buzzes muted. As usual, the unrhythm forced by stepping over tree-roots and under branches on the overgrown trail made her think of the deserts on Arrakis in Frank Herbert's *Dune*, where the *fedayeen* kept their steps irregular to avoid summoning sandworms. She had no need to chatter, and Andrew O'Connell seemed content to poke along at her pace. Now that she'd made her mind up, her thoughts were peaceful: she wasn't sorry he'd come—and would be equally glad to see him return to his gaudy world to stay.

On one of the narrow parts they moved out of the trees, and, after a steep erratic bit across a rock face on their right with a drop-off on their left, she paused to catch her breath. Finding a perch, she monitored her heart rate by reflex, was conscious of it slowing. She patted the outcropping. "Susan calls my hill 'the National Granite Reserve,' says we'll never run out." Her hill: solid, dependable, here today and tomorrow—safe.

He found himself a chunk of rock for a seat, gazed around the clearing and out at the horizon with approval. "Good spot."

"Will you get blisters from those boots?"

"They're all right—but I can see proper hiking gear's better." He eyed her curiously. "Mind if I ask ye a question?"

Why the diffidence? "Shoot."

"Ye're climbing pretty steadily here..."

"How does that fit in with the whole 'Chronic Fatigue Syndrome' bit?" *Fair enough.* "Eight years."

"Ah...?"

"At first I'd do half a block." She remembered those years, increasing her expenditure by dribs and drabs on the flats of Princeton and Hanover, stoically keeping herself motivated during the relapses. "I added a minute or a short distance when I could." She shrugged. "Careful management—I can usually go an hour or so. If I overdo it, I take extra rest." *If I'm unlucky, I lose several days—I learned the hard way not to push my limits.* It didn't seem relevant to mention that sometimes nothing helped—and today would almost certainly be one of those times.

"Ah." His gaze veered from the clearing out to the distant hazy line between green and blue. "Can ye see the town from here?"

The topic switch disconcerted her. She'd half-expected to be grilled—he hadn't been reticent before, and the insatiable curiosity of storing everything he learned in a database for later mining made sense for an actor. What deflected him? She'd probably never know. *Ah, well.* For response, she pointed west. "If you could, it would be somewhere out there. Why?"

He crossed his arms over his chest. "It is so tranquil up here."

"I'm sorry."

He looked straight at her. "Come again?"

She had responded impulsively to his body language, tone added to his words. She felt her cheeks coloring. "You said that as if Hanover were especially *not* tranquil."

"I'll have to be on guard round ye." He leaned forward, shielding his eyes with a palm from the brightness. "What? No questions?"

"Everyone is entitled to secrets." What could possibly be bothering him? *Drop it.* She stretched her arms out sideways, hard, tugging on the muscles in her shoulder blades; the daypack wasn't heavy, but its pressure on her shoulders encouraged the muscles to knot. "My bad habit. When Ethan was in the hospital, and even— *after*, his friends would sometimes talk to me—because their parents couldn't..." *It was my privilege.* She stood, dusted her hands on her jeans. "I was honored." She smiled at the memory. She re-tied the arms of her windbreaker around her waist. "Ready?"

She turned once more toward the summit, determined not to pry. Up here, the vegetation became sparser and the breeze stiffened, scuttling a leaf across the path. She picked her way over the alternating patches of soil and granite, alert to the loose scree which might cause a foot to slip. The mindfulness of focusing on each step gradually restored, as it had countless times before, the quiet in her mind. The little climb had been a good idea.

A final turn, a detour around a precarious boulder which might dislodge thousands of years from now, and they were at the crest, standing on bald rock. She luxuriated in the now-familiar happiness of earned tiredness combined with a glorious view.

"Wow!" Andrew rotated slowly, surveying the whole horizon, mountains to the east, fainter mountain ranges further west. "Ye set this up!"

His evident pleasure made her grin. "I do know my trails."

"How high are we?" He surveyed the valleys around them and the taller mountains in the distance.

"Not very. Below two thousand feet—Mount Cardigan is over three thousand." She indicated the remote eastern peak. "But we didn't start at sea-level; we're only a thousand or so higher than the house."

"Impressive, having yer own mountain."

"I love it." She hummed the tune from the *Peer Gynt Suite.*

He smiled recognition. "'In the Hall of the Mountain King.' Or Queen?"

"Except that his hall was *inside* the mountain. It runs through my head, gets me over the rough spots." *Keep it light.* "I was told the campers had a tradition—they left camp in darkness, carried their supplies, and reached the top right before dawn." She tipped her head toward the eastern sky, then to a soot-darkened semi-circle of stones forming a natural fire pit. "You can still see where they cooked breakfast." She selected a boulder, put the pack down, and wriggled into the windbreaker. Sitting on the boulder with the sun on her face, she finger-combed from memory. "Do me a favor, would you?" She dug out her camera, noted his sudden immobility. *Relax—I couldn't handle having a photograph of you up here.* "Susan doesn't believe I ever get out. Would you snap a picture? My friend Zoë's too lazy to hike here with me."

He snapped several shots, handed her the camera when she put out her hand, made no comment when she zipped it into the compartment.

"Thanks." She extracted bottles of spring water, passed him one. She unscrewed the cap on hers, sipped the still-cool water. "Doesn't get better than this."

"Water?" Mock consternation.

"Good for you. Besides, if I'd fetched beer, it'd be all shooken up by now."

He nodded sagely, took a swig, tucked the bottle into his jacket pocket. "Good point. Ye hike up here often?"

"Couple of times a week, weather permitting, though I don't always come this high. There's always something new to see."

"Snow?"

"Snowshoes."

"Alone?"

"Usually. But there are cell towers on Mount Kearsarge," she pointed to the southeast peak, "and Mount Cardigan. I leave a message for Zoë, send her another when I'm back without incident. I'm not reckless." And I time myself, and monitor my energy, and take a very long nap when I get home. *Could I be more boring?* Boring was good.

Andrew paced, examining the view in all directions. He halted before her abruptly, looming over her, backlit by the rising sun. "Wise." He dropped into a crouch beside her, forearms on his knees and hands clasped. He reached forward, hefted an egg-sized stone.

"Boring." She shifted her position to face him directly, and almost missed his next words.

He tossed the stone up, caught it, gazed at her through narrowed eyes. "Two night ago there was a young girl staked out in me bed."

Kary's breath hissed in past her teeth. Bad. *That would hurt.* "On your set."

"In me trailer. Yes." Dead flat affect, words infused with venom. He tossed the stone, caught it, tossed, caught...

"Oh, God." *This shouldn't happen to anyone.* She watched the stone, exhaled heavy air. *If the media got hold of it...* "A local?"

"Huh?"

"Not sophisticated?" Her mind created damaging rumor scenarios like cracks spreading on winter pond ice. *Not fair.* No way to counter, a faint taint left on the palimpsest of the public mind forever. Stalking went with the fame... "What did you do?"

"She's been cautioned—it'll blow up in her face if word gets out." He stood, threw the stone at a boulder on the other side of the hilltop, where it popped straight up at impact before clattering down to the boulder's base. "They put new locks on me cage, beefed up security."

"How do you deal with... with all of it?"

"Ignore it, for the better part." He cracked his neck, shook himself. "Are ye coming?"

A damn shame. She chose a different path back, down the far side of the hill, heading for one of her favorite stops. The route was longer but less steep, so she didn't need to watch her step as carefully, and her mind insisted on arguing: This is *not* your problem. *This shouldn't be how he remembers New Hampshire.* Since when is it your job to protect New Hampshire? *I can offer him a break.* Don't; he won't take it—and you'll look idiotic for offering. *There's a reason he mentioned it to me—he knows it won't go any further.* It was an accident—you were at the right place at the right time, and he's feeling all fuzzy because you told him about Ethan. *Ethan doesn't come into this!* Kary, listen to yourself. *He'll say no—but at least I've offered.* Right—he'll say no—but you've offered. *Aargh!* Do *not* feel sorry for someone far more able to take care of himself than you are. *Fine. I'm a fool, but I won't.*

The freedom had gone out of the hike. The day's heat increased and movement brought the large muscles into play. She made a quick stop, slipped the jacket into her backpack. Wordlessly, he helped with the zipper when it caught, followed her again when she took off. Gradually, the trees thickened, and by the time they reached the shaded bower where fallen trunks were benches by a rivulet burbling into a hollow in the exposed granite, she was calm. "Three-quarter mark," she announced. "Last stop."

He extricated his water bottle from his jacket. "Blecch!"

"Not so cold? Pour it into the stream." She drank from her bottle. Water was water. The lilt which was as much part of his voice as its pitch was moving from the category of instantly unsettling to familiar, losing its power. *Stick to the plan.*

Andrew kept his gaze on the drops as he dribbled the water onto a flat rock. "Didn't mean to drop me piddling problem in yer lap."

"A year ago I wouldn't have understood." Gravity pushed the trickle into the hollow to join seamlessly with the other water molecules on their long journey to the Atlantic. The gentle breeze rustled the leaves into and out of the dappled sunlight, changing one green for another. Her fingers caressed the velvet moss on the log. The very peace she depended on challenged her. *I must—because I can.* He would never agree; maybe he would feel better because she offered. That would suffice. "Don't be too hard on her, the girl."

"What?"

"When I was young like her I had a crush on Paul McCartney." She felt heat over her cheekbones, didn't trust herself to meet his gaze. "Of course every girl my age did, but I didn't know that. I was a solitary child, interested in books, not rock-and-roll. But their music played on the radio, even I heard it. I was madly in love, puppy love, the worst kind. He was singing only to me." She risked a glance.

"And?" His eyes were kind.

"Well, I realized it would never work."

"Why?"

"Because I had nothing to offer *him*." *And I'm completely over that, aren't I?* "There must be reciprocity in relationships." She picked up a twig with two leaves on it. *Which is why you and I can never be more than friends.*

"Very mature for a teen."

"Of course I own every Beatles' album ever made. Even the bad ones."

"Aye." He chuckled. "Me too."

She fan-folded one of the leaves, breaking it into narrow slices. *He need never know my petty secret—millions saw and loved* Roland. "It'll get worse."

"And the solution is?"

He was too intent. Doubt gnawed. *Last chance.* "What makes you think I have one?"

"Cough it up."

She scattered the fragments of leaf onto the pine needles at her feet, decided. "Andrew, you'll need safe havens where you can be yourself without watching your back and every word you say." Her throat required clearing. "I might be one for you."

"Here?"

In for a penny... "There are two extra bedrooms for when the girls come. No one would bother you."

Especially not me.

✎ CHAPTER EIGHT ✐
Lord of the Dance

Only the wise man
chooses to walk away from
a fight he would win.

Tahiro Mizuki,
trans. by R. Heath

ANDREW O'CONNELL'S mere presence in GRANT SYKES' latest flick should guarantee BIANCA DOYLE the hit she desperately needs after recent box office duds: publicists remember award nominations—but no one else does. The current crop of dewy replacements for the title of AMERICA'S SWEETHEART wait in the wings—and *they* won't mind signing autographs.

Screen Gold magazine, April 2005

ANDREW
Sanctuary; April 29; 10 A.M. (cont.)

ANDREW'S HEAD JERKED back. Warning bells rang, the defensive wall rose. He was caught unprepared. Why? *Because I expected platitudes.* "That's very generous of ye, but I couldn't."

"Okay."

No drama? An offer from obligation, then. "I truly appreciate the offer, but it's too big an imposition." He glanced around; he would remember this glade. *Pity.* "Our hours are crazy."

"You're worried about disturbing my work?"

"I *know* it would disturb yer work—Christ!" He watched her eyes, wondered what went on behind the cool composure. "Ye can't even have music on when ye're writing!"

She capped her water bottle, stored it in the backpack. She paused with her fingers grasping the zipper pull. "Maybe I gave you

~ 131 ~

the wrong impression of how I work. I start writing soon after the sun wakes me. Two, three hours if I'm very lucky. With a nap in the middle. Or two. *Nothing* stops me until the muse quits."

"Houseguests stink." *No way around that.*

She zipped the pack in her lap. "Unless you choose to come into my office when the door is closed—and somehow I can't imagine you being that insensitive—I won't even be aware you're here. I write when the girls come—Stephen watches cartoons upstairs because 'Mam Mam' is writing."

Damn b.s. radar—always on. "Ye were writing Monday afternoon."

"Far worse. Editing. A job I relegate to the lowest point of my day." She chuckled, wiped her hands on her jeans, and started to rise. "The more exhausted I am, the less garbage passes muster—" Her head turned abruptly and she stooped back down.

He followed the direction of her gaze: in the little pool a moth struggled, rippling the surface and scattering bits of light.

"Wait! It's still alive." She scooped it out. "Rats. It's plastered to my finger."

"Ye're afraid of moths?" He reached over to brush it off.

"Don't! Its wings'll shred like wet tissue paper." She examined the moth closely. She brought it to her lips and blew a soft steady air stream.

"What in heaven's name are ye doing?" Was she trying to blow it off?

"Evaporating the water." She returned to blowing.

Of course.

She held the moth up. "See? His antennae are coming unstuck. Drat! I don't know if I can get him off in one piece."

Not yer usual entertainment? "Need help?"

"If I try too soon I'll rip his wing right off." She used the tip of her nail to raise the edge of the wing. "It's drying." She sounded satisfied. She lifted the opposite wing's edge, blew, made a frustrated humph. "My damned nails are too short. Do you have a key—anything sharp?"

He brought out his Swiss Army knife, unfolded a blade.

"Perfect!" She blew, alternated with freeing the wings with a jeweler's precision, until all four quivered in the gentle breeze. "Look. He left moth dust on my finger." The minuscule scales refracted the sunlight. "Hope he doesn't need all his dust to fly. Oops, wait a minute, little fellow!" A bit of wind bore the insect aloft; it fluttered awkwardly to the ground.

"Good job. He can fly." She'd rescue baby wildlife for her kids. Like the bunny he stole from his Sheltie. Hopeless. Mostly they died anyway.

"Not quite. That right front wing is kinked. He's flying lopsided." She coaxed the moth onto her finger. "Just a second, little guy." With the blade tip, she positioned the front wing over the back one at the wing notch.

She showed him the moth. "See how the front wings fold over the back wings when he's at rest?"

He kept a straight face while he inspected it. "It's a *moth*, Kary."

"I know. They have such brief lives, it's a shame to cut them short. And they don't eat humans." She scooted the now-reluctant moth onto a leaf. A gust got the moth airborne again; it flitted to a low-hanging branch to perch, glittery wings fluttering in a spot of sun. "Stay away from water, you hear?" She handed him his knife back. "Thank you. It has now saved a life."

Did she really care that much? "It's only a *moth*, Kary."

"Makes up for all the mosquitoes I've slaughtered," she said sensibly.

"Ye know, ye just performed mouth-to-moth resuscitation."

"Aargh! You're absolutely awful. I rescind my invitation." She stood, shouldered the pack. "Come on, you need to get going."

He followed her down the mountain, crunching the occasional pine cone, catching his balance on a muddy section through slippery moss. Sure-footed, she didn't pause until they reached her drive and emerged from dappled shade into midmorning sun. It gave him time to think. Could he accept the offered safety valve? She was so sure it wouldn't interrupt her work; her offhand manner—take it or leave it—reassured him. And she was right: having to be 'on' all the time was taking a toll on his work; even Boston had been a nightmare of dodging paparazzi. *I needn't come 'less I want to. It's worth a try—I can always stop.*

"You should make it in time with no trouble." She had turned when they reached the house. "Careful on the curves: we do all our roadwork in the summer—a pile of gravel can block the road without warning."

He hesitated, but the alarms had packed up and gone home. He took the plunge. "I thought about yer safe haven, Kary. I like the idea of having one, even if I don't use it often. Is that all right?"

She seemed surprised, then tilted her head in acceptance. "If I hear the cycle, I'll know you've come. Knock if my light is on and you want to talk." Womanlike, she arranged all the details. "If you don't come, I'll know things are going well."

He felt buoyant, free. "It's like plotting an escape."

As if she had just thought of something, she raised a finger. "Wait. What's your home phone number?"

"Come again?" Red flags went up. *Damn his hair triggers.*

"Last four digits." She walked into the house, stood poised by the security panel.

"Ah. Four nine aught six."

She keyed it in, showed him how to use the system, house and gate. "I set repairmen a temporary code; the easiest number to remember is their own. Anything else?"

"One last thing." Awkward to word it.

The thick soles on her hiking boots raised her gray-green eyes almost level with his. Her attitude was a query.

"Yer reputation?"

Her laugh dismissed the absurdity. "Thank you." She inclined her head. "I consider myself forewarned. Now go play. *I'm* going to take a nap before work. Elise left a message she needs a complete treatment; thinks she has a publisher for Akiiya's story. Will wonders never cease?"

It felt natural to lean in and kiss her cheek as Paalo had, before swinging his leg over the big Harley, and kicking it into action.

He negotiated the winding road back to Hanover with the wind whipping his long hair stingingly along the helmet's rim. *Plenty of time.* He hadn't been this relaxed since he boarded the plane for America. He found himself singing a bar ditty about a one-armed sailor.

His lines were there, solid. He was ready to be a good father to the lovely Bianca—surely she must see the colonies' treason as he did? A tiny spark of guilt assailed: Why hadn't he told Bianca about the girl in his bed? *Keep it strictly professional, lad.* And why had he told Kary?

It had a good sound: Sanctuary.

KARY

May 3

KARY WRESTLED WITH the Angel of Doubt. Her battleground was the dining room table late in the day, her weapon the mighty pen. Why were her words lying dead on the page? Granted, Akiiya's story, which Kary working-titled *Hostages to Fortuna* in honor of Sir Francis Bacon, encompassed both parts of the quotation, in that wives (husbands) and children were impediments, and that Akiiya and her work were worth her sacrifice. But if there were to be no womb-children for the fiery mercenary with the long red braid and the damaged psyche, saving the postulant-planet K'Tae would save many children and Akiiya would be planet-mother to a generation. *Surely adequate stakes?*

But for all the bloodshed on K'Tae, the writing had come bloodless, friable, from Kary's fingertips each morning now for four days. Her mind drifted to the distinct absence of motorcycle din on her drive. Every afternoon, she forced it back to the editing task before her. *He said he might not come often. I said that would mean things were going well.* The filming must be going well. *He has no need of Sanctuary.* He isn't coming, Kary, and you need to accept that, deal with it, and get back to work: the film crew will be out of New Hampshire soon, and you'll have either written for a month—or wasted a month. Choose. *How?*

She chose, settled down, and found Akiiya's story sweeping over her and out her fingertips.

Outside her den, spring rains made everything bloom that was not already covered in green. She wondered briefly about outdoor filming, put the whole thing out of her mind.

When the phone finally rang for a promised call from Zoë, Kary had earned the interruption. "Hi, Zoë—long time no hear."

"Sorry—first examinations this Friday. God, I need a break!"

You and me both. "Worse than usual?"

"An undergraduate with a high fever and a diagnosis of swine flu right before exams enough for you?"

"You don't sound convinced."

"It wasn't, of course—the poor girl had Lyme's she caught here—but by the time they figured it out she'd been quarantined because she just came back from China—and there's all that movie silliness, with half the drama department part-timing it on the set and the other half getting in the way—imagine if there was swine flu on campus!—and the poor girl didn't have her textbooks and with the wrong meds for a week and now she's suicidal because... Oh well, why doesn't matter—I keep telling the students—but only in cases like these, of course—wouldn't do for it to get around as an easy out when they haven't studied—we'll figure it out somehow and they haven't blown the term and—"

"You should have called."

"Why? Were you going to rush in and fix things? God, sorry, I didn't mean that."

"For your *own* sanity?" No, she never meant it.

"You know I hate to disturb you when you're working."

Working. That's what they call it. "I was expecting your call."

"Yeah, sorry I was late—and I can't talk for long. A *huge* stack of papers to grade to give back tomorrow and for some stupid reason the husband can't take the boys to practice." Zoë made a pfft of disgust. "So how's it going?"

Going? Swimmingly—through formless chaos. "When do I get to read this year's new mystery?"

"Uh—wait right there, missy. Are you putting me off?" *Zoë, bloodhound.* "What's wrong?"

Impossible to share: I've invited a movie star to stay, but he may not come. "The usual—plotting—starting new characters."

"Nothing you haven't done before. How's the genre switch?"

"God knows I loved enough SF in my misspent youth—that's not it."

"Then?"

"Not sure yet—it'll work its way out." *Easy as birthin' a babe. Tell the new mother in labor for thirty-six hours.*

"I can come and whack it out with you..."

Right. "Think I can handle it. But you gave me an idea." She'd done it before. *Stop running. Face it head-on. Fight it out.*

"Oh?" Sounds from Zoë's background. "Listen, sorry, gotta go— the boys are standing here with that *look* on their faces—I'll call you later—I want pages, though—I'm *coming*—"

Kary replaced the handset into its kitchen cradle, stared at it. She *did* know: Zoë kneaded it together, enough verve for everything: students, family, house, writing. *But I can't—energy dumped into life comes from somewhere—and won't last.* She had been robbing Akiiya to brood when she should have been dumping every shred of emotion *into* Akiiya. *Just divert the river of blood back to its proper course.*

A million cuts, her badly-suppressed emotions dripped lifeblood. First step: get them out of her head onto paper. Fresh emotions were manna for a writer. *Why do you keep forgetting that?* She started listing: pride, false dignity, forced hospitality, deceit, lust—*lust? Yes, throw in lust*—fear, obsession… 'Inappropriateness'—that was nicely modern—how old were the husbands of the Wife of Bath?… After a scathing ten minutes, she set the list aside—more would come later. Bloodletting weakened her—but it also relieved the pressure, and the image got her thinking. What kind of medicine did the future have? K'Tae? The different ethnic groups? Who controlled it? Who paid?… *Elise will be pleased—if I ever catch her in.* The cuts scabbed and dried, and the blood flowed once more in the story's veins.

When she looked up from consulting her list, scribbling further entries, and marking up her printouts, the sun had set without fanfare outside the lighted circle from the chandelier, the table was littered with charts and lists and pages with more penciled notes than black letters, and Kary was spent—in the right way. She glanced at the mantel clock behind her, askew so she could see it. Time for one more tedious chore before she heated some dinner and crashed.

The ultimate acceptance of reality: she had been postponing the duty since the day the black rider showed up on her screen. Tired and raw in all the muscle fibers that kept her vertical, she dialed Susan—not Ronnie, Ronnie would be sympathetic, would sense something, would ferret out undesirable confidences. It was late enough—Susan would be home, surrounded by the evening craziness of a household with a small child—which would allow no chance to 'chat.'

"Mom? Hi. Fancy hearing from you."

"Don't be silly, Susan. And you can call any time."

"Any time I don't mind interrupting—"

"This will be short; I know you have to get Stephen to bed." She didn't *want* to talk to Susan. "I'm going to be crashing soon, anyway. Let me say 'hi' to my baby."

Four-year-old enthusiasm took several minutes while diplomatic relations were reestablished, until at last Susan set the boy down and sent him to his father for the last rough-and-tumble of the evening which would make Stephen hyper and hard to handle… Susan was back. "Happy now?"

"Of course, honey. He's a sweetheart." Kary breathed deeply, exhaled. "I'm also confirming you girls are coming in August—you said you were." Tempting fate? Possibly—but a woman with grown daughters is safe. *Protective coloration.*

"Well, about that. I've been meaning to call you. Is it okay if we come earlier?"

"Earlier?"

"Well it's not like you usually have plans to go somewhere, is it?"

"I'm not planning to go anywhere." *Literal truth is not truth, Kary Ashe.*

"Greg has this conference, and I thought I'd come out, leave him alone to get ready. He gets so..."

Uh oh. "When is the conference?"

"Does it matter?" Susan did annoyed really well. "Mid-summer, I think. Something about Bastille Day. I'll check."

Mid-July. He *will be gone by then.* "I'll buy a kiddie pool—the inflatable kind. And Zoë has a pool. She's always trying to get me in it."

"I'll arrange for tickets, and Ronnie said she might be able to come then, too. Princeton first," Susan hesitated, "then out to you."

"I'll pick you up in Manchester, so email the arrival info, okay?" They never spoke of Charles—or Amanda and little Thaddeus Charles Renton—Tad the Usurper—but the dust had settled quietly on that front before Ethan, and Kary hoped Stephen and Tad would grow up untainted. Not their fault. None of it was their fault. They were 'family'—not *her* family, but family. Animosity took energy—gave nothing. If she found any she would put it in Akiiya.

Never begrudge family.

ANDREW

Hanover; May 10

"YOU CAN'T GO AROUND making commitments without even consulting me! I'm your agent!"

"Maury, Maury." Andrew held the receiver away from his ear to keep from being blasted out of existence. He dropped into one of the trailer's armchairs. He thudded his boots onto the end table as he mimed at George, puffing with two fingers to his lips. Maury's call had caught him five minutes before early morning wakeup, with rosy dawn promised through the windows.

George shoved up from the couch and rummaged for a pack and lighter, handed him a lit cigarette.

"I just got the script for this *Dodgson* thing from Bianca Doyle— she says you agreed to play the title role!"

For Crissakes. Had she no brains? Of all the boneheaded— "I'll be considering it—if and when I scrounge up two minutes to me-self." Why hadn't she said any— *Hold on.* "What did ye get from her?"

The script draft—and a cover letter.

"What *exactly* does the letter say?"

Blah blah—consulting with her on the script—blah blah—interested in the role.

"That's it?" He visualized Maury Gibbs's head on the body of a frantically bouncing Chihuahua. Why did he keep the bloody annoying little bugger around? Ah, right. Connections. "I *said* it sounded *intriguing*—she gave me a copy of the script."

"This stuff has to go through channels!"

And be stuck there for how long? "Did ye *read* the script?"

"You can't do this—I have other plans for you! Much, much better."

Define 'better.' "Such as?" What had the blighter been holding out on? The restraint of a cold iron collar around his neck made him immediately cautious. He'd seen the cliché too many times: one or two good roles, but never the solid bankable leading man—and another promising career dissipated into the ether of sidekicks and character roles. *I need the little prick.* The man was supposed to be a Hollywood insider. Just until—

"Can't tell you yet! I'm sworn to confidentiality! Trust me—you don't want to be locked in somewhere else piddling. Your fans want to see you headlining blockbusters."

Aye. Blockbusters equaled huge commissions—for agents. *Good fans don't want me typecast.* But stupid, *stupid*—to pay an agent and ignore his advice. "What *can* ye tell me, Maury?"

"Don't sign anything!"

"Wouldn't dream of it."

"And don't make any plans—when is this *Bunker Hill* thing done?"

Andrew's hackles rose. "I'll be decompressing in Ireland." *Don't try to talk me out of it.*

"You still have commitments for *Roland*!"

"Cool yer heels, Maury—we'll do what we can." If Grant let the outside world intrude on his shoots, Maury'd have him doing dog-and-pony shows for publicity—in New Hampshire. He'd known in his bones *Roland* would be the one, bad luck though it was to think so, but the magnitude of the feeding frenzy still amazed him: George refused six requests for interviews a day. He listened to the agent's shrill yapping. He grabbed the phone pad, pinched the phone 'twixt shoulder and ear, fumbled for a pen. He gestured his thanks when George flicked him one before he could get up, scratched down notes. "All right, dammit. Whatever ye say. But home first—before yer damn tour."

Maury had the sense to wrap it up; Andrew replaced the receiver in its cradle, admiring his own self-control, storing the exasperation up for Grant...

George eyed him thoughtfully. "I thought ye weren't too thrilled with the *Dodgson* script."

"I'm not. But the concept—and the role..." He shook his head in frustration—the chance he'd actually get to do it was miniscule. *I want the soul of this repressed Victorian cleric.*

"But?"

"*If* I get script approval; *if* the finished script fulfills the possibilities; *if* she keeps it from imploding in editing— hell, if *she's* any good..."

"A lot of ifs—ye really think Bianca can keep control?"

"Small cast, short shoot, tiny budget, script control, in and out before anybody interferes—straight to Cannes? She's a bigger stake in it than I do."

"Art film." George chuckled. "But does she have the pull to hold off the studio?"

Andrew shrugged. "I want to watch her try." He wasn't quite old enough to stop working in front of the camera—*yet.* But she was.

"Ye're the spittin' image of Lewis Carroll—and shy, like the man—but it'll blow with the fans if she screws up."

"They're just happy to see me naked." *Damn.* Now he really wanted it. If he could fit it in, if she didn't have somebody else lined up—Plan B—*and she's only waiting for me to say no.* It was a wonder anything got made, ever. *I can't say yes, not with the script as it is—but what if someone else does?*

George's gaze was speculative. "So. Anything I need to be doing—for Maury? Ye signing on for his tour?"

"And lose me leverage? Not bloody likely! I *need* home, *need* to work on the CD." Best thing about George: he didn't pry. *Damn. A man shouldn't leech off his friends.* He handed George the scribbles. "Maury will fax ye the schedule—he's a fool to think *any* dates are sacred until Grant has it in the can." *Though if anyone could...* "Tell him no a lot."

George's eyes had aged: the price of coming with. "Be good getting home a while."

"Always the diplomat, eh?" *Good old George.* "We'll not be finishing the CD at this rate." Andrew ground the cig out. Last one till the day's filming was over. *Me and me stupid rules—even if nicotine withdrawal's giving me a fine edge.* Why didn't Colonel Strathmore smoke the Virginia barn-cured Broadleaf of his time? *Fastidious bastard Englishman.* Jittery anticipation pulled him to vertical. This life he could handle. "We'll work it in somewhere. I promise."

"It'll wait. Ye'll be wanting it done right."

That's me problem. "I want everything done right."

BIANCA

May 11

BIANCA FLIPPED FROM deep slumber to instant awareness, as always; Michael insisted he remembered dreams, but she never did. Only two people had the number to the cellphone bleeping on the nightstand: her agent—and Michael. The clock's LEDs read four-fifty. She clicked the alarm off; she had lost ten minutes of needed sleep.

"Mornin', beautiful." Michael.

"Hi, yourself." Why had she ever found being addressed like one of his chippies charming? Andrew always called her Bianca, three slow Irish syllables full of grave courtesy. She hadn't caught the brunt of his legendary scorn, but it was early yet. Their father-daughter relationship was about to turn adversarial. She shivered—standing up to him would be delicious.

She stuck her tongue out at the mirror in her trailer's bedroom, turned sideways to verify the tight curve of her neck. "Wait a sec."

She flicked the lights on so the production assistant wouldn't dare barge in to wake her like on the first day. *'Never be late for cues, princess,' Papi said. 'Makes them think you're not professional.'*

She slipped into a rose peignoir and matching mules. *Shit.* She'd snagged the edge of a nail on the satin robe, pulled a thread loop. Well, forget that one; she made a mental note for her assistant to ship a replacement out from California. She rummaged around on the dressing table, located an emery board before retrieving the phone. "What's up?"

"I wanted you to know—the Henson deal came through."

"The documentary?"

"Yeah. But they've extended it—they want a miniseries." Michael's tedious tone begged for praise like a dog with a stick.

Why should she remember all his deals? "Right." She put in as much warmth as she could manage first thing in the morning. "Congratulations." *It's TV, Michael, for God's sake.*

She filed the ragged nail edge on her left pinkie, careful not to disturb the clear enamel. She couldn't wait to grow real nails again. "When?"

"We're heading to Calgary; we'll be more or less stationed there."

"So you won't be around when I get back?" *Who the hell is going to take me to the stupid Liver Fund dinner?* And what the hell would she talk about—how Papi ruined a perfectly good liver by drinking?

"I'll be bopping back and forth. Wouldn't want to neglect my girl. How's it going?"

"I'm having piles of fun."

"Is the great one as prickly as they say?"

Prickly. Long spines made close approaches tricky. *What was that old joke—how do porcupines make love?* "He's okay. We're all working pretty hard."

"Any luck getting him to do *Dodgson*?"

"It would help if Francis stopped sending me half-baked drafts." *Damn Francis anyway.* 'There's something missing,' Andrew said, forcing her to agree it wasn't quite finished.

"I thought you liked the script."

"Andrew says it's too unfocused." He'd done his homework, dragged out his notes with his copy of the script draft. Damn artistic integrity. No matter; when they filmed, she'd have the last word. But it *proved* Andrew was attracted, for all his hedging. "But I *know* he's interested."

"You picking up tips?"

"Can't wait to work with Grant. I've about bled the Second Unit Director dry." *It's not that hard.* She'd shadowed him doing town scenes and other fill, compared scenes taking shape in front of and behind the camera. As she did, and even with the script unfinished, *Dodgson* had gelled in her mind. *I'll make it work.* She wouldn't let the studio butcher it; she would take her cut straight to Cannes. *Directing myself is the only way I'm going to twist it right, make them notice.* Grant always did his own sex scenes—she'd learn as she bedded young John. *And then I'll turn the heat way up for the Rev.* She could taste the perfect role.

Hell, even *Bunker Hill* should be hers: Sarah was the new American, the survivor left standing once Winston died of his war wounds and her colonel father retreated to England with his tail between his legs. But get Grant to see it that way? Fat chance.

"You sure you really want to do this, babe? It's a big step for you."

"What? Honestly, Michael? *Now?*" *I'm working my rear end off—and you don't get it?* Wasn't he supposed to be *supportive?* She clamped down on every muscle in her body to contain the rising fury. *'Never show men your anger,'* Papi said. *'Hollywood will crucify you.'* Her clenched hands shook as she forced her voice into control. "You think I can't direct."

"I didn't say that."

Her gut ached from the effort. "I will handle it, Michael."

"Well, I'm sure you'll work it out. And speaking of working it out, Bi, I've been thinking, when we're done in Banff, whether," Michael's voice was hesitant, "...whether we shouldn't take some time off together, make it permanent, think about kids..."

Now? Right after he insulted her? *Sheesh, Michael—could you be more clueless?* "Listen, sweetie. I'd really rather not discuss it unless we're together. Didn't you just tell me it won't be long?"

"With the company doing so well now, I thought—"

You'll protect and defend me? The stupid company—that would deflect him. "I'm proud of you for getting the Henson job, Michael. It's what you've always wished for."

"Want me to come out there first?"

Oh, God, no! That was the *last* thing she wanted to cope with. "No, Michael. You know I can't take that kind of pressure. It's too important a decision."

"Grant will understand."

And I don't matter? "Don't even think of coming, Michael. You know how I get with the sex scenes. You'd shut me down completely." *Shit.* She needed bigger guns. "Besides, Grant won't let you on the closed set, anyway. And John is so spanking new at this all he needs is my boyfriend hanging around. I have to focus on work." Beautiful hunk-of-muscles-and-insecurities John. She relaxed as her mind threw up defenses. *'Boyfriend'—that should mollify Michael.*

"Did Grant finally decide to sex it up?"

"No—but he has to film both versions. He won't commit to a final cut until they run it past test audiences. You know that." She found herself fiddling with the emery board again, but its rasp irritated her; she jammed it back in with its fellows. She demolished the offending nail bit with the razor edge of her teeth. Coffee. Her stomach rumbled. She needed coffee. Mainlined.

"But—"

"Hear that? There's the makeup call. Gotta go." *Safe—for now?* Had she passed up the opportunity to break up with Michael, get it over with? *Not yet. The publicity would kill her.* "I promise I'll think about it." *Like hell.* Her arms shielded her flat belly—she couldn't go through *that* again. "Goodbye, Michael."

We are so over— As soon as I have Andrew hooked.

ANDREW

Denny's Disco, Hanover; May 18; 9 P.M.

"WHAT A DUMP!" BIANCA was waiting for him to open the limo's back door. She sat poised to exit with one hand on the doorframe as she looked up at him.

He followed her gaze at the dilapidated entrance behind him, with *Denny's Disco* flashing in neon colors below an ancient awning. He flicked the fag he'd been smoking while waiting for the limo to catch up to his 'cycle, now parked around back, extended his hand.

She startled as the New England thunderstorm flashed the unprepossessing exterior for a second's stark relief with a bolt of light. George rounded the boot, She glanced at George. "This is the place?"

"Yeah. George scouted it out for us." *Good thing he had, too,* since the heavy showers made tonight's shoot impossible. *We were wanting some serious partying anyway.* What better way to spend lost work time? "Are ye coming?"

"You're certain it's safe?" Bianca took his hand, scooched close to him under the awning. She wore a silk shawl over something short, strapless, and spangly, not appropriate to the raw wet night. She shivered. "You said 'disco.'"

"Inside's probably better." *Relax. She's only putting everybody's thought into words.* He shrugged out of his damp leather jacket, settled it about her shoulders; in this country, inside would be heated. She clutched the jacket's front edges as if to avoid touching unclean walls.

The rest of the group gathered with Grant and Johnnie in a knot nearby—curious how Bianca's space was respected, even on a democratic night out—waiting for him to make the first move. He opened the door for Bianca. "In for a penny…"

"I'm game if you are." She laughed up at him and scurried inside.

"Aah!" The cool dim inner sanctum welcomed him like the pubs they played in Ireland. She handed his jacket back with a tentative smile as she looked around; he slung it over his arm.

George scooted past them. "Come." He brought over a stocky hippie-type with a graying ponytail and beard. "This is Stewart. He kept Denny's name when he bought the place."

And obviously Denny's psychedelic decor. "Not bad." Andrew shook hands with Stewart, put an arm around Bianca's shoulders. "This lovely young one here is Bianca."

Stewart gravely carded Bianca—"For your own protection." He pointed to an art deco sign behind the bar which announced: *Don't be offended: Anyone even looking younger than thirty must prove age.*

"You're sweet. It's my twenty-first birthday."

"Happy Birthday." Stewart filled her request for a Daiquiri. "Now that you're old enough."

Andrew settled them at a table with Grant opposite, hung the leather jacket over his seat back. He accepted Stewart's offer of draught Mountain Stout. Johnnie claimed the other chair next to Bianca, and George conscripted one from the next table.

Andrew let his gaze wander around the room as he savored the bitter undertones bottled beer never quite got right, drew in the calming nicotine. On a weeknight, half the scarred wire-spool tables were empty. The kiddies from the crew crowded around a couple, locals occupied a few more. His attention was drawn momentarily to a booth where a man and a woman, in their late twenties by the looks of them, whispered angrily, heads close together. But they were paying no attention to the new arrivals. *Lover's spat?* He dismissed them from his mind, continued his survey of the perimeter, noting potential trouble spots: entrance, dance floor, corner booths, bar. And the back exit, where he'd left the motorcycle.

He monitored desultorily the Hollywood gossip Bianca was engaging in with Grant, punctuated by an occasional comment from Johnnie, adoring from afar. An expensive whiff floated over occasionally from Bianca's direction, braided invisibly with the aroma of bar. Scattered thunder crashed at intervals, shaking the building like a terrier a rat.

His gaze paused for a moment on George, whose hand was curled around a *Franconia Notch* microbrew Stewart recommended, and whose roving gaze alertly encompassed the room while he listened to the insider talk. George kept his own counsel when Bianca was around; they didn't have much in common. His promise to George—*we'll write for the new album*—was unfulfilled. *There just isn't time.* George teased him he channelled Col. Strathmore, rather than playing the colonel. *He had a point.* George alleged he was pig-headed about staying in character. 'Strathmore's tone-deaf,' he'd told George, making it Gospel true. 'But he likes Bach. For the complex rhythms.'

"Good choice, George." He forced his skull toward each shoulder until he got a satisfying crack. "How'd ye find this place?"

"One of the gaffers is local."

Their director pushed his chair back. "Gotta go talk to the producer." Grant grabbed his ale, rose. "Good job."

George grunted in acknowledgment.

Bianca, a bundle of nervous energy, eyed the dance floor. Music from the 70s mixed with more recent tunes, and the boys and girls of the crew headed out. She bounced up, extended fingertips. "Come on, Andrew. Dance with me."

"Never turn a lady down." He drank up. "But I warn ye, I'm not as good as young Johnnie here."

"I've seen you move. Shut up and come." Bianca bent to Johnnie, kissed his cheek; the lad went crimson. "I'll get *you* later."

She led him out. Even in four-inch heels she was doll-sized next to him. Midnight blue suited her. She tucked her hair, loosed from Sarah's ringlets, behind her ears, sliding red-tipped talons through black silk. The strapless was modest enough—until she moved. She was the one with the wild steps; it took little to show her off. She didn't need a spotlight: every man in the room knew she was there.

The music slowed. He wove Bianca around the floor using the other couples as warp. He kept his amusement from showing on his face. Old neon lights sputtered as lightning earthed too near.

He escorted her back, fetched her a drink, himself another draught in a frosted mug. *Americans—and their passion for cold.*

Johnnie waited for Bianca to take a sip. "You promised me a dance."

She glanced at Andrew; he gestured 'go on' with his mug. Standard problem on films with a single leading female role—not enough women to go around.

Her exquisitely bare shoulders shrugged consent as she turned her brilliant smile on Johnnie—she handled it well, no favourites. "You're on!"

Johnnie was a smooth and inventive dancer. But he was no match for electrified Bianca. He looked unhappy; he was out of his league. *Kid owes a few years' dues.*

George nursed his brew, eyes nictitating, a crocodile at river's edge watching the other carnivores and their prey. "She wants ye to watch her."

Andrew tipped his chair back, yawned, gripped his left elbow, stretched his arm down toward his back; the cigarette butt nestled familiarly between his left third and fourth fingers came perilously close to lighting his hair on fire. *Live dangerously.* "Grant said she's taken—lives with some producer in Los Angeles." He scarfed up a greasy handful of popcorn from the basket on the table, wished he hadn't. As old as the posters of Jimi Hendrix and less well preserved. American junk—they'd never serve this at McDuff's.

"Ye checked. Hmm." George turned his attention to Bianca. "Hard to imagine her with kids. Not that ye have to have any."

"Try that on Fiona!" Andrew chuckled. "Doesn't matter. Off limits."

"Ye're dense sometimes, ye know, Andy boy?"

"Anyhow, she's dancing with Johnnie," he said logically.

George's gaze shifted to him, back to Bianca. "She's dancing for ye."

"Hmm." Andrew's eyes narrowed. He saw Bianca in profile as the camera saw her: shimmery, animated, remote; perfect. George was a cynic. *She just likes to dance.*

His hand retained an impression of the small of Bianca's back. How would she look in a pink negligée? Woman's body, when even a childish one had stirred him for a thoughtless second?

No poaching, remember? Bridget was yer fault, not Fitz's. Ye were never there; she couldn't wait forever.

He pushed the memories further, used them: how would the colonel react to a woman in his bed? One of the slave girls, or a camp follower—a woman of his own class would never sully herself. He'd made Strathmore fastidious: the colonel would order her out. No woman could replace his Emily, extinguished in childbirth by the son meant to follow a Sarah who had so grown to resemble her mother it hurt his chest...

What did he really know about Bianca? Competent, beautiful, string of increasing ingénue roles; the dramatic ones had been less successful at the box office. On the older edge of the ten young Hollywood actresses who could headline a major film. He never scrutinized his costars' work when preparing for a role: he didn't want his reactions tainted. She was right to add directing to the mix—maybe. She couldn't have a better mentor than Grant.

Only two of their scenes were in the can so far, one a minor pivot: 'Good eve, Mistress Strathmore,' from John's gentleman farmer Winston earned a coy 'Miss' from Sarah, acting as hostess for the colonel. Bianca played it with a shy sidewise glance at her father. Exactly what Grant and the script called for, perfectly executed— but it could have been anyone.

He drained the coffee-touched stout, ground out the fag. The heft of Stewart's good Irish pint glass made him homesick. Restless, he shoved away from the table, prowled. Seventies hippie paraphernalia on the walls. A framed newspaper article—Woodstock happened nearby. The storm-front thunder resolved into a steady rainbeat on the flat roof, reminding him of the scenes of hippies in mud. Tough week; he was almost too tired to party.

On a microscopic stage behind the tiny dance floor, the weekend band's instruments languished against the wall. His fingers stretched out to a battered Gibson, still plugged in to the amplifier by its long cable. George's sly observation about Bianca festered under his skin; but that was their arrangement: 'The day I can't speak me mind is the day I leave.' 'Wouldn't have it any other way.' Life was complicated; music was easy. He sought Stewart's eye, cocked his chin at the guitar.

Stewart meandered over. "Want it on?"

"Aye. I left mine home."

"How many you got?" Stewart reached over and flipped the amp's switch.

"Ten or twelve." Andrew fingered the strings, adjusted the tuning pegs. He played a little melody, ran it back in a discordant version, screeched the guitar, picked soft bits. "Hey. Not bad." The rush started. "What do ye play?"

"Keyboards," Stewart said. "Classical pianist, long time ago. How'd you know?"

"Yer eyes."

Stewart killed the tape, set another stout in reach.

Andrew twisted round, bellowed, "Hey, George!" George turned. Andrew motioned him over. "We got any frustrated drummers?"

"I'll check," George said. He canvassed the crew, co-opted a kid with copper pot scrubber hair. He picked up the bass with a deep sigh of bliss.

Andrew's fingers itched. He peeled off his sweater, tossed it over the end of the bar. He knew he was pulling rank, didn't care; there had to be some perks.

Steel strings bit into his fingertips. Chords—A, G7, C#m—formed without conscious thought. Fatigue leached from his blood. He concentrated—the key to lyrics was memorizing the start of the next line—repetition engraved the rest on yer brain.

The small crowd moved to anything with a beat. Bianca danced with whoever asked her, even dragged Grant out. Johnnie squired her as often as she allowed.

Andrew kept her in sight as he seduced the microphone.

She likes to boogie; that's all.

BIANCA

I DIDN'T COME TO DANCE with John.

Bianca fumed, forced her smile friendly and impartial, accepted every chance to do what she was supposed to do: flaunt the toned body, the silky flowing mane.

What the hell would Andrew want? Exclusivity—her attention only on him? Or competition—to cut *his* woman out of a herd? *I thought I had him on the dance floor—and then he picks up some stupid old guitar.*

She maneuvered her partners where Andrew had no trouble seeing her. She remembered to '*Sparkle, Bibi,*' as her Papi said when she was six, pudgy, her first dance recital—the last one he'd been around for. If Andrew, standing there in an old frayed Beatles T-shirt, insisted on playing at rock star, she could add a studio to her house. She wasn't pudgy anymore; she *knew* he was watching her...

Raised voices behind her. Bianca tensed. Before she could locate the source, a scuffle, then a thud. An overturned chair? An enormous black shape bumped into her, wrenched a squeak from her throat. Six-foot-five? Six-foot-six? A long-haired biker-type from nowhere. Panic strangled her; she couldn't breathe. *All that training—for nothing.*

But he wasn't after her: he headed across the dance floor, half dragging a girl in a black leather miniskirt who clung to his tattooed arm. "Hey, you—big shot," he slurred. *Thoroughly plastered.* Flashed image: Mother, crossed-arm in contempt for Papi's drinking.

The sound level plummeted. Where was Andrew? Had Grant even thought about bringing bodyguards? Andrew would save her. Her eyes zeroed in on center stage. On Andrew, his head lit from behind by the spotlight, his eyes in shadow.

"Hey, you. Jeannie here wants your autograph." The drunk thrust the girl stagewards. "She thinks you're something special."

"It's okay." The girl dug her heels in. "I don't need an autograph. Let's go home, Mark." She pulled futilely at his arm.

Bianca's gaze locked on Andrew. Her eyes narrowed, her gut relaxed. *Moment of truth.*

Andrew slipped the guitar strap over his head, held the instrument out to freeze George in place. He stepped forwards, into the light, his eyes terrifying slits in an amiable mask. His stance put the whole band behind him. Under protection. He smiled at the girl.

Every hair on Bianca's forearms stood painfully on end. *How easily he takes control.*

"Sure thing, Jeannie." He reached for the paper in the girl Jeannie's hand, signed it, held it out to her with a polite inclination of his head. "Good luck to ye."

That's it? Bianca's certainty faltered. He'd pitched his voice low and slow. *Appeasing? He's a coward?*

The girl took it, turned, put her palm flat on her date's chest. "Can we go now, Mark?"

Mark snatched the paper, tore it to shreds, and dumped it on the floor. "Satisfied? Got your big shot autograph?" He sneered at her, grabbed her arm and twisted her around. "Get going." He turned to Andrew. "Keep your goddam autograph. She don't need it."

Jeannie whimpered.

Bianca shivered, scrunched herself tinier. *Now he'd be forced to...*

"Let her go." Andrew's voice carried weight, authority, calm—menace. "Ye're hurting her."

"Don't tell me what to do with my woman!" Mark whirled, more agile than a drunk should be, shoved the petrified Jeannie behind him. He lashed out.

Andrew was ready—and not drunk. He caught the larger man's fist, spun him round, Mark's arm at an impossible angle.

Ahhh...

Jeannie screamed as Mark feigned a kick, ducked, writhed out of Andrew's grasp. He made a wild grab, latched onto a fistful of Andrew's T-shirt. It ripped; Mark staggered back, knocking a tray of beer glasses off the bar with a loud crash.

Bianca exhaled, straightened. An odd thought intruded: only movie T-shirts rip without great force. *Or very loved ones.* She identified Andrew's look: housecat with mouse. Excitement flushed her skin. *He's been waiting for an excuse.*

Mark bounded up with a shriek of fury, lunged.

So little sound, such a tiny motion to pin a man bigger and taller than himself: Andrew grabbed Mark's wrist, yanked, *placed* him face down on a table as neatly as hitting a mark. *Over way too soon.* Bianca tasted her own blood—she'd bitten her lip.

Stewart and George took over, hustled Mark out the door, followed by a sobbing Jeannie. Grant hurried over. Andrew jerked his head towards the door; Grant followed the commotion out.

The slamming door cracked the spell. Bianca went to him. "You okay?" She took his bloodied right fist. Real violence, not choreographed into routine. The heavy ring on his left would have done even more damage had Andrew thrown a punch. *Why didn't he?* Her nipples tingled. What would it taste like, his blood?

"Split me knuckles. Damn drunks." Andrew glanced at the soaked returning bouncers. "Sorry," he said to Stewart.

Stewart dredged up a battered first aid kit. "Happens. Don't sweat it."

"And...?"

"Neighborhood cops—he'll spend the night at the station—no need to get involved."

"Thanks, man."

Bianca claimed the kit. She extracted cotton, hydrogen peroxide, gauze, tape. Playing a trauma nurse on a soap opera had its benefits. She reached for Andrew's hand.

It jerked in hers at the sting of the antiseptic. She knew he was watching her, kept her eyes focused on his weathered hand, dabbed as efficiently as any real nurse. Real blood was less sticky than fake—it needed a lighter touch. When she finished, she lifted her eyes to look at him. He smiled back sardonically. Her heart still pounded. *Everything happened so fast.* What if the drunk had pulled a knife?

He broke eye contact as Grant interfered to inspect the split skin. "Let me see. You're lucky. Probably won't need stitches."

"Is Jeannie all right?" Andrew's gaze was back on Bianca.

"Sent her to her mother's in a cab," Grant said.

Bianca turned her palm up.

Andrew replaced his hand in hers, let her bandage it. "Thanks. Lovely job." He reached for his sweater.

Surely he felt the same tension she did. *If we were alone...* She helped him ease the soft wool sleeve over the taped gauze. She held the sweater's neck open while he ducked his head through, slid the sweater over his torn T-shirt through which tanned taut skin showed, over muscles resilient to her fingertips.

She blinked, busied her hands with the first aid debris on the table. She had no idea what to do with it.

Stewart took over the menial task. "The girl let slip he's been in scrapes before; can't imagine he'll make trouble." He took one look at Bianca's face, went to fetch her brandy.

It made her cough.

Andrew reached out his unbandaged hand to pat her.

His hand was warm on her naked back. *It begins...*

ঙ CHAPTER NINE ঙ
I put my hand in the fire for no man

...Bad boy Andrew O'Connell is doing it again! Seems he can't keep his hands off girls in bars. When he got fresh and started pawing a Dartmouth coed, her boyfriend protested, and our Knight Errant flattened the poor guy. Handlers hustled him out before police got there, but there may yet be charges filed. Watch this spot!...

www.wayneblackburn, May 20

Andrew and crew from *Bunker Hill* were spotted dancing at a popular watering hole in Hanover. A few lucky patrons caught Andrew and *Deadly Nightshades* bassist George Cosgrave in impromptu jam. Photo link <kev.grasshutmonkey> (Thanks to Kevin S.)
WARNING: major distortion in gossip mills: Wayne Blackburn took his weekly potshot at Andrew. Apparently there was an altercation when a disgruntled local drunk took a swing at Andrew. Swallow with large dose of salt.

www.AOCORNER, May 21

The critical consensus is a Triple Fail: viewers like America's Sweetheart with a big dose of sugar—and sweetness was conspicuously missing from this role. Those who want women in gritty roles wondered, Why her? And the box office was dismal. Stick to what you do well, Bianca Doyle.

www.RottenReviews, Archives, 2004

ANDREW
Sanctuary; **Wednesday, May 18; 11:30** P.M.

I MUST BE CRAZY. SHE'S an early riser—probably in bed.

The black cycle shuddered rhythmically beneath him where he stopped just below the top of Kary Ashe's drive. Before him, the halogen headlight illuminated a hedge-hogish creature which lumbered off the drive like a grumpy pensioner in a zebra crossing, just slow enough to force him to brake. The trees dripped in the mist, shadows cast by an almost full moon appearing prophetically at her gate as the light shower paused long enough for him to punch in his familiar code on the keypad. The gates had swung shut behind him on ghost hinges.

All he'd wanted was to get away when his mere presence caused a mess in a quiet New Hampshire bar, where Stewart's matter-of-factness about the fight—'It happens'—simply increased Andrew's disgust. *I should have been able to head it off.*

He'd poured the adrenaline into maneuvering the beast on the eerie dark twisty hairpin turns in the lashing rain, his only thought fear, not of death, but of an accident which would delay Grant on *Bunker Hill.* A ride on a night like this at home meant familiar country lanes and an uncovered head, and laughing because ye're wet, and drying off by a fire in the pub with yer mates and good music and the owner's daughter with her full tray of pints. Here it was an adventure—into what?

Sleeping here was the beer's idea. He could always reverse, return to his trailer on set, to Grant, George...? To Bianca, pale, shocked, eyes too wide. She shouldn't have to deal with blood and bandages. He'd heard some rumor about a paparazzo, or a crazed fan stalking her... The night out should have been safe. *Damn—we needed the break in the filming.*

Up the last bit of hill to his left, light suffused from the great room, spilled out onto the deck where the closed picnic-table umbrella stood striped sentry duty. No reason she should close her blinds—ye couldn't see in through the sliding glass doors except from the verandah, accessible only through the house—but he felt a voyeur.

He paused on her front stoop. *This is how ye seek Sanctuary.* A thief. In the middle of the night. From people rooted to the land. To move, she'd need to move her mountain. *His* profession defaulted to rootlessness. Smoke rose, signaling from the chimney. Fire—and warmth. He'd have to go in now, or she'd worry about prowlers. Or did she sleep with the lights on? In which case he might wake her...

Get on with it, man. He punched the code, opened the door.

Paper piles, stacks of folders surrounded her on the couch and floor; a half-dozen sheets touched edges in a row on the coffee table.

"Hey!" Kary turned, glanced at his hand. "Look what the cat dragged in. Still pouring?"

"Just stopped." *She wasn't waiting, on the off chance...?* "Isn't it past yer turn-in time?"

"Muse delivered a puzzle piece as I was dropping off. Didn't dare offend her; besides, it fit so perfectly I couldn't risk losing it." She patted the sheaf of lined yellow pages covered with scribbles in her lap.

"Shall I go away then?"

"No need. Almost done." She hid a jaw-cracking yawn with the back of her hand, glanced at him. "Hungry? Thirsty?"

His stomach growled; his yawn echoed hers. "Maybe." But he didn't want to put her to any trouble.

"Can you scrounge? Or—I'll be at a stopping point in a couple minutes...?"

So *that* was the reason she seemed stiff, nervy. "I'll go a'foragin'."

"Thanks. Fridge's full—cold cuts in drawer—more substantial stuff in—"

"Beer in cave. I can handle meself in a kitchen. Ye want anything?"

"Hot cocoa—mix in cupboard—"

"With the cups. Aye." He tossed his jacket over the chairback.

She nodded satisfaction, bent to her scribbling.

Odd sensation? He pinned it down: more like good old times? *Fool. Women never ignore ye anymore.*

He cobbled together a sandwich, couldn't locate mayo, found himself whistling as he poked through her pantry and refrigerator. Which door had she opened for a tray? Aah! The gigantic room gleamed white as an operating theatre, except for the north window over the sink, full of...philodendrons? 'Not enough sun for flowers,' Kary'd said.

He carried the tray out without spilling the cocoa in twin mugs labelled '#1 MOM.'

Kary tucked the last pages into the top folder. "Need anything else?"

"Nope. Here."

"Thanks." She sank back, put feet with short pink socks on the table's edge, yawned ferociously.

It was past midnight. He yawned back. "I can't eat if ye do that."

"Sorry. I'll stop." She sipped, her eyelids half-masted.

Spicy brown mustard, horseradish bite that cleared his sinuses, teared his eyes.

She shook her head violently. "Even Calliope can't keep me up." She stretched, suppressed a yawn as pledged, ran her fingers through already mussed hair. "Poke around in the far guest room if you need anything. It's there someplace. Come some time when I'm awake?"

Damn. She sensed something was wrong. He forced a chuckle. "Party pooper." *Will she really go?*

She raised her eyebrows. "Want me to get out the toothpicks?"

"G'night, Kary."

"I have caffeine tablets somewhere—"

"G'night, Kary."

"Okay, okay. Don't pick up—I'll never find anything again—leave it on the counter—"

"G'night, Kary."

She headed for the stairs, bent down near the top. "Light switch by the security panel."

"And I'll put out the cat. G'night, Kary."

Fingertips waggled; she disappeared.

Tomorrow he'd deal with the bar aftermath, insist on paying for the damage—no reason Stewart should get shafted.

Damn. It had been a fine night—until the drunk.

He kept his mouth shut when Grant mopped up, sent everyone to the trailers with a joke about being *in loco parentis.* Maury'd manage media repercussions—that was his job.

But tonight he was a field mouse safe in a shoebox, cocooned in lamb's wool. She hadn't asked why he came, what was wrong with his hand. She didn't fuss. And she left him in possession without a second thought.

He poked the fire, set the grate. *Safe—to sleep ye need to feel safe.*

He'd not relaxed this completely since home.

KARY

Sanctuary; **Saturday, May 21**

HE NEEDED PEACE; HE came here. Once.
Good enough. "That's why we keep regular hours," Kary told her bleary-eyed mirror-twin. *Did we imagine him?*

She glanced toward the far bedroom before heading for her kitchen. The door was open, still—nothing had changed in two days since he'd left without her seeing him Thursday morning. She hadn't expected otherwise; he'd said something on his first visit about early makeup calls. *Was cycling out from Hanover worth a few hours sleep?* She stifled disappointment along with the yawn. At least she hadn't kept him up that night.

She poured water over crushed ice in the giant plastic tumbler, decided food would make her more sluggish. Sluggisher?

Akiiya awaited her on K'Tae, crouched on one knee; the sand beneath the rebels' campfire was still warm. *Akiiya's Story is my salvation.*

Kary took her seat at her control panel in her inner sanctum, docked the tumbler into its own special place above her computer, blocked the internet. In her outline, the scene was labeled 'Akiiya captured by rebels.' Kary visualized the scene from her printout of the previous day's work:

> Akiiya dusted her palms off impatiently. She issued orders to the squad of Techtarch Lyonis's guards detailed to 'assist' her. Her report was in the wordcom, ready for hypertrans.

Kary opened the scene's computer files: text, structure, notes.

> Akiiya activated TRANSMIT, re-examined her brief audience with the K'Tae ruler while she waited out the timelag. 'My job is to make K'Tae very, very prosperous, an industrial diamond in this sector,' Lyonis said. He pressed his request for assistance from GalCen. 'When the rebels disrupt trade, their own people suffer most.'

Kary watched Akiiya, severely military in her GalCen uniform; Akiiya knew the value of symbols. It wouldn't do to pace in front of underlings. Akiiya's lower-left eyelid fluttered once; she blinked. Stress. Akiiya wasn't aware of the tic; her superior would have yanked her on the spot.

"Problems personnel section." The ear-speaker regenerated Col. Ermire's curt tone from his voiceprofile. Akiiya had stated her single qualm 'for your ears only.' "Permission denied. Father Damien LeRoux professional agitator. Repeat, permission to pursue conspiracy genocide theory expressly denied." I get it. Damn Franciscans. "Execute program. Report pacification next transmission. Message over." Her carefully-expressed doubt would leave a blot on her record.

It had been so hard to make Akiiya consider listening to Father Damien; her transformation had to be justified, motivated, pre-figured, a one-degree shift at a time in Akiiya's iron GalCen conditioning.

The big scenes were hard to write. Kary was attracted to Akiiya's strength, repelled by her character's predatory side; ergo, Akiiya must suffer—one person tortured to save a world. Kary sketched out the rest of the scene: Akiiya's anger pushed her into taking the risky chance of tackling the school in the rebel-sympathizer village on her own; her fury when she was captured and disarmed; her first dismissive meeting with Reyker, on her knees; the intended humiliation of being given over to the women to guard—women whose necks she could snap in an instant. Akiiya *mastered* her rage, *used it* to formulate a better plan—*this could work.* Little did they know the viper they had allowed into their midst...

The timer startled Kary—three hours gone without notice. On cue, the internet blocking software offered escape. She backed up the files, took another moment to print; paper was cheap. Rough cut; much too long; the editing, revising, polishing might take a week for this one scene. *Tough.* The scene was a crucial link, a tactical change and a step out of character—it would be good.

She stretched the kinks out of her spine and shoulders. *What next?* Start a second writing period after a short nap? *No.* She knew her body—it couldn't reprise what it had just done. Not today. Not with the adrenaline kick of finishing the draft.

So. Hike? Breakfast? *Who are we kidding—nap.* She resented the discipline—and reminded herself for the millionth time that pushing the limits cost her writing days—and never helped.

A tiny self-indulgence? Followed *immediately* by the hated nap. She wouldn't *read* her emails, just check if any required attention.

Okay; Ronnie's message could probably wait—she'd emailed late last night—but *I've earned it.*

> Mom -
> Can't wait to see you! Have my ticket for June 11, just a couple things to do after exams. Susan's bringing Stephen because Greg has some poetry convention in Paris, and she doesn't want to be stuck in a hotel room.
> So excited! So much to tell you!
> All my love. V.

Like old times. Plus Stephen—little bundle of boy clinging monkey-like, fascinated by every creature under a rock.

Something was off. *June?* Not July? But Susan said— Bastille Day—misassociation with Paris?

But what about Andrew?

You got yourself into this, kiddo. He'd understand—ask him not to come while the girls were here? And what would she tell *them*? Ronnie'd bubble, want to meet him. Susan? And a little boy? End of Sanctuary.

Wait. Andrew said beginning days of June. *Bunker Hill* would be over, he'd be gone, she wouldn't have to 'fess up. Just hide any jangled moodiness from having him so close—and then even more gone than before. She had three weeks until the girls arrived. No need to ask; a quick anonymous peek at AOCORNER would confirm when the filming ended. She typed in the URL.

Confronted with Andrew's brooding *Roland* image on the site's front page, and the constriction in her pericardium, she wished she hadn't broken her interdiction. She'd find the date, get off.

Right. Impossible to ignore the link—she knew where *Denny's* was. Crew excursion? *There's always someone with a camera phone.* Goofy group in the silly poses of kids at school picnics: George's tongue lolled while Andrew pantomimed a chokehold.

Altercation? Which one of the jackals was Blackburn? *Guilty until proven innocent?* AOCORNER always took Andrew's side; prudently eschewed linking to avoid giving the critic's site more traffic. She typed 'www.wayneblackburn' into her browser's address bar, read the entry.

A kernel of truth? Charles always called her naive. 'You believe any story your interns hand you.' *Actors are temperamental—they get into brawls...*

She drew a sharp breath, withdrew her hands from the keyboard into her lap, bowed her head, closed her eyes. Heat charged up the back of her neck. *Et tu...? You're as bad as the rest.* A link to a bear-baiting, and you jump in with a stereotype and a judgment and a morbid fascination so quickly I can *hear* 'Off with his head!'

With you for a friend, he doesn't need enemies. You didn't even give him a fair hearing first. You *wallowed.*

Kary abandoned her office; she needed cleaner air. *Serves me right.*

Ronnie might still be in her dorm room—but she couldn't risk waking her, could she? Ronnie'd think it was an emergency... The kitchen phone made the decision: Ronnie.

"Hi, Mom."

"How did you know I was thinking about you, honey?" *Damn.* She'd neglected to confirm the date.

"Did you get my email? You never pick up when you're writing; I took a chance."

"Just read it. Done for the day. Need money?"

"Mother!"

"How much?"

"It's just that we're getting one last ski trip in next weekend—"

"Couple thou?"

"Way too much!"

"Then you won't need another transfusion for a while." One of the small pleasures of having money; those years in Princeton on disability had galled for many reasons. "Take lots of pictures."

"Okey-dokey. How are you, Mom? Anything new going on?"

"I'm fine." She hesitated. *Tell her.* "Writing."

"Can I read some?"

"Maybe when you come."

"Tease."

Their always game. Why could she never let go until the first draft was complete? *Because I'm afraid to lose it.* Zoë sees the pages when you write them. *Zoë trades—she gives me* her *life's blood.*

It had been hideously hard, that first time sharing. *I ran a fever.* "Don't forget your long johns for skiing, sweetpea." "Never. Give Lucy a kiss for me. Bet she has my room all ready." *This is going to blow up on me. Sooner rather than later.* "We've got some catching up to do, don't we?" What would their Goldilocks say when she found out who had been sleeping in *her* bed? *TELL her. NOW.*

"Talk to you later, Mom. Gotta run. Something about actually going to study, my roommate's dragging me out the door." Sounds of laughing, an insistent 'Come on!' "Love ya, Mom."

Building on half-truths was erecting on slowsand: trapped—and sinking—without even the possibility of swift extinction. "Love you, too."

You lost your one opening to be truthful. 'Truthful'? Blurt out, with no background or subtlety, 'there's a movie star staying in Susan's room,' or 'my friend Andrew O'Connell has been by, you know, from the show?' Anything I say needs so much explanation to give it the right nuance it's futile. Better to say nothing—and then what? Hope they didn't find out? Why had she asked him to stay? That was the moment she had slipped over the line. But she had something he needed.

Stop. If you *have* to, for any reason, make it a non-event, a common courtesy to let him know, a change in plans. He'll understand. *I can protect him.*

But she shouldn't need to. There should still be a gap. At best, the girls wouldn't find out—he'd be on his way with no further thought as soon as the filming was over, before they came. She didn't examine what 'at worst' might be: it wasn't going to happen... She jumped as the dead phone in her hand beeped, asked her to redial if she wanted to make a call.

For what I have done, for what I have failed to do...

ANDREW

Sanctuary; Monday, May 23; 11:50 A.M.

ANDREW WHISTLED 'KAREN'S Song' from *Exodus* under his breath as he descended, revitalized, after a second night's dreamless sleep in Kary's spare bedroom. He loved not having to disturb her—she hadn't even heard him come in. Her stone steps were silent—no need to walk on the left, skip the third tread like his ma's house. His damp hair hung loose—the stylist didn't want crimps except where *she* put them.

"You still here?" Kary, holding a fat box topped by a pile of folders and a loaded clipboard.

Up from her dungeon already? "And top o' a very fine Monday mornin' to ye, m'lady." His gaze flicked to his wrist. Close, but ten minutes gab with his phantom hostess was small payment for sleeping like the dead after a Sunday's filming that lasted well after sunset. He startled her by taking the stack. "Where do ye need these?"

"Dining room table."

Three words and an amused look to make him feel like a Boy Scout who forced an old lady across the street. "Day's output?" *No, eejit—this year's taxes.*

"Aren't you late?"

Guest's needs first, of course. His glance hadn't been surreptitious enough. The mantelpiece clock slowly bonged twelve strokes. "Not needed till one."

"Nice to have seen you, then." She pulled out the armchair at the foot of the table, the ladyseat.

"Are *ye* in a hurry?" He hesitated, gestured at the papers.

"God, no!"

"Join ye for a few minutes?"

"Thought you'd never ask."

"Writing going well?" He draped himself over a well-padded chair. Everything in this house was built for creature comfort.

"Very. I'm closing in on the ending. First draft, but it helps to know how it comes out." She lifted the clipboard to the heavens, dropped it on the folders. "I'm knee deep in half-formed ideas."

He chuckled. Writers!

"Acting going well?" she inquired politely.

Had she heard about *Denny*'s? Or was she ignoring the whole episode? Either way, he was just as happy not to bring it up. "Biggest turkey of all time takes as much effort as—"

"As the biggest blockbuster?" She shook her head, cocked it. "The proof is in the eating?"

"Something like that. But ye can hear little motors humming contented in Grant's skull."

She drew up straighter. "How's your timeline? Progressing?"

She seemed tense. "Aye. More or less." *Ye could always hope.* He couldn't wait to get back to Ireland. "We're scheduled to be done by the end of next week." *Am I in her way?*

"Ah."

"Do *ye* write to a deadline?"

"They've learned not to push." She stifled a yawn behind her fist, leaned back into the armchair. "It's the greatest of luxuries." She stretched out her arms, widened her fingers on the table's edge.

"*I* need the pressure." He wondered what the aftermath had been of her outing herself. He wouldn't add to it by asking—it couldn't possibly affect *him*.

She dipped her head in acknowledgment, grinned. "*I* crack like an egg!"

He made a face at the image of splattered brains. "Listen. I've been meaning to find some time—"

"This isn't a quid pro quo, you know." Something guarded in her manner. "You've been absolutely no bother."

"Didn't mean it that way. Just don't want to leave without knowing ye a bit better." There, he'd said the right thing. She relaxed again, the shadow gone from her eyes.

"You're the one with the schedule."

"Would ye be free Friday afternoon?"

"Think so." She tapped her pursed lips with her knuckle, nodded. "What did you have in mind?"

He opened his hands, left the matter to her local experience. "Another hike? Assuming yer blasted monsoons hold off?"

"It *is* spring, you know. Crops?" She considered. "Heard of Mount Kearsarge or Mount Cardigan?"

"And the difference is...?"

"They're both around three thousand feet, but the hike up Cardigan starts from the bottom and takes a mile and a half; for Kearsarge you start at a parking lot—with a great view—three quarters of the way up; it's about a half-mile climb. Both are straight up, over granite, easy hikes."

Hiking with a friend. *The extravagance.* And he'd not see an article with photographs—'movie star on hike with local writer'— friends never betray ye, gossip to the media. "Can ye manage the longer one? I'm getting sluggish from all the sit around and wait. Two-ish?" He glanced at his watch.

"I'll pack lunch." She inspected the clock pointedly.

"I'm goin', I'm goin'!" *Fair's fair.* She hadn't asked, but if experience'd taught him anything... "One more thing?"

"You're going to be late."

He watched her eyes. "Would ye like to see a bit of the shooting?"

"Oh." She stared out the window a moment, considering. "I would. Very much."

Most people went all blathery about whether it was convenient, whether they would interrupt, requiring reassurances all round. *This is much better.* "Wednesday afternoon?"

Again the moment of thought, then a grave nod. "Certainly. Thank you." She cast a significant glance at the clock again.

"I'm goin', I'm goin'!"

He had plenty of time while navigating her drive: it had been on his mind, it was taken care of. He grinned through the visor, heard the soft click as the gate closed behind him, checked both ways before roaring out onto the road. The long rest had done immense good; the afternoon lines came easily; he saw how to make the colonel's farewell speech tighter, let the troops hear his absolute faith they would follow him.

Maybe Grant *would* be able to stick to his production schedule—it *would* be a first—but one could dream. The much-maligned New Hampshire weather was perfect: clear skies and low humidity. *Today.*

No complaint; the Fates were being kind.

BIANCA

Bunker Hill **set, Hanover; 3** P.M.

"CUT! TAKE FIVE, PEOPLE." Grant ambled over. Freed temporarily, the crew dispersed. "Bianca? A word?"

I'm in for it now. She squared her chin, adjusted her cleavage so the girls popped. She gave Andrew credit—he hadn't moved a muscle. Better still, he'd reacted with cold fury when she pulled her little stunt. John, now—his mouth gaped. *Damn it—take the risks—or get out of the business.* "Yessir, Mr. Director, Sir?"

Grant shook his head theatrically. "Bianca, Bianca, Bianca." His eyes narrowed, but the smile crept up. "What the *hell* do you think you're doing?"

"Did I miss a line?"

"You know damn well you didn't miss a line."

Because I never *miss lines.* She batted her eyelashes with their oh-so-subtle darkening. "You like?"

Grant did the cougar thing he did when he was frustrated, growling wordlessly with his hands clawed out to strangle her.

She bowed her head, bared her neck in submission. "I took a chance. A microsecond worth of chance." She straightened, locked gazes with her director. *And I'm right.* "That's what you *pay* me for."

"Defiance. Really?" At least he did her the honor of taking her seriously. Or was he exhibiting his legendary temper control? Here. With John watching, before Andrew in full dress uniform by the carriage, ready to set out for the loyalists' ball. Everyone else—from extras through lighting techs and animal handlers—discreetly moved out of earshot. *But they are not blind—I am center stage.* "We discussed this. Proper British young ladies did *not* defy their fathers."

"Not openly. But she's going to." She lifted her shoulders in a demure shrug. "It seemed a good place to foreshadow."

"She has her chance for that later." Grant turned, consulted the alpha male. "Colonel?"

Bianca kept her gaze on Grant, jumped when she heard the suppressed rage in her father's voice. "No daughter of mine would dare flout me, much less in front of servants." His hulking presence, at the edge of her peripheral field of vision, was as real as concrete.

"Andrew?" Grant raised his left eyebrow which furrowed his forehead unsymmetrically.

"Eh. She has a point, Grant." The hulk hesitated. "Not sure I agree with her timing."

Bianca exhaled. *Weasel.* At least he hadn't dismissed her out of hand. *Solidarity?* Safe though, given how Grant catered to him. Another small step in the right direction: if he won't side with me now...

"A bit of warning, missy. Next time, bring it up in rehearsal." Grant gave her a last look, headed back towards the power seat on the camera crane. He spoke over his shoulder. "Places everyone. Do it *my* way."

Then it wouldn't be on film. Where he could use it during editing if he wanted to. She turned to Andrew. "Thanks?" She couldn't read him. Amusement? Or did he think her a fool? And where the hell was he this morning? He kept disappearing on her, like after the bar fight, just when she thought she was getting through. Last night, after dinner, they'd run lines, she'd had plans...

"Don't thank me. Grant knows what he wants."

"It's *my* role." Something different in how he looked at her with those disconcerting eyes. *Respect?*

"Thin ice." The corner of his mouth curled. "Young Johnnie here is going to get a *handful*."

Young John is out of his league. "Relax, John. Grant doesn't bite." She inclined her head sweetly at her husband-to-be. "A proper colonial wife would never *dream* of defying her husband."

The makeup girl's powder took care of the fine sheen of perspiration on her upper lip. Her stomach unknotted. She ticked off another item on her mental list: *Andrew will take my side in a pinch.* Her skin tingled with prickly points of stress, her groin had a not-unpleasant heaviness.

Her hand was steady as she let Andrew help her back up to the seat of the carriage for the beginning of the scene. Grant was about to get exactly what he wanted. She owed him.

As long as the director wins in the end.

KARY

Sanctuary; 7 P.M.

SOMETIMES THE IRON discipline of ritual wasn't enough.

Kary evaluated her day, sitting quietly surrounded by papers at the dining room table, the mechanical pencil in her hand too heavy to lift. When Andrew left, she'd edited—successfully—for another hour, rested, but not slept, doing yoga breathing exercises slowly and consciously, aiming for a quiet mind. Lunch—in the warm protected spot on the deck. A short hike to stretch her legs, and to see and photograph the dogwood blooms at the little clearing she'd named King's Landing, a third of the way up her hill. Another rest, and a half hour of pleasurable reading noting the kinds of scene openings in some of her favorite science fiction novels: she knew now how to start Akiiya's next scene. *And for what? Another day safely spent without crashing?*

And throughout, right behind her third eye, the consciousness of ignoring the really big gorilla sitting in the exact center of her mind: *I'll be visiting the set of* Incident at Bunker Hill *as Andrew O'Connell's guest.*

She could think of it as 'the landlady guilt visit' or 'the landlady I'm-being-nice visit.' Either sufficed, kept things evenly keeled, allowed her to appreciate the sights and sounds, meet a few of the indubitably fascinating high-energy people he worked with, and satisfy any curiosity *they* might have about her. *And then, all verities satisfied, to slink back under my rock.*

Ritual discipline did not allow for visiting movie stars with real lives. Nor for obsessions, however well controlled. *But the ritual is mine, it is what I have.* And it preserved the one thing nothing else could in her tiny restricted locked-in life: the ability to write.

Outside, the last of the daylight was fading. It didn't help to know it had a name—'sundowning'—depression setting in because the day was now gone forever. The later it got, the more energy it took to do battle.

She faced the facts: to protect the life she had created for herself out of the shambles of the old, the burden needed sharing. *For the sake of my eternal soul.* Choose your audience: someone who would endorse no judgment and, if anyone could, understand.

She invoked more ritual, laying a fire from the supplies Lucy always left close at hand, accepting the pleasure of the lighting, staring at the flames. *As on that night...* The mantelpiece clock chimed the half-hour. It was time. In California, the retirement home residents would be settled, the next item on their schedules a leisurely dinner served in the graceful dining room at five, a useful endpoint if the conversation got awkward.

She dialed Aunt Ruth's number by heart.

"Kary! What a wonderful surprise! I thought of you this weekend."

"You can call me, too, you know."

"I don't like disturbing you while you write."

"If I answer the phone, I'm not writing."

"That's what you always say when I disturb you."

"People first. Especially you." *Capturing words next, above everything else.*

"How *is* the writing going, my dear?"

"Very well. The new story is coming almost faster than I can capture it." Their formal jousting, as ritualized as a quadrille. She exhaled. *I haven't committed—yet.*

"What is it, dear?"

"You know me too well, Aunt Ruth. More of the same, I'm afraid."

"I knew there was a reason to worry. Are you ready to talk?"

Am I ready to talk? Anyone else would push, demand. "No, but I need to." *I should have thought this out, decided where to start—*

She ran her fingers through her hair, tugged, impatient with herself. "Remember the last time we talked?"

"Stop me if I'm crazy. I'm getting senile in my old age." She hesitated. "Is it the same man?"

Kary visualized Ruth in her favorite armchair, taking a moment to think before speaking: losing marbles was *not* a family trait. "Here I thought I was keeping you from worrying. Yes. The same man."

"Ah. The actor, then. Andrew Connor, or something?"

Am I this horribly transparent to everyone? "It's complicated." *So, uncomplicate it.* "You always get it. O'Connell. He's a house guest. Part of the time. They're filming his next movie in town." *See? Was that so hard?* "I've been invited to watch them film Wednesday afternoon."

"He's disturbing your peace."

Aunt Ruth radar. "Not intentionally. He's been the perfect guest. But…" *Get it all out at once, like an afterbirth.* "But yes. Just by existing. The reality is overwhelming…"

"It always is, dear. Good *and* bad. He is young, for a man. And healthy, isn't he? They take up so much more space than you think, all that vitality." Ruth hesitated again. "You are sure…?"

Bless her. "Nothing. Don't worry." *Lord, the temptation.* Enough fascination to pull her hand into his fire. But no, nothing there. "If I were younger." And beautiful. Beauty deserves beauty. *If I weren't sick.*

"A cat is allowed to look at the Queen, Kary."

"A cat is *not* allowed to want to *be* Queen."

"Better not to want?"

"Better not to want." *It hurt.* In the background she heard sounds of people approaching Ruth, asking if she was ready to go in to dinner. *Salvation.* Kary let out all the air she had been holding in.

"I can eat later—"

"No. Don't. I just wanted—" needed "—someone to talk to. You're my someone."

"I love you, Kary."

"I know." *It was done.* "Now go get your dinner. I'll call you when it's over. Promise."

"Promise accepted."

The very last part. He certainly needed no more publicity. "You won't tell anyone."

"You have to ask?"

And that's why I love you.

✨ CHAPTER TEN ✨
"O yes, I saw sweet beauty in her face"
(Wm. Shakespeare, *The Taming of the Shrew*)

Action Star MICHAEL HENDRICKS spotted by fans at the tiny LEBANON, NH airport! Can rumors of an engagement be true this time?
Star!, State of the Union, May 26

...accompanying pic is the lovely BIANCA DOYLE from the upcoming BUNKER HILL. The young man with the enviable task of kissing her hand is up-and-coming revelation, Australian JOHN ROBBINS.
Sources report ANDREW O'CONNELL arguing with director GRANT SYKES about production delays, some say caused by the actor's own interference...
www.wayneblackburn, May 26

VIOLA
About your years, my lord.
DUKE ORSINO
Too old by heaven: let still the woman take
An elder than herself...
Wm. Shakespeare, *Twelfth Night*

BIANCA
Bunker Hill; **Wednesday, May 25; 1** P.M.

EIGHTH TAKE. THE FOCUS would be close up, on John's face. The cameras were now behind her. All she had to do was repeat her lines exactly as for her side of their shot; the marks were the same. To get the best reaction out of John, she'd let him see how much she loved him. If he didn't blow *this* take, they'd be done. Bianca smiled up at John's young foolish ardent face.

"ACTION."

She peeked beyond John's shoulder at Grant. Something was wrong. *Oh, no.* A familiar bulk stood next to—and dwarfed—that gnome, Grant. What the hell was *Michael* doing here? *Shit! Now look what you made me do!*

She gave John credit—he, aware of the cameras and his own work, didn't acknowledge her momentary loss of concentration, and he would never say anything, but she *knew* he noticed...

She compartmentalized. She turned her full attention on John— young Winston—made it easier for him. Her gaze roved over his handsome, beloved features. He would be gone for months, might never come back: it was imperative they find a way to marry, and if Father wouldn't allow it, well, Father didn't *understand*... When Winston bent his head to hers, the kiss he found was real, tender— unlike the one a few minutes before, on her take, where his awkwardness had almost cost her a split lip.

That ought to shut Grant up.

"AND CUT."

Grant's assistant on the megaphone released them.

"IT'S A WRAP, FOLKS. TEN MINUTES."

Where was Andrew? The next scene was a continuation—no change of dress or set—he should be here already. Shit again. She was going to have to manage Michael with Andrew hovering in the vicinity? *Shit!*

And John, too? *Do I have to live my whole life publicly?* She brushed him off with a quick sincere smile, deliberate warmth in her eyes. "Nice job." She touched his arm. "I'll be right back."

Thank God Grant wandered off! She knew he hated unplanned breaks—but whether he was condoning Michael's breach of manners, or truly had things to deal with this very instant, she didn't care. She lifted the confining skirt, marched purposefully to where Michael stood in isolation by the gantry. She recoiled when he inclined his head. "Don't. Makeup." He could make of that what he wished. "What are you doing here?"

"Hey. Just thought I'd stop by and see my girl."

"In the middle of filming? Are you nuts?"

"It's okay. Grant understands."

"Understands what? You nearly made me blow the scene!"

"C'mon. That kiss looked pretty good to me. Will I have to duke it out with Robbins over you?"

"*John* just kept me from looking like an amateur."

Michael had the grace to look sheepish. "Aren't you going to ask me why I came?" His hand went to his jacket pocket.

Oh, God, no! She was abruptly conscious of the multitudes ogling their little unscripted scene: crew, food handlers, the guy gentling John's horse, the Assistant Director... and somewhere the last person she wanted watching. *Damn it Michael—did you count on an audience?* And someone was bound to have a camera phone already framing them. *You are* not *going to pull this one.* It would *ruin* the box office, kill the titillating rumors of her and John... "Don't. Just don't."

Michael's hand came out holding a tiny jeweler's box. "Bianca Doyle, will you...," he opened the box, held it out for her inspection, "promise to wait until I get back from Canada?"

Is that *what you staged this little drama for? A* promise *ring?* She held herself rigid. All eyes *must* be on her. *You put me through this...? Are you insane? What is* he *going to think...?* She resisted briefly as Michael reached for her right hand, slipped the ring on her middle finger. She glanced down, where her other hand toyed with what better be a star sapphire, up at him. "It's too big."

"Damn. I forgot how you starve yourself when you're working."

"I don't *starve* myself." Dangerous ground. "I eat healthy, and I lose a few pounds for the camera."

"Whatever." He leaned in, kissed her cheek before she could react. "Sorry, babe, gotta go. Say goodbye to Grant for me, will you?"

"Michael—"

"I'll call you—they're waiting for me."

"*Michael*—" He'd pay for this. Stock-still—she'd be damned to let all these people see any reaction—she watched him leave like the coward he was, turning for a little wave just before he disappeared around a corner.

"Yer man?"

Andrew. When had he crept up on her? She felt the heat rise in her cheeks—would the makeup hide it? "Ah— Yes. That was Michael."

"He's not staying to cheer for ye?"

"I can't— Not with an audience!"

Andrew chuckled, looked around. "Broken fourth wall?"

"Broken concentration." She used it. "He should know. By now."

"New bauble?"

Damn. Andrew'd seen Michael insist on shoving the ring onto her finger. She hoped he'd also seen her drag it off; it was a turd

clenched in her fist. "I can't wear it in costume! And this thing—"
she opened her arms wide and stared down at her tight bodice, "—
has no pockets!"

"Give it here." He tucked the ring into his breeches-pocket. "Remind me later."

How to explain? A *promise* ring? Thank God it wasn't— Michael
would be sorry— Her mind came to her rescue under pressure, as it
always did. *Here goes.* "Way to mess up an *apology.*" Did that explain the gift, the little scene Michael put her through? Damn Michael to hell. "He had to run."

"Leaving ye in a bit of a state, it seems."

"You understand." *Had it served?* And now here was that weasel
Grant Sykes again, wanting her to work. She reined herself in,
forced the tainted air from her lungs. "Very bad timing." *The absolute worst.* Everyone was looking at her, even that irritating George
who was always hanging around Andrew.

Fine. Watch me. See how it's done.

KARY

THE CHAMPAGNE FROTH threatened to bubble over again. A
steel band encircled Kary's chest. She drove around a corner,
parked the pickup on Adams Lane in the mottled sunlight under a
cool sweetgum. Bark mulch dampened by an oscillating sprinkler
gave off the odor of licorice. The humidity was increasing. *A perfect time for war.*

She was thankful she'd worn sturdy walking sandals, and, over
tinted sunscreen, the minimum: mascara on pale lashes, the permanent curse of the blonde. She wasn't used to being 'in public' any
more. She put on sunglasses, girded her loins. Her hand crept to the
outer pocket of the lightweight nylon bag slung over her shoulder:
Andrew's note.

Come any time after lunch. Ask for Ted Silver in
Security. Slept like the dead. Thanks. Andrew.

She'd seen him last night for all of thirty seconds. *I'm getting
quite blasé.* He had repeated his invitation by reminding her to wear
'sunburn stuff.' He'd told her to use the Parrish Street entrance. She
approached a knot of people leaning against a red-and-white striped
barricade, craning for a glimpse of the filming. *At least in a college
town crowds are well behaved.*

Anticipation warred with nerves. She resolutely ignored the question of whether Andrew had talked about her. Possibly she wouldn't even meet anyone, just observe from afar. Under foot, dogwood-petal confetti littered the sidewalk, pink organic trash.

"Why are they here? Bunker Hill is in Massachusetts."

"They already filmed there—here's cheaper."

"Andrew O'Connell's in it, and Bianca Doyle."

"I tried out to be an extra but they never called."

"Have you seen him?"

"Nah. Too far away—but he signs autographs if you wait till the end."

"Are they done?"

"It took forever yesterday—was here until seven."

Kary took a deep breath. "Excuse me." She edged through the onlookers who swiveled, curious, as she passed.

At the barricade, a uniformed guard held a clipboard. "Can I help you?"

She cleared her throat. "Hi. Kary Ashe. I was told to ask for Mr. Silver at Security. Ted Silver?"

"I'm sorry, miss. Captain Silver's not available right now." The face under the cap was young, beefy, unconcerned. "Could *I* help you?"

The crowd was a vise.

Hi. I'm Andrew O'Connell's guest. Kary clenched her hand, to forestall reaching for the note. *I could never use it.* She fought the impulse to thank the guard, slink away through the crowd. *And then explain to Andrew why I didn't show up?* Now what? Leave a note for Silver?

Eyes drilled into her back.

The security guard blinked. Stubby eyelashes. A tightening of his forehead as intelligence clicked on. "You wouldn't be *Dr.* Ashe, would you?"

Saved! Involuntary nod. "Yes. I'm Karenna Ashe."

The onlookers murmured behind her.

"Who's that?"

"Dr. Ashe?"

"Do they need a doctor?"

"The captain told me to expect you, Dr. Ashe." The guard motioned her around the barrier with officious alacrity.

Bless Andrew's sweet heart and his compulsive attention to detail. She shivered. *Safe!* As the fear quelled, still sparking, the excited bubbling returned, intensified: she would be watching him act for real, witness the raw fabric of dreams.

The walkie-talkie crackled, received an unintelligible reply. "Someone will be here for you in a moment, Dr. Ashe."

His switch to instant deference made her uncomfortable. *And does he have to keep repeating my name?*

"How come she gets in?"

"Doesn't look like anybody important."

"Must be somebody's relative."

Kary *knew* the last one was the fifty-ish woman with the high bun, large arms in a sleeveless print shift. The one who had just taken her picture. *Thank God I didn't use Andrew's name—that's all he needs.*

She twisted round at a tap on her shoulder. With cargo shorts and a windbreaker's sleeves tied around his waist, reddish-brown hair curled thickly between shorts and high socks laced into boots, and almost as thickly down his arms, the man could have passed for a Dartmouth grad student or young professor. She felt the tight muscles in her face relax as she exhaled, smiled. "It's Mr. Cosgrove, isn't it?"

"Cosgrave. With an 'a'. Ye remembered me." He sounded pleased. "Call me George."

"Of course. We had a nice talk at the restaurant. How are you, George?" Her stomach was reacting uncooperatively to new situations. She told her body to cut it out.

"Topping. Today's set's a short walk. Are ye okay? I can fetch a golf cart..."

While I wait here until you get it? Where they were the most interesting thing the crowd had seen all day? "That's fine." She would pay for the aftereffects of the adrenaline overload for days as it was. *If I keep overreacting like this, they'll be sending the ambulance for me.* The sooner they got away... "I walk a lot, and I've had my morning nap." *First nap—but who's counting?*

"Good. Carts are noisy." He glanced at the people behind the barricade. "They have to block off a fairly large area to keep some control over the sounds that get to the mikes." He inclined his head, led the way. "It's unfortunate. Grant said he'd like to let folks up closer—makes for good publicity—but he's on a pretty packed timetable."

Walking soothed the flutterers in her stomach. She soaked up details. She approved—their choice of location was impeccable. The houses on Parrish Street, many in the National Registry of Historic Homes, were a treasure trove of russet and Federal blue. She took mental notes of the signs of the shoot, which were everywhere on the cordoned off several-block segment: cameras, microphones, dollies, carts loaded with unfathomable equipment. Thick black cables with color-coded connectors snaked in all directions in sets of four. *In case I need color for a book.* "So much to take in."

"Aye. Boggles the mind to know there will be a line in the credits listing me name as 'Assistant to Mr. O'Connell.'" George shook his head wryly. "We've been at it—they've been at it—since early March. It still feels new every day."

He was gone before I came up from my shortened writing schedule. She managed *not* to say 'I was in a movie once.' "What does the Assistant do?"

"Oh, the usual. All-tasks gofer. Coffee. Lunch. Anything and everything. Mostly hurry up and wait, with occasional frantic bits." He shrugged. "Missing items. Though Andrew is so professional he rarely forgets a thing."

Right. *Andrew.* Listening intently to George, she had almost forgotten.

They rounded a corner to come on a tableau set out on the far side of a square block of park, actors in period costume, one of them mounted. Beyond them, a house with weathered shutters, stable on its left—repurposed garage?—big trees to its right. Around them in expanding concentric arcs, a backdrop of crew and equipment, motionless, trained on the small cast.

"Ye get used to the chaos. Hold a sec—" George froze, put out a hand in a warning gesture. He tapped a forefinger to his lips.

Not quite a 'shush.' *I was getting* comfortable, *dammit.* Halted obediently, she let her gaze rove, noticing light reflector panels, positioned to provide better-than-sunlight on the scene being filmed; an overhead boom mike; a camera on a track trundling toward the actors.

Far right, what must be the caterer's setup: coffee urns, water bottles, and circular trays of brightly hued objects—probably fruit—and sandwiches? Pastries? *Glad I ate, dragged along a couple of protein bars.* She remembered: everyone on a set knows the not-so-subtle hierarchy of who eats where—and when. This was not for extras. *It's for him.* For the figure center stage before them, with the ramrod-straight bearing of authority. Acting.

"CUT! TAKE FIVE!"

Released, George resumed moving. Up closer, everything attracted her scrutiny. Her guide aimed for a white canvas canopy to their left, set up adjacent to the track-mounted camera. She turned to better listen to him as they walked. Something caught her toe; she stumbled. George reached out instinctively to steady her. At her feet lay one of the ubiquitous black cable bunches, hidden by the long grass. All heads turned toward her. *Just great—why not call attention to yourself with a megaphone and be done with it?*

"They get everyone at least once." George's face was a study in concern. "Yer ankle okay?"

"I'm fine. Really." She excoriated herself for clumsiness. Brains were wired to detect erratic behavior in their peripheral vision field: for a predator it can mean an easy meal; for prey, life.

George took her elbow. "Watch yer step." He grabbed a pair of tall yellow canvas chairs under the canopy, *'Bunker Hill'* stenciled on the back in black. "Okay now. We have a couple minutes while they reset." He pointed to a short man in khakis with longish salt-and-pepper hair gesticulating and weaving between the actors in the area defined by the light-reflector panels. "There's Grant. He gives them a quick review before each take—what he wants different."

"I feel conspicuous—everyone else has a job to do."

George chuckled. "They're about to go at it."

She wondered how hard it was to maintain concentration with so many people watching their every move. No castles here, just balmy New England planting weather alternating rain with sun, and prosperous gentlemen-farmers. Best not to see movies being made. *Like politics and sausage.* On *Roland*'s set, would those scenes have lost their power had she watched them over and over?

She dug out her pen and small spiral-bound notebook. Crew members stood mindful by their equipment. Her heart raced with an undercurrent of excitement, no more than twenty feet from the eye of the storm: Andrew in period military uniform, a young man on horseback, and a tall older black man in breeches holding the horse's reins, a delicate woman in gown and wide-brimmed hat that shielded her face. *This was his reality: attention, fawning, work—and beautiful women.*

"ROLLING FILM!"

Kary located the source of the sound: the assistant with clipboard and bullhorn.

She held her breath and forced calm. *This is where the magic begins.*

ANDREW

"OVER MY DYING BODY!" Col. Strathmore, commanding officer, meant what he said. This young whipper-snapper, Winston, riding off on the bay mare without a backward glance, would *not* court Sarah, not while loyal officers of the King stood ready to offer her their hearts and lands. He *refused* to allow it. She would do as she was told—and thank him later, when she came to her senses. His obedient daughter, who revelled in the latest fashions from England, consider life as the wife of even a prosperous colonial mountebank? *Poppycock!*

A stiff breezelet lifted the wide brim of Sarah's hat, its emerald ribbon matched perfectly to the green silk of her gown. *She will not find the homespun to her liking.* His daughter raised her eyes, so like his dear Emily's. But Emily never defied him, and here was both defiance and—pity? How dare she—

"*AND—CUT!*"

The tinny megaphone burst Andrew's fictive bubble, let in cameras, crew, caterers... It took so much work to reconstruct; he longed to be left in the colonel's world to finish his story.

Bianca hadn't moved. The ghost of a smile flitted about her lips, and she was no longer his Sarah, but an actress on her mark, where she had positioned her body exquisitely to milk the rise of her bosom, brimming as much as Grant allowed. Thank God she seemed to have an instinctive knowledge of camera lines of sight; she never interrupted a shoot with the petty time-wasting complaints of many a starlet. If she kept it up as a director: ye either *knew* sightlines—or ye could not be taught. Her smile for him turned modern, and she broke character along with eye contact. She picked her way with delicacy to the makeup girl's stool waiting in the shade of a monstrous beech. "Aargh! Somebody take this hat! I swear the hatpin is going through my skull!"

He watched Johnnie canter back on the big bay for Grant's instructions. *Good man.* He knew Grant would be anxious over the mare shying, spooked by Bianca's hat. *With live animals ye take what ye get, animal trainers notwithstanding.*

Peter Hyland stood waiting to receive the reins, like the good servant he portrayed. He stroked the mare's nose, and she whinnied with anticipation as he pulled a lump of sugar from somewhere within the folds of his breeches.

In the background, the animal handler hovered.

Grant joined them. "Perfecto. Be sure on the next take that you turn," he gestured with his hands, "a smidge into the sun."

Robbins turned.

"Perfect," said Grant. "A bit more. *Perfecto.* We'll have this light for just long enough to get the scene, so don't dilly-dally. Okay, folks. Take ten." He walked off briskly to talk to the AD who was gesturing frantically with her clipboard.

Andrew's gaze followed— *Shite.* His eyes closed a moment in frustration. He'd forgotten. Kary Ashe. In quiet conversation with George. *Shite.* One *more* thing to tax his concentration, destroy his focus. But he owed her. She was *his* guest—better go make her feel welcome. He handed the tricorn to one of the wardrobe girls, strode toward the canopy. He'd invaded her peaceable kingdom to seek refuge—the least he could do was to share his. Might be worth—in some future book. *Reciprocity runs both ways.*

He'd gotten used to the sense of royal progression whenever he crossed the set. Everyone had a job to do. *Equals—but not.* He was about to confer the center of attention on Dr. Karenna Ashe; he hoped she was up to it. *Ye never know.* She looked up, attuned to the intangible in the air.

He would have sworn he caught dread. The set was noisy, crowded, exciting—the antithesis of her peaceful sanctuary. Was she hoping just to watch? *Too late to change course.* Damn, he should have asked ahead of time. No choice, now. Keep it short, stupid. "Come meet the posse."

George shooed them off. She took a moment to thank him. *Of course—impeccable manners.* Then she inspected Andrew. "You look—old?"

"The colonel is forty."

"An awfully weatherbeaten forty."

He held out a hand. "Man spends his life in the saddle."

Again, the impression of 'dancer': she took his hand to rise, released it to sling her bag over her shoulder, laid her arm naturally in the crook of the one he proffered. She listened attentively as he pointed out what was 'beyond' the set: the farm down the lane where Robbins rode off, the town setting implied by the houses around the park, the stables attached to his town house. As they neared Robbins and Hyland, her grip tightened.

Don't worry—we're just folk. But he knew it wasn't true.

He introduced John Robbins to Kary. Robbins kissed her hand, bowing low, "Charmed."

Flustered, she examined the delicate embroidery of John's egg-shell silk vest. "What gorgeous fabric."

"I'm being upstaged by my clothes," Johnnie complained.

"She never reacts normally." *Better than blathering.*

"I'm sorry." Sincere. "What a gorgeous young man. But aren't you a bit tall for a colonial?"

"That's why we always give him the shortest horse!" He stopped worrying. *She'll do.*

The makeup artist discreetly placed a tall stool. Andrew took the seat to let her perform her job with small brushes and sponges in quick, feathery dabs. The woman fussed with getting his long hair slicked down, pulling strands out of place with the end of a rat-tailed comb. Finally he reached up and tousled the mess, and he and the woman agreed they had achieved the correct effect.

He looked up at Kary. "What do ye think?" Before she could answer, he sensed an approach. *Ah.* "Peter! Come meet Kary." He turned to Kary. "Kary, meet Peter Hyland."

"This is an honor." A small strangled sound came from deep in her throat. "*Cover the Moon* is one of my favorite movies of all times."

"One of mine, too." She was in a pro's hands: Peter was always gracious putting fans at ease. "I'm glad you liked *Moon*."

"Are you playing Peter Salem or Salem Poor?"

"Ah! The lady knows her history." He smiled, pleased. "Peter. But of course the character is largely a construct. Not much actual documentation to base him on."

"People should leave more written records." She sounded wistful.

Images of Irish medieval monks copying texts by candlelight... *Americans—history babies.* "Aye. Even if they only go back two hundred years. In Ireland—"

"In Ireland what?"

Ah. Grant had returned, break over. Introduce her to Grant, hand her back to George... *Interlude accompli.* They needed to get back to work. "Dr. Karenna Ashe, this is Grant Sykes, our director."

"Nice to meet you, Grant." Kary offered her hand. "Please call me Kary."

Grant grinned as he shook it. "The pleasure is mine, Kary. Andrew mentioned you." He released her hand. "Wait just one minute!" He peered at her more closely. "You wrote *Prairie Fires*, didn't you?" he said, wagging his forefinger. "My brain *never* lets go of faces. Drives me nuts. You were on that show with Andrew.

My wife grabbed me—I'm usually asleep by that time, if I'm in New York—but she called me because Andrew was on. She's read your book, wouldn't stop talking about it for weeks—not that that's bad, you understand. I get a lot of good ideas from my wife."

"Shut up, Grant."

Grant pointed the finger at him. "You told me you had a 'friend' in these parts," Grant accused. "You didn't say it was Margaret *Mitchell.*" Grant addressed Kary. "She read me pieces. Said I should film it. Are you interested?"

Kary startled. "It was optioned, but nothing further happened. I suppose…"

"Who's your agent?"

"Elise Carter."

"Make a note—Elise Carter!" Grant yelled to his assistant.

"Copy that!"

Grant eyed Kary speculatively. "Ever considered doing the screenplay yourself?"

"I've never written one. Might be an interesting challenge."

"Ah…" Grant hesitated. "Maybe it would be better to get someone—ah, more experienced?"

The little minx has been keeping secrets from me. Respect from Grant put her in a completely different category. He'd have to find time to read her book. "Kary told me she hadn't written *anything* before *Prairie Fires*, Grant."

Grant stared at her. "That was your first?"

She nodded.

"She can learn," Grant decided. "Got a computer?"

"Settle down, Grant." *More and more interesting.* So modest and unassuming she looked. She'd never alluded to being optioned. *A whole new line of conversation—* Andrew noticed the AD waving, attracted Grant's attention, jerked his head toward the waiting crew. "Later?"

"We'll talk—you *will* be available later?" Grant's face screwed up in sudden worry.

"She lives in the neighborhood, Grant."

Motion by his elbow.

"Andrew? Aren't you going to introduce me?"

He'd forgotten her. Bianca was back.

BIANCA

WHO IS *THIS WOMAN stopping progress?*

She took the invader in with one glance: too tall, washed-out hair, gray eyes, no makeup, white sleeveless blouse and a mid-calf denim skirt buttoned up the front, sandals but no pedicure, no jewelry except tiny gold earrings. Damn aristocratic bones. *Vaguely familiar?* Whose relative was she? Absolutely *no* sex appeal.

Everyone seemed at ease, so—in some small way an insider. But why didn't Grant move things along? When she directed, she'd keep better control.

"Men!" She rolled her eyes, smiled exasperatedly. "I'm Bianca."

She caught the quick look the visitor gave Andrew. *A warning?*

"Kary," Andrew said gravely, "this is Bianca Doyle. Bianca, Kary."

What was he concealing? *Later.* She held out her hand for a handshake that was firm but gentle. "My pleasure."

"Kary is a novelist," said Peter Hyland.

Bianca glanced at him. *Am I supposed to know everyone?* Men! They kept you in the dark, never brought you up to speed—and then acted like you're an idiot if you asked. Trust Hyland to give her too little information. Grant was just as bad. Her eyes narrowed. She made the connection. She smiled again, warily. "I remember now. You were on TV with Andrew."

Kary's smile was crooked. "I give one interview in eight years, and everybody sees it."

Nervous. One interview—that meant the writer wasn't used to being center stage. She herself hadn't actually *heard* the interview. *Michael's hands were roaming...* Michael was in the doghouse. But what was the woman doing *here?*

"Kary's Andrew's friend," said John.

Thank you, Captain Obvious. "Oh?" *What the hell is Andrew's interest?*

"Grant wants to option Kary's story." From his tone, Andrew was *way* too invested in the outcome. Waiting for Grant's reaction?

Kary spoke up. "There may be a problem."

"I thought you said..." Grant was atwitter with anxiety.

What on earth are they talking about?

"I want to be consulted on the actors, and I'd like to approve the script."

"That's probably why the option wasn't exercised." John dismissed the idea with a laugh.

Ah. The writer shoots herself in the foot. Definitely not a professional.

Grant's face did not display 'happy.' "Not many authors get that kind of power."

"Too many movies have the wrong actors. And fail."

That old fool Hyland was nodding.

"Such as?" asked John.

Bianca cringed. *Shut up, John.* The question was going to prolong the break. She chafed in the stays, while he had on comfortable breeches.

"*The Godfather*—Part III. *Robin Hood: Prince of Thieves. The Phantom Menace.*" Kary had a mulish look on her face.

Grant inclined his head to her. "She does know film."

When Bianca shifted her gaze to silent Andrew, she sensed... agreement? Curiosity? Of course—he likely wanted to direct some day, too.

"A trivial example: BBC cast Ian Carmichael as Lord Peter Wimsey in the Masterpiece Theatre adaptations—*knowing* he was completely unsuitable for the remaining stories. Edward Petherbridge *was* Peter Wimsey. And he should have done *all* of them." Kary shrugged. "Pet peeve."

Wimsey? BBC? Petherbridge? How long ago was that? *She's crazy. Nobody* gets script approval. And Casting would have a cow. *Not a chance in hell.* "Creative control is a tough issue, isn't it?" She smiled to take the sting out of the truth.

"If Carole Lombard had been cast as Scarlett O'Hara, it would be blamed on Margaret Mitchell. Who had *no* say."

"Regrettably, we'll have to continue this." Grant was comical with his dithering. "Some other time?"

"Oh, I'm holding you up!" Kary had the grace to be embarrassed.

"Kary lives in New Hampshire," John said unnecessarily to Bianca.

"Ah, New Hampshire." *She really has no idea we're all waiting on her?* "It's lovely." The local yokels always wanted to hear that. *None of this is important!* Could we *please* get back to work?

"And this being New England, we can't count on it staying that way, so... later?" Grant finally seized his opportunity. He nodded to Kary. "Okay, people, let's get going."

Bianca's head itched and her shoes pinched. *About time!* She turned to Andrew, but Andrew's attention was on his embarrassing guest. Why hadn't *he* said a word? She minded her manners. "Very nice meeting you, Kary. Best of luck."

Like I would give Francis control of anything.

KARY

"YE MADE AN IMPRESSION." George had appeared from somewhere to walk her back to the canopy.

Can't have random outsiders walking around the set, can we? Kary took her seat, leaned into the canvas chair's welcoming arms. The knot in her gut refused to loosen. *I kept a hundred people waiting while I stated an opinion so amateurish even John knew I'm crazy.* "Grant expressed a mild interest in Prairie Fires."

George's eyebrows arched. "Movie people are always looking for the next great property."

The whole option possibility had blindsided her. *At this late date?* "I—"

"*LOCK IT UP!*"

"Ah! Ready to shoot," George whispered, as the tinny reverberations of the megaphone died away. He turned away from her to watch the scene.

Right; I made quite an impression. Her mother used to say, 'No one wants to hear your opinions, Kary—not all of them, anyway.' Mother meant it kindly. It always stung. Half her life was spent trying to think before she spoke. *And the minute I'm in a new situation, everything I've learned goes into the trashcan.*

The actors moved apart, each taking an expectant position. Young Winston mounted, rode the mare down the lane to the left. Col. Strathmore and his daughter stood before their house, their servant behind them to the right.

"*ROLLING FILM!*"

The low-level hum ceased. Crew members made tiny adjustments to headphones and control panels. *King Lion is ready.*

"*ACTION.*"

Winston cantered up to the colonel and his Sarah. The young colonial's words floated clearly in the quiet afternoon air as he began his greeting while sweeping his tricorn hat off.

The motion must have startled the horse because it reared suddenly. Kary heard George's sharp intake of breath. *Ah. Unexpected, then.* Emily flinched, while the colonel held his ground.

The director made a vertical circling gesture, and the camera continued its slow trundle toward the actors.

Winston regained mastery of his horse. He dismounted, gave the horse's nose a careless pat while handing the reins to the servant who stepped forward for them, returned to his lines.

Even Emily's flinch had been in character. Winston had words with the colonel, starting with a simple request to escort Emily to church, leading to an increasingly heated interaction with an attempt by Emily to mediate, anger and refusal from her father, ending with a barely civil, "Good day to you, sir!" from the young man, who remounted, slammed his tricorn on, and rode off in the direction from whence he'd come.

The moving camera reached its final position at the end of its track, held. Emily expostulated gently and unsuccessfully with her father. The scene ended with the colonel's curt reply.

With cameras rolling, the actors *became* their characters. *How do they do that?* Except for actors taking turns and enunciating distinctly, it might have been real. Kary shivered. Smoke and mirrors. *Impossible to know when a truly good actor was being deceitful.*

"CUT!"

The air circle Grant Sykes drew this time was horizontal.

"GOING AROUND!"

George answered her non-verbal question. "Minimum set up time—they'll do the next take immediately." He scrunched his shoulders, relaxed. "Which means in a couple of minutes."

"That was intense." Kary blew out the breath she had been holding.

"First take always is."

"Was the horse...?"

"Aye. Have to love horses. Very visual. John's a good horseman—didn't faze him. Andrew, too—grew up with 'em on the farm."

"Does Bianca ride?"

"Part of the job description, I believe, though she gets a double when they do long shots. Too risky—what if she broke a leg? Pisses Andrew off—they won't let him gallop."

"Too valuable?"

"Aye—"

"ROLLING."

The announcement came quietly this time, and George interrupted his answer automatically.

"ACTION."

The repeat did not include the horse rearing. Subtly different, though the actor's words were the same as Winston began his request...

No moviegoer wants to see this part. She laughed at herself: two takes and already her mind wandered. *Why?* Because watching ruined the story, yanked the observer out of the process of creating a single coherent story, the one true version.

Nobody wants to see my ditherings, either. Scenes, words, paragraphs changed, scratched out, moved around, edited, revised. Grant had his job—creating enough pieces on film so he could walk his viewers through the story. But no viewer would have to choose. No different than what she did, but her ramblings were solitary—and private. *And just as excruciatingly boring to watch.* Fabric of dreams? *Raw material for nightmares.*

"CUT! GOING AROUND."

She was beginning to anticipate the rhythm of the production. *Stop and start.* "Am I keeping you from doing your job, George?"

"Ye're me job right now." George pressed his lips together, shrugged. "I do whatever Andrew needs. But never fear, if they need something they'll grab me quick."

"There are a lot of people involved." Their world—jobs to do, camaraderie born of shared work, a group energy she was not part of. With a pang she remembered med school: group studying, rounds with ever-present pressure to diagnose first, days on call. *Couldn't work in this zoo now if I tried.*

"This? This is the minimum for an outdoor scene—what ye'll get if ye let them make yer book into a movie." He chuckled. "Don't worry. Grant's filming only *seems* chaotic—he's in control."

"ROLLING!"

It freed her from small talk. *My book. I never thought when I blithely authorized Elise to offer it to the whole movie world.* To see some actor overlay his interpretation of Jake on the one she had lovingly created over years—and supplant it. Even Andrew? *Even Andrew. It cuts both ways.* To see an actor create a Roland more real than any she had imagined while reading the poem. She would never write her own version of the *Roland* epic without conjuring Andrew's face…

Control. Was that why Grant was so distressed an outsider might have the right to meddle with his vision? *I didn't think.*

Which made me look even more foolish when I insisted. They'd all been so polite—which made it worse. *Humoring me like a small child.* John's reaction was unguarded—and the most honest. Peter Hyland managed a sympathetic nod. *Andrew was there.* He listened, to see how it would play out. Amused? *Bianca might as well have reached up and patted my head.* Normal people would laugh it off. Did Grant consider the option seriously? Maybe. *Until I opened my mouth.*

It's mine—I don't need the money. Share her story with millions worldwide who would never read the book? *Not if it isn't* my *story any more.*

"CUT! TAKE FIVE."

"Kary?" George had gotten up. "Sorry to disturb. But we have a couple minutes—horses need their breaks." He peered at her through solicitous eyes. "I'm getting meself tea. What would ye like?"

Typical of me—lost in thought. She smiled for him. "Cold water?"

"Indubitably. Right back."

She watched him join a general exodus toward the catering stand.

"Are ye filling up notebooks?" said a voice.

Andrew. He'd made no noise.

"Sorry, m'luv! Didn't mean to make ye jump."

"In my own little world, as usual." She ignored the painful thud of her heart. Startling did that. "There's a lot to take in."

"Bored yet?"

"Done yet?"

"They give me the playing. Every other body here has to work."

"Don't tell Grant. He'll charge you."

"Right." Andrew's head swiveled as he caught some signal she didn't see. "Off to the sandbox!" And he was gone. Her gaze followed his back as he sidestepped through the parting crew, nodding and joking as he went—to *his* little world.

George followed her gaze as he handed her a bottled water. "Ah, Andrew made it round." He sat, tapped a packet of sugar into his tea, made a vortex with a wooden stirrer.

And every eye was on us. Which she never noticed until Andrew left, same as at *Mallory*'s in New York. "Having a guest on set is disruptive."

"Think this is bad? Should've been here this morning when Bianca's *boyfriend* stopped by." George shook his head. "Half expected the man to drop to one knee."

The bottle was icy, drops condensing on its surface. It soothed where she held it against her skin.

"ROLLING."

I would have sworn there was something *between Bianca and Andrew.* She sipped chilled water, replaced the cap.

"ACTION."

Pay attention. She filched pen and notebook from her bag. Best take advantage of what *must* be a one-time event. She noted the leaves of the oaks shimmered in the faint breeze, and the sky was a painted corn-flower blue belying the weatherman's promise of 'scattered thunderstorms.' The sun had not moved appreciably, but a hasty glance at her wristwatch confirmed her instincts: two hours had passed since she left the pickup at Adams Lane. *My time runneth out.*

She focused, and, now that she had the flow down and needed to listen only peripherally, found notes easier. Sketchy sentence fragments—in a clear rapid handwriting she had invented to take notes in medical school. Unslanted, stubby, pedestrian, accurate—even at speed. Andrew first, of course. John. Peter. Little frantic gray mouse Grant Sykes; but she skipped 'frantic gray mouse' and categorized his movements, as he set up each take with the actors, solely by their visual manifestations—a trick from attending to patients. *Old Doc Forsythe drilled that one in—'Once you start judging, you stop observing. Tell me what you see.'*

Kary watched Bianca the longest, struggled with the words to portray Bianca who transitioned effortlessly, from a relaxed and playful modern hamming it up between takes, to the subdued and submissive body language of an obedient young lady of the period. Andrew looked on ramrod straight—or turned away. Different processes; was it a huge relief to put the whole characterization aside at day's end?

"CUT!"

During the next two takes, Kary moved on to the crew, noting clothing, tics, headgear, steel-toe'd workboots versus sandals, hats... each choice revealing. Body language equaled subconscious choice: posture, attitude, eye contact—hierarchy, dominance, competence. The female crew members were almost as fascinating as the actors, the male more predictable. Too many to capture. She made choices, regretting she did not have the entire scene before her on tape for later dissection, and her brain was so much slower than when she could diagnose a patient in minutes. An old gaffer. The girl assisting Bianca with her clothing. The chunky cameraman with a headset propped in his wild hair. George seemed content to watch, except that twice when she looked up, she found him looking at *her.*

"CUT! GOING AROUND."

Something was different. Grant, talking earnestly to John, made new gestures. He had brought the animal handler in from the background. When *'ACTION'* was called again, she found she had guessed correctly: Grant made John intentionally repeat the horse's rearing from the first take. She added notes to Grant's page.

"CUT! IT'S A WRAP!"

Phew! Another hour gone: for a segment which would last less than five minutes in the final film—if not abandoned on the cutting room floor—a hundred people spent four hours, not counting considerable prep time, working out-of-doors on a hot New Hampshire afternoon. *I didn't even move, and I'm exhausted.*

She stared hard at the actors animatedly centered around Grant, engraving the tableau in her memory. Andrew argued with Grant, dipped his chin in acquiescence to something Grant said. Bianca's laughter carried over the crew's din, her hand rested on Andrew's arm, her face was lifted to him. Ice constricted Kary's veins. *Remember who you are. Remember what* he *is. This is what he gets whenever he wants.* If not Bianca, any one of a million perfect young beauties who shared his world and its stresses. *It is right and just.*

And time to go. *Thank George, ask him to say my goodbyes, slip out, and make it to bed before I crash.*

"Ready?" George waited patiently while she stored her notes. "Andrew said to bring ye over."

She stood. *Did you really think you could escape that easily?*

Oh God, I want to go home.

ᔕ CHAPTER ELEVEN ᔓ
"And I will put enmity between thee and the woman..."
(Genesis 3:15, KJV)

Often missed in critiques of Bianca Doyle's performances is how much her stunning looks overshadow the subtlety and power of her characterizations. Not since Vivien Leigh in *GWTW* has an actress fulfilled the expectations of incarnating a beloved character with such complete aplomb. Bianca Doyle IS Nurse Althea Sweeney in *Corregidor* (she lost so much weight she ended up in the hospital), a film leaving little behind but her haunting eyes. Women in Hollywood fight the stereotypes; Bianca Doyle wins.

www.insidefilms, Archives 2004

CUCKOO'S EGG: The female cuckoo bird lays her egg in the nest of unsuspecting hosts of another species; when the chick hatches, it pecks and pushes the hosts' chicks out of the nest, so it can be the sole beneficiary of its hosts' frantic efforts to feed it. It is often much larger than them.

www.brownschildrensencyclopedia

ANDREW
Bunker Hill; Wednesday, May 25 (cont.)

ANDREW LOST COLONEL Strathmore. Again. *Being a father is tough.* He needed to save the impressions he'd had as Winston rode angrily away, of keeping his daughter Sarah from making a terrible mistake. He closed his eyes a moment to block out Grant. Grant had notes—Grant *always* had notes.

And now George had brought Kary, and was standing discreetly his usual pace back. Kary fumbled her notebook out of her bag, held it like a shield. *Are we that intimidating?*

Grant gave the dispersing crew a fleeting glance. "Want to see the night shooting, Kary?"

Curious. Andrew assessed the director's body language: in one of the sheep dogs it said 'submission.' *Very* interesting. Grant must want that option badly. *Curioser and curioser.* "Ye might—"

"Don't do it." Bianca shook her pretty curls with an expression of exasperation. "Night shooting is even worse than this afternoon— and you really won't be able to see a thing because of all the lighting equipment."

"She's right. And we'll be at it quite late." *Sweet of Bianca to make the effort to be inclusive.* He liked his women to get along. A clap of distant thunder belied the clear skies. All heads swivelled momentarily toward the sound, like compass needles to north. The forecast was 'scattered thunderstorms.' Portents? *Might end up postponed again anyway.* Part of the game, but shooting delays frustrated his concentration. And cloudbursts wreaked havoc with Sarah's gown. "Grant's a perfectionist."

"Look who's talking!" Grant's accusatorial finger wagged at him. "I refuse to take all the blame."

"I think the results justify it." Kary shivered. "I get chills from the alien abduction scene in *Valerian*."

"That was *years* ago!" said Grant.

She'd said, 'I don't get out much.' Including flicks? But *Valerian* was one of the reasons he worked for Grant.

"Still one of my favorite movies." Kary settled the shoulder bag's strap as if carrying something far heavier, shrugged. "Thanks, but if my treatment isn't finished Elise will have my neck. I told her not to promise, but the publisher *is* getting restless."

"Ye should've said something—I've taken a whole afternoon." Kary had the thin edge of tightness around the eyes and the body stillness he now recognized as exhaustion. *Time to get her home safe.* He chastised himself for allowing it to go this far. "Get us a picture, George, would ye?" They scooched together around the guest with practiced speed for George's three quick snaps, separated again.

"I wouldn't have missed today for anything." Kary patted the notebook. "I'm glad I got to watch a pivotal scene."

It was—but how did she know? He hadn't discussed *Bunker Hill* with her, beyond a general outline.

Grant's eyebrows rose. "Are you sure you haven't done this before?"

"What's in there?" Peter's measured voice expressed curiosity, as his head nod indicated Kary's notebook.

And neatly changed the subject. Thanks, Peter. It was odd to feel protective of a woman who was obviously doing just fine.

"Word portraits," Kary explained, as a third-grader might discuss her poem with the visiting president. "I've captured you on paper."

"Of course," said Peter. "Words for a wordsmith."

"Can I see one?" John asked.

"Johnnie." Andrew added a warning tone to his voice.

"No, it's okay. Would you like to see your own?"

She took the upstart too seriously—she'd never handle crowds that way. *Needs a thick skin—like mine.*

"May I?"

"It's meant to be accurate rather than flattering," she cautioned. "I hope you can read my handwriting." She flipped the notebook to the right page, handed it to Johnnie.

"Read it out loud," Bianca said.

"Handwriting's perfectly legible." Johnnie read out loud, "'Reddish blond hair, tall, slim, reddish gold hair on the back of his arms, large hands and feet.'" He laughed. "Got that one right! That's what the wardrobe people said." He read again, "'Shy smile, longish face, straight nose, long sideburns, square jaw, slightly narrow, lanky when not acting, controlled otherwise, reddish knuckles, freckles, narrow face—look of a greyhound, long square fingers, nails cut straight across, slightly stoop-shouldered, genetic ancestry probably Celtic—from the fairness of the skin. Eyes set perfect number of millimeters from the nose.'"

"Johnnie, ye're blushing!" *Tease the lad. Easy prey.*

"I missed a few things." Kary took the notebook from Johnnie, retrieved her pen. "What color are your eyes?"

The lad met her gaze, his cheeks still ruddy.

"Ah, yes, I remember now." Kary made a note. "Hershey's-chocolate brown."

Andrew became aware Bianca was scrutinizing Kary with intense interest. *Time to get Kary disentangled.* "George, could ye—"

"May I see mine?" Bianca asked gingerly.

Kary hesitated. She flipped the pages, gave the notebook to Bianca.

Bianca didn't read out loud. She glanced up at Kary. "It's very…," she searched for the right word, "generous," she said finally, handing it back. "You've made me out a porcelain doll. I'm really much sturdier."

"I was reacting to your portrayal of Sarah," Kary said. "I liked it very much."

Bianca smiled. "Thank you."

"You're welcome." Kary turned to Grant. "Thank you for letting me watch. It's been fascinating."

"Least we could do to thank you for keeping Andrew here sane." Grant jerked his head toward Andrew with a grin. "Kind of wish I could get away, too. There's no one on the set who doesn't feel *completely* comfortable calling me when they need something, even at three in the morning."

"That's yer *job*." Andrew's brain pounced on perceived weaknesses. *Goes with the territory, Grant.*

"Want it?" Grant asked.

"Yes." *Of course.*

"Yes," echoed Bianca.

"Well you can't have it." Grant skewered the sentiment conclusively. "But that doesn't mean I can't wish for peace, does it?" he said, returning his attention to Kary and taking her hand. "Andrew says you have no one for miles."

For a moment, Kary's smile stiffened.

Andrew found no answer for her questioning glance. Oblivious Grant. *Unintentional idiocy—and me own fault?* The damn locatability clause Grant demanded to counter the motorcycle requirement Andrew had insisted on. He'd told Grant where to find him as a matter of courtesy; he'd never thought to ask Grant to keep it secret. *Hindsight…*

Bianca laughed, turning to face him. "So *that's* where you've been disappearing to."

BIANCA

AND THAT'S *WHY YOU haven't been around when I wanted to talk to you.*

Andrew stiffened. His hand made an abortive 'Stop' gesture: palm down, then clawed, then fisted.

For one unguarded moment before he realized he couldn't stop Grant? *A confidence?* Grant got in his business? She felt the skin around her eyes tighten and her forehead pull down. *Focus, Bianca.* What *was* that reaction? Her eyebrows rose: Andrew wanted to strangle sweet little blabbermouth Grant.

What's going on here? Her mind went into overdrive. She had to get to this place. "Did you come very far?" She faced the writer, and did 'ingenuous.' Beside her Andrew smoldered; she could practically smell brimstone.

"I'm afraid it's just a hermit's writing retreat." Kary smiled and shrugged. "Little less than half an hour."

"I'm always curious how writers work." Bianca mirrored the shrug. "Ours go away, new pages appear." She snapped her fingers.

"Kary probably works longer hours than we do." Andrew had his voice under his usual tight control again.

Bianca grinned at him. "I have trouble writing a long e-mail," she turned back to Kary, "and you write thousands of words—like magic." She gave it her best smile, the one that lit up the corners of her eyes. "Does your house help your writing?"

"I think so." Kary's expression was amused. "Would you like to see?"

This is what I do best. She clinched the devil's bargain. "Could I? That's one of the things I regret about our shooting schedules—we never see much of the countryside we're filming in."

"Make Andrew bring you over some time."

Better and better. She lifted her lashes, smiled at Andrew. "I'll do that."

"Better still—"

Bianca's elation hesitated. *Now what?*

"—would you *all* like to come? It *is* quite peaceful," Kary said to Grant. "And I'd love having you over for dinner."

The rest waited for Andrew, tongues hanging out like a pack of jackals.

"That's a lot of work, Kary. We're a pretty rambunctious bunch."

"What are caterers for?"

"Can we, Andrew?" Bianca put wistful into her voice. Had Kary seen through her? Even Michael might have—but he wasn't here. Well, it would be almost as good. *Always easier to get forgiveness than permission.*

Andrew glanced at George. "I've a better idea. George, can ye arrange food? We'll bring it—that way ye won't have to do anything."

George said, "Sure. Can do." He stood there, waiting for his master's orders, as always.

"I'll make dessert." Kary looked at Grant. "Monday's Memorial Day—do you have plans?"

"Crew picnic at noon—fireworks in town are the night before."

"Any time after six?"

John turned to Bianca. "I, uh…" Using his own words to her frequently made him stutter. *I could probably make him swallow his tongue if I tried.* "Will…," he cleared his throat awkwardly, "will it make us later?"

"Later?" *So irritating, puppy love.*

"Uh, well… You already knew Grant extended the shoot by two weeks, didn't you?"

No, I did not. "I—"

Andrew flared, "Since when?"

Stress again—just a note in his voice. Well, at least the party was a done deal. *He can't back out now.* "Of course I did. We all get two more weeks together." Easy to smile genuinely at John's gift. "Delays are in your contract." *And thank you, Grant—two more weeks to get in Andrew's pants.*

Grant nodded. "I *posted* it this morning—didn't George tell you? Hope to budget we won't need more—June 16 is bad enough already."

"I'd be telling ye at dinnertime," George said.

After the day's work. Bianca kept her gaze on Andrew. *Wonder what's eating him.*

"Weather, weather, weather…" John's bobble-headed motion underlined his happiness at the delay. "In the contract."

Peter Hyland joined in, exasperated. "If you'd stop praying for rain…"

"Fine. It won't be pouring Monday—because it's one of your American holidays." Andrew addressed Kary again. "Don't do any unnecessary cleaning, or anything fancy, right?"

Bianca registered the undertone, kept her mouth shut. *Awfully domestic, isn't he?*

"Don't worry," Kary said. "I promise I won't fuss. Can't, anyway. Elise is waiting."

"Settled then. *Perfecto.*" Grant nodded his thanks. He motioned significantly with his eyebrows to his actors. "Get some grub, put your tootsies up, report back at seven—it'll be dark by nine."

As Bianca sauntered away, waving goodbye with her hat, she went over the little scene, poking for flaws. *Not exactly what I had in mind. Very* close to the line—Michael would've over-thought it, never moved; at least she had done *something. Like Papi never could, either, leaving Mother with three kids and then dying on her.* Power—it soothed her soul.

Shower. Dinner. Makeup for night shooting. No more thunder after the first rumbles—storm averted, back to work. Right next to *him.* For hours. Talking back, making him mad. *Perfect.*

What *was* Andrew's relationship with that woman? She was so much older—houseguest? Sleeping with her? Not possible! *Why can't I get to first base with him?* She forced herself not to look back, pushed 'breezy' into her step. *Stupid sleepy little town.* But she'd make it happen for her. Everything in due time.

I have to see for myself.

KARY

"YE DIDN'T NEED TO INVITE the clan, luv." Andrew was looking at her with that damned intelligent sympathy. The soft Irish accent was incongruous in the red-coated English colonel. Cast, crew, and director had abandoned the field to them, and the lengthening shadows underlined the passage of time. The sky had reset to the pastels of sunset.

He was right. *What was I thinking?* Had she been manipulated? No—her perpetual caution and exhaustion had lost to the equally strong longing to be 'normal.' *A normal hospitable visitor would invite them over.* "I don't think it'll be all that much trouble—and I *should* take Memorial Day off from writing, shouldn't I?" *Fun to have them over—just this once.*

George grinned.

Andrew's head was shaking in the almost imperceptible movement which, along with a compressed smile and crinkles around his eyes, implied amusement. His gaze went momentarily to the departing figure of Bianca Doyle with hat.

"It just sort of happened!" *Because I never thought it might.*

"Things do, don't they? Ye turn around, and ye're up to yer neck in unplanned." He cocked his eyebrows, raised his shoulders.

"Like Grant?" If it was real, it would take some adjusting to. *Later.*

"Like Grant."

"Right." *And Elise's expectations—pfft! No way today.* "I'd better get going, then—thanks for an interesting afternoon. Can't see how you do it day in and day out."

"It's only the working. No worries." He stood up straighter, made a parental face. "Have yer keys? George here'll go bring the truck round."

"It's no problem—just point me in the right direction." *The sooner, the better.* The adrenaline surge crested; she felt the beginnings of the crash. The overtaxed muscles at the top of her spine protested at the weight of her head.

"Ye're not leaving until we get some dinner in ye." He patted his pocket as if looking for smokes. "That would help, would it not? I was not paying attention, but ye're in no shape to drive."

"I have a protein bar somewhere... enough to get me home." She put finality into her voice with the last of her reserves. *And a nap in the cab.* Did she need to invoke the Zoë card and stay in town? So *many* additional complications attached. *Just leave.*

He put out his hand. "Keys. Food will help—ye didn't eat anything, did ye now?" He glanced at George, got ratification. "Ye know I'm right."

"Fine." Surrender breath. *Recognize the inevitable.* A quick snack—they had to get ready for the night's filming, didn't they? She fished out the keys, gave them to George instead. "Adams Lane. Blue pickup. Thanks. It'll save walking back."

George bowed.

"George'll get it. Come here to me. I need a quick bathe—fresh start for the makeup trowel. Ye can visit me digs."

I can visit a movie star's trailer, and wait while he showers. More and more ludicrous by the second. Charles would have a cat. *'You never see the implications!'* Charles could shove his implications. "Then I can go?"

"When I know ye're safe on the road." He inclined his head toward the right.

A brief walk round a couple of corners took them to an area with a number of trailers big enough to be called mobile homes. Moving the large muscles in the legs helped—she had been sitting for too long. And food *would* help. Was he being welcoming or meddlesome? She didn't care. *The minute I get home, straight to bed.*

Someone had bracketed the bottom step with wooden tubs of deep fuchsia pansies with black faces, giving an appearance of permanence, and they'd given him the good spot, under a spreading oak. "This one's mine." Andrew tapped the keypad next to the door. Six beeps. "They added it—since..."

She nodded. *Since the girl in his bed.* That one he *had* told her about. She wondered who else knew. *Harder and harder to separate what he told her from what she'd read...* And what had *he* told Grant about *her*? "Does George know?"

Andrew's eyes narrowed, his gaze fixed on her. "George handled the whole mess. Grant knows. Security."

She only dared nod. *His business.* Too close for comfort.

He escorted her into a luxurious but impersonal trailer, deep navy carpeting, leather couches, wood cabinets, random throw pillows. Barren of photographs or obvious keepsakes. A stack of papers waited neatly on the table; clean generic black bakelite ashtrays, more than she would have expected. Someone did the place up while the actors were working. *Does that someone fold his clothes—or is he neat?* So many things she didn't know.

He got her settled in a corner armchair, headed to the tiny kitchen, opened the fridge. He brought her a water bottle, himself a beer. "Replenishes the electrolytes."

"Of course." He hadn't offered her beer. *Of course.*

He rolled the bottle in his hands, showed relief when the beeping sound was followed by the door opening as George came back. "I won't be half a mo. George'll keep ye company."

"We'll be fine. Go." *I'm a grown woman. I can keep myself company.* The idea of food had taken hold more than she was willing to admit. Then home. *And I won't have to choose between fixing myself something and sleep.* No fire tonight—just collapse, preferably in her own bed rather than the couch. With luck she'd be out for the night.

"Get me clothes, George?"

"As soon as ye're out of them."

She rested, observing, while Andrew hoofed it down the short hall. George followed, returned in moments with the colonel's gear over his arm and the colonel's boots in his left hand. She waved him off when he seemed unable to decide between small talk and his duties. *Ah, manners.* "I'm fine, George. Go." It made sense: give the stars some privacy for wardrobe—not the bullpen she remembered with the racks and racks of period clothing, and the flimsy dressing rooms nearby. *We will all be teddibly civilized.* She closed her eyes, too tired to care. In the background, the faint buzz of an electric razor was succeeded by the clunk of a shower faucet and the sound of rushing water.

A door sound—she shook herself back to consciousness.

"Was I so long?" Andrew, in crisply ironed jeans and open-necked polo, barefoot. Wet hair loosed about his shoulders. Not weatherbeaten—and not forty. The clean sharp scent of *Irish Spring.* She wondered whose idea *that* was.

Before she could answer, the beeping sounded, and George was back with another armful of military accouterments. "Set these up for ye on the bed?"

"Thanks, man." Andrew perched on the edge of a kitchen chair to lace up sock-less sneakers, scrambled to his feet. "Let's get this traveling circus going, shall we now?" He held out a hand for Kary.

"You look refreshed." She spoke lightly, adjusted her shoulder bag. "Shall we?" But she wasn't fooling him.

He inspected her face, inches from his in the confines of the trailer. "I've been thinking. Hear me out, woman."

She braced herself. *I should have left when I could.* Why had she let curiosity overcome her better instincts? "I'll be fine. Really. Don't worry."

"Ye fell asleep when I left ye for ten minutes."

"I—"

"It's me fault. I should've known better. I forget." He pressed his lips together, came to a decision. "Don't be foolish. I'll send George to drive ye—"

"Way too much trouble! I'll be *fine.*"

"Or... ye can come back with me after dinner, take a rest, and leave after. It's early—ye'll still make home in excellent time—but I won't worry ye're smashed up somewhere on those twisty roads ye call highways." He lifted his right shoulder, raised both hands with fingers splayed. "It'll save sending someone out to bring George back. Spare everyone a lot of bother." He brought his chin down in emphasis. *"I'll* be out of yer way as soon as I get me togs on. George'll come back when ye need a wake-up, get ye on yer way."

Breathe; think, brain. "You're right, of course. Thank you." He *was* right, dammit. *I should have left—* But you didn't, and now you're going to inconvenience *someone.* Accept consequences,

Kary Ashe. He's trying very hard here, and he's right. Stupid to let yourself get so tired. Even stupider not to deal with it. *If I had just left and rested in the back seat... He won't even be here.* Such a small request—why couldn't she resist? Ironic—she'd have a perfectly innocent reason to be in his bed... She faced George. "That won't be inconvenient?"

"Less than driving ye home, but of course I'll drive ye if—" George angled his head. "The pickup's already parked out back."

"Not necessary. A rest will get me home in good condition." *And I won't get myself into these situations again.* She faced reality as if it had been her plan all along. Her stomach grumbled—it *had* been a long afternoon. "As will dinner."

George's gaze—his whole attention—shifted to Andrew's hand. "What are ye doing?"

Andrew had moved to the kitchen as she spoke with George. He blew out an exasperated puff. "Thanks, man. Not thinking clearly." He slipped the heavy ring back off his finger. "Forgot—but we'll be back."

George raised eyebrows. "And in a big hurry."

"Ye are as usual correct." Andrew paused a moment at what turned out to be a small wall safe in a cabinet, stowed the ring. "Now?"

"Stepping on yer heels, lad."

"Shall we, Kary?"

He'd worn the ring on Night Talk—*she had almost touched it.* "All right to leave my bag here?"

And get myself out of this as quickly as I decently can.

ANDREW

"IS THAT ALL YE'RE EATING?" Andrew compared the tray Kary had just set down with the contents of his own—steak, baked potato, onion rings, butter 'n' buns, two glasses of sugared ice tea, and the amazing American pecan pie the cute girls from catering had amongst their selections. He could feel himself rolling around fat and complacent.

"It's all I need?" Her chicken displayed appetizing grill marks, and the steamed vegetables were... colorful? She was smiling, a slight edge to her tone.

Women! Always dieting. As far as he was concerned, she needn't worry. "I could tell ye horror stories about the catering..."

"You worked all afternoon—I sat." She inhaled the savory aromas, smiled broadly, attacked. "Don't you ever eat anything green?"

He crunched an onion ring, tackled the char-broiled steak. "No."

She ate tidily, using knife and fork in the American way, switching the fork to her right hand to spear each bite. Differences in table manners still amused him. He had selected the far end of an isolated table from which to survey the whole of the huge white canvas commissary tents, their sides rolled up to let the cooling evening breeze circulate. A hint of mugginess was all that remained of the spring rains which persisted in interfering with their outdoor shoots. *Eh. Good for the crops.*

Kary gazed around; staffers at far tables minded their own business. "You're sure I'm not intruding?"

"Will ye get it through yer head? I ask for dancing girls, Grant asks how many, what colors. They spoil me unmercifully to keep me happy."

"Are you?"

"When working, aye." He shrugged. "Can't explain it. Everything quiet, the camera rolls, endorphins flow like water." *Aha!* The figure he awaited approached: Bianca, in white shorts, navy polo shirt, sandals. Glass in hand, her hair silky and sleek, she appeared crisp, clean, and refreshed.

She ensconced herself on the adjacent chair. "There you are," she said, including Kary in her greeting. "Staying to watch the night filming?"

"Heavens, no!" Kary's smile was wan. "Home for me. Andrew insisted on feeding me first. Have you eaten already?"

"She doesn't eat."

"I do, too," said Bianca, raising her glass. "One hundred percent of my nutritional requirements, with no effort on my part. Chocolate."

"How do ye survive on milkshakes?" *Damn the camera-added weight.*

Bianca laughed. "I'm never hungry when I'm working. If I didn't drink this stuff I'd probably pass out." She deferred to Kary with a graceful nod. "You?"

"When I'm writing, water. Period." Kary waved her hand, her fork forgotten on the plate. "When I'm getting enough exercise, I'm ravenous. Otherwise not. After New York I don't eat for days—

Elise drags me out to lunch. 'Marketing, marketing!' She complains I'm a recluse."

He loved watching women interact. Bianca had a deep attractive laugh. *When Ma and me sisters get together...*

"I want to apologize." Bianca dipped her chin, stiffened her back. "For inviting myself to your house." Bianca gripped the glass with both hands. "I thought about it—I was incredibly pushy."

He glanced from Bianca to Kary. *A little belated, but—properly penitent.*

"I'm glad you did." Kary's voice went grave, formal. "I should have suggested myself. It will be fun having you all come."

She means it. He liked forging connections between friends. *She's right—it'll be a blast.* "I'll make certain George—"

"You worry too much." She carved out a bite of the chicken, conveyed it to her mouth. The muscles worked along her delicate jawline. Exhaustion limned her stillness.

"I saved you pie."

The voice at his shoulder made him jump—he hadn't expected ambush here, in the mess, where most people were now used to having him around and almost ostentatiously didn't fuss. He raised his gaze. "Ye startled me. Penny, right?"

"I saved it for you. The pecan pie goes fast, and I noticed you like it." She set the plate alongside his tray. "Oh. I see. You already got some." Disappointment tinged her voice.

"What station do ye work, Penny?"

"Desserts." She pointed.

"Tell ye what. Next time, I'll get it from ye. Good?"

Her face lit up. "Sure. That'd be fine. I'll make sure we have some. Shall I—?" She reached for the plate.

"Not so fast!" He laughed with her. "But ye can't give me two any more—or they'll be pouring me into the colonel's breeches, ye understand? Wardrobe will have a—a conniption?"

"Yes, sir!"

He watched her walk away with a bounce to her step. *Such a small thing.* Beautiful American girl, skin the color of Dutch roast with real cream.

"You made her day." Kary's voice brought him back to the table.

"She'll tell all her friends," agreed Bianca. "Fan for life."

"Charmin' young one—she'll be having me as big as a house." He inspected the extra pie. "Ladies?"

"Give me a small piece." Kary held out her plate. "I'm afraid you'll have to handle the rest."

"She took a big chance." Bianca's jaw emphasized her tiny head shake. "Grant instructed the staff. I know I will."

Which is one reason ye might be an adequate director—attention to detail. "Ye crave recognition, but it flipflops from 'no one cares' to 'leave me alone' overnight." He speared a bite from the second slice of pie. *Too sweet? Right on the edge.* "She seems normal."

"She'll be crushed if you don't accept pecan pie from her every meal for the remainder of the shoot." Bianca punctuated her words with a sip from her straw.

"What should fans do? Especially when they see bolder ones rewarded?" Kary broke off a tiny piece of pie, and closed her eyes and smiled beatifically. "Excellent pie!"

"Not cross over the line." He cracked his neck to each side, refrained from stretching himself at the dinner table. "Unfair, but safer."

"We *have* to be able to work." Bianca pushed the glass away. "Fans are dangerous. Because they're unpredictable."

"All?" Kary's hands went to her lap.

Something there—what? She had mentioned neither the man who invaded her home, nor the girl in his bed, here and now when it would have been *à propos*, and so easy to slip into the conversation. *A rare treasure—the woman who doesn't gossip.*

"Even the 'good' ones go too far. Which is why I am not filming in America." A determined nod of Bianca's chin sealed the pronouncement.

He kept his mouth shut, waited. *Here we go.*

Kary took the bait. "Is the choice yours?"

"It will be, when I direct."

"Soon?"

"When I can get Andrew to sign the contract!"

"Andrew?" Kary's gaze questioned.

Made by a leprechaun tailor to measure. "Bianca is referring to a role she wants me to do for her."

"*With* me. He's perfect! You know who Charles Lutwidge Dodgson is, right?"

Kary assented. "We've always loved *Alice*."

"It seems the Rev. Mr. Dodgson was a fascinating character himself. Can't you just see Andrew as a clergyman?"

"Telling stories to little girls in a punt on the Thames? Logical segue from the English Army, I dare say." Kary's eyes narrowed; she scrutinized him. "Is this a role you want?"

"We're negotiating." *Continuing now.* "Strong concept—the life of an interesting man. But— well— it's not quite there yet." He shrugged for emphasis. *Stick a few more hurdles in there.* "And me agent—ye remember Maury— ye met in New York? He's not happy."

Bianca didn't look happy, either. "Francis— Francis Matt, Kary— he wrote the script for *Red Horizons*? He was on the team for *Back From Blue*—on TV? I think this will be really, really good, but—" her shoulders carried regret, "if Andrew isn't interested, I have a bunch of people next on the list."

She does, does she? "Might end up good. Isn't yet." *Important to get that in.* "I'd like to run it past some experienced writers. I was wondering if ye'd take a look, Kary, maybe give us some pointers." *There. Done.*

"Me?" Kary sat up straighter, focused.

Next to him, he knew Bianca's mouth was agape. "I don't—"

He turned to Bianca. "What would be the problem? Maury's seen a draft."

"I'll check with Francis..."

"You *do* realize I've never even seen a movie script?" Kary's expression was stern, but he'd anticipated the reaction. "And the media are quite different?"

"Doesn't take many before ye start to see the movie in the mind." Kary shouldn't take pity on Bianca, particularly since he was *not* on board. *Not until I'm completely satisfied, not until I can shut down Maury's objections.* With an unproven director—it had to be unimpeachable. *Kary's vote could clinch the deal.* "Didn't Grant say he was going to train ye up?"

Her head pulled back and tilted; her hands, the heels resting on the table, spread out in a 'wait!' gesture. Her gaze went from Andrew to Bianca and back. She shook her head. "Way too fast there. You want me to read a script and give you an opinion as to what? The story? The characters?"

"Whether ye think it all hangs together, makes sense." *Whether it's right.*

Kary consulted Bianca. "He's bullying you. Doesn't sound like you require me—or anyone—involved in this." She paused, attentive.

"It's not that— though I really need to ask Francis first—" Bianca blew a breath out noisily. "I wish…"

"…he'd discussed it with you privately." Kary eyed him sternly. "As you should have."

"There wouldn't be any harm in it… I guess." Bianca controlled her voice.

She knows I mean it. He wasn't leaving her any space under the paddock gate.

But it was Kary who thought it through. "I understand there's something called a non-disclosure agreement? If I get you one of those would it satisfy your writer?"

"Get one of what?" George set his tray down next to Kary's mostly empty one. "Isn't it about time for ye folk…? Ye have about ten minutes, lad." He walked around the end of the table, put something discreetly in Andrew's hand. "Found this." George walked back, sat beside Kary, dipped some kind of fried appetizer into a container of sauce.

Andrew'd forgotten—thank God George checked. *And Kary needs to get home.* He wished he'd found a time for this later, but there *was* no time, not even with the schedule extension. Dammit-all, this *was* the right time, they were all here, and it wasn't that big a deal. "A non-disclose." He faced Bianca. "Ye can trust Kary. She'll not steal the idea, m'luv— she has plenty of her own." This was not Kary's initiative, which made it all the more valuable: she'd appraise the script dispassionately.

"I suppose so." Bianca conceded graciously enough. "That should work. I'd love to hear your thoughts, Kary. Fresh eyes."

Finally. "Can ye get us one, George? Get Kary's signature and give it here?" He glanced at Bianca. "Fetch Kary me copy of the script—from the trailer." *Done.* He'd make amends to Kary later for dumping his doubts in her lap.

"Let the man eat his dinner? We'll get it done—before I leave." Kary's face was unreadable.

A weight off his mind, starting another hare. "Shall we, daughter?" He rose, pulled Bianca's folding chair out for her. *Least ye can do after running roughshod over her like that, ye pig.* Did Alexander the Great feel guilt for cutting the Gordian knot? *He did not.*

"Samantha Taylor isn't coming," George announced. "Fell off a horse." He looked at Kary as if to say 'I told ye so.' He put away spaghetti and meatballs like a true Italian, with a spoon to guide the wrapping of the pasta around his fork.

Bianca exhaled in a huff. "Great— The shoot will be even longer now. While casting sends Grant a replacement."

Andrew saw Kary's confusion. "Samantha was to play Sarah's mother, Emily. Memory scenes. We've been waiting for her to get here. Not good. More delays."

Kary's brow furrowed. "Didn't Emily die in childbirth?"

"Yes." *So?*

"Well, wouldn't she be about her daughter's age now?"

"A bit older. And?"

"Except for clothes, maybe hair, wouldn't she look just *like* Sarah...?"

He grinned at her, shook his head with rue. He addressed his little costar. "Why didn't *I* think of that?" He returned his gaze to Kary. "Exactly why I want *ye* to assess the *Dodgson* script. Wait'll Grant hears what he's been missing all along." He extended Bianca his hand. "This is yers." He placed her man's ring George rescued from the colonel's breeches—and the washer people—into her palm.

Bianca scowled. She clenched her hand, shoved the expensive bauble into the pocket of her shorts.

What was that about? "Come, me dear. *We* have love scenes to discuss."

ᕫ CHAPTER TWELVE ᕬ
"... one of you shall betray me"
(John 13:21, KJV)

He that covereth his sins shall not prosper: but whoso
confesseth and forsaketh them shall have mercy.
                                        Proverbs 28:13, KJV

CASSIUS
The fault, dear Brutus, is not in our stars
But in ourselves...
                        Wm. Shakespeare, *Julius Caesar*

CAESAR
Et tu, Brute! Then fall, Caesar.
                        Wm. Shakespeare, *Julius Caesar*

KARY
Sanctuary; Friday, May 27; 1 P.M.

SUCH A PERFECT DAY FOR a hike.

Kary'd swallowed two extra-strength headache tablets, the bitter
verboten ones with caffeine. *Just this once.*

She locked her front door, took a deep breath of outside-clean air.
Her little entry clearing always pleased her, wild yet controlled. The
mountain laurel and the rhododendra would blossom soon: their
buds were full and set.

Maybe the extra excitement in her life had translated into more
ideas. *It is not necessarily good that the woman should be alone.*
Surely a happy medium lurked between total isolation and being
subjected constantly to other people? One which would still enable
her to write in the mornings? *Dream on.*

Nice to have some time to hike with Andrew. *Ignoring that the last time escalated into inviting him to stay?*

She got into the pickup, set her armload upright on the seat. *I need to get out more.* One o'clock. More than enough time for a half-hour trip.

She'd awoken from her morning nap to raucous rock on the clock radio, groggy from a deeper sleep than she usually managed during daytime naps: she had fallen into a dreaming state almost immediately, had dreamed of hiking Kearsarge with Ethan and the girls, but Ethan turned into Stephen, last summer, and the shorter hike up the south trail with a four-year-old that had taken them all afternoon. Dreams did that when you worried. *The first sleep cycle takes an hour.* Seconds later her wristwatch beeped its now-unnecessary backup alarm.

They'd agreed on two o'clock, Winslow parking lot; the hour's rest would have to do.

The nap had followed an intense writing period again this morning: the draft of Akiiya's capture scene was finished, stored and backed up, printed. *Ready for editing when I get back.* Akiiya was a smart-bomb with a self-timer: Akiiya would decide when to explode—and who to take down. *What could go wrong?*

Kary turned the key.

The short drive down to her gate enhanced a sense of adventure and well-being. The weather could not have been more fortuitous, New Hampshire at its late spring best. The East Coast mugginess was bearable, good for skin protected by a tinted sunscreen barrier: there was little shade on the road this close to noon, under a fierce cloudless azure sky.

I did everything right: I earned this break.

Last night she'd set out jeans, long-sleeved shirt, cotton T, hiking boots, flannel-lined windbreaker—there was no rain in the forecast, but the mountain summit winds never ceased. Their lunch was basic—water, sandwiches, Clementines, cookies—and ready to stuff into her pack, with the light-weight binoculars, an emergency compass on an inch-long cylindrical case containing waterproof matches, and the mylar survival tarp which weighed an ounce. The cellphone camera would do if she needed photos.

She'd almost forgotten: he'd be asking about the *Dodgson* script. She read the screenplay through after supper, and thought she picked up an uneasiness he might share: the script hinted at an unsavory underside to the Reverend, but did not fully commit, and the interpretation was left to the viewer. Yes, actions seemed strained, but then Victorian England *had* its constraints. Separating private life from church advancement, especially for a cleric for whom marriage was not automatically proscribed, would have been a difficult decision in any age. What was Carroll really like? She'd reserved several books with the public library's online system; if the answer wasn't there, she'd brave Zoë and her access to Dartmouth's Library. And she knew why Bianca wanted to do the film.

Studded with sticky notes and protectively packed into a padded manila envelope, the precious script awaited sedately under the backpack.

Kary opened the gate with the remote. She told herself paranoia was unattractive as she waited on the sketchy shoulder until the gate swung shut before heading east down NH Route 4A, a scenic two-lane highway recently re-paved. She drove carefully—they hadn't repainted the lines.

The blue pickup bounced along a quarter mile when the low-fuel alarm binged loudly: the truck was running on fumes. *Damn!*

She pulled over, inspected the dashboard: well below the eighth of a tank mark. *When...?* It didn't matter. *Now what?* This was what safety margins were for. She'd counted on getting to the park early. Route 4A was shorter on paper, but Route 4 went through towns. With gas stations. She executed the U-turn, briefly considered the single-gallon red can in her storage room as she passed her incongruous armored gate, decided that would only postpone the problem, continued toward Enfield. *Plenty of time.*

On the outskirts of Enfield she glanced at the pickup's clock as she slowed to the strictly-enforced 25 mph speed limit; she had made good time. She stopped at the first gas station, surprised to find two cars before her in each of the lanes. She wished she were back in New Jersey where an attendant would fill the tank. As she extracted her wallet from the pack's outer pocket, the manila envelope reminded her she should give it to him after the hike. She put it in the back seat, face down, made a mental note with an image of her saying goodbye while handing it over for Bianca.

She was glad she had spent the rest of yesterday afternoon pleasantly weeding the flower beds which encircled her yard—a task she'd been postponing, but which needed doing before the *Bunker Hill* bunch descended on her Monday. Music from *The Wiz* played into her headphones. Was she crazy? Too late to cancel. *Stop worrying—the party will be fine.*

Yesterday morning, and not for the first time, she'd invoked the iron discipline of the writing room: show up, write. Anything. Rigid routine had failed her only once since she set it up: after *Roland*. Actors are told to wait seven years before they use personal incidents—maybe then she'd look back and be able to control that power... She blocked the thoughts: she promised herself an afternoon on the film set would not be permitted to derail Akiiya's story.

Failure came close—before writing Akiiya she needed to clear her head, transcribing her notes from the set verbatim and dumping several thousand words into a file to get them out of her memory.

Then, blessedly, the writing she'd outlined drew her in, filling the recesses of her brain with the scene in which Akiiya was captured by rebels from the village school where she taught cyphering as cover story to justify her presence on K'Tae. Writing an action scene was engrossing: choreography, shouted dialogue, and Akiiya's feelings and fears—would her infiltration plans work or would the rebels do the safe thing and execute her?—were more real to Kary than the day in man territory, now safely stashed in a dated file under 'Imponderables.' Akiiya consumed her remaining timed writing period, went over. Kary broke the writing off, placed a start-up note for next time. *Thank God for work.*

The car in front of her finally drove off. Kary got out, ignored the gasoline fumes as best she could, plunged the spout into the pickup's intake. The sign on the pump said, 'NO OPEN FLAMES ALLOWED.'

Wednesday night after she returned from the set, she found the fire Lucy had left ready in her fireplace for a single match to bring to flames. Kary gazed longingly at her living room, and made the adult choice: she dragged herself upstairs, and collapsed. She didn't think she'd brushed her teeth.

One tiny problem remained: after what Grant said about extending the shoot. *Now I have to discuss logistics—* The gas pump handle jerked in Kary's hand as the automatic shutoff valve kicked in.

She checked the time, retrieved her credit card and receipt from the slot. She had lost another ten minutes.

Drivers seemed particularly inept. She approached the critical junction at the end of a long line of cars at the moment the light turned red. If they had moved, she would have scuttled across the intersection on the next cycle. Stuck in front of *Woody's Antiques* as a jaywalker took his life in his hands, her eye was diverted to a scarlet stadium blanket arranged artistically over a cane rocking chair jutted out onto the sidewalk so as to block easy passage and tempt a tourist.

The spot of color yanked her mind back to the variegated-yarn crocheted throw on Andrew's bed. And the oddness of sleeping in a man's bedroom when he wasn't there: she hadn't opened the closet door to tuck in the corner of his leather jacket, hung up too hastily; the bed had a duvet and the kind of goose-feather pillows she hated because their support was illusory; using his bathroom, with its shaving kit contents spread over the counter, shampoo tube in the shower, damp towels haphazardly tossed over the shower rod and hanging from the hook on the door—and wondering whether it would be proper to leave the seat she found up, up or down. Clock-radio; an enameled wooden tray with the usual keys, coins, slips of paper; a dresser with six drawers; a long pillow with a russet sham. An undertone of cigarette smoke—acceptable because it was his? She left the room as untouched as she could manage, the throw folded neatly where she found it. The word-picture she recorded on her computer would take her back to Andrew's lair as clearly as if she had photographed every item. *Intensity makes a good focus.*

The car behind her had the temerity to honk. She made it through the intersection and out onto Route 4; he did not.

Served him right. *But it was my fault.*

ANDREW

1:30 P.M.

IF ESCAPING WERE NOT possible once in a while, me head would explode.

The Harley belonged between his thighs, zooming out with the slightest touch on the throttle to pass a car that poked along at 65 mph. He would miss this one, and it was glorious to let the steed have its head on the perfect road surface this fine day.

Not that he'd change a thing: when the set went quiet, and the cameras rolled, he was top dog—and he knew it, craved it, *deserved* it. And would do it again tonight, as he had in the mornin'. That one was in the can. Tonight's would be, too, regardless how late it went.

'Time will be tight,' she said. 'You'll want to be able to get back straight away.' Her justification for indulging him, for telling him to ride the bike to the mountain, not to stop and fetch her and the pickup, and drive her both ways. Even if she didn't have a yen for roaring down the American Interstate motorway I-89 with the wind in her hair, she understood.

Even if she didn't yearn for repeating words not her own for the camera, as many times as they needed him to, she understood. Curious how naturally she fit in with his bunch. And how they warmed to her, even little Bianca. George got her off safely, while he and Bianca had at it on the set that was starting to feel a lot like home.

He was going to miss Kary. *Make sure she lifted not a finger on Monday.*

His reverie was interrupted as he poured around a wide curve and had to slam on the brakes. The eternally unpredictable: road work. The traffic had slowed to a snail's pace, channelled into a single lane by orange-and-white striped cones protecting both the shoulder and the high-speed left lane which was currently occupied by an asphalt-spreader and the lorry feeding it hot tar.

He put a foot down to steady the machine as the queue halted; far up ahead the spare asphalt lorry beeped as it backed out of the construction lane. Gone to procure another load, no doubt.

Now he'd be late; he'd left it too close, but there was always something doing on set, and Grant had wanted a word...

The line crept forward to the end of the blockage, and he saw his opportunity as the car preceding him was slow resuming speed. He slipped round it with the nimbleness of his steed, throttling it into high gear and pushing the petrol. He gave himself a few seconds at top velocity to relieve the pressure in his skull, and reluctantly brought it back down within 10 mph of the speed limit, as insisted on in his contract. As much Maury as Grant? At this point it would be incredibly expensive for Grant to replace him, and it wasn't fair to take undue risks with his employer's overpriced 'merchandise.' *Not if ye want to work again.* Interesting to see oneself in such a light.

Around the next bend, a State Patrol car had pulled over one of the cars that passed him by, hell bent to make up lost time.

He chuckled self-righteously as he toodled on by.

Now for the intersection with Route 11. 'The *second* exit for Route 11. You need east, toward Andover.'

The adrenaline heightened his sense of well-being. He was the freest thing in the universe and it felt good, right down to his core, the road open before him to infinity. *Life doesn't get better than this.*

His truant run ended at the intersection; he took all required precautions, feeling virtuous, and moved smoothly onto the narrower state road bordered by the occasional dwelling typical of rural America. *Definitely not Ireland.* He proceeded at the sedate posted limit. This seemed to be taking longer than he'd expected; he found himself suddenly in more of a town than she led him to anticipate, and when he looked about for signage found he was on 'Main Street.'

A block or two down the street he realized that the road markers now read Route 4 *and* Route 11, and he remembered her last bit: 'If you get to 4, you've gone too far.' *Shite.*

Standard instructions—or just for him? She knew there was a lot on his mind, and filming tonight. *Generalissima* Kary. And try not to keep Grant waiting. *The break will do ye good, boyo.*

He found a place to retrace from, paid more attention on the return trip, and located the entrance to the park marked by a brown sign and not much else, with a nondescript road petering off into trees. Now he *was* late, but it couldn't be much farther, so 'twas best not to get out of the slow-moving line to call.

Remember to leave earlier than ye planned, mate.

KARY

2:05 P.M.

IF THE CARS IN FRONT OF me drive any slower, it'll be faster to walk.

She turned off at the entrance to Winslow State Park on Mt. Kearsarge's northwestern slope, wondered about politics, nepotism, and the finances of having two parks on the same mountain. Anything to keep from focusing on the time. *A bad start.*

Did he managed to find his way to the northern park from I-89? The signage only made sense if you already knew where to go, and the entrance was iffy. *He has your cellphone number; he's an adult.* She'd asked George to get him maps online...

Now through the toll booth, she chafed at the park's low speed limit: she hadn't expected this much traffic, and the trip took twice as long as it should have. The ribbon of road sloped gently up through a wide expanse of meadow and wildflowers. Framed without the access road, would it serve to film a prairie?

Damn Grant: she was beginning to get glimmerings of how *Prairie Fires'* broad scope might be condensed into a screenplay, but the image lodged in her psyche, of Andrew as Jake and Bianca as Meggie, could not be allowed. The minute she had time, she would dig out the Jake and Meggie images she originally sketched for her files, and pick suitable actors to cast. Damn Grant—and damn images; images were more stubborn than words. *Damn this brain.*

At twenty after two, she pulled up to the far end of the crowded parking lot nearest the trailhead at the Winslow Picnic Area, picking a spot in the sun which would be shaded two hours later. The truck-engine rumble ceased, but opening the door dumped her next to a noisy picnic area where most of the tables—and all the shaded ones—were occupied.

And no Andrew or motorcycle anywhere she could see.

Now what? And why hadn't she considered the possibility?

Relax. And energy-conservation mode. First, air-conditioning. She turned the engine back on. Better to stay with the pickup—he recognized it. Second, actually check her cellphone—instead of worrying what she might find; she had deliberately checked the house's answering machine before she left—no messages. *So whatever happened was after you left.* The cellphone displayed several bars, but no messages icon.

What's the absolute worst that can happen? She'd rest in the truck for a half hour, drive home—and would find out later what kept him. It was not the end of the world. She adjusted the AC control to its lowest, reclined the seat, closed her eyes.

And was yanked out of a deep sleep what seemed moments later by a tap on the window.

Andrew, in aviator sunglasses. "I almost let ye sleep," he said as she joined him. He leaned against a split-rail fence and wiggled legs ending in a serviceable pair of hiking boots. His long hair was tied back with a yellow bandana.

"I'm fine. Why waste perfectly good time? Everything okay?"

"Sorry, luv. Road building on yer perfect highways, and a mess of cars on the way in."

Stupid again. The crowd would be horrid for him. "Friday's usually deserted—I forgot it's the Memorial Day weekend."

"No problem." He jerked his head toward the motorcycle, parked in shade. "Ready for a quick getaway."

It will be in full sun, metal-hot when he leaves. She bit her tongue. "You're sure you want to risk this?"

A trio of teenage girls in shorts and sandals brushed past them to the trail, followed by a short round woman with a pink daisy on her sunhat and a stocky tanned man with tree-trunk legs wearing a sleeveless undershirt. None of them stopped talking long enough to look at Andrew.

"The key is not being where they expect ye, not looking like they expect ye to."

"Act normal?" *When a single teeny-bopper could ruin his day.* He saw the direction of her gaze. "Not one of those."

Easy now; his choice. "Did you manage to keep it out of the papers?" *And don't mention the bar brawl.* A mental cog slipped—did his friends visit AOCORNER?

"I'm assuming she was embarrassed enough to keep her mouth shut."

"That's all you need—being accused of statutory rape." *That did not come out right.*

"I don't touch children!"

This was going to be harder than she thought. An iron band constricted her forehead. She packed her windbreaker around the water and sandwiches in her backpack. Dread settled into her intercostal spaces, shallowing her breathing. "Takes a while to get to the top." She hauled her tone back to 'conversational.' "But it's worth it."

"We're too close to civilization." He followed her to the trailhead sign. "I don't like filming in America; the exotic shoots are better. The locals aren't so star-struck, and the obsessive fans can't stalk."

Change subject. "Shall we? The firetower at the top won't march down like an Ent." She led off onto the switchback start. They hiked in silence through air which carried the subtle pine scent industrial cleaners failed to duplicate. She relished the hypnotic sway, paying attention only to the next rock to place a foot on.

They passed a white-haired couple in head-to-toe Eddie Bauer. They were passed by families with lanky boys in dilapidated running shoes announcing their presence by disrupting the peace with their calls and challenges; the sound approached and retreated, changing pitch like the whistle from a train.

In a half hour they came to a boulder-lined clearing, and she called a rest. Altitude gave them an expanding horizon through a gap: green hills far into the western distance.

"Breathtaking, isn't it?" She perched on a rock with spruce needles and dry shreds of tree-flower litter in the crevices, stretched her muscles and tendons. The lined jacket which seemed excessive in the parking lot barely kept her from shivering. Better than summer mugginess and bugs.

She glanced at him. Odd. He hadn't dragged out smokes to defile the crisp mountain breeze.

"Aye." He pried a stone from the path, threw it hard. It skipped among the boulders. The soil of the path retained a damp-dark shadowed impression of the stone, like a photograph's negative.

I've overstepped my bounds. "Look, I'm sorry, about what I said—"

He whirled and glared at her. "Damn it, Kary. Ye were right! If that *child* had been a little older, a little more devious...?" He resumed pacing. "The only thing it's good for is the part." He snorted bitterly. "Grant says if that's what it takes, he'll arrange for a steady supply. I almost chewed his head off; he laughed at me."

"Fans buy tickets." *Cautious enough?*

"Ye heard I was in a bar fight in Hanover?"

He'd put the glasses on in the sun; she couldn't see if his gaze was on her. "I'm not sure...?" Was it in the paper? *Damn.* Did he *assume* she knew?

"A drunk with a girl to impress." His voice was dead. "Things have escalated. I've been a real bear. Grant pooh-poohed it."

"He's not afraid of bad publicity?" *Safe topic?*

"Grant's good. Nothing fazes him." Wry smile. "He knows half the gossip in the tabloids is leaked to give people morbid curiosity about the movie."

"Intentionally?"

"Not by him."

"Friends?" *Wrong answer.* Mirrored lenses swung toward her.

He straightened, hardened like wet cement into concrete. He took forever to reply; when he spoke, his tone was atavistic. "It's freaky, people hounding every step. I'm feeling a caged beast."

"Obsessions aren't all bad." She'd been an utter fool to think she could play this game. *I don't know how not to set off his deception monitors.* She stood, shouldered the pack. "It's what you do with them." Her knotted stomach would not release. *I am an adult; it is the adult thing to do; he will understand. Maybe.* She started up the trail.

I have *to tell him. And it won't be pretty.*

ANDREW

HE TEASED KARY GENTLY. "Are ye ready to talk about what's bothering ye?"

"Talk about what?" she said, not turning her head.

"Ye've hardly said a real word since that crack about obsessions." He chuckled, raised his eyebrows at her. "I have eyes. It's not like ye not to blurt it out."

They sat on cut logs in a protected spot off the trail, down a hundred feet or so from the exposed mountaintop. Out of the sun, it was cooler, but sheltered from the worst of the gusts. Before them was spread out the whole of the valley between Mt. Kearsarge and the next state west. If the hills had been bare, he might've been able to see all the way to Hanover, to their set on the outskirts of town. But by winter they'd be gone, and the evergreens—spruce, pine, Douglas fir—would still be in the way.

The sandwiches she brought—honeyed ham and American Cheddar and a spicy brown mustard—were good, if mushed. He had to admit even tepid water was welcome. The chattering squirrels were not quite tame enough to take the crumbs from their hands. Contentment filled his soul, met his expectations: a break from the intensity of filming. Grand to have a friend in the area. *Fine choice, the hike, the mountain.*

He'd followed her, hiking at a steady irregular pace up the uneven path, which alternated rock, log steps created by the volunteers to stem erosion, and dirt with leaves which were slippery where wet. He fell into her businesslike, quiet rhythm until they reached, at one turn round a giant boulder, the top of the mountain. Not a peak, the top was a broad mound of mostly-bare granite, with a fire-tower at the highest part; a microwave tower to one side; and a number of small park or maintenance shacks, tucked into the lower, more wind-screened coves among the few scattered evergreens hardy enough for the peak.

"We're not above the tree-line, are we?"

"Seems that way, doesn't it? But no. A fire burned off most of the vegetation a couple of centuries ago, the soil eroded, and hasn't recovered yet."

They climbed as far as permitted on the open staircase of the fire-tower before retreating to the enclosed observation platform built into it, where they were afforded almost-as-full a view, but the wind was forced to fight harder to pelt them with air which could travel from the eastern coast. Kary'd pointed out a few named mountain-tops, the White Mountains, and the distant peak of Mt. Cardigan closer to Hanover, but it was mostly a sea of green. She'd said that on the right mornings, only a few peaks would stand high above the mist, like islands. Some other day. Maybe.

"Too bad Bianca missed it!"

"Bianca?"

"She wanted to come, had to work at the last minute. Thought she might use some exercise not connected to a machine." He grinned—remembered Bianca's annoyance at the aide who brought her the news. "A scene or two where she's her own mother—Grant found a schedule hole for the second unit to do them in." He shook his head. "She had her boots on by that time."

"Does she exercise?"

"Obsessively." *If ye ask me.* "Says it gives her energy."

"Complicated to fit it in? I imagine she has a busy schedule, costume changes and all." Was her expression guilt? "I started looking at her script. I'm doing a bit of research first, before I tell you what I think. I've got an idea or two."

"Don't put yerself out. Didn't expect it finalized this soon anyway. I'm most sorry—Bianca's in a hurry, but I'm not." Ack. Another distraction to worry about. *If it's not one ewe lambing, it's another.* "Has to be right—a debut film has to make everyone stand and take notice."

"She sounded determined," she spoke in the tone of cool analysis he had come to associate with her, "for you to play the Reverend Mr. Dodgson. A few scenes will be—scorchers?"

"In the way of scorchers, Grant said ye are a genius."

"Must be hard for men who rear daughters by themselves, particularly if the daughter favors her mother." She scanned the horizon for answers. "If he wasn't so preoccupied, he would have thought of it himself."

Or I should have. "Aye."

They'd been considering whether to eat lunch in the glassed-in observation room, with the 360° view, when the sound of plastic slapping wood announced a young woman descending the stairs from the roof, laughing and chattering with the boyfriend who came behind her, and who peered at him so keenly he could sense what she'd say next, the 'Don't I know you?' and 'Wait, I know who you are…'

The boyfriend gallantly gave up his red and black flannel shirt to her shivers, and in the confusion of the small disturbance, Andrew gestured toward the entry, and Kary nodded and came out after. They moved far enough down the mountain to be partially hidden from the path, sat facing out.

"That girl—" he began.

"Did you see she made the whole climb in flip-flops?" Kary shook her head in exasperation, but her statement was strangely without heat.

And then he'd asked his innocuous question. "It's not like ye not to blurt it out."

As if an unseen hand had wiped off all expression, Kary's face went blank. Her shoulders dropped with the expelled breath. "You're not going to like this."

Eh? Not a promising beginning. *What did I do?* Was she going to tell him he was taking too much of her time? Interfering with her work? "Try me. I'll get me head round it."

"Will you?" She straightened, tossed the last crust to the bravest of the rodents. She turned to him, her eyes slits in a mask. She hunkered into her jacket like a foxhole. "It's becoming a dead cow in the middle of the living room." She broke eye contact to stare at the world beyond the mountain. "What is your greatest fear, Andrew?"

He didn't like the way she said his name. "I'm not sure. Bad directors. Not getting a part I know I can do better than anyone else. Doesn't matter now. They're all survivable." *Even Bridget.* "Yer biggest worry?"

"I fear what every woman my age fears: making myself look ridiculous."

"Ye'd never look ridiculous." A cold gust whipped his jacket. The inkling grew.

She took a deep breath, held it, blew it out slowly, faced him again. She stared intently, that memorizing thing she did. "I have a problem. It's not fair to you, but I have to tell you something."

"Why?"

"Because it's going to come out, one way or another." She shrugged, hunched over. "I can't keep things straight any more."

Straight? What things? "I will understand." Would he? His skin prickled.

She shook her head, a tiny motion which gave away her disbelief. "I 'know' too much about you, *Andrew*—" She turned away.

Last time she can call me by name? He picked up cues she was not giving. *Damn me overactive imagination.*

"—but I can't always remember where it came from, whether you told me or someone else or I read it somewhere." She shoved her hands into her pockets, became immobile, a rock addressing the valley.

His stomach knotted. *Get on with it.* "I got the distinct impression ye'd never heard of me when we met on the show."

In profile, her lips formed a crooked moué. "I hadn't. I don't get out much."

"So? It made ye more interesting." The muscles around his eyes tightened, narrowing his field of vision. *But something's changed.*

"I don't follow papers or magazines, especially not about movie stars. It is energy I don't possess. I had no idea who you were..." She hazarded a brief look at his face, hastily turned away from what she saw. "Some weeks after the show, Dana sent me a DVD. I— I hadn't seen the clip from *Roland*— in New York." She took another breath, measured out the words. "I went to see it—because I couldn't *not* go."

"I see." *Why do people always feel they must tell me their stories?* He wished to God he didn't know what was coming.

"I don't think you do. I saw it, over and over." She shrugged again. "I couldn't write. I couldn't sleep." The tiny head shake again. "I *let* myself become obsessed by it. By Roland. It had been a long time since something that— that *strong* came into my life."

"It's a bloody *movie*." *And ye are bloody ordinary.*

"It didn't stop there." Her voice was catching, making it rough. She cleared her throat. "I watched every single one of your movies." She laughed mirthlessly. "Except *Angels*. I couldn't get *Angels*."

"I'll make sure ye get a copy." He felt himself withdrawing into politeness. "It was not 'critically acclaimed.' Ye won't like it."

"It's part of the set." She glanced at him; returned her gaze to the horizon. "You don't understand. I *watched* them. Two or three times each, straight through. Then in pieces, only *your* scenes, over and over, looking for false moves, a fragment out of place, something not perfect. I never found any."

"Film editors." *They bloody well earn their pay.* "I've blown me share of takes."

"They can't put in what isn't on the film."

"Ye are very methodical in yer obsessions." It wasn't a compliment.

"I'm not finished." Her chin lifted. "If there's a site on the web with anything about you, I've seen it. I can't separate out what's true."

A wet, squirmy mess. "Most is gossip, publicity. Why would ye read that crap?"

"That's how my brain does research. So I gave it free rein. Until I saturated." She pulled both hands from her pockets, kneaded her forehead. "I had to get you out of my head. I wanted— I needed to get back to work. It didn't seemed important— I never expected to see you again..." She was quiet for a moment, remembering. "Exhilarating, like riding a wild horse. But an absurd thing for a grown woman to do." She clasped her hands tightly, gripped them between her thighs. "So don't tell me I would never be ridiculous."

"Except that I showed up at yer gate." Had he a forewarning then? *She should have told me.*

"Which was a shock."

"I'm very flattered." His gut clutched. Muted shufflings and talking marked hikers passing on the trail. *Back into dealing-with-the-public mode, boyo.* The wind whistled cold through the spruce tops. He pulled his leather jacket to against the chill. He had opened a birthday present to find a wriggling mass of roundworms. Sanctuary had kicked him out.

The woman he didn't know at all sat rocking almost imperceptibly, mute.

She should have told me! How could he be so stupid—he allowed her in. *But she let me think she was—what? She's made a royal eejit of me—with me own help.* He was a fool for being so gullible, not seeing it coming. *Ye can never trust new people—none of them—not ever again.* Because he was too dense to know when he was being deceived. *Ye only found out because it suited* her.

Worse, he'd vouched for her to Grant. To Bianca. *To Peter!* She manipulated him right to where she wanted him.

What damage had she done so far? Who did she gossip to? The daughters? The friends? What had he told her he couldn't have bandied about? She'd seemed so fragile, so innocent, so safe. He hadn't seen how an isolated writer could be dangerous. An isolated *best-selling* writer— *Blessed Mary and all the saints!* His right hand grabbed the back of his neck, while the left balled into a fist. "So why tell me now?"

"You asked me if I knew about a bar fight in Hanover…"

Trying to squirm off the hook? "There might've been something in the paper."

"I almost never read the paper. But there was an item on your fan website. About distortions. And a photo."

"Ye said ye'd stopped— *researching* me. Before I came." *Lying again?* Stop feeling stalked, man, laid bare on her dissecting table for her amusement. *Ye should be accustomed to this by now.*

"I needed to find out when the filming would be over."

And I would be out of yer life before ye… "I'm that big of a dead cow."

"My daughters are coming." Monotone.

And ye're ashamed of me. "I won't be in yer way." *Bad to worse.* He took a deep breath, let the air out between clenched teeth. *Be careful, man.* He let go of his neck, used the hand to still his left arm, forced himself to open the fingers of his fisted left hand. A flash of red from the path on his right, and the couple from the fire-tower slowed—but mercifully didn't stop. He unpursed his lips. *Keep it civil. Ye* are *in public.* But he couldn't quite control the harshness in his voice yet. "What do ye believe ye know?"

She jumped at the tone. "I—"

"Who have ye told?" What had he mentioned, in passing, which would add to the misery of misunderstanding already out there? *Get to the bottom of it.* "What have ye told them?"

"I haven't… Why would—" She gave him an unreadable glance, turned away. "That's not—"

His eyes narrowed. "Begin with me family."

He could see her eyes were closed. "This may take a while."

"Ye have something *better* to do?"

Her head bent, came back up. "You are the youngest, by ten years. You have two older sisters, married, with two children each." Her words were mechanical, detached. "They—and your parents— run farms in County Galway. When you can, you go home to Ireland, and help around the farm, which is remote and difficult to find. The villagers are protective, and can't remember where O'Connell's is. There are horses; you grew up riding and herding sheep and cattle with a whistle and dogs. Your roots are Irish— back to the days of William of Orange. Every couple generations or so, your family throws up a black sheep. The one before you was your Great Uncle Giles; he studied drama at Trinity College. Dublin. Before it was a formal drama program. You wear his ring." Her shoulders rose, dropped. "The ringstone is a garnet. You keep pigs. You've modified the house to add a recording studio for your childhood band—they were on the show. I have listened to the songs on all three of your CDs." The dispassionate recital halted, as if she were unsure how to proceed.

"What do ye think of them?" Damn reporters had shadowed him, friendly-like, asking their incessant questions. *Giving their 'articles' the slant they selected before they ever met me.* He remembered the blonde: fascinated by his ring to the point of making him uncomfortable; he hadn't yet figured out how she discovered which of his uncles gave it him. Uncanny guesses, published as certainty. He'd learned—to be engaging. And vague.

She sighed. "Some of the pieces are surprisingly good. With intricate harmonies you don't pursue."

Eh? "The rest?"

"Some are primitive, derivative, and self-indulgent."

Which got a harsh laugh from him. He granted her point with a sideways jerk of his head. "Me career? Me *love* life?"

Her profile remained inscrutable. "You made yourself useful on movie sets when you were old enough to lie about driving. Farm machinery would explain driving. Left school as soon as you could support yourself. There were jobs as a gofer. Extra. Bit parts. The first speaking part picked up by the microphone was on *Angels*. It was not 'critically acclaimed,' but your tiny part was. It led to bigger parts." She was answering his questions impassively, narrating a documentary. "You have a hot head, get into bar brawls. You drink. You can hurt people—if you want to. Made trouble at an award ceremony over..." her voice faltered, "...a minor writing credit you thought had been mishandled by the producers."

"It had."

"You hadn't read the writer's contract; they were legally within their prerogatives."

"'Twasn't right."

"I assume much of what Hollywood does isn't. The writer was blacklisted; they thought he had instigated your outburst." She sighed deeply, continued in a wooden voice. "Your love life? You've been fairly discreet—for a movie star. No known wives or children. The paparazzi tail you if they can, but you've gotten a lot better at hiding in private clubs. The media likes to propose affairs with your costars; they rarely have any definitive photos, but it isn't hard to locate pictures of you with them at…"

"At the damn premieres!"

"Not hard." She paused. Her body language gave him nothing. "I suppose you want to know what I've read about your Bridget?"

"Damn it all! What do ye know about Bridget?"

She had startled momentarily from her immobility, but resumed speaking without further prodding, wanting to be released from duty? "Truly know? Nothing. Existence." He was starting to have difficulty hearing her, but she cleared her throat again, and raised her volume to the previous. "You wrote songs to her. About her. You were together for many years before she married someone else. The rest is innuendo. Your main fan website is remarkably close-mouthed about your personal history, about *all* your dalliances. But you have many female fans. Some of them are more… speculative. None of my business."

None of it is yer business. He reached the limit of his gorge. "She's not a subject for idle talk."

"No."

"I'll be needing to go." On the mountain top he was far from safety, cut off, trapped. *Safety?* Behind the walls of a metal home? *Not a good time to talk to folks here.*

"Of course."

He stood carefully to one side as she shouldered her pack. His muscles ached as they had the summer week he'd spent at fifteen carrying stones to wall off his ma's garden from the hares. Before him the green hills hurt his throat: they were not Ireland. He set off after her as she headed down the path without a backward glance.

He couldn't wait to get off the mountain.

KARY

Sanctuary; 8:15 P.M.

KARY POSTPONED THE inevitable as long as possible.

She hadn't expected to conk out so long. Outside, dusk afforded her enough light to gather an armful from the woodpile. She placed each twig in the kindling teepee she was building in her living room's fireplace with microscopic precision. One match—to light one purifying fire.

Food didn't appeal to her. She brought hot chocolate to the living room: the mug cooled on its coaster.

Pride had not allowed her to admit exhaustion when he'd asked, forcing himself to be polite, 'Will ye be okay driving?'

As if there was anything he might do.

She couldn't have faced accepting help. Not then. It was easy. He was in such a hurry to leave, cyborg-like once he put the black helmet over those eyes, that he skidded, spraying parking-lot gravel, when reaching the road. But her body was relentless. Before attempting to drive home safely, she clambered into the pickup's rear seat, grateful for dark windowglass, grateful she had parked with the hood toward the woods edging the lot—harder for passersby to peer in. Grateful for the shade. *If you have to sleep in public, at least do so discreetly.*

Just make it home. She drove with a drunk's methodical exactness. There would be time to think, but this was neither time nor place. The imperative was to go to ground, return to the den to recoup. A half hour rest was barely enough for a half hour's driving, no more. Eight years' illness had taught her hard boundaries, Ethan's death how to stem the emotional tide until it was safe to let the floodgates open. The plan to go home by the scenic route was ditched by default: it would tax her resources enough to remember the tricky junctions and the speed limits in the towns, to reverse the roads and turns she had taken a lifetime ago.

Mechanically, she watched the gate shut behind her. She pulled up to the house, parked by rote.

She abandoned her pack on the kitchen counter.

The granite steps were regular, polished, wide—so unlike the ones on the trail to— She made it upstairs, changed into soft and non-binding, crashed. For two hours. Until near dark.

The wood in the fire before her, turning to ashes with each pop and crackle, might as well be the timbers of the bridge she thought she could build. She had inched too close to Promethean fire, and the gods handed out their terrible retribution: annihilation in the cleansing flames. The embers of her reputation mocked her. *It is over.*

Time to face the music. You can't hide any more, Kary.

I'm not hiding. I know full well what I've done.

Your mother warned you. Think carefully before you speak: you can be forgiven, maybe, for your words—but you can never *unsay* them.

I thought I could control myself, I thought I could offer him a quiet place, a safe place. Because he needed it.

You were weak. You were *prideful*. You *know* your limitations, and you willfully disregarded them. You should not have gone to *Night Talk*, nor to the his party afterward. You couldn't *abide* being ordinary. You should never have invited him back after he showed up on your doorstep. You should never have gone to the set. You had no business pretending to be normal, being on that mountain with him. And now you've accomplished the exact opposite of what you say you wanted. He will be even *more* wary in the future, more distrustful of people he meets, because he was starting to get comfortable with you—and it blew up in his face. *Friendly* fire.

At least I kept it private.

And if Bianca had been there? That's Envy. Wanting what women like her get.

I couldn't have said anything in front of her.

If she'd been there, you would have been even *more* likely to say something awkward and expose your stalking. Public disgrace may still be in the works for you.

It is his right.

And even now you are still protecting your greatest sin: Lust.

I can't help myself.

You are *never* to let him know.

It's not like I'll ever get the chance...

The phone rang, startling in its echo in the granite-backed space. She considered ignoring it. *What if one of the girls needs me?* She made herself pick up the handset. *Thank goodness for Caller ID.* She grimaced. Pitch black out—wasn't it late for an agent to be calling? *Damage control already?* "Hi, Elise."

"I was hoping to find you in."

Where would I be? "What can I do you for?" She dumped the contents of the backpack on the countertop, dealt with them while Elise went through her laundry list. The water bottle with Andrew's fingerprints went into the recycling bin as Elise nattered on about statements and royalties.

"Uh-huh. Sounds good. I'll leave it up to you." Kary reached for pain tablets, poured herself water to gulp them down. Elise employed the Oreo method: sandwich bad news between two good 'bits.' *We're not done yet.* "Anything else?"

"You sound funny."

"Wiped. I'm going to shower, head to bed." *And pretend this afternoon didn't happen.*

Elise hmm'd. "I have a small confession."

"Oh?"

"Have you gotten anything special in the mail?"

Get on with it, Elise. "No. Why? What did you send me?" He'd charmed Elise into giving him her address. *Bet he rues that impulse.*

"Well, it was more of a who... He said... It's just that I feel guilty I didn't tell you..." Elise took an audible breath. "Andrew O'Connell called, said he wanted to send you something—after the show, you know?—and I let him have your address. They're filming up in New Hampshire somewhere. I was curious—did he contact you?"

And I made the biggest fool in the world of myself. He couldn't get away from me fast enough.

"Kary? Are you there?"

"It's all right, Elise. I'm sure he has no intention of contacting me." *Ever again.* "They must be quite busy filming."

"Oh. Well, then. It probably slipped his mind."

"I wouldn't worry." It was good Elise couldn't see the color that crept up the back of her neck. *I certainly won't bring it up; he...?* Just deserts? "Anything else?"

"That reporter from the New York Times still wants—"

To make my humiliation national news? "Not yet. I'm unbelievably exhausted, Elise." At least that part wasn't a lie.

"That's too bad. Rest up." Elise's voice altered somehow. "I have amazingly good news for you."

"Oh?"

"You should sound more excited," Elise reproved. "I received an option request for *Prairie Fires*, and this one looks legit."

"Who from?"

"Isn't it 'whom from'? Never mind. Some Hollywood agent who specializes in these things. I looked him up. He's real." Bottom of the Oreo slapped on.

Grant? "Did he say who wanted it?"

"Very cagey about the whole thing. I'm getting the paperwork ready. I'll express it to you."

"I'm not getting excited. This has happened, what, three times now?"

"I smell it. Said they had a particular interest."

"Do I have to? I thought that possibility was dead."

"I always knew you were crazy. When you finally give an interview, and the world notices, you go hide under a rock. This is big, Kary." Elise sighed. "But I'll never understand *you*. By the way, are you doing anything special Memorial Day?"

The picnic! Did Elise have radar? *Get off the damned phone, Kary Ashe.* "Don't think so. Writing. Resting. But have a good holiday weekend with your family, Elise."

Elise eventually ran out of pleasantries. Kary placed the phone back in its holder by the fireplace. She sipped the lukewarm chocolate, willing calories into her bloodstream: she shouldn't be empty, but the thought of anything solid nauseated her. It was going to be a battle to get herself to sleep, back to work tomorrow morning; an empty stomach would make it worse. *As if anything could— Stop it! You* knew *there would be consequences.*

She put two more split logs on the fire, rearranged them carefully with the poker. *You just lied to Elise. How will she feel when she finds out?* Would Elise be another burnt bridge? It didn't matter. Elise wasn't entitled to personal information, she just liked it. Kary evaluated the effort necessary to reheat the chocolate in the microwave. *Too tired.* Room temp it was.

She jumped when the phone rang. *Have to stop doing that.* Zoë. Now what? If she didn't answer, would this be the time Zoë climbed in her car and came all the way out to ensure Kary was okay? Zoë had the house code. *Talk to her.* "Hi, Zoë. What's up?"

"I should have called you sooner. Sorry. Are you coming on Monday?"

"Monday?"

"Memorial Day."

Zoë's annual picnic!

"We're having the usual people over—they like you. Then fireworks at the park—I know you don't usually stay for those, but the boys enjoy them, and they're doing the *1812 Overture* with real cannons, and this may be the last time they go with us—you never know with teenagers—"

Zoë's work colleagues, friends from town... *I can't be with people now.* "I don't think I'll make it this year. I— uh—"

"But you always come! And I haven't seen you in forever! Everyone will be so disappointed."

Everyone will be relieved. "We must get together soon. I'm sorry. Just too tired."

"How's about I dispatch the spousal unit to pick you up and take you back."

Zoë would. *And I'd be stuck in the car with him for half an hour each way.* "Thanks. Sorry to crap out on you. Too tired." *At least that's true. Say it enough, and she'll get the hint.*

"He won't mind."

That's the worst part—he wouldn't. And she'd have to make inane conversation with him. "No. Don't, please. Sorry—"

"—You're too tired. I get it. What's going on? The new book? I told you, you should have stuck to tried-and-true. What are you doing researching a completely different area? Science fiction! What were you thinking?"

"Margaret Atwood did it." *How do I get her off the phone?* "I'm fine. Really. Just need some extra rest."

"Okay then, but I'm calling Monday to see if you've changed your mind."

"I won't. I'll probably be asleep."

"Fine! But we'll miss you."

"Give my regards to spousal unit and the boys. Have a great time at the fireworks."

"OK. Bye for now."

The click and the white noise on the line freed her from further inanities. *Now you've lied to your best friend. Becoming quite the little liar, are we not?* Why wasn't Deceit one of the seven deadly sins? *Because it's already included in Pride.* The flush on her cheeks had to be the fire.

The phone rang. *Again? What kind of vibrations am I giving off?* "Hi, Susan, honey. What's up?" She forced verve into her voice—Susan always had sharp ears.

"I wanted to confirm our dates—and ask you if it's okay for Stephen and I to stay a little longer.

'Stephen and me.' But she'd stopped trying to fix other people's grammar. "Sure, baby. Troubles?"

"Why would you assume that? Of course not. Greg's going to the conference—by the way, it's June, not July—and I haven't spent time with you in ages—thought I'd give us more time for catching up. Why? Is it a problem?"

Exactly what my pride needs: to fill my daughter in on her mother's ridiculous behavior. "None at all. Ronnie gave me the dates." *And destroyed my world.* "Stay as long as you like. I'll get extra Cocoa Crunches—"

"Oh, he's over that phase now—"

"—or whatever it is he eats. You can go with me to the store—"

"Just wanted to check with you first, before I get the tickets. I swear, sometimes you're lost in your own little bubble. You should come out here, live closer to us. Stephen could see you all the time. He misses you."

For my sins. "I'll think about it."

"That's what you always say."

"We'll talk when you come."

"Yes, we will." Susan sounded irritated, as she did so often now. *Do I worry about* her *marriage now?*

"Okay then, honey. Bye."

"Love you, Mom."

"Love you, too. Kiss Stephen." She didn't add 'Kiss Greg.'

'Thou shalt deny me thrice.' Three times have I lied. To the women who will stand by me no matter what. She turned the ringer off. No one else would call.

She thought of the perfect summary in the Spanish version of the Confiteor at Mass: *'He pecado de pensamiento, palabra, obra, y omisión.'* Not as sonorous in English: 'I have sinned by thought, word, deed, and omission.' You had to fight hard for poetry in English. *'Por mi culpa, por mi culpa, por mi más grande culpa.'* '...through my most grievous fault.'

'Lust.' She stirred the fire, and the word danced before her eyes along with the flames. *Is there anything more foolish than the woman who wants a man she cannot have, should not have? He will marry. Yes, someone like Bianca. Young and beautiful and healthy. Who will bear him the children he wants. Deserves.* Which would be her salvation: she had no interest in married men.

The fire was burning out. Put on more logs? Or be an adult, and take the required actions. Cauterize the stump, learn to walk with a limp. *Get my self back.* Did you learn nothing from the *Roland* fiasco? You have your work. *It is a dry consolation.* Nevertheless, it is *yours.*

She dug her emergency recovery measures out of her fogged brain—that always helped: start with food, ice-cream if necessary. *Like I need a reward.* Be still. Ten minutes in the hot tub, no more. And turn the heated mattress pad on to warm the bed. Clean pjs— different ones. Fuzzy socks. Meds—'not habit-forming if used in moderation.' She'd pay the piper with a day's grogginess, but she couldn't afford to lose her sleep cycle. *Not when work is all I have left.*

And in the morning: wake up, breakfast, work. With her tattered shreds of dignity.

She could never tell another soul what happened on the mountain.

BIANCA

Bunker Hill; 9 P.M.

BIANCA WATCHED ANDREW pace the narrow corridor between the dolly and the lighting panels. *What's eating him?*

Grant consulted in low tones with the cinematographer and the cameraman. Bianca wished she were closer so she could hear, and not encumbered by her hat and fur-trimmed cape, but she couldn't have it all. *Not at the same time.*

They were used to her attention and questions, but the job came first. Always first. When the camera rolled, she would be alone until Father barged in to *forbid* her to speak to her Winston. Women in the audience—like the small crowd allowed onto the set for the evening—would unite with her to *be* Sarah Emilia Swarthmore taking her stand against patriarchy and an oppressive King George. But *she* would be the one to allow Sarah to possess her willing body and speak, and *her* image would be on the screen for those precious seconds. As close as she got to pure happiness. *This is what I was born for.*

She had persuaded wardrobe to let her wear the rose gown with the cape; the color matched the background azaleas, even in the dim light. And warmed her skintones. The blue the costumer declared historically accurate made her skin sallow. She wouldn't wear the blue at all if she had a say. Well, maybe in one of the scenes where she had to look ill. The old woman caved when Bianca inquired about her grandson—the snapshot on the corkboard displayed a skinny older teen with dark hair—and the requisite zits. She shuddered at the memory.

"ONCE AROUND. PLACES."
Andrew snapped to attention. Sometimes she thought he sought drama just to get into the mood. *I should have been on that hike.* She'd figure him out later. Whatever the reason, he'd come back charged with tension that crackled through the necessary blocking and rehearsals; Grant was a perfectionist. *Well, so am I.*

Her skin prickled with the knowledge that now , when things were perfect and right, the cameras would roll, and she would step into the role she had been created for, the representative of Every-woman.

Grant spoke into his megaphone. "From 'Father, Winston has asked…,' Bianca. When you're ready." Grant raise his finger in his signature 'Quiet!' gesture, and everything—crew, extras, cameras with film rolling—froze into position, waiting for her curtain to rise. Grant's gift to his actors; when filming it ruined a few feet of celluloid, but Grant maintained it saved far more in wasted takes. She knew she owned fifteen seconds, longer if she needed, where no one was allowed to break into her concentration; she'd already stolen the idea for her own. Fifteen seconds was a very long time. Andrew waited impatiently, primed to explode at her command.

She raised her eyes, released him, shrank back when he came on, as he did, in full furor.

"Father, Winston has asked me to marry—and I have accepted him."

The Colonel made fun of her love of finery: dress, hat, fur cape. "You'll not see the same as wife to a penniless farmer."

"He will become prosperous."

"He will be in gaol in chains for treason to his King." His interaction with her, as she shrank from her father's verbal assault, had been choreographed to the T; muscle memory would show better on film than awkward spontaneity. "You have not my sanc-tion to marry!"

"Winston says I do not need your consent, Father. But I would have your blessing."

Bianca flinched as Andrew lifted his hand to her.
"AND CUT."

Grant approached, brow furrowed. His voice was matter-of-fact. "Bianca, you okay?"

He's concerned? Heck, I'm concerned. Where did that come from? "We're fine. He didn't touch me."

"I don't strike women." Andrew cocked his head. "Unless it's in the script."

"Tone it down a bit?" Grant stood protectively to Bianca's side, scowled up at Andrew.

"Really, Grant?" She turned to face the colonel, her beloved father. She narrowed her eyes, let a wisp of a smile settle on her lips. He was so close she had to tilt her chin. "I rather liked it."

Andrew scrutinized her.

"He's been holding back." She locked gazes with him. She knew he liked what he saw. "I only want you to be happy, *Father*. I can take it." *And give as good as I get.* Whatever the reason, he was finally looking at her the way she wanted him to: as prey. Fully engaged. Like it was personal. This, she could handle. The arms-length distant thing, where he treated her like a child? That drove her crazy. She tugged provocatively at the idiot stays in her gown, readjusting its tight top. *Shove the PG rating.*

The powerful lights stippled the shadows under the leafy sugar maples and sweetgums; the slow oaks, starting to fill in, appeared skeletal in the reflected light. Bianca longed for the drier air of home as the makeup person blotted her face.

"Let's do it again," said Grant. "And Andrew, try not taking her head off, okay? This is your only daughter."

Andrew's eyes became slits. "She'll be on the next ship to England."

"But you will miss her, okay?"

"Bloody women," Andrew muttered. "Next thing they'll be wanting to govern the country." He jammed the plumed hat back on, stalked back to his mark.

Bianca glared at his receding back. And what's wrong with that? *I can never tell when he's acting.* Even his banter on the set stayed in character. At least he was better than Michael—who couldn't act his way out of a paper bag. And better than Zed, who wanted her to give up on their mutual dream of acting. *As soon as the brat came on scene...*

They ran the scene five times in rehearsal before Grant was satisfied. With the crew in place they did three more for camera placement and light reflector adjustment. At dark began the painstaking process of locking the takes on film, reshooting each from the opposite angle so the editors could cut back and forth between Sarah and her father. Bianca ignored boom mikes, lights, camera, and watchers, focused on Andrew and his glowering face. Her spine tingled each time she stood up to him. His eyes warned her how near he was to slapping her for insolence. She dared him to. She loved this part: if a scene was good, once was not nearly enough. She stayed Sarah as Andrew's Swarthmore stormed away—his technique, not hers—she was beginning to understand its possibilities. *We'll do it your way—for now.* Her heart ached as the aloof father she adored confirmed how desperately he would have preferred a son.

During a short break she startled him by crouching at his feet. "Father? Are you unwell?"

He reached his hand towards her, dropped it with a sigh. "You are so beautiful, my little Sarah. A sight for sore eyes." He smiled sadly. "So like your mother."

Fine. Back to work. *Wait*— She had it: what Grant was looking for—and verbalized as 'short of insolence.' When a man raised his hand to a woman, there was history between them. She visualized it in her mind's eye: Mother's body attitude when she defied Papi— who came close to hitting, but never did. She would have lost all respect for him, but the drink made him angry, and he struggled to control himself: somewhere there had always been love, but Mother's 'American wife' never satisfied his Latin temperament. He'd been a naturalized citizen, but she could have easily been his child with his Mexican whore, only suitable for maid roles, too Mexican for Hollywood. *If not for Mother's Nordic genes...* Words from one of her teachers floated through her head: *Be happy when bad things befall you—good actors with idyllic childhoods don't exist.*

She was disappointed when the scene finally wrapped. And exhausted. And happy. *And I am the one who owns it all.* No matter how much they storyboarded and scripted and planned, it always came down to a live actor in front of a live camera where anything might happen. *And when I direct myself, I'll never have to settle.*

She'd show Hollywood. *Incident at Bunker Hill* was *working.* She didn't have the sinking feeling from the previous flicks, doing her utmost to deliver what the director claimed to want, knowing it was *not* her, and yet she would be blamed—because the only thing critics every remembered were the actors' performances.

"That was good." Andrew never permitted himself to look tired until the end of the day, but even he showed wear—and he wasn't even involved in the morning's shoot. "At least *something* is going right. Ye're coming, right?"

Coming? Her heart gave a painful beat. Until he jerked his head towards the edge of the set, where a small group of fans were *still* standing or sitting on the grass. But still *there*. He couldn't be serious. She needed out of the dress before she went under: the adrenaline she banked on vanished with '*It's a wrap.*' Couldn't the locals just fade away quietly into the night and leave them alone? But he was waiting expectantly; she pasted a smile on her face, and took his arm. At least that forced him to walk at petticoat speed.

"Shouldn't take long; then we'll all crash—the rooster crows at four."

"You're kidding. Since when?"

"I am learning to check the notices. Grant said the weather report is good for the morning. Best to stay busy." That last had an edge to it.

"We're not busy enough?" She said it with a laugh, got a moment's hard stare in return. The 'something' was still eating him. "Problems?"

"Why do ye ask?"

"I have eyes, Andrew." She stumbled—they *would* leave their stupid equipment laying around—gripped his arm hard. *Damn these shoes!* When she glanced back he was gazing towards the fans, preparing to do his charm thing, and the moment was lost.

She pretended delight and smiled until her cheeks hurt.

When the last fan and his camera was at long last escorted off set, she was annoyed to find Andrew had reverted to his black mood. *After I just stood here for you for hours?* "You okay?" She took his arm again as they headed for wardrobe's white tents.

"Beg pardon?"

"You haven't stopped scowling since you got here." She had to tip her chin up to make eye contact; he could hardly avoid looking down her bodice. "You look like you've lost your last friend."

"Ye're right." He smiled wryly at her. "I'm sorry. I shouldn't take it out on ye. When ye're an actor, ye think ye can take everything…"

Small triumph: she could coax him out of his moods. Was it that woman and their little hike? *What the hell did she say to him?* "I'm not tough, but I can take it." *Everything but indifference.* "What gives?"

"Can't talk about it." He shrugged. "Maybe some day."

He thought too much. *It won't make any difference.* She toed his stupid line. "You let me do what I do tonight." *Sincere flattery usually worked.* "I'm still hyped."

He gave a half-snort, shook his head slowly. "Glutton."

"Yes." Seducing a man in public was the greatest challenge—and she was up to it. If not her, who? Unless he was gay... there *was* that movie, and he was so damned good kissing another man... "*I'm* the one left standing when my husband is dead, and my father is sent back to England in disgrace."

"I like gluttons." His tongue touched the rim of his front teeth and his gaze was speculative again.

No mistaking *that* look. *Tip him over the edge?* Damn; they were at Wardrobe, and the minions were swarming. It would do him good to wait a night, now that she commanded his full attention. And there was their early call... *Tomorrow...* She let herself be divested of hat and cape. *The world will forgive me dumping Michael—as soon as I have Andrew locked up.*

He wouldn't know what hit him. *Tomorrow will be soon enough...*

❧ CHAPTER THIRTEEN ❧
Friendship be the most dangerous game

POLONIUS
…Those friends thou hast, and their adoption tried,
Grapple them unto thy soul with hoops of steel…
Wm. Shakespeare, *Hamlet*

Father Damien's eyes were shadowed with sadness.
"You're their friend." Akiiya faced the coward.
"They need you."
"If a friend is close enough to save you, he is close
enough to destroy you."
Kary Ashe (as K. Beth Winter),
Hostages to Fortuna

KARY
Sanctuary; Saturday May 28; 5 A.M.

IN HER OFFICE, KARY stared at the email in horror. *All my little
chickens coming home to roost.* A more innocuous content was not
possible:

Dear Kary -
Thank you for your kind words about our fan site
AOCORNER. We do indeed take great pride in maintaining a site full of 'true facts,' while striving to keep
it free of the kind of gossip and rumors that afflict the
web.
We are only interested in giving the fans the latest
scoop on Andrew O'Connell's movies and appear-
ances—things that are public and commonly available—in one organized place. We strive to keep

AOCORNER a place Andrew would not be embarrassed to visit—he's been kind enough to give us an exclusive from time to time.

Please let us know if you have any knowledge in that vein from his visit to your state—he is filming in Hanover, N.H., and we don't always see all the items in the local papers.

Thanks again for your interest.

Sal and Dave, Moderators, AOCORNER

They know you. They know where you live. They know you're a fan. They have your email address and your real name. What on earth was she thinking when she fired off a little note of appreciation to the site, back in the remote past of two months ago when her obsession drove her in an unseemly search for—what? Her cheeks crimsoned. Her instinct as a writer was to leave a thank you for the efforts of others online who helped with research or provided sources of otherwise-unavailable information. *Every time you do something, it comes back to bite you. Internet trails are forever.*

She'd broken her rule—'don't look at email until the day's writing is over.' She'd have to stop using physical pain—and waiting for meds to kick in—as an excuse. *Just punishment. The wages of sin...*

It wouldn't have made it easier to discover this later. Running from consequences was not her style. Deal with it: no more outreach of any kind in connection with Andrew O'Connell. *Leave the man strictly alone—you've done enough damage.* She filed their missive away with its offending trigger, her initial email to them, dug out of her files, as proof of what stupidity would get her. *No more.*

She had to get back to work, to the even larger horror which woke her, and got her to her desk this morning: the realization that she had let Andrew O'Connell deep into her work, in the form of a model for Reyker, the rebel leader on K'Tae. How could she not have seen it? *There are a lot of things you're not seeing lately.* The character was a thinly-disguised clone. Without meaning to, she imbued Reyker with everything but Andrew's coloring. *As if that would make him different.* Reyker moved like Andrew. Reyker spoke like Andrew. He thought like Andrew. *No. He thought as I imagine Andrew thinks—and my record there is abysmal.*

She started taking notes, going through every chapter already written marking each place where she lazily reached for the nearest example of a man of action—and inserted her crazy simulacrum of a real human being, a model to which she had no right.

It would take days, days of re-inventing Reyker, of making him his own man. Days of rewriting. More delays to explain to Elise. More pain. Eventually the land mines would all be exploded. *Better now, so very much better than having some astute reader point out the likenesses when the book came out.* Work was the solution to all her problems. Work was all she had that was her own.

The solution to his *problems is to get as far away from me as he can.* She would hurt if he was not happy, if he didn't attain his goal—*the goal you perceived when he sang Mother of My Child.* She was adult enough to know that his goal could never include her—the very idea was ludicrous. *You were burned by having him near. Now your betrayal, yes, betrayal, will make it harder for him to achieve happiness—because he will distrust the world more.* The world isn't trustworthy: he shouldn't trust it—the world eats the unwary. But she didn't want to be the cause of his misgivings. *You should have thought of that.*

And prepare yourself: there will *be a polite call canceling your party.*

The shiny promised by the world was tin foil, not polished silver: it reflected the light almost as well, but had no inherent value. She had to stay away from shiny—it served her right because she let herself be distracted by the flash of sunlight into her darkened corner. The passing sun had no reason to shine in her corner ever again. For the first time since she moved into *Sanctuary*, she wished she owned thick light-blocking drapes to draw over the blinds.

She stored her feelings of having let out a sordid secret—*my feelings, to which I am entitled*—for her scene in which the biogenetic experiment being conducted on the rebel populations was disowned in disgust by the Techtarch's son.

Lazy, lazy! You had no right. She used all her self-discipline to focus, to make a list.

She began the long process of stripping all traces of Andrew O'Connell from her work.

BIANCA

Bunker Hill; 6:45 A.M.

"DAUGHTER..."

The voice croaked at her, and Bianca whirled, stared. *Damn his silent approaches.* Andrew's appearance in torn uniform, stubble, and stained bandages shocked her. A flash of fear recalled her own dead Papi lying in his casket, the first time she had seen him in three years. She fought the memory—it was too fresh, too real to use. She focused on Andrew's haggard face, his hollow eyes. How much was the Colonel who inhabited him, how much himself? "What happened to you?"

"Like it?" His smile broke wide, and he looked immensely pleased with himself. "Full out—told the makeup guy not to make me pretty."

Idiot! "You look like the walking dead." Stupid prank, but of course makeup—for a war wound and a week in a hastily-contrived jail—was always finalized only for the actual shoot. Her pulse slowed. "Congratulate him. For a minute there, I thought it was *real.*"

"Ye care. Me heart is touched."

"Of course I care, *Father.*"

"Touché!"

"Wondered where you were—Grant's been spitting nails." *And I'm learning how to handle actors like you by watching him and listening.* It stung, comparing Grant with some of *her* directors— but Grant didn't shoot flops.

"Took a wee bit longer."

"After yesterday, I was expecting you to show up hung over." *Poke the bear.* She had seconds to crack his composure; Grant was yards away.

"We'll not talk of yesterday, *daughter.*" His pleasure in his appearance vanished in a scowl. 'Predator' returned to his eyes. "I don't get hungover. Drop by for a beer tonight if ye like. I'll show ye."

Tonight. She held his gaze, bit her lower lip gently to plump it for the camera, licked it with the tip of her tongue. *After you've had a couple—and I'm ready.* She was glad 'yesterday' was in no way her fault. She deliberately turned her back to him, curtsied to their director. "Good morrow, Sirrah."

"Professional, as always, Miss." Grant bowed. "And you," he turned to Andrew, "we'll talk later. The makeup man said you wouldn't let him call me."

"Ten minutes grace, boss."

Grant was not amused, examined his actor from bandaged head to blood-stained boot. "At least I won't have to beat you up myself. Scat!" For a short man, he managed quite well. Andrew scatted.

"PLACES, EVERYONE!"

John materialized in noisy high spirits from wherever he'd been hiding. *Puppy!* She gave him a warm maternal smile; she wished he would shut up. She faced Andrew. *The big scene makes or breaks.* Both of them knew it was forever: the emotional core of the movie. *How ironic: I have to choose John over Andrew.*

Her excitement built, that energy she lived off and for. Whatever his choices in the scene, she would send sparks back. She would pour herself into Sarah, her longings into Sarah's fateful choices.

"We're rolling," came from Grant's megaphone, oddly calm. For battle scenes he got wildly excited, like a little kid. For these, his voice was grave-steady. The boy with the clapper held it before the camera.

"ACTION."

In the blank time, Bianca offered up her body and her willing soul; then Sarah stepped forwards, put her hand hesitantly on the ragged officer's arm. How could she make him understand she had made her decision to be an American? "Father…"

The gaunt Colonel turned slowly. His eyes drank her in. He reeked of exhaustion, pain. Then, as if he'd seen a ghost, the eyes hardened and narrowed. "I have no daughter," he said, turning a ramrod-straight back on her.

Sarah wept, beseeched him, would have fallen had not her young patriot *husband* supported her. She could not take her eyes off her father.

The Colonel gave not a rearwards glance as he marched away with the British prisoners.

"CUT. AGAIN."

She looked up to catch a tiny nod of acknowledgement from Peter. It warmed her spirit. Too bad his part was so tiny—he brought fans to the theaters. She made a point to be pleasant to Peter—you always wanted Peter on your side. She focused, ready.

It was setting out to be a perfect day. Grant was right; in the early morning the weather had come up crisp before the inevitable bright sun and heat and humidity of the East Coast. Another long day's work—and they would have two whole days to recover—and learn their lines for Tuesday, but who was counting? She'd find a way to separate him from the acting.

Andrew scowled, ready on his mark.

"ACTION."

Fifteen seconds was an eternity. *Too little sleep? Someone keep you up talking?* A hard day's filming would burn the residue right out; she'd make damn sure he slept well tonight. She wasn't planning to drink much of the promised beer.

I'll show you something better than talk.

ANDREW

Hanover; 8 P.M.

THANK THE GOOD LORD for work—unless work failed ye!

Andrew had walled the whole fiasco off, managed to sleep. But now it appeared work, mind-numbing work, would be denied him tonight. All dressed up and nowhere to go... *Damn.*

The clear weather mocked him. The set was a coffin, closed and dark in the setting sun until someone on the crew resuscitated the auxiliary generator that sputtered and roared to a flickering life. And died. Only Peter stayed behind with him; Bianca and most of the other actors sensibly headed for the showers and dinner the instant Grant released them. Johnnie looked torn—but decided to follow his wife. The lad was coming along nicely, showing more steel than expected, at least when the cameras rolled.

There was always more prep to do, but he hadn't planned on doing it tonight. Tonight was slated for work. Well, George always had beer. Poor Grant.

He commiserated with Grant, but had the good Irish sense his mother sometimes credited him to do so in silence. Grant's Chief Electrician went off muttering to order overnight air express delivery of replacement parts that should be available, but mysteriously were not.

Peter, in the livery of the colonel's household, handed the reins of the dogcart to the stablehand, patted the dappled gray mare's nose, and fished out her sugar cube. The mare snorted softly and accepted the gift with slobbering dignity. Peter shrugged fatalistically. Peter took everything with a lump of sugar.

"Darn it anyway," Grant grumbled through clenched teeth. "There's no way it'll fly tonight."

Andrew pressed his lips together; wouldn't do to laugh. "If ye'll just let me take a looksee...?"

Grant faced him, exasperated. "If you don't get yourself off this set and out of my hair, I'm going to end up shooting *you*."

"Trying to be helpful, man." He tried to look useful. *If not for American unions, I could be. Back in Ireland...* Behind him Peter made a small sound like a muffled snicker. His cheek muscles struggled to suppress its echo.

"Go play or something. Leave my crew alone. We'll fix this if it takes all night."

"Aye, aye, *mon capitain*." Andrew saluted. But the elation was fading, as was the possibility of hard physical labour, and the trainer was long gone for the day. *Damn.* He was getting exactly what he didn't want: time to think, to feel justified. Peter was looking at him oddly. Talk to Peter? On *Roland* Peter had been a mentor; on the *Bunker Hill* set, he'd welcomed Andrew as an equal—tested, proven, annealed—starting to get respect. Not that Peter slacked off; instead, each film was ineffably better. He'd be learning from Peter forever. A long haul, and Peter'd managed not making any of the really stupid mistakes: alcohol, drugs, women, entitlement. *What's the right step for me here?* What control did he have? What was he supposed to do, to be? *Peter will commiserate—he has his share of crazed fans.* "Come on, Peter, I'll buy ye a drink."

They dumped their costumes, corralled George, scrounged up beers, and dragged plastic lounge chairs out to watch the orange-and-mauve sunset from under the massive oak that shaded his trailer. *It took a long time to grow an oak this size, a lot of disasters survived.* Cicadas droned, and a swift flying object revealed itself a bat, not a bird.

He slammed into the trailer for cigs, lighter, retrieved his beer from George's hand. Once they were settled, the idea of talking seemed less viable. *Damn her*—he would've taken something like this to Kary.

George's face was studiedly non-committal. "Staying home tonight again?"

He heard the question behind George's question. He glanced at Peter, who was peaceably sipping his lager and minding his own business. He drew on his cigarette, blew smoke rings at the persistent gnats. *In for a pence...* "Tell me, Peter. Would ye rather know something about a *friend*, even if ye didn't like it—or not know, and wonder why they were acting peculiar?"

Peter's eyebrows rose. His hands encircled the beer can in his lap like a chalice. "Peculiar how?"

How indeed? "Jumpy when certain topics come up innocently in conversation."

"This person owe you money?"

"Money? Lord, no. Money would be easy." *Money I could write off, hope friendship didn't leave with the money.* Out of the corner of his eye he could see George give him a long sideways look. *Best thing about friends like ye, George: we've known each other so long neither of us needs hurry.*

The skin around Peter's eyes crinkled, kind. "What do you consider unforgivable?"

Do I consider this *unforgivable?* The plastic chairs were hard, unyielding. "Deceit. Prejudice. Hurting others."

"Good list." Peter nodded in agreement. "I would add self-righteousness."

Ouch.

A burst of machine-gun pops and a faint whiff of cordite drifted from the munitions testing out behind the last trailers. He focused his gaze on the dissipating puffs of white smoke.

Peter ignored his lack of response. "None of my friends are perfect. And most of them are irreplaceable. They provide the mirror when I get too big for my britches. New ones are hard to find." He squinted at the dying sun. "I need them far more than they need me."

"So ye'll be the one making the accommodations?"

"I'm the one who went and changed." Peter's gaze pierced armor. "What did this 'friend' do—talk to the press? Drag you somewhere to show you off? Overstep the boundaries and want something from you you're not prepared to give?" Peter's glance flicked curiously at George.

No way—George would never... His breath came out in a huff. "It'll sound unbelievably idiotic."

Neither George nor Peter interrupted while he took his time.

She invited me to stay under false pretenses. She as much as admitted that she... what? Admired me work? This was turning out to be less than obvious. *Dammit. All she did was make me troubled.* A drop of condensate from his bottle landed on his thigh. He brushed it off before it sank in; it left a tiny damp spot. "It's hard to explain. Thought it was one way; turned out to be another."

"Ah. Thought something was going on."

"Why? Is it affecting me work?"

Peter deliberated, squinty-eyed, "No. Or better, not yet. But I can see the effort it's costing you. You've been nervy, keyed up, short—and then you have to apologize. You almost took the head off the guy who bumped you with the boom mike. You're wearing yourself out."

"That's what I want."

Peter acknowledged the wisdom of that with a quick sideways head jerk. "It's not sustainable."

"The hell it isn't."

"You're not giving me much to work with." Peter leaned back onto hands intertwined behind his head, peered up at the darkening sky. "Did your 'friend'—and note that *you're* still using the term—do you any actual damage?"

That's the crux of it. "No."

"Tell you something about yourself you didn't want to hear?"

"No. T'other way round." *How the hell do I say this?* "She told me something about herself I'd rather not know."

"She, eh?" Peter took a long moment to think. "Did she have a choice in the matter?"

Choice. What would've happened if she hadn't said what she did? Image of Kary on the rock, staring into space: couldn't have been easy for her. *I refuse to tell Peter she said she'd been obsessed with me but it was over.* So many things wrong with that he wouldn't know where to start. "She said it was a dead cow in the middle of the room."

George stifled a snort, got beer up his nose, straightened up choking and brushing spray from his shirt.

"Serves ye right for making merry of me problems."

Peter was not diverted. "I take it this is some small form of personal betrayal, but without any bad intentions or consequences except hurt feelings."

Peter is too damn psychic. He stalled. "How do ye figure?"

"Well, it's bothering you, but it's bothering you that it's bothering you."

"Clear as mud."

"If there were bad intentions, you would dump her without the slightest qualms."

"Actually, she intended to help me." *She said she gouged it out long before I came on the scene. And* I *was the one who looked* her *up.* "The lack of consequences?"

Peter raised his eyebrows, stroked his chin. "That's what's vexing you—you have nothing objective to complain about in her actions, or we wouldn't be having this conversation. Am I right?"

"Uncanny, ye are. Her behavior has been impeccable." So far— and George's radar hadn't caught anything. *She's been dignified, warm, hospitable, and welcoming. She's made no demands, done all she could for me comfort, stayed out of me way, and been true to her statement that she had her own life to take account of, thank ye very much.*

"So how bad was the betrayal?"

Ah. The heart of the matter. He squirmed—why didn't the chair have a more comfortable position? It struck him: Kary asked nothing of him. Not bragging rights. Not publicity. The offer had been safe haven. *What if I jumped the gun?* She possessed the brains to realize being on guard every moment would be constraining. So she'd done the adult thing. Her medical mind dissected out a painful nerve, determined to expose it cleanly from end to end, excise it after careful examination, and discard it.

She was angry at herself for liking me. No. For allowing a childish behavior to have any sway over her. *She nipped it in the bud, took the risk I would be offended.* It put her in a very different category from the gushers and the sycophants. 'It's what you *do* with an obsession that counts,' she'd said.

"If you'll allow?" Peter waited for his acquiescing nod. "I've had my share of crap to swallow—"

"I didn't mean to—" Saracen chief or freed slave, Peter brought a quiet gravitas to the role. What had it cost him, a black man in America? How much had he choked down?

"Let me finish?"

Andrew let the man talk.

"*As* I was saying. Crap to swallow. My dear wife Cassandra took me aside one day and told me that if I didn't learn to manage, I would end up having a heart attack, and she and the kids would have to survive on my life insurance, and that she would be happy to spend it with the next man—but I should ensure there was a quite large sum." He chuckled at the memory. "In the long run it has been easier—and a lot cheaper—to pick my battles, and to let the rest slide into so deep a pool, with a sack of rocks tied to it, that it would never surface to bother me. A *lot* of crap."

Have I been a total eejit? Suddenly he wanted very much to talk with her. If he ever became even *half* the man Peter was. "Thanks, Peter."

"Glad to be of service." Peter got up, folded his chair against the side of the trailer, touched his forehead to George. "Just let Uncle Peter know when you have another problem as simple as this. 'Night, gentlemen." He walked away without looking back, whistling, his hands in his pockets.

In the dimming light he could see the half-smile on George's face. And still no questions. Good ol' George. He shoved out of the lounge chair and headed to the trailer. "We good, George?"

George didn't look surprised when he came back out holding his helmet under his arm.

KARY

"IT CAN'T BE THAT GOOD if it puts *ye* to sleep." Andrew stood in her bedroom doorway. "I saw light."

Kary had startled awake to an unexpected shriek of wind in her carefully quietized bedroom, where clocks, lights, heating system were fine-tuned for the absolute silence she needed to sleep. Her frontal lobes went blank, and all she could manage was, "I didn't expect to see you." *Tonight. Ever.*

"Ye didn't change the gate code." He stared at her, the black motorcycle jacket looped over his left arm, with his right—and the treacherous garnet gleaming dully—pressing the jacket into his midriff, a shield.

Her traitorous body had overwhelmed her with its stupid need for rest, rest, and more rest. And left her vulnerable, sitting up in bed in less-than-decorous pajamas and an old hooded sweatshirt, surrounded by her first twenty chapters scribbled over with pencil scratches, fast asleep. A hell of a way to receive guests. *Especially this one.* And why hadn't she reset the code? Hope? Stupid, stupid hope? *Focus, Kary.* "Do I need to?"

"Not for the sake of me."

Careful, careful, said the feral brain. *You are getting one of his rare second chances. Don't screw it up.* No pressure—the next few words would change her life. But no pressure. Wind gusts hit the windows hard enough for the howl to make it past the lined drapes. "No filming tonight?"

He angled his head, listening. "Not the wind. Broken generator—and backup generator." His eyes were unexpressive. Driven rain peppered the windowpanes. "The wind came later—front moving through. Near blew me off the bike."

The accidental nap had done *some* good: she could feel her wits gathering. *Breathe.* "Why are you here?"

"I reacted— On the mountain—" He shrugged. "Then I had some time to think."

"And?"

"May I come in?"

"Certainly." She pointed to the divan. *Moving closer—a good sign?*

He perched, tense, at the edge, incongruous on rose brocaded silk. "I haven't been fair."

"You don't owe me anything."

"Common courtesy?"

"Not even. I weirded you out."

"That ye did."

"So— what now?"

"We're even? I know more about ye—and ye're not too happy about that."

"I wasn't planning to tell you."

"We know how that one went."

"Yes."

His arms relaxed, and his jacket seemed to become an encumbrance. He set it next to him on the divan. "This is a very ungainly chair."

"Unless you're leaning into the back support, yes. I use it for reading." She indicated the reading lamp. "With my feet up."

"I liked it better when ye didn't know who I was."

She sighed. "Humpty Dumpty."

"Aye. That egg shattered." He stretched, craning his neck to each side until it cracked. "Speaking of— Have ye eaten?"

"Not lately."

He got up. "Scrambled?" He turned toward the door. "I'll get them started."

Just like that? She heard her mother's voice: *Kary, can't you just shut up?* A major failing, wanting to make things right once and for all, poking the beast with a stick when it was lying quietly. *I can't.* "Sit."

"Excuse me?"

"Sit down. Please."

He returned to the edge of the divan, his gaze locked on her, as stiff and guarded as when he stood in her doorway.

"I was going to mail Bianca's script back when I figured out—"

"Bianca's script be damned."

Can't leave bacteria in a wound to fester. It would have to be scrubbed clean. Against raw flesh, without anesthesia for either of them. "You asked me a question, back on the mountain—" She faltered. His features were set again in the hard lines of disgust she had glanced at from her rock perch, only this time he was four feet from her face, and head on.

"Ye don't have to."

But I do. "Who I talked to about you, when."

He nodded, kept his gaze on her eyes.

Be extremely careful. "My world has few people. Elise. My daughters. Zoë. My housekeeper. My lawyer in town." Why didn't she say Joe's name? Too personal? *No matter.* "I told no one. It— It seemed important to— to protect your privacy." She hesitated. She'd been less terrified when she spoke on the mountain. "But my Aunt Ruth in California—guessed."

He had turned to stone.

What exactly did she tell Ruth? She knew there was no unease in her mind when she'd hung up the receiver, no wondering if she had told Ruth more than she should have. Ruth had been there, always, her rock when Kary's parents died together in a plane crash on a medical mission of mercy in a remote area of the Amazon, two months before Ethan... Ruth said, when it was all over, that her parents would take care of Ethan for her in Heaven until she arrived. No, Aunt Ruth would not gossip to anyone, not even if the story broke out in the *L. A. Times* above the fold. "I told her you were a houseguest. Ruth is— a black hole. What goes in never comes out. She's the only person in the world I'd put my hand in the fire for."

"Not yer girls?" His eyes watched her with the intensity of the predator.

"You never told your mother and dad a fib?" Her lip twitched at the memory of some of the whoppers she'd heard from her three over the years, when 'The dog knocked the lid off' covered for 'I'm sorry, Mommy, I let the garter snake escape in the back yard by accident.' "Just-in-time honesty. If and when the girls need to know, I'll tell them."

"When they come?"

"When they need to know."

"Point. And thanks to Grant, the other isn't precisely a secret." He made a wry face, wary. "Is *that* all?"

"Yes." The other was irrelevant—buried so deep it would never see daylight. *Never from my lips.*

"Are we done, then?" Something ineffable had altered in his manner. "I'm still hungry." He cocked his head significantly at the door.

"I'll be right down." She released him with a nod, and he bounded away like a large puppy let off a leash. She heard him clatter down the stairs, followed by the metallic clang of the drawer under the stove opening and the skillet rattling onto the burner.

Her body shook in reaction to the adrenaline, the good aftereffects of the nap already used up. Her heart thudded loudly. Outside, the stormfront had moved on, settling the air into stillness, the wind roar vanishing as abruptly as it came. Her body needed food, whether she wanted it or not.

I made the right choice. You took a harebrained risk. *I took a chance on* him. She *knew* both that she would never blurt out indiscretions about Andrew—and that her very awkwardness would give away the game: lying smoothly and efficiently depended on practice—or an agile mind. If he hadn't responded as he did, she would have let it go. She would have been free, politely free. Instead of still being friends with a fascinating, mercurial man. *Whatever 'friends' means.*

She pushed the lap-desk aside, rose quickly and closed her door. *Time to put things on a more dignified footing.* Each of her muscle fibers ached separately, and every joint where bone grated on bone. She rummaged in her dresser, chose jeans and a turquoise cotton-knit sweater. At least she had showered before falling asleep, stretching under the hot stream as long as she dared. Being fully dressed was a lot more proper. *What would Susan say?* Funny, it hadn't seemed to bother him. No sense of modesty. Actors!

She scooped up his forgotten jacket; its hangar, in her hall closet with the girls' parkas pushed to the side, still waited. The compression under her breastbone was loosed in a froth of tiny bubbles such as hydrogen peroxide made disinfecting a wound.

The wound could heal now, clean. *You did the right thing.*

ANDREW

"I DIDN'T EXPECT SUCH service." She joined him in the kitchen where he'd assembled his ingredients on the counter.

Three eggs broken into a bowl, a whisk at hand; three more waiting in inanimate patience their turn to become irreparable. Sliced Swiss. A spice bottle, turner, loaf of Jewish rye. He'd remembered she kept the butter soft on the table. "Hope ye don't mind—I went a'diggin' through the cabinets and such..."

"Mind? The man cooks."

"Reminds me of when I lived in Dublin in a little hole in the wall with a tiny cooker and no fridge. We ate a lot of eggs—cheap." *And Bridget was a worse cook than me.*

"What can I do?"

"Push the lever-thingy on the toaster." He turned the fire up under the skillet, set a square of butter to foaming, took up the whisk. "Done in a minute." He'd located plates; she finished setting the table in the dining room. He watched her out of the corner of his eye whilst she gathered supplies from the kitchen drawers: something, something microscopic, was wrong.

His hands moved among the utensils; his mind searched for the incongruity. He had it. *She got dressed—why?* Not the robe and fluffy slippers he'd expected for late night grub. Meaningless, for certain, but he hadn't survived this far without radar, and it asked him why she needed armour. *Leave it be, lad.* He couldn't, damn him. "Kary..."

"That one ready? Here, I'll take it." The toaster popped, she busied herself with the butter knife. "It works best if it's hot."

Ye'll hate yerself. He cracked the remaining eggs into the bowl while butter melted, whisked, poured. "Go. I'll join ye. This one's almost done." When the eggs set, he filled the omelet with a jigsaw of Swiss slices, sprinkled on some of the caraway seeds, folded the yellow curds with their tantalizing aroma to expose the browned underside, slid the whole onto a plate. He joined her in the dining room, where she'd lit two blue tapers at one end of the table. Their light reflected off the black of the windows, making them four. *Eat first—ye're not making sense.* But he had the same foreboding as the last time he'd made an omelet for Bridget. And he'd been right then, too.

"You're awfully quiet." It was a statement, not a question.

"Years of meals eaten on the run—teaches ye not to bolt yer food if ye don't have to." He compressed an errant caraway with the edge of his teeth, releasing the fragrant oil without splitting the delicate fibrous seed casing. Tactile *and* aromatic.

"When I first came, I'd eat in the kitchen with a book, then wonder why I took a pleasurable moment and tried to get it out of the way as quickly as possible." She gestured at the rich room which suited her so well, a jewel in a crown. "Now I take my time. Being alone can be sybaritic."

"Didn't figure ye for a hedonist." Dressing for dinner, even when alone—part of the same? Habit? *Then it won't make any difference, and I'll know.*

"One way, I'm the writer, secluded by choice. The other, one step from the crazy hermit lady, babbling in the back woods."

"Can I ask ye a question?"

She stiffened. "On one condition."

"And that is…?"

"I've been thinking about it. I'll answer any question you care to ask, literally, and on the spot—*if* that's what you want. But don't try to surprise me into blurting something out. I don't have the mental quickness for games any more, and I'll look the fool."

Damn. Handcuffs. "I don't—"

"You do. You live by your wits, by the word." She inclined her head, smiled to take out the sting. "I used to, and it's great fun—I miss it. But I can't. Do we have a deal? Oh, and one other thing. You *will* find a time and place, and ask? If something is bothering you? Don't let it fester."

"Fair enough."

"You have something you want to ask me. Go ahead."

"Ye're the devil." He fidgeted, cracked neck and shoulders. "Do I get a moment to think?"

"As long as you need." She got up, took their empty plates to the kitchen, where he heard the small clatterings of cleanup; doors opened and closed: dishwasher, fridge, presses; rush of water from the faucet.

She caught ye fair and square, lad. What *did* he want to ask? 'Why did ye dress for dinner?' which would get him 'I always dress for dinner.' Literal. Factual. Or 'Is there something ye haven't told me?' Which would result in a raised eyebrow. Or 'This obsession of yers—did ye have designs on me body?' The answer to that one was of no consequence—all women had designs on his body; he banked on it; it was fantasy: he'd watch her face when she answered, embarrass her by the asking, and have a useless piece of information.

Kary was back. "Still thinking? Hmm. It must be a doozy." She took her seat, looked at him expectantly. "You don't have to do this tonight, you know. Or ever." She shook her head, smiling ruefully. "I'm sorry. I meant to help, not drive you nuts. And would you mind not doing that infernal cracking? As a former physician, I'm pretty sure it's not good for you in the long run. Here, let me." She walked around behind him, put her thumbs on his spine knobs just below his neck, her fingers feather-like on his shoulders, intuiting the knots. "Relax. You're tight as—" She probed and he flinched. "What on earth have you been doing?"

"Ye don't—"

"Bend your neck."

She pressed and his back arched, but it stayed short of pain as she manipulated muscles and vertebrae. "Ah. Magic fingers."

"Don't they have someone to do this for you?"

"Yes, but he hurts."

"Seems counterproductive."

"Ye think? Does the job." He winced as she hit a nerve. "Ack. I can't do this this way."

He started to straighten. "It's fine—"

"No. I need you lying down to do a proper job. Come."

Just like that? He followed her up the stairs, not surprised when she led him to her bedroom. "Where?"

"You have a couple of choices. I can do this with your shirt on— or you can take it off, and I'll use baby oil."

"The difference is?"

"Well, the oil is a bit messier, but you end up with soft skin. It's not important—I just need something so my hands won't stick."

Hell of a seduction scene? He was almost disappointed. "Oil."

She made a face. "You would."

What does it matter? He kept his expression carefully neutral, awaited her cues. *Shouldn't dissatisfy a lady.* He pulled the polo shirt over his head.

She took the shirt from him. "Take your belt and boots off."

He unbuckled the leather belt, slid it out from the belt loops. He sat on the edge of her bed to remove his boots.

She placed shirt and belt on the divan, boots under. "Lie down on this side. I need a towel." She pushed the covers out of his way.

When she came back holding a towel and a plastic bottle with the picture of a baby on it, he was splayed out on his stomach on the king-size bed, arms overhead on the pillow, his skin taut with anticipation, wondering how he'd gotten himself into this exact state.

"Scooch over a bit more. I need some room."

He scooched. He closed his eyes.

The bed gave as she sat down. He heard a click as she lifted the fliptop on the bottle, jumped as she poured oil in the depression at the bottom of his spine. "Cold!"

"Baby." She put her hands on the oil, moved in circles, sliding easily over his sensitized skin. "Ease up. You're a bundle of nerves." She adjusted her position, massaging the oil into the base of his skull.

He chewed his lip, made the effort. *She said she wasn't good at games.* Was he missing something? Tread *very* softly. The room was no help. She had dimmed the lights—to help him unwind. Hands against skin made the faintest of sounds against the total silence. He heard her unlabored breathing, his own. The baby oil wafted the lightest of scents, but against the lack of perfume or room odors, it smelled as clean and ascetic as the sheets. His senses struggled overtime in the silence.

"This isn't working. Hold still." He heard clunks as she slipped off her loafers. Faint sound of hands against towel. In one fluid motion she pivoted, shifted her weight so the bed creaked, and straddled him. Denim caught on denim. "Much better. Don't flail about."

He heard the bottletop click. This time she poured the oil into her palm to warm it, and when she transferred it to his back he didn't startle. But every nerve in his body knew exactly where she was as she stroked his back from the top cervical vertebrae to the last lumbar one, expertly following and loosening the myriad strands of the *multifidus*. *Finish this.* "Can I ask ye that question now?"

"If you promise not to tense up." Her thumbs pressed harder into the space between the shoulderblades, where the last knot always lurked.

"I'm curious. Ye were thorough, right? In yer searches?"

"Right."

"What is out there on the great wide web—" *Commit, dammit.* "—about me sex life?" If that didn't pick a fork on this maddening road, nothing would.

She hesitated, pulled back, took her hands off.

"Don't stop." She placed her hands on his shoulders, resumed the probing. Was her pressure heavier? Could he feel a lie?

"It's all gossip, is that okay? None of your girlfriends seems to talk. I checked."

"Very thorough."

"Shh. I'm thinking."

The strokes were long and impersonal. *Over the line?* Where the hell *was* the line? "If ye'd rather not—"

"Shh." Quiet stroking, but he felt the tenseness in her inner thighs. When she spoke again, it was the analytical tone. "If I didn't know you, I'd think it was all for show—and that you're gay."

"What?" From his pinned position he twisted to face her. "I'm *not* gay!"

"I said *I* didn't think so, but it's not that important, is it?" She pushed him gently back down with the hard heel of her hand. "You're tensing up. You asked about research. I just answered your question."

Like hell ye did. He started laughing, deep huffing chuckles that shook him from the inside out.

She waited patiently, sunk back on her heels—perched on his rear.

He spoke into the pillow. "Why the hell would I live with a woman for ten years if I was gay?"

"To avoid professional suicide?"

"Ye did see me portray a gay teacher in *First at Lies?*"

"Yes, but—"

"For show. Right."

"Actors do all kinds of roles."

"I can't believe we're having this conversation."

"You asked."

He wriggled out from under her, stood them both up by the side of the bed. He held her by her upper arms, looked at her sternly. "I am not gay."

"It doesn't matter."

He leaned forward, and kissed her lightly on the lips.

She tasted him back, cocked her head when he released her. "Acting?"

"Oh, God, Kary. This is why I love coming here." He shook his head, with the laughter threatening to erupt again. *Aye. Hell of a seduction.* "Go. Change back into jammies. I rub backs as good as ye do."

"You don't need to—"

"Go." *Final test: lie naked under me hands.* He had to know.

She came back obediently, lay prone in the center of the big bed. She turned her face toward him, closed her eyes. "You can't press."

"I know." What did he know about her?

"At all. I can't take it."

"I know. Oil?"

Her eyes scrunched up as she considered. "No. The flannel is smooth enough."

Coward. He sat astride her, but kept his weight on his knees. He ran his fingers over her upper back, searching for tender spots. No bra. *Hmm. Not* that *dressed, then.* Her back spasmed, twitchy.

"Stroke as if you were fingerpainting. There won't be any knots, but all the little fibers need to let go. I'll relax where you touch."

He started circling motions on her shoulders. *Ye got into this one all on ye're own, lad.*

"Slower."

He slowed.

"Do you know where the seams are on a shirt back?"

"Uh. Yes."

"Top of the shoulders, neck seam, sides, and the waist."

"Right."

"Pretend you're smoothing out the paint uniformly all the way to each seam."

"Right."

"Still slower."

"Right." He finally got the rhythm and the pressure: she settled down, stopped squirming under his touch.

"Mmm."

What had he gained by risking his inane rule not to get involved with women when on a shoot? The woman whose narrow back he stroked wanted nothing from him. He was only partly ashamed of himself: he couldn't have crap hanging over him. *Waiting in ambush.* Dammit, he needed space to create, freedom from unexpressed expectations, to focus his efforts on the career that was at long last taking off. He deserved every speck of it—it cost him everything he had. He couldn't live in the ordinary world and produce a damn thing.

If he had to be a bastard to be a good actor, well, at least he was a good actor. His needs came first—friends were the ones who got that, who respected that, who didn't bind him or hold him down.

His rules were for his own protection. *But still a burden.* She passed every test he'd thrown at her with flying colours, thwarting him at every turn, by simply being who she was: a friend he could trust— and as big an enigma as when she'd memorized his hands.

She was asleep and slack when he kissed her cheek, tugged the blankets up, turned off the lights. He shook his head still chuckling, collected his discards, pulled the door to quietly, and headed for the bedroom at the end of the hall.

KARY

11:30 P.M.

SHE WOKE, UNNATURALLY lying on her stomach and with a cold foot out from under the covers, fear gripping her heart and making her mouth dry. *The children—* Why? Something had dragged her out of a too-light sleep. Intruder? Wind?

The sound repeated: a low moan. She scrambled to a sitting position, listened hard. It came again. Human. Unless an intruder had tripped in the dark and hurt himself, surely he would be silent? So, not an intruder. *Stop that; you can't live alone if you jump at every sound.* Her heart slowed. She reached into the drawer beside her bed for the metal 4 D-cell flashlight she kept for when the power went out. Its heft reassured her.

She slipped into terrycloth mules, snatched her robe from the closet and belted it around her waist. Her ears stretched as large as a bat's toward the sound. Not a moan this time, but definitely sounds of movement.

She headed into the upstairs hallway, found her door ajar—that explained it. The door didn't always latch without an extra push. He couldn't have known.

The evening's events came back to her, in reverse order from when she had fallen asleep grateful to have survived his little test: once you made your mind up, further actions in support of a decision were automatic. Silly man: he thought he was being subtle—as subtle as one of his broadswords.

She rapped on his door, got no answer, pushed it open cautiously. He lay on his back, tangled in the sheets, struggling—that was the other sound. Another strangled groan escaped his throat. Pale green light from the bathroom nightlight illuminated obstacles. She trod carefully: boots and a belt buckle lurked somewhere in the room to trip over.

She leaned down, shook his naked shoulder. It scalded her cold fingers. "Andrew. Wake up. You're having a nightmare." She drew back when he seemed to go into fighting mode, stiff and alert.

"Who's there?"

"It's me. Kary." She pitched her voice lower. "It's okay. You were having a bad dream."

"Wha—"

"I don't know. It sounded as if you were battling the demons of hell." She sat, facing him sideways on the edge of the bed, hands crossed in her lap over the cold flashlight. "If it matters, I think you were winning."

"Horse was crushing me. Couldn't get out from under. Heavy." His eyes focused. "Oh. Sorry I woke ye."

She loaded her tone with maternal authority. "The kids had nightmares sometimes. If you close your eyes, you'll go right back to sleep." Her mind served up Ethan, afraid— *No. Not Ethan.* Stephen, then, curled into a ball. She babysat for him when Susan went out for an anniversary night dinner with Greg. "You'll be fine now." She started to rise.

He reached out, grabbed her wrist. "Stay with me a while?"

She settled back down, stretched with her other arm to set the flashlight on the dresser. His hand burned in painful contrast to her chilled skin where it encircled her wrist. *It won't take more than a moment.* "As long as you need."

He closed his eyes.

His wariness calmed. She breathed with him, letting him hear the regular sighing of her slow exhalations, willed herself to be still. It worked—as it always did with the children: his agitated breathing slowed, synched to hers, took on the quiet rhythm of pre-sleep.

His hand would release her as he slid into a deeper sleep; no need to move and risk waking him.

Too much time to think. *He kissed me.* Even joking, it was an offer, and he was the devil, tempting her—with empty promises. It hadn't been hard: he offered, she refused, he was content. This was the way it must be between them for her to maintain her self-respect, to be able to live in her own home, with life a long string of like days. And her work. *The work which is always mine, always there.*

Traitorously, her own mind now presented her with the supine body of her enemy. No, he was not the enemy. Temptation came from her, not him. Any med student who couldn't put up an impenetrable wall around her reactions never survived first year, and, as by far the youngest in her class, she'd needed it the most: calm was a cloak that allowed her to focus on her patient, not herself.

Lust broke over her in waves, driven by sight and sound and smell, touch and kinesthesia and the taste of his lips. *Last chance.* She could slip in beside him, he would turn to her... Only chance. Ever. To fulfill the fantasy, to sate the body's lust. *His skin, the sound of his breath in the throat's hollow.* Something to remember on the cold, lonely nights. *A 'screw you' to Charles.* Proof that you are desirable. And woman.

Hush. He will feel you, he will sense you've changed, he will draw you in.

She took 'Lust' out of the box and examined its passion. He fed his effect on women, his stock in trade: of course he oozed raw sexuality—worth millions of dollars. Natural, fake, or unconscious—it didn't matter.

She counted time by her heartbeats.

Ridiculous to be so affected by pheromones; gorgeous as he was, it was his mind that attracted her, the brooding and calculated intelligence he worked to conceal—only intelligence could have produced the character of Marney, the guileless lovable simpleton. A stupid actor could not play Roland or a doomed IRA terrorist who broke your heart—only one who understood those characters down to their bones. The combination—brains and body—was devastating.

But sex changes everything. It could never be undone. It would make him far warier of offers from such as she, would cement in another brick in the wall he built to block the world. It would make him cynical. Show her to be only one of many. *And I don't— can't—share.*

Absurd principles. For just once more in her lifetime could she throw caution to the wind, go with the flow, let consequences sort themselves out after, instead of empowering them before?

Isn't that what every man wants? King's Gambit? A sexually repressed woman who opens only for him? One-sided exclusivity?

It doesn't matter what he *wants; only what* I *want.* Reciprocated—or nothing—too high a cost for him.

Regret reared its ugly head, but it had already lost. She had bitten her lip, the blood coppery on her tongue. Once again she stood alone on the plain of the vanquished. She quelled her shivers as she coffined Lust, and buried it, like Hope and Pandora's box. King's Gambit, declined.

His death-grip on her wrist slackened. Soon, very soon. *You won.*

Drained to the core, she fought to avoid shivering. The thermostat was set low for sleeping, her feet in the backless slippers were blocks of ice. Only her wrist, captured by the hand of high male metabolism, was ablaze.

As if sensing her decision, Andrew released her wrist, rolled over exposing a naked back, and flung his arm over a pillow.

Free.

And the last tiny temptation hit with a nuclear force: human warmth. *Slide into bed behind him; curl up like spoons; steal some of his waste heat; go back to your own bed warmed. Simple elemental survival.* Stephen went back to sleep when she climbed in next to him in the youth bed where she lay drinking in the little-boy smell of clean hair and fresh pajamas. *But this man will not. And he will still leave.*

She dared not tuck the covers around his shoulders. She arose, as frozen as a robot. The furnace kicked on.

It took all she had left to walk away from his bedroom, leaving the door open a crack—so she could hear him if he needed her.

❧ CHAPTER FOURTEEN ❧
"... by their fruits ye shall know them."
(Matthew 7:20, KJV)

A true man must own
even the unintended
consequence of choice.

Tahiro Mizuki,
trans. by R. Heath

"Must you go?" Meggie stood by the great roan as
Jake mounted, gathered the reins in hand. A full moon
limned his saddlebags. Behind her the fiddlers played
tunes in the distance for those who danced around the
bonfire, and the children from the wagon train already
played with the children of the settlement, long past their
time for bed.

"The snow will come early this winter, and I must
o'er the mountains before it falls. Settlers await back
East."

"As we did, Jeremiah and I."

The silence grew between them, too long until Jake
spoke again. "May he rest in peace."

"Amen." In Heaven, Lord, not where the river flooded, and took his soul.

Jake raised his gaze over Meggie's head as a dark
figure joined them. "Evenin', Matthias." He touched his
hat brim to the both of them.

"You will not stay? We have need of men." Matthias
put his arm round Meggie's shoulder, lifted Meggie's
smallest boy who had found them in the darkness.

Jake tousled the boy's hair. "You have need of farmers." He wheeled the stallion, waved as he galloped into
the night.

Meggie's heart stopped beating. She set her chin, and rejoined the feast on the arm of the man she would take on the morrow to husband, with a smile upon her face.

Prairie Fires, Epilogue

Then came there [...] all they that had been of his acquaintance before, and did eat bread with him in his house.

Job 42:11, KJV

BIANCA

Sanctuary; **Memorial Day, May 30; 7** P.M.

THIS IS THE DEFINITION *of irony: I'm sitting here, pressed thigh to thigh against Andrew—and we couldn't be farther apart.* Bianca was squished into the leather back seat of the limo, Andrew to her right, and Peter Hyland to her left. Before them, facing backwards, George and Grant squeezed John between them. As for George, there was no punishment sufficient for the look on his face when she'd arrived on Saturday evening, primped, for the promised beer with Andrew—and had to share it with George.

Andrew leaned forwards, forearms on his knees, participating in the headache-inducing adolescent-male ritual of topping each other's stories. A sea of testosterone was palpable, and her face hurt from smiling at their stupid jokes.

The limousine halted at a wrought-iron gate set into tall pillars of stone, and Andrew popped out to type in a code on a panel on one of the pillars. *Couldn't he just give the code to the driver?*

"Sorry." Andrew had let the driver pull through and the gate clank shut before he hopped in beside her, taking up, as usual, more than his fair share of the seat.

"I'm fine." She added a winsome smile, patted his leg. Once. Lightly. "Almost there? I can't wait." *To see what you two have going.* Impossible that it meant something, but she had to see for herself.

"Top of the drive." He settled back, finally silent, warm in solid contact shoulder to knee.

On either side of the gravel driveway trees encroached untidily, with occasional touches of white or pink blossoms on overgrown bushes. *Too rustic for me—it could use a good gardener.* In a moment she'd see what this Kary woman lived in—houses didn't lie.

The limo backed to take a tight turn, halted itself before the stoop. A fortress-like mountain house as primitive as its approach greeted her, dark timbers and granite blocks, with a glimpse of a second-floor balcony. Minimal landscaping. Few windows on this side. Evening drifted over the hilltop whose shadow lengthened as the sun sank behind it, leaving the cul-de-sac in deepening shade under a paling blue sky. No other vehicles but a blue pickup. *No locals for me to be gracious to—didn't Kary have any friends?*

Before the driver could reach for the door handle, Andrew bounced out, buddy-buddy. *Let the man open the damned door.* She suppressed a small sigh at Andrew's ubiquitous Irish sweater. *He'll learn to dress up more in Hollywood.* She gave him a quick smile, and leaned heavily on his proffered hand as her heeled sandal caught in the gravel, minutely marring the graceful rise-and-exit she had planned.

His face gave no indication that he noticed; he turned as the door swung open.

There stood the enigma, Kary Ashe. Short-sleeved gray angora turtleneck, long flowered skirt. Hair soft, muted makeup. On one of those tall, lanky WASP bodies which had never had a weight problem. *The exact same clothes she wore on TV? Who does that?*

The enigma spoke. "You made it."

"It took Bianca forever to get ready," Andrew exaggerated.

"Did not!" *'Every minute was necessary,'* Papi would say as he emerged showered, shaved, and splashed with Old Spice from one bathroom, while the rest of them made do with the other.

"You should all be glad at the trouble she took for you." Kary extended her hand to Bianca. She sniffed. "Is that *Joy*? You look lovely."

Had any of the men even noticed? Bianca detected no undertones in the older woman's compliment. "Thank you." She pirouetted easily on the wide stone stoop. Her motors hummed happily. One of the benefits of her rigorous exercise schedule was the luxury of living in a finely-tuned machine. *I work at it, I earned it, and by God, I'm going to enjoy it.*

"Come on in."

Bianca followed her hostess, surrendered the bolero jacket with the intricate braid edging and frog, conscious that her dress's spaghetti-strap bandeau top emphasized her slim arms, and its body-skimming skirt showed her legs off to great advantage. Better than that monstrosity of Emily's with petticoats. *Even if it does squeeze my waist down to nothing.* It wasn't hard to say the right thing, as her gaze darted about the open floorplan room—granite fireplace and sitting area, and beyond, a long dining table and a glass wall overlooking a wall of trees. She turned to Andrew. "So this is where you've been hiding out. It's beautiful."

"If it weren't for those shoes, we could hike up the mountain."

Are you serious? She pouted prettily. "But I like these shoes."

"Stop teasing her." Kary led them farther in, and Grant followed.

"We'll get the food." George. Being responsible. Andrew bounded after him, leaving the rest of them to follow Kary on a brief tour of the view. *Why does he always disappear?*

Bianca took in her surroundings, as Kary answered questions from Grant and Hyland, and John tagged along quietly. No photographs, except of landscapes. *Curious—no people in Kary's life?* Expensively comfortable couches and chairs, in golden oak with rounded edges and earth-tone cushions; throw pillows in warm shades which brought out the brilliance of the Navajo rug, pricey but not extravagant. A fire was set but not lit in the fireplace, with a collection of sea-shells on the mantelpiece. Shelves book-loaded with hardcovers; figurines and statuettes and pottery from extensive travel—hers? Framed and mounted textiles. Bianca made a note to check whether the desert paintings on the walls were originals. A hand-high bronze sculpture of a horse on the coffee table would be. The unsophisticated arrangement of clusters of mountain laurel blossoms, tiny six-sided white cups with deep lavender creases, must be Kary's work. *Taste—or a good decorator?* Bianca didn't expect this level of polish out here in the wilds of New Hampshire, and it unsettled her. *More money than meets the eye.* Dangerous? Or purely self-indulgent? A minor annoyance: once she got Andrew locked down, Kary Ashe would vanish from the scene; Kary Ashe wouldn't go back with them to Hollywood when the movie was over; Kary Ashe was not from their world.

They followed Kary out to the encircling deck; it overlooked a garden backed by trees on all sides. Upper windows overlooking the deck were dark. *Where did Andrew sleep?*

"I like it!" Grant leaned on the balustrade bordering the deck and giving the house his seal of approval.

"I'm glad you do." Kary laughed. "I was planning to keep it."

"Do you get much wildlife?" Peter gestured at the shiny ravens which fled just out of reach as the guests trooped out onto the deck.

Like Nevermore. So noisy in a bunch.

"They'd better be careful, there's a gray wolf around these parts—and she eats them. In winter. If she can catch them."

"She?" Peter's eyebrows went up.

"I've seen her with cubs."

"Ah."

John surveyed the surroundings with an appreciative nod. "Can you see Hanover from here?"

"From the top, if it's dark, sometimes there's a glow in the sky in that direction." Kary pointed over the house and hill. "But it would be too far to see."

"Good." John spoke with unexpected conviction. "I think I've gotten enough of Hanover for a while."

I know what you mean. Bianca shivered. *Since Emily isn't making any progress with her papa, maybe I'll have better luck here.*

"Goosebumps? Come back inside." Kary opened the sliding-glass door and they traipsed in.

Bianca, intrigued, studied Grant and Hyland chatting with Kary. Grant wasn't merely being polite—egomaniac little Grant was being *deferential.* And standoffish Hyland spoke to her as an equal. Bianca's hackles rose again—she desperately wished she'd made time to look Kary Ashe up. All Andrew said in the car was that Kary had some illness that made her tired. *Hell,* I'm *tired.*

The talk turned to old movies, with Hyland starting in on the anecdotes, John wide-eyed, and Grant chiming in. If Bianca wasn't careful, this would degenerate into a free-for-all which could go anywhere. *And waste my opportunity.*

She waited for an opening. "I love what you've done here, Kary. What's the rest of your house like?"

"Nothing much. Bedrooms upstairs, my office downstairs." Kary waved the rest of the house off dismissively.

Rats—no tour up those enticing granite steps.

An ominous clatter issued from the kitchen. Kary stopped midsentence. "Excuse me, I'd better go see."

Bianca forced herself. "Can I help?" She wasn't sure her nylon nails could take much stress. *Does Andrew like his women domestic or decorative?* She was only partly relieved when Kary declined.

Because classy or not, Kary *was* a threat. Andrew came here willingly Saturday night.

Nothing so far quieted Bianca's instincts. *This is a bigger potential mess than I thought.*

KARY

WHAT IN THE WORLD have they gotten up to? But Kary was grinning as she headed to the kitchen—it hadn't been necessary to cancel the party after… No; better not to follow that line of thought. Better to deal with the here-and-now.

Andrew stuck his head out. "Anybody hungry?" He blocked the door casually but effectively.

A cat who swallowed a vulture. She shook her head ruefully. "What did you guys drop?"

"Nothing that isn't almost cleaned up." He checked over his shoulder before stepping aside.

The three of them—she suspected it'd been mostly George and the driver—had set up a buffet arrangement of containers on the long white counter. At least one of them possessed some household sense—any incriminating evidence was hastily concealed in the trash can, with only a piece of white paper sticking out as a flag of surrender.

"Good job." She nodded approval. "Where's the driver?"

"He was here a minute ago." Andrew located the high-tech corkscrew Susan gave her for Christmas, didn't seem to need instructions as he tackled the first of the bottles. "Must've gone back out for something."

She wished now Zoë or Joe were there to represent New Hampshire and Hanover. *And make it seem as if I have friends and a life.* Zoë could be wickedly funny—Zoë owned a doctorate and half-jokingly expressed a wish to be German so she would be addressed as Frau Professor Doktor Wilkins. But Zoë had her own energetic annual picnic plans.

And Kary hadn't contacted Joe or members of their support group, either: she knew *her* limits—the three hours she'd allotted for the party were a stretch, even with the long nap before and the one she promised herself afterward—and many in the group were far worse off than she. *An excuse? Too late now.*

She bent to prop the kitchen door open with a wooden wedge, stood in the doorway to include both groups. She raised her voice. "Attention, folks." Conversations dribbled off as heads turned toward her. "Now, dishes and silverware are on the dining room table, food is in here, wine's in the cooling buckets. Ice, glasses are on the counter, and Andrew, will you show everyone where the beer is?"

"Certainly, luv."

She'd let her peacock guests do the work, relax, and enjoy the flammable mixture of personalities. *And be glad it happened at all.* "Grant, would you lead the charge?"

Grant inclined his head and initiated the exodus.

Choose the right leader, and the rest will follow. She stepped back into the kitchen, out of their way. "You can sit at the dining table, or out on the deck—but I warn you, there *are* mosquitoes, so keep the screen door closed—or in the living room. Make yourselves at home. You've brought enough food for the entire Russian Army, and there's no way you're going to leave it behind."

She made sure there were salt and pepper shakers, and sufficient serving spoons. Behind her she heard Andrew taking orders for beer.

She peeked out the kitchen window—the driver had not returned; he sat in the limo reading a book. *One last battle to win.*

ANDREW

WE'RE LIKE GYPSIES COME to town. How did I let Bianca...? Andrew watched Johnnie, the last one in the buffet line, head for the dining room. He wondered why Kary hadn't invited any locals. *Respect for me privacy?*

He opened a couple of beers with the churchkey from Kary's 'miscellanea' drawer, paused as the kitchen became quiet. He knew that sound, checked outside the screened kitchen window over the sink: a crested juvenile male cardinal chirped away at the birdfeeder, as proud in its own existence as if it had created the world. Andrew also knew that other sound—the solid clunk of Kary's front door.

Andrew froze, the bottles cool and slippery between his fingers, as he espied Kary approach the limousine and tap the driver's window. 'Eavesdropping is the devil's work,' his mother always said when she found him, her youngest, tucked away in odd corners listening to his elders. It drove his sisters crazy, especially when he learned the devastating effect of dropping precisely the right nugget into a conversation.

Their driver, a tall man with a ruddy complexion and snow white hair, startled and rolled the window down. "What can I do for you, miss?"

"You can come in and join the party." She bent to put her face at the same level as his, rested fingertips on the lowered glass. "My name is Kary."

"I don't think I'm supposed to do that."

"This is my house and I'm inviting you to the party." She dipped her head. "Please come in—I wouldn't enjoy my own party if I knew you were sitting out here."

"I don't mind. It's part of the job. I brought a book." He held it up. "See?"

"You'll get hungry."

"No, Ma'am—I brought a sandwich." The man reached to his right, turned back with something in his hand.

"We'll stick it in the fridge. You don't mind, but I do." Kary's tone held just enough authority. "Humor me."

"Well, that's very kind of you, miss." The driver opened the car door and unfolded himself.

"Kary."

The man's strong yellow teeth gleamed in the overhead flood-light. "I'm Frank McCauley, Kary."

Andrew's conscience pricked him. *I should have done that. I'm part host here.* He remembered Dublin, holding down a bartending job to keep body and soul together while auditioning for bit parts. Just such a small kindness from an established actress gave him one of his first breaks: a recurring spot on her soap. She took a liking to him, asserted he was right for the part even when the director egged him into flubbing the two lines he'd been given. He hadn't thought of her in years, but the memory was warm and sharp. *From those to whom...*

Kary escorted the driver into the house. The kitchen door to the entrance had been left open when they fetched the food in; Andrew saw her encounter Grant Sykes in the narrow hall.

"Oh, there you are." Grant beamed at Kary. "I see you beat me to it." He conducted his quarry into the dining area where Peter and Johnnie, plates in hand, stood talking and not eating. "Listen up, gang. This is Frank McCauley." He swung round to the driver. "Do you know everyone, Frank?"

Andrew slid in unobtrusively, delivering a bottle to George on his way. He took a sip of his own: cold, smooth, familiar. *Grant will put the man at ease.*

"I haven't met the lady, but I know who she is." Frank nodded to Bianca. "Evenin', Miss Doyle."

"Bianca, please." Bianca gave the driver a wide smile from her seat at the dining room table.

Good girl.

"I'm Grant, and this is John." Robbins shifted his plate awkwardly, shook hands. "You know Peter." Hyland nodded. "And this is George."

"We've met already."

"And Andrew..."

"He gave us a hand with the baskets." Frank smiled at Andrew, bobbed his head in acknowledgment.

"Gave us a hand! I practically carried the whole load in single-handed." Andrew put indignation into his voice. They'd had a chat back when Frank picked him up at the airport. He told the driver to call him 'Andrew,' whereupon the man nodded. *But he never used me name.* So many people, so many sets. Business acquaintances. Colleagues. Workers. Crew. So many... The constant battle: he needed isolation, peace, and quiet to be able to think, to do his *job. But am I letting the hierarchy of the set—and me on the top of the heap—affect me judgment?*

"Come on, Frank." Kary inclined her head toward the kitchen door. "They've gotten a head start on the goodies, and I need something to eat *now*." She made sure Frank followed her through the extensive selection of salads and cold dishes, breads and dips. She led him into the dining room, chose the seat at the head of the table, and indicated he should sit at her left side.

Andrew grabbed his plate, took the empty seat to Kary's right, next to Bianca. Kary made her own decisions, went straight to the heart of the matter. She didn't ask anyone's permission, didn't consult Grant—just did the right thing. He relaxed, enjoyed the fading of the sunset through the plate glass windows. *She's far stronger than she looks.*

The party would be a success. *Thanks to me women.*

BIANCA

"YOU HAVE A BEAUTIFUL home here, Kary." From her seat at the long table next to Andrew, Bianca let herself nod approval. "You must come visit me when you're in Los Angeles."

"If I'm ever out that way, I'll let you know."

Across from Bianca, next to the driver, Grant spoke up. "If you come, my wife will be beside herself if you stop by, so she can introduce you to all her literary friends. We'll give you a tour..."

"Whoa there, Grant." Andrew shook his head. "Aren't ye putting cart before bullocks here?"

"Could happen—if Kary…"

"If I come to L. A., I will let you know."

"You said if!"

"I haven't made any decisions. May I remind you we're not likely to agree on terms?"

Grant waved dollars. "It could be very lucrative."

"Fortunately, I don't need money."

"Unfair!"

"But true." Kary smiled at the driver and asked him if he needed anything, dipped a broccoli spear into the calorie-laden dressing Bianca shied from in horror, and munched it with an air of finality.

Bianca searched Kary's face for signs of coyness. *Either she's a master negotiator—or she really doesn't care.* Time to get some information. "I'm curious, Kary. Did you know Andrew before you did that TV interview with him?"

"I'm afraid I hadn't had the pleasure."

Was that a hesitation? Kary's demeanor didn't change, but she gave Andrew a quick glance before returning her gaze to the driver. Bianca *knew* that behavior—morning-after behavior: wordplay, little glances, and a general air of happiness and goodwill. *It can't be… He couldn't… What the hell is going on?* She *should* have found time somewhere to research Kary Ashe. *Careful—these waters are mined.* She switched tactics. "Grant, what is this you want so desperately? Maybe Kary will let *me* direct it. A woman's touch, you know."

Grant gaped at her. "But— we talked about it on the set— you were there!"

Andrew jumped in. "Ye really don't know?"

If someone bothered to clue me in? She put on her most conciliatory smile. "I believe I came in halfway on that conversation. What did I miss?"

Grant's face got redder than was good for him. "Kary wrote *Prairie Fires*!"

"Really." Bianca concealed surprise—a lifetime of practice protected her. Now Kary was looking uncomfortable. "I wondered why you had several copies in hardcover on the shelf in the living room. I am so sorry, I *didn't* know. Which makes me feel stupid—it was one of my favorite reads when it came out."

"No reason you should know—that's the whole point of pseudonyms."

Andrew looked confused. "Didn't ye say ye watched the show?"

"I caught a bit of it—the part where you sang with the acoustic guitar—" She nodded to Kary. "And I saw Kary..." *Michael's roving hands...* "But I had an early morning meeting—to work out the *Dodgson* financing—I didn't catch the end." *Another meddling interference to chalk up on Michael's tab.* And it didn't help to have to 'fess up before the driver's air of concern.

"Didn't catch the end of what?" John traipsed in, followed by Peter and George. "We decided to join you—it was getting lonely in the living room."

Andrew took it upon himself to be helpful. "Bianca didn't know Kary wrote *Prairie Fires.*"

"Ah." Hyland selected the seat at the foot of the table, flanked by Clown John on his right and Clown George to his left. "Well, that's all clear now."

"It is, Peter. It is." Bianca thought furiously—had she said anything to screw the pooch? "And Grant wants Kary to do the screenplay adaptation, too." She put on her most beseeching woman-to-woman face for Kary. "I've *always* wanted to play Meggie. Ever since it first came out, when I was too young." She glanced at Grant. "And you're trying to make Grant give you the final word in selecting the actors."

"Meggie? But she's too old for you." Kary looked flustered. "I mean, you're too glamorous for Meggie..."

Bianca laughed. "I dirty up good."

Andrew piped up. "Who's Meggie?"

"Don't you ever read?" *At least I read the damned book.* "Have some respect for your hostess! Meggie is the main character in the story. She births the babies and buries the dead, holds the women together, consoles the widows. She's tough as nails. But soft inside. And she prevails."

"I can see why ye'd like to play her." Andrew's face assumed an appearance of penitence. "I promise to read it."

"Women have a hard time in a man's world." Peter's deep voice lent his statement gravity.

Kary rose, and returned from the bookcase with a white-spined volume. She rummaged for a pen in the breakfront drawer, inscribed the book on the flyleaf, presented it to Andrew.

Bianca peered over Andrew's arm. "What did she write?"

Andrew laughed, handed it to her.

Bianca read out loud, "'To Andrew. For when you need to sleep. Love, K. Beth Winter.'" She chuckled. "You have a treat coming."

"Am I the only one at this table who hasn't read it?"

"'Fraid so." Grant glanced around and counted nods. "Except that my wife digested it for me, so I didn't read all of it. But I know the story. Kary's going to let me do it, aren't you?" He squinted at her. "I'm intrigued. How did you write that powerful a book first time out?"

"I was in the grip of an obsession for three years." Kary's voice was composed, dry.

"Best way." Grant turned to Andrew. "You okay?"

Andrew was choking. "I'm fine." He met Kary's gaze, said nothing further. George, who had risen, sat back down.

Bianca sensed collusion. *What was that all about?*

Kary laughed. "It was very erratic because of my illness. I'd read stuff, write like crazy, be wiped out for three days, go back and do it again. Exhilarating." She shook her head, remembering. "And stupid. I've learned to pace myself."

"Were you that passionate about medicine?" Peter's resonant tone removed any sting from the personal question.

"God, yes…" Kary faltered. She took a deep breath. "Medicine was my first love. Worked ninety, a hundred hours a week when I first started." She shook her head as if to free it, ran fingers through her hair.

"Can't you go back?" Bianca wondered what nerve Peter hit. *Clearly, I'm still missing something important.*

Kary's laugh was short and bitter. "Even if my brain could stand the retraining, I'm ten years out of date, and much too old for school. Oh, the basics are there. But the fine details—diagnoses, pharmaceuticals—irretrievably gone." She collected herself, smiled ironically. "But I had a good run. How many people get two such different careers in the same lifetime? And—for what it's worth— I'm good at first aid."

Bianca agreed. Useful for a hermit. She'd underestimated Kary Ashe. *Dr.* Kary Ashe. *What* other *skills do I have to worry about?*

Peter nodded. "'*Ode on a Grecian Urn* is worth any number of old ladies.'" At John's puzzled expression, he added. "William Faulkner. About Keats."

If Peter was going to go all wise and literary... "Would anyone like something to drink?" She rose.

Andrew wagged his empty bottle. "If ye're offering, another beer would sit right."

Bianca carried her plate to the kitchen. She had eaten as much as she allowed herself. At Kary's clever cave, she located an identical beer for Andrew. *One more—perfectly safe?* She'd never seen him drunk—he seemed to use beer as a lubricant, not an anesthetic as her Papi did. She went back to the kitchen to open the beer, poured herself a glass of white wine.

Andrew broke off what he was saying to Peter, got to his feet, and accepted the beer with thanks as he held her chair.

Good little hostess Kary included her in the conversation. "We were talking choices. I always thought that Taylor and Burton were made for each other—their on-screen chemistry was incredible— but they couldn't manage to stay together."

"You don't know what they were like in private." Bianca glanced curiously at Andrew. His rugged looks and easy manner reminded her of Burton. She liked this private Andrew. He hadn't lit one of his endless cigarettes, except for the one she saw him sneak on the deck, though Kary provided him with an ashtray and a red ceramic lighter in the shape of an apple—the forbidden fruit?

Kary seemed to have gotten a bug up her ass. "Fiery? Passionate? They tried to make it work twice. I think they got seduced by fame, and were unwilling to make the hard decisions necessary to shut the world out."

Andrew sipped his beer, smiled tolerantly. "What decisions might these be?"

"To put each other first. They had plenty of money, I'm sure. But they could have been a team. Who would understand the pressures an actor feels better than another actor?"

Bianca's eyes narrowed. *That was going to be my argument.* Or was Kary setting up a house of cards? Bianca sipped her wine, gazed lazily at Andrew over the rim. The tabloids had linked him with a dozen actresses and celebrities in the past year—none stuck. *Why?* A quick back issue check turned up an ex-girlfriend in Ireland who'd lived with him in his twenties, but they'd broken up years before and the girl was married, with two small children. Bridget something. She'd *had* him. *How could anyone give up An-*

drew? He *wasn't ready?* Bianca embraced Fate's opening. "What do you think, Andrew?"

Andrew shrugged. "Their careers went in different directions."

"That's silly," said Kary. "They both had enough star power to make their careers go wherever they wanted. Other couples manage. Look at Paul Newman and Joanne Woodward."

"Does not always work. Bruce Willis and Demi Moore?" Andrew rolled the beer bottle back and forth between his palms. "Huge egos. Make God laugh. Tell Him yer plans."

The back of Bianca's neck prickled. *He regrets whatever it was that didn't work. He's goddam* wistful.

"But you *choose* how to respond." Kary lightened up. "I'm an incurable romantic."

"I'm with you, miss." Silent Frank opened his mouth. "The missus and I were married for fifty-nine years when she passed. Was never a day I didn't thank the good Lord for her."

Bianca saw the old man's eyes mist. "How about you, Kary?" Without turning her head, Bianca sensed she had overstepped: Andrew abruptly stopped the annoying noise with the bottle. *Shit.*

"Divorced, unfortunately. Three kids. Long time ago." Kary picked up her plate, stood. "Seconds? You are *not* leaving until it's gone. Peter?"

"Yes, Ma'am."

"Grant?"

"Right behind you."

Incurable romantic? *Shit. And double shit.*

ANDREW

ANDREW, PLATE LOADED up with the wee green cheesy tarts at the kitchen counter, wondered where Kary had gotten herself to after the awkwardness in the dining room. *Damn Bianca anyway.* He'd apologize... Later.

Kary wasn't in the kitchen. He peered into the dining room to an unexpected sight: Kary had moved into his seat next to Bianca, and was gesturing with the wine glass he knew contained water, sitting pulled close with something on the table between them.

Conspiring like schoolgirls. He slid into the armchair at the head of the table.

Kary turned round. "Oh, hi. I was just giving Bianca her script back, and she asked some questions..."

Bianca looked up guiltily. "She gave me notes."

"The pink stickies are plot questions, the blue ones are suggestions for characters, et cetera."

Grant returned from the buffet, put his plate down, and resumed his seat across from Bianca. "Whatcha doin'?"

Andrew met Kary's questioning glance. "Kary, do ye know what script notes are?"

"Not exactly. This is how I annotate my manuscripts when I'm not sure." She shivered, grimaced. "I hated when teachers scribbled on my nice clean pages with an indelible red *pen*."

Grant's bushy salt-and-pepper eyebrows arched. "We have a procedure for notes."

"Oh, this isn't the *Bunker Hill* script. I'd need a non-disclosure from you for that, wouldn't I?" Kary glanced at Bianca, held Grant's gaze. "Andrew asked me to take a peek. Why? Something wrong?"

Bianca piped up. "You know I'm doing *Dodgson*, Grant. I told you about it."

"Yes, you did. I wasn't aware you were doing it on my time."

"I'm not!"

"We're not." *Dammit.* The last thing he wanted to do was antagonize Grant.

"Oh, stop teasing them, Grant." Kary exaggerated an exasperated expression. "The subject came up. I offered. It's *my* time. Besides, today's a holiday."

"Then you have my official blessing."

"Blessing for what, Grant?" Peter rejoined them, followed by the pack.

"Bianca's got Kary reviewing her script."

"Got a role for me?"

Bianca looked flustered. "Sorry, Peter. It's pretty white Victorian London."

"Which is too bad. Because you'd make a splendid English Dean Liddell. Except the Tenniel illustrations have Alice Liddell as a blue-eyed blonde." Kary shrugged. "What do you think, Bianca? Talk to your screenwriter?"

Peter snorted, and let out a belly laugh which grew in intensity as he watched all their faces. Infectious, it had them all joining in by the time he wiped his eyes. "Nope. If I can't be Lewis Carroll himself, you'll have to do without me. And I'd need way too much makeup for that."

Good egg, Peter. "Ahem. Ye are poaching on me intended role, Peter. I believe the lady is offering the position to me?"

"Broadswords at dawn."

"If ye're challenging me, I am most certain the choice of weapons is mine?"

"A million pardons."

"Pistols at twenty paces. Broadswords are so untidy."

"Seven a.m.?"

Andrew scrutinized Grant's mock scowl. "Better make it six. Yer replacement will require time for costume adjustment."

"Six it is."

"What's going on?"

"Ah, Johnnie. Pay attention. Our good friend here," Andrew indicated Peter with a sweeping gesture, "has challenged me to a duel for the role of the Reverend Dodgson in Bianca's eponymous film, tomorrow at six a.m." He had a brilliant idea. "Ye can be me second."

"I thought that was me *job*." George sounded peeved.

"Sorry, me man, the young one needs practice. But ye may second Peter, if ye like."

Peter drew himself to his full sitting height. "Don't I get a say?"

"Very well, Peter. I'd rather not have George incapacitated, in any case. Ye may choose Grant instead if ye like, but I warn ye he is quite grumpy at that hour."

"I'm glad that's all settled." Grant bestowed his benediction by nods at each of the participants. "Now, may I finish my dinner?"

"And while you're doing that, I'll get coffee started. Regular?" Kary counted hands. "Decaf? George, would you give me a hand?"

"Can I help ye?"

"No. You have to rest up for your duel at daybreak." Kary escaped with her dinner plate, and George did likewise.

Grant conferred quietly with Frank, who rose and left the table. Clattering sounds ensued from the kitchen until George swung the door shut.

Andrew savoured both tarts and company for the next few minutes. Pleasantly full, he pondered a postprandial cigarette. *Always want something, even if it's only a fag.* Or brandy. Or a little beauty. Bianca eyed him speculatively back, but said nothing. He sighed. *Remember the fine thing is spoken for. Pity...*

Generalissima Kary returned. "We'll have dessert. In here. *If* you'd be so kind as to take your plates to the counter next to the sink? I'll deal with it later." She placed the dessert plates and utensils she carried in on the table. She nodded to George, who set a cake in the shape of a heart before Grant.

"That's..."

"Yes. Plates to the kitchen, first?"

"Yes, mistress." "Ma'am." "*Tout de suite.*" Andrew scooped up the absent Frank's plate with his own, followed.

When they were all back at the cleared table, cups and coffee paraphernalia were at hand, with a large bowl of the jewel-like fruit salad he'd become accustomed to on the set of this movie. *No, not all.* Where had Frank disappeared to?

Kary had taken the empty seat to Grant's left. "This cake is special. Julia Child calls it *Le Succès.* I thought it appropriate for *Bunker Hill.*"

"It looks beautiful." George said. "What's in it?"

"Hazelnuts, almonds, eggs, butter, sugar, milk, and chocolate." Kary reached for a long knife. "I'm afraid it's not exactly heart-healthy."

Bianca's face was a study in horror. "That must have a billion calories!"

Andrew watched her in amusement. *Women. Always dieting.*

"Probably." Kary laughed. "I don't dare make it often. Grant, you have another surprise for us."

"Ah, yes." He turned his head. "Come on in, Frank."

All heads turned as Frank carried in a bakery cake, a single candle alight on its center, and set it in front of Bianca. "Happy Birthday, miss."

"How did you know?"

Frank inclined his head at Grant. "He blabbed."

"Not taking credit. George clued me in—arranged the whole thing." Grant nodded credit where due.

"It's not until tomorrow..."

"You're welcome. Thought it would be more of a surprise that way." Grant looked quite satisfied.

"That's so sweet of you. Thanks, Grant, George." Bianca's generous smile included the whole table.

"We must sing." Peter rose, lifted his wineglass, led them on a rousing rendition of the American 'Happy Birthday' song, ending with a deep, 'And many *moooore.*'

Bianca blew out the single candle to applause.

"How many years is it?"

"Johnnie, Johnnie—didn't yer mother teach ye not to ask a lady that question?" The lad needed to think before opening his mouth. *Old enough.*

Kary drew the heart cake closer. "Who wants what? Bianca, would you do the honors with that one, and I'll serve this one?"

Bianca nodded, reached for a server and a knife.

Kary put a slice of the heart cake on the plate Bianca passed her for Grant, added a dessert fork. "My daughters say it has the required proportion of sugar to fat: fifty-fifty."

Grant took a small bite, closed his eyes, smiled beatifically. "I've had it in Paris. Yours is better."

Kary placed a thin slice on Bianca plate. "New Hampshire cows."

"Sarah's dress is already too tight!" Bianca added a token amount of the fruit salad, micro-sampled each cake. "Mmmm."

Kary fetched milk for herself and Johnnie.

Andrew switched reluctantly to coffee; a swallow of bitter cleared his palate. He wasn't usually a sweets man, but... He let it melt on his tongue, surprised. "Ye're right, Grant. This is incredible."

"Thanks, Kary. It'll keep him manageable. Fat, but manageable."

"He can work it off." Kary's raised eyebrows accompanied her smile. "Were it so simple."

Andrew took another bite. *Were it.* He liked this kind of conversation, which ebbed and flowed around the dessert plates and the coffee cups, touching on the topics of his field: rumors of roles, stories of ego and power and studio executives with less sense than newborn babes, budgets and scandals and the latest in Hollywood gossip, all comfortably about *other* people.

At a suitable point Kary tapped Grant's shoulder, showed him to the breakfront section with her extensive collection of brandies and liqueurs, glassware from tiny crystal liqueur glasses to brandy snifters large enough for goldfish, put him in charge, and left him to deal with the duty of host.

Andrew let Grant serve him *Calvados*, rolled the dark liquid around on his tongue and the roof of his mouth. *Smart of her to preserve her energy by delegating the small tasks; anyone else would hover.* He sensed the fey: the house and its hostess were *Brigadoon*, and this was the hundred-year mark. One for the reminiscences.

Grant broke his reverie. "Refills? Anyone? All righty then—I abdicate." He bowed to Kary. "You all know where the grog is." He poured himself a second dose of *Galliano* from the tall tapered bottle, reoccupied his seat between Frank and Kary. "Excellent selection, Kary."

"I wouldn't have picked you for a *Galliano* man."

"It's the bouquet." Grant raised the glass, sniffed appreciatively. "Lily and I fell in love with it on our honeymoon cruise to Italy. Now it's linked to celebrations and memories of milestones."

"Glad I had some, then. Have you been married long?"

"Forty years this September. And what that woman has put up with from me." Grant shook his head, grinned widely. "Couldn't survive without Lily."

"Now there's a patient woman." Andrew's eyes narrowed. *Too good to be true?* "She doesn't make ye pay for being away?"

"Not yet. Maybe it'll all come due at the end, a giant balloon payment."

Johnnie glanced sideways at Bianca. "Head in the sand, eh?"

Bianca rewarded him with a neutral smile which didn't include her eyes. "I've met her at award ceremonies, Grant. She worships the ground you walk on."

"T'other way around."

Kary's brow wrinkled. "Why doesn't she travel with you?"

"She's on so many boards she can't leave Los Angeles; when I'm gone I'm busy every minute, anyway, and she'd have nothing to do here. Now it doesn't matter, but she used to say the children needed at least one parent to survive."

The table suddenly became very quiet.

Grant turned to Peter Hyland. "Oh, God, Peter. That was amazingly insensitive of me."

The plane carrying Arianna Hyland back to their children after visiting Peter on location crashed and burned at an African airport. Andrew's speech center failed him.

Kary found the words. "I heard about it back... I am so sorry, Peter."

"It's a long time ago, Kary." Peter faced Grant with a half smile. "It exactly proved Lily's point." He returned to Kary. "The kids and I have made our peace."

"How many children?"

"Arianna and I had two boys. Luke and Ben have made me a grandfather several times over. Cassandra and I have Chantelle. She's thirteen."

"A lovely family. You must be proud."

"I am blessed."

"Children are the most important thing in the world." Kary's tone conveyed deep conviction. "Choices have consequences. *Nothing else is as crucial as protecting the children.*" She turned toward Andrew. "You have a song about wanting children."

Andrew closed his eyes a moment. *Bullseye.* "Some day. With the right woman." He shook his head. "Our profession has a lousy track record." *The right woman.* He made eye contact with Bianca. "Ye're awfully quiet, Bianca. What's yer take on the mushy stuff?"

"Michael's away for months. I suspect things will be very different when he returns." Sad smile. "You, George?"

"He's taken." Andrew preempted George's reply. "The fiery Fiona has arranged for Mother Church to nail his boots to her floor."

General laughter.

Bianca lifted the tablecloth to stare at George's boots.

George blushed.

"Children? I'm not done growing up."

Chuckles all around greeted Johnnie's outburst.

"To families." Kary raised her liqueur glass—*Crème de Cassis.* He'd seen her pour it. *Less alcohol than beer.*

"Hear, hear." "*Salud.*" "Cheers."

'He who hath wife and children hath given hostages to fortune…'

KARY

I KNOW SO LITTLE ABOUT this raucous coterie of tropical birds perching at my table before flying off to wherever Destiny scatters them.

Time for the homesteader. Kary picked up the platter with the remains of the heart, its softening layers of meringue and buttercream visible at the cut. She headed for the kitchen and its buffet spread. Better to get the mess under control before the edges of exhaustion furled around her, weighed her down.

Bianca pushed her chair back. "What should I bring?"

"Oh, no. You sit. I'm not having the women clean up. Sends totally the wrong message." She caught motion in her peripheral vision field. "Frank, don't you dare move."

George rose at the other end of the table, retrieved the birthday cake and coffee pot.

"As you were, the rest of you. The bar is open. One helper is all I need." She held the door for George, and was safe in the kitchen with the door closed behind them in a moment. "Thanks, George."

He set the cake on the counter. "Tell me what ye need."

"Open the drawer to the right—"

The door swung open and Andrew sidled in.

She put a severe expression on her face. "I said—"

"Don't send me away, mistress. I need to move."

Probably true. "You could take yourself out onto the deck with those filthy cigarettes."

He bowed his head and raised hangdog eyes. "The mosquitoes will eat me, mistress." His lower lip quivered.

Ham. "Very well, but only if you do what George tells you. I think you've gotten entirely into the wrong relationship with George."

"Yes, mistress."

"George, you will give him all the dirty work."

"With pleasure, m'lady." George furrowed his brow at Andrew. "What would that be, precisely?"

"Send him out with the garbage."

"He loves mucking about."

"We can redirect some of that boundless energy."

Andrew grinned as he collected the bags, replaced the liner. "With pleasure, mistress."

"It won't seem so thrilling after you do it for the thousandth time. Make sure you put the lid on tight. I have raccoons."

"The little masked bandit things?" Andrew looked ready to do battle with the wildlife.

"Bandit is about right. And if you don't cover the cans securely, *you* will be cleaning up their mess."

"Yes, mistress."

They watched him go. "Here, help me get the dishwasher loaded before he comes back, George."

"I can load it."

"Would you?" She sat on the kitchen stool, chuckled. "Surely you've learned to manage him by now?" *For his own good?*

The door swung open again: Bianca with coffee cups and dessert plates. Bianca glanced around the kitchen.

"Thank you, my dear. Put them on the counter. Now scoot."

"But—"

"I have to take a stand somewhere. I'm not letting you get all sweaty. We're fine."

Bianca scooted.

Regardless how much fun it would have been to watch Andrew and Bianca, like puppies, playing 'kitchen cleanup.' That's what he needed: a helpmate from his circle to riff off, healthy and young and able to give him *many* children. *No—not Bianca. Hadn't she mentioned a 'Michael'? Husband? Boyfriend?* Someone *like* Bianca, then. "Everyone wants to help today."

"It's Andy. As irresistible as gravity."

Kary was startled at his ironic tone as he competently loaded the dishwasher. That's what she'd been watching at the dinner table. The heavenly order. Stars vying with each other to accrete celestial material to themselves to increase their magnitude. Normal people like Frank stayed out of the fray, oohed at the Northern lights; George—George was a planetoid quietly circling a nova. It was amusing to watch John try to break out of last place, not so much to find Bianca relegated to the status of 'women and children last' *with* John. No wonder Bianca wanted to direct—only that would give her the next step up with this stellar company—that, or a major blockbuster. *In the unlikely case* Prairie Fires *gets filmed and I negotiate any say in the matter, and she's still young enough—a lot of ifs—she should get a crack at it.* For being in at the beginning. Not that Kary could make any promises—Joe had taught her to be cautious about anything verbal which might be construed as a contractual obligation. No point in raising Bianca's expectations. *But I will remember.*

George finished loading dessert plates into the dishwasher. "Shall I start the machine?"

"Too noisy—I'll run it later. Put the platters by the dishpan—and make Andrew do them."

"Yes, Ma'am!" He set to, with her direction, locating the right size containers in the drawer, putting the remainder of the food away.

A movie Prairie Fires *is a pipe dream.* It was fun to see Grant's face when she told him she didn't need money. She'd just rather not look the fool. *I will return to my hermit ways, but we all like to go to a party sometimes, even if we sit on the sidelines.*

Andrew returned noisily from his expedition with the bags. "All locked down, mistress."

"George?"

"Yes, Ma'am!" He got Andrew organized at the sink, took the other stool, and presided with contentment on his freckled face.

Andrew chortled. "I have gone from the exalted position of house guest to barely tolerated family member, George." He rolled up his sleeves, slipped his signet ring into his jeans pocket, plunged nylon brush into dishpan.

"One step up for ye."

Such a small thing. Andrew threw himself into dishwashing with such gusto it was like watching a large child allowed to wash pots for the first time: bubbles everywhere, and no heart to chide him. She reached past him to quell the flood. She put the image of Ethan at five doing the same chore in the wood-paneled kitchen in Princeton, her blue flowered apron to his knees, firmly out of her mind.

ANDREW

ANOTHER JOB WELL DONE—nothing to this domestic stuff. Andrew, wiping his hands on his jeans, let himself be shooed out of the kitchen.

George followed. Behind them, Kary reached back to flip the light switch and close the door.

The gang had relocated to Kary's comfortable couches, with Grant and Peter holding court, as incongruous a pair as Danny DeVito and Arnold Schwarzenegger in *Twins.*

Kary settled into one of the armchairs with her drink.

Grant beamed. "Perfecto. We were just talking about you."

"Nothing good, I'm hoping?" Andrew glanced at the clock—8:30. *Not late, but keep an eye on it.* Time went too fast.

"You took so long I was about to send in the cavalry." Grant waved his liqueur glass in John's direction, almost sending the golden liquid over the rim.

"The bear is skinned, smoked, and stored away for winter, sir!" saluted Andrew, clicking his heels. He bowed low, ogling Bianca. "Bearskin to follow." He grinned at the memory of the famous pinup of her prone on a bear rug, concealing arms crossed coyly on its head with a tulip-bowled champagne goblet in her fingers, wearing nothing but pink high-heeled mules—and a pink ribbon around her neck.

Bianca laughed coquettishly, raised her liqueur glass of emerald-green liquid to him. "You wish!"

"What man would not?" *And how many lads have ye on their wall?* Even though he'd leaned forward in the car to give her space, the impression of her body against his thigh still burned. *Lucky man, her Michael.* He roosted on the arm of Kary's chair.

"I own that poster!"

Everyone laughed at John's outburst, while the lad blushed cherry red.

"That's so sweet of you, John." Bianca's whole face was illuminated by her pleasure.

"Stop teasing her," said Kary. "Even I've seen that one. It was a very modest pose." She gave a little chuckle. "I have almost identical pictures of the girls. A bit younger, of course."

Bianca jutted her chin defiantly. "I'm proud of that picture."

"You have a right to be," said Kary. "Talent includes using the gifts God gives you."

"Speaking of talent..." Grant peered at Andrew. "What's this about touring with your band? Movies not enough for you?"

"You wouldn't say that if you'd heard him sing," Kary said.

Andrew glanced down at her. She stiffened.

"Actually, I have." Grant's eyes flickered from Andrew to Kary. "Does a good job on some of those plaintive Irish melodies."

"The rock stuff is more fun." Andrew shrugged. "Movies take years. Music is now."

"Too bad you didn't bring your guitar," Bianca said.

Kary lifted her gaze to challenge Andrew. "I have a guitar."

Andrew looked down at her. *Of course ye do.*

She held his gaze, her cheekbones tinged with red. "Would you like it?"

"Put your money where your mouth is." From Johnnie.

"You're in for it now, lad," said Peter.

"George, would you open that long drawer behind you? Sorry, I only have the one." Kary pointed. "There's a capo, too."

"No worries. He can manage fine without me."

Andrew reached for the acoustic guitar George brought him. Light, inexpensive, with a colorful bit of inlaid wood around the sound hole. "Nice. Where'd ye get it?" He strummed an Am7-chord experimentally. "Ye have it tuned very low."

"It suits my voice. Fourth fret gives you fairly standard tuning. We—I—bought it for one of the kids on a trip to Mexico." Her eyes glistened. She blinked quickly a couple of times.

Ethan's guitar? He cradled its waist gently on his knee. "What shall we sing?"

"Something old, Irish, which we might all know," Kary said. "'I'll take you home again, Kathleen,' that sort. I have a songbook up here somewhere."

"Can I get it for you?" Bianca got to her feet.

"Sure. It's right behind you. The tall book with the yellow spine." When Kary turned back to him, her face and voice were serene. "Some of the loveliest songs are Irish."

Bianca located the songbook. She drew her Early American wooden armchair from next to the fireplace to a spot closer to his free side. "Here. I'll hold it for you." She scanned the table of contents. "One of my favorites! Can you sing *The Highwayman*?"

"If ye help with the chorus?"

"I don't sing—they kicked me out of choir in high school. My voice cracks."

"Really? Doesn't affect yer speaking."

"Voice coach." Bianca's shoulders raised and dropped gracefully.

"Then the rest of ye need to help." He glanced around, caught nods. "Frank?"

"The missus was the singer." Frank shrugged. "You need an audience. I'm practiced at that."

"Peter?"

"We'll see."

Andrew chose '*Kathleen*.' Good enough for this bunch—funny how Americans got misty-eyed about Ireland: around him, half of them claimed an Irish ancestor.

A couple of songs later Bianca said, "Sing one of your songs, Andrew."

"Ye'll have me cryin' in me beer before long. It's not a pretty sight."

"You just don't want to."

"Women are hard, hard." Andrew, glancing from Kary to Bianca. He strummed lightly, settling the guitar in. "No wonder Irish men never marry." He eyed Kary. "I heard ye singing along. *Mountain-top*?"

"You want me in on it?"

"I do." He watched her face closely, prepared to accept her response. *Will she?*

"On your head be it."

"George?"

"Sitting this one out."

"Yer funeral, George." Andrew strummed the four-chord introduction they'd used on the CD version.

Kary joined in on the beat, locked exactly onto his voice, in tune, clear, but distinct. She matched the odd rhythm of the refrain, watched and listened as he picked out the bridge notes to the next verse. But on the second verse she came in a third above, stuck with him with adjustments for the minor chords in a paced harmony rather than a perfect mirror. She did the same for the refrain.

His spine prickled, and his fingers stumbled on the unfamiliar nylon-stringed guitar. As on the CD, he picked a whole verse and refrain; she waited, a cat watching her mouse.

In the third verse she let go, and the harmony kicked and teased as she wove tendrils around his simple tune, below, above, in syncopation and back in lockstep. His own music, his own lyrics, transmogrified, subtle, stretched to limits he'd never heard. She climbed effortlessly to the octave for the last note of the repeated refrain's '...*back in time,*' held it exactly as long as he did, their gazes locked.

At the spontaneous applause, she startled, embarrassed.

"Brava!" from Peter, with a quizzical expression.

George said, "Ye didn't need me for that one."

"He writes good songs. I just decorated a bit."

Ye turned a simple ballad into music.

Bianca turned to Andrew from his side where she held the songbook closed in her lap. "That was lovely. You two must have been practicing."

"A lot." Kary leaned forward, turned to face Bianca, nodded sideways. "It's not traditional; in Irish ballads the singer is solo, and there are no harmonies." Her tone gave Andrew no hint of their shared secret—'*I have listened to the songs on all three of your CDs.*'

Listened, hell. She added dimensions—to his own song. '*Intricate harmonies*'? She came in so easily to disturb the sleeping beast at the bottom of the well—and slipped out as delicately. *Why did I invite her in?* He was so good at being self-sufficient—was it that few people dared him back? *Me own song.*

Bianca spoke again. "Do another one, Kary."

Kary shook her head. "You want to hear him sing, not me."

"I know just the song," Andrew said, conscious of a wicked impulse. *Lucky choice—or can ye do it again, luv?* "Sing *Galway Summer* with me, Kary."

"I have one." Grant rose, gestured dramatically with his hands over his heart. *"Should auld acquaintance be forgot..."*

"It's not even ten," Johnnie protested. "The night is young."

"Sorry to pour cold water on your fun, boys and girls, but—"

They responded in chorus, "—but we have an early start."

Bianca shook her head so her ringlets bobbed. "You're getting so predictable, Grant."

"What? You've all had your break."

"We're not your...serfs!"

Ah, finally, Johnnie is learning to think before he speaks. Peter's mere presence changed their language—he was pretty sure Johnnie had been about to say something else. Peter's cool facade told him Peter was used to the reaction.

"Grant's right," Peter said. "The *children* need to go to bed."

Frank stood. "I'll get the car warmed."

Andrew searched for what he hadn't heard: any loudly stated wishes from their hostess that they all remain and the party continue. Kary relaxed below him in the plush chair, with a faint smile across her face, and her goblet of deep maroon liqueur barely touched.

Time for them to go.

BIANCA

WHAT EXACTLY JUST happened here?

As the limo pulled away, Bianca stared through the tinted-glass rear window to where Andrew, standing with his arm around Kary's shoulder on the stoop, waved.

Not here, next to me. She was *beyond* swearing.

What just happened? She had been standing between Andrew and Grant in the little entrance hall. The singalong had been ridiculously quaint, but it allowed her to sit next to Andrew as he sang, close enough for his scratchy sweater to brush her arm, with her bare shoulders on display.

Kary said some hostess-y thing about how she hated it when things were over, and handed Bianca her jacket. The driver opened the front door, and Bianca remembered goosebumps in the sudden breeze—the black evening sky held none of the daytime warmth. She turned to Andrew with her wrap. 'Would you?'

'With pleasure.' His eyes crinkled at the corners when he smiled.

She felt his hand linger a moment on her shoulder. She turned to her hostess, tiptoed to brush Kary's cheek. 'It was a great party.

Thanks for having us. You won't forget the rest of my little script?'
She cradled it. Light pooled around the entrance, a stark theater in
the round.

Kary shook her head, raised three fingers, thumb over pinkie.
'Scout's honor. As soon as I finish writing tomorrow.'

'And you'll remember me for Meggie?'

'If Grant is truly interested, I'll put in a good word.'

Then the driver opened the limousine door for her, held out his
hand. She stepped lightly into the limo, and settled in the center of
the rear seat. She remembered noting that the leather was soft and
cool on the back of her legs.

Then Grant climbed in, followed by Peter; the men shared the
rear-facing seat, leaving John to sit next to her. George went up
front with the driver and the food packages Kary insisted the driver
take home with him.

And then Andrew popped his head in and said he'd see them all
tomorrow. And closed the door, leaving her sitting with that puppy
John—and no warm Andrew bulk next to her where she'd saved
him a seat. And no one seemed to think it was the least bit unusual!

Kary bent and said goodbye—to the driver, who said something
about 'Any time you need a driver,' and handed Kary his card. Andrew said, 'Good night, Frank,' shaking his hand. The driver said,
'It was a real pleasure, Mr. O'Connell,' slipping back into his proper place. But Andrew insisted stupidly on democracy: 'Andrew.'
'Andrew it is,' said the driver, and with a 'Good night,' he pulled
away.

What had Andrew replied when she'd leaned forwards, showing
cleavage, and said, 'You're not coming, Andrew?' with as much
disappointment as she dared show?

He met her gaze with a sheepish grin and a shrug. 'I think I'd better stay—help Kary with the mess.'

What mess? Didn't the woman have a housekeeper? It made no
sense—why would he pick that precise moment to be a gentleman?
I thought I had him.

She'd had it all planned: as long as he was next to her in the limo,
she would give him the little signals a woman uses. A light touch
on his thigh, the special laugh, intimate eye contact. Then she
would figure out some unobtrusive way to get the driver to drop the
last three of them off, 'to walk it off,' and she and Andrew would
leave John behind at his trailer, and she'd have Andrew walk her
home, and...

"Bianca? *Bianca?*"

Instead of sitting oh so close to Andrew again in the back of the limo, she was sitting here with *John*. She was going to have to strangle John. She warmed her face and her smile, and turned to her *husband*. "What is it, dear?"

John blushed and sputtered.

Grant took pity on him. "I think the lad wants to know what you're thinking."

Bianca widened her smile, included Peter. "Me? Oh, I'm just sitting here rehearsing my lines for tomorrow morning." She batted her eyelashes at John, halfway between Sarah's demure character and her own voracious mood. "You aren't nervous about it, are you, dear?" She had *planned* to expend her sexual tension on... And that wouldn't happen tonight. She ached. The next morning's scheduled bedroom scene with her new husband would demand every acting chop she possessed.

"Only a little." John made a gallant effort, took her hand and kissed it.

Take him to bed? He would be a poor substitute, and, sadly, she needed all that fumbling youthfulness in the morning to be real before the cameras with this inexperienced child. *Or is he?* He was over eighteen. *But...* She couldn't risk it. She lowered her eyes.

Peter laughed.

Grant said, "Save it."

A *most* useful profession. She pretended to be captivated by the conversation that resumed around her. But her mind wouldn't quit. *What went wrong?* What had she missed at the party? Because she must have missed *something*.

But he'd been in high spirits at the party, helpful, chatty, then entertaining when he sang. Nothing she could put her finger on—a rousing triumph for this egomaniac bunch, except for the awkwardness with Peter, but Peter handled that well. After the bearskin commentary... A million teenage boys had caressed her naked back—and she couldn't land one adult male? *A man who isn't intrigued doesn't mention photos of you nude.*

How about before? What did Andrew say in the limo on their way *to* the party? Something very minor... About Kary having some illness that robbed her of energy? But Kary looked perfectly healthy, managed the party with aplomb, acted as if it were normal for her to have a crowd in a house clearly designed for such. Kary didn't look ill in any way. She had traveled to NY, been on TV. *So, she's always tired. So am I.*

Bianca knew 'tired'—her mom's exhaustion, and the bags under her mom's eyes, when she came home from working the second job to feed them all. Papi—the morning after one of his parties—when he drank a bit too much, and looked like death. Kary? Kary looked fine. She should get more exercise.

Hypochondriac? That must be it. *And she uses it as an excuse when she wants Andrew to stay.*

The same way she manipulated Andrew into singing with her. That whole little scene played out in front of Bianca's excellent memory: the guitar, the setup, the telegraphing glances, leaving George—George who sang in Andrew's stupid band—out, the single perfect performance piece, the coy refusal to sing anything more. What was that about?

Sitting quietly in the back of the limo speeding down the back roads of New Hampshire, surrounded by the jabbering idiots she was ignoring without their even being aware of it, Bianca examined the evidence. Fury had burned to cold ashes, and she could think. *Kary and Andrew?* She would eat one of her hats if Andrew O'Connell was sleeping with Kary Ashe. A woman *knows*.

But whatever was going on was disturbing, because the potential for *something* was there, and it was just a matter of time. *While they are wasting* my *time.* Because the shoot would be coming to an end soon, there was an enormous amount of work yet to be done, as always, and the cast would scatter to the ends of the Earth—and her opportunity would be lost.

And not just the personal chance, but the professional chance to lock Andrew down, make *Dodgson* the success it had to be for her. He *would* do every movie he could, to solidify his position, but she had to get him to sign before someone else did. *If you're not with him, in the middle of the pressure cooker, you stand no chance.*

The limousine full of chattering monkeys slowed, turned into the warren of Hanover streets leading to the trailers.

Her face was tired. The script in her lap was dead weight. She needed far more power—it *had* to be a success. Even Kary had said, 'This is a good script for Andrew.' *How the hell did she know?* And why was it taking her so long—what else would she change? Could Kary's intervention really help? If *Bunker Hill* failed? *Nobody gets a third flop before being declared DOA.*

Those flops weren't my fault! It didn't matter. The actors' names were forever associated, like for *Heaven's Gate*, with the box-office disaster. Nobody else's. *The turkey Bianca Doyle made.* Hollywood would be crowning its new queen from among the ladies-in-waiting. To be used up and chewed up and spit out, like so many before them. *The vultures-in-waiting.*

The limo pulled up to her trailer first. John jumped out to open the door for her, offer his hand. He still had a faint blush on his cheeks. *Good boy.* And, since tomorrow was critical to the success of *Incident at Bunker Hill*, and she was a true professional, she lifted her lips to touch his. *I don't need you tangled in knots.* If Grant didn't like it—tough cookies. "Sleep well—tomorrow will be fine. You'll get me pregnant in no time, *Husband.*"

She typed in her code, let John open her door. She waved as they left, leaned against the cool interior of the metal door with her eyes closed. *Too bad; malleable, beautiful John was going places.* Just not yet—and she couldn't wait. Nor was it certain—John could turn out to be as big a fail as Michael. No, it had to be Andrew. *It* will *be Andrew.*

She hadn't the faintest idea how she was going to separate the two they had left behind, but it had to be soon. And it had to be explosive.

And it can't possibly be traced to me.

ANDREW

IF I DIDN'T KNOW BETTER, I'd be thinking Bianca was available. What a mess that would make of their professional relationship—Grant would kill him. Exquisite little thing. *Better to bottle it, use it—we have scenes to shoot.*

The instinct had been sudden, strong, irrational—and he followed his gut, and stayed behind, because it had gotten him out of trouble so many times before.

Though the few times he'd been wrong, he'd been spectacularly wrong.

Women! The muffled rumble of the motor faded as the limo disappeared down the drive. Andrew's nerves were jangled; at home he would have taken Midnight out for a long ride. Why? A simple enough party, good food, friends one could let down one's guard with. Kary was looking at him quizzically. He suddenly felt awkward, removed his arm from her shoulders, opened the door for her, closed it after them against the night.

The kitchen counter was clear, and no one had smoked inside so there was no cigarette debris to deal with. The sight of clean ashtrays made him irritable for a smoke. *Later.*

"There isn't much cleanup." Kary fetched the dishwasher detergent from under the sink and filled the dispenser. "This part's easier to do than explain."

Makes sense. The signs were there—if he paid attention: talk cost effort, too. A quick calculation—and energy calibrated in teaspoonfuls, rather than squandered with a prodigal hand. In stark contrast to his mother and his sisters who bustled about doing all the work when the farmhouse was full of people, and fussed over the menfolk who retreated quite happily to their own company, Kary had quietly accepted help and been content to supervise from her own kitchen stool—when it would save her strength.

She ran the hot water, started the machine. "I'll put those away tomorrow. Or not." She yawned, stretched arms above her head, each arm tugging the opposite wrist in turn.

"It *was* a nice party, Kary. Ye made everyone welcome." The dishwasher clunked and whirred as water flowed noisily in the pipes.

"It was, wasn't it? You were spared the locals. I couldn't get anyone to come—they all had plans."

So, she did try. "Sorry we cost ye a writing day."

"Oh, but you didn't. I always write—it's too important to skip." She yawned again. "But partying wipes me out. Which is the difference between an extrovert like you and an introvert like me."

Slings and arrows... "*I'm* an introvert."

She laughed as if she were humoring a small child. "Yes. A very *aggressive* one. You can't wait to do it again." She rotated shoulder muscles, neck. She glanced at the clock. "Told you there wasn't much to do."

Not like her to stand irresolute in her own living room. He nodded at the grate, laid out with split logs and tinder. "Would ye like me to light the fire?"

"It's too late for me—I'd fall asleep by the fire. But feel free. Just prop the screen in front when you're done; no need to put the fire out."

I'm missing something. "What would ye have done if Grant hadn't gone all parental? Kicked us out?"

"Leave you in possession, head for bed." Her gaze flicked to the clock and back.

She's trying to get away from me. "I'm in yer way. Good night, Kary. I didn't even ask if it was right to stay. I'll be gone before ye get up. George is sending a car."

"You're never in the way—I'm fading." She opened her mouth, closed it again.

"It's me, Kary. Say it. What would ye be doing if I were on me way back to town?"

She inhaled, let the air out, decided. "Come, I'll show you." And headed up the stairs.

To her room. The hairs on the back of his hands tingled. *A pass— at this late date?* But she went on, through her bathroom, to a tiled room with floor to ceiling windows.

"It came with the house."

"A Jacuzzi! Woman, what other secrets are ye hiding from me?" His guard was still up. *Other women, other pools.*

"Lots. Most of them none of your business. I figured I'd be wound up. I put it on the timer." She angled her head toward the hot tub. "Would you like to try it?"

"I didn't bring a suit, Kary..." He knew uncertainty was written on his face. *Damn!* She unbalanced him.

"Susan's husband Gregory left one last time he was here. I washed it for him—it's in your room. He's a big man. It should fit fine."

"Is there anything ye don't think of?" Paranoia again.

"I can't help it if I'm blessed with a logical mind, now can I?" She grinned. "Scoot!"

The suit was navy, nylon, the kind a father would wear to the beach. When he returned, the door was ajar. He knocked lightly.

She was already submerged in the swirling bubbles, wearing a plain black tanksuit. She waved him in. "Is it too hot?"

He held a beer, handed her a plastic mug of ice water. He slid into the green faux-marble tub. "No. Aargh." He exhaled deeply, reaching his arms out and leaning back.

Her eyes closed, and she sank deeper into the foam. The white noise of the jets made it easier not to talk.

Just as well. His eyes half closed, unfocused. He immersed himself to the base of his skull, let the bubbles swirl round him. Nudged by the bubbles, his thoughts wandered. He was getting to his usual itchy point: this show was wrapping up in the usual subtle ways— shooting the breeze about next films; vacation plans which substituted for 'No new contract yet'; talk of getting together, of awards, of rumours, of scandals—all indicators that the hold of the present was loosening, had to loosen. Keeping the colonel fully alive long enough to finish, while also exploring new characters. Unsettling. Painful…

The bubble-chatter stopped.

"Better?"

His eyes opened wide; he remembered where he was. "Pardon?"

"Sorry. I should have let you fall asleep."

"No. Ye're right. Much better." He reached for one of her feet. She stiffened. He kneaded it, stretching tendons and muscles.

"Aah." A beatific smile spread across her face. "Sybarite!"

He gave her foot back, took the other. She relaxed, let him work the kinks out with small crackings he felt as he bent the ligaments and tendons supporting the metatarsals.

She wiggled her toes when he release the foot. "Gimme." She reached for his foot.

"Ye don't have to."

"After making you do all that fetching and carrying? It's my responsibility."

He winced as she stretched the stiffness out. "Where did ye get such strong hands?"

"Did I hurt you? Sorry." She worked her thumbs into the ball of his foot, moved down toward his heel.

"I can take it." He grasped her forearm. "Yer muscles are like iron bands! What do ye *do*?"

"Well," she said guiltily, "this afternoon I disassembled the washing machine. But I had to wrestle it out to work on it."

"Ye should have waited till I got here. I noticed earlier ye hurt yerself." He indicated a deep angry scratch on the back of her right hand.

"Soaking in hot water makes it look worse than it is. Damn washers have sharp bolts inside."

"They're not meant to be taken apart by the homeowner." He imagined her with the washer dismantled, tools spread out in the upstairs hall, swearing.

"Works fine now," she said defensively. "Otherwise I'd have to wait for a repairman. In case you wondered, I did call, and they can't come out until next week—I couldn't wait."

"What was the problem?"

"Sock in the pump."

He laughed, shook his head. "Just when I think I've got ye figured out, ye twist again."

"That's silly." Her eyes half-closed. "I'm exactly what you see, a woman who has found what she wants in life, and is fortunate enough to indulge herself."

"A woman who sings."

"I'm never going to live that down, am I?" She closed her eyes, leaned back into the sculpted seat.

He shook his head. "No, Ma'am."

She reached for the recessed button which turned the bubble jets on, effectively squelching *that* line of conversation.

He allowed himself a small smirk. *Coward.* She was right, of course. It was a time for winding down, letting the water do its work. His thoughts drifted back to the party conversation, with its talk of songs, children, dead wives. Peter had truly got on with his life after the tragedy: he talked about his families easily, without regrets. *'Wisdom to know the difference.'* Ye couldn't change what ye were. When Bridget had told him she'd lost their unplanned baby, his feeling of relief—relief that the forced path into marriage and fatherhood for which he was not ready had been avoided— showed in his face barely long enough for her to see. She knew him for what he was—in the brief moment he was too inexperienced, too new as an actor to hide it. Words had not helped; that was the beginning of the end for her. *'Time heals all wounds.'* Time hadn't gotten a chance. He poured himself with ferocity into *Angels*; she, disillusioned, looked for a man who *was* ready. Now that he could offer her everything she wanted, that path was blocked. And now that the impulse to stability dogged his heels, finding a woman who would take him as he was, who could fit into his crazy schedule, manage his absences and his demons—that path seemed blocked as well. As he said tonight, the *right* woman. He envied Kary—her choices were behind her... He pushed the thoughts back where they belonged, drowsed, stretched his toes and fingers...

The water jets stopped. "What are you doing?"

He raised eyes widened at the sharpness of her tone. "Eh...?"

"With the water. What are you doing?"

"It's a stupid game I amuse meself with when I'm bored?"

"Sorry." She broke eye contact.

"Something wrong? Kary? It's only a stupid game." *First thing out of yer mouth is 'bored'?*

"I'd forgotten." Her eyes were haunted. "You think you have it all under control." She shook her head to clear it. "I should thank you for triggering a memory… I'd forgotten."

"Can ye share?" He waited, prepared to drag the conversation somewhere else, somewhere safe.

She took a long time. "The summer of '95…" She covered her face with her hands; she brought her hands down until her thumbs rested under her chin, with her steepled index fingers pressing on her lips as if to bar words from coming out. When she seemed to realize what she was doing, she tucked her hands under the water. "It's okay. That was the year when everything was still all right. We knew the kids would be out on their own soon—Susan was almost sixteen, pushing boundaries in all directions as she struggled to define herself." She smiled, shook her head again. "So Charles and I took them on a tour of the West. We did Yosemite, hiked in the giant redwoods at Sequoia, and got as far as Gray's Peak in the Colorado Rockies. I had made them each bring an extra bottle of water. I told them it was for a 'secret experiment.'

"When they were as wound up as I could get them—I know, torturing your children—I took them on the trail to a brass plaque marking the Continental Divide, and I explained watersheds and gravity and I told them how a drop of water released on one side of the Great Divide will eventually find its way to the Atlantic, while one a millimeter to the other side will go its merry path—to the Pacific. They spent a quarter hour testing the theory, until they'd used up their 'special' water, and as much of our reserves as I would let them expend, and then they tired of the 'experiment.'

"But later that day, at the hotel, where I was allowing Ethan to sit a short while in the Jacuzzi under strict supervision—he was only eight, and the hotel had rules—he sat there, dribbling water on his arm as you did, giggling, watching the droplets choose sides to slide down." She exhaled sharply. "I don't know how I forgot." She looked at him from that place people go when the memory is good. "You couldn't have given me a better gift." Her gaze drifted far away…

The timer dinged.

"And that's my limit, but you can stay as long as you like." She pointed. "That door goes out to the hall."

Dismissed as superfluous. But she was right.

KARY

THIS IS WHAT HAVING A friend does: it exposes all the raw.

Time to walk away. Kary used the handrail Susan had insisted on—*'The last thing you need with that thing is to fall on a slippery tile floor and break your neck, Mother'*—grateful that rising from the waters was steady and unambiguous. She stepped out of the Jacuzzi, reached for her navy terrycloth robe, and enveloped herself under Andrew's watchful gaze. "I mean it. The off switch—"

"Here, let me get it." He rose like the cat he was, stepped over the edge.

Kary handed him one of the thick striped pool towels.

"What?"

"I'm sorry—" *And I'm staring at your chest...* "but you've got an interesting collection of repairs there." She stared at a scar several inches long much too close to where his liver was, a vertical line which started an inch above his waist... brought her gaze up to the largest, a jagged line on his upper chest.

"That one? Me own damn fault. Josh warned me to keep me shield up. I swear I dropped me guard but for an instant—he lunged."

"Unfair. But I supposed that means he expected you to react more quickly. It's a compliment, really."

He laughed. "And he got in *so* much trouble for trusting me not to be a bloody fool." He shook his head. "No matter what I said to defend him—and of course everything comes to a rip-roaring halt while the medics swarm everywhere."

"Defend him?"

"I didn't do me job. Cardinal sin. Ye can't coddle yer actors *and* make them any good." He shrugged. "Josh was better'n me. He shouldn't have had to hold back, not at that stage, not with cameras rolling." His eyes narrowed. "It didn't happen again."

"On a real battlefield they wouldn't have done such a tidy job. It might have gotten infected, needed cauterizing... It would strike terror in all your opponents *because* you survived."

He threw his head back and roared. "It hurt like bloody hell!"

"Big baby. And now you sport this lovely scar to remember by. May I?"

He watched her with an expression of vast amusement.

She ran her finger along the edge of his right pectoral. "That must have hurt. Too bad it's so pretty."

"Come again?"

"See? It's a clean thin line…"

"So yer interest is purely professional? Haven't ye seen plenty of wounds and scars?"

"Well, yes—but not for a while, and I need—" She followed the scar toward his side, feeling the collagen thickening where the stitches must have been.

"Ye need a fresh wound because ye're writing a fight scene?" He stuck a thumb in the waistband by the vertical scar. "Good God, Kary, do ye want to see the rest? Maybe ye'll like one of the others better? I haven't been stabbed in the back much."

"Ah, no… I think I have what I need for a visual."

"Ye have the hand." He indicated the raised crimson slash on the back of her hand.

Her hand—with its index finger still resting on his chest. *Kary Elizabeth Ashe—what do you think you're doing?* She looked at the back of her own hand as if she'd never seen it before. His laughing eyes were inches from her own… "I am *so* sorry. You're getting cold."

He took the hand gently, kissed the scarlet line. "Ye see? All better now."

Get control of yourself. She forced a smile, took her hand back. "This? I'll be lucky if I get a pale white line. But I'll put some scar gel on it, I promise." *Think, Kary, think.* "What *do* they do when you get a wound like that," she pointed from a safe distance, "during the course of a movie, but you're filming the scenes out of order?" *The Beast settled back on its haunches.*

"Somebody from Continuity looks at it, and then they make it worse. Adds to the rugged image. They want me pretty, Makeup covers them up."

The Beast put its huge head down on its paws. "Body image is such a weird thing, isn't it?" She reached for the lever to drain the spa. "Take Bianca's. She probably works like hell to stay that way. I think she likes you." *Careful, Kary—you really don't want to know.*

"I'm shocked, Kary, she's me daughter!" He exaggerated an offended expression.

"Tell me you haven't thought about it." *The Beast closed its eyes, disappointed, went back to sleep.*

"Hmm." His eyelids drooped slyly, he hid his mouth behind his hand. "On the *other* hand, he's a widower of long standing. I wonder...a touch of incest?"

"Grant will have my head." Safe topic. "Save it for the next one. Are you really going to let her direct you as Lewis Carroll?"

"It could be a perfect little gem." He shrugged. "The script is rough—ye saw it. From long experience I'm leery of projects where I sign me soul over before I find out they want me to jump into the North Sea in the buff."

"Can they do that?"

"It's not uncommon."

"What do you do?"

"Hope they consider doing the water scenes in a Hollywood tank. Grit me teeth and jump. It's not so bad after the fourth take—ye're frozen solid."

She shivered. "My job's easier. Which reminds me: I have writing to do in the morning." Game, set, match. "And I promised Bianca my final notes on said script afterward." She pulled the robe closer and shivered again. "Don't *you* have an early call?"

He leaned over with a grin and kissed her cheek. "Good night, Kary. Thanks—for everything." He went off rubbing the damp hair at the nape of his neck with a corner of the towel. He shut the outer door as he left.

She stared at the door. She could feel the capacity for rational thought draining out of her like the water from the tub. *You won, Kary.* Wonderful. When they had risen to leave, she had been so happy the party was over; they would all be gone soon from her neighborhood—as if they had never been. *Envy Bianca?* Might as well envy the hummingbirds which came to her feeder, or the ravens with their glossy feathers.

A man in a bathing suit was both completely naked and fully clothed. He was her guest—that was the touchstone; she would have offered the same hospitality to Susan's Gregory.

She took control grimly: if she missed this sleep cycle, she'd have to wait another hour—or all night. Shower tomorrow—right now it would wake her up, waste the hot tub; get the last pain pill for the day in—before the relaxation faded and the pain came roaring back; postpone the extra stretching until morning.

She climbed into her pre-warmed bed, forced her attention back to K'Tae so her subconscious would work on it overnight. She turned off the light, had to turn it back on to capture an idea of how to use…

Her eyelids got very heavy as she started the patterned breathing which blocked all thoughts.

BIANCA

Bunker Hill

THAT WOMAN HAS HER claws in Andrew. It stops now.

Bianca put the drink down hard. She had to keep her mind completely clear. But what could she *do*?

Round and round it had gone for hours now— Pacing the trailer. She knew how to do this: the glass she had shattered was into the trashcan. You didn't let underlings see your rage, not if you wanted to work.

See what delay cost me? I should have gone on that damn hike!

What had he said? *Think, Bianca, think.* 'Some day. With the right woman.' As he was looking directly at *her*. *So why…?*

Her body ached…

If she didn't get some sleep, her scenes, her *stupid* scenes with John, would be fried in the morning. The clock showed 11:30.

She had even considered—God help her!—*calling* the little prick. He was eager enough, she could seduce him, get rid of the horrible sexual tension, *think*.

But if the twerp gave off one hint, one solitary smirk tomorrow, and Andrew happened to notice, he would *know* immediately, and all her careful plans would—

But her careful plans were failing anyway, and she couldn't see *why*.

I can't, for the life of me, see what he sees in her. She's old. Lives in this backwater. Has *no* connections.

I don't care if she had some good ideas for Dodgson.

I don't even care—careful now, she *did* care—about Meggie. *I want Meggie. I deserve Meggie.* Whatever she did, Kary must never know.

Andrew staying behind with his arm—*his arm!*—around that whore's shoulders—was the last straw. Bianca saw the handwriting clearly on the wall: whatever they have—as temporary as it *must* be—has to go.

Now.

And it can't be traced back to me.

Of that last she was very, very sure.

Tomorrow was another day. She'd figure it out tomorrow. She *had* to sleep. She stumbled to the bathroom in the stupid trailer, found the bottle of Seconal, counted the pills as she always did to make sure the cleaners hadn't stolen any of them. *I should put them in the safe—but then they'd be hard to get to in the middle of the night.* Washed two down with the whiskey in her glass. *That* she knew how to fight: coming back from drugged sleep was a skill she'd acquired as a child by watching two of the best at it. *If it worked for them...*

She had about ten minutes.

Wearily, she brushed her teeth, removed the remainder of her careful makeup for Andrew, stared at her baffled reflection in the inadequate lighting. There was *nothing* wrong with her. *Nothing.*

The booze made her stupid, but she *wasn't* stupid. *I am smart.*

A little question popped up as she stared: What does a woman like that *fear*? What would destroy her, distance her from Andrew? *Make her hide?*

Why didn't I watch her idiotic interview? Because she had no idea. *Add up the pieces:* the whore lived in the countryside away from everything. She only came into town for Andrew, and then made as little fuss as possible on the set. She gave the distinct impression she didn't want anyone to know who she was—anyone else would have made *sure* Bianca knew she had written *Prairie Fires* by dragging it into the conversation, if not on the set then at her house. *I felt like such a fool.* She is sick somehow—or at least she thinks she is. She doesn't drink—she barely touched her drink—but she didn't want to advertise the fact, so she held one in her hand. She has Andrew trained to come at her beck and call. *Grant* thinks she walks on water, but *she* made that asinine comment about not wanting money.

She made a mental note to insult Kary by sending her money for her *Dodgson* help anyway.

Think, Bi...

She looked at the bathroom clock and the answer stared back at her: Hell. For the first time since she arrived in this god-forsaken place, she thanked her lucky stars she was on the *East* coast: it was three hours earlier in Hollywood, and Hell's deadline for tips was midnight.

Get it right, dammit, she told her brain which kept trying to close her down. She read the email three times before she dared click 'Send.' What was the point of setting up untraceable email accounts and establishing stature as a CI if you never used them? It was going straight to Hell. And Hell would know *exactly* what she was getting.

Andrew would react like a gentleman, and leave the whore alone to sulk and hide in her precious house.

Bianca would step in, all sympathetic when he was a bear—she had plenty of practice—and *there*. On the set. Until the end of the show. No way it wouldn't work. Now she could sleep like a baby.

As long as it never comes back to me.

❧ CHAPTER FIFTEEN ❧
"A false witness shall not be unpunished, and he that speaketh lies shall not escape."
(Proverbs 19:5, KJV)

Oh, what a tangled web we weave,
when first we practice to deceive.
Sir Walter Scott, *Marmion*, 1808

Who provideth for the raven his food? when his young
ones cry unto God, they wander for lack of meat.
Job 38:41, KJV

Life must run beside
the edge of the precipice,
one step from the fall.
Tahiro Mizuki,
trans. by R. Heath

ANDREW
Bunker Hill; **Wednesday, June 1; 6** A.M.

IT'S STILL TOO EARLY. Andrew's jaw cracked with his yawn.
Late night shoot yesterday, early morning call didn't leave time for
anything but exhausted sleep. The makeup trailer was cool in the
dawn of another cloudless day, and he wore sweatpants and a tatty
hooded sweatshirt with a zippered front under the protective cape
Carmella, the makeup artist, had whisked around his neck. Her
hands were as gnarled as her face, and as light and careless as but-
terfly wings. Coffee, ignored, sat near her right elbow slowly becoming mud.

He didn't mind makeup too much; over the years he'd gotten
used to the feeling of cosmetics on his skin while he worked, paid it

as little attention as he would a layer of sweat and dirt when clipping sheep—except that he refrained from using his sleeve to wipe it off. He'd made an agreement with Carm to leave his eyes for last. He preferred to be the first one ready, and usually managed to sleep upright through most of the process, waking as his alter ego. The other actors came in later, and Bianca's elaborate costumes and hairdos required she be assigned her own special dressing room. *Just as well—she'd been on fire yesterday—the party did her good.* She could wait. He smiled inside his head, careful not to move a muscle.

Carm would rather he not talk as she worked: makeup went faster, and she had fewer repairs to make. She was a thorough pro, a veteran of ten Grant Sykes films; Andrew suspected she had gotten over any thrill from being close to famous faces before he was born, and liked him because he was as stationary as one of her practice dummies in long-ago school.

He opened his eyes when he heard the door of the trailer open and shut and Carm stopped dabbing at him and did not resume immediately. *George?* George was always up as early as he was, but with a thousand things on his list, he didn't normally come by for idle chitchat. He had a newspaper in hand, and he didn't look happy. Carm queried George with raised grizzled eyebrows and a jerk of her chin.

"Gotta talk to Andrew, Carm. Can I steal him a minute?"

"Sure." She took a moment to put her trade tools in order on her cart. "I'll grab a fresh cup."

George waited until she clicked the door closed.

Something bad. "Out with it."

"Ye're not going to like this." George handed him the national daily *State of the Union*, folded to a rectangle of an interior page.

It said, under the attribution *Hell's Angeles*, bylined Helena Van Sant:

NOTES FROM HELL

Irish heartthrob, ANDREW O'CONNELL, star of ROLAND, has a new focus. In New Hampshire filming INCIDENT AT BUNKER HILL, directed by GRANT SYKES, is his beautiful and talented costar, BIANCA DOYLE, his current interest? Or is it local author KARENNA ASHE, paired with him since their NY NIGHT TALK interview, whose mountain compound he has been visiting at very ODD hours of the day and night? Watch this space—you'll know as soon as we do.

"Dammit, George!" Andrew jerked his other arm out from the cape to check his wristwatch. Five-thirty. Kary would be getting up to write soon, if she hadn't already.

George fielded his glare. "There's no way ye can keep it from her—ye know that."

Damn! Damn, damn, damn! Andrew paced the limited corridor behind the chairs at the makeup counter, glad no one else was there. Especially not Bianca: she'd warned him about this kind of crap, but the last thing he wanted was her intelligent sympathy. *Who did this?* The trailer door opened behind him and he whirled, his fists balled. He battled the urge to rip the makeup chair from the floor and hurl it through the thin metal wall.

"And a good morning to you, too." Peter Hyland's deep voice filled the room as he sauntered in for his turn with Carm. His gaze flicked from Andrew to George and back. "Something is wrong." It wasn't a question.

George handed over the paper.

Hyland scanned the page, tsk-tsked. He raised eyes to Andrew, shook his head. "It is always a pity."

"What do I do?"

Hyland's expression bore deep regret. "I am sorry. There is nothing you *can* do."

Andrew met George's gaze. "Give me yer phone." *She can't see this.*

KARY

Sanctuary; **11 A.M.**

WE ARE FINALLY *GETTING there.*

Kary stretched luxuriously in her computer chair, then straightened the thick sheaf of papers which represented her day's output. Yesterday had been bad; today was tolerable, tomorrow would be better, and by Friday she should feel in control again. She shrugged. *Cost of the party—so I lied.*

She opened the drapes. The deck off the main level almost blocked the sun, and rays streamed through the glass illuminating the odd dust mote and warming the room. The new chapter, a crucial contest for Akiiya's rebel captors, had flowed from her subconscious fully formed, sixteen pages of stealth and forays, assault and counterassault, culminating in a brief battering bloody strike; Athena, goddess of warfare and wisdom, must have been pleased to so bless her words.

She reread the draft, shadowing her characters over the cragged and gullied mountainscape so different from the smooth hills of New Hampshire. She jotted penciled notes in the margin to mark small changes, tucked the printout into a newly-labeled hanging folder in the file drawer. *A very tolerable day.*

She shut the computer down. Even the quietest hardware on the market, and scarcely audible fluorescent lights, eventually affected her capability to concentrate, and especially to plot. The next piece, a pair of pivotal chapters, would require much digging: good place to stop. *Nap, lunch—or lunch, nap?* Hollow but not hungry. Nap. *Down here, or all the way up?* The master bed beckoned. Outside in the garden, something white attracted her attention at the base of the farthest dogwood; she made a mental note to investigate when she went out later to put her tools away.

Water. And ice. She climbed to the kitchen—to an unusual phenomenon: the message light on the answering machine, on the counter by the toaster, blinked so many times she couldn't count them. *The girls? Stephen?*

She pushed the machine's buttons with shaky fingers to display the numbers: twenty-two messages. Two from Elise, two from Zoë, three from Susan, and five, spaced an hour apart starting at six, with the number Andrew had given her for George's cellphone. Of the rest, a couple were local, most were not. Her abdominals spasmed.

She clicked to George's first message.

Andrew's deep voice played back clearly. "Kary, don't read the paper. I'll talk to ye later. Do *not* read it."

She rarely read the paper; she preferred her news predigested by *Newsweek*. She leaned on the counter, dizzy. Her father had done that with her diminutive mother: telling her not to read articles in the paper which might upset her, as if she were a child to be protected. *'Never stopped me,'* her mother confided, *'but he has his ideas.'* A bygone generation. Kary missed them so much.

The paper would be there already; if she didn't have the energy to hike down later for the mail, she'd take the pickup. The nap would wait. *Just this once?* She changed her slippers for boots.

The azaleas she'd had planted, flanking the gate to mask the chainlink fence and raw earth, bloomed fuchsia and lavender; she wondered how they could be so lovely but have no scent. No mail yet. She scanned the paper's front page: the world still turned. Rummage around in the rest? *Not here.* Her body warned her: *You're on borrowed time.*

In the kitchen she poured herself water, spread the newspaper on the countertop. *Borrowed time, Kary.* A few more minutes couldn't hurt, could they?

It took but one to find the offending column. She stared, her chest constricting. '*Even forewarned, a mule kick hurts.*'

Who told them? And what did that matter? You knew this would happen when you invited him to stay. *Could happen.* No; if you're going to lie, Karenna Ashe, at least don't lie to yourself. *This is* my *just punishment for pride.* The avalanche had been accumulating over her head—*his* head—from the first moment she offered him Sanctuary: a Sanctuary she had no ability to guarantee. *Nothing can be the same from here on forward.* Her map of the known universe had just run out. The kitchen stool caught her as her knees released.

She re-examined the excrement she had brought into her home. She couldn't read it, didn't *need* to read it again. Her fingertips touched it: black ink on grayish newsprint, the non-odor of the press. Which was wrong. The worst part about medicine and babies was the smell. Hospitals, medications, sick people, pus, vomit, diarrhea. Ordinary shit gave *warning.* Such a small thing: a column-inch. Of words. *To rip Sanctuary to shreds.* Really, Kary—if anyone should know the power of the printed word... *I was prepared for something dramatic.* The... *paragraph* was the blob of snow which falls from a pine branch. *And triggers the avalanche.*

She remembered his plea—don't read it. He *lives* in avalanche territory. *He is poised, ready to ski away.* You are not. She stared at the silenced phone as another incoming message registered. Her hand reached for the phone—

Stop.

You can't. Other people can, but you can't. You cannot talk to anyone in this shape. You knew that when you stubbornly squandered energy—you barely made it back from the gate. What do you do now? What is the default response? *To do what I should do.* Which is? *Rest first; the problem will still be there.* Unless it is a physical emergency...? *Get the brain in the best possible condition to handle the problem.* When? *Now.* Does it feel good? *No.* Does it work? *It always works.*

Upstairs? No. You wasted the energy. *The couch, then.*

She carried the water with her to the living room. From the drawer she retrieved the blanket and the pillow and the eye-mask and the tiny red-and-green kitchen timer set for thirty-five minutes stashed there exactly for this situation. She lay down on the couch, her fading rational mind screaming that she needed to do something, *anything!* She ignored it, grimly started the ritual: breathe in through the nose, filling every alveolus, stretching to maximum air capacity; hold, counting two beats as soon as she detected her pulse in her jugular; release the air in a giant uncontrolled whoosh; two more counts with the pulse, and release the muscles again, letting the easy air out; another two counts, push the remaining air out *hard.* Put off *every* thought—thinking could wait until she breathed three more times, couldn't it? *It can't!* It will. Breathe in… Repeat until the end of the world if necessary…

The timer went off *ta ta ta ta…ta ta ta ta…* She stopped it, stunned for a moment.

She sat up, drank more water. The clamoring multitudes rushed back, but dampened, strangely civil. *And you can think.*

In the kitchen, she reached again for the phone, startled as it rang under her hand.

She picked it up. "George?"

"It's Andrew, Kary, I need—"

She deliberately ignored the paper splayed out before her on the counter. "It's okay, Andrew. I already saw it."

BIANCA

Bunker Hill; 11:15 A.M.

BREAK OVER. SHE SMILED and lied through her teeth, batting her eyelids gently at her spanking new husband. "I await your pleasure, my love."

"Cut it out, Bianca." Grant exuded eau d'exasperation as the shoot dragged on.

"Yes, Lord and Master." Sarah demurely lowered her eyes, her hand clutching the top of the incredibly inadequate cotton shift. Bianca raised the same eyes. "'Tone it down.' We'll be fine, Grant."

"And John—Winston—do it like Bianca rehearsed with you yesterday, okay?"

"PLACES, EVERYONE."

Yesterday. The most frustrating day of her life. *I met her stupid deadline.* There was *nothing* in Hell's column yesterday, and this morning she hadn't found a paper before the early call, the one she was almost late for—it went to her second backup alarm before she dragged herself out of drugged sleep and got her ass ready for Makeup, literally ready for makeup—and now here she was, the only practically naked woman on the set, in front of a bunch of middle-aged men with headphones with mikes, clipboards, and studiously averted gazes. Kudos to Grant for clearing it down to the absolute minimum—and keeping the assistants and hangers-on off the closed set—*only* the minimum necessary—to man two cameras where the fourth wall should be, and one overhead. *Pervs.*

This is standard, *people. Nothing to see here.* Like a million other love scenes being filmed right this minute to fool the rubes into thinking they're seeing something. *It would be* easier *to do porn.*

Tone it down. Even if John needs more help than a real twenty-year-old farmer. *Sheesh. He* has to be in charge, leading the waltz, even if he can't put one foot in front of the other at the ball. *Man up, John.* She smiled, sweet-Sarah-smile, shyly took his hand and brushed her lips lightly over his knuckles...

"AND CUT!"

Grant approached. "That was *much* better, John." Grant looked worried. "Good for another round after the break, Bianca?"

"Good to go, Grant." Pretending to let John deflower her bore all the marks of high comedy, and this time was no different from a dozen different flicks before: the ridiculous thong which barely covered pubic hair, camera shots that maintained PG-13 status a millimeter from an aureola—but only after severe frame-by-frame editing, sounds to utter worthy of the great Linda Lovelace. Was there a screenwriter anywhere who didn't want his leading lady naked and in chains? *Damn adolescent male fantasies.* You want to work in this business? You put out, and put out, and put out. *And smile.* Audiences didn't pay for Vivien Leigh's acting, they paid for the rape scene which started on the grand circular staircase. "Just let me get the shoulder retouched, 'kay?"

"Perfecto." Grant addressed John. "Not so hard, lad. Sarah wouldn't have had re-dos."

"He's fine, Grant. I can take it." She smiled at John, slipped her arms into the kimono held out to her, belted it around her waist before escaping to the sidelines. To the next pimply-faced minion. Honestly, couldn't they let the babies practice on the extras if they needed to learn someplace? She met his gaze. *Yes, I'm nearly naked under this robe. Deal.* She lifted her eyebrows. "You Makeup?"

"Yes, Miss Doyle."

"Water bottle, please?"

He turned to go. His back pocket bulged.

"Wait. Is that today's paper?"

His hand went guiltily to the folded newsprint, and he tried to shove it deeper in his pocket.

"May I?" *Could it be...?*

"Uh. I don't— Grant said not to—"

He knew what was in it. She put on her most charming winsome smile. "Give."

"Grant said—"

"Really? I'll take it up with him." *If you value your life...*

"He said you'd be upset—"

Enough. She flitted behind him, took the paper from his pocket.

He turned bright red.

The paper was folded to Hell's column. It *had* to be... *Thank God I practiced!* This gangly boy was about to get the private show of his life. Her eyes quickly scanned the lines. Contribution from Hell? A reference to *Night Talk*. Bianca caught her breath, closed her eyes. *Nice!* She opened her eyes, made a tiny head shake of incredulity, read it slowly again, let her face, when she lifted her gaze to the perfect witness, display hurt, disbelief, innocence. *Watch your timing—no retakes here.* She thrust the paper at his clumsy hands. "That's— that's horrible." *Careful. Underplay, underplay—* this *is the report that goes out to the whole set.* She raised her head, glanced around. Not a single person would make eye contact; each one had found something very important to do. *Perfect. Quit while you're ahead.*

He stood there looking like a puppet with cut strings, his mouth open.

"Do you think you could find me that—water?" Her hand went to the back of the makeup chair to steady herself. She clutched the kimono close to her chest with the other hand, turned and slowly climbed into the chair. *What did that stupid woman do all day yesterday?* Run it through their Legal Department? Consult some stupid boss? Rumor generates revenue. *As if that anonymous email address has* ever *sent her something unreliable.*

Bianca sat up very straight, a tiny waif in the huge chair.

ANDREW

HE HEARD, "IT'S OKAY, Andrew. I already saw it." All his plans crumbled to a heap of rubbish. "Kary, I am so sorry."

"You wrote that?"

His head jerked involuntarily. "I—" Out of the corner of his eye he caught George's significant glance at the suddenly hushed set around him. "Hang on." *Shite.* He turned his back on the crew who, along with a crowd of redcoats and Hessian extras in hunter green in the background, had been avoiding his gaze all morning. The backs of his hands tingled.

She didn't chatter while he withdrew a few paces.

He lowered his voice. "Kary, how could ye think...?"

"You can't apologize for what you didn't do. It makes no sense."

"It's still me fault. If I hadn't come— I am so very sorry someone took a potshot at ye because of me." *Get on with it, man.* "Listen, the best way to deal with this crap is for me not to show up any more, not give them any more ammunition to misfire."

A long pause. "Certainly. For the good of the film."

What? "Film be damned. I don't want ye dragged through this."

Another pause. "Are you on set?"

"Yes. Ten minute break. Ye didn't pick up."

"There was a small but finite chance something like this would happen. And it has. That is all."

"Ye knew that, and ye asked me back?" *Brave? Obsession? Foolish?*

"I didn't intend to set it off." Her voice was cool. "And yes, there may be fallout, but I can't live my life worrying about what people think."

His fist balled. "When I find out who—"

"You will do nothing."

"It's libel—somebody from this set—"

"Whoever this Helena person is, she knows what she's doing. It's innuendo. Every word, every sentence, is literally true. This was written by an expert. Don't you see?"

His breath whooshed out in frustrated fury. "So what—?"

"She wants to see you explode. So you...?"

Listen to Kary. "Ignore the bitch."

"She needs to enhance her reputation by taking you down—that's how people like her get their creds. No gossip, no revenue."

"Someone *here* told her."

"And you know who that person is? For certain?"

"I can track it down."

"Wouldn't Peter say that doing an investigation on the set would *prove* you have something to hide?"

"Fine. Maury can find out from his end."

"Yes, that would do it—and do you really want it out there that your agent is digging into who fed this tidbit to a gossip columnist? Do you want to give this—and Maury—that much power?"

"Ye're boxing me in, Kary."

"*If* there were a photograph—which there isn't—and *if* it could be determined that the person took it on my property, the most I might be able to *prove* is criminal trespass. My lawyer demands a perfectly clean chain of evidence before we're certain enough for a court of law—and then he strikes."

"Ye're taking an awfully high-road approach to this."

"May I say something?"

It brought him up short. *She is far more affected than me.* He exhaled, glanced around. They were waiting for him. *Après moi, le déluge.* He was the cause of the flood. "The damage is done."

"You are the rock tossed in the pond, not I. When you leave, the ripples damp out."

He saw her in his mind's eye, leaning against the counter in her kitchen, willing him calm. *She is right, of course.* Thanks to her cooler head, the avalanche had been averted. "I—"

"Goodbye, Andrew. Ignore it."

The phone went silent as she clicked off. *Brazen it out.* He still wanted to put his fist through something. Someone. So what else was new? Be damned if he changed his behavior one iota for this eejit.

He knows who he is. *If I ever get me hands on that sonofabitch...*

KARY

STOP IT, KARY. ENOUGH. She stared at her hand, still on the cradled phone. *No. Simply no.* She hadn't done anything wrong, wasn't about to do anything wrong, and that sick bit of trash from a random troll was not going to score its desired effect.

Even with her fake bravado when Andrew called, her predictable mind had screamed at her: *'For the good of the film'*? That's the best you could do? You blew it. He gave you the perfect opportunity to disengage, and you *blew* it.

Enough. The good sense to rest her brain, to purge the debris from her cerebral fluid before talking, had restored her ability to make good decisions. It served no purpose to berate herself. Nothing had changed. She still wanted what she would not take. It was none of the world's business. Her fingers reached out with longing. She curled them back into a fist. *And I still won't touch him.*

She picked the handset up again, turned the counter stool so she could look out the breakfast nook windows to the birdfeeder. And the baffled squirrels, little kamikaze thieves. She'd never seen the white squirrel again. *Predators? When the snow stopped hiding its winter-favorable mutation?*

She punched Elise's number on speed dial.

"Kary! Thank God! Where have you been?"

"Writing." *And going through a black hole in the space-time continuum.* "Where would I be? Good morning to you, too."

Silence on the other end.

"Elise? You there?" Mean, mean, to let Elise think she hadn't seen. *I* feel *mean.*

"Kary— Did you—? Have you—?"

"I was hoping you were calling to tell me you found a publisher for Akiiya's story. Did you?"

"Ah— Well— There are one or two distinct possibilities there, but—"

"I thought you were hoping for an auction."

"Well, I am, but I'm waiting for the full final outline—and some finished chapters—it's a departure, Kary. No one will touch it until they can hold it in their hands. Not in this climate. Not even from you. *Are* you writing?"

"I'm working on it. In fact—" *and it wasn't even a lie* "—I was just finishing one of the early chapters this morning, and I can't wait to send it to you, and the outline is done but it needs a couple tweaks after this morning." *I am a bad, bad person.* "If I don't suffer any major distractions, I should be able to get it to you by the end of the week." *Which* is *a lie, because this is going to cost me, no matter what I say.*

"Ah—" Long silence. "That will be really good."

"You don't sound convinced, Elise. What's up?"

"Kary, I hate to be the one to tell you this..."

Two can play at this game. "Tell me what?"

~ 315 ~

"Do you get the *State of the Union*?"

"I glance at it sometimes for national news. Why?"

"Did you read it today?"

"Elise, you're scaring me."

"There's— uh— something you should see."

"Why?"

"Because— I think you should see it."

"I usually pick up the paper when I go down for the mail." *Literally true. Sin of omission.* "What is it? Read it to me." You are going to hell. *Very funny.*

"It's just that your name came up— In one of the Hollywood gossip columns—"

"Really? Because of the possible option for *Prairie Fires*? You haven't sent me anything on that yet, have you?"

"It's just about ready for the mail—have to get the lawyer to take a quick look." Pause. "Listen, Kary. There's gossip about you in the paper—and you need to know about it." The last bit came out all of a rush.

"Read me the gossip." She put the kind of authority into the words which she would use with an intern who was hiding lab results.

"I—"

"Read it, Elise."

Elise complied, with stops and starts, tripping over 'mountain compound' and going silent after 'you'll know as soon as we do.'

Kary let Elise hear her sigh. "Is that all?" *I am* really *going to hell.*

"But— You told me he never— Kary, what's going on over there? Is this *true*?"

"Does it matter? It's gossip, Elise. Get your mind out of the gutter."

"But—"

The nature of the professional relationship—Elise was not her friend: Elise was her *agent*—struck Kary as it hadn't before. *True friends come down on your side—by default.* Huge mistake, thinking of a friendly relationship as friendship. She leaned wearily on the kitchen counter. "But you are worried how this will affect my sales."

"Well, of course. That's my *job*, Kary. You know that. I have a long list of calls waiting to be returned. This could give you the publicity that would make sales skyrocket, give you an in with some of the biggest publishers, as long as we respond quickly."

I know now. "'Respond'? To what? No."

"So you *have* seen him?"

You had your fun; now consequences. "Not that it's any of your *business*, Elise, but yes, several people from the film, including Grant Sykes, have been to my home. Which is why you got the contact for the option."

"Has he come by himself? At '*odd* hours of the day and night'?" Elise spoke clearly and deliberately.

Elise is not your friend. Elise is your *agent*. It is professional, and always must be. *I liked it better before.* This is the present: you don't have the luxury of remaining always loyal—to an agent. *Only as long as she's on my side.* She may not even be the agent for Akiiya—this may be the time to find another agent, before Elise can send anything out. "Elise, listen. Listen carefully. I'm only saying this once."

"It's my fault. I should never have given him your address."

She visualized Elise at the big cluttered desk in the Manhattan office, dirty sky hovering to the horizon, instead of the twin towers, air which never completely lost its aroma of exhaust. The room was so Elise, cluttered, but somehow organized, under control. She had never figured out whether Elise's frantic *modus operandi* was real or whether Elise found it a convenient facade to hide behind. But it worked. Heart-stopping the negotiations had been each time Elise had put her books out for auction, and each time the financial rewards had almost blown her mind. *Our relationship has been based on my anonymity.*

"I'll make this perfectly clear. Again." *Exactly as I did after I met Andrew.* "It is the deal-breaker, understand? My personal life is off limits." *However uninteresting.* "I don't give interviews. *Night Talk* was one-of-a-kind, and won't be repeated. For now, you do *not* have my permission to send out *anything* to *anyone* regarding Akiiya's story. You will make no promises as my agent, and I will consider carefully what I want to do when *I* am ready to start selling it. My plan *changed*: I won't be marketing it at all until it is finished, which may take *years*. Repeat that back to me." She waited for the too-precise echo. "Send it to me, *in writing*, with your signature. Two copies. I will return one copy, signed, so that we are in perfect agreement."

"Are you canceling our agency agreement?" Elise's voice went faint, as if she were very far away.

"No." *Yes. Maybe.* "Not for now. You are my agent of record." Well-rewarded, ever since Zoë's agent recommended the manuscript for *Prairie Fires. Would I have even made it through Elise's slushpile?* "I can't take the pressure, and you know it." Nasty, but necessary.

And I couldn't have done this eight years ago. "I'm tired now, Elise. Goodbye."

~ ~ ~

AT LEAST THIS MORNING'S work is salvaged from the wreckage. Her favorite sunny breakfast nook was suddenly too bright.

Had it been only a few short months since the fateful decision to go on a NY talk show?

She had changed so much and so wrenchingly inside. Hard to remember how she had needed her family and her friends so much to keep her from being a totally isolated hermit, when they had been her sole contact with the world—and she had been aware of how much more she needed them than they—each of them with a busy bustling life—had needed her. How she felt grateful and then resentful when any one had given her a crumb of attention. Yes. Even Elise.

And how even the crumb felt like it was crammed down her throat, too much to swallow—because they were heedless of her time and energy when they *did* call or come. Feast—famine. Drought—monsoon. And then they were annoyed when she couldn't keep up. *Healthy people have no idea what it really means.* They couldn't fathom. They seemed surprised, each time she talked to them, that she was still ill. *Is the word 'chronic' now marked 'Archaic' in the dictionary?* If she'd been in the hospital, they would have been at her bedside for weeks. *They don't understand how long a life sentence is. Stupid medical research can't even agree on a definition.* And she had to pretend, each time, to be 'as well as possible'—to reassure *them.*

She shook her head ruefully. Now she almost resented the time and effort it took to talk each one of her supporters off the ledge. *If I can call Elise a supporter any more.*

She stood up, walked the few steps to the answering machine to cradle the handset.

Two more weeks. If the column had not been published... He would have been gone tomorrow and the tip worthless, a more-current scandal in its place. If the original estimate for the end of the movie hadn't been extended. If. If. *If.*

She knew, deep in her bones, she'd been wrong to not say anything sooner—just as much as it had been the right instinct to let no one in on her obsession or her offer of Sanctuary. *Great: irreconcilable conflicting moral positions.*

The rest of the phone calls? *I have to.* They loved her and would be there for her after... *Derail that thought.* It was her obligation as a member of a societal unit. Hiding wouldn't help. *Or I'd be sorely tempted to not answer the phone.* For a month? After she'd just burned a bridge with Elise. Lovely. Fine. *Sucks being a grownup.* And where the hell had she picked up 'sucks'?

She would pour it into Akiiya. And, if anyone read her in the far future, some pedantic academic would investigate, and make the connection and state, in a dry academic paper long after Kary was dead, that *'the timeline of this novel* clearly *shows the link between the petty life of the now-elderly recluse author and the bright movie star who dropped into her life for a brief shining moment'*—or some other crap. *So I can roll over in my grave.*

Cut it out, Kary. Mine the despair, and the whatever-you-called-this, save it in notes and characters and novels. It hurts too much otherwise.

Now get out of the kitchen—it's getting depressing in here.

She grabbed the wireless receiver from the dining room, set grimly to her task: who first?

Call Aunt Ruth? *And say what?* Would staff or cousins dare show her the article—because she and Ruth shared a last name? *Shit.* Ruth was forewarned, would act mildly interested and change the subject. *There is nothing going on, Aunt Ruth.* Was that what made it so unfair? No, there would be time later for Ruth. It wouldn't matter one whit—what was a whit, anyway?—once he returned to the Heavens, leaving her not even in Hell, or in Purgatory serving her time, but in long-discredited Limbo from which there was no exit. *I will be stranded in an alternate universe far from my former peace, with no way to return, and no peace ahead.*

Not Susan. Not yet. Zoë.

Out on the deck. It would be cooler, less stuffy on the deck. She fetched more seed for the feeder. Darn the acrobatic squirrels—they managed to dump a bite of seed when they set it swinging. Typical:

causing chaos to get a trifle for themselves. Such a clear drama-less day: no wind, no clouds, no storms—no day to expect an avalanche—but that's when they were most treacherous—when you never thought they'd happen.

A raven cawed loudly at the feeder as she approached, and flapped off in annoyance. Kary stared: under the feeder, at the very edge of the deck railing, was a soft white pile. Her shoulders slumped. It wasn't moving. She closed her eyes, steeled herself. It had come when Andrew came, and now it was dead at her feet. Tears threatened, rose. She suppressed them savagely. She had obligations. The bird would be back, with reinforcements; she would have but a moment if she wanted to protect the little body, deprive its murderer of the prize. She whirled, returned quickly with her choice of shroud: one of the new dishtowels from her stash, white with a narrow band of blue at the hem. The thought of allowing the garden soil to befoul the white fur, meticulously cleaned in life by the tiny tongue, was wrong.

She sunk cross-legged to the deck, laid the cloth out, lifted the small stiff body with its neck at an awkward, loose angle. She laid it with care on the towel, marveling at the fur, coarse outer strands over the silky undercoat. Its eyes were dull, the red of the true albino. Had it not seen the crow? The genetic weakness might have cost it life. Or was it no longer hidden against the snow, and thus easy prey? It didn't matter. Nothing mattered for it any more—its one chance was over.

She blinked the stupid tears away again, set to her final task for the little omen. She had known the right box, had picked it and a pen up on her way through the living room where it awaited more of the photographs which now came from the girls in digital form instead of printed. A silly, gaudy box the size of a small shoebox, with a metal insert on the front holding a blank label for its contents. She placed the squirrel gently in the box, tucking the towel around it to fill the space. She wrote, 'White Squirrel,' and the date.

She carried the box out to the garden, supervised by the gathering murder, dug a hole deep into the friable loam under the rhododendron. There were no words: either God took His creatures home, or He didn't. She wasn't a pet person.

She went back up to the deck where she'd left the phone, and called Zoë. Zoë had cats. Zoë would understand.

At least Zoë would care little about the negative publicity—it would float serenely, unexamined and unexplored over Zoë's colleagues—Zoë hadn't talked much about her friend, writer K. Beth Winter, and they might not have made the connection even if one of them had watched *Night Talk*. Ivory tower inhabitants all—or just most? *Without Zoë's rock-solid support, I wouldn't have made it this far.* "Zoë? It's me, Kary. Can you talk?"

Zoë was sarcastic, curious, oddly compassionate. "You old dog."

"I *tried* to invite you on Memorial Day; I couldn't get a word in edgewise."

"Try harder."

"You would have fit right in." *If I were sleeping with him, this would have been so much harder. Small consolation. I'll take what I can get right now.* "Grant Sykes talked about optioning *Fires*."

"Really? That's wonderful."

"He wants me to take a stab at the screenplay."

"Not bad, not bad. You really should. You're not taking enough chances professionally."

"If he decides to go ahead." *Grant's faith in her ability might falter when the press dug up gossip if the project went ahead—he had financing considerations. But I could walk away—satisfy contractual obligations if any—disengage.*

"You'd be perfect." But Zoë was chuckling. *My status with Zoë has changed.*

Kary visualized her friend—Zoë's defense against the chaos of two teenage boys was a cleaning service and an attitude and a pristine office on campus. And a mantra: 'If you can't find it, it's your problem. We're leaving.' For hockey or school or swimming class. Somehow it worked. For her. "I love you, too." *Another one down.*

Susan next? No. *Coward.* Ronnie first, but Ronnie was probably in class. Or at the apartment? Ronnie's untidy apartment with friends? She shuddered. Ronnie knew where everything *was*—but she didn't need to have it *in* organized containers. *I use to have that kind of total recall—what I'd do to get it back.* Kary returned to the kitchen to locate her cellphone on its charger, accommodating to Ronnie's preference for text. *Who cares about my preferences?* Oh, shut up—you're getting tired, and it shows. Handle the whole thing with a quick text? Maybe. What was it with the preference for texting? You lost all nuance. Maybe that *was* the point.

She shut her eyes for a moment before turning the cellphone on, refusing the adrenaline which threatened, slowing her thoughts down viciously and deliberately, wondering again how this very useful physical process had no negative repercussions. *Odd. Un-*

Freudian. If I am thinking the elephant is blue, I can't also think the elephant is yellow. Psychology wasn't yet as 'science' as it would like to claim to be, but it was definitely useful to 'know yourself.' To make the conscious choice to block her own emotions. *Like a Vulcan.* She *felt* like a Vulcan.

Not fair to prefer talking to Ronnie—just because she is easier than Susan right now. Not fair to either. She planned her message to Ronnie: 'Call me when you want to chat.' Which she knew perfectly well Ronnie wouldn't do unless Kary called her first. *I'm feeling fragile and worn and vulnerable.* Too much power for one pint-sized hand-held apparatus. She clicked the monster to 'on.'

Ronnie beat her to it:

> mom one of my friends asked if andrew oconnell is going to be my stepdad. i popped him one. i told him i have a father. sheesh.
> really need to talk to you

Kary texted back:

> Hi honey. Ignore rumors. Will explain when I see you.
> Love you.

It would have been good to connect with Veronica. Ronnie was level-headed—she would understand. *I have gone from nonentity to gossip fodder in one well-timed tip.* So close to perceived reality—so far from truth. One thought niggled: Ronnie *never* 'needed' to talk. *Am I imagining things because my nerves are raw?* Peace, Kary. Peace. She blew the tension out, slowly, three long surrender breaths.

Susan now? Susan. Then another nap? *We'll see.* Kary walked slowly to the living room, propped herself comfortably in a nest of pillows. She needed support when talking to Susan these days. *Is there is something wrong with Greg?* If Susan divorced him, Susan would want to come live with her mother. Kary would be very happy to take her in, and love her and Stephen, and help her get her life in order—but the very thought of the energy it would require to deal with the drama was daunting. And there was nothing in it for Kary, because the minute Susan could stand on her own two feet, she would be pushing her mother away again. *Sigh. Just doing my job.* Kary would handle it. Somehow, she always handled it. *So far.*

But if Susan moved in, Kary would get attached to Stephen, and then her heart would be ripped out again when Susan took Stephen with her to their new lives. *Stop it, Kary.* None of this is happening. You are just being a writer. *Real life drama.* Soap opera, you mean. *Oh, shut up.*

From her nest on the couch she could see the family picture Andrew picked up: Susan before new adulthood hit, before she was a mother herself, before... everything. Beautiful blonde Susan with the perfect long straight hair and perfect cheerleader smile, even at that age. Susan shimmering.

Maybe she won't be in, and I can leave voicemail. She hadn't bothered to listen to Susan's likely hysterical messages. The thought made her tired. *How did I produce such a reactionary daughter?*

No such luck. Kary dialed her eldest's cellphone; it answered on the first ring. She braced herself. "Susan, it's Mom."

"I called three times! Where *were* you?"

"Where I always am at this time of day. Writing. You know that."

"Mom, what is going on? All our friends are calling me about that *thing* in the paper. They all wanted to know if it was true."

Kary didn't have the stomach to pretend not to know what Susan was talking about. *It would only prolong the agony.* "Well, it's partially true. Mr. O'Connell stays here sometimes."

"You hardly know him!"

Really, Susan. "He's a very nice young man, and I offered him a place to get away from nosy strangers. He comes when he needs to hide out."

"Mother! I can't believe you'd do this! Think how this makes me look! You're old enough to be his mother!"

"I'm needing a moment to think about what you just said, honey." She paused, not to consider the alternatives—those were clear—but to regain control of her voice. Her most vulnerable spot. "That's enough, Susan. I am perfectly competent to make my own decisions. Won't you be here soon? We can talk then."

"I'm in Princeton with Daddy. He said he ran into one of *my* friends at the grocery store and she asked—"

In Princeton already? *And Charles grocery shopping? Now that's—*

"Mother! Are you listening?"

"Of course, baby. But you have to stop this nonsense right now. Whatever your father said—"

"He said, 'First the trashy novels, and now your slut of a mother's sleeping around with movie stars!'" Susan's voice faltered. "And then he raved on about how you're ruining his life and making him a laughingstock..."

And you repeat this to me—why? "I thought we were past this, Susan. I thought we agreed—" She closed her eyes wearily, sighed. "You can't let your father's opinion of me—" *No, that wasn't going right.* "Don't repeat what he says. Don't answer him—"

"I didn't!"

"Let it go by you, like—"

"—water off a duck's back. I *know*, Mother."

But you keep doing it. "Good girl. Now, if there were anything going on, don't you think I'd tell my own daughter?"

"Well, yes, but—"

"There is *nothing* going on, honey. People are busybodies and gossips and...?"

"And I shouldn't give them anything but a blank stare." Susan's voice was calmer. "I'm sorry, Mom."

"You don't have to apologize, honey. You know I love you more than anything."

"Me, too, Mom."

"Call me when you have some time to chat?" *About Greg?* "Not now—Elise is really pushing for the outline for the new book..." *If Elise is speaking to me at all.*

"I will. Love you, Mom. Gotta go."

Talking to Susan left her drained. *'You're only as happy as your least happy child.'* The stages of a child's life could be tedious. Susan's effort to free herself as a wife and mother from the taint of her parents' divorce was one such tedious stage. And the divorce happened just as Susan was pushing her mother away to become her own independent self. *She is right to be angry with me, wrong to take it out on me, and too young to see it yet.* She couldn't love Susan any less, but it was sometimes hard to like Susan. Which makes you a bad mother. *No. Stop.* Automatic negative thought. *It merely makes me a mother.* Susan would learn not to be affected by her mother's life.

Kary's own mother warned her: don't marry a surgeon, a politician, or a pilot. *'Their work requires them to be God, and you don't have the temperament of a Handmaiden.'* She'd forgotten about Charles—none of the blinking lights on the answering machine displayed the Princeton phone number still engraved in her psyche. Trust Charles to take a shot at her; it wasn't as if *he'd* ever done anything unconventional, say, taking up with a student nurse? *Careful, Kary, that path is mined. And you officially don't care what Charles does.*

Charles played into the idolatrous unconditional love of 'Daddy's girl.' When he filed for divorce, Kary had gone from incredulous, to hurt, to not wanting anything to do with him, to a level of civility because Amanda tried, and because of Ethan. *But this is the last straw.*

Not through Susan.

It would take time to heal what Charles had carelessly done to Susan in one stupid rant. She wanted to strangle Charles's aristocratic neck with his non-Princeton tie.

So one more thing—before the *required* extra rest. Gathering snow and speed, the avalanche roared down the mountain. She barely managed to slip aside while it thundered by.

She called, gave Joseph Farentz, Esq., very precise instructions. *Not through my cubs, Charles.*

BIANCA

Bunker Hill; 7 P.M.

DID I LOSE? DAMN ALPHA male. *I'll know—the moment I see him.*

If nothing else, she'd ramped up the voltage on this set, and everyone would be watching her. And him. It bought respect, functioning professionally under stress.

Bianca opened her well-stocked refrigerator, perused the row of protein shakes with their lying labels, selected the container of Double Fudge Caramel Chocolate, grimaced. She cracked the plastic screwtop, took a whiff. 'Artificial flavors' greeted her nose like the impostors they were.

Where was the bastard? She knew he had major scenes all day with the second unit. Grant liked to do his own sex scenes so he could 'protect' his leading ladies. *Supervise, more likely.*

She'd walked back to her trailer in a transparent bubble, leaving the moment Grant released them, remembering to smile warmly for her co-star. *He worked his sexy butt off.* Shower. Moisturizer. Clean

Dior jeans, polo shirt in the deep rose that made her glow, Versace sandals later, she felt almost human.

What if Andrew found out? Relax, it *always* functioned flawlessly before. *Hell owes me for the tips over the years.* No point in having a computer hacker brother if he couldn't set it up. If Andrew roared off on that stupid motorcycle at 'odd hours of the day and night,' anyone could follow him. *What if Andrew is sleeping with the whore?* It would explain his attitude—maybe she'd find out. *In which case I'm screwed anyway.*

She filled herself a large goblet with crushed ice, eyed the shake with something near revulsion. She was trapped in this hell-hole prison with nowhere safe to go. *If I had a hog like Andrew's for a ride in the countryside.* Or they would let her borrow a horse, but after what happened to her 'mother'—*send her flowers, by the way*—there was no way in hell Grant would let her ride a horse.

She took the glass and the shake container to the dreadful 'breakfast nook,' set them down next to her copy of the script with its multicolored change pages. She was starving, hollow, but it wasn't for food, and her lines for the next two days were already memorized. The fastest way to ruin a career was to fluff lines; she had no patience for actors who were unprepared, a trait she was happy to share with Andrew. *'Is work, Bibi. They wanna see you make it look easy, and that's the hardest thing, but you never disappoint. Do your homework.'*

Doing his homework. That's what Papi called the hours of singing, practice, and lessons that came first in his life. *When he wasn't quite handsome enough, quite good enough, quite* white *enough.* She could see him in her mind's eye vocalizing in front of the mirror to make himself conscious of the position of every facial muscle that affected the quality of the sound.

Once more can't hurt. She opened the laptop, prepared to record herself for fine-tuning. Check first—had Tonya answered her email from last night? Text—not email. Hmm. She brought up the Message program. *Shit—video message from Michael.*

Michael's vapid handsome face. Short. Vague. *'Hope you're okay—what the Hell is going on down there? We need to talk. I'm here for you.'* The big black fly in the ointment buzzed again. Twelve hours ago. She jabbed Delete. Her stomach clenched. *Be careful, Bi—the whole world watches.*

No. Wait. Survival. Always survival. *'Don't burn the bridges, Bibi. Not before the war is over.'* Other than the purely physical need now for Andrew O'Connell, alpha male, bastard, what else was at stake here? *My survival.* Where? *Here, where I can work, be the best.*

And? *Michael isn't allowed to jump ship unless I release him.* She just might get him now. But not video—that took more effort. Grab cell. Dial.

"Hi, babe. What's up?"

"You're not telling me somebody in Canada has time to read that crap?" Incredulity into the voice. Warmth. "You're not keeping them busy enough."

"Whatcha doin'?"

"Running lines?"

"Alone?"

"And then bed. The usual boring."

"What's got Hell in a snit?"

"Damned if I know—it couldn't be more normal here. Chaos." Divert. *'Bird in hand, princess. Bird in hand.'* "The *last* thing I need tonight is sex."

"Oh? You sure? I could be there in a couple of hours."

"After I spent the day coaxing my new husband to actually touch me? I don't think so."

Michael laughed. "John any good faking it?"

"I think he's a camera-virgin. Was." *He is so young.* She had reached for his hand, put it on her breast. 'This isn't fake.' He had gone scarlet. Malleable.

"Usual crowd ogling?"

"Grant runs a tight ship."

"Learning?"

"He wanted it filmed both ways, brazen new lover, nervous awkward new husband, so he can choose in editing—if he uses it at all." *I learned: low-budget films like Dodgson can't afford Grant's indecision.*

"What a waste." Michael cleared his throat. "You know—we should talk."

Shit. SHIT. Attack. "You telling me you have something on the side up there?"

"What?"

"See what I mean? We can't 'talk' this way." *Good enough?*

"Fine. But I can't wait to get you home. Snip this PR mess in the bud, you know, make an announcement—?"

"Good." *Over my dead body.* She put her hand around her own delicate neck, wondered what Andrew would do if he found out what she'd been up to? She *knew* what Michael would do—and so far, she'd let him. "How's the documentary coming? Are you capturing the light?" Let Michael jabber. *Michael is so over.* She made the right responses automatically, helped him end it when he ran out of 'sharing.' She couldn't wait to get off the phone.

But had it been enough? She stared at the 'shake.'

Check the text from Tonya first. *I need—what?*

Tonya IM'd: 'Been trying to reach you all day. Show's at 8. Text me. Love, Toe.'

Oh, right. They were both on East coast time. 7:15—Tonya would be fiddling with makeup in her dressing room, ready, even though they wouldn't actually need her on stage for almost an hour. She texted back: 'Toe? You alone?'

The phone in her hand rang. "Hey, Bi. Yeah, alone. What gives? You know this bunch—anything with a whiff of New York catches their eye."

"New York?" She'd forgotten Hell's little addition. "Oh, right. You know what they're like out in L. A.—if they don't get something for a while, they make it up. Grant's ignoring the whole thing."

"Goings on with the local author?"

Bianca gave her throwaway laugh. "How should I know? He disappears every once in a while, goes motorcycle riding in the hinterlands." *That was the right tone—uninterested in the extreme.* "She's nice—had us all over Memorial Day. She's even looking at *Dodgson* for me."

"That a good idea?"

"Andrew suggested it—she's a writer. Can't hurt—I don't have to pay attention to anything she suggests."

"Getting work for his girlfriend? Kinda ballsy of him."

"Grant seems to think she's the cat's pajamas. He's really quite comical—wants her to write him a screenplay. Oh, God. Don't tell anyone that—it's supersecret right now."

"My lips are sealed—until you tell me."

"Thanks, Toe. Grant'd kill me."

"This wasn't Grant's little publicity scheme for your movie, was it?"

Diversion—gift from the gods? "I don't think so. It's not really Grant's style—he was very close-mouthed today. Didn't mention it to any of us."

"Which reminds me. Has Andrew signed on the dotted line?"

"I think Andrew's agent is trying to avoid the whole deal—I'm casting alternates." *Be careful—I was an imbecile to even talk to her about Andrew.*

"You're better off without him then. Wimp. What's the excuse—I thought he was interested?"

"Something more lucrative lined up?"

"Andrew needs a lesson on the fine art of dumping an agent who thinks he owns you. And how's your love life?"

Bianca heard *'Five minutes, Ms. Illstrom,'* and a door shut at Tonya's end. "Michael says hello." *Close enough.*

"Did you talk to him?"

"Ten minutes ago."

"Give him my love." Chair drag sounds—Tonya was getting up. "He isn't going to wait forever, Bi."

"What's the big rush? Now? So the gossips can have their 'rebound wedding' after that stupid rumor? Get serious, Toe."

"Later, okay?"

"Later. Go. Break a leg."

A graceful way out if I need one? Where was that bastard Andrew tonight, anyway? Mess tent? Trailer? *I cannot go out looking.* Another trip for a 'beer'—out of the question. She picked up the stupid shake. Add Vodka? Call it a Black Russian—to match her mood?

Andrew's fans were probably up in arms. *My fans?* She could already see the reaction—rampant innuendo, rabid support. Some still followed her from her soap opera days. *As long as I perform.* Does that woman even have fans? Probably—reader types. *Tread carefully.*

Something caught her ear outside her trailer, and was followed almost immediately by a loud knocking on the door. She went to open it, found she was still carrying the despised 'Gourmet meal replacement.'

The whole lot of them stood there sheepishly, Andrew on her top step with the expression of a naughty teenager on Halloween. "M'lady. Yer loyal servants have come to take ye to dinner."

What is going on? "I have my dinner," she held it up. "I was about to pour it over ice."

"We have decided," Andrew included John, George, Peter, and Grant in his royal 'we,' "that after all yer *hard* work today," he winked in John's general direction, "ye should be feted properly tonight and come to dinner with yer clan."

Testosterone? Cologne? Pheromones? It didn't matter. Even in a crowd, even playing the buffoon. *The alpha male protects what's his.* The smell was power—and she understood power. She glanced back at the table. "I think my ice has melted."

"Give it here." Andrew took the shake, opened it, sniffed, made a face, screwed the lid back on. He offered his arm.

At the mess tent, after a walk with the rowdy bunch cavorting like jesters for their queen, Andrew made a show of fetching a goblet of crushed ice, and pouring for her. He lifted the glass ceremoniously. "To *Bunker Hill*."

She accepted it solemnly, acknowledged the toast with an inclination, took the first sip of ambrosia as the 'gourmet' on the label came to life. "To us. To *Bunker Hill*."

Inner circle. Not just colleague, but protected friend. Her heart pounded solidly in her chest, the backs of her arms tingled. She'd been right to act. He was *here* and not there. She loses. *I win.*

But I still have to cut him *from this herd—does he have to be such a blasted extrovert?*

KARY

Sanctuary; 8:30 P.M.

THE BELL RANG. NOT THE phone, the doorbell. *What?*

Not what. Who? *Oh, God—if it's Andrew...* But it wouldn't be. He didn't need to ring—

The bell rang again. Insistently. She went to the intercom. Joseph Farentz, Esquire. *What now?* She pushed the button. "I was waiting for your call." *Stupid. He was here.*

"May I come up?"

"Um. Sorry. Of course." *Why couldn't you do this my way?* She clicked the gate button, watched Joe's gray Lincoln Continental edge through, pass off the screen. The gates swung shut.

She could hear the crackling of the fire she'd been lighting when the bell rang, took the few steps back, checked to make sure it was contained. The clean smell of wood smoke greeted her with its familiar comfort. She glanced around the living room; as usual since she started living alone, nothing out of place beyond what she brought out. She checked her laptop, open on the dining room table, its software ready, legal pads and several pens next to it. She took her dinner plate to the kitchen counter, noted that the last vestiges of day had faded, returned to open the door before Joe could knock.

She inspected the man who stood on her doorstep looking oddly determined, and who had taken the trouble to wear a suit and tie under a navy cashmere peacoat. *No plaid?* "You drove all the way out here, at night, to dissuade me?"

"Can we talk?"

Kary led him wordlessly to the living room.

He unbuttoned his coat when he sat, but did not remove it. "I'm here as your counsel, Kary, but I'm also here as your friend."

"A friend who wants to keep me from doing something rash."

"Which may have negative consequences, yes." He brought his interlaced hands up to point at her with the index fingers. "First, let me ask. Is this in reaction to the, ah, *item*, in the paper today?"

"Are you going to ask me if it's true?"

"Ah, no." He looked around, pursed his lips, fidgeted. "But that *is* the inciting incident, is it not?"

"You could call it that."

"Is there any possibility Charles originated it?" He dipped his head. "In which case, you need to be careful how you react to his bait."

"What? No. There's no way he'd have the contacts—he despises the whole 'Hollywood scene.' And he'd need someone watching me." Her brow furrowed. *Can I please just make the call?* "Why would he do that?"

"A hunch?"

"Which makes no sense."

"Where there's smoke, there's fire. Is there something he still wants at this late date?"

She leaned back into the cushions, stared at the fire. "Yeah. Vindication. He's always known the mess he made of our lives and our family was his fault, and now he can blame it on me." She turned to her friend. "But it seems so unlikely."

"I'm only trying to tease out why that item, and why today."

"I've been doing the same all day. It has to be someone from the crew, but I can't see who benefits. Do they pay people for these 'tips'?"

"Not enough to risk losing your job over. It seemed rather protective of Miss Doyle."

One of her fans? "Bianca? It implies she's been cast aside. For what purpose?"

"A boyfriend with connections to someone on set? He'd want to drive a wedge between her and anyone he sees as competition—what better way than to put her on notice he has eyes everywhere?"

"Which seems pretty farfetched, Joe." *Even for a conspiracy theorist.* "You're getting me tired and confused. And none of this excuses Charles's comments to Susan. Which is why I'm calling him tonight. Regardless of what you say. Did you at least bring the recording equipment I asked you about?"

"Kary, we have a problem."

"Why?"

"I can't. It is illegal to record a conversation in New Hampshire unless *all* parties know and agree to the recording. I'd face disbarment."

"But I'm calling Charles, and he's in New Jersey. Only one person need give consent in New Jersey. I looked it up. Or maybe, because it's between states, Federal law applies."

"If you want to use the recording in court, he needs to know. If you want an injunction. If you want to sue him…" He shrugged delicately, hands outstretched. "Unless you go back, and make this call in New Jersey…?"

"Get real. I'm doing this now." She sighed. "*If* I take notes, and I transcribe them later, can you attest that the transcript is an accurate rendition of the conversation? Will that work?"

"It might. Depends on the court, and the reasons… You know I can't answer those questions. Some things are proscribed by the law—"

"—and everything else is open to interpretation. In court. At great expense and time."

"It's for your protection."

It is for the protection of the guilty. "Does he need to know you're sitting here with me?"

"No. But if he asks, and it matters exactly what he asks, and you lie to him…"

She rolled her eyes. "But him slandering me to our daughter is okay?"

"Did he talk to her in front of witnesses? Witnesses who will testify?"

"Of course not; he's not that stupid."

"Then it's he said/she said—and the credibility of the accuser…"

"She would never testify against her father, and I wouldn't ask her to."

"Then what is the point of this little exercise?"

"Taking a stand, Joe. Taking a stand *somewhere*. He told our friends—*our* friends—that we had amicably decided to separate. I didn't contradict him—what was the point?" *And it was the early days, before I learned to deal with some of the exhaustion, and I was simply too tired to care.* "Charles took a chance, not much of one in his mind. He needs to find out it is *not* okay. Trust me on this one? For Susan?"

"Of course. But wouldn't it be better for you earlier in the day?"

When I'm more coherent? "Charles is never available during the day; he takes his work seriously. He'd be at the hospital." *Dedication—above everything, including wife and children.* She grimaced, wondered how Amanda liked it. Or did she have more power over him? A second divorce would prove he was the one at fault for the first, wouldn't it? *A hit to his precious reputation.* "He didn't like it when I went on TV."

"Hardly his business."

"'People' asked him about it; suddenly, I was a minor celebrity, instead of the woman he cast off as unsuitable. He called. I told him it wasn't a good time, and hung up on him, but he got a few choice words in first."

"Did you record him then?"

"It was over too quickly. I didn't even think to. Then."

She got Joe settled catty-corner from her at the dining room table, slid a yellow legal pad and a pen his way. She didn't need to, but she checked the number she hadn't dialed in half a decade in her laptop's address book. She typed it carefully into Skype, clicked buttons.

"Hello. Renton residence."

"Amanda, it's Kary." She heard TV sounds in the background. "I need to speak to Charles."

"Oh." Long pause; the television sound muted. "He's in his study. I'll tell him."

Moments later Kary heard Amanda talking to Charles, followed by 'Amanda, would you please take Tad to bed? It's late.' Kary heard a door close, recognized the heavy clunk. Charles came on the line. "You interrupted my play time with my son."

Letting Ethan—or Tad—be in the study while you work is not the same as playing with him, Charles. "I'll keep this brief." Kary

~ 333 ~

squared her shoulders. "I will not allow you to slander me and agitate Susan, and if I ever hear of you doing it again, I will take you to court. Is that brief enough?"

"I don't know what the hell you're talking about."

Really, Charles? "She called me, very upset. She told me you said, and I quote: 'First the trashy novels, and now your slut of a mother's sleeping around with movie stars!'"

"She's exaggerating. I meant—"

"Did you slander me to my daughter? Did you say those words?"

"Well, I must have said something about your new friend—"

"In those words? To my daughter?"

He exhaled sharply. "Yes, I did. Susan is a Renton. She is *my* daughter." His tone was utter contempt, the cutting tone of the head of the Department of Neurosurgery dressing down a lowly intern for a beginner's clumsiness. "And you've made both of us—*and* Veronica—a laughingstock. There. Are you satisfied?"

"Until now, I never told the children what you did, because I knew we would all have to live with the aftermath of whatever was said during that time." *Peace at any price—for the children.* "But even Ethan knew. You are a very foolish man, Charles, and I am fortunate to be rid of you." Something—her trampled vows, her allegiance to Mother Church, her good Catholic guilt—cracked and gave way. *What did I ever see in him?* "I will be happy to mail your lawyer a copy of this conversation." She ignored Joe's horrified gestures.

"You're not recording this!"

"It is recorded. I don't trust you any more." *And I am recorded telling the whole world there is nothing between Andrew and me.*

"You can't use that in a court of law!"

"My lawyer is shaking his head. I have no intention of using it— in a court of law." The surface of the newly-halted snow mass was untracked wilderness in all directions—only the mountain peak remained in its former place. And, after the chaos, she could not remember how high it was before, and whether the avalanche had now reached the piedmont and used up its potential energy in fury—or whether, instead, it had paused on a high ledge, and was even now accumulating mass and instability for another roar. *If Charles chooses to escalate...*

"There are other Courts. Goodbye, Charles." *Go to hell, Charles.*

๑ **CHAPTER SIXTEEN** ๑

"...a time to mourn, and a time to dance..."
(Ecclesiastes 3:4, KJV)

Word has it that fans lucky enough to be in Hanover,
N.H., USA, may wait long hours (check the daily shooting schedule at www.BunkerHillIncident), but are rewarded with an appearance by Andrew and other members of the cast, sometimes including director Grant
Sykes. Be warned, however, that the shoots can end in
the very wee hours. Completion of main photography fast
approaching June 16.
Thanks to Jonathan H. for the pics.

www.AOCORNER

And see, and, behold, if the daughters of Shiloh come out
to dance in dances [...] and catch you every man his wife
of the daughters of Shiloh...

Judges 21:21, KJV

KARY

Sanctuary; **Tue., June 7; 3 P.M.**

THERE ARE NO ANSWERS on the mountaintop. On her granite
throne, Kary surveyed her domain, Queen of green in every direction. *Maybe the questions will be clearer?*

Insects buzzed, and the only other sound was a faint rustling of
leaves in the overhead pin oak which thrived on in the dominant
position on her hill's crest, its one scar from lightning almost hidden in dense late-spring foliage.

She extracted the letter from her backpack, turned it round and
round in her hands. Heavy cream-colored paper, full of its own self-
importance, its ability to strike fear in the heart of the recipient.

Law offices of Laurence Binkman, III. The crest in the corner was embossed in orange and black: he *had* gone to Princeton. Charles's prep school classmate of hated memory, the 'family friend' with the capacity to confuse her during the divorce hearings, twist her words, make her look stupid on the stand. *Renton* family friend.

This is my *home.* Charles wasn't supposed to be able to reach in here and twist her soul.

The thing with Charles—she'd known, from the instant she hung up on him, that he wouldn't be able to let it go.

Choose your behavior, Kary, choose your consequences.

It had been the writing day from hell. Well, maybe Hell was the trigger, but there *must* be more powerful forces at play than a columnist thousands of miles away scratching in dirt.

Last night's emails from the girls? They were *both* in Princeton now, visiting Charles and their half-brother, Tad the Invader. She calculated: Tad would be eight now. She wondered how they described Amanda, who was too young to be called 'stepmother' except in derision. Susan forwarded, in her orderly fashion, a copy of their airline itinerary. Ronnie repeated, 'cant wait need to talk,' the wriggling worm in the ointment.

Kary had borne the impending doom into the writing room, a burden she tried to give to Akiiya: Akiiya went up, not down, when she retook her freedom, to the parched rocky peak of The Sentinel, on K'Tae, to put her thoughts in order. Once Akiiya got off the mountain, she would have decisions to make, plans to set in motion, the last major battle of her private conflict to deal with in the middle of a war between worlds.

Kary couldn't write it. She did everything right: timer set, notebook on the clear desk, files open for any thought her mind would care to drop. When it made no difference, she blamed lack of sleep, forced herself to get out the emergency cot from the closet in the moving room, breathed through the rarity of an extra nap to clear her mind of everything but the writing. To no avail.

It happened, less frequently now that she was her own mistress, but she reminded herself every writer faced blank screens at one time or another. Even more unusual, her usual solution, to write out why she could *not* write, also failed. But her contract with herself was time, not words, for this very reason. Process didn't fail. Process would work tomorrow. *No cause to panic. Yet.*

When the last timer released her, she pushed away from the desk.

Rest? The cot was still out. Another rest, after the failed writing session, would clear her mind. *Discipline.*

It didn't. She folded the cot into its cubby, closed the door, her mind still chasing from crag to crag like a mountain goat.

Safety in routine—food first? Emptiness could always be starvation—she had a bad tendency to let herself get too empty to note hunger.

She postponed the kitchen visit on a thought: the postman might happily provide junk mail to distract herself with over lunch. She tied her boots, tucked her cellphone into the outer pocket of the small backpack with its half-finished bottle of water and dried out emergency granola bars, and hiked down to the gate.

Good. She'd been afraid he would be late today, depriving her of circulars and the local throwaway with the baseball scores for the middle school in Enfield, football and basketball and track results for the farther district high school in Hanover.

The metal bin yielded a surprise cardboard box, its weight and shape an indicator for books she didn't remember ordering. Curious, she used a sharp-edged rock to slit the plastic tape: four fat trade paperbacks on screenwriting, with a note on the invoice where the online bookstore provided space for the customer's message which said, 'Get to work. Love, Grant.' A ray of warmth on a gloomy writing day. *He was serious, then.*

She put the package into the backpack. She faced the next task: the IED she had been waiting for.

Not here.

She placed the envelope along with the rest of the junk mail into the backpack, headed for home.

But when she got to her stoop, she couldn't face taking the garbage into her home.

Instead, she abandoned the heavy books on the granite step, shouldered the pack again, and emulated Akiiya's climb. For women, there was no guru on the mountain, only time and space to think.

Akiiya had to make do with the stark shade of the crag; Kary got her scarred oak.

And the heavy cream envelope which was her due for defiance.

She fought the impulse to shred the unopened missive, to reduce it to a powder so fine it could be used, without further processing, as raw material for toilet paper. *Consequences, Kary.* The humiliation of having to ask Binkman for a second copy? Of not facing whatever nonsense they concocted?

She set the envelope on a round flat stone and stared at it. Consequences. That's what it was all about, what it had *always* been about. The consequences of standing up in front of half of Princeton at Saint Augustine's modernistic altar, Charles's parents in one front pew, hers in the other. The consequences of taking vows for all eternity, in the bosom of Holy Mother Church. The consequences of belief in the sanctity of marriage, deep in her soul. For better or for worse. In richer and in poorer—which was a laugh after the settlement Binkman extorted. In sickness and in health—*but not if I got ill.* Bound, in her own mind—what had she said to Dr. Moreno? 'According to the Church, I'm still married.'

Was there any meat on that picked-over carcass?

Consequences for her, seemingly no consequences for him. *I consider myself married—he does not? He moves on easily—I cannot?* Scruples?

Excessive scruples are bad.

Holding myself to a higher standard.

Being more Catholic than the Pope.

I know that sin: it's called Pride. Pride in its most virulent and insidious form, the Pride of the Fallen One.

In desperation she worked the ground she had scraped over with her hoe and rake, cultivator and harrow, so many times before. *What did I miss?*

Her head hurt. Her theology was out of date, shaky, overly fundamentalist.

She had refused to testify at the Ecclesiastical Tribunal—Charles had gotten an annulment hearing, anyway. Apparently, her absence wasn't an impediment for the Tribunal.

So they sent a priest round from the Diocese of Trenton, a roly-poly man from Goa with a sing-song accent, to 'talk to you.' 'The Church has two requirements for a valid marriage: that you be free to marry, and that you intend to commit to each other only, until death do you part.'

What else did the priest say? 'It is my duty only to collect the best evidence I can—and your husband—or I should say, your *putative* husband, is alleging you were too young and immature to truly understand what you were promising when you married him. You were, ah, how old...?'

She stared at him. 'I was twenty-two.' She skewered him with her gaze. 'I understand the age of consent for women is fourteen?'

'Twelve, actually, with parental approval. I, ah, would not advise it.' He smiled as if he disagreed with official teachings. 'Would you, ah, consider that you were certain, in your own mind? You were not *immature*?'

'He said what?' She stared at the priest in disbelief. 'I had just finished *medical* school. Hardly a child not to know my own mind.'

'You had sufficient time to consider, ah, the *gravity* of your commitment?'

Was he offering her an out? 'No way in hell, Father. I had the mental capacity to make the decision. I had every intention,' she spoke distinctly, enunciating, 'of marrying Charles Renton and of keeping my vows *forever.*' It took all her civility. Charles, with a child on the way, requesting permission to marry his mistress in the Church, blamed *her?* 'And now, would you please leave?'

Had fury kept her from seeing things clearly?

Two people. They were both free to marry: of sound mind, with no previous marriages.

Her intent had been clear.

But was his?

Had she missed that? Did *he* go through the motions, a farce to satisfy his parents, while reserving the right to do as he pleased—from the very beginning? She ignored the rumors, of dalliances even as they prepared for the wedding, believed him when he said it was malicious gossip. Had he never *intended* monogamy?

Why on earth hadn't he told the Tribunal? Their deliberations were confidential. *Pride?* Had he lied to them, taken no responsibility, assumed he could blame it on her? *He did blame it on me.* And then it was too late, because he had perjured himself?

Did Charles unwittingly block his own annulment? *Ultimate irony.*

She released all the air in her lungs; stared, blind, at the horizon.

You did your best. It wasn't your fault, Kary.

I was never married. She laughed mirthlessly. The civil wedding was valid—all the requirements of the State had been met—she was dumped from that by divorce. *But the one which mattered, the sacramental marriage I have been faithful to all these years?* That *never existed.* The Roman Catholic Church didn't allow dissolution of a valid marriage in cases of adultery, only separation. *My 'marriage' simply never was.*

You've been hiding behind your faith.

Why?

To avoid dating Zoë's colleague, men, getting hurt again.

To justify myself as the injured party.

Pride—again.

She could not admit *she* made a mistake, chose the father of her children unwisely, hadn't seen what kind of a person he was when it should have been obvious: 'dating' one of his students? Pressuring to lock her down before she was finished with med school and training? He didn't care about her—she was 'a presentable candidate' for the job of wife to the great Dr. Charles Renton—and should be happy for the honor. That she was Catholic—his mother's requirement—made her suitable. *I almost ruined his plans when I applied to NASA, but then they turned me down, and he made sure to initiate the next stage in his life—producing offspring. His* life. With whatever *he* wanted on the side. *'Yo soy soltero; la casada es mi mujer.'* 'Me, I'm single; the married one is my wife.'

I have never been validly married to Charles Renton. Would she have found out if she hadn't gotten sick? Had the stress contributed to her illness? And letting Charles have this much sway over her all these years?

I am a fool.

The urge to shred the letter overwhelmed. She ripped off a corner. *Wait.* It would give more pleasure to destroy the envelope and each sheet inside separately. She slid her finger under the flap.

Put it down, Kary. What are you doing?

Damn. She looked around, but she had subliminally noted the fallen branch on her way to the summit; she found it easily, a few steps down the trail. Sturdy, a good four inches in diameter, a yard long. She hefted it; not too heavy—it had already started the decomposition process, losing moisture from its cells; it was lighter than she'd expected. And the granite outcropping gave her a perfect target. She swung the tree limb tentatively, got a satisfying crack! out of the boulder. She hit it again, harder…

She demolished the tree branch methodically, hitting the rock over and over as more wood chunks chipped off, using her energy carefully for maximum thwack, pausing to reposition her hands, choose a different section of rock.

First Charles, then the Church, and then herself. Not God. If there was a God, He was unknowable: does an ant rage against the boot-ed monster on the garden trail which destroys her sisters?

She found herself breathing in hard huffs, with a tingling in her hands, and knotted torso muscles where ribs joined spinal column to sacrum. Scattered wood chips lay at her feet. The remainder of the branch was too short for leverage. She had damaged the granite less than herself.

Enough?

Enough.

She set the stump down, retrieved the envelope.

She opened the letter dispassionately, read through the legalese: Binkman was appalled that she recorded their conversation without his client's permission. Binkman demanded a copy of the recording. Binkman wanted the original and all copies destroyed or handed over. Binkman warned the full weight of the law would fall on her should she not accede immediately to his demands or should she ever attempt to record his client's words again without his client's express permission. Binkman threatened legal action should she be so misguided as to attempt to use the illegally-obtained recording in any way.

What? No fear?

Binkman was so predictable. *Charles* was so predictable.

And he'll never affect me again.

Oh? Except for one tiny detail. *Exquisitely my own fault.* In a hot-headed moment, you accused Charles of slander—and he's not go-ing to let it go.

She closed her eyes for a moment, sighed. *Must I always pay for my sins?* She opened her eyes—the external world had not changed.

You made it impossible to ever touch Andrew O'Connell.

I wasn't going to; let him at least leave this place in peace.

But now you can't. Ever.

I can't.

Because when Charles takes you to court to fight your charge of slander, the only thing which will save you is your ability to state unambiguously that you've never slept with Andrew O'Connell; if Binkman gets you on the stand, if he can get you to admit to *ever* sleeping with Andrew, no one will believe you didn't do it *before.*

She wasn't, especially under pressure, that good an actress. *I promised Andrew safe haven.*

She hung her head, raised it. *I will not lie in a court of law.*

Which keeps him safe from you.

She imagined Joe's horrified face, sighed, took out the cellphone, dialed Joe.

"Joseph Farentz, Esquire. Anneliesl speaking. How may I direct your call?"

Really? They must have Caller ID. *Anneliesl thinks I'm bad for Joe as a client.* Anneliesl was probably right. "May I speak to Joe, please, Anneliesl?"

"He's with a client. May I ask him to call you back later?" Anneliesl's tone made her expectations clear.

"No. I need him now. Please tell him—" She stopped playing games with underlings. "No. Put me through." She gritted her teeth, waited.

"Kary! What a pleasure." Joe's voice boomed through the connection. "What can I do for you?"

"You're not busy?"

"Nah. Just sitting here working on papers—someone's buying the old Fennelly mansion, wants to turn it into a B&B. Why?"

Good to know. Tell him about his secretary, the one who was in love with him...? *Focus, Kary.* "I got the letter today, Joe."

"From your ex's attorney."

"Yes."

"Read it to me—or do you want me to come around and get it?"

"Not necessary." She read it to him, slowly, so he could take notes. "I just want to know one thing."

"Shoot."

Wish I could. "Do I need to *do* anything right away?"

"Why?"

She pictured him hemming and hawing in his executive office chair, spoke clearly and deliberately. "Do I *have* to respond, in any way, immediately?"

"I'd say no; there is no specific legal threat, no court date, no imminent action on their part. I can draft an answer for you, let them stew for a month or so, send it on its way..."

"A month?" *All I need is ten days; even if the girls are still here,* he *will be safely away.* "Thanks, Joe."

"I'll see you before then, right? We have our meeting on the third Sunday coming up. It's Father's Day."

"Father's Day?"

"We meet *every* third Sunday—Easter, Passover, Father's Day—I'll be there." Joe's tone tried hard not to lay on guilt, failed infinitesimally. "You missed the last one."

Father's Day—how appropriate. "Fine. I'll bring it then."

She hung up the cell.

Her insides were hollow. A sip from the water bottle helped marginally.

Questions didn't go away: they lay in wait. What are you doing, Kary?

Trying to survive. For ten days. Until Andrew leaves. He was so excited to be going home. Home to Ireland.

My home is here. Sanctuary.

Which felt like prison. What was the difference?

Home is where the heart is. Home is where you're safe.

Stupid granola bars. Stupid *ancient* granola bars. Stupid *necessary* granola bars.

She picked her way down with care, barely made it to the couch, crashed.

Her last thought? *This is getting ridiculous.*

BIANCA

Bunker Hill; 6 P.M.

THIS IS THE SCENE THE Academy will show at the awards ceremony. Her killer scene, her sure thing for the Academy nomination for 'Best Actress,' the reason Grant paid her a star's full price. The scene she searched for in every script she read—a tearful Sarah, carrying her dead husband's unborn child, begging her father the colonel to stay, become an American, join the side sure to win. *And no one is going to take this one away from me.*

She would be on the red carpet, on Andrew's arm in the most gorgeous dress—to contrast with the mended rags she wore today. Would John's performance be strong enough to threaten Andrew's nomination for 'Best Actor,' to divide the voters? *If it did, it's due to me.* There were advantages to being the only female character—no dilution of effort, no splitting of the vote. Always a crapshoot, the Academy voting.

Bianca smoothed the shapeless gown the colonists would have considered suitable for a woman 'in the family way.' *If I get it right.*

Grant approached. "Just do it like we played, we'll get the remaining angles." He glanced at the sun, here in front of the makeshift barracks where the extras in tattered Revolutionary 'uniforms' stood ready to guard the British prisoners being exchanged and returned to England.

A truly perfect day, not a cloud in sight. Endless Grant reshoots all day. Stupid directors, like the last two. No usable directions. *What the hell do you want?* She nodded, not trusting her voice.

"We can get in this last run after the break, wrap it up. Good job."

Which was the problem. It *felt* wrong. Competence, being on the mark, letter-perfect memorization—and all the emoting in the world—and there was still something wrong. And it was driving her crazy. Worse, the crew knew; standing around focused on their jobs, the air of 'get this over with' was palpable. Andrew was going to claim this one. And there was nothing she could do. *This is mine. He doesn't get to take it from me.*

"Problems?" The enemy stood before her with that speculative look he got. The man had the most finely-honed trouble sense she'd ever acted opposite.

None of your business. "No." Andrew didn't have to play against type—he always got hero characters, hard men of action and decision, with a bit of a soft side and a bit of tail—but nothing like her constraints. *'Nobody pays good money to see a hard woman, princess.'* Men made the movie decisions—and wanted to see what their girlfriends would later fulfill for them in their beds. *Fortunately, it is so damn easy to give it to them.* She had to fit the rest, mother/whore/sister/lover around the titillation. Look at *Monster's Ball*—it made no sense. Icky little movie, icky people, and Halle Berry banged, naked, by a succession of men. Where was the art in that? And yet the Academy…

"Missed ye this weekend."

I will have to kill Grant. "Grant lent me his plane—and John—big fund-raising dinner for the Liver Foundation." When she was planning to send her regrets and a donation instead, citing 'scheduling conflicts due to filming.' *Everybody drops out of these things at the last minute.* There was always some B-list celebrity available at the last minute to fill in—the people who ran those things expected their awardees to have other commitments, and 'work' trumped everything else. "Sweet of Grant."

"Jet-lagged?"

"A bit." She would wait until the film was in the can, and then strangle Grant—the Academy voters were suckers for tragedy—they could award him 'Best Director'—posthumously. She would reminisce as she lifted the Oscar to the gods of film in earnest tribute. She did 'teary earnest tribute' exceedingly well. "I slept on the plane." *When John stopped bouncing.* It was like Grant had some plan to keep her apart from Andrew—or was she getting paranoid? "A bit."

"Ah. Yer man still up in Canada?"

If you don't stop calling Michael that— She laughed. "I'm sure he was too busy—'scheduling conflicts.'"

The break was almost over. The sound tech was always the first one back, endlessly messing with his headphones and switches. At least he only spoke to request sound levels.

"Ready, daughter?" Something odd flitted through Andrew's eyes. "May I, for luck?"

She craved him, she hated him... She flinched as he reached out, caressed the small bump made by the pillow under her dress the costumers insisted on... *What the hell?* "I don't think you would have done that in colonial times, *Father...*"

"No." He rubbed his chest with his fist as if to relieve pain. "More loss to him. He'll miss his grandson."

What the hell? "Or granddaughter."

"A man can hope." He blinked. "Ye and yer man, are ye thinking of offspring—?"

That song refrain on the NY talk show—him singing about the 'mother of my child.' His attention to the dinner discussion at Kary's house—he'd been wistful about marriage, kids. *He's broody.*

Grant signaled to his assistant.

"READY ON SET!"

The tough colonel with the unwavering loyalty to King returned to Andrew's eyes. He resumed his mark between the guards. "Any time, Grant."

Andrew O'Connell is broody. But the colonel's daughter is damaged goods. She saw in a flash what she was missing. *I am not Sarah.* Somehow she had let her own utter disregard for the child slip into Sarah—but Sarah, stupid little Sarah, wanted that child with all her heart, wanted the stupid young farmer she lost, was willing to stay and slave on the farm for her in-laws, put her heart and soul into rearing the little American. Sarah was secondary—to herself. Sarah didn't matter—except in as far as she was necessary to her child's survival. Sarah changed from spoiled brat to patriot. *I am a fool.* That would make it fly: want what Sarah wants. *But I will get what I want, and without the mewling infant like an anchor around my neck.*

"ACTION!"

She waved to Grant. *Sarah* will not cry or beg. *I will kill Grant later.* But first…

"Father."

"How the devil did you get in here?"

"Our widows have standing to petition, Father."

"What the deuce? Standing—with whom?"

"With the authorities who hold you prisoner, Father. We need officers. They believe I will persuade you to change your stripes."

"And my loyalties?" The colonel's voice dripped bitterness.

Bianca stiffened her spine and raise her chin. Andrew sensed her shift, responded by mirroring her stance. *Good—I can count on him.*

"Yes."

"The day will come when your 'authorities' will be hanged."

"We are winning the war."

"Are you daft? Winning a battle has given the rebels but a higher platform for their eventual gallows."

"General Washington is at Princeton. We will prevail."

"We sail on the morrow's tide. 'On my honour' to not return. Honour! From rebels! We have been given leave to ship our families; in England you will be safe, wed to a decent officer, loyal to the King."

She pushed it, replaced the previous soft entreaty with Sarah's new resolve.

"I am an American, Father. I have no home in England."

"Your husband is dead. You have no safety here."

"Father, I go to my husband's parents, to our farm."

"An indentured servant!"

In the groove, her voice modulated by itself.

"You would have me undertake an ocean voyage... in my condition?" Sarah lowered her gaze.

"A child...? It will not be a hindrance. Mayhap it will perish on the sea. 'Twould be for the best. There will be more—with a suitable husband. In England."

"Stay, Father. Learn to be kind to— to Winston's child, as you were not to him in this life. We will find you a place—"

"You have cast your lot." Col. Strathmore's visage hardened. "On your head be it."

"I will pray for you, Father." Sarah, dry-eyed, stood her ground.

Sarah's hands protected the child. From her own father, if necessary. *How dare he?*

Andrew's eyes narrowed. *He* turned his back on her, on the camera, marched away.

Bianca shook, her skin clammy. She defied the camera's slow approach.

"AND CUT!"

With all eyes on him, Grant hesitated, paused, spoke. "It's a wrap. Good work, everyone."

"IT'S A WRAP! THANK YOU, EVERYONE."

The silence had changed flavor. Not everybody knew; the girl with the mike went about her business, wrapping the cord around her elbow and through the space between thumb and forefinger, over and over as she took up the line. But most of the crew took its cues from Grant. And Grant knew; this silence was respect. And Andrew did. Even John, watching, dead, from the sidelines knew. *I know.*

Grant was oddly tender. He summoned an assistant with a golf cart. "Take Ms. Doyle to Wardrobe. Wait for her. Then take her home." He turned to Bianca. "Want something delivered?"

"Thanks. I don't think I'll need anything—and there's stuff in the fridge." He had his points. Maybe she would let him live. She grimaced. Andrew would have to wait. "I'm going to crash."

I earned it—I delivered. When it counts.

ANDREW

Sanctuary; 9 P.M.

HAD IT REALLY BEEN almost a week since he'd had a night off after Grant's mad run to completion added Sundays to their schedule? He stopped at the crest of Kary's drive, put his foot down to steady the black machine. *Since I proposed getting out of her life— and she told me no worries?*

He'd had thinking time on the ride over, though he'd almost hit one of the gravel piles she'd warned him about—road repairs. Always obstacles. All that drama with Bianca to sort out. *Hollywood stars have runs of bad luck, same as us probies from the sticks.* No wonder she was so desperate to do *Dodgson.* At least she had the long-established boyfriend. Not that *Dodgson* wasn't shaping up nicely, but he bet she was having producer trouble. Better her... *Shame, really; great role—for me.* He needed to be free to follow his path. *When tendered Starship Captain, do ye damned all to Alpha Centauri.*

Making sure he wasn't followed—easier in the gathering dusk. There'd been no further gossip—he asked George to keep watch. The shoot went back to whatever passed for normal lately; end of principal photography was always hurry-up-and-wait, long days without a break—interspersed with unpredictable stretches of exquisite utter boredom whilst talent waited for crew to fix tech mistakes. Except for tonight, this week was shot. *Should've managed to ring Kary up.* But he couldn't bear the artifice of the wireless phones, not for...

He gazed at the house with affection—and tendrils of nostalgia; few homes graced as natural a setting, granite and dark beams growing out of her mountain. The light over the front stoop clicked on as he rode up; the kitchen window radiated a cool fluorescent glow. A shadow moved across it. *Good; she's up.*

He waddled the bike over next to the pickup truck, silenced the throttle and kicked out the stand. Had she heard him? No matter. But he gave the bell a courtesy ring before he opened the door.

"Ah. There you are." Kary looked as if she would tell him to wash his hands and behind his ears. "I was finishing up. Have you eaten?"

Just like that? It was eerie, how easily he slipped back into her serene life in its mountain holdfast. "Might I scrounge?"

"I can do you one better. There's sauce simmering on the stove, linguini in the colander, broccoli in the microwave." She lifted her shoulders daintily. "I felt Italian. Here, I'll get the Parmesan out again."

"Broccoli?"

"It's good for you. Or do you have the gene which makes it taste bitter?"

"Broccoli it is." He served himself while she fished the cheese out of the fridge, nodded when she offered to grate it for him over the fragrant meat sauce, redolent of garlic and onions and sun. "Ye sound happy."

"I had a good writing day, and— well, I resolved some problems." She did not elaborate. "Come on out to the living room when you're ready. I was about to build a fire."

She left him in the disconcertingly non-hovering way of her which made him feel very much a household member. He poured himself Chianti from the winebox, helped himself to garlic bread from the rack on the counter. *Comfort food?*

He settled on the couch next to where she'd set up a work station on the coffee table—pens, printouts, colourful stickies, several books—and ate unhurriedly while she went through the firestarter routine with the teepee of twigs... "Editing?"

She looked guilty. "I had some more ideas for your script."

"*Dodgson*? I thought ye'd given it back to Bianca."

"I did. That's not the original—she took that—but we didn't have enough time at the party, so I worked on it this afternoon, and now I think I've *finally* done all the damage I can." Her eyebrows arched at a thought. "Can you take it back for me?"

"Certainly. More notes?"

"She can transfer them to her copy." She cocked her head toward the script. "I'm not sure I understand why there are two endings."

He shrugged. "Different audiences." At her look of confusion he explained. "She's aiming at *Cannes*—art film, artsy ending…"

"And then the more conventional one, for a mass audience?"

"Aye. World audiences don't like ambiguity—they want to cheer for someone. Which did ye prefer?"

"Oh, no. Skewer me and make me declare myself elitist *or* proletarian? Not on your life."

I'll miss the banter. "Ye caught me out."

"You?"

"I like happy endings. They rarely come to pass."

"Cynic."

"Realist." *Right; 'incurable romantic' were her words.*

She sat back on her heels. "I promised myself ice cream. Would you like some?"

"Knotty problem solved?"

"Believe so. If it would only *stay* dead."

"No, thanks. I think I'll just finish me Chianti." He stared at the dancing flames until she returned, mellowing as he allowed the wine to relax into his veins.

She sat cross-legged on the rug, set the cup with the ice cream on the coffee table. "You've had a good day, too?" She replied to his quizzical glance at the cup. "Moose Tracks. Peanuts, chocolate. They make it in Hanover. Out of this world." She spooned up tiny bits of the dessert, savoured them with obvious enjoyment.

"Ah." Which accounted for the brown lumps. "'Twas an odd day. Take after take—not really a critical scene, either. Something going on. I didn't think she'd get it—I don't think Grant did, either, not that he was any help—and then the girl pulled it out."

"Bianca."

"I could have sworn she had no idea, that it was going to go down as one of those things the editor cobbles together in post." Bianca's part was peripheral, even the coming awkward scene with her playing his beloved Emily. He shook his head, remembering the frustration evident in her whole manner. *We'd've slugged it out had she not played truant all weekend.*

"Did you say something to her?" Kary set the half-full cup on the table. "Is that even done?"

"Must've, but for the life of me I can't figure out *what*. Doesn't matter—but it was like a top flipping upside down when it spins." He sipped the Chianti. "Sometimes it takes hours of crap before ye find the— the right interpretation?" *Whilst the rest of us wait.*

"I'm glad for her."

At her easy tone, the muscles around his eyes tightened speculatively. *She means it.* He relished the rough red wine as he evaluated her over the rim of his wineglass. He knew few people with the ability to accept which seemed native to her; no comment limned with sarcasm or *schadenfreude* or envy or disbelief. No edge—and no curiosity. A simple acceptance of another's success which required no analysis. "Probably sleeping like a milk-drunk babe. When she's good, she's good." *Eventually.*

"And Grant got it all on film?"

"He did." Knew it immediately, too. Gratifying to work with Grant's solid intuition. *Not a struggle.*

"Ah." Satisfaction filled her voice and illuminated her smile. "So things are going well."

"Dangerously well." He rapped solidly on the coffee table.

She dug out the last of her indulgence, licked the spoon. "It can't just be that everything is clicking, and the movie is getting its final pieces—because of good planning?"

He snorted. "Is that how ye write?" He knew his face was in full skeptic mode.

She clunked the cup down, chuckling hard. "Oh, God—no. I wish. More like exploring a field with unexploded land mines." She looked at him ruefully. "You're right. That was silly of me. It's how it looks in retrospect, all tidied up." She seated herself on the armchair across from him. "So the film will be finished."

"Likely; but we're running out of time. Today's shoot took far longer than it should've. There's much to do, the money starts draining out of the coffers, shortcuts happen."

"You have to settle for 'good enough.'"

"Ye don't?"

"No." Her hands struggled to encompass her meaning, fingers spread wide, then fisted. "I can't produce under those conditions. So I don't let them push me. I accede to no deadlines. I would miss them for sure, and it won't help any of us."

"Sometimes ye don't get choices."

"And in those cases I cope. Somehow. For the duration." Her head wagged slowly, side to side. "But I can't write that way."

"Ye don't come through in a pinch?"

"Not in writing. I freeze."

"Inconvenient."

"For them. Which is why I'm terrified of taking on a screenplay. Don't tell Grant."

"No chance." *Uncommonly shrewd of ye.* He thrived on tension, sought it out, provoked it when it wasn't there. She... crumpled? When writing, in any case. Quick vision of her on the mountain, answering his wounded questions... She hadn't crumpled there. *No.* He swept his arm wide, gesturing with the wineglass at the fireplace. "I'll be missing the fires soon enough. Ten days—and home to Ireland with me. A bit longer, if Maury gets his way. Ye must visit—"

She startled, exhaled noisily. "Oh, God. I almost forgot. Not that you're not welcome to the fire..."

"But?"

"The girls are coming. Saturday. With Stephen..."

Her world: one small boy. Could she look at him and not think of hers? Regret stabbed; the pinprick popped Andrew's balloon and all his hazy plans escaped. *Time to make the best of it.* "Good thing then it's Tuesday."

She tilted her head, confused. "Tuesday?"

"Lucy comes tomorrow." Kary made the effort, because he came, but he'd already detected one suppressed yawn. *Wrap it up, boyo; she writes at dawn.* "Ye won't have to lift a finger."

"You haven't been any bother... You occupy the tiniest footprint of any house guest I've ever had. Three hours after Stephen arrives..." She shook her head with forbearance. "You'll have to come meet them..."

And see ye in the different context? "If time allows, for certain." He cursed himself for the instinctive withdrawal. *Spoiled ye've been, lad.* "It's been grand. Grant's fault, really. We should've been out of here by now."

"I'm not sorry." She said it quietly, hands in her lap, one side of her face in dark, the other illumined by the shifting firelight. "It's only Tuesday."

"The rest of *this* week... The schedule..." He'd hoped to find time the following week. He shrugged fatalistically. *Ends always come.*

"Damn New Hampshire spring weather."

"Aye. Blame the crazy rain. Grant's fault, picking an outdoor show."

"It'll be good."

"As long as there's no thundering and storming for the big battle scenes we're working up to."

"Should he've left them for the end?"

"Not his choosing."

"Ah." She tried to hide the yawn, laughed at herself.

"Scoot, m'lady. I won't be having ye drag out the toothpicks."

"Sorry." The contagious yawn leaked out from behind her hand. "Don't—"

"—forget to put the grate before the fire. I won't." As a reminder, the fire spat out a spark and a whiff of resinous pine.

"I meant to say don't worry about it, but that'll do."

"Good night, Kary. I'll pick up." He indicated the cup, his plate.

"Lucy will be here..."

"Good night, Kary." He rose, extended his hand. "It's time."

"It's time." Her smile was wide and generous—and remote. "It has truly been a pleasure."

"Trying to get rid of me again, are ye?" He shook his head, raised her hand to his lips. *It ends—with an infinity of questions and the closing of doors.* He hadn't even asked whether there'd been any aftermath to Hell's spite-filled column. *So like her not to share demons.* He held her gaze a moment longer. "Goodnight, Kary."

She didn't turn back as she ascended the granite staircase.

Why hadn't she told him before *when* her family was coming? He reached for the fire tongs, stopped short as the answer came: because he hadn't seen her since her party. *And I haven't talked to her since she told me not to worry about Hell.*

He leaned in, restive, inspecting the flames, until only embers remained.

BIANCA

Bunker Hill; **Wed., June 8; 1** A.M.

THE CRACK OF THUNDER woke her from a nightmare.

Bianca sat upright in bed, heart pounding alongside the reverberations of the storm. Outside her trailer windows, rain pelted against the metal siding; she could have sworn there was a brief period of hail.

The LEDs on the clock blinked '12:00' in the annoying way they did when power got interrupted; she had no idea what time it was, except that no light crept around the edges of the black-out curtains after the bolts of lightning moved away with the diminishing thunderclaps.

She fumbled for the cellphone. 3 a.m. *Shit.* She really needed to get back to sleep, but there was no way the rumble in her stomach would quit if she didn't eat something.

The lights worked. *Thank God for something.* She used the dimmer, kept it low—too much light would wake her up to full consciousness—killing all hope of rest.

She reset her clock to stop the flashing. She padded over to the little refrigerator, grimaced as she examined the selection, chose the only protein shake with no caffeine: Silky Royal Caramel Vanilla. Who named these things? She resisted the chocolate and the mocha—one of those, and she wouldn't get back to sleep for *sure.* If she did everything exactly right, she'd get another full sleep-cycle in before her phone's backup alarm, and she needed that sleep.

Read her lines again? No. That would engage her brain.

She took the container with her—with a sudden fear of finding that her laptop, plugged in for charging, was fried—sighed in relief when the screen lit. She unscrewed the container's top, swallowed enough to get the process of transferring protein into her bloodstream started, noted and set aside her reaction to the intense artificial bouquet. She typed in her password—'KillMichaelSoon'—unlocked her email.

Oh, joy. She opened the missive from Tonya, who must've sent it after last night's show.

> WE'VE BEEN NOMINATED FOR A TONY!!!
> Pumped! ttyl Love, Toe

Whoopee-do. Good for her and all that. She sent the obligatory reply—Congratulations! Woo hoo! You deserve it!—ignored the stab of envy.

That reminded her: time for a bout of Broadway—and the blessing of the critics for 'the legitimate stage'? A stint of New York City—and eight shows a week? The same thing every night for the three-month star engagement—thunderous applause night after night sounded pretty good right about now, but could she afford the time off? *At least I'd be away from Michael...*

Bianca yawned, stretched. She froze abruptly at half-stretch. Michael. The nightmare was about Michael. It flooded back: Michael drowning her, accidentally holding her head under water while he grinned like a moron and talked gibberish at her, not seeing that she needed air because he was so excited about— what? The fact that she was pregnant. Stupid Michael—if she drowned, the kid would drown with her. *Let go, Michael.*

She stared at the screen with Tonya's open email, but her mind was inside itself. In the dream she hadn't wanted Michael's child, didn't want *any* child. But Michael did.

And Andrew does.

She let all the air in her lungs out in one long slow exhalation of tension. She hugged herself, cold. *He wants a son.* The magical switch that made men desire to leave their earthly treasures to their heirs had clicked.

She groaned, frustrated. *I don't want another child.*

But he did. He was sending out baby signals loud and clear. *And if I don't answer them, someone else will.*

It was worse than that: Andrew already assumed she and Michael—'her *man*'—were at the same stupid life stage. 'Wanting a little one to complete their lives.'

The thought made her physically ill. The months of nausea. The bloating. The stupid doctor's appointments. The *blob* destroying her body contours—her perfect body contours. Trying to work with hormone brain. Losing *Glass Menagerie* because, well, '*We can't really have a pregnant Laura, can we?*' The sleepless nights with Zed insisting she breast-feed the colicky baby she wanted to throw against the wall. The relief of leaving the howling brat with Zed when she left for work... *I can't, not again.*

And on the other hand... It wasn't Strathmore yesterday reaching out to pat a baby bump. Strathmore wasn't even supposed to know about the baby when they started that scene. *It was Andrew.* It was a tell. The frustration of the shoot not going well led Andrew to an unconscious gesture, but it fit.

She was going about things all wrong. Andrew didn't want a playmate. Andrew needed a *family*. So her job had doubled: not only did she have to convince Andrew that she and Michael were over, but she had to make him want *her*—as a brood mare. *Revolting.* A guaranteed breeder. She revised the mental image: on the red carpet she'd be standing next to a protective Andrew all aglow with impending fatherhood, a Balenciaga gown with a discreet empire waist covering a slight swell. He had to see her as the perfect mate—what was more perfect than a vessel for his seed? *Ugh.* He had to be 'in love'—not merely in heat—and firmly committed, because the world had to blame him for stepping in between her and Michael. Stupid world. And she had barely enough time to complete the process between now and the end of *Bunker Hill*: she needed every second.

The computer screen reminded her: she couldn't tell Tonya anything—Tonya was Michael's friend. *Just as well; I can't tell anyone.*

Thank God for the final gift. Grant left the dream sequence for last, because she transitioned from being Sarah to being Strathmore's beloved Emily. Innocent but sensual. Fans loved the story of stars who fell for each other on a shoot—the ultimate passion on screen had to come from somewhere. Their right and their destiny. Well, it did—but the fans would never understand *how* it did. Paradoxically, fans couldn't wait to forgive Pitt for exchanging Aniston for the more powerful Angelina, either.

Decisions taken, she craved sleep; a quick glance at the clock told her she had plenty of time before the alarm. She would sleep like a baby should.

But at least now I know what I need to do.

ANDREW

Sanctuary; **7 A.M.**

THIS IS THE LAST TIME I ride the bike away from Kary's.

The 'lasts' were piling up, the part he hated. Across the road from her drive, he pulled over to wait for her gate to close securely, the portcullis drawn up.

They'd gotten into a rhythm—she ignored him when she was writing as she must be now, chatted if she was up when he came, never let him feel unwelcome, but never fussed. She'd become a good friend in what—Sanctuary's forty days? He chuckled as he revved the engine, peered both ways before roaring out onto the rural road. He might as well be the house cat.

The road was deserted this early, as usual. The sky held no hint of clouds. He should be in Hanover with time to spare—they had a packed day, followed by several more, as Grant crammed everything left into this week, holding their few days the next in reserve for the inevitable after Monday's epic battle. *Glad it's not me bailiwick.*

Which was disingenuous: Grant's track record was sound, back thirty-odd years. Grant was making movies when he, Andrew, was in nappies.

He needed the world's forbearance. *Me pick of every role from now until I die.* Problem? *Everyone wants their pound of flesh.* Solution? Go home, boss the pigs around, wait for Maury and the next show. Something would come.

But not quite yet. And there was still the fair Bianca to bed.

Bianca. *Shite.* He examined the roadbed, found a gravelled turnabout off the edge of the shoulderless road. He *knew* there was something he missed. *Kary asked one thing of ye.* He checked his watch. *Plenty of time.* He'd sneak back in, grab the sheaf of papers with her notes, be on his way again in three shakes of a lambín's tail. He pushed the throttle and the speed limit.

Last time, eh? Eejit. Nothing like making the grand exit, and then having to slink back... He shook his head at himself, more irritated than amused, as he parked the bike by the stoop. *In and out, no harm done.*

He traversed the living room to where the position of the script copy had registered subliminally, picked it up by the metal spring clip. His ears pricked. Music. From the stairwell, bouncing off the granite walls. American country ballad. Woman's voice. Deep, mellow, smooth, the words indistinguishable.

What the...? This was not a house with constant music. His watch said he had a few spare minutes yet before makeup call. A quick peek, and back on the road.

He cat-footed down the granite staircase to a spot two-thirds of the way down where the stairwell wall opened up to the lower floor. He sank to his haunches to survey the 'moving room.'

To a completely unexpected view.

Kary Ashe was dancing.

He froze. *What else of her don't I know?*

Kary moved to the solid beat. The sunlight streaming through the plate glass wall silhouetted loose black pants and black leotard, ballet slippers. She was not singing with the CD, but appeared to know the music, anticipate its rhythms. She was intent on step, arm placement fluidly melded to turns. She worked the sunlit floor by the windows in improvisational, syncopated movements—not repeated but of a kind and pattern. *Whitewater on a river's boulders.*

He was an interloper in a private ritual, transfixed on the dark stairs where he had no right to be.

He rose quickly, intending to withdraw as silently as he arrived, leaving no disturbance in her field. But his boot snagged the script, kicking it down a step, clattering clip on stone step, at the exact moment she revolved in a graceful arc.

She halted all of a piece, spun to face the noise, stood shock-still with the music blaring. "Who's there?" There was fear in her voice. "Who is it?"

He descended, stooping to retrieve the script with its offending clip, came hesitantly into the room, stopped where she could see him. "I... I forgot *Dodgson*." He gestured with the script. "I heard music... Didn't mean to startle ye." *Lame.* "I'm sorry, Kary."

For response, she strode to the CD player, shut down the stereo system.

"Who's the singer?"

"Emmylou Harris."

She wasn't going to help him. Her cheeks were scarlet. Embarrassment or exertion? *None of yer business, boyo.* "Beautiful song."

"I like a lot of hers. I think my heart stopped." She took a deep breath, exhaled. "Your door was open. I was sure you were gone."

"I know. I was. Got half-way there..." He raised the script.

"You'll be late." She crossed her arms self-protectively. Her eyes broke contact, looked at the floor, where her foot traced small circles.

Schoolgirl, caught in a misdemeanor. "I didn't mean to intrude."

"It's okay." She gave a small laugh, met his gaze, glanced away again. "It's something I do when the blood threatens to coagulate in my veins and the words won't come." She shrugged, faced him, squared her chin. "You scared me. I thought one of the lunatics got in. You'd think I'd be used to living on my own by now." Her customary composure returned to envelop her like a cape; she waved him out. "I'm fine. The blood is moving nicely now; I have to write."

He hesitated. "Forgive me?"

"Of course." She nodded gravely. "Shoo."

He felt her watching as he climbed the stairs.

The images would not fade for the rest of the ride. He scarcely noticed the countryside.

The most erotic thing a woman can do for a man is to dance for him alone.

❧ CHAPTER SEVENTEEN ❧
A daughter's your daughter the rest of your life

Illusion or real?
Both happen in the same mind,
but are not diff'rent.
Tahiro Mizuki,
trans. by R. Heath

"...Daughters of Jerusalem, [...] weep for yourselves,
and for your children..."
Luke 23:28, KJV

"...Rachel [wept] for her children, and would not be
comforted, because they are not."
Matthew 2:18, KJV

KARY

Sanctuary; Saturday, June 11; 2 P.M.

SHE WOULD HAVE TO stop thinking of it as 'Andrew's room.'

She stood in the doorway before entering, remembering. The room was full of light now. Lucy had thrown back the curtains, done the weekly dusting and vacuuming, re-made the bed with fresh sheets and draped the bedspread, and the room was as empty as a hotel room, in spite of fresh hydrangea blossoms in white, pink, and blue, already starting to fade on the dresser in a crystal vase.

She slid the volume of *The Poetry of Robert Frost*, with its stark winter cover, from the nightstand into its home among Susan's other poetry books on the bookshelf. An inspection of the bathroom revealed a stack of clean towels, topped by Stephen's favorite Bert-and-Ernie beach towel. And nothing to indicate a man other than

Greg ever occupied the space. She gave the bedspread an unnecessary tug.

Quick check of the time; she needed to leave for the airport, an hour away, within the next fifteen minutes to be early enough to rest in the car before the plane landed at Manchester from Logan International. The girls had a convoluted trip—Princeton to Boston to New Hampshire—with a four-year-old; they would be tired. *Enough to deal with without me being exhausted, too.* Had the girls respected her morning writing time—or was it happenstance? When in doubt, give them credit. They were good girls.

She opened each drawer in the closet and the dresser, making sure there was room for Susan to unpack. When she opened the last bottom drawer, her hand retracted as if scalded. There, next to the extra blankets, sat an unexpected stowaway: carelessly folded— Andrew, not Lucy—a hand-knit Irish crewneck, cream and cableknit and heart-stopping.

She sat down abruptly on the bed, staring.

Her fingers dared. She pulled the rough heavy sweater into her lap, tidied the folds, tucked the long sleeves neatly into the bundle. The faint aroma of lanolin thrust her backbrain into memories of nursing... Such a long time ago. She restrained herself from burying her face in the woolen bulk. She refused to name the other scent. *It will have to go back.*

A phone jangled downstairs. Her left hand reached for the bedside handset reflexively, turned it on. Good thing she hadn't left yet. *Something wrong with the flight?*

"Dr. Ashe, it's George Cosgrave."

Her heart skipped a beat; she suppressed the reaction with annoyance. "George, if you're going to be formal, I'm not letting you wash my dishes any more."

"Sorry! Can I start over?"

"Try me."

"Kary, it's George."

"I recognized your voice. What's up?" Calling to say goodbye so soon? *Stop jumping like a cricket on a hot griddle.* "Is everyone okay?" *Stupid.* Why wouldn't they be? And if they weren't, why would George phone *you*?

"Never better. Andrew's up to his ears in horse, ah, dung. He said yer kids were coming today, and would they like to come see the big battle scene Monday afternoon?"

He remembered. She couldn't find her voice.

George spoke again, softer. "Andy thought the little guy might like it. Easy enough to slip out early if he gets tired."

If I get tired. She cleared her throat. "He probably won't remember it when he's grown up, but—" *Irritating throat!* "—I'm sure he'll love it."

"Stephen will remember his whole life. Which is how Andy got hooked on films." George paused. "Maybe ye don't want that for the lad?" There was a moment's silence on the line. "It's just an idea; himself will understand. He'll be busy most of the time; ye'll have to make do with me."

Find the words, Kary. What would she have said if Grant had been the one to invite them? "Nonsense. It will be amazing." *Public display of 'friend' with her whole family, including a grandson, on the set—his way to leave me free of rumors? Genius?* She ran the sensitive back of her hand over the sweater in her lap: supple fibers, coarse weave. She excoriated herself for her weakness. *Susan can have a migraine if she likes; Ronnie will watch Stephen.* "We'd love to. How's it going?"

"So far so good. We're into the third day of battles, and nobody's been hurt, except John, and he gets to ride with a real bandage instead of a fake one."

"What happened?" *I wasn't supposed to ever see him again.* She'd guiltily allowed herself a single visit to AOCORNER— notices of *Roland* openings in Europe with Andrew slated to be present; a reminder of their policy of reporting on Andrew as an actor, his private life off limits; a link to candid shots from the BagelCam website, Andrew clowning on a break with Peter Hyland to see who could wear more bagels on his fingers; a report from a reenactor/extra with minor quibbles about historical inaccuracies—but nothing about John.

"He got too close to the mare when she spooked, and she kicked him in the shoulder."

"Is he all right?" *Poor John.* He was on his way to Andrew's gallery of scars.

"They wrote it into the script." George's voice radiated amusement. "Grant's not about to let that slow things down, and John's game. But I warn ye, the lad'll be bending yer ear with the story."

She hugged the folded sweater, hunching her shoulder to hold the phone. "John wouldn't let anything stop him. Not on his first big break." From where she sat, she reached into the bottom of the closet for a spare nylon gym bag and tucked the sweater in, reluctant to release roughness or pale essence. "What time would be best?"

"Can ye make two o'clock? They're setting up all day tomorrow, makeup and last minute things Monday morning, and Grant said only a major thunderstorm—not a minor one, ye understand—will stop him from filming. By major thunderstorm he means one where the animal trainers won't let him use the horses. He doesn't care about the people."

"Sure he does." Grant wasn't really a monster. "But it's all the same to him if they're wet or dry—and wet is more dramatic. If less historically accurate—in those days they couldn't fight in the rain. Wet powder."

"The weatherman *guaranteed* dry."

"Fine. We'll be there at two, sharp. Same entrance?"

"Andrew's sending Frank, Kary. The windows in the back of the limo are darkened glass."

"Oh." Fans. The real world intruded itself into her fantasy. She damned the encroachment. "Tell him thanks."

~ ~ ~

I SHOULD HAVE LEFT FOR the airport already.

She'd checked—the flight's arrival was still listed at three forty-five, and the Manchester airport was an hour's drive on the quicker back roads. *No; don't take chances—stick to the Interstate.* It would be tight now: she'd barely sneak in a short break after driving before she had to deal with... *It will be so good hugging Stephen again.*

The dashboard clock displayed '2:15' as she turned the key in the ignition. Clear skies—no rain delays to stress about. A two-hour round trip was a little longer than she usually drove—she'd ask Ronnie to drive back. Not Susan—Susan insisted on driving *at* the speed limit on Interstate 89. She'd ride shotgun next to Ronnie, and Susan could tend to her little bundle of energy in the back seat. She didn't want to talk to Susan about Greg in front of Stephen. *And we'll all survive, and it'll be a nice visit.*

Thank goodness the girls were so self-sufficient—Susan would cook and the house would fill with the odor of garlic and sautéed onions and basil, and Ronnie would talk and keep them in stitches, and Stephen would be in two places at once. The right ratio: three grownups to one small boy. Ronnie could play with him, give her sister a break. Some day, when Ronnie settled down, she'd be a great mother. *As she was a great sister to Ethan when I needed her because the others were falling apart.*

She slammed on the brakes: the tractor-trailer before her had slowed to a crawl. *Pay attention!* Off to the side, pavers and a backhoe loader, a roller and a grader and an asphalt distributor— thank you, Richard Scarry and innumerable re-readings of *Cars and Trucks and Things That Go*—idled abandoned by the road crew for the weekend, and the road ahead narrowed to a single lane marked by orange plastic traffic cones. Asphalt aroma penetrated the cab. *I'll be lucky now if I arrive before they land.*

She blasted her horn at the Mini-Cooper which tried to cut in, shook in reaction. *What idiot gets between a pickup and a semi—in a tin can?*

Disruption. She'd forgotten how close to the edge it was, always, in spite of her hiding away. She drove slowly, concentrating on keeping pace with her new best friend. Behind her, the Mini-Cooper tailgated. *If I stop suddenly, as he deserves, he'll crumple like an empty soda can without even denting my bumper.* Which will make you even later. *If I didn't hate paperwork...*

Five miles at twenty-five per later had her gripping the steering wheel, reminding herself to breathe. *Adrenaline is not my friend.* It didn't matter if she was late. They would worry, but Susan would call, and Kary'd pull over and explain, and it would be an inconvenience, not Armageddon. *All the wisdom of age, and you can't even drive to the airport without making it drama.* That helped— poking fun at herself always did.

It's not the drive. It was the indeterminate amount of time spent with people, however beloved, invading her fortress. Entertaining them—keeping Stephen happily occupied. The invitation to the shoot was convenient—even well-behaved children need to leave the house, to move. Andrew *would* charm them...

And it wouldn't hurt the girls to know their mother was not an old fogey who did nothing but sit around and wait to die—or quietly and anonymously write novels. They could be healthy and secure—because they were loved and supported in childhood. *I disrupted their life enough by divorcing their father—but that is past.*

Finally! The end of the endless procession of tipsy orange cones. Three-fifteen; she sped around the semi grinding its gears up the incline. She waved to the trucker, wondered if he listened to Books on Tape—or a long-winded preacher—to while away the miles. *Some of my best fans are long-haul truckers.*

Parking in the short-term lot opposite the entrance was anticlimactic: ten minutes to touchdown. She left the safety of the pickup, ordered her eyes to stay open, slipped into energy-conserving mode. If she shortened the time between rests for the remainder of the day, she wouldn't cause the girls concern. *We can talk tomorrow—we have plenty of time.*

She faced the Arrivals Board uncomprehendingly: DELAYED.

"Excuse me, miss. Do you know what time the plane lands here from Boston?"

The uniformed blonde girl at the counter pivoted to inspect the board behind her, which still listed the original arrival time. "Sorry, Ma'am. The computer will post the time when the information is available."

"You don't have updated flight information on your screen?"

"Every single one of them has the same information. I'm sorry," brilliant smile, all orthodontia. "You can watch the landings from the restaurant, if you like."

"Can you tell if they've left?"

The girl shook her bouncy mane. "But as soon as they're in the air, the board will announce the arrival time. Sometimes they can make up time in flight."

"Thank you." She got out of the way of the next customer. *Now what?* Damn. She should have asked if it was mechanical trouble. What if they didn't fix it right? What if the courteous smile became a concerned smile, a smile which gathered all the people whose loved ones were on a flight into an out-of-the-way lounge to be 'handled'? *I can't do this again.* She should have told them to take the train, to rent a car. The view before her—bustling local airport, people and luggage and the electric carts which beeped—took on a quality of impermanence...

Breathe, Kary. There is nothing wrong. *Not yet.* You are hyperventilating; stop it. Sit down. It's a perfectly ordinary flight delay on a day with perfectly clear skies. Being ridiculous won't make the plane fly faster. Nobody is panicking but you. There is no need to imagine engine parts spread over half of New Hampshire. *Like Peter's wife.*

On the tarmac, a droning mosquito Piper Cub taxied toward the far end of the runway. The digital clock display changed to three-forty. She sat down on a hard green plastic tubular armchair in a row of the same, closed her eyes. From here she could keep an eye on the board, watch the arrivals. *And be even tireder when they get here.* Willing it wouldn't keep the plane in the air.

The sane thing is to go wait in the pickup, and take the nap you thought you wouldn't have time for. *But I won't be able to see the Arrivals display.* You know it will make no difference: they'll get here when they get here, and you can choose between being rested—or even more frazzled. Susan will call if she doesn't find you standing there at Baggage Claim. *But normal people would go buy a cup of coffee and a newspaper.*

She walked leadenly back to the short-term lot, moved the pickup to a spot with half shade. She crawled into the back seat, curled up as comfortably as possible with her pillow and the fuzzy maroon stadium blanket. She let her eyelids relax...

"Mom! Are you there?" Banging on the window. "Honestly, Mom. Don't you ever check your phone?" Susan. Peering through the darkened glass with her hands making a shadowed circle.

Kary rolled the window down. "Why didn't you call? I made sure my phone was charged before I left home."

"Here. Let me have it." Susan took the cellphone impatiently from Kary's hand. "I've been calling for ten minutes. You sleep like the dead." She poked at the tiny buttons. "Why did you turn your volume down?"

Stupidly, "I didn't."

"Well, it was. You must've butt-dialed."

"I didn't— Let me see." Guilt. She hadn't raised the volume back up after church last Sunday. *A whole week.* At least she'd checked for texts.

"I changed it back for you." Susan handed her the cellphone. "Doesn't matter. We're here, and Ronnie is standing at the curb with the bags trying to keep Stephen from running out into the road."

"Doesn't he—"

"Of course he knows better, *Mom.* Don't you think I try? You know you can't trust four-year-olds in new situations." Susan shook her head in exasperation. "Unless you want flat four-year-olds."

"Don't. I already worried enough about you."

"Not the airplane panic again, Mom? Airplanes are *safer* than most anything else. You know that. Even... even with what happened to granma and granpa. That was a badly-maintained four-seater in the rainforest; this was a modern jet in the States. You don't want Stephen afraid of flying, do you?" Susan peered at her. "Are you okay?"

Unless they aren't safe. "Just a little groggy. Here, let me out. I'll be fine."

"I'll drive. Give me the car keys."

"I'm *fine*, Susan." She gave Susan an awkward hug, walked around to the driver's side, slid in. "We'll be on our way in minutes."

"Mam Mam! Mam Mam!" At the curb, the running bear hug from Stephen almost bowled her over. She scrunched down to enfold him, comparing every feature against her memory of him. He smelled of baby shampoo and baby sweat, the hair damp and curled on the back of his neck. Each time she saw him he was more defined, more boy. "How's my little man?"

"I'm not little any more."

"Oh?"

"I'm 'most five now, and I'm a big boy, and I get to go to school now, Mam Mam. Mom said so."

"If Mom said, it must be so."

Ronnie was quiet, embraced Kary and lay her head on Kary's shoulder for a moment. "Good to be here, Mom." She held eye contact with Susan for a moment.

Ronnie will tell me what's wrong with Susan and Greg in her own time. "When do you have to be back at school?"

"Not until after Labor Day." Ronnie shrugged. "There's a summer program, but I wasn't planning to go."

"Good. We'll have a nice long visit. Let's take you home first, feed you something. Unless you guys need to eat before…"

"I brought sandwiches for the plane, Mom." Susan had stopped bustling. "I can't let Stephen get too hungry—makes him go all hyper. Can we go?"

What is the right thing to do? "Will you drive, Veronica? Susan can sit with Stephen in the back seat."

Ronnie looked *wrong*.

"Here, Mom. Let me do it." Susan gave her sister a quick glance. "She can navigate. You remember the landmarks, right, Ronnie?"

Ronnie nodded.

"Would you mind sitting with Stephen, Mom? He's been so looking forward to seeing you." A request, not Susan's usual 'people managing.'

Kary stared at Susan. "Sure, honey." *Susan is getting her support from Ronnie so she doesn't bother me.* She focused on her favorite grandson to hide the stab of regret over Susan. "Come on, Stephen. Let's get you fastened in. How do you like pickup trucks?"

"I want to sit in the front seat!"

"Maybe next time? Keep me company back here?" She opened the door. "You can have the pillow."

"I'm not tired!"

"Did you manage to sleep much on the plane?" She diverted Stephen's attention to the seat buckle. "You put—"

"I can do it myself! Just like the plane!"

"Did you? Oh, good. Now you can remember to fasten your seatbelt like all the grownups." She supervised and admired as he made the tab click into the buckle.

"Not a whole lot, Mom. Ronnie and I talked, he colored—and bounced."

"We'll have time, honey. Where's his backpack?" She helped Stephen extract his coloring book out of the pack as Susan eased them out of the parking spot, followed the signs, drove them out of the airport lot and onto the secondary highway. *Too bad—but it isn't worth the aggravation just to let Stephen enjoy the construction machines.* "It's so good to see you. I've missed you. How's Amanda?" She knew she meant, *How is your father?*

"Me 'n' Tad catched pollywogs." Stephen's face lit up.

"Pollywogs? I remember pollywogs." And a bullfrog tadpole which almost made it.

"She and Tad are fine." Ronnie looked at her sideways. "She really does love Dad, you know."

"I know, honey." After a brief glance at her daughter, she returned her gaze to the highway.

Susan kept her eyes on the road as she spoke. "I blame Dad."

Kary sighed. "It's over, sweetheart, water under the bridge." Another lifetime, so long ago it happened to someone else.

"I don't care. He shouldn't have a son almost the same age as mine."

Kary sighed again. "Guess what?"

Stephen lifted his face to her. "What?"

"Zoë—you remember my friend Zoë?—she's having us all over for a picnic tomorrow. She has a pool; did you bring suits?"

Susan's voice tightened. "We always do, Mom." She braked hard as the car before them turned onto a side road. "She has a couple of boys, right? Cute little boys?"

"They're the stars of the high school hockey team."

"You're kidding."

"Nope. Sixteen and seventeen."

"Time passes. I remember them in our sandbox."

"Faster than you know."

"Do we have to, Mom?" Ronnie gazed out the side window as if the current green wall was somehow special.

"If you guys are tired, I'll take Stephen so you can rest...?" They would sit on Zoë's patio, watching her boys and dogs romp with Stephen, while politely avoiding the subject of Andrew O'Connell; Andrew couldn't help being the center of chaos, even when being kind. She wouldn't tell Zoë they were going to watch the filming— because she wouldn't want Zoë's sons to hear; she wouldn't be able to invite... *I'm going to need a lot of naps this week.*

Susan spoke. "I'll go with you. Stephen loves swimming."

"Can I decide tomorrow, Mom?"

Something wrong at school? "Sure, Ronnie. No rush." The silence lengthened into miles.

"So—how's the book going, Mom?" Susan spoke without turning her head, seemingly determined to keep a conversation going.

Kary glanced at her uncharacteristically silent other daughter. "It's going well. Thanks. I wrote this morning."

"What does Elise say? Didn't you tell me you were going out on a limb with this one?"

"She hasn't seen it yet." *She may never see it.*

"What's it called?"

"*Hostages to Fortuna*—working title."

"Sounds like a book about mercenaries. Is that what it is?"

Kary laughed; Stephen looked up at her, bent his head to his coloring. "Not exactly. It depends on your point of view."

"When are we allowed to read it?"

"When it's a little closer to finished?"

"Stop being cryptic, Mom. What's your hero like?"

Encapsulate Akiiya in ten words. "She's a soldier, sent to pacify a rebel planet."

Susan started to turn her head, restrained herself. Her surprise showed in her voice. "What do you know about soldiers, Mom?"

"It's science fiction—I don't *have* to know anything."

"Do you even read the stuff?"

"I read widely—before you three came along."

"Yeah, blame it on us." In the passenger seat, Ronnie stared out the side window. The back of her head was entirely devoid of emotion.

"What's her name? Your heroine?" Susan accelerated, and actually passed the poky Volvo station-wagon they were following.

"My hero's name is Akiiya."

"Spell it?" When Kary did, Susan waggled her head. "Why that? Sounds Hawaiian."

"I liked the sound. '*Ah—keee—yah.*'"

"Huh."

The back of the pickup in motion was noisier than Kary remembered. She adjusted her seatbelt where it cut into the side of her neck. Stephen's head lolled on his shoulder, the crayon still gripped in his little fist. She put the pillow between them to prop him up. She placed her forefinger and thumb on the crayon, tugged. His grip tightened reflexively; when it loosened, she slipped the crayon out and replaced it in the box with its companions-in-color. The yellow cardboard box with the familiar green edges went back into his backpack along with the Winnie-the-Pooh coloring book. The pickup truck was warm. She yawned...

Susan's voice interrupted. "Mom. Wake up. There's a gate. You didn't tell me about a gate. When did you acquire a gate?"

The pickup was stopped. Beside Kary, Stephen stirred and stretched.

"Mom?" Ronnie twisted, leaned an arm on the back of the front seat. "Why do you have a gate?"

~ ~ ~

IF YOU HADN'T GOTTEN sick, you wouldn't be divorced. *And if I hadn't gotten divorced, I would have been a better role model for Susan.* And now you're going to have to pay for it. Children break your heart simply because they exist—and don't always make the right decisions. *Whatever Susan says, remember she is hurting, and the last thing she needs is a judgmental mother.*

Kary stared into her open refrigerator. But for now, a moment's peace to gather her thoughts while the girls unpacked. *Time to get dinner started.* She extracted the container of spaghetti sauce she'd made the day before, poured the sauce into a small pot she set on the range, adjusted the flame to simmer—

"Mom, can we talk?"

Kary jumped. *Susan.* Alone. "Where's Stephen? This really isn't a house for children."

"You think I don't know that? The guardrails on the deck are an invitation to climbing, and those stone steps of yours are a disaster waiting to happen."

"He was fine when you came two years ago." She took the Italian bread loaf from the breadbox, placed it on a cutting board.

"Yes, but I never let him out of my sight. Now he's a determined little monkey."

"I do remember what it's like to have small boys around."

"I'm sorry, Mom. I didn't mean—"

"Don't apologize. You're right to be vigilant. By the way, where *is* Stephen now?"

"Very funny, Mom." Susan reached into her pocket, put Kary's hot tub timer on the counter. "Ronnie took him into the Jacuzzi— it's all he wanted. 'With bubbles, Aunt Ronnie.'"

"Only fifteen minutes—"

"I know the rules, Mother." Susan exhaled, irritated. "Stop stalling. Can we talk? To start with, what is going on here?"

Ease into what's bothering you? Fine. "Nothing." *I killed any chance I might have had quite effectively.*

"There's all this stuff in the papers about you, and we get here, and there's a gate across the entrance like some medieval fortress—" Susan squared her shoulders, set her chin. "Is the gate because of him?"

"Him who?" Kary positioned the serrated bread knife lengthwise on the board.

"Are we going to talk about this like adults?"

Him. *Now?* "No. It went up before… Joe recommended it. Joe. My lawyer."

"Out of the blue?"

Kary took a deep breath. *I should have told them.* "I had a little problem with a fan showing up unannounced, a while back—"

"After you were on that TV show?"

"He tracked me down somehow—"

"Why didn't you tell us?" Susan exhaled with a hiss, threw up her hands. "No. I don't even know why I ask that question any more. Of course you didn't tell us. You didn't want to bother us."

"It's taken care of, and nothing happened—" *Turned out I didn't need to disembowel him with my kitchen knife.*

"Nothing happened, but you went out and spent umpty-frat dollars on a secured gateway." Susan's brows drew together, her face tight. "Greg and I are worried—"

Decision point? Kary found she didn't want to know about Greg. "And I need to get dinner ready, because a small boy is going to emerge pink and clean and *hungry*. Wouldn't it be better to do this later?"

"Stephen will be around, and then we'll eat, and... You know perfectly well that you'll put it off later because you 'have to get a good night's sleep before writing in the morning,' and then it won't be until tomorrow."

"Am I that bad?"

Susan's lowered chin and lifted eyebrows exaggerated the exasperated look. "You need to ask?"

Bit between the teeth—you need to talk? "Sorry, baby. I guess I'm postponing the bad news as long as possible. Ronnie's worried—what does she know I don't?" She took a deep breath. "What is going on between you and Greg?"

"Me and Greg?" Susan's face scrunched up. "What does Greg have to do with this?" She closed her eyes. "Not that again. Why don't you like Greg, Mother?"

"I like him fine if he treats my baby right—"

"But you've never understood him, and worse than that, you've never understood what I *see* in him."

"I *had* hoped you would marry someone—"

"Someone who doesn't have his head in the clouds?" Susan forced a laugh. "He suits me. I have him wrapped around my little finger, and he worships the ground I walk on."

"Greg?"

"Oh, yes. I express the tiniest desire—it happens. I can have whatever I want." Susan's voice took up a hint of desperation. "I just don't know what I want.

"That's it?" *I've been agonizing about you—* "If he were teaching engineering mechanics to boys, instead of English poetry to girls."

"Not that again! And besides, they have women engineering students now." Susan held Kary's gaze. "And he knows anything like that 'happens,' I go after him with a knife." Susan's voice dripped judgment. "I picked Greg *after* you divorced. Not everyone is a good Catholic man like Dad, Mom."

"Susan!"

"I love Dad, Mom, but I don't respect him. Amanda's crazy to put up with him. I can see why you divorced him."

"I didn't—"

"Fine. *Technically*, he divorced *you*. Big deal. You didn't fight him very hard. Big fat lot he cared about being Catholic then."

"Why all this now, Susan?"

"Because you're always faulting Greg for not being Catholic, *Mom*."

"Oh, honey. No. I worry about *you*. And Stephen. It's harder when parents don't agree about on basic issues. Do you even go to church any more, Suzy Q? Is Stephen going to Catholic school? He's so excited about starting. Like you at his age."

"If you must know, I go—when I can. He comes with me sometimes."

"Stephen?"

"No, Mom, Greg. He wants Stephen to go to Catholic school."

"*Greg?*"

"Yes, Greg. He says our Saint Bartholomew's is great, academically."

"Stephen will barely be five when school starts. Isn't he too young to sit still so long?"

"He's already reading, Mom. How long do you want me to keep him back?"

Just like you. "Can't you keep him home, do a lot of things with him this year?" *Have another baby?*

"So he's even more advanced when he goes to Kindergarten next year?"

"You survived. Was it so horrible?"

"No. I don't get all the people who hate nuns. Saint Augustine's was a wonderful place to grow up in. Well, at least until my parents got divorced *my senior year*." Susan's blaming face was her least attractive feature.

Kary sighed. "Your father couldn't wait." *After he announced he had a baby on the way and was going to marry Amanda.*

"Yeah. The *baby* had to be born legit." Susan pressed her hands against her abdomen, her voice flat, emotionless.

"Don't, Susan. That baby is innocent. He didn't ask for this."

"That baby's name is Thaddeus, Mom. Thaddeus Charles Renton. And he's not a baby any more. He's eight."

Tad the Interloper. "Yes. Tad."

"Stephen adores him. They just had the best week together." Susan shook her head, her eyebrows raised, her eyes wide with disbelief. "Tad is Jewish. *And* Catholic. I have no idea how they're going to make *that* work. They circumcised him *and* baptized him. They'll be lucky if he believes *anything* when he grows up. He's in Saint Augustine's. *And* goes to synagogue with *her*."

"I should count my blessings—at least Greg's Christian."

"Grant him that, Mom. I told him Stephen could go to Saint Bartholomew's *after* Kindergarten. They don't have a full-day Kindergarten. The public school has full days. I need more time to myself."

Good enough for now? Or would there be another excuse next year? "You're guaranteed a place?"

"It's our parish. Father Wayne likes Greg."

"What kind of a Catholic name is Wayne?"

"Mother!"

"What? I've never heard of a Saint Wayne."

"You take the cake, Mom. Now you're questioning the orthodoxy of a *priest*? You're a good one to talk. *I've* never heard of a Saint Karenna. So there."

"My middle name is Elizabeth."

"His is *Rosario.* Rosary."

"You asked?"

"I asked—when he baptized Stephen."

"He understands about the public school Kindergarten? Are you sure there will still be a place in first grade? Catholic schools can be very hard to get into."

"Let it go, Mom." Susan's tone seconded the warning.

Kary took a deep breath, blew the air out. *How you rear children matters, Susan.* "Letting go. It's none of my business." She pulled a bag of fresh green beans from the vegetable crisper, put the colander in the sink.

Susan pulled the kitchen stool to where she could watch Kary work. "You think? And you didn't even ask what I need time for."

Feeling like a shuttlecock here. She deposited a saucepan with salted water on the stove, turned the burner on. "Tell me."

"I want to move on in my life, get work, a job. I have a degree in Computer Science—and I've never even used it, what with Greg moving around, and Stephen…"

With scissors from the drawer, Kary began to trim the ends off the beans, a bundle at a time, and cut them into halves. *I don't get it...* "You're worried about your *career*?" She was sure the confusion showed on her face. "Why now?"

"I watch you—and you had Dad, and the three of us, and a career, and now you have an even better one, and I, well, I can't even decide what to do. Especially now that Stephen is old enough for school."

"You have a full life. Isn't that enough for now?"

"Isn't that enough? You always said we could do anything we wanted—and I can't figure out what that is?" Susan struck the counter with both fists. "I've been helping the IT department for the public school—they're hopeless. You can learn anything on the internet now—I keep up."

"You know my choices haven't been perfect, Suzy. Maybe if I hadn't been working sixty hours a week with small children, I wouldn't have been so stressed—" She rinsed the beans, dumped them in the saucepan.

"And you might not have gotten sick." Susan retrieved a long spoon from the rotating container on the corner of the counter; she gestured pointedly with it. "I don't see why you insist on living out here in the middle of nowhere—behind a *gate*—instead of moving closer to me and Stephen. I was going to tell you—there's a really nice house for sale on the next block, beautiful view, enough land so you wouldn't have near neighbors... I miss you Mom, and so does Stephen. You're losing out on his best years."

"And you want me to babysit in the afternoons so you can work." *Why do I always see the downsides?*

"Would that be so bad?"

Act normal? "No, of course it wouldn't. Are you telling me Greg got tenure?" *And will stay in one place the rest of his academic career?*

"You know it hasn't been seven years, Mom. But it looks really good—he's got the best student evaluations in his department, and..." She stirred the beans, turned the flame down.

"Which means exactly nothing. Even tenure is worth nothing if their enrollment declines." *And if Greg has to move on in a year, two?* Kary leaned on the counter, waved at the view beyond the breakfast nook and the deck. "I can't, baby. This is me."

"You're serious. After all that's been in the papers?" Susan shook her head in exasperation. "None of this would have happened in Colorado—whatever this is. And by the by, you are very nicely managing to turn this discussion *away* from what I want to talk about, namely, what the *hell* is going on in this mountain retreat of yours?"

"Language, Susan!"

"Language be *damned*, Mom. What am I supposed to think when the papers imply my *mother* is having an affair with a movie star?"

"Honey, I'm not." Barely. *By the grace of God.* In the words of the sacrament of penance: *'to avoid the narrow occasion of sin.'* "It really is none of your business, Suzy Q."

"It is my business. You're my mother. And if you're sleeping with some actor, I think I have the right to know."

"Suzy, dear. In the first place, I am not 'sleeping with some actor.'" Reality was bitter. *I was so close to giving in.* "I find that offensive of you. And even if I were, surely it would be only between him and me?"

"It would be, if it didn't appear in the papers. Honestly, Mother. What were you thinking?"

Susan knows all my buttons. "Actually, I was thinking of him. Your kind of attitude makes it impossible for people like him to lead a normal life. Relax, Susan. He's an occasional house guest. Even when he's here, he's gone before I finish writing." She went to the cupboard for plates, laid them on the breakfast table, added silverware and napkins to the placemats. "He has a job to do, you know." She gave her stiff daughter a little hug. Susan resisted, and Kary shrugged. "Thanks for worrying about my reputation, but it really isn't necessary."

"I have to. I don't think you do."

Kary sampled the spaghetti sauce, stirred. "If you think about it, it's quite flattering."

"Mother!"

"He's very charming. You're meeting him Monday." *Damn. You weren't going to tell them until tomorrow night—remember?*

"Mother!"

"He's invited all of us to watch them shooting a Revolutionary War battle."

"Mother! I—"

"That's enough, Susan. Stephen will love it." *And I can't back out of public display now, can I?*

Ta-ta-ta-ta. The timer on the counter startled both of them. Susan gaped.

Kary reached, pushed the button. *Silence.* "Don't you have to…?"

"A minute won't hurt. Much." Susan pocketed the silent timer. "All he could talk about on the plane was that hot tub."

"I'm surprised he remembered."

"Children remember odd things." Susan's face compressed stubbornly making her look five again. "We're not done, Mom."

"Go get your cherub out of the water. I promise I'll make time later." Saved by the bell? *We are getting more and more ridiculous.*

Duty won. "I'm going."

Kary stopped Susan before she got halfway to the steps. "Wait. But if Greg isn't…" *Crunch of fear.* "What is wrong with your sister?"

Susan faced her, discomfort crossing her face. She opened her mouth, thought better of it, pressed her lips together. She exhaled heavily. "It's personal. I don't have all the details."

I should have called Ronnie, insisted. "How long have you known what's going on?"

"Only since the plane. She broke up with her boyfriend…"

Heaviness settled in a knot under Kary's breastbone. "That's all? She's so… damped."

"She flew in to Princeton days later than we did. I think she doesn't want to talk trash about him because she isn't sure if they'll get back together… So she's been moody and weepy and wouldn't say anything. Maybe you can get some sense out of her."

"We'll have plenty of time. Go." *Not your job, baby.*

~ ~ ~

LET IT BE. *RONNIE WILL tell you when* she's *ready.*

Kary blocked the thought of rest, was infinitely glad she'd fallen asleep in the car. She pulled pre-cut salad greens from the bin, set them on the counter next to her wooden bowl. She turned the oven to 'warm.' The Parmesan came out to join the grater. She gave the sauce a stir, releasing a bubble which carried the acidic tang of tomatoes and reminded her to add a teaspoonful of sugar. Then the salad dressing from the fridge. Vinaigrette. And a memory of Stephen's face on his last trip, unchildlike, as he made a face at the tartness of the raspberry vinegar on his tongue, and asked for more. *So like Susan.*

"What can I do?"

Kary whirled. "You startled me." Ronnie. "You can—take out the pasta pot, fill it with four quarts of water—"

"—Four quarts of *cold* water and a teaspoon of salt."

Kary grabbed the dressing, closed the refrigerator door. "Some things never change, do they?"

"Everything changes." Ronnie set the pot on the stove, fiddled with the controls until she had the flame adjusted. "I wish I had a gas stove like yours." She took the other kitchen stool, reached out for Kary's hand, examined the back. "Don't tell me. Tree limbs, garden implements, or something on a tall ladder."

"I'm careful!"

"Tree limbs—"

"The washing machine, if you *must* know. What?" She studied her daughter's disapproving face: Ronnie's eyebrows were arched, her brow accordioned. "I'm careful!"

"Uh huh. Of course you are."

"Stephen still loves 'paghetti and meatballs, right?" *Too much drama with Susan.* She could feel the crash coming. *Get dinner over, find an excuse…*

"As far as I know…" Ronnie stared out the deck glass door, her voice wistful. "I love this house, Mom. It's so peaceful here. You can hide away and never come out."

Twenty-two-year-olds shouldn't need to run and hide. "Susan thinks I should move to Colorado."

"Susan thinks she can keep everyone safe. She's a lot like you, Mom."

The knot in her gut tightened into a noose. "Ronnie, what's wrong?"

"You really want to know?"

"Susan said you broke up?"

"I might as well tell you." Ronnie's voice was defeated in a way Kary hadn't heard since Ethan's death.

"Whatever it is, we'll deal with it, sweetheart."

Ronnie looked at her as if it might be the last time. "Yeah?" She turned away, focused on the Ruby-throated hummingbirds buzzing each other for control of the feeder on the deck. "Mom, I got pregnant."

Oh, God. What could possibly be the right thing to say? "You wouldn't be the first girl to graduate from college married, with a baby. Susan managed."

"Married?" Ronnie's lips pinched in a sneer. "He ran, Mom. Like a scared rabbit. I can't stand the thought of him."

Kary waited for the other shoe.

"I made an appointment, Mom. At the clinic." Ronnie laughed mirthlessly. "Alone. And you know the worst part?"

Kary didn't dare move a muscle. *How do you react when your child aborts your grandchild?*

"My body aborted the baby, Mom. I made it happen." Repeat of the painful laugh. "'Spontaneously.'"

Not—? "You can't, Ronnie. Listen to me—"

"I did! I'm not pregnant any more."

"Ronnie, listen to me." She found the teaching voice. "If women were able to abort their babies that easily, they would. In droves. The ones who didn't want to be married, or were forced, or were raped by advancing armies? The ones who know the next baby will kill them? Women whose husbands are running around? The ones whose husbands will know for certain the baby isn't theirs?"

"You don't understand, Mom. I *prayed* for this baby to die, and God *heard* me." Ronnie's gaze was full of misery. "I didn't even get to the clinic for the appointment I made." She stared at Kary defiantly, rigid.

Kary opened her arms. Ronnie clung to her, her dark head grinding into Kary's shoulder. It was a moment before Kary dared speak. "How long...?"

"A week ago."

"No, how—"

"You mean how pregnant was I?" Ronnie pulled back, glared at her. "Does it matter?"

"You should have let me help."

"I prayed for God to kill the child I was carrying, and He did. I was so relieved." Ronnie's tears were stuck, her voice strangled. "And I can't forgive myself."

"Ronnie, sweetheart—"

Ronnie breath hissed out between her teeth. "The worst part?"

It was like holding wood. *There is worse?*

"I can't stop thinking, what if something went wrong? With *me*. What if that was the only child I'll ever conceive?"

"Listen to me, Ronnie. If you miscarried—" She started again. "Sometimes keeping a fetus alive is well nigh impossible."

"I know. You've told us: Mother Nature getting rid of her mistakes, because the baby is unsuited for life in this world."

"At the hospital, we kept those babies alive at great cost—to both family and baby, sometimes in great pain. Most still didn't make it."

"But some did, Mom! What if I'd had proper pre-natal care—"

She kept her voice calm, reasonable. "Which is why I asked how far along you were."

"Five goddamned weeks."

"Ronnie: listen to me. That fetus was gone before you knew it. *Nobody* could have saved it."

Ronnie collapsed in tears while Kary held her awkwardly half-on, half-off the kitchen stool until she could speak. "Mom, I miss the baby. After all that." *Rachel mourning for her children.*

"I know, honey." She patted Ronnie's back, reached for a tissue, waited until Ronnie blew her nose several times. "Come. Sit on the couch with me." She remembered to turn off the burners, brought along the tissue box and placed it on the coffee table between them.

Ronnie pressed into the curve of Kary's side and arm, blew her nose again noisily.

Kary glanced at the photo on the mantel, found her words. "I miscarried, before Ethan. I often wonder what that baby would have been like, whether it was a boy or another one of you girls, whether I would have even *had* Ethan, whether everything would have been different…"

"Not have Ethan?"

God chose, not I. "Three is a lot of children for a working mother."

Ronnie followed her gaze. "I can't imagine not having Ethan."

The tears released again, and Kary gathered her in like the lost child she was at that moment. Kary let the sobs come until Ronnie hiccoughed. She stroked Ronnie's back. "How do you comfort a grammar nerd?"

Ronnie pulled back in confusion. "What?"

"There, their, they're." Kary cocked her head, shrugged. "It works better written."

"Oh, Mom!"

"Come here, baby." *Where I can't make anything right.*

Ronnie cried herself out, snuffled. "I'm okay, Mom. It's not as if there was something I could *do*."

Learn? Kary held her daughter. She said nothing, holding that which was broken, not trusting the platitudes which came to her mind. *There is nothing so divisive as the simple birth of the next generation.*

"I'm hungry, Mam Mam." Stephen had come quietly into the living room, stood, eyes wide, at the end of the couch.

Kary reached her free arm out to him, and he crawled into their embrace. His hair was slicked down, damp, and he smelled of baby shampoo, soap, and dryer sheets. *How far we have come since morning.*

Stephen patted Ronnie's arm. "Why are you crying again, Aunt Ronnie?"

BIANCA

Bunker Hill; 9 P.M.

THE DIFFERENCE BETWEEN Andrew and John was palpable. *Andrew's mere presence dominates the set.*

Now that it was time, Bianca rocked impatiently on the tall stool reserved for her, almost wishing she wasn't about to film Emily's deflowering dream sequence. Her first sex with Andrew would have the force of natural awkwardness—not necessarily bad. But she would have infinitely preferred it be private. Worse, it was her last big scene with Andrew. Grant, talking in cahoots with Andrew just out of her hearing range, would've postponed this scene even further—'Don't want your father/daughter relationship with Strathmore contaminated. I know you can handle Emily as well as Sarah, Bianca. Humor me,' Grant had said—but even he had the sense not to push filming critical scenes too late. *And I only have until Thursday with Andrew.*

John she'd had to coax along, encourage, tease into relaxing, in-cite ardor in—it was *work.* But now, standing here in newly-wed Emily Strathmore's thin chemise in this bedroom in her father's English country house after a London wedding, watching Andrew talk to Grant, she was finding it near-impossible to keep her racing pulse anywhere near normal. *Father assured me the servants were far away and asleep in their own wing.*

It was going to be *hard* filming this the way Grant wanted first: demure, frightened young bride learns what is expected of her in her marriage bed— *Oh, please.* Did all men have the 'first night' fantasy? His money, his film, his script—and none of them thought about, or cared about, the fantasies of women watching some night a few months later in a darkened theater.

What is taking them so long?

Finally, Andrew gave a last nod, and peeled off. *Something's different.* As he came towards her, she realized with a shock that he'd taken years off the Colonel. There was a spring in his step, energy in his bearing the war-weary Colonel had lost. He wasn't *playing* the younger Strathmore—he *was* twenty-year-old Strathmore. Was that a whiff of the clean smell of saddle soap? She imagined him shaving in the room over the stables where Father had quartered him— *'Until he* becomes *my son-in-law.'*

He grinned at her. "Evening, Mistress Strathmore."

She felt heat rise up the back of her neck, lowered her gaze, didn't resist when he offered his arm. *And she was sixteen again.* Before the soap opera's recurring 'plot' hardened her, before even Zed, before the brat... She raised her eyes defiantly, to find her spanking new husband gazing so earnestly at her she did not know where to look...

"Keep it for the cameras, you two. Places, everyone." Grant checked his watch, said something to an assistant who scuttled to do his bidding.

"ROLLING!"

Two hours later, Andrew/William was exactly the same man— but she was ready to scream in frustration. She buttonholed him as they came back from a break. "It's okay to touch your new wife, you know."

"Overdoing it, am I, mistress?"

"I get it; you're nervous—"

For a moment something ancient stared out at her from his eyes. "And ye, m'love, are too bold."

Chilled, she broke eye contact first, signaled to a minion with an unnecessary rat-tailed comb in one hand, brush in the other, had her perfect curls retouched while Andrew, not William, stared. *Damn!* She had broken the unwritten rule: don't tell your costar what to do—and the steel fist snaked out of the velvet glove in an instant. It stung; but it was good to be reminded. *And when I'm your director, you'll give me what Grant gets: anything he asks for.*

"PLACES!"

She played it straight, strangled all but the young girl William had courted. She mined memories of her first time, scared and ex- cited and stubborn—poured them into Emily. She ignored everyone and everything—crew, lights, the stupid mike-on-a-boom that dan- gled overhead just out of frame. Grant wanted 'demure'? She saved everything else for the other version, gave Grant 'demure,' made Andrew work for every gasp and twitch. She pushed it to the limits of PG-13—and stretched those limits as far as she dared.

Want it to sell tickets, Grant? This was the night William would plant the seed that became Sarah? *So be it.* She'd bring back a ghost for Strathmore. She cooperated with her new husband as well as a new colt takes to the rope harness placed around its neck. A gentleman would have reacted as Scarlett O'Hara's first husband did, and retreated from the battlefield for the night. Andrew was no gentleman...

"AND CUT!"

She sat on the edge of the bed, breathing hard, her gaze on the crown molding decorating the ceiling's border. Andrew sat down next to her, giving her six inches of space, with the sense not to open his mouth. Grant and his cinematographer consulted in whispers around the playback screen.

For better or for worse, everyone on a set *knew* when the stars slept together. *Maybe it's better this way.* Acutely aware of the man on the bed, she waited impatiently for Grant to release them—do it again, or move on to the version he *knew* the fans would never see in theaters? Reserved for the director's cut? *Bring it on, Grant.*

Her heart-rate slowed. Almost without taking his eyes off the screen, Grant made a quick throwaway gesture, and a minion scampered away from the herd, fetched a robe and put it around her shivering shoulders; she jumped as Andrew tucked it around her, ignored him. *This is taking far too long.*

Finally, the cinematographer nodded, and Grant echoed the motion. They pulled back from the screen, talked quietly a moment longer.

She recognized the next movements, and her heart raced. Grant was moving to the setup for the same scene, second version, checking the timing, consulting with the key grip... She let herself become the other Emily, the one with the buried passion men so loved to think they brought out in women. How little did they know it was not them, but *in* the woman—they could get out of its way, or they could hamper it—but it wasn't up to them. Oh, no. It wasn't up to men.

Emily would have to hide it, to not seem a tramp. Emily would pay for it by dying in childbirth to give this man a son, and Strathmore would end up with nothing but memories like this one, and a young Sarah to raise by himself in the New World. But she, Bianca? She would harness her own power, and bring him to his knees.

Newly-wed Emily Strathmore set her chin. He wouldn't know what hit him...

"THAT'S A WRAP."

What the hell? Her breath caught as the crew started the takedown, rolling up the mic cables, hitting the off switches on equipment, securing cameras and rolling stock.

Grant headed their way.

He crouched at her feet, with his headphones dangling around his neck, clipboard in hand. "You okay?"

She stared down into Grant's wary eyes. "Why wouldn't I be?" *Shit. Where was this going?*

"That was very, very good, Bi." His tone was gentler than usual.

It brought back memories of the director on her first soap. *The one I kicked in the groin so he'd stop pawing me.* "So—when are we doing the... the *other* version?"

"I'm not sure we need the other version." Grant tapped his watch. "It's past eleven-thirty. Long day for the crew."

"But—" *Give me my chance, you bastard.*

"If I decide we want it—after Monday's battle—there's time."

"I *have* to leave before Thursday. I'm way overextended. Wouldn't tomorrow be better?" She glanced to Andrew for support, puzzled at his blank expression. *Surely he'd want it on celluloid?*

"I can't, Grant." Andrew's tone held regret. He shrugged. "To-morrow is scheduled to the second— For the battle prep—"

"Tuesday. Wednesday. There's time." Grant mirrored the shrug. "Besides, I'm not even sure I'll need to use it."

You're blowing me off, you bastard. There wouldn't *be* any time. And Andrew *knew.* Fury rose. Both men's gazes were on her flushed face. *Be very, very careful, Bi. 'Never let the bastards see you hurt.'* She could shrug, too. "Tuesday. Or Wednesday. Your call, Grant." She nodded in agreement for public consumption, sensed rather than saw a slight relaxation of tension. *They'll pay for this.* But not at the box office, and not now. The only difference would be that, after Wednesday, there might not be a scorching vision of perfection stored unseen in a film vault somewhere.

So I explode it out of the gate with Dodgson—Andrew was so close to signing she could smell it. The thought cheered her immensely. The tip of her tongue touched her front teeth. *I am still in the game.*

She glanced pointedly over Andrew's shoulder, motioned to the waiting staff. *Anyone. Get the fuck over here.* Released, Makeup, Hair, and Costume suddenly came to life, like ball boys at a tennis tournament after the star aces a serve, and scurried over *en masse.*

She smiled graciously as Grant uncrouched. Andrew got to his feet, his eyes narrowed speculatively. She liked the feral way he was looking at her. Did he have *any* idea what he'd missed?

She nodded to Grant, allowed herself to be ministered to and led away. She forced herself to be *particularly* benevolent to the innocent children poking at her with sponge and cloth. Out of the corner of her eye, she saw Andrew already deep in conversation with the waiting horse trainer. *That's how little this means to you?*

She made herself smile patiently on the tall stool, surrounded by worker bees. *Monday, eh? Just as well.* She'd've had to fake it tonight, anyway. Besides, there was something so unfinished after filming war that came from exciting the pitched fervor of warfare and damping it with the unions' demand they not actually injure anyone. Especially not horses. *PETA didn't care about the humans.* It was after precisely such a fake battle that Michael Henderson had seen the light. And if her fuzzy history served her right, wasn't Arthur Pendragon seduced by his half-sister the same way in *Camelot*? Fake or real, something about surviving combat made men weak.

The minions finished retrieving the last hairpins. Driver and cart waited in the shadows. Reaction was a bitch. She was drained beyond exhaustion.

Monday night is soon enough—and I won't be tired then.

CHAPTER EIGHTEEN ❧

"... no atheists in foxholes."

Love's not Time's fool, though rosy lips and cheeks
within his bending sickle's compass come.
Wm. Shakespeare, *Sonnet 116*

> "If only you had been alive in Charlemagne's time. What a magnificent Roland you would have made!"
> "Madam, you forget my profession. Had I been alive in the time of the great Charles, I would have been his court jester."
> Andrew O'Connell to Lady Cockett-Smythe,
> London premiere

KARY

Sanctuary

"YOU'RE SURE YOU WANT us to go, Ronnie?"

On the small CCTV screen by Kary's front door, the gates were swinging inward to admit the limousine. Kary glanced at her daughter, opened the door.

"I'll be *fine*, Mom. I'm going to read, sit in the garden, maybe take a nap." Ronnie shrugged. Her tone was flat, her demeanor closed.

Stephen ran outside, and Susan, bag in hand, brushed between them sideways to follow him out of the quiet dim of the house into brilliant sunlight.

Kary shouldered her bag, stepped over the threshold. For once, the weatherman had guessed right. Days were *supposed* to be like this, like the ones she grew up with in Southern California: sunny and warm, with low humidity good for actors and horses, colors too bright. She stood with her right hand rigidly clasping her left wrist, as if she could forcibly contain her apprehensions. *It is so ordinary, standing on my own stoop.*

Ronnie joined her.

No one knew where the stone would be thrown into the space-time continuum to start the outward ripples. *My worlds are about to collide.*

The limousine rounded the last turn up the drive, emerging into the clearing in front of the house. Susan reached for Stephen's hand in the universal protective gesture of mothers thinking ahead. Ordinary people getting ready to leave the house for a trip—to another world, a world with a different timeline, a world which, like *Brigadoon*, was about to disappear.

The decisions had been made: Kary was not permitted to cancel. Ronnie, who had spent the day at Zoë's playing in the pool with Stephen, aided by Zoë's boys, one of the kids rather than one of the grownups chatting on the deck, was remote but calm. Ronnie insisted on going to Zoë's—and was equally insistent on remaining at home today. *Parental obligation: I have let her—as if I had a choice.*

The limo didn't halt. Purring quietly, it began a slow, precise K-turn.

Kary felt soiled, compromised. This morning, with one stroke of the metaphorical pen, she had let Akiiya's bastard story-child live. *Because I can't face Ronnie asking later if I based Akiiya's miscarriage on hers.* What did it matter? All the writing in the world would not bring back Ronnie's child. *There has been enough death.*

The black vehicle avoided the pickup by inches. They watched the balletic turn of the impossibly long vehicle in the erratic non-quiet of the countryside: a cicada rubbed its legs, the leaves made a fretting sound rubbing together in a puff of breeze.

George had said only strong winds would stop the shoot on a cloudless day, and there was no front due: she'd checked the weather. Grant was damned lucky. *I guess we're really doing this.*

The limousine stopped, pointed toward the drive. George hopped out. "Afternoon, ladies—and gentleman," he nodded toward Stephen.

Stephen's eyes were all agog. "Are you the movie man?"

"No, son." George crouched eye-level with Stephen. "I'm the movie man's assistant."

"What's a 'sistant?"

"His helper." Susan, thawing slightly.

"We're going to go see the movie man make a movie." George looked up at Susan, back at Stephen. "Would ye like that?"

Stephen nodded vigorously.

"Okay, then. Ready?" George stood.

"You've met Stephen. This is Susan."

George shook.

"And Ronnie."

"Me pleasure."

"Are we keeping you from your work, George?" Kary regretted the words instantly. *Relax.*

"Believe it or not, days like these I really don't have much to do. All the animal stuff is done by professionals with special credentials. And the explosives are handled by experts. All I usually do is stay out of the way. This actually gives me something useful to do."

Susan spoke. "What will it be like?"

"There are seven camera crews for this one, and they will shoot it all the way through only once, because it is too big to repeat, and everything gets blown up. One go.

"Then Grant and the editor will take the shots they need and piece together a battle sequence they like. It's apparently rare that they don't get everything they need, but if they don't, the computer graphics team will patch it up. After the main battle, they'll be shooting three separate extra pieces, specific to the three battles in the movie—ye know, the parts which are different in each. And then we're done. All the hard prep work is done already; but they won't have anything to show for it until this afternoon is over. Any questions?"

"How long will it take?" Ronnie.

Being polite?

"They never seem to start on time. Everything's been tested for weeks, but something always needs last minute attention—half of this stuff is held together by string and sealing wax. But they have to be done before five-thirty, Grant said, to keep the light. And the horses are only allowed to work so many hours. Me guess is they'll actually start filming around three, and Grant will cut his losses and go with what he has around five."

"Will they let us know when to be quiet?" Susan, worried tone. "If there are going to be explosions, I may need to remove Stephen."

"Each of the cameras has mikes near it, and there are a dozens of extra mikes all around the battlefield. The editor will be choosing sounds independently from all the tape recorded. Don't worry about it—I can't believe he's louder than cannon."

Frank came around the car, opened the back door. He touched his cap. "Kary."

"You haven't heard him," Susan said.

"Don't worry, Ma'am." George peeked at his wristwatch. "We all ready?"

Now is the time to explain Ronnie isn't coming. Kary opened her mouth to speak, "Those of us who—"

"I can make my own excuses, *Mom*." Ronnie addressed George. "It's very nice to meet you. Please tell Mr. O'Connell—"

Stephen's voice piped up clear and loud and high. "I want to ride in the front!"

"I'm afraid not." Frank peered at Susan. "Airbags, Ma'am. Can't have little ones in the front seat."

"I'm not little!" Stephen insisted. "I'm big!"

"Okay." George spoke directly to Stephen. "How much do ye weigh?"

"I dunno. Six *hundred* pounds."

"Do ye have a scale, Kary?" George's face was grave.

She nodded. She refused permission to the smile which tried to lift the corners of her lips. "Upstairs. In the bathroom. End of the hall to your right, through the bedroom." *Andrew's room.* No, Susan's room.

George spoke to Stephen, man to man. "I'll make ye a deal, right? We'll go up to the scale, and if it says ye weigh over one hundred pounds, Frank'll let ye ride up front. All right?" He caught Frank's eye. "Okay?"

Frank said, "One hundred pounds." He returned to the idling limo, leaned against the hood.

Stephen nodded, his little face reflecting the seriousness of the bargain. They climbed the granite steps side by side.

Susan smiled. "If he doesn't have kids, he ought to."

They were back in minutes, Stephen solemn, George pursing his lips.

"The scale says I'm *almost* big enough," Stephen said. "I ride up front *next* time. Right, George?"

"Right." George was expectant, but unhurried.

Ronnie's cellphone rang. She took it out, glanced at the screen, tapped an icon.

Kary met Ronnie's gaze. "Do you need to answer?"

Ronnie shook her head. "It's Amanda. Must've left something in Princeton. I'll call her later."

"Which reminds me." Kary took out her cellphone, turned it off. "Can't have it going off during a battle."

"Good idea." Susan tapped the screen on her own phone several times. "You won't be able to reach us, Ronnie."

"I'll be fine—" Ronnie gazed over at Stephen, who was already 'helping' Frank open the limo's back door. She duplicated Susan's motions on her own cellphone, slipped it back into her pocket. "Wait a minute, Mom. I think I'll grab my backpack and come. Susan will need a hand."

BIANCA

Storrs Pond Recreational Area, Hanover; 2:45 P.M.

TONIGHT! TONIGHT! Sometimes musicals were so appropriate.

The van driven by the girl minion trundled up the back road to the ridiculously-named Balch Hill where the battle would be filmed. Where *did* these yokels get their names? She was surprised originally to find out that the battle of Bunker Hill was fought on Breed Hill because some idiot Col. Bridley? Gridley? changed his mind at the last minute. *Men.*

She'd guessed right. The memo from Grant—'rushes of Saturday's scenes were satisfactory'—meant no more 'Emily' relationship to respect.

Andrew would be tired after the battle—and wired. The tip of her tongue wet her upper lip. *He won't know what hit him.*

The explosives techs had been practicing—with the van's driverside window wide open, there were already, as they approached the huge zoo-like battle set, the aromas of sulfur and cordite—from fake smoke and safe explosions. *I love the smell of napalm in the morning.*

What had Alan Alda said in *Sweet Liberty?* 'Defiance of authority, nudity, and explosions.' *That's what the American moviegoer wants to see.* Defiance and nudity were in the can; now Grant would lock in 'explosions' and all the tension on the set would have somewhere to rest. *If he doesn't screw it up in post—and Grant never screws up in post—we have ourselves a hit.*

And she wouldn't even have to do anything today. Her schedule for the next two filming days was packed to the gills with fill-ins and retakes—but today not a body nor a camera could be spared, and she could just look beautiful—and watch. She took great care—and slept late. Her hair was glossy, her pert navy skort and feminine sleeveless not-quite-Polo shirt were cut to show off legs and tanned bare arms, and the thought of *after* the battle—well, she knew her lips were plumped to perfection. *America's Sweetheart*—a sight for sore eyes. *If I do say so myself.*

Camera mounts encircled the battlefield like alien watchtowers. The minion drove around the back of the extras' holding pen, stopped too far from the white awning with some lame story about how they didn't allow the vans closer.

Bianca had expected the tall canvas-backed stools to be empty, but there were figures under the awning. Did Grant invite local dignitaries to watch the big battle? Damn him. He'd expect her to make nice—last thing in the world she wanted right now. A man—and several women, one in the classic pose of mother clasping child on hip. An uncomfortable echo—her last 'family' picture with Zed—and Nate on her hip, in that exact pose.

Who the hell brought a kid to a shoot?

Too late. She was trapped. That idiot George turned, was looking straight at her. *Shit.* No chance in hell he couldn't see her. *Shit, shit, shit!*

And then the woman with George turned, and the shit hit the fan and went splattering all over the field: what the *hell* was Kary Ashe doing, standing by the chairs, holding a little boy?

Bianca covered her shock by detouring to grab a couple of water bottles, put the 'delight smile' on her face, walked up and offered the little guy the cold bottle. "Hello, little man. And who might you be?"

"I'm not little. I'm big," the kid said petulantly. But he took the bottle.

"My bad. Let's start over, okay? Hi. I'm Bianca." She smiled at Kary. *And I have just stepped into a large pile of poo.*

"These are Kary's daughters," George indicated, "Veronica..."

"Ronnie. Hi."

Bianca nodded at the dark-haired one.

"And Susan." George nodded. "Ye've met Stephen."

The blonde, not quite as tall as Kary, smiled and held out her hand. "Susan Mancuzzi."

Bianca did 'fan-dazzling smile.' "Nice to meet you, Susan, Ronnie. Kary told us about you." People either went all babbly or all shy when they met movie stars—thank God these weren't the running-off-at-the-mouth kind. She glanced around. No dignitaries? Good. *Just the witch and her brood.* "Welcome to our little Armageddon." *Now what?*

George saved her. "Uh, we're getting pretty close to..." He shrugged, inclined his head significantly towards the boy. "If there's anything anyone needs? We don't talk once they start."

The blonde one took the hint. "Excuse us. George, would you mind showing me the facilities?"

"I don't need to go!"

"Well, I do. Let's go check them out." Susan took the boy from Kary, put him down, held out her hand. "And you can run around a bit. Because you have to be very quiet when the horses start, or you'll spook them. Right?"

Solemn nod. The boy gave Kary his bottle of water to hold.

"I'll come with you," Ronnie said.

"Lovely family, Kary. You must be proud." She took her seat next to Kary, made the best of a bad situation. "I'm glad you're here. I can thank you personally for the extra work you did on the *Dodgson* script. You didn't have to do that."

"I had one or two thoughts after you left; nothing important. It's shaping up to be a curious story." Kary's eyes narrowed in speculation. "Your screenwriter friend has an interesting mind."

"Felix? We go way back. This would be a big break for him, *if* I can get it made." *Sufficiently off-handed?*

"I thought it was already approved."

"Nothing's a done deal until you're spending the money." *And things can still fall apart.* "Hollywood is littered with dead projects."

"Ah." Kary glanced in the direction George went. "When should I pencil it in for viewing?"

"At the very best, sometime next year. *If* Andrew signs on, and everything goes smoothly."

"He hasn't signed?" Surprised.

So they don't talk about me. "Negotiations are a pain." *The less said, the better.* She glanced around, checked her watch. The horses were restless; one reared in the holding pen. She realized she was rocking softly, stopped herself.

"Ah." Kary reached into her bag for the pen and small notebook, waited to see if Bianca would speak, and, when she didn't, opened the booklet, scribbled a few lines.

Good; she can entertain herself. The air was charged. Bianca felt the electricity kissing her skin. The well-oiled machine that was a Grant Sykes's shoot proceeded inexorably, stretching like a dragon waking up—a claw here where a troop of redcoats clambered into the saddle, scales where the assistant directors broke like a football huddle and headed for their posts on foot or in golf carts, the head— *Where was Andrew?*

George came up from behind, answering the questions of his charges in a low voice, placing the boy between himself and Susan, to Kary's far side.

They are moving to my heartbeat. Everything rested on the next few hours, and Grant couldn't have gotten a more ideal day if he'd paid for it. *Maybe he's just damn lucky.* Over-and-over lucky. *I need some of that luck.* Finally! Andrew, mounted, taking command of his troops as if he were real. Reaching down to reassure his steed. Another one of his little competencies, horses. Was there anything he *couldn't* do?

Support personnel began their retreat at the signal. They were committed. The dragon was preparing to take flight. *And breathe fire.*

ROLLING!

Grant signaled the order to go into battle. The first cannonade made her jump. She'd been trying to follow Andrew, but the firing came from the other side of the gigantic set, spread before them like a museum display of toy soldiers.

The armies charged behind their officers, standards snapping. Cannon boomed, spewing gray smoke which drifted across the plain. The first volley, and the first dead crumpled to the field. A shrieking horse reared. She knew the smoke plumes came from canisters, and not the combustion of dirty 18th century powder, but her eyes told her otherwise. The smoke hid Andrew's horse from view, and her heart clenched.

Relentless pounding went on for hours, until her head felt like the kettledrum after the *1812 Overture*. Her eyes ached from the chemicals, and the strain of peering through the billowing clouds from the smoke machines trying to keep Andrew in view—so she could praise him appropriately later, and not sound like an idiot. The finale went off, slowly building after more rounds than were probably fired in the *real* battle, until, *finally*, they were done, and the last sonic boom was not followed by another, but faded from the scene, echoing.

It seemed the whole world held its breath while the cameras silently recorded the plumes sifted over the scene by an errant breeze. One second—two—an eternity—

"CUT!"

She couldn't hear the repeats at each station; she didn't need to. The cheering began far to their left, where Grant directed the battle, while supervising Andrew's shots himself. *Of course.* She'd lost sight momentarily, but there he was. Leaping back into the saddle, standing in the stirrups, roaring, his fist pumping, troops rallying round him. She would've thought the British won the war. *The big ham.*

"The reenactors had a good time," said Kary.

Ya think? At least the kid hadn't made a fuss the whole time. *Time to be 'nice' again.* She got up. The panorama before them was of purposeful work, shifting people and equipment, and, for once, she had nothing in particular to do. "I don't think I remembered to breathe in hours."

"They'll be telling their grandchildren about it," George said.

"What's next?" Kary again. Her daughters flanked her, curious but silent.

George answered. "There's a short break while they clear the extras who won't be needed, which is most of the locals; they've been here since early morning; they'll be wanting to go home."

"And Grant doesn't pay overtime if he doesn't have to." *Did I sound too snarky?*

"It most likely ensures him funding for the next one, doesn't it?"

Perceptive. "Some directors have a legendary habit of going over budget; the money wasted could fund many more films." She laughed. "Do I sound bitter?"

"No. Wise." Kary stood quietly, her gaze roving over the set.

George spoke again. "Now comes the good part. Who do ye want to watch die?"

Kary's attention focused on George. "Excuse me?"

"They're setting up to film the last battle parts, while the cannon are still on the field," George said. "Peter's dying, John is dying, and Andrew is getting a tearing big war wound."

"You can't tell anyone what you'll see." Bianca paused for the solemn head-shakes. "My husband dies, and our favorite servant dies trying to protect him. John's lucky—he's perfect. Those cheekbones! He dies a noble death on the battlefield."

Susan spoke to her boy. "Many people died for our country."

"They say over a thousand British troops died—and almost 150 colonials, so, yeah, noble death." *Idiots.* "He doesn't even try to get out of the fighting, not even with a pregnant wife." Did the kid know 'pregnant'? "And I get to raise his son with my in-laws overseeing every step. Whoopee." She said it with a smile.

"Everyone made sacrifices." Susan. With a disapproving mouth.

"Where will we be least in the way?" Kary, changing the subject.

"Actually, ye have to watch all three from back here," George said. "There isn't time to move, and there's nowhere closer ye can watch from."

"Here will be fine."

Always so damn agreeable.

"I think I'll take the little guy for some ice cream." George looked up in alarm. "Pending permission from his ma?"

"Do your worst." Susan shook her head. "And thanks."

Ronnie spoke. "Do you mind if I come with...?"

"The more the merrier. Do any of ye need ...?"

Heads shook. George headed off to wherever the ice cream was with the two of them. The boy hung from their hands, swinging like a monkey. *Where was Andrew? And why, oh Lord in Heaven, did you stick me with these rubes?*

"He's been very helpful," said Susan.

Oh, great. Women talk. But she might as well take the opportunity. "George is always there." She gave her tone an appreciative ironic twist. She turned to Kary. "Have you given any more consideration to Grant's request?"

"What request, Mom?" Susan said.

Bianca made her eyes wide. "Oh, your mother didn't tell you? Grant wants her to do the screenplay for *Prairie Fires*."

"Mom, you never mentioned that."

"We haven't even agreed to an option." Kary sounded prim.

You ruin my plans, I'll ruin yours. "Are you *still* dickering with him? I thought it was a done deal. What Grant asks for, Grant usually gets." She laughed to take the sting out of it. Her gaze went from daughter to mother. "She didn't tell you? Oops, Kary. Sorry I let the cat out of the bag."

Kary shrugged. "It would have come out sooner or later."

"Tell me, Mom." The tone suggested annoyance with secrets kept.

"Not much to tell, really. I told him no, but he keeps sending me books on screenwriting."

"But that would be so exciting for you, Mom!"

"*And* an enormous amount of work in a discipline I know nothing about."

"Mom, you don't *have* to do it yourself. Couldn't you just supervise?"

"Which brings up its own problems."

So intent was Bianca on stirring her little cauldron, that she jumped at hoofbeats as Andrew cantered up on the big black stallion, encrusted with grime and fake blood. Behind her, George walked up with his little entourage in tow.

The boy's eyes looked ready to pop as he stared up at Andrew.

"Would ye like to come up?"

The boy nodded, speechless. George handed him up. *What had Andrew said about having a special rapport with kids—'never worry about one of them sandbagging me.'*

"Take us a picture, would ye, George?" Andrew posed with the kid in the saddle, and the daughters standing with Kary at the horse's head while George snapped several quick shots.

"Scooch into the picture, Bianca, would ye?"

Just what I need. She smiled with them when instructed to 'Say horse.' *You don't say no to Andrew in host mood.*

Andrew passed the boy down to Kary. "Gotta take Alhambra back to the trainers for his dinner. Be right back." He pulled the big horse's reins around, and galloped off towards the animal corrals at the far side of the battlefield.

"Whew!" Susan reached out for the kid.

"I wanna ride the horsie."

"When ye're a little bigger, son," said George.

"I *am* bigger."

"That was amazing!" Ronnie.

"Thank you, George," Kary said. "It made the whole thing extra special having you here to explain it for us." She nodded towards her grandson. "You've made his day."

What am I? Chopped liver?

"And you, too, Bianca."

Of course. Didn't the woman ever get tired of acting 'gracious'?

Grant was back at his station, megaphones crackled into life, and, in the distance, now split into three widely-separated sets, three units used the battlefield backdrop to film the separate pieces. *And if these intruders hadn't been here, I could have meandered over to watch Andrew.*

By the time they finished filming the remaining segments, the boy was restless and squirming on his seat, and the mother was finding it difficult to keep him quiet; not that it mattered—there wasn't a microphone near enough to pick up their voices. At least they kept silent, not sure, and Bianca didn't have to reply to questions.

She itched to escape. Dust and smoke left a fine gritty layer on her skin—she should have expected it. *Not a biggie—he saw me sitting here all afternoon watching him film.* It would have to do.

"IT'S A WRAP! THANK YOU, EVERYONE."

They were back to normal, the extra crowds long gone, and there were no cheers. Grant took as long as he needed. After the long day, all the crew wanted was to stow gear, and pack it off the outside set and back into the trucks and vans, so the local—who'd made a bundle—could have his bare hill back intact. The back-breaking labor would go on for hours yet.

Thank God—not my problem. Her watch read half past five. Her face hurt from smiling and feigning interest in the fate of her menfolk. The *only* good thing about the watchers he'd invited to screw up her afternoon, was that Andrew would come the hell over to say goodbye.

Kary *had* to be wiped. The brat, too. They *must* have the sense not to accept if Andrew was stupid enough to invite them to dinner. *I can stand next to him and wave goodbye.*

And here he was. Dust, dirt, sweat, blood, and bandages caked his makeup. Even at a distance he *smelled.* "Did ye get enough?" Huge grin. *Men.*

"Where's the horsie?" The interrupting midget.

"Long gone, lad. He's back at the stable, feasting on oats and hay. He needed a good brushing. Beautiful, isn't he?"

As you are. Damn it. He positively thrummed with high spirits.

"C'mere, Daughter."

"Yes, Father?"

He opened his arms wide. His eye twinkled and his grin was totally evil. "Give us a hug."

She moved towards him obediently, made sure her gaze told him she knew exactly what he was doing. *What the hell—I need a shower anyway.*

Kary put a hand on her shoulder to stop her. "Don't be mean, Andrew. You stink."

Not again, the miserable woman. *Would you* please *stop interfering in my life?*

ANDREW

DEPRIVE ME OF ME PREY, will ye, m'dear? "Aha, Kary. Then *ye* give us a hug." He opened his arms wider. The aftermath—so different from the anticipation of battle—was settling like lead, and he would not permit it. The sun was barely beginning its descent from the apparent zenith where it had hung just long enough for Grant's perfect shoot. *I am King of this hill, and will not be denied.* "Come to me, m'luv."

"Not on your life." She gave him a stern look. "We were waiting to say goodbye and thank you." The light broke out on her countenance. "That was *amazing.*"

"*Thousands*, not counting extras..." He smiled as she caught the reference. *Well, boyo, another one gone without making too big an ass of yerself.* But no actual damage—God be praised. No broken bones to be taken care of in CGI, always a potential problem with the fight scenes—getting it to the razor's edge without cutting himself. There would be sore muscles—tomorrow. Today, adrenaline coursed his veins like quicksilver.

"Where's your horsie, Mr. Movie Man?" The boy Stephen's upturned face was full of wonder. *Inviting them was the right move.*

He reached down and swooped the child up, rotated and pointed to the far side of the field. "Do ye see that covered box on wheels, there, by the blue truck? Where they're loading the cannon on the flatbeds?"

The boy nodded.

"That's Alhambra's. He worked hard today." Hierarchy was setting in: crew and cast went through the same battle—only everyone else, including Grant, had *work* to do. *Except me.* "He's going home now."

"Are you going home?"

"Soon, lad. Soon." Too soon. The reenactors had walked off arm in arm to head for their local pub—and their familiar conversations. He would have been the center of attention had he shown, was not

~ 397 ~

missed at all when he didn't—he'd made *that* mistake before, been pitied by the extras—ouch, when George explained it to him. *The end is beginning.*

"When do you ride the horsie again?" The child's face was inches from his.

"The next time we're in a movie together." *Never.* But the boy would have no concept of 'never.' "Did ye have fun?"

The boy nodded vigorously, and Andrew set him down. Kary's girls chimed in with thanks, and he answered the small talk on autopilot, in the middle of a scene which would pop like a soap bubble in seconds. All he'd done was to prolong the end.

Bianca standing patiently, smiling, next to the girl, Ronnie.

Susan retrieving her little one.

"*As* I was saying…" Kary.

Serene. Matriarch. *The last time I saw ye, luv, ye were dancing.* He *knew* she must be tired, but her face did not reveal it. She had gone mysterious on him again, and he knew he was intruding. George was approaching in a bee line from where the limo waited, Frank leaning on the hood, on the field side where the horse trailers loaded. Time hung in his heightened consciousness, and words failed him.

"…I'm sure you have a lot to do." Kary's gaze flickered to George, returned. "We'll get out of your hair."

He found his voice. "Actually—" *Think quick.* "Ye're looking at the most expensive piece of superfluous equipment on this set. They can finish the whole thing without me now. Grant won't even have rushes for me until late tomorrow." He grinned at Bianca. "This little lady now gets *all* of Grant's attention, and he has been shamefully neglecting her for days."

"It's not quite that bad." Bianca laughed. "*We* call it 'prep time.' It's in the schedule."

"Then we'll let you get to it." Was there desperation in Kary's voice?

"Ye won't hit the commissary with us?" *Best ye can do? Let her go.*

"I think not. *Stephen* needs bedtime and a bath." She forestalled the boy's protests. "In the *hot tub*, Stephen. With boats. The movie people have a lot of work to do, and here comes George. You get to ride in the limo again with Frank."

"And Chinese food." The little guy's voice was stubborn. "Aunt Ronnie promised."

Ronnie indulged him. "I'll go fetch it while you have your bath."

"Chinese food. Me favorite. Ye're a lucky boy. Do ye know how to use chopsticks?"

"Yes." Balky expression.

"He's learning." Susan.

"Keep at it, lad—I was a lot older than ye when I had me first Chinese food."

"Come eat with *us*, Mr. Movie Man." Stephen turned to Susan. "Can he, Mommy?"

"I think he's very busy—"

"Why don't you?" Ronnie chose that moment to join the conversation, surprising him. "You said you had nothing to do here."

Leave them be. Make an excuse. *"Thanks—I really can't."* *"Maybe some other time."* Empty social constructs. Kary is dead on her feet, and ye know it. "Are ye sure?" Coward that he was, he crouched down and addressed the boy. "Are ye going to leave enough egg roll for me?"

"Yes! Mam Mam, can we get *lots* of egg rolls?"

George arrived. "Are we ready?"

Ronnie spoke again. "Will you come, too, George?"

"Come too, where?"

"We're all going to Kary's to eat Chinese food." *And I am going to hell.* "Bianca, ye'll come with, right?"

Her composure shifted for a moment—something flitted in the back of her eyes and was gone. "I would love to, but I can't. Unlike *you*, I have work to do tonight."

"Ah, *damn*—" Remorse hit him. "We were going to talk about *Dodgson* tonight, after dinner." *Think fast.* "Will ye be available after—?"

Bianca indulged him with the throaty laugh. "Go have your fun. Come talk when you're back. I'll be up. *Working.*" She smiled dazzlingly. "Don't let him stay too long, Kary. We have *piles* to go over."

"I won't. I'll send him right back to you after the last bite of almond cookie." Kary's look told him, *"I'll talk to you later."*

Bianca smiled again, said her goodbyes, headed toward the parking area.

He watched her walk away. *A fluid, classy stride.* She'd make a nice little director—not take any shite from him. It would be a good night.

"I think I'm going to bail, too, Kary—if ye don't mind?" George spoke with regret. "Frank can do the honours."

"It has been quite lovely, George. Thank you for everything."

"And who have we here?" Peter Hyland's deep voice joined the conversation from behind Andrew's head.

And ye didn't hear him approach—ye're losing it, lad. "Ye done, Peter?"

"I'm as thoroughly dead as I can be. John's *almost* dead." Peter smiled, indicated the far left of the field, where a camera crew still worked under Grant's exacting direction, with a wave of his hand. "Hi there, Kary. These your girls?"

"And me!"

"And you, of course." Peter shook hands gravely with Stephen.

"Would you like to join us for dinner, Mr. Hyland?" Ronnie's voice was full of the respect Peter commanded.

"Ah, I would love to, my dear—but I must pack."

"Leaving tonight, Peter? Surely ye must eat." And now ye're trying to hide behind Peter. *Have ye no shame?*

Peter's glance pierced him. "A quick bite at the commissary while my assistant finishes packing, *then* a talk with Grant, and he's sending me back to L. A. on his plane—it's going to fetch something he needs before Wednesday, and I'm catching a ride."

"Ye won't be here for the wrap party?" *Damn; it won't be the same without Peter.*

"Regrettably not. Cassandra awaits; we have obligations." Peter shook Kary's hand. "Dinner next time. If you're in Los Angeles?"

"I will." Kary inclined her head. "If I'm ever in Los Angeles."

The adrenaline didn't let him down. "Peter—have ye got ten minutes?"

"Ten? Certainly. Why?"

"Kary, come." He put out his hand, and she took it. He seated her in one of the tall chairs. "Keep Kary entertained while I hop on the bike and go remove this goop," he indicated the torn and stained uniform, "and George, send Frank with them after me in exactly ten minutes."

George's eyebrows went up. "Ye can't make it in ten."

"Standard bet?"

George checked his watch, pushed a button. "Go."

Finally. A place for the adrenaline. He sprinted toward the bike, parked across the field near the edge of the road. He reached it with the first minute going, kicked the stand out, and the machine roared to life. He scooted carefully through the surprised crew, headed down the road toward the shower and clean clothes. He promised himself no more than a family dinner—then say goodbye again, but that was hours away. *I can go to hell after dinner just as well.*

He was sitting on his steps, still toweling his hair dry, when the limo arrived.

"I'm impressed," said George.

"I win?"

"Ye win. I'm sure ye cheated somewhere, but ye win." George held the limo door for him, accepted the soggy towel. "Send him back early, Kary. He claims to have nothing to do, but *I* have a long list for him."

"Will do. Bye, George." Echoed by the chorus.

George closed the door after they piled into the limo, waved them off.

And now for amends. He turned, slid the panel between him and Frank to one side, got his answer in the form of a lap blanket Frank pulled from somewhere in the front compartment. "Did ye order, Ronnie?"

"George ordered while we waited."

"Here, luv." He handed Kary the blanket. "Pull a hedgehog. I'll keep the family entertained."

"I'm absolutely sure you will."

He heard the gratitude in her voice, kicked himself again. *No more than a quick dinner, ye heel.*

Kary pulled an eye-mask from her bag, inserted earplugs from its tiny pocket, let Susan wrap the blanket around her and tuck her in.

A mask focuses attention on the half-smile below. How did she make the taboo, sleeping in public, vanish? *Because we allow small children and the sick to violate it when necessary.* Wise of her; the household would not come to a complete stop until the little one crashed.

He was as good as his word all the way to Enfield, where they stopped for Ronnie and Frank to retrieve the ordered 'banquet for eight with extra egg rolls,' and on the final approach to Kary's gate and house. The now-familiar landscape slipped by beyond tinted windows. *A good solid forty minutes—hadn't she claimed the re-storative value of a half hour?*

He lazed in the limo's back seat while Stephen asked enough questions for a whole Kindergarten.

Simple, easy questions.

KARY

MY LIFE HAS BECOME FARCE.

Before her, at the head of her dining room table, Andrew O'Connell, Emperor of China, held court.

Controlled chaos, car, to kitchen, to dining room in world record haste. She'd helped the girls collect plates and chopsticks, and forks—*'just in case'*—fetched a beer for Andrew and Ronnie and water for the rest of them, brewed tea.

Stephen bounced at Andrew's left, Susan next, then Frank. On Kary's side, Ronnie sat handmaiden at Andrew's right hand. Kary had left the chair between them empty, so she could capture the scene—and face Frank across the broad expanse whose only concession to propriety was individual plates under the army of open wire-handled white cartons.

I close my eyes for two minutes...

The problem? That he looked so natural, filled the entire house with Andrew-ness, but still *had* to leave. He kept digging the empty hole deeper. She hadn't taken off the eye-mask, but she woke when the limo stopped at Enfield for the whispered drama:

'I'll gather the goodies.' Andrew.

'You have to be kidding—we'd never get out of there with hot food. Frank will help.' Ronnie.

'Can I go, Mommy?' Stephen.

'Next time. Shush—you'll wake Mam Mam.' Susan.

Kary promised herself she'd help him escape gracefully as soon as dinner was over.

He can't help it any more than a black hole can. Two days ago Susan believed he was the devil. In the car, she'd been scandalized at Kary's critical examination—*'A lot better cleaned up. Quickest shower on record?'* And now Susan was eating out of his hand.

Stephen was in his glory: two adult men were treating him as one of them.

And Ronnie. Had she invited Andrew to dinner to see for herself what the relationship between this *Man* and her *mother* was? Brittle Ronnie, not quite herself. The bubbly self-assured, no-trouble child. *The one I trusted to work out her problems. The one I hoped would* never have to suffer. That was stupid: everybody suffers. *My sunny middle child has turned into someone I don't even know.*

"More egg roll, Kary?" Frank, limned by the light of the long day approaching the solstice, smiled at her, a beardless Santa Claus in a dark suit.

She shook her head. "You'd have to roll *me* into the kitchen."

"Will you miss New Hampshire?" Ronnie. The determined tone.

Kary's head snapped toward her daughter, just quickly enough to see Andrew's gaze return from her to his questioner. *He came of his own free will.*

"What say ye, Kary? Will I miss it?"

"Like a gypsy campsite—here today, gone tomorrow. Movie people. *Actors*." She didn't like the constriction under the center of her sternum. *And I will miss you more than I've missed anyone in a very long time.*

"Mr. O'Connell, can I ask you a question? Off the record?" Ronnie squared her shoulders.

"Record?"

Oh, God. No. She's not going to ask Andrew what his intentions are, is she?

"She's a journalism major." Susan answered. "They drill it into the students. It means she won't ambush you in print."

"Aha." Andrew peered at Ronnie with renewed interest. "Only if you call me Andrew."

"What happens next?"

"That is a *wee* bit open-ended, is it not?"

Ronnie tucked her hair over her ears, clasped her hands in her lap, in the tell Kary knew meant Ronnie was figuring out how to procure something she wanted. "Mom said the filming is wrapping up."

"Aye. Me last day is Thursday, then some promo for Maury, and home to Ireland. Ten more days. Why do ye ask?"

"After today's battle, I was wondering what you'll miss the most."

Protecting me?

"That one's easy, girl." Andrew glanced at Kary, back at Ronnie. "Carm, of course. A special lady."

"Carm?"

"Me makeup lady. We've become— intimate."

Kary stopped breathing.

Ronnie was confused. "Ah—?"

"She's the last to touch me face before every scene." He considered, nodded his head. "Poor dear— She's getting along in years. She told me this is her last shoot for Grant. Too much for her rheumatism." He nodded again. "Ye saw her—I trotted meself over to her every break in the action for a touchup."

"The lady with the brushes?"

"Aye. Carm."

From her side vantage point, Kary noticed the subtle tightening of jawline as Ronnie clenched her teeth. Andrew vs. the bulldog. *Even money.*

"I'll miss Kary. This. Yer mother—" slight emphasis on the noun "—is a fascinating woman." He indicated house and view with a vague gesture without breaking eye contact. "*On* the record. But ye know that."

Ronnie's jaw relaxed. "May I ask another question?"

His body was completely still. Full alert. "Shoot."

"What is it you notice most different between the finished film and your memories of shooting?" Ronnie placed her hands, loose, on the edge of the table.

Andrew contemplated, breath indrawn; exhaled. "Good one, m'dear." He wore the air of approving of her as an interviewer. "The sounds." He nodded slowly several times. "Aye. After the wrap the sounds are… calm. Businesslike. People go back to whatever they need to do, they talk, there's shouted instructions—all very… mundane." His gaze went deep inside for a moment. "Even in the rushes, the sound is missing or rudimentary. But when ye see it, at the premiere, it's shocking, because sound makes it real. Battle, sounds of the dying, shrieking of horses…" He shook himself. "And the music, of course. Layered in later."

Kary pulled herself together. *And I will miss this, the easy talking.* Time to send him back to camp. She stood. "Don't get up; entertain the kiddies. Frank, would you give me a hand?"

"Surely."

She escaped to the kitchen with plates, Frank following with the first of the open cartons. It could never be awkward around Andrew. He wouldn't allow it. *I needn't have worried.*

Did Ronnie want to know if Andrew and her mother would see each other again before he left? Kary chuckled grimly; instead of the light private goodbye they'd already executed, his invitation arranged a ridiculous set piece: waving goodbye to the mother of adult women in front of her whole family and staff. Only Lucy and Joe were missing to make it the perfect theater of the absurd. *Oh, and maybe Charles.* After the ludicrous spectacle of a grown woman sleeping on full display in the corner of the back seat of a limousine.

But it reset my brain. She sighed. Everyone would think it cute if Ronnie had a crush on Andrew. Actors past forty routinely displayed 'costars' half their age kissing them for half the movie. Was it in their contracts? Or were they just too stupid to be good actors until they were that old—while all the actresses had to do was to look pretty and be themselves? Ouch, Kary! Feeling our age? *Fool.*

She closed the leftovers: Ronnie would have the Sesame Beef, fiery version, for breakfast; Susan would munch on the shrimp; and Stephen had claimed the Chicken with Cashews before they'd even opened it. *So predictable!* She loved predictable.

"Ready for you, Kary." Frank had lined up the cartons, neatly labeled by Andrew with black marker, on the counter next to the refrigerator.

"Sure you won't take some of this home?"

"No, Ma'am. Done enough damage for one day." He patted his ample stomach, looked around for more items to tidy away. "Did you notice your answering machine is blinking?" He pulled it out from where she'd shoved it behind the toaster.

She stared at it stupidly, harbinger of bad news. Another gossip column already? While the girls were still here? *Damn.*

She forced herself to scroll through the numbers. All from the 609 Princeton number she shared for nineteen years. A blip on the machine every half hour. *Later. After he leaves.*

But wasn't there a call from Amanda—what did Ronnie said on their way out? *'Probably something I left in Princeton.'*

Had Ronnie turned her phone back on? She wouldn't have been so rude—she hadn't been out of Peter Hyland's sight, and then Andrew's in the car... *No one* turned a cellphone on in Andrew O'Connell's presence.

She put her hand on the phone. *Don't.* But she'd be too tired later. What if it was important? *Get it over with.*

It rang while she hesitated.

She picked the snake up. "Hello?"

Amanda. "Kary? It's me. Is Susan there? I've been trying to reach the girls for *hours*." Amanda's voice was far higher than usual.

Put the phone down, and the girls won't need to know. "They're here with me, Amanda." Had the girls not told Amanda where they were going, to spare her feelings? *Don't ask.*

"Mom?" Ronnie held the house's stash of extra chopsticks, and the stack of extra napkins from Enfield's China House. She was followed by Susan, with Andrew right behind Stephen whose tongue stuck out, clamped between his baby teeth from the honor of carrying the teapot.

No. Not now. "What is it, Amanda?"

"Mom!" Ronnie was reaching for the handset.

Kary ignored her.

"It's Charles." Amanda's voice dropped an octave, slowed.

Kary could *see* petulance on the redhead's pointed chin. She closed, opened her eyes. "What?"

"He—he collapsed. This afternoon! I called!"

Careful, Kary. Keep your tone absolutely neutral. "Is he all right?"

"No, he's *not* all right, Kary. He's *dead*!" Amanda wept and hiccoughed on the phone.

That wasn't possible. *He's not that old.*

"Wait one second, Amanda." She pressed the handset against her chest.

She bypassed the girls' questioning faces, sought Andrew's concerned gaze. "Could you and Frank take Stephen to the living room and build a fire? Carefully?"

Andrew nodded. "Hey, Stephen. I bet they never let ye light the match, do they?"

Stephen's face brightened.

She waited until the kitchen door swung closed behind them.

"Amanda, get a grip. What happened?"

"I don't know!" Amanda wailed. "He was playing squash at the gym with Larry, Larry Binkman. Larry said Charles clutched his head and crumpled. He said Charles was conscious long enough to look him in the eye, tell him it was a cerebral aneurysm, and nothing could be done. The ER said it would have been too late even if they got him to Princeton Medical Center faster. He *knew*. It was horrible."

Intraparenchymal hemorrhage.

She found herself shaking—with anger. She'd been so over him—and he'd reached out to ruin her peace, her life, even her last moments with Andrew. *Andrew will leave—and I have to deal with this mess dropped in my lap.*

Breathe.

She couldn't shield the girls from this—even though she knew their world would change forever the instant she told them. "Amanda, I'm sorry."

She took another deep breath, gazed at each daughter in turn. "I am so sorry. Your father died this afternoon." Ronnie was closest. Kary handed her the phone with its coiled line anchored to the answering machine.

And leaned on the counter, helpless, as first Ronnie, and then Susan spoke with their stepmother.

Her right hand fingers circled the base of her left ring finger, where a faint indentation remained even after eight years.

When Susan gazed at her, distraught, she took the handset back. "When are the services, Amanda?" She listened. "So soon?" More listening. "We will be there." She hung up the phone.

Wordlessly, she gathered Ronnie into her arms, reached for her eldest to pull Susan close.

Final judgment is out of my hands. A chill straightened her spine.

Ronnie's words: God chose.

Charles had gone before the Omniscient Judge. *All I can do is pray for mercy.*

Would his Purgatory be longer because of his weakness? Or shorter because he had no capacity to realize how weak he was?

Look to your own soul, Kary. Because by those standards you will be judged.

The world will now know I'm free. And it made not the slightest difference.

It got so confusing.

Which is why you leave it to Him.

ANDREW

WHATEVER HAPPENED WAS bad. He'd seen that look on Kary's face only once before, when he abandoned her on Mt. Kearsarge. *'Will ye be okay driving?'*

It would forever sear his conscience, the last blank wall when she said she'd be fine, and he roared off, like the selfish bastard he was, without a backward glance, because *his* vanity was affronted.

He broke the silence for them. "Who is Amanda?" He kept his gaze on Kary who glanced quickly at Stephen before her gaze returned to lock to his. She held herself stiffly, rigid in the shoulders. *Right when she should've been getting rid of me and taking herself to bed.*

But Ronnie replied first. "The other woman."

"My father's second wife." Susan.

"My other grandma." Stephen slipped out from under Andrew's hands on his shoulders to run to his mother.

Kary never mentioned the name. Kary never talked about her divorce, period. *Damn that Charles.*

Only Susan moved. "Sit here, Stephen. I have to tell you something." She sat Stephen on the couch, crouched to his level. "Something very bad happened to my Daddy today, and we are all going to be very sad."

Stephen's eyes were round and subdued. "Is Pap Pap okay, Mommy?"

"No, honey, I'm so sorry. Pap Pap..." She choked. "Do you remember when Buster..."

"Is Pap Pap dead like Buster, Mommy? Are we going to put him in the ground in the back yard?"

No one could make me believe Grandda was gone, and I was nine. But when...? They wouldn't have come watch if they'd been called...?

"Something like that. You need to be brave. Amanda and Tad are going to need you to be very strong, and so am I. Do you understand?"

Stephen nodded solemnly. "Is it okay to cry, Mommy?"

"Of course, honey. We cry when we are very sad." She sat next to him, took him into her arms and pressed his head into her shoulder.

Andrew's eyes took a 360° pan of the scene. Sudden death hung palpably in the air, changing the house—the one he never thought he'd see again—to a house of mourning. The woman with the child in her lap. Frank leaning forward from the other couch, his hands clasped. Ronnie standing by the armchair, looking at the boy, her hands in helpless fists. Kary holding lightly to the back of the couch. Himself with the matchbox still in his hand. And on the shelf behind Kary's head, the photograph of the family smiling, at the beach.

He set the matches on the mantelpiece.

Frank rose, addressed Susan. "My deepest sympathies, Ma'am." He turned to Ronnie. "Miss."

Susan thanked him; Ronnie nodded.

Andrew followed the example of his better, forced himself to speak to each daughter in turn, a mechanical robot. "I'm most sorry, Susan. Ronnie." *That ye were watching me prancing about the field on Alhambra when yer father lay dead. Christ.*

Ronnie's clenched jaw and intense stare were pure hate. "He was only sixty-one!"

No. Not hate. Anguish. But they couldn't have reached Princeton even had they known. *Nothing any of them could've done.*

Frank spoke to Kary. "Please accept my prayers for you and the family." He moved the box of tissues from the wall unit to the coffee table. "Is there anything I can do?"

"Thank you, Frank," Kary said. "It's most kind of you, but I don't think we need do anything except show up. Amanda's made the arrangements—the funeral is at eleven tomorrow. I'll call the airline in a minute, we'll book a flight first thing in the morning."

"That's soon."

Kary would go? Why...? *Of course she would—for her daughters.* 'Twere it himself, he'd be wanting to make certain his enemy was dead. *But Kary?*

"Yes. She's Jewish. It's her preference."

"Where, Mom?" Susan looked anguished. "Dad's Catholic."

Ronnie answered instead. "Saint Augustine's. Amanda told me burial will be with Grandma and Grandpa behind the church. His good friend Father Royce is still pastor. He arranged everything."

A good Catholic funeral for the man who cast aside a sick wife? He caught himself. Say goodnight, Andrew. Let the women deal with the mourning. This is not yer concern. *Take meself out of her way.*

Ronnie pulled her cellphone out, poked viciously at the screen. "I'll get the times, Mom."

Something skittered across the recesses of his mind. A faint but recent memory. "May I borrow yer phone, Frank? Left me own."

"Certainly."

He went back into the kitchen, let the door swing shut behind him. *Ah, yes. Frank's phone had Grant's number.*

He clicked, waiting impatiently, until Grant's exasperated voice answered. "Grant Sykes, here. What is it, Frank? I'm in the middle of something."

"It's me, Grant."

"It would be. Where the hell are you?"

"Did ye need me?"

"No. I just like to know where you are."

He didn't answer. "Is Peter there with ye?"

"Why?"

Christ, Grant. Can ye never trust me? He took the time, brought Grant up to speed as swiftly as he could, asked his question. "Right, then. Owe ye one."

"One? Stay out of my hair, we'll call it even."

He heard the hangup, stood for a moment in thought. It required some planning, and he had *one* chance. By all rights he should take Kary aside, tell her quietly. *So she has the proper chance to refuse yer meddlin'.*

But it made such perfect sense...

Ye didn't arrive where ye are by balking at the fences, boyo. He played out a couple of scenarios, settled on one—he didn't have much time. Ronnie was already making reservations...

In for a pence...

He pushed through the door silently.

Ronnie was speaking into the phone. "Master Card number three-four-oh—"

He moved briskly to her side, put out a hand over the phone.

She looked up, annoyed. "What?"

"A moment, please?" He glanced at Kary. "I have a plan."

"This is not a good—"

"Hear me out."

Ronnie rolled her eyes, spoke into the phone. "Hold the reservation, would you? *Renton.*" She spelled it out. "I'll call you right back."

Shortest number of words, eejit. Ye can do this. "I just spoke to Grant. Do ye remember Peter is going out to L. A. tonight?"

"Peter?" Kary nodded. "But what—?"

Spill it. Fait accompli. But only the basics. "We'll take ye to the Lebanon airport now, Frank and I. Get all packed. Peter will meet ye there, and the plane will make a quick stop at the Princeton airport, and drop ye off on the way." *They don't need to know...* "Can ye hire a taxi from there?"

"Tonight?"

"Ye said the funeral's at eleven tomorrow." He jerked his head at the plate glass windows, where the day dimmed. "It's still light. Ye won't be much late tonight."

Susan said, "We can rent a car at the Princeton airport."

"Whatever works for ye." *First ally.* He made eye contact with Susan, cocked his head. "Ye could be there for yer stepmom tonight." *Coward.*

"But—" Ronnie gaped at him.

"No buts. It's making no practical difference to the pilot."

"Mom—" Susan hugged Stephen. Her eyes pleaded.

"Of course, honey. We are very grateful to Mr. Sykes." She waited until he had turned to her with his best hangdog eyes. Her mild gaze penetrated all the way to his backbone. "It is unbelievably sweet of you, Andrew." She went all the way. "I was not looking forward to the travel. Even if I'd considered chartering a plane— which I should have—I could never arrange anything so fast."

"The plane's ready; Peter'll be leaving for the airport in a short bit."

She turned to Ronnie. "Could you let Amanda know—" she made calculations "—you should be at the house by, say, it's eight now, so, say, before midnight?"

Generalissima Ashe. She could sleep on the plane. But for the phone call, he would have helped tidy up, said goodbye to everyone, and then Kary again, in the presence of her family. Frank would cart him off—the house disappearing theatrically in the rear view as the limo slunk down the drive. *Exeunt.*

He excused himself to call George.

Time enough later to tell her there would be one more passenger.

CHAPTER NINETEEN

"Parting is such sweet sorrow"

(Wm. Shakespeare, *Romeo and Juliet*)

On one knee, Reyker wiped the soil of K'Tae from
his hands. *Goodbye, comrade Merton. Mentor. Friend.*
He looked up to find Akiiya watching him for signs of
weakness; a painful smile twisted the corner of his
mouth. He addressed the heavens: "Father, if Thou art,
add this man's blood to the price of Thy forsaken planet."
He rose, shouldered his weapon.

Hostages to Fortuna

LADY CONSTANCE
Grief fills the room up of my absent child,
Lies in his bed, walks up and down with me,
Puts on his pretty looks, repeats his words,
…my fair son!
My life, my joy, my food, my all the world!
My widow-comfort, and my sorrows' cure!

Wm. Shakespeare, *King John*

KARY

Sanctuary

*ALL I HAVE TO DO IS DECIDE what the spurned wife wears to
her ex-husband's funeral.*

Shock, of course. This was what ritual was for. Packing away relationships. All the girls had to do was to put every single item they
brought with them back into their suitcases.

Her favorite deep maroon suit would get her through another life
event. She added it to the go-bag kept packed by a woman who
never went anywhere, wheeled it out onto the landing. *We are all
being very proper in the face of sudden death.*

Andrew took the case from her before she reached the lower level, returned for the girls' bags, wordlessly carted them all out to Frank.

She locked her house, let Frank hand her into the limo after Ronnie, noted incuriously that Andrew chose to ride up front to give them privacy. Susan and Ronnie put Stephen between them, as it should be.

She told her fear of flying: we won't make it any other way.

She closed her eyes for a moment, woke as the limo slowed down and turned onto the tarmac at the tiny Lebanon International Airport. *'A fat lot of help I am, asleep every time they need me,'* warred with *'Rest when you can,'* as usual. She ignored the skirmish.

As they approached, George and Peter clambered out of the van parked by the executive jet.

Peter directed his condolences to Susan. "I am so very sorry to hear about your father."

"Thank you."

He shook Ronnie's hand, squatted to Stephen. "Sorry about your grandpa, son."

"Shake Mr. Hyland's hand and say thank you, Stephen." Susan's hand rested on his head.

Stephen's entire body was subdued as he executed the unwelcome social grace.

Never too early to learn. "I hope we didn't keep you waiting, Peter."

"Nope. No problem."

"We'll easily make up the time in flight, Ma'am." The pilot.

"Ah." *'Ma'am.'* Another of Grant's packages to transport, nothing more. She shuddered at what she had escaped: two long drives, three airports, Security, interminable waits. *I didn't have the brains to charter a plane—when am I going to learn I have money?* "How long to Princeton?"

"A little under an hour, Ma'am, once we're airborne. In another fifteen minutes, copilot tells me."

"Thank you." Chief mourner? Head of bereaved household? Eleanor of Aquitaine, mother of the king's sons? *What the hell... Language. What am I?*

The pilot nodded, tapped his hat's visor with two fingers, excused himself to ascend the short ladder into the jet.

"I loaded yer bag on with Peter's," George told Andrew.

Kary stared at Andrew.

George saw the change on Andrew's face, turned to Kary, turned back to Andrew, closed his gaping mouth.

"Grant doesn't need me," Andrew said. "I cleared it with him, and the plane'll stop on the way back to fetch me."

She couldn't find words.

"Ye might need someone along who isn't, ah, emotionally involved." He made an odd gesture, not quite a shrug. "Unless ye have friends awaitin'?"

Waiting? All eyes were focused on her face. "Amanda has room for... family." She indicated the waiting trio. "I was going to call Marge... Maybe stay a couple of days..."

"But not tonight."

"No. There's an Inn." This was true madness. *I shouldn't even be going.*

"It's settled, then."

Nothing was settled. *I have no business going to Princeton, much less with Andrew.* Man up, Kary. Do the right thing. Kiss the girls and Stephen goodbye, send them off to Princeton with Peter and the pilot; they'll be fine. Thank Andrew; let him and Frank go back to the set where they belong. Take a cab home. Go to bed.

"We're ready, Ma'am. Sir." To Andrew.

Where had the pilot appeared from? And how was Andrew now in charge? Thoughts swirled, refused to gel, as she tried to imagine consequences. *Everyone is looking at me.* Andrew awaited her response with the attitude of a penitent schoolboy; all he needed was to wring a cap in his hands. *It is truly my choice.* "Do you know how to drive on the right side of the road?"

"*With* traffic?" He cocked his head, held her gaze. "They let me drive in rush-hour Marseilles."

"Ah." She would never be able to pay him back. She took a deep breath. "You are a true friend." *And I am certifiable.* "Peter, shall we?"

It was so easy to let the men *handle* everything: load the luggage, plan quietly as men do in a crisis, and help the women and child into and out of vehicles.

The copilot, a young woman in navy blue slacks with a military bearing, came out to make sure their seatbelts were fastened; the plane taxied to the end of the runway, the jet engines came on with a rising pitch, and they were airborne with less fuss than it had taken to retrieve the kids at the Manchester Airport parking lot. Behind her, low frequencies from Andrew rumbling to Peter; before her,

Susan read to Stephen, while Ronnie gazed out the window at the setting sun on their horizon. Once they reached flight altitude, the copilot materialized with a pillow, and a blanket she tucked around Kary with a smile. The copilot brought drinks, disappeared back into the cockpit. Soft white leather seats... *Don't get used to this.*

"Ye should rest, Kary." Andrew.

"Yes, Mom." She closed her eyes obediently, ignoring the little voice: *'You just took a nap!'* A ridiculous way to cope. But there was nothing she could do right now, and this *might* ameliorate the enormous rest debt coming.

She opened her eyes when the engine pitch altered and the nose lowered. The sunset hadn't changed; they had flown at about its speed, due southwest. Below them, brake- and headlights twinkled, traffic lights changed; ahead, the landing lights sketched out a runway, with the last daylight and the red Mercury-vapor streetlights giving the blue Princeton Airport buildings a ruddy glow.

"George called. It's all arranged."

As Andrew loaded their bags with Ronnie's insistent help into the blue minivan which drove out to meet them, Kary turned: the jet carrying Peter to L. A. alongside Grant's mysterious errands was already lifting into the skies. *I* could *get used to* this.

"Where to, Ma'am?"

It would have made more sense for Ronnie to drive. "Right out of the airport onto Rt. 206; ten, maybe fifteen minutes total." She directed him at the left onto what would become Harrison Street, warned him about the Princeton police's penchant for enforcing 25 mile-an-hour speed limits, guided him through the narrow street where turn lanes had been carved out of non-existent space at the intersections, turned them left onto Prospect Ave., and showed him where to pull up to the house on River Road she hadn't been to since Amanda moved in. The déjà-vu was crushing.

Andrew located the right suitcases, deposited them on the broad front porch, recused himself to the darkened car.

Kary pressed the doorbell. They must have heard. The door opened immediately, and Kary stood by as Amanda received 'her' daughters' embraces, knelt to hug Stephen.

"Come in, please. Janet's here." Amanda ushered them inside, shut the door.

"I'm very sorry, Amanda." Kary stood in her entrance hall after a quick clasp, infinitely glad of Amanda's taste in bunnies and pictures of pastel birds. Not home any more. *Mother Renton would have had a cat.* Mother Renton was thankfully not with them any more.

"Thank you so much for bringing the kids."

And the anticipated awkwardness made its appearance with Amanda's sister. *Final exam time at etiquette school, a proper way to do anything.* Blood ties and marriage ties. *What is Janet to me— ex-husband's second wife's younger sister?*

"Hello, Kary," Janet said. "How nice of you to come." Janet's embrace was as wooden as the one at Ethan's grave.

"Hello, Janet."

"Where is your suitcase? We have room..." Amanda's voice trailed off.

Miss Manners, tackle this one. "Thanks, but I would be an awkward houseguest. My hours are non-standard. I'm staying at the Washington Inn."

Amanda's relief was too palpable. "They're lovely."

"They are." They would do, whatever they were after all these years. You couldn't get more 'Princeton' if you tried. "I just wanted to check out the arrangements. What time tomorrow...?"

When Kary had given her diminutive supplanter another short hug on the porch, the door to Maison Renton shut behind her; the van headlights came on just as the porchlight failed. *The last time I touched Amanda was at Ethan's funeral.*

"Done?"

"Done."

"Fancy place."

"Very Princeton." In-laws in residence. Marriage. Children. A career. Illness. Minefields all. *I made it a home. Sometimes.*

"Where to?" He peered at her in the dim light. "Are ye all right?"

"I think so." Her gaze was on the house. "She didn't ask how we got here."

"Shock."

"Yes. It has strange effects on people."

He turned the key.

"I don't think I said thank you." *I'm not alone.* Ronnie had told her on the plane, *'I am so glad you're here, Mom.'* And Ronnie asked, when they arrived at Amanda's, *'Do you want me to come with you to the Inn, Mom?'* But Amanda needed them. *Amanda doesn't need or want me.*

"Ye're welcome."

How refreshing. He *knew* what he'd done, didn't need to talk about it.

They had pulled into the Washington Inn court, registered, checked out rooms on the third floor, and were sitting in the bar, with whiskey and lemonade, before eleven.

"Seems I've done nothing today but sleep," Kary said.

"One of the oddest days in me recalling," Andrew replied. "So. Tomorrow?"

"I told Amanda I'd come by for the girls and Stephen at ten, take them to the funeral home by ten-thirty. They'll go from there to Saint Augustine's, service at eleven-thirty, interment at noon behind the church. It's a bit of a mishmash, but she promised in writing he'd be laid to rest next to his parents, so there will be a Memorial Service, but no Funeral Mass. I don't know what Amanda's mother will do—not my problem—but the rest of them will sit respectfully in the front pews and listen to Father Royce's words—Bill's known Charles since they were kids. I don't know how many people will be there, or who, at short notice, and on a weekday."

"Will ye go in?"

"To the funeral home, only for a moment. To the church? Yes, and sit in the back. I owe him that much. To be there for our girls. To take Stephen out if necessary—Susan and Ronnie will sit with Amanda." She rubbed her aching forehead. "It will be over soon enough. What time is the pilot coming back for you?"

"I'll be meeting him at four."

"Plenty of time." She looked at her watch. "I'm going to take melatonin, so I *will* be groggy, but I'll manage some sleep. The brain will be confused, but it can't be helped." She buried her face in her hands, then folded her hands under her chin. "I can't think straight any more. Will you be all right?"

"Kary."

"Well, you *were* fighting a war all afternoon."

"I'll be fine. I conked out on the plane. I have a book. And there's always the telly idiocy."

"Oh, good." She reached out, squeezed his arm lightly, kept the unnecessary thanks to herself. When she glanced back from the foyer, he was still sitting in the armchair, sipping the whiskey with a pensive air.

In her room, she hung the maroon suit in the little bathroom, brushed her teeth, swallowed extra pain meds and the hated melatonin, forced herself to lie down in the darkened room with her eye-mask compensating for the inevitable light leaks around the curtains in hotel rooms, did a few careful stretches at half speed so as not to raise her pulse. Considered again how wildly inappropriate it was to be staying at the same hotel with the man she had just touched.

She prayed, drowsed.

She was back in Central Park; maybe this time she would actually be able to hug Ethan. His mouth was visible, and his lower face conveyed sorrow. The horses clopped in a gentle rhythm along the curb lane on the south side of the park where the shadows always obscured the rest of Ethan's face. But if she reached out... He spoke!

"Kary. *Kary*." Someone was shaking her shoulder. Her eyes wouldn't open. "Kary. It's nine. Ye need to get ready."

"Ethan?" Her eyelids fought, won. Why was *Andrew* sitting on her bed? How...? *What did I do?*

"Ye're dreaming, Kary. And ye didn't lock the door."

She expelled her breath hard. "Thank God."

"Thank God?"

Her mind wrestled to untangle her tongue for speaking. "You didn't have to locate the manager."

"No." He chuckled. "Yer reputation is intact."

"Don't like to appear *too* stupid." She struggled to sit up in the bed.

"No. Of course ye don't." He pulled back, rearranged himself so he could face her better. "Are ye awake now? Is it safe to leave ye? I waited as long as I dared."

"I'm awake."

"Sleeping stuff."

"I'm not using *that* again." How could she have forgotten to wind the alarm clock the Inn clerk handed over when they asked about wakeup calls? *'No phones in the rooms, Ma'am.'* She shook her head to clear the cobwebs, opened her eyes to their widest. "I'm okay."

"Downstairs in thirty."

She nodded. The formal rituals were about to begin. He left, closing the door softly behind him. She clamped down, hard, on her heart.

The spot on the bed where Andrew had sat slowly decompressed.

ANDREW

UNDUE HASTE? *GUY DIDN'T even get a decent wake.*

Not that he deserved one; a selfish man, by all accounts. *But are ye not being selfish, too?*

Kary was next to him, toward the rear of Saint Augustine's Roman Catholic Church. Her whole being focused on the ceremonies at the altar. Upstart country; their churches were not a candle-lit dark with damp and moldy stone which never quite dried, but open and brilliant with light and color. Not conducive to proper sentiment at a funeral.

Reading, in the car parked in the shade at the back of the church lot bordering the cemetery, had proved untenable, and walking about fitfully was no better, so he had taken the step not taken in years except for the christenings of nieces and nephews, and had opened the side door cautiously, looked for Kary, and gone pussyfooting to sit with her in the pew. She had granted him a single glance of acknowledgement.

He willed himself to stop fidgeting at readings almost familiar, but in some new translation without the sonorous musicality of the old. The organist alternated. Latin responses came unbidden to his rusty tongue.

Nowhere better to watch a woman under stress. Knowing that he added to that stress by his mere presence. *She is an odd duck.* He'd invaded her last safe bastion—sleep—and she'd taken it well. When she was awake, she was so—alive. And then it went, and she stumbled with words, and he could see there was nothing left. *Painful to watch; she doesn't complain.* For that matter, she didn't complain about the man they were there to memorialize—and bury.

Did she need to *see* him buried? Closed casket, no embalming. Didn't they always do autopsies for sudden deaths? What strings did the second Mrs. Charles Renton pull? They could always dig him up later if they suspected foul play, right? Cynic. *Ghoul.* Well. He would've liked to see whether life had been kind to the man in the photo—not that he could have finagled a peek. Was *she* like that? He wouldn't blame her. Younger replacement wife, and another child? That must have galled. Or didn't she care? She was sick by then—maybe it was easier? Unless the eejit was a real bastard about it.

The acrid odor he'd choked on as an altar boy, of the incense censed at the white-draped coffin, finally drifted to the back of the church. Coming later like thunder lagging lightning. Sweetening the dead.

The priest chose to deliver his homily from the aisle, not the pulpit. He intoned the *Ave: "...pray for us now and at the hour of our death. Amen."* He faced Amanda. "Charles Renton was my friend..."

Somehow, he wove Charles into the lessons for the Memorial Service. A pillar of the community. A paragon of professional virtue and skill. A loving father and family man; the priest had the grace not to say 'husband.' How had the good Father taken it when his childhood pal abandoned a lawful wife and took a concubine? "Not an easy man." *Ye got that right, priest.*

Charles's daughters sat in the first pew with Amanda, with the heir-apparent and the grandson between them. He couldn't tell much from this angle—and he sure as hell wasn't going to meet the wife—but she was attractive and well-groomed on the morning of the funeral of the suddenly-dead husband. A step-mother who would decide whether they saw their half-brother again. They must be fond of the poor kid, and the uncomprehending little Stephen held his young uncle's hand like an anchor whenever they stood.

I was like them. He'd hated his Grandda's funeral. The priest then had intoned a list of virtues nowhere near the real Alexander O'Connell, who would have been scandalized he was being blessed and buried out of a church. Even after a decent Irish wake. *That's what 'dead' means: no more control.*

That funeral had been fire and brimstone and dark, the beloved Grandda who smelled of pipe tobacco and grog gone to judgment and purgatory as a warning to all. Somewhere in there a young boy's faith died, too.

This priest fellow was different, give him that. He spoke of funerals being an occasion to examine beliefs, faith, church, God. Pain. Atonement. The suffering of children allowed by a loving God. Lazarus and the daughter of Jairus coming back from the dead. He spoke of finality, but also of hope and mercy. Friendship and not being perfect. *Better for the collection plate?*

"And what do Catholics believe about death? That we will be judged fairly and with great mercy by the God who created us and loves us more than anyone can imagine, so much so that he sent His only Son to redeem us from that death."

Andrew shifted uncomfortably. He stretched back, forearms reaching for the top of the low padded pew. Not like deep foreboding prison benches carved from dark wood and polished by centuries.

Kary glanced at him, said nothing.

He straightened, put his hands in his lap. *Ceremonies of Mother Church to support the bereaved.* His agnosticism raised more questions than it answered.

The priest moved on to the Communion. He explained that non-Catholics were welcome to come up for a blessing, and should cross their arms over their heart. In the gentlest possible way he told this group half of heathens not to partake of what they did not believe in. Andrew wondered about the boy Tad, conferring with his mother before heading the line with Susan. Catholic school, here in the same parish, the priest said. Old enough to have made his First Communion. Would this day, honoring his father, be his last time? Taste of host lo these many years, *'centuries of Jews forced to pretend,'* swam in his memory.

The organist sang as she played. Kary sang quietly at his side.

Kary put her hymnal in the pocket, slipped out, walked unselfconsciously down the side aisle, arriving as the last communicant. The priest turned, smiled at her, placed the host in her hand. The deacon attended while she drank from the chalice. Priest and deacon returned to the altar, and Kary the way she had gone. A few heads turned her way briefly, returned to their prayers. She knelt at his side, bent her neck. *Brilliant timing. How does she always manage that serenity?*

Kary's head jerked up as the organist began *Ave Maria,* stared as Veronica Renton's pure tight voice reached for the highs, all eyes on the girl as she managed to keep from tears to the last note and resume her seat visibly shaking to a hug from Susan. *Gutsy girl.*

He heard Kary's breath released.

The priest blessed everyone, believers and non-believers alike, and made a small announcement: they would be following the pallbearers... *Time to sneak out before someone recognized him, and tied him to Kary.*

But curiosity stopped him at the side door when it became apparent the cortege would be exiting through the main entrance. A perfect observation post. *Allot it to Mother Church to orchestrate the heck out of the opportunities.*

He watched idly as □Ronnie stepped quickly to her mother's side, and huddled in whispered consultation for several moments. Interesting body language: Kary drew herself into a statue, unbent awkwardly to her daughter's quick embrace. Ronnie returned to stand with the bereaved after Kary nodded acquiescence.

Then the organist started the recessional, and Andrew got himself out of there, went to sit in the car to wait for her. The day outside was brilliant to the point of pain and he was glad George packed sunglasses.

"What was that all about?" he asked when she joined him.

"Ronnie? Logistics."

Nothing more? All righty. "Where to, m'lady? Are ye...?" He gestured with his shoulder toward the cemetery behind the church.

"Not until they leave. Would you mind if I rest here until it's over? Ronnie said they're all going back to the house."

'The' house. "I have a book."

"Poke me?"

"For certain."

"Pop the hatch, would you?"

"Would ye like me to...?"

She shrugged, smiled deprecatingly. "I just need a sweater. My body temperature drops..."

And ye keep putting her in positions where she has to explain. But she hadn't needed it for her first nap, whilst they waited for the procession from the funeral home with the hearse. Unpredictable, then. He searched for the boot lever, found it.

She was back in a few moments, opened the side sliding door instead of the passenger door, climbed in. She reclined the seat, took her eye-mask out of her handbag, tucked the sweater over herself. "It shouldn't be too long."

He glanced at his wristwatch. Not quite noon. "Out ye go." From his vantage point he watched the funeral cortege stop. The slow spreading of mourners around the site with the earth mound had the set-piece feel of every movie funeral he'd ever watched. The only shade trees were on the very border of the property. It wouldn't do to have roots poking through the blacktop. Or mixing with the bones. The searingly-lit scene contrasted sharply with that dreary misty day in Ireland among the crumbling ancient headstones at Saint Brendan's. He reached for his book. *But it makes no difference that matters to the dead.*

He was engrossed in his reading when motion in his side window, and the sound of a car door slamming, reminded him where he was. Almost half past already.

He waited until the cars finished exiting, and the car park was mostly deserted, giving her a few more minutes. "Kary?"

"Yes. I heard them. What time is it?"

"Half past."

"That was a good nap." She put the seatback up. "I'll be right back."

"I'll come with."

"Thank you."

They walked in companionable silence to where the gravediggers and their miniature backhoe were starting their cleansing task. "Give us a moment, fellows?"

The man checked his cellphone for the time, spoke with his companion. "We'll finish up after lunch, then. C'mon, Karl."

"Thanks." All the same to them, must be. They stuck their shovels in the dirt in the manner of gravediggers everywhere. He was amused when 'Karl' hopped onto the running board of the little construction vehicle, and it slowly rumbled toward where the lorry with the trailer waited at the side. They could've walked faster.

"He's with his dad now."

Ah. Family plot. He inspected the dates on the headstone, but of course the new one wouldn't be chiselled on yet... And saw what she meant. *Shite.* He strangled the reply that had come to mind— *'best a man rest with his parents.'* "Ah..."

Kary knelt on the section of artificial turf by the headstone, traced the letters with her finger. "He loved his dad." She sighed. "Charles wasn't a bad man, you know? Just weak."

He didn't belong here; too many undercurrents.

And how can ye be such a bloody clueless fool?

KARY

IT'S A BEAUTIFUL BALMY spring day in Princeton, and all I feel is cold.

"I used to walk here, from my apartment on Witherspoon." She stood up, brushed her fingertips reflexively against her skirt, though they weren't dirty. The headstone was cool, dry.

Andrew's warm respectful bulk had given her his hand automatically, as she rose.

She watched him read, but she knew the words by heart:

ETHAN CHARLES RENTON
Dec. 10, 1986 ~ Dec. 14, 1999

~

Surely goodness and mercy shall follow me
all the days of my life:
and I will dwell in the
house of the LORD for ever

~

PSALMS 23:6, KJV

"He picked the verse himself."

"What was he like, yer boy?"

"He wanted a horse, you know? But Charles didn't want him spending time on that, so he got Ethan riding lessons instead. Said Ethan had better things to do than muck out stables."

"Every boy needs a horse."

She glanced at him: he was serious. "The lessons were boring, Ethan said. He stopped going when the set was finished, and Charles took it to mean he'd gotten over another 'phase.'"

"They didn't talk." It wasn't a question.

"No."

"So ye did."

Perceptive. "For hours. Late at night in the hospital when he couldn't sleep." Those last few weeks it had been their routine. "He planned his funeral. He was so worried about everyone else. His sisters. Tad. Charles. Amanda. His friends from school. He knew it was going to be very hard for them."

"How did ye cope?" he asked quietly. He stood next to her in the dark suit, with Col. Strathmore's ridiculous dark brown ponytail neatly pulled back. One hand held the opposite wrist, and his gaze was on the headstone, not on her.

"He would be annoyed at me if I hadn't." Her shoulders shrugged. "He orchestrated the whole thing. He persuaded Susan to get married."

"What?"

"Oh, yes. Over the American Thanksgiving holiday, the final Saturday that November. Greg let him be best man." He had looked so adorable in his tuxedo you almost didn't notice the wheelchair. "It was the last time he left the hospital. And he was grinning ear to ear the whole time." *The little schemer.* "He nagged Ronnie to send her college application essays in—he wanted to know where she'd go."

"Did she?"

"Of course. He told her she'd be a fool if she didn't go to California, like she always wanted, that he wanted to visit. She applied to Annenberg; got in early admission. He was proud as Punch."

"Wasn't this all extra hard on ye?"

"We took so many naps together, him in that hospital bed, me in the recliner." Ethan insisted. *'I'm tired, Mom.'* "Everyone thinks I'm so cold. Because I kept it together before he died. And didn't fall apart afterward." She stroked the glands in her neck which persisted in aching. "The thing is, there is nothing you can do, is there?" *All the raging in the world wouldn't bring my baby back.*

"Ye're not cold."

"There were things which had to be done. Charles fell apart, wanted to keep trying new cancer drugs, things which would have—" *Calm.* She blew the air out slowly, found her voice. "Things which would have prolonged his... pain without curing. The girls were devastated; at least they had each other." She chuckled. "Susan came back pregnant from her honeymoon. He was the only one she told." *And he told me in 'complete confidence.'*

"Does it help to talk about it? I don't want to pry."

"Do you mind?"

"Not at all. That's what friends are for?"

"Ethan said he wanted to make sure he didn't miss anything. It's amazing, what he accomplished. He had his heart set on becoming a teenager. He hung on until Susan came back, and we all celebrated that birthday, and I am pretty sure he talked one of the student nurses into kissing him." *Men!* "I found one of them sobbing in the corridor, gave her a hug. But I didn't have the heart to chastise him, when I went in later, and he looked so proud of himself."

"A bucket list."

"He wanted to reach the year 2000 so badly, and then some idiot..."

"Told him the new millennium didn't start until 2001."

"One of his school friends." *Who was horrified when he realized what he'd done.* "We thought he would make it to Christmas. But I think he got tired, and he'd done all he realistically could, and then it just got tedious and he was worried about pain, about becoming a drooling baby in diapers, about not being a coward. Imagine that. Worrying about how *we* would remember *him*... I think he stopped fighting, somewhere deep inside."

"Was he at hospital?"

"I— We didn't have a home where— where we could *all* visit him." *One of the many unforeseen consequences of divorce.*

"He saw the toll it took on ye?"

"When I took the funeral director in to see him—Ethan insisted— he asked if there was a place I could take naps at— at their place, for the viewings, and there was. I sneaked away when I needed to. And at the hospital, too. There always seemed to be somewhere— there are certain privileges extended—"

"To doctors?"

"To the parents of dying children."

"Kary, are ye sure...?" She could hear the concern in his voice. He shook his head. "Of course ye're sure."

I'm almost finished. "After— after his birthday party, he faded. Spent most of the time asleep." She cleared her throat. "I was there. Right before dawn. There were blips on the heart monitor. And then there weren't." She located a tissue, blew. "We played all his favorite music; the kids brought hundreds of origami cranes—we got a special coated paper—they folded them for hours, the kids did, and it snowed, which it never does that early in Princeton." His classmates standing around with their breath—their breath!—making plumes in the cold, sharp paper birds of all colors on the soft white blanket which covered Ethan's bed. She remembered their concerned little faces, even the tough guys on Ethan's soccer team. *They tried so hard to make it better for me.* "Most of them had never been to a funeral. We gave him the best going-away party we could imagine."

He stood there, rock solid, seeing it with her.

Only a little more. "I must have slept for a week. Ronnie brought groceries, and we talked, and then I'd go back to sleep." And Charles went right back to being Charles. *He petitioned successfully to have child support reduced.*

"And ye moved."

Was there an implied question? "All the next spring, while Ronnie was still in high school, she'd come to my apartment after school. I started writing more—it kept me sane. This was my triangle: the apartment, here, and the Princeton Public Library. All within blocks." *Such an odd routine.* "And then Ronnie had the chance to go early, some kind of special summer program, and I encouraged her to go. And she said she didn't want to leave Ethan, but I told her—and I realized it then, and made my own plans to go."

"Realized—?" He sounded confused.

"I was only staying for Ronnie. Ethan isn't here."

She indicated the stone. "He doesn't need them any more. The only thing here are his bones."

ANDREW

AT LEAST YE KNEW YER child.

"He was excited about going to Heaven." Her voice was too calm. "The hospice nurses, they told me only to promise him I'd be there as long as he needed me, not to get his hopes up. 'That's what children need,' they said.

"But Ethan wasn't concerned with not growing up, not marrying, not going to college—all the things we knew would hit us. He was only concerned with being a kid again, with playing soccer. And if his body was quitting on him, well, there was a better one waiting." A hard exhalation.

True faith in times of crisis must be an immense comfort to her. Andrew made the huge effort. "He believed."

"He knew he was dying. 'Don't tell Amanda and Dad,' he said. 'They can't take it.' I told him it would be our secret."

"A tough kid." At zenith the harsh American sun made compact puddles of shadow at their feet. Rows of headstones with no character, not like back at Saint Brendan's where individuality was preserved even in death. From the back border of the cemetery came the tyre-sound of a passing car. An errant zephyr wafted a sniff of something sweet from the massed flowers at graveshead, the smell of tilled earth. Men didn't rate flowers unless... *For Grandda, a boutonnière at me sisters' weddings, lilies only when dead.*

She moved closer to the open grave, peered in. "You know the worst part?"

He joined her. *There* is *no answer.*

"Charles knows now." She hugged herself as if she were very cold. "It isn't fair, is it? I'm still here. And *he's* with Ethan."

Or in hell. He wanted to hold her, to tell her it was not fair, to smooth the anguish which had crept into her voice. He dared not move, break the spell. *She'll never be this vulnerable again.* "Yer girls needed ye."

"I know. It's a good thing suicide is a mortal sin—you don't end up with the one you're trying to follow."

"Only if done with intention!"

"There was a moment, after— I was *so* tired. But Ethan would've been shocked at me." She inhaled sharply, shook her head. "You don't know what it's like to lose your baby."

Forgive me, Lord. I was relieved—and Bridget grieved. Stop it. A speck of tissue was *not* a baby. "Ye stayed strong, until he didn't need ye."

"And the girls did."

"Besides, you wouldn't want *him*—" he jerked his chin toward the coffin, "to have the satisfaction."

"Never thought of that one." A tiny explosive chuff. "And you're right—it would have vindicated him somehow. Can't have that."

"Why'd ye marry him?"

She took forever to answer. Finally, she spoke. "It may have been an accident."

Rows on rows of clipped grass, mute headstones, a robin hopping and listening for grubs. He had the horse-sense to keep his trap shut.

"I was a very young doctor, doing my Residency in Pediatrics at Saint Peter's Children's Hospital in Newark, about an hour north of here. He was hard on me—the Attendings always are—but when I wasn't on his service any more, I kept running into him. I was so naive, I was grateful I'd found a mentor. Lunches at the hospital, took me to a charity event, dinner one night late..."

If the bastard weren't already dead... "He was grooming ye."

"And I was too stupid to know. You get hit on a lot, there's a lot of casual..." She shrugged. "I should have just slept with him—it would have been over. He had a bit of a reputation..."

"Instead, ye told him it wasn't going to happen."

"Because I was a good Catholic girl. My standard excuse. Honestly, it was true. I didn't want anything getting in my way, not until I finished my specialty, got established."

"Principles?"

She laughed. "Pretext? Justification? Easier to avoid entanglements. But the idea— Ick. A string of men in my past? No thanks."

Her expression challenged him. "Ick?"

She colored. "Yes. I am *not* 'modern.'"

Quaint. It suited her. "Ye are what ye are." *And what ye are is safe.* "He told ye he admired that in a woman."

She stared at him.

"Men are cads."

"He told me his mother would approve. He implied *he* approved."

She would have been irresistible, even more stunning then. A younger gawkier version of the long-legged dancer he'd startled under the granite steps. Focused on her work with no self-awareness of... *Watch it, lad.* "And when he got nowhere, he proposed."

"He brought me down here to meet his parents."

"The cad."

"I don't think I was good enough for Mother Renton."

"What the hell did *she* want?"

"I think she had a couple of Junior League types lined up. Like my friend Marge..." She inhaled, held, blew the breath out. "I'm sorry, I shouldn't be..."

"Let it out. It's not doing ye any good bur— stuck inside ye." *Damn.*

Her arms clasped tightly, she shrugged. "He was older— thirteen years. My mother warned me. 'He'll have bad habits,' she said. But my Dad was tickled with the idea of me marrying a surgeon, and he and Charles got on..." She paused. "And Mother Renton gave in, I was acceptably Catholic, he was settling down at long last, and when I had a baby on the way, well, then it became all right with her. She wanted someone to carry on the family name."

"Did she..."

"They both died the year before Ethan did. As far as they knew, their mission had been accomplished."

And their mission was still *accomplished, with the new heir—but the non-Catholic second wife bit would have galled.* Was arrogant doctor already too jaded in his tastes for the young Kary when he married her? So glutted he couldn't make it work? *And what does that say about me?* "It must've been hard, when the kiddies came."

"Oh, I think it was okay with Charles. He didn't have that much to do with them. Not day to day. I did my best, but the hospital was a demanding place. Best not show weakness, you know. Other women coped."

"With three?"

She acknowledged with a side nod. "Usually only one."

"But he wanted a son." It wasn't a question. *All men want a son.*

"If Susan had been a boy..." Her shoulders rose, fell. "Stupid, really. It's daughters who care for you in your old age."

"Me sisters'll save me." A quick glance around confirmed their isolation. He shifted position. *If ye live that long.*

"Am I making you uncomfortable?"

"I'm being me terminally-nosy self."

"Do you want the rest?" Her tone carried a note like the gritting of teeth.

"I can guess." *Get it all out, shall we, m'luv?* "He started running around on ye when ye were expecting Susan..."

"Before. The 'wife' bit only made it more fun. I tried. We took vacations. With the kids. I did far more than my share of childcare—figured he was more important, more advanced in his career. We managed. We both worked too hard. I truly imagined we were coping. Together. We didn't talk much. I had invested everything in 'family,' kept cutting him slack due to circumstances— And I was so stupid, and so busy, so determined to be the perfect working wife and mother, I missed all the signs."

"And then..." *And then the best intentions of one party were no guarantee.*

"And then I got sick. I couldn't care for patients, stay awake in meetings. I had to stop working—though we felt it would be only for a short time, until..."

"But ye didn't get better."

"If anything, I tried harder. I was home—I could supervise the help, ensure he never lifted a finger. But he didn't seem happy." The laugh was bitter. "Which is ironic, because, if I did *one* thing right, I thought, it was to make sure *he* didn't suffer."

Overhead a jet passed, leaving a high white chalkmark across the painful blue. Insects whirred gently in the midday sun. "But ye started noticing the little things..."

"Where were you when I needed you?" She gave him a sharp glance, looked away. "I was trying to hold on, keep it together until we figured out what the hell was wrong with me—"

Nothing, luv. "He started 'working late,' not calling ye."

"And he came home that night, told me about Amanda... You want to hear the best part?"

Eejit. He gave ye *up.* He inclined his head, let her talk.

"I offered to adopt the child." A long pause. "I've never felt a bigger fool than when he said it was quite noble of me, but I had it all backward."

Bridget walking away from me, carrying what she said was another man's child. At least she'd had the grace to leave him first. "Backward?"

"I'm pretty sure it was an accident—he was too careful. But she put her foot down, his career was at stake, his reputation— At the hospital, he blamed me; I wasn't around to contradict him; that was that."

"How long were ye… together?"

"Almost twenty years."

Son. Profession. Marriage. Flushed down the crapper. "Ye would have reared his illegitimate child."

"Women have done so throughout history."

"With varying degrees of success." *If her husband had honoured his vows,* she *would have pressed down her humiliation, done her duty.*

"You forget. The child was innocent."

"A constant reminder."

"Moot. It's just as well. He got what he wanted— and I'm still sick. So you could say he made the better choice."

"Are ye forgiving him?" Something in her tone of calm acceptance rubbed him wrong.

"I forgave *him* a very long time ago."

"Why?"

"Because it only hurt me not to?" She bowed her head. "The illness… it doesn't allow me strong emotions." She glanced back at Ethan's headstone, lifted her gaze from the pit to stare into the distance. "It took me a lot longer to forgive myself."

"That makes no sense, m'luv. Ye did nothing wrong."

"I made the most basic mistake a woman can make: I picked the wrong father for my children."

"But—"

"I know what you're thinking. That they are wonderful children. That God meant these children to be from the very beginning of the world—and that meant marrying Charles. *These* children, not just any children."

"*Yer* children."

"His children." Pause. "And Tad. Not Ethan. How wrong is that?" A longer pause. "But *Tad* is right."

"It's a random universe, Kary." *Where yer forgiveness and commitment are admirable—and unrewarded.* He wanted to touch her, to envelop her in his embrace, to protect her. *A fool's impulse—there is nothing ye can fix.*

"I can't believe that. I have to believe that children *matter*." Minuscule shakes of her head. "And it matters who loves them and who rears them, and what they're taught."

"Can't argue with ye there." *It matters. Bridget's second son was as unlike the first—stop.*

She blew out a long exhalation. "It just barely kept me from bad-mouthing him."

"Provocation?"

Her eyebrows rose, she jerked her head in a sideways acknowledgment. "He was getting ready to sue me."

"Ye're joking."

"Hard to kid about that one." She seemed to reach some sort of resolution, relaxed her stiff pose, turned square to face him. "That's quite enough of that. You are a good friend—I don't think I've dumped the whole thing on anyone. I don't know what got into me."

"In any case, ye're a widow now. In the eyes of the Church. Will ye remarry?" *And ye are way over bounds, lad.*

She gave that a consideration it didn't deserve. "Me? No. Far too much baggage. I am content with my writing." She looked down a final time. "Goodbye, Charles. Take care of our boy. I hope you find peace."

They walked side-by-side to the rental van, but they might have been on opposite sides of an abyss.

Door slammed, lock turned, throw away the key.

ೋ CHAPTER TWENTY ೪
The Scattering

He beholdeth all high things: he is a king over all the children of pride.

Job 41:34, KJV

JUNE 12: A list of current and future projects starring Andrew O'Connell:
Incident at Bunker Hill (in production—2005)
Leviathan (planned, 2006)
Dodgson (rumored, 2006)
If you know of any others, let us know, and we'll add them to the list.

www.AOCORNER/movie_schedule/

New friends become old
When enough time each has spent
In the other's soul.

Tahiro Mizuki,
trans. by R. Heath

KARY

Princeton

ANDREW TURNED THE KEY in the ignition. "Where to, m'lady?"

To where I can suture the wounded psyche I should have never let you see. Where to, indeed. "Turn right onto Nassau Street. Head downtown. Stop for pedestrians."

"All of them?"

"All of them. And don't go over twenty-five. Princeton's cops are very particular."

"Yes, m'lady."

But when she had located a shaded parking spot on a side street downtown and fed the meter, she hesitated. *I need distance.* "Would you like the nickel tour? I have the feeling you aren't going to be back here for a long time." *If ever.*

"'Twould be a pleasure. Not too tired?"

"Too much sitting." *And standing still.* "It's nothing like what you're used to. Dublin. Paris. London."

"I'll be judging it on its own merits."

"We treat things as old if they're pre-revolutionary; you think of things as old if they're pre-Roman."

"Understood."

He didn't say, 'Like Hanover.' He made her awkward, uncertain. Not fair. *He makes me aware.*

They followed the cross street back to Nassau, took their time walking up the west side of the street, by the shops, as she pointed out the Princeton landmarks—and where the landmark shops *had* been. "Even here, things change."

At the Garden Theater, they crossed Nassau to the University side with a small contingent of walkers with strollers, and a well-dressed couple speaking Japanese with their teen daughter. When the family group continued down Nassau, she turned them into the short walk up to the Firestone Library and the Princeton chapel. "We get a lot of tourists—they come to see Princeton, scope it out for their children."

In the chapel, she knelt for a moment to pray. The ghosts were everywhere. You couldn't live in a town twenty years and not see ghosts: taking the kids to play at Marquand Park, and hoping they wouldn't hit their heads or skin their knees on the boulders surrounding the sandpit. The Nutcracker at McCarter. Visiting the Mercer Oak at the Battlefield Park, and learning about the real revolutionary history which flowed through Princeton and made it once the nation's capital. Watching the reenactment of Washington crossing the Delaware down in Trenton. Brunch at the Faculty Club with Laurence Binkman, who *had* gone to Princeton. The sense of loss when exhaustion prevented her from enjoying more of the town—after she was forced to stop working the long hours, and was sick and 'at home' in Princeton and finally had time. *I have sung 'All is well with my soul' in this House of God.*

She had come to Princeton a young bride, determined to fit in. And left when there were too many ghosts, each one tarnished by the overlay of betrayal and illness. She crossed herself and rose, stood uncertain and silent in the cool nave, empty but for a gaggle of teens with cameras.

"Memories?"

"Too many to share." *And I will not, or I will cry.*

"Beautiful," he said, when she had walked him around the nave, showed him names of famous alumni chiseled into blocks of the granite walls.

"It's the largest university chapel of its kind in the States." *And I have no need to defend this simply because he has seen far older.* "If you come at the right time of year, you can see the stained-glass windows illuminated by the rising or setting sun. Ready?"

As they crossed the campus roughly parallel to the street, she pointed. "They filmed *A Beautiful Mind* here. I was gone by then, but several people I knew auditioned as extras. Big fuss." Her voice was doing odd things. *I hadn't realized how much I missed home.*

"Ah. Which explains why it feels familiar." His tone was puzzled. "Not many students."

"Too hot and muggy for a summer term. Grad students—and faculty on grants." *Just as well—undergrads'd be much more likely to recognize you.* She found herself walking more briskly. "If we had time," she indicated Maclean House as they passed, "we'd sign you up for the Orange Key tour, and you could hear a student tell you everything you never wanted to know." They reached the sidewalk. "Lunch?"

"The airport isn't far, if me geographical sense is correct."

"Plenty of time—nothing is very far in Princeton." *And that was the problem.*

They re-crossed Nassau at Witherspoon, and she halted at a building which would have been at home in *Bunker Hill.* He held the door for her.

"I'll be right with you folks." The harried young waiter found them a corner table by the street window, scooted off to deal with checks for the thinning lunch crowd.

When he arrived with his order pad, she asked Andrew, "Would you mind if I order for you?" and at his interested nod, pointed to what she wanted on the menu. "Two, please?"

The waiter lit up. "Splendid. I believe we still have some today." He scurried off, returned with steaming ramekins and a basket of soda bread. He fetched a pot of tea, disappeared.

"I'm thinking this is what you'd call your 'local.'" She was taking a big chance here, but the day could not become any more surreal. *And it matters not one whit whether I fall flat on my face.* "The last day I would ever have imagined, sitting in the *Alchemist & Barrister* in Princeton, eating Irish stew with an incognito movie star, with Charles dead and buried." And grateful she wouldn't have to play Charles's taped words to the girls. *They can keep whatever illusions they have left.*

"I'm not incognito."

"Okay, I take that back. I think our waiter was eyeing you, and hasn't figured out that he has to alter the hair color and remove the ponytail. He'll get it."

"And then he'll whip out the phone, and me pic will be all over the internet, 'lunching with a mystery woman' in New Jersey, in the middle of nowhere."

"They might object to that characterization." *We aren't doing anything wrong.* She watched him take the first bite.

A expression of pure bliss suffused his features.

"I know you're going home, and I was afraid it wouldn't be as good…"

"Me Grannie couldn't do better."

"The last time I was here, Ronnie was sitting where you are, and she was going off to California the next day." *I was already half-packed.* She hugged herself, remembering.

"Kary?"

"Sorry." *It takes such an effort, and he is so full of intelligent sympathy.* Why was it that with him it all seemed so possible? *In short bursts, even I can fake it.* How can you ignore burdening him for the rest of your life? Charles got your 'good time'; yay, Charles. *I am selfish.*

"Ye vanished on me for a moment there."

For reply, she took another bite of the fragrant lamb. She realized she was starving. Detach—that was the key. Drop him off at the airport. *Figure out what to do with myself and my dead fantasies.* "I wouldn't worry about the waiter. Odds are, he's a double major graduate student in Philosophy and Epidemiology, and will end up as President of the World Bank."

Andrew raised his eyebrows.

"This is Princeton. It *could* happen. No one fusses over celebrities; the university provides a steady stream. Pay attention. He's not *just* a waiter. The bearing, the attitude of complete concentration when he took our order. As if he's researching, waiting to write a book."

"Or he's doing the job so he can *be* a waiter in a production..."

"A production of what?"

"That's the problem—can't think of a role which requires a waiter."

"*Down and Out in Paris and London?*"

"Ah, excellent. Ye know yer Orwell."

I could reach out and touch his face, put my hand on his arm. He was too near, Princeton was too small. A bigger table would have set her at her ease, put white linen and flowers and stemware between them, random food without emotional connotations. Her stomach shut down. Had they been closer, she would have offered him the rest of the stew. Had they been more distant, the matter wouldn't have come up at all, and she would not have felt guilty about the lamb which... *Stop it!* You are so close to free.

"Kary?"

"Was I wandering again? Sorry. It's been a long day."

He leaned forward, reached across the table to take her hand. "Kary, we have to talk."

She froze. "We *are* talking."

"Ye've been a bit preoccupied." He lowered his head, made sure she was looking into his eyes. "I crave a boon of ye."

"A favor?" *And this is why we are saying goodbye, because I cannot deny you.* "What do you need?" *That I could possibly provide?*

"I've fallen in love—" he released her, leaned back, clasped his hands before him, "—with Jake. And I want ye to write it for Grant. Then I'll wheedle him unmercifully into letting me do it."

"What are you talking about?" *For one split second... Fool!*

"I had me readin' time. *Prairie Fires.* Ye gave it me?" He shrugged. "I have a whole new appreciation of ye. Ye know what ye're doing." His head did the little sideways jerk, his tell for things which intrigued him. His eyes held her gaze speculatively.

"Thank you?" But no. Just no. *I could not live with Andrew being Jake.* She hadn't even known Andrew when she wrote Jake—and he would be so perfect it would hurt. *I can't.*

"Ye can put in the good word for me with Grant."

She stared at him stupidly.

"It's the worst possible time to ask ye, but we've run out, and I had no idea until last night. Stayed up half..." He shrugged. "I'll be getting too old. Jake is a young man... These things take time to develop... Forgive me."

You are perfect right now. She closed her eyes, captured the memory forever: Andrew—Jake—begging—for her work. Impossibility helped her focus. "You might as well ask for a Broadway musical! I'm not a screenwriter. You've seen my life…" She shook her head. "I can't. It's that simple."

"Ye could help someone write the screenplay."

"It'd be a full-time job. For a well person. *In* Hollywood. *With* meetings. And pressure. Deadlines. And…" She'd even considered it briefly—when Grant's books arrived. Done some online research, read what healthy young male screenwriters wrote about being ground into big studio sausage. Hopeless. *It is easy—when you can't.* She steeled herself. "No."

"I'd be a fool if I didn't ask."

"Ask for something I *can* give." *Not years of my life. Not this way.*

"Yer story *needs* the big screen."

"People still read."

"Tell me, how does it end?"

Like this. "I won't spoil it. You'd stop reading." She had to laugh. "You can skip to the end."

"Not bloody likely."

"Thanks?"

He leaned back, making the chair creak. He peered at the ceiling, composed himself, blew it out. "Karenna Elizabeth Ashe. Ye are a good person to ride the wind with."

"Once."

"If ye change…?"

"You'll be the first to know."

With impeccable timing, now that she didn't need saving, her cellphone rang.

He raised eyebrows.

"It's Ronnie. Just a minute." She listened. "Do you need me?" More. "All right, then. I will. Call me." She sat still for a moment, the cellphone cradled in her hands. The elevator had stopped with a jerk at the wrong floor.

"Troubles?"

"Ronnie said to say goodbye and thank you." *You can't. Not after…*

"Kary, what is it?" He read her face. "Take yer time."

With you of all people watching me. The scenarios played out in her head: ask—or stand on her dignity, keep quiet, take the very long road home. *But what if he can't?* You have to ask. *I can't.* Not after... *Especially after.* "I— I didn't think it through when we came."

"Ye came for yer girls—what else could ye do?"

"And then you offered..." *I'm still in shock about the whole thing.*

"Not me. Grant."

Worse. He's a big boy, Kary. He *can* say no. If he did not one more thing... *Ask.* "They're staying with Amanda. They don't need me. And Marge has gone over to the dark side." *Let the consequences begin.* "When I take you to the airport, is there any way I can hitch a ride back to New Hampshire?"

"Is that all? Of course—" His gaze met hers as implications registered. "This *is* awkward. Ye are right. I don't actually know who..."

"Or how many..." *And you* must *be on it.*

"The plane's in the air. Let me call Grant..."

"I'll be right back." *At least I can give him privacy.* She located the tiny immaculate restroom past the bar in the cool dim interior, stared at her face in the mirror. Funny. It was the same as the last time she'd really looked at herself. At home. *You used to be so proud of your ability to handle anything life threw at you.* All she wanted was to go home, get back to K'Tae. Dig deep into the politics and greed and survival on a terraformed fringe planet with an obvious genetic solution. *And forget I ever...*

The waiter had brought the check and was chatting with Andrew about local beers when she returned. The table had been blessedly cleared of debris with its residual aroma. The waiter pulled the chair out for her with a flourish as Andrew rose from his seat.

She smiled at the young man, remained standing. "Thank you, but we need to leave."

"I'm a huge fan, Ms. von," he said.

Her smile froze.

He turned to Andrew. "You were brilliant in *First At Lies*, sir. I think you were channeling one of my professors."

"Aye. 'Twas a good 'un." Andrew shook the waiter's hand. "Kary? Shall we?"

ANDREW

CAN'T LEAVE HER HERE alone.

He'd insisted on driving back to the airport—save her energy. But the right side of the road always felt wrong. As had this oddest of twenty-four hour periods in a long time—yesterday at this time he'd been filming in another state on a horse he'd never see again either.

And if there was no room on the plane, he had no other option: he'd already put Grant to major inconvenience by his Galahad act, and he couldn't ask someone from the cleaner crew to stay behind to bring a friend back with him without acquiring a reputation, nor could he charter her a flight back. Ruddy mess.

"Everything okay?" Kary had navigated him out to Route 206, but kept an eye on his maneuvering.

"Just admiring yer mountains." The vehicle's compass kept shifting between N and NE as the road twisted. "Didn't expect so much snow this time of the year. Looks like Everest, but they can't be that high."

"Mountains?"

He pointed down the street they were passing, to their left.

"Ah."

He glanced her way. "What?"

"New Jersey is flat. Those aren't real. I call them cloud illusions. '*Both Sides Now*' song? Joni Mitchell?" She peered past him down the next cross street. "I love mountains. Which is why…"

"Ye moved to New Hampshire."

"I grew up in California, between the mountains and the ocean. When the weather is right here, and the clouds come in from the west, if you squint down the street at the right time, it could be snow-capped mountains. Made it feel like home." She sighed. "They'll be gone with the next brisk wind. Water vapor and turbulent air. I've always wanted to see Everest."

"Some day ye will."

"Sure." She breathed deeply. "And India. And the Ganges. And the Taj Mahal. Maybe after Akiiya. I gave Akiiya mountains." Her tone was dead.

"Ye'll get there." Their surroundings changed to professional buildings and small shops. "This seems familiar."

"The airport's just ahead, on the left. But you have to do a jughandle to cross—right lane before the traffic light."

"Righty-o."

"Jersey's famous: each intersection is unique."

His phone rang as he was executing the required maneuver, cautious of cars from the car park to his right as he merged. "Might ye get it? In me back pocket." *Damn. Should have left it out where she could reach it.*

The traffic signal cycled to yellow. He curbed his urge to floor it, used the brake pedal as leverage to lift from the seat enough to let her slide the phone out. *What say ye, Fates?*

"You *could* call back, you know." She put it to her ear. "Hello? Oh, hi, Grant. It's Kary. He's, uh, driving—and I won't let him talk and drive at the same time."

Let me?

"Yes." She listened. "Thanks so much. Yes." She listened longer. "I'd like that. Goodbye."

The signal went to green, and he drove onto the airport access road. The relief had been patent in her voice. *Must've been hard to ask. And no hurried farewell at Airport Security, me looking like an eejit.* He owed the Fates another one. "We're good then?"

"He said there were only four in the cleaner crew?"

"His specialty—he brings in a fresh team to close things down, stay behind in case anything's needed. The regulars can all go home after the wrap party tomorrow night. Includin' Grant."

"Ah. Nice."

"He's thoughtful that way." And many others. *Interesting guy, Grant.*

"The personal touch."

"Aye."

He pulled the car into the rental car slot, got their bags out. "Here. Let me. It'll be faster." He hoisted a bag in each hand, and they strode through the terminal; in a few minutes they were watching the jet approach and land.

He handed off the cases after extracting Kary's book, clattered up the fold-out staircase after her. She hesitated at the entrance, said hi to the four faces which turned to examine them, two men and two women who smiled back. He motioned her toward the rear. The cleaners went back to their muted conversation, quietly excited as kids on a promised school outing.

"Take that one." He indicated the seat which would recline fully. He located a blanket, tucked it round her, and they were rolling out and airborne in minutes. He watched out the window at the clouds massing behind them—New Jersey *was* flat. When he turned back to Kary, she had pulled a hedgehog again, and didn't protest much when he pushed the button to recline her seat.

He opened the hardcover to where he'd shoved an American dollar as bookmark, but *Prairie Fires* lay unread in his lap as he stared straight ahead. *A lot to process.*

And a lot to hand to George when we land.

'Just let me know,' George had said. 'Any photos of ye out there which might be made to look compromising. Best forewarned.' *Shite.* They'd been in the Princeton airport lobby for departure no more than ten minutes, but he was sure he'd heard a click somewhere—might've been something else.

When they'd arrived last night? He'd handed over his international driver's license along with hers, had it scrutinized and the details recorded, but the baby-cheeked clerk seemed more concerned with selling them insurance. He could usually tell from the change in behavior when someone recognized *him*; they'd have far less reason to know *her*.

The waiter? Kary's instinct there was probably trustworthy; but it went on the list, though he'd not noticed anything resembling a cellphone pulled out in the restaurant.

The funeral and the memorial? A few heads had turned to Kary when she went to Communion, but they quickly went back to their mourning, and no one blatantly turned around to stare *or* photograph. He was pretty sure Karl and his colleague at the cemetery were more interested in lunch than in them.

The Inn? The bar? Quick in-and-out, and be where they don't expect ye—nothing obvious. He hated that damage control had become automatic. *Ye wanted to be infamous.*

A thought occurred to him; he popped up to the captain with his request, stopped to chat with the cleaners about their up-coming work. Good bunch; exuded quiet competence, used to far bigger talent than he was. Might've recognized Kary, might not've—but it wouldn't matter: Grant's crews were solid.

She hadn't moved. He opened the book again, reread the inscription. '*For when you need to sleep.*' Where did the gentle self-deprecating humour come from? He'd almost missed this— this whole— And all because a small boy demanded the Chinese food he'd been promised. Children don't forget. His ma's voice: '*Never break promises to a child.*'

He'd taken advantage of her vulnerability to pry. Or had he just let her talk because she needed to? He knew things about her which were none of his business; when she'd caught herself, the flood-gates slammed shut. Faith—and fragility. He understood the writing better now: her underpinning was survival, family, society—at the cost of individuals, individual happiness. Meeting her daughters emphasized that strength. She'd said on the interview aeons ago that she couldn't do what the survivors of the great wave across the plains did—but she was still standing, strong, able to do, same as them, whatever was necessary to maintain a center for what was left of her family. And not collapse until it was over. She had found her own balance, in a blank computer room. *'I'm not here,'* she said. She'd found a way to still make a contribution to society...

The plane hit a spot of turbulence. This country's wide spaces let the wind build up too much speed. Presaging a wet wrap party? But not the final battle yesterday, rain date today. Grant was damned lucky. But neither of them would get *Prairie Fires. Shame, really.*

The engines' pitch changed and the nose dipped, interrupting his reverie.

The future was only postponed. He closed the book; he'd find out later how it ended. They landed with a small bump as a crosswind lifted the wing at the last moment. This was the part he always hat-ed, endings.

Kary woke and straightened as they taxied from the end of the runway. "What'd I miss?"

"Not much."

Three minivans, a limousine, and a motorcycle awaited. George chatted with Frank by the limo's bonnet.

The cleaners trooped down the ladder, separated into pairs by sex, and began signing paperwork passed to them on clipboards by the drivers of the minivans. Kary walked with him to meet George, and behind them the pilot and copilot tended to additional papers and arranged hangar space.

Small house; he counted onlookers at a baker's dozen.

Time to say goodbye. With one clean take. "We set, George?"

For reply, George presented him the black helmet. "I'll fetch the bags."

"Thanks, man."

"Hello, Frank," Kary said.

"Grant owns me hide, and he can't wait to slice it off me. George is taking ye home."

"You know this makes me look entitled," she said sternly.

"I do. But 'twas yer pride or mine—" he did 'sad puppy' eyes for her, "and I hope ye are generous enough to spare mine."

"You promise not to make a habit of it."

"No, Ma'am."

"And it's okay with Grant—it's an hour's round trip for Frank?"

"Dancing girls?"

"I remember. How many, what colors." *Grant wants you happy.* She made her face serious. "You're *sure* you can manage without George?"

"Wouldn't be safe for him without a helmet, now would it? And Grant would have me neck if I lent him mine." He shrugged. "Leaves no choice."

She compressed her lips as she shook her head. "If you say so."

"I'll help Frank with these bags," George said.

"Ye do that." They watched George remove himself. "It's only equitable. Ye kept me sane for Grant. He should pay for it."

She inclined her head. "I think this is finally it. Thank you for taking me." She held her suit jacket in clasped arms. Maroon suited her fair coloring. Her gold earrings caught the afternoon sun.

"'Twas nothing. Ye would have done the same." He was acutely conscious of their audience, but no one was in earshot. *Keep yer bloody body language restrained.*

"You could have stayed in the van at the church."

"'Twouldn't be right."

"I'll miss you, Andrew."

"Ye must visit me in Ireland." *Fat chance.*

"Let me know when you're going to be there a while." She tipped her head toward the limousine. In the light, the gray-green eyes held specks of gold. "Shall we?" She moved toward the limo stretched out sparkling in the sunlight, shiny and black as the asphalt.

He followed, got the door, gave her his free hand for a moment as she got in. Hers was dry, cool. She released him, settled onto the back seat. *Choreographed like a ballet, we are.* He leaned on the door frame.

"Goodbye, Andrew." Her smile made tiny crinkles at the corners of her eyes.

He took the chance. "We'll always have Princeton."

Her pale eyebrows arched, and she laughed. "We will."

"Until next time."

She held his gaze. "Don't you have somewhere you're supposed to be? I'm going to sleep for two days, catch up on writing. Have a safe trip home."

'Don't call me' writ large. "Will do." After the dozens of promos Maury had him booked for. He set her back on the mantel like one of the Dresden china shepherdesses his mother so loved, graceful and frozen in time. He closed the car door. George and Frank moved to passenger and driver doors, got in.

The limousine glided off. He watched her slip out of his life. He'd lucked out. She'd offered Sanctuary and stability, an oasis of calm in the chaos. An image of her came into his mind: on her deck, leaning on the railing to watch the sunset. 'Friend of Kary' was a good thing. *She keeps her promises—good to know.*

He slipped the helmet on, swung his leg over the bike, adjusted the mirrors. Behind him on the tarmac sound and motion resumed. The mugginess increased with the gathering thunderheads which had followed them east.

He shook off the sense of regret. He'd cut the margin of safety to the bone, and there were no further options. A billion things to do with Grant before tomorrow's wrap party. And he'd have to report back to Grant about her script—maybe Grant would have better powers of persuasion. *Unlikely—but possible?*

He turn toward town, in the opposite direction from the limo. Meanwhile, he'd b.s. with talk show hosts of the boring male variety, see what Maury had bubbling in the pot—

Crap! Simmering on the back burner was a perfect little gem—and he'd forgotten completely about its owner. Bianca was going to be *pissed.*

Dammit. He *wanted* that role, the Reverend Charles Lutwidge Dodgson. What was it with the 'Charles' bits in his life lately? That chapel in Princeton had reminded him, and now that Kary'd put the kibosh on *Prairie Fires*, he couldn't afford to forfeit *Dodgson.*

He would have to be extra endearing to Bianca. Ask George to send roses, write, 'Unavoidably called away.'

Something like that. *Damn.*

KARY

I COULD GET USED TO THIS.

Outside the limo's tinted glass, the world she'd left yesterday slipped quietly back into place. Inside, air-conditioning to remove the residual humidity, a blanket to remove the residual chill. Tired always made her cold. She wrapped the soft periwinkle-blue blanket around herself, wondered why George had chosen to ride up front.

You could buy it for yourself.

It wouldn't be the same without the cabana boys.

I don't know why I even try.

She had to admit it felt good, relinquishing all responsibility. And every little courtesy saved her energy, preserved a writing day. Except for 'all the rest,' she would be writing again very soon. *Whoopee.*

Quite a nice little scene you pulled at the airport, the self-sacrificing farewell. Too bad it isn't recorded on film for all time.

He's leaving. I said goodbye.

You pushed him away so hard you left indentations on his chest.

It was the right thing to do.

You are a coward.

I am not wife-of-Andrew material!

He deserves young, beautiful, fertile, healthy. He needs children, a helpmate.

We are not doing this now. There was still a short coda to this extraordinary adventure. There would be plenty of time later for self-flagellation. *Pretend I have dignity.* She closed her eyes for a moment, began the patterned breathing. There was nothing in the world which couldn't wait for three breaths…

"Kary." George's voice. She opened her eyes to find him twisted around to talk to her through the sliding glass partition between the compartments. "We're here. I need the code to open yer gate."

"Ah, home." She told him.

"Andy's number."

"Easy to remember." She folded the blanket, put it on the seat, and was ready when Frank pulled the limo up to her doorstep after turning it to face outward.

George offered his hand.

"Thanks." She was starting to feel either like visiting royalty—or someone's ancient mater. *A few more minutes, a few more meaningless politenesses…* "Same code for the door."

"Don't forget to change it."

"I won't." She stopped to thank Frank, followed George into her own hall.

"I'll take this up for ye," George said. "After ye."

"Thank you."

At the top of the stairs, he stood aside so she could precede him. "Where would ye like it?"

Did I leave a mess when I packed? It would be awkward to ask him to leave the case in the upstairs landing. "Could you bring it in here?" She did the absurd porter-at-a-hotel-room dance, only without key or tip.

"Wow. What a view to wake up to."

"I think this is what sold me on the house." *Inane Conversation in a Bedroom 101.* But it had.

"Okay, then. Anything we can do for ye before we leave?"

Ah, right. Work. "I'll come down with you. Can I offer you a drink? Leftover Chinese food?"

"I think I'm good, but thanks." He turned to go.

Conscience pinched her. Hard. She *had* forgotten. *Must I?* You must. "Wait. I forgot."

He watched, interested, as she opened her closet, took out the other bag.

She put it on the bed. "I found it after he left. In Susan's room." *And why did I add that?* "Before the girls came." *Shut up, Kary.* "Here. I wouldn't have known where to mail it."

"Excellent. Himself would definitely miss this. His ma knit him the two, herself." George accepted the folded fisherman's sweater. "Ye know the tradition, do ye?"

"That they're used to identify the bodies of men lost at sea?" *When their decomposing bodies wash up on the beach.* "Or that wool is warm even when wet?"

He laughed. "I'll be handing him his estate back intact then, when I go."

"You aren't going with him?"

"Ah, ye wouldn't know. Me da's had a turn. Me ma needs me to come lend a hand." He shrugged. "Can't say Fiona's displeased, neither."

"Does he know?" *None of your business.* It had slipped out.

"He will when I see him; Ma called last night." George shifted from one foot to the other, and back, as if the sweater were a heavy burden.

"I'm sorry."

"I'm the son. Fi and me, we're talking. We'll be putting the banns up, moving in with the folks." His face turned ruddier.

"That's wonderful. Congratulations." She smiled at his happiness. "We better get you back to camp then. You must have a million things to do." Accidentally-acquired knowledge she could do nothing about. *He won't be there for Andrew.*

Andrew is a big boy.

"A few." George gestured with the sweater.

She indicated the door, followed him down, shook hands, closed the door after he clattered down the steps.

She opened the gate remotely for them, leaned her back against the door until the screen showed the limousine pulling out onto the highway. She secured the gate.

Now?

No, not yet. They had all the time in the world.

She stood in front of the open refrigerator door staring at Andrew's blocky print lettering, in grease pencil, on the white cartons. She poured herself cold water, added ice, shut the door. Whatever she'd eaten of the lamb would have to suffice. Food was not an option after all.

Penumbra faded to umbra outside the plate glass. The first flecks of the gathering storm made their falling tracks. A thunderclap startled her.

The phone would not ring, but she clicked the ringer off. Thought it through. Clicked it back on. The girls might call.

She didn't remember having laid a fire. It bore his stamp: the tiny teepee of kindling was boxed in by a precision grate of twigs, the back log flanked neatly by medium-sized sticks of firewood. She hesitated, swore at herself, put a match to his handiwork.

She rocked gently in place, exhaustion a pain in her very bones.

Editing? She laughed at herself. Editing—reading. They would require she focus on a page.

Tomorrow she would write. She'd say to this one: do this. And he does. And to another: go there. And he goes. And she'd be powerful. Writing she could do.

Who do I think I'm kidding?

Now?

Might as well. A good excoriation would lead to hollowed-out peace. Peace to dancing. Dance to sleep. Eventually.

Okay, now. First, the things you somehow managed to do right.

As good a place as any.

You managed to behave yourself. Amazing.

I did, didn't I?

You managed not to embarrass him *or* yourself in public.

Only in private.

There are no smoking guns.

Nothing happened!

And that matters... how? Now let us discuss rationally the irrational hopes...

I have no hopes.

You have been searching for a way in which your many disadvantages could be overcome. Well, now you have proof it *can* be done. He provided it himself. You went to Princeton. You survived. You managed to find little holes to take naps in, times to rest. You guided him all over Princeton.

Because he did all the work! And I cheated at every turn!

My point precisely.

Why would anyone take on such a burden?

He didn't seem to mind.

For one *day. Once. For a friend.*

And what did he gain?

A chance to repay minor hospitality, which he had already done ten times over.

For better or for worse?

For heaven's sake. Charles got all that.

Lucky Charles.

You know perfectly well that no one expects 'worse' when they start.

Again, my point.

First a relationship, then all the good parts, then get sick and still deserve the good parts. You don't start this way, sick and useless.

So *Jane Eyre* of you.

Which part?

What, sick people can't be worthwhile?

Sure.

Just not you. Easy to say 'everyone is worthwhile, even if they're sick and disabled.'

I'm not everyone.

Your standards are so warped it's ridiculous.

I have nothing to give him.

He asked for *one* thing.

No.

Then we're done here?

I see nothing but dead soldiers.

She changed upstairs into the worn black sweats she wore for writing. She gazed with yearning at her bed, wished for the surcease of a short deep sleep, knew it would leave her unable to sleep through the night without drugs.

She went down the two flights to her moving room, pulled out the cot and got it ready just in case.

Just in case?

Fine.

She chose her favorites, slow ballads of love and longing and loss. She adjusted the volume to somewhere between 'too loud for thought' and 'painful.'

When there was no more left than she could afford, she slid between the sheets on the cot, hugged the extra pillows close.

Outside, occasional lightning, and the rain pelted the windows with white noise. She breathed, let go.

Whatever it costs, I'll deal with it tomorrow.

BIANCA

Bunker Hill

I LOOK LIKE SHIT.

Bianca stared at her image in her dressing trailer's mirror.

Behind her she overheard the makeup guy, Reggie something, speaking in lowered tones with whoever had come to deliver her to the next scene—her last for this shoot. 'She's in the chair.' 'How much longer?' 'Ten, maybe fifteen.' 'Van's waiting; gimme a call.'

He returned. "Sorry, Ms. Doyle. They are—"

She used her most neutral tone. "I look like shit."

It rattled him. "I am so sorry, Ms. Doyle, but you are so terribly thin since we started and I—"

She swiveled her head one way, then another, inspecting. "It's perfect, Reggie. Maybe even a little more on the hollows...?"

She squinted, assayed a smile at her reflection. "I look like a death's head. Weeks of short rations because of the redcoats stationed in our farmhouse— I *would* look famished. Do you think I looked famished, Reggie?"

"You look ravishing, as always, Ms. Doyle," he sputtered. "But famished, yes. Famished. Definitely famished."

"Good. Do your worst."

She relaxed, responded to his ministrations like an automaton, not listening to the patter he kept going with himself and his brushes and paint pots.

The call list for the past two days had been impossible: all the transitions Grant shot film on in case the editor wanted them, plus the whole plot line with her living with her in-laws while Winston was off at Valley Forge and the Brits illegally quartered troops on the area farms, eating into the stores the colonists needed to survive the winter.

And I have been so very cooperative for Grant. Not one single tantrum or harsh word while she filmed fill shot after fill shot, crap they should have shot earlier, with the second-unit director. Papi had trained her well. *'They will remember only the final days, princess.'* And the results. If she trusted anyone, it was Grant Sykes. She learned so much on this shoot, whenever they let her, by watching one of the best. But the weather strained even his management skills, or they wouldn't be working back-to-back fourteen hour days. She was so tired. *A few more hours...*

'Above all, do your job, Bibi. Or they will find someone who will.'

Si, papi. *I'm ready.*

Reggie began removing the thin cloths protecting her worn gown from his spillage, gently replacing them with fresh ones.

She read concern in his attentive eyes and hesitant movements. *Good. My legacy begins.* "Thank you, Reggie." She made her eyes mist. "For everything."

He gathered his kit, assisted her out of the chair, opened the door, and they descended to the waiting vehicle.

She was startled to see the spring green of the rolling hills of New Hampshire, closed her eyes when strapped in to replace the view with hard-falling, blown and drifting snow. An odd thought struck her. *Today is the last day of Sarah's life.*

Either Father would be there, and this would go live, or...

When she'd woken up yesterday with a start at the assistant's cautious knock on her door, still wearing the makeup she left on for *him*, and knowing he had stood her up, her self-preservation kicked in and she blocked all thoughts of him. So completely that, when between scenes the same assistant carried in the huge bouquet of red roses with its insulting typed card, *'Sorry - unavoidably absent, Andrew,'* she smiled sweetly, admired the blooms, and allowed them to be placed on her coffee table instead of making the assistant eat them.

She *knew* he was back on set; the rest was not her worry, nor would it be if, when she was primed, the scene was canceled with no reason given. *Director's problem; Grant's problem.* But *if* they shot it, her one chore was to give a performance so memorable Grant could not conceivably leave it on the cutting room floor.

Trust the process, Bi. She let resentment, at the arrogant enemy occupation of *her* home, begin to build.

The van came to a complete stop, and its side door opened. "It's only a few steps up into the farmhouse, Ms. Doyle."

She raised her eyelids enough to make the steps, maintaining her illusion of winter until the kitchen door was pulled to, and the snow on the windowsills battled the miserable fire on the hearth and won. She shivered. The farmhouse kitchen, a reluctant loan from the local historical society, reeked of woodsmoke ingrained in the heavy overhead beams. The cauldron simmered; the techs put apple-scent, possibly real apples in the pot.

'STANDING BY FOR ROOM TONE.'

In her chair, she rested her eyes again while the murmuring voices muted for the sound check.

Grant came in asking for Andrew's whereabouts.

'WALKING' crackled from the scratchy walkie talkie.

It was peaceful here with her eyes closed.

"Bianca, ready?"

She opened her eyes. "When you are." Reggie respectfully removed his protective cloths from her neckline, tut-tutted at the waist's looseness, tightened her stays, fastened a thin cloak around her shoulders. She heard the door open, ignored it.

"Ah, there you are." Grant's voice. "We're running behind."

"Set to go." Andrew's voice. No, *Father's* voice.

Muscle memory took over. Having rehearsed with a stand-in as stiff as a dressmaker's dummy actually helped. She took her mark in the passageway, awaited the gruff cue from the invader demanding service. A prop girl handed her a meager basket of firewood, sprayed her cape with artificial snow, gave the signal.

'ROLLING.'

Minimum crew in the cramped spaces of the log structure. Grant's assistant made the calls unamplified. The cameras focused on her first. She didn't know whether to be offended. She paid them no attention from long habit.

Colonel Strathmore slumped, exhausted, battleworn. His boots trailed muck into her kitchen...

"What in tarnation takes so long?" His accent disconcerted her, reminded Sarah how things had changed since she was his little girl. She entered the kitchen, hung her cloak on the peg. Without a word, she fed the fire, stirred the pot.

"I say, what—" He bestirred himself, tensed, pushed away from the rough table. "Where is the old woman?"

"I sent her to bed."

He sprang up, wary, shrank the distance, dragged her up to face him. Stared at her, stunned.

"You are hurting me, Father..."

Pent-up frustration drove her, and the words came roiling as she tasked him with the depredations of the troops under his command, the plight of the farmers.

He retorted that insurrectionists deserved no mercy, but he would attempt to save her neck from the hangman for her mother's sake.

Sarah's denunciation rose to a crescendo as she fought to keep her tongue civil, lest he penalize the colonists for her impertinence.

"Good day, Madam. The cavalry will be relocated to your neighbor's farm, with your compliments," he said coldly, bowing stiffly, and reaching for his hat. He stomped out.

She remembered, aghast, the pitiful circumstances at the next farm, where the father and two older boys served with General Washington, while the mother tried her best to run a farm in wintertime with boys of eleven, nine, and five, and a girlchild of two.

The door slammed shut.

'CUT.'

Grant peered at her. "Ready to go again? Or do you need a break?" He waited.

He asked me. "A minor touch-up first? I think I smeared something." The cold kitchen got inexplicably warm.

Grant motioned with his head towards her chair, called Andrew over into consultation.

She ignored them, had Reggie position her facing the window with its snowy ledge and green baize background. He brought her much welcome water, fussed over her, but didn't speak except to have her turn her head as he needed. She heard rearrangement of cameras and equipment behind her, disregarded the racket—and charged pause—when some klutz jostled cookware. In an eternity, the bustle hushed. She faced them, removed the last of the cloths.

"Ready to finish this up, missy?" Grant.

"I was born ready."

"That you were. That you were. Andrew—?"

"At yer command, Lord and Master, *sir*." Andrew saluted.

For response, she resumed her mark.

Grant nodded.

'LOCK IT UP.'

'WE'RE ROLLING.'

The second take, with the cameras on Andrew, went quickly. She would feel the effects tomorrow, but the adrenaline high flushed her cheeks, and she gave him everything she had left, energy she hadn't known she'd saved.

'CUT.'

She went to the chair for makeup repair. The shortened call list set aside two hours for this shot. It would allow them several more full runs through—

'THAT'S A WRAP, FOLKS. THANK YOU.'

Grant was at her chair. "I'm fine, Grant."

"Join me outside?" Grant signaled to Reggie. "We're done here."

Now what? Could be good, could be bad, could be Grant wanted some other scene more. But the crew were collecting equipment and taking up the camera rails. Grant lifted a finger at her, requesting patience, bent his head in consultation with his assistants and the cinematographer. *Could be he's cutting his losses...*

She permitted Andrew to lead her outside. Someone fetched her chair and Andrew's, set up Grant's facing them under a leafy oak with a plaque stating something historical. Gathering clouds dimmed the sunshine. Maybe he'd get soaked galloping away from the farmhouse. She'd be glad to dump the eighteenth century and its ridiculous constraints on women: making them do all that work while pregnant and wrapped in miles of skirt.

"Ye're done."

All her work locked tight on celluloid, safe. *I am.* "You?"

"Couple more, but Grant wants to do them personally."

"Ah." Of course. If the shots were still on the list this late on the last day, Grant would be in charge. Not relevant for *Dodgson*—she wasn't planning on a second director, not on her budget. But noteworthy.

The makeup man approached diffidently, cleaned off the bulk of the cosmetics with his lemon-aloe-impregnated linen wipes. At her mild request, he stopped fretting, went to wait for her in the van.

"I feel naked without makeup."

"Ye look younger." Andrew shrugged.

Where was Grant? *And why is he making me wait?* "Men don't like makeup."

He let that one lie.

"I got your flowers. They're lovely." *They're back in my trailer, proof I have self-control.* She had quietly contemplated whether the trailer would look like a proper cockfight if she severed each rose-head and shredded it, but decided the effect would be wrong—boudoir rather than crime scene, beauty rather than blood. Her fingers twitched.

He found the grace to look sheepish. "I had to make a quick trip. And Grant's kept me busy every second since I got back."

"Oh? Where did you go? Grant said there was an emergency."

"A funeral."

"I'm so sorry." She put as much warmth and concern as possible into the automatic response. Grant released him to go to a funeral? *Who important enough died?* "Were you close?"

The sheepish flustered expression again. He shuffled his feet, his eyes remote. "We, uh— Went to Princeton. New Jersey?"

She raised eyebrows, prepared to offer words of comfort.

"Kary's ex died; Grant lent them his plane. To take the girls there in time. It was already taking Peter back to Los Angeles."

Kary. Again. *I cannot fight Fate.* "And you went along." She forced 'nonchalant,' glanced around, *anywhere*, gestured to Grant who was closing in. "Kind of you."

"Grant's idea."

That damn witch has interfered every step of the way. Plan B it was. "Oh?"

"He rearranged the schedule a little for me."

"I noticed." She couldn't afford to tell *either* off. She bit her tongue until it throbbed. *They'd pay—some day.*

Grant was smiling. He plunked himself down in the director's chair he rarely used while filming, with a flourish of satisfaction. "A few minutes? The plane's waiting when you're ready."

"For you." She let her voice trail. What did he need?

"It has been a real pleasure."

"Thanks for getting me home for my backers' meeting tomorrow." The next was insurance; technically, she'd been finished from the moment he called it a wrap. "Sure you don't need anything else?"

"No, no. All in the can. Well, all of *yours*." He jerked his chin towards Andrew. "This lug has a couple more hours for me."

Andrew fake-pouted.

Except for me naked with Andrew. In front of a crew of only thirty. Just as well. "Thanks for mentoring as we went, Grant." After she wore him down. *Let him think it was his idea.*

"Ah! No problemo. Always a pleasure." He checked his watch.

Can I go, please? Didn't he have work to do? "It'll reassure the backers." *And that bastard, Tom Pentell.* She caught the tiny nod Grant gave Andrew. To her shock, Andrew dropped to one knee and took her hand.

"*Mistress* Doyle, I beg indulgence of ye. I must be yer Reverend Dodgson."

"But—"

"No buts, Mistress. I *must* be yer man."

She stared hard, fighting for control. "I dunno. I really wanted a blond. There are *several* under consideration."

"But Mistress—I can play blond!"

She spoke sternly to Grant, but the exultation was already making her chest hurt. "Are you a party to this foolishness, Grant?"

"Who, me? Not at all. My role was merely to keep you here so Johnnie can say goodbye. You've made quite an impression on young Johnnie. Ah, there he is." He beckoned to the approaching actor.

With *another* load of roses. "You may rise now," she told Andrew.

"Not until ye say ye will be me— director."

Two could play at this. "And my ring?"

"Alas, I bear no ring. But I will purchase a pretty forthwith."

Did he read her elation? She kept her face severe. "And I *may* accept you when I have it *in hand*."

He got up, dusted off his trousers with exaggerated gestures, bowed.

She took no notice of him, faced John.

"Here," said John. "And I'm to tell you that I can be packed in ten minutes to escort you home."

Andrew picked John up by the elbows, moved him two feet sideways, occupied his place and glared at her. "Ye are not missing the wrap party?"

She waved him aside; he went, disgruntled. She addressed John. "Very sweet of you, John. I can't stay," she returned her attention to Andrew, "I have urgent *grownup* business," she turned back to John, "but you should stay. It will be quite a party."

John would learn to conceal his relief better. "I will pine for you, wife."

"Pine away." She got to her feet holding the bouquet awkwardly, kissed his baby-soft cheek. Predictably, he blushed. She made herself find it charming. "Goodbye, husband." *Forever.*

Grant bounded out of his chair, opened his arms wide.

She submitted to the hug, kissed both of his cheeks. *Respect— from Grant. Not bad.* "You behave yourself, now."

"Still have work to do."

"I know." She turned to Andrew. "You'll hear from me."

"Soon?"

"Soon." She tiptoed to brush his cheek with hers. Had she really just landed *the* essential element? The backers would be thrilled. Andrew was huge—and thank God, Irish—which practically assured lucrative foreign distribution. One more bargaining chip to inch them up on their estimate. "No rest for the wicked."

"No rest for the *weary.*"

You could've had Monday night. Her body ached. No slam-bam-thank you-Ma'am for *your* convenience, not now. "Goodbye, Andrew."

"Hasta luego, señorita." Solemn bow.

"Till we meet again." *You have no idea what you missed.*

ANDREW

THE MOMENT HAD WEIGHT. The crowd standing around was much larger than it needed to be.

"THAT'S A WRAP."

"THANK YOU, EVERYONE. GOOD JOB."

The crew broke into a round of spontaneous applause.

Andrew handed his sword off to the props guy. He ambled over to where Grant was making final notes with the cinematographer, along with the editor who had become almost as much part of the filming as the cameras. "Are ye sure? There's an hour left in the schedule..."

Grant raised his eyebrows pointedly. "Are you questioning my judgement?"

"No, *sir.* Avoidin' additional dialogue sessions. Be tough to schedule them in later."

"Just worried about *me*, right?"

"No, *sir.* Me." That got a satisfying chuckle from the crew—his reputation was safe. The tension broken, crew and staff began the process of cleaning up after the final shot, and the cinematographer walked away in deep heads-together consultation with the editor. "Got a minute, sir?"

"You 'sir' me again, I'll enlist you somewhere. What, going to miss the colonel?"

"This?" Andrew removed the hat, accepted wipes from the makeup man. New paint smell permeated the background: the owner let them borrow this house—on a promise of getting it fully repainted, *all* sides, when they stopped needing something weatherbeaten. New lawn, too. He sighed. *It begins.* "What? Me miss ye olde English bastard?"

"I knew there was a reason I picked me an Irishman." Grant addressed the men preparing to take down the awning. "Could you guys take this down last?" At their nods, and a chorus of 'Sure, boss,' he pulled Andrew over to sit for the last time in the chairs stenciled with their names. "What's on your mind, soldier?"

So many things. "Feedback? It's me last chance to be chewed out proper."

Grant peered at him from under the bushy excrescences. "You're serious."

"Aye, boss. Wrap party starts in an hour, and every minute from then on is pinched till it squeals."

Grant conferred the benediction. "You did good, boy."

"Ye'd let me play in yer yard again?"

"I would." Grant nodded his chin slowly. "It wasn't *quite* as bad as I expected. Won't know for sure until the rough cut, but..." He pursed his lips. "Might take you on again."

"Means a lot coming from ye, boss." They sat in a companionable quietude, watching the takedown.

Grant broke the silence. "You're not going to lead young Johnnie astray, are you?"

"Me?"

"He's a little high-strung; it's his first at the top. Go easy on him?"

"Peter's not here, so he'll be me own little lambín."

"That's what I'm afraid of."

"Ye wound me deeply." Andrew thumped his chest with a closed fist. "All this time together, and ye still don't trust me."

The location manager—a burly Sudanese from South Texas with the softest, most persuasive voice Andrew had ever heard, perfect for his job sweet-talking reluctant owners of desirable real estate—had something on his clipboard for Grant which couldn't wait.

Guy should've been an actor. *Speaking of which.* His lips curled in anticipation of the traditional razzing awaiting young Johnnie's first appearance above the title. *Baptism by fire.* It practically guaranteed the lad being able to handle the pressure, the roles, the women, the wild life, the friendships. Johnnie would remember tonight. *He* could still remember…

The LM departed with a wave, and a 'later, mon.'

"About the lad, now," Grant resumed. "After all this time together, I know you *too* well."

"Have I given ye a lick o' trouble?"

"You were awful easy to work with these last couple days. I thought you'd been taken over by aliens." Grant's brows were permanently stuck in skeptic mode.

"Couldn't give ye a hard time, not after…"

"I kinda liked it."

"Won't happen again. I have me pride."

"Figured."

"We'll go easy on the lad. Cross me heart—" He inclined his head, put on his most innocent look, all open and trusting and—

"I promised his agent."

"He's over eighteen, Grant. Ye sound like ye promised his *mother.*" He evaluated Grant's eyebrows. He balanced them against the hallucinogenic visions in his head of endless drink and dancing and himself in photos with at least a thousand people, most he'd never see again, promised himself not to act too big the fool for those he would. "Fine. Easy." *As easy as possible.*

"Just a sec." A frantic call on Grant's cell had the director holding the phone away from his ear, speaking soothing words in between.

Nobody knows where I am. Very peaceful when the rushing about had nothing to do with him. An aberration. *Better soak it in—won't last.*

"Hollywood—it can wait." From where they were bustling, packing their lorries, Catering brought over water at Grant's signal. "What next for Andrew O'Connell, movie star? More *Roland* gigs?"

He rehydrated. *Blech.* "Maury's having kittens. He's got me booked solid. Ye ran late, ye know."

"It's in the contract."

"Only way he'd keep his paws off me. A car takes me to Boston tomorrow. He wants China—told him China'll still be there; they won't be opening for months. I'm at his mercy till Dublin in a couple o' weeks—and there we part ways." Indentured servitude. *And I go home.*

"And after that? Just a mo."

He waited out the brief consult with the executive producer, watched Grant: these were Grant's peeps, trusted to do their job whenever Grant needed them, a tight web of recurrent camaraderie, lacking the scattering and the emotional letdown.

Grant climbed up into his chair again. "Have another gig locked down?"

"We're in negotiations. Working title *Leviathan*. World War II. Submarines. Norway. Fjords. Not till next year. Spring."

"Maybe I'll see you when you come to Hollywood to record additional dialogue for me."

"Maybe ye'll come to Norway to get yer ADR. Might be cheaper."

"Maybe we won't *need* ADR."

Fat chance. "Haven't I done every one of yer lines two thousand different ways?" With only a little arguin' in between. *That* was one of the few problems Grant *shouldn't* have. "Hope there's no other fallout. The, uh, *teen*—?"

"George didn't tell you?"

"He said there was a police report."

"In gory detail, with photos, parent statements, policewoman statements... Which will be given out to the press with a request to keep the minor's name out of for *her* sake, if necessary."

"Sorry, man."

"Security's fault. You did the right thing. Forget it." The Assistant Director and her clipboard needed Grant's attention.

A good AD held shoots together; one bad scandal could bring all Grant's work down. *Or drive them to the theaters to see for themselves?*

George taxied up on the big motorbike with the spare helmet on back, kicked out the stand.

Another thing I'll never see again. "Hullo. Not a pumpkin and six, but it'll do."

"Just got the signal it's over." George removed his helmet, handed it over. "Leave it by the trailer. Most stuff's packed. Kary remembered the sweater ye left."

"Thanks, man." He *knew* there was something he'd forgotten. "Ready to party?"

"About that—"

Grant wandered back from his talk with the AD. "Hullo, George. Ready for some beer? I think there'll be grub there somewhere, too." He clambered into his chair, made himself comfy.

"Actually, I can't stay. Didn't want to disturb Andy with him working." George faced Andrew. "Got to go. Tonight. Me da's ticker—it's not doing well."

"Ye're not coming to Boston." His gut tightened.

"Can't, man."

"Wish ye'd told me sooner." *It'd change everything.*

"Only just found out." George's brow was furrowed. "Nothing ye can do. It's me himself needs."

"Give 'im me best, will ye?" Without George, Maury's tour would be a whole other brute. *Dammit.* "Keep me posted?"

George nodded.

"Been a pleasure," Grant said. They shook on it.

"Anything ye want. I'm on the phone." Andrew stood to pull George into an awkward bear hug. "Give Fi a kiss."

"Kiss her yerself. Ye're to be best man."

"Ye devil!"

"Three weeks?"

He reflected. *Just.* "Aye, then."

"Time we settled down. For Da."

"Da? For Ma." *'For Fiona'* hung between them. He heard Grant's chuckle. A van pulled up to the back of the set. He watched George go. Shite. *And shite on me for being a selfish bastard.*

Grant was in deep conversation again, this time with the second unit director. Andrew waited until the man walked off with his clipboard tucked under his arm. "They don't really need ye, do they?"

"Nope. Just bad habit."

"Anything ye *must* do between now and the party?"

"Call Lily, tell her I'm coming home. She says she misses me. Why?"

"Come along." He tossed the water bottle. There were better ways to absorb moisture. He presented Grant with the extra helmet. "If it's critical, they'll call. Ye never got a ride. Buy ye a beer?"

Grant stared at the foreign object in his hands. "Why not?"

He waited while Grant got comfortable before revving up the great black Harley, and headed back toward the town center of Hanover. He chuckled as Grant clutched him convulsively when he roared around a corner, throttled back a bit to a steady throb for the too-short ride through the splendid sun-drenched afternoon.

He pulled into the postage-stamp carpark behind *Denny's Disco*, cut the engine. Grant scrambled off.

He kicked the stand out, set his helmet on the seat. *One more ride, and this one fades to history, like all the others.* He ignored the morbid thought, pulled open the bar's back door.

Stuart was pulling a foamy one for a guy at the bar. He glanced up, nodded, came around to the table in the back. "What'll it be?"

"Sorry I didn't make it back sooner."

"No worries—we've been full every weekend since your bunch first came in. Lot of crew, too. What'll you have?"

"The *Franconia* microbrew?"

"Done."

Stuart returned with two frosted mugs of the dark stout. He refused payment. "On the house."

"Thanks, man."

Grant spoke up. "Is that a new photo of me behind the register?"

Stuart beamed. "From that night. Came in about a week after."

George. Always thinking. "Want it autographed?" Andrew scrawled his signature next to 'George Cosgrave' and passed the black marker to Grant to do the same. He doubted it would ever sport Bianca's, but ye never knew. *Halfway to L. A. by now.*

"Come any time." Stuart took the glossy back to the bar, replaced the glass in the frame, hung it back on the wall, and went back to polishing glasses.

"Star spoor," Grant said.

"How do ye do it?"

"What?"

"Switch gears. Bites me every time." The bitter hit his tongue. "They say taste and smell make the strongest memories."

"You're done. I'm not. I'll get a couple of days, interrupted every fifteen minutes on the phone, and then there'll be six months or more of post-production, and then the premieres..."

"Right."

Grant squinted at him. "Don't go maudlin on me until *after* the party."

"Me?"

"You going to do Bianca's little movie?" Grant jerked his head toward the bar. "I hired her for fireworks on this one. Got them. Buried depths, that one."

"If I can— I meant what I said. Nothing signed yet, ye know. It's not the money—after what ye pay me, I can afford her art film. I'd work for scale—the script's perfect for me."

"If I'd known you'd work for scale, you would *not* be getting whatever I'm paying you."

"That's why I didn't tell ye."

"I'll remember."

"Don't tell anyone else, and we're good. Ye know it's about the roles."

"Yeah, yeah, yeah. That's what they all say."

"It's the agents who are mercenary. They badger us."

"Right. And be careful with her—we may grumble about the lovely Miss Bianca Doyle all we like, but Hollywood will close around her like a vise if you screw with her."

"She's the insider, I'm the upstart foreigner."

"Unless your movie brings in far more money."

"Sigh. Always about the money."

"You knew that from Day 1."

"One hopes to remain pure."

"I call b.s." Grant took a long drag at his mug. "Bianca's a fine intuitive actress; she goes directly for the gut. You, you're more analytical. You think through all the possibilities, then you choose. Then you work yourself into a lather about it. She's more all or nothing—she can flame out, but when she's on, she's on, and you'll find yourself scorched. This directing thing. She's incredibly ambitious."

"I like ambitious. I'm a bit that way meself."

"Watch yourself with that one."

"She's taken."

As sole response, Grant scrunched his brow, took an appreciative slurp of his stout.

"Do ye know the boyfriend?"

"He used to do villains in B-action flicks. Another power-hungry one, like Stallone, only I don't think he can write."

"Good pair? I'll keep me eye on her if they split up."

"Apply a little leverage?"

"Not me style."

"How about the other one? She more your style? You invite her to the wrap?" Grant was peering at him with those shiny black beady eyes under their bushy tents.

"Kary? Lord, no. Not her style." But he had a flash of her at *Mallory*'s, in New York, holding calm muted court in the middle of the melee, with Dana and Dana's sister. *And George.* "She's probably happy to see me gone from her life. She couldn't wait to get back to her book, she said."

"Speaking of...?"

"Ah..." *He's going to kill me.* "I, uh..."

"You asked her." Grant interpreted his face. "She said no." Grant laughed, took a big swig. "You *do* know I expected that?"

"Ah, no?"

"There isn't a novelist out there with anything worth filming who doesn't think the movies will screw it up royally." Grant shook his head. "The ones who think 'it will make a wonderful film' are usually dead wrong. It's practically a tell."

"Ye're not looking to kill me?"

"What'd you do? Why?"

"I got to reading?"

"Reading. Reading. Reading. Such a terrible habit. You do that, the story's in your head in a few hours, and I can't dislodge it. All my backing and all my people, and you went ahead and did a little movie in your head, and now what am I going to do with you?"

He laughed. *Going to miss this guy.* "Black magic."

"Oh, yeah. Black-and-white magic." Grant was still shaking his head. "So, what'd you say to her?"

"Eh— Something about wanting to play Jake."

"Now you've gone and done it! You told her exactly where to grab— You can hardly complain when she pinches."

"Ye're acting as if this were all quite comical."

"She said no. To me! In her own home." Grant stared owlishly over the brew after a long swallow. "Because I have nothing she wants. *Yet.* Mark my words, one of these days she'll need access. Money. The kind of public attention you can't buy. Then she'll remember me."

"This happen to ye a lot?"

"Not so far," Grant said with elaborate dignity.

"She said she doesn't need the money." What could she spend it on she didn't own? Privacy? Serenity? *She already lives in an impregnable fortress.*

"She will go down in history as 'the one who got away.' Unless, of course, she comes crawling to me." Grant enunciated consonants with care. "And then I will be *magnanimous*."

"Are ye maybe just a wee bit drunk? On *one* beer?"

"I haven't exactly been sleeping much. Not to worry—I will be *perfecto*. Principal photography on major motion picture, you know. No problemo."

"Maybe we should be getting ye back." *Tuck him in for one of Kary's little restoratives.*

"*You* get to be the pretty boy in front of the camera. Somebody has to do the grownup work, you know. Three years, now. Three *years* I've been working on this one."

'The one who got away.' All the way back to the set, where he dropped Grant off with a frantic assistant who glared at them, but agreed to fill the little director with black coffee and something to hold it down, he rolled Grant's words around in his head.

He parked the cycle for the last time, realized he was still wearing the colonel's boots. Someone from Costuming would fetch them. George had left clean duds, neatly packed bags.

He headed for the shower, prepared to torture Johnnie. One last good night.

The one who got away.

KARY

Sanctuary; **Thursday, June 16, 2005; 8 A.M.**

AM I ALLOWED TO GRIEVE?

Grieve what?

If you cover a wound, it festers.

Scrub it out with lye soap, then. A sure cautery.

It had to be done. But it would hurt. A lot.

She couldn't afford to lose more time to *l'affaire Andrew*.

Which wasn't!

She'd already lost the whole of Wednesday unable to write. Unable to think. Unable to do much more than stare at the fire she'd lit to counter the cool front moving through with its wind and its rain and its *Sturm und Drang*. Just as well: she knew the instinct to hike up her mountain was the worst thing she could do to her body after the stress she had heaped on it, curse the disease. Rest, rest, and more rest was the only thing which might work. At least the front left behind clean air.

He would be leaving sometime today, if he hadn't left yet.

No business of yours. Necessary goodbyes were said on the tarmac at the airport, in person.

He won't call.

But she had been at the computer for two hours, starting to read her notes for Akiiya, and then finding she couldn't make herself concentrate.

She tried all the usual tricks from her list: read the last chapter. Check the plotting software for the scene. Become Akiiya. Pick up the threads of where the story was. Travel to K'Tae and visualize the harsh landscape.

But Akiiya kept sliding away from her.

And she knew why.

I was going to do this later.

Really?

Am I allowed to grieve?

You survived illness, divorce, Ethan's death. This is nothing by comparison.

If you cover a wound, it festers.

She smiled. Logical techniques for emotional distress—counterintuitive. *A normal person gets to cry.*

You're not normal.

She put Akiiya's files away. This would take however long it took. It always worked, once she put in the time. The other way, the endless circular thinking, never resolved because it encompassed no mechanism for resolution. Its mechanisms were all about perpetuation of pain so as not to lose memories, cement them into storage...

Self-indulgence.

I know.

She sighed, closed her eyes. Calm required many sets of three breaths; how many didn't matter—counting the sets was not part of the process, only the clean clearer state at the end which always came. Eventually.

Just shoot me.

Nope. No easy outs.

'Do your breathing, mom,' Ethan would say, holding her hand.

Are we ready?

She opened her eyes. *We are ready.*

> *Step one: write everything out.*

She created a new file, encrypted it—usual password, dated it, labeled it, *'Getting back to normal after Andrew left.'*

Close enough.

The tale came out, taking words from her head and painting them on the page in chaotic paragraphs of roughly-related topics, double-space and new paragraph when the ideas morphed.

Gathering stage.

Wish I could write fiction this fast.

Gathering didn't hurt: she permitted herself no judgement, only inclusivity. *The feelings are mine, and I am entitled to my feelings.*

No argument.

So many new people. Too many people. Grant, George, Peter and John and Bianca.

Peter said I was good for him.

Peter Hyland is a sweetheart. Don't get sidetracked.

The security guard and the people watching her at the barrier. The crew and the caterers eyeing her on the set, naturally curious. Frank. The pilots. The smirking clerk at the Inn asking how many rooms they wanted and not quite managing to hide his surprise. The people at the church surrounding the grieving widow, many of them people she collaborated with for years who had never called. Their waiter at the *Alchemist & Barrister*, and wondering whether he was a time bomb. The incurious gravediggers. The woman with the blue baseball cap who retrieved the rental car. More people than she'd seen in the previous year, all at once.

Too many holdover people.

Zoë would say this meant Kary *could* meet new people, if she wanted. After all these years, Zoë still didn't understand. But maybe she could let Zoë introduce her to…? *Solving exactly nothing.* Later. After Akiiya. Maybe.

Joe would understand; the backlash from overdoing, and the relapse, and the slow recovery were all boring perennial topics at their CFS meetings, one of the reasons she often skipped.

Elise—do I need to mend fences? Not unless Grant pursued *Prairie Fires*, and she nixed that option pretty solidly. *Another pipe dream.*

Ronnie and Susan and Stephen and Greg and Amanda and Tad the Infiltrator. *I must stop referring to him like that—he's a child.* Her way of insulating herself from memories of Tad, at four, who would not be consoled when no one would answer his question, '*Where is Efan? Want Efan.*'

Ronnie had texted, "*i learned my lesson. going back to school, masters, focus on work. be less stupid next time.*" Kary sent back,

"I'm here, I love you," frustrated at not finding better words. And received, *"i know love you too."*

The past Sunday was their first Father's Day without a father.

She didn't stint. The file lengthened.

When the energy flagged, she took a nap on the emergency cot. The process worked best if she finished in one fell swoop. *What is a fell swoop, anyway?*

Research that later.

Real food would have been better, but she didn't want to climb the stairs, risk blinking lights on the answering machine. *Not yet.* She laughed at herself: the only reason she was eating was because otherwise she would collapse. But it wouldn't do any harm to improve the stale emergency stash.

The consequences, she hoped, would not be as bad as might be anticipated. She didn't examine the emotions, thoughts, and words, but only recorded them. And she knew this stuff—nothing was new.

It has been clogging my brain, begging for attention. But mostly it wanted acknowledgement, not sentiment.

She left *him* for last.

After Second Nap. After stretching and twisting to loosen the kinks.

Now?

Rather waste another day?

Writing doesn't matter; I'll get back to it in time.

Hate to tell you this, but writing's all you have.

Right. I keep trying to squirm away from that hard truth.

Get it over with, then.

Clean file. Date. Label '*Andrew.*' There wouldn't be any confusion.

She sat for several minutes with the discomfort of beginning. Subduing the craving to do something, anything, to avoid the task at hand—and not let the compulsion win—was a subject mastered in college, when she was sixteen and everyone else was dating and learning to drink. Like a feral cat attracted by a bit of kindness, procrastination always came back. *Give in once, and it knows you will.*

A simple chronology would require less effort.

Start? Dana's show. Easy. Woman in a mindless panic. She had never heard of him before, nor *Roland*, much less an Irish pub band. Be careful not to mix the memories of that February night with the memories created when she watched Dana's DVD: that was later.

She took notes: first noticed were those eyes, with the black lashes making the vivid blue startling against healthy white. Healthy? Yes; he exuded vitality, an impression which only got stronger as she came to know him. Energy. Extrovert. Wary. She'd wondered at the time about 'wary,' watched Dana try to push him over the edge, noted his habit of hesitating long enough for a quick thought. Unusual in a give-and-take; he must have been burned...

How little control she'd exerted. She could have said thanks, but no thanks, to *Mallory*'s after *Night Talk. And none of this would have happened.*

She didn't bother with her obsessive stalking online—she knew what she'd done; this part wasn't about her.

The brief nasty gossip interlude? Those worries would fade: gossip followed him, not her.

In the two months they'd been filming in New Hampshire after a month in Boston, fewer than a dozen interactions. *Feels like far more.*

Conversations: it irked her to remember what they'd talked about, and what was said, but not the extra, the Irish word choice and order and intonation which engendered a hefty portion of the charm he used expertly but with abandon. He was being himself—she let herself be enthralled.

Intelligence is an aphrodisiac in men. What a stupid statement. But, like many a tired cliche, it gained currency by being irreplaceable. How else would you say it?

Fine.

An obtuse man was easy to ignore.

Another huge file grew. Details accumulated: she would add to the file if she came up with anything later, but it was important to pin down as much as possible before her stupid brain forgot critical particularities, such as the sound which turned her heart to ice when he dropped something on her stairs, and she caught him watching her dance.

What a collection of images of her *he* would have.

And they ended with me being weird over my ex-husband's open grave. Which should stop any man short. Again, just as well: he knew her far better than he would have otherwise, all putting her in the innocuous category of 'too much baggage.' *Too old, too ill.*

She carefully listed each minute instance of physical contact: riding pillion on the cycle; touching his scars; his hand encircling her wrist when he slept. And the places where he had preternaturally avoided contact: at the cemetery; at her party; saying a public goodbye at the airport. Intuition welded to intelligence—a rare combination in a man. *Making him more dangerous.*

The data multiplied, as accurate a record of research as any of her books.

Step two: analyze.

She evaluated the file clinically when she was finished. After Ethan died, she listed the few things she could do for her daughters and his friends at school; she did them. *They're so right about me: I'm stone-cold.*

A few minor questions and they'd be done. She laughed mirthlessly.

Executive summary?

She'd believed she was happy, secure, productive—until he came, and reminded her of the great big world out there she didn't have access to. It was hard to come, again, to the conclusion that she was doing the right thing for herself. *What the hell would I do out in the world?* He'd disturbed her fragile peace, but nothing changed, nothing was changeable, nothing *would* change—except she now possessed a tiny useless shred of knowledge: whatever was in her which longed for something—or someone—was not yet dead.

The yearnings were caged. She *chose* to pour them into characters.

Step three: conclusions.

Do you love him?

I love him. It felt so right to simply admit that, here alone in her own sanctuary, in the best condition she could be, given the extraordinary life of the past several months. She would always have a soft spot for him in her heart. *I love him.*

Does he love you?

The tough one: No. He thinks of me as a friend.

There is the truth, then: you are friends. Lowest common denominator. Good friends.

Maybe the stupid CFS will go away as stealthily as it came.

And maybe the next generation of pigs will crossbreed with eagles.

I don't want to do this any more.

Finish it, Lady of Shallot.

Do I have to?

You do. If you love him, what do you want for him?

Whatever he needs to be happy: a rewarding career, a woman to love him and bear his children and laugh with him in the night.

Aunt Ruth would ask the right question: are you that woman?

She crossed her arms, considered the inquiry for a moment. The telling fact that he arranged so much to enable her to mimic his pace for one day—unsustainable. He needed a mate to egg him on, ski down the mountain on the black diamond trail with him, match him in intensity—not someone to bring him down way below boring average human to her level. *Not under any circumstances I can foresee.*

Short answer?

The short answer is 'No.' I am not that woman.

'Are you sure, dear?' Ruth would have concern for me, and distress, and faith.

'My best evaluation,' I'd answer, and she'd believe me.

Then we are done here.

Not quite.

To finish the catharsis, she typed again:

> *Blessings on you, Andrew O'Connell. May God's favor shine upon you. May you be happy. May you have a wife worthy of you and children you love. May you have peace and freedom. May your responsibilities lie lightly on your shoulders, your pleasures be safe, lawful, and many. May the Lord grant you long life, many wonderful friends, jobs which challenge you, and a wonderful sweetness—and take you home when you are ready for Him.*

He is not religious; you know that.

He was born Irish Catholic; it would have to suffice. *Besides, this isn't about him.*

But it *would* be easier once he found someone; she had no interest in married men.

Not my problem.

She thought for a long time, decided not to change a word. She smiled, sniffed. Melodramatic as all get out. *I'll keep this to remind me of who I am, and what I am, and be satisfied with what I can legitimately expect, the friendship of a fascinating man.*

She added the date to the top and 'Dr. Karenna Elizabeth Ashe' to the bottom, printed it out, and put the single sheet in a file she marked 'Andrew O'Connell', placing it in the rear of the lower drawer of her file cabinet.

She was home, in her hidey-hole. She was safe.

Charles was gone.

Andrew was now behind her. She was responsible only to herself for herself.

Regrets? *None.* She wouldn't have done anything differently. No shame in accepting what must happen. *As long as I am exceedingly clear about my choice.*

She locked herself in the tower, threw away the key. The whole ludicrous episode was over.

She had contributed her small stab for CFS.

She was driven, but the only contribution she could make to the world now was in her stories.

If the girls truly needed her, she'd find a way to manage somehow. But, absent their need, nothing in the world pulled her in. *Go back to work, back to who I am.*

She'd gotten out alive—taken the win, and run. She rescued herself; she would not look to any more from him. As long as she kept within her limits, she was all right, capable of running her own life. She was endowed with a satisfactory job, and a family who loved her and would see her more often—if she could take it.

Her *vocation* demanded making the best of what she was given, no more, no less.

It could have been far worse. The *certainty* that she couldn't ever have him meant nothing. This was about *her.* *Any pain is my own damned fault.*

She was grateful she had met him. She never expected to see him again.

Fool—to be attracted to any man, *especially* this one.

Whatever illusions she'd held before, they were thoroughly exposed to the merciless light of reason. *I tried, and now I* know *it can't work.* She could not be part of his world, no matter how successful she'd been at faking.

But he left me better at handling mine.

She woke up the next morning starving.

And found she could write. Akiiya awaited.

   Step four: move on.

TO BE CONTINUED.

WHAT NEXT?

The website for the books is PridesChildren.wordpress.com. Please follow, and you will be informed when Book 2 and Book 3 area available, or when there are special discounts.

Additional content related to the books will be added there, and a contact form for the author.

I will not share your email address with anyone, and will be *very* parsimonious about sending you emails.

Books 2 and 3 are complete in rough draft; I am working hard to revise, edit, and polish the rest of the story.

If you are moved to leave a review on Amazon, it will be much appreciated.

But what makes me happiest is when readers recommend me to their friends.

Alicia Butcher Ehrhardt
November, 2015.

DESIGN NOTES

Made in the USA
San Bernardino, CA
18 February 2017